PRAISE FOR THE LAST BALLAD SERIES

Winner of the FanFiAddict Indie Novel of the Year, the Pencraft Award for Literary Excellence, and the Literary Titan Gold Book Award

"A monumental, unyielding, and gut-wrenching sequel to one of the best debuts I've ever read." — **FanFiAddict**

"Scott Palmer is a Rising indie star in the epic fantasy arena." — **SFF Insiders**

"A sweepingly epic yet character driven Norse-flavoured fantasy that will make any dark fantasy lover's heart sing with both joy and sorrow." — **Grimdark Magazine**

By Scott Palmer

<u>The Last Ballad Series</u>
A Memory of Song
The Sound of Starfall
A Chorus of War

A
Chorus
Of
War

SECOND VERSE OF THE LAST BALLAD

SCOTT PALMER

THE NYTEWOOD PRESS

Edited by Kelley Tai, https://www.bramblecrowbooks.com/

Proofread by Dom McDermott, https://www.dominishbooks.com/

Cover design © Stuart Bache, https://www.stuartbache.co.uk/

Chapter headings, scene break, and logo by Brian Vandevelde, https://brianvandevelde.ca/

Interior design and formatting by Scott Palmer, https://www.scottpalmerauthor.com/

Maps by Joshua Hoskins, @Noctua_Cartography, https://www.deviantart.com/noctuacartogy

Story Recap: HornedGodSlaine - Creative Commons Attribution-ShareAlike 3.0 License .https://www.deviantart.com/hornedgodslaine/art/Old-Scroll-360124397

(**NOTE**: ORIGINAL MATERIAL HAS BEEN MODIFIED)

Digitized Wax Seal and "the song so far" by Adrian Marc Gibson, https://adrianmgibson.com/

Palmer, Scott. (A Chorus of War, The Last Ballad 2.0) Paperback Edition.

To Sydney, who makes it all easier than it should be.

To Indie, for being the reason to never give up, it's all for you baby girl.

And to Sandy Wright, who said more without words than any person I have
ever known. Whose legacy was love and respect. There she be.

CONTENTS

A Note on Maps

There are full maps in this book, but you can find full-colour, zoomable maps of the entire Remembered Lands on my website at scottpalmeraut hor.com/maps

There is also a full glossary in the back of this book with terms and pronunciations, but you can find the glossaries for the entire Last Ballad Series at scottpalmerauthor.com/glossary

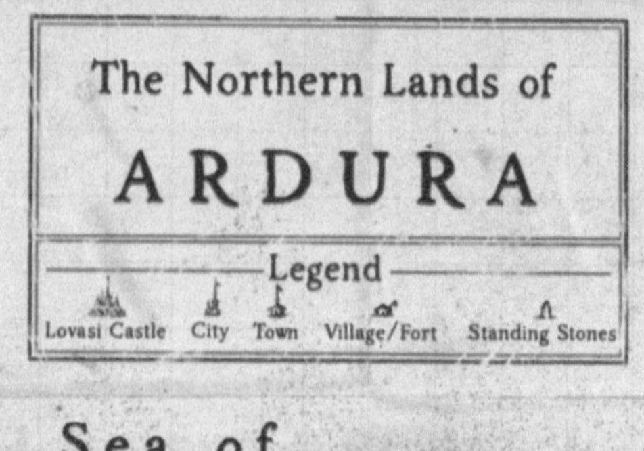

The Northern Lands of
ARDURA
Legend
Lovasi Castle
City
Town
Village/Fort
Standing Stones

Sea of Stars
N
Mountains of the Mother
Kallahorn
The Fell Mountains
THE FELLS
Isle of Darra
Wick
Pool
The Old Arbor
MAL HALLOW
Rosen
Icewall Falls
Dark Water Lake
Fever
Oster
Beauty
Glennish Flats
Wick Arbor
Till
Lorne
Foulds
THE GLENN
Maple
Dawning
Petty Fords
Hallow Hills
Ockam
Tide
Barley
Dark Arbor
Bay of Trees
Oldwood
Glenn Arbor
Isle of Scales
Elurra
Tusk
RYNE
Silverwood
Lone Keep
Ardeen
Whitewatch
Blackstone
Lake of Scales
The Channel of Krakens
Ramstone
Brey
Sheed Mountains
Canter
Edell Mountains
Hearthill
Sheed Arbor
The Gorge
Crossroads Inn
Gale
Blackwood Arbor
Ilbury
Glavelin
Lost Arbor
Leveny
Honeywell
Morland
Timpany
AYELAND
The Hesterlands
Severn
Harbourtown
Carisfield
Bralter
King's Arbor
Solace
Cheston Peake
Bastil
Red Eagle Falls
Moonfort
Roaring Sea
The Starfall Isles
Mirerock
The Cackle Mire
Valence
Hest
Carl
Logan's Rock
Talonsford
The Ayelish Channel
Mountains of Soma
Hammerstone
Boretta
Lazuli Mountains
Roen
Blacksilver Bay
Blackshire Inn
Asuri
Darry

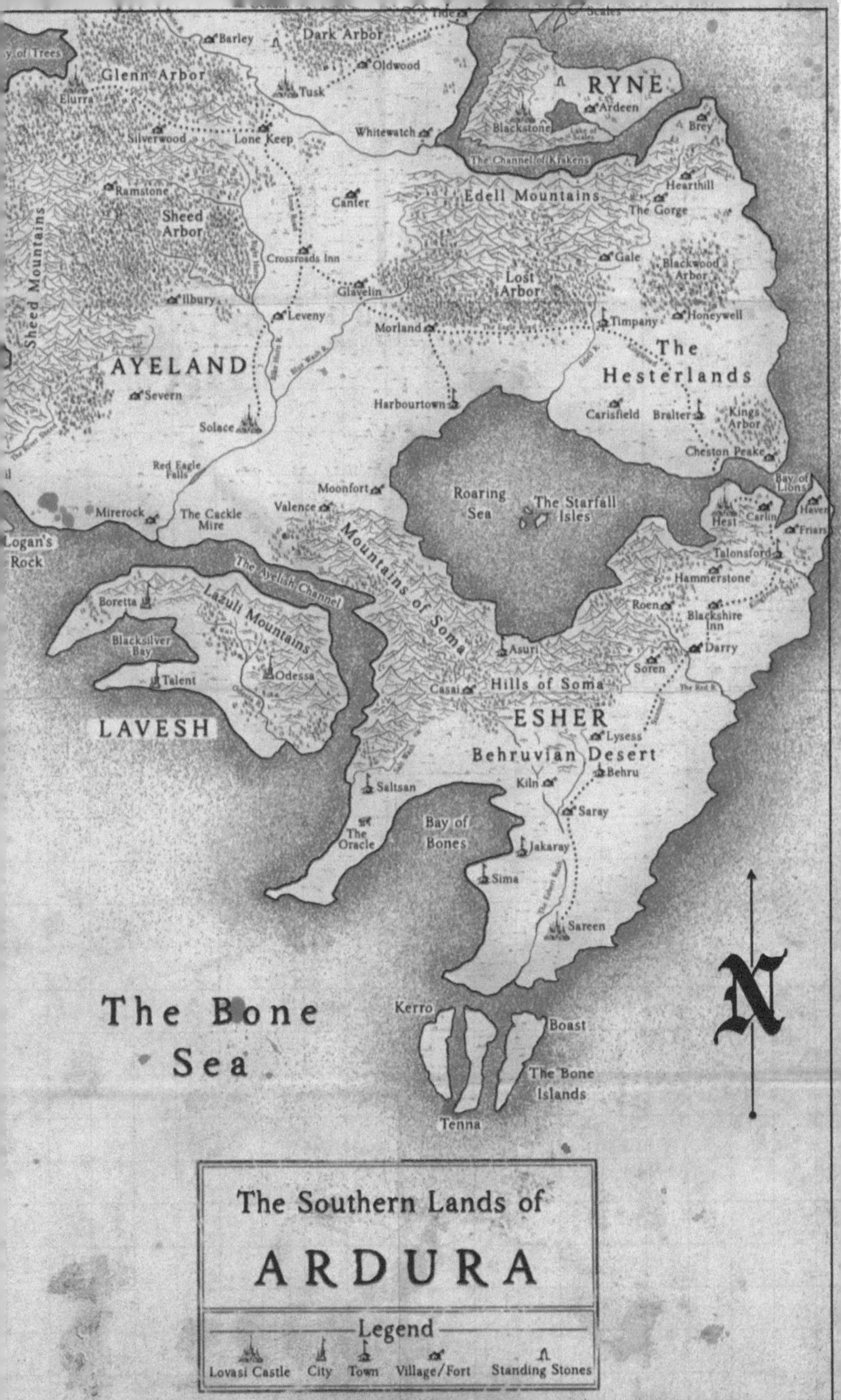

Glenn Arbor
Barley
Dark Arbor
Oldwood
Tusk
RYNE
Ardeen
Blackstone
Lake of Scales
Brey
Elurra
Silverwood
Lone Keep
Whitewatch
The Channel of Krakens
Hearthill
The Gorge
Ramstone
Canter
Edell Mountains
Gale
Blackwood Arbor
Sheed Arbor
Sheed Mountains
Crossroads Inn
Lost Arbor
Ilbury
Glavelin
Leveny
Timpany
Honeywell
AYELAND
Morland
The Eagle Wind
The Hesterlands
Severn
Carisfield
Bralter
Kings Arbor
Solace
Harbourtown
Cheston Peake
Red Eagle Falls
Bay of Lions
Moonfort
Roaring Sea
The Starfall Isles
Hest
Carlin
Haven
Mirerock
Valence
Friars
The Cackle Mire
Mountains of Soma
Talonsford
Logan's Rock
The Ayelish Channel
Hammerstone
Boretta
Lazuli Mountains
Roen
Blackshire Inn
Blacksilver Bay
Asuri
Darry
Talent
Odessa
Soren
The Red R.
Casai
Hills of Soma
LAVESH
ESHER
Lysess
Behruvian Desert
Behru
Saltsan
Kiln
Saray
The Oracle
Bay of Bones
Jakaray
Sima
Sareen
The Bone Sea
Kerro
Boast
The Bone Islands
Tenna
N
The Southern Lands of
ARDURA
Legend
Lovasi Castle
City
Town
Village/Fort
Standing Stones

OLDSTONE
Ash Mountains
Old Mountains
The Black Strait
Hearthspear
Hall
Ash Valley
Whale
Rock
Ironhowe
Hall
Farrock
Bay
Ash R.
Omenhall
Cape
Massey
Bay
Old Fen
Hall
Witch
The Serpant
Mire
The Lighthouse
Cape of Krakens
Ardura
Sea of

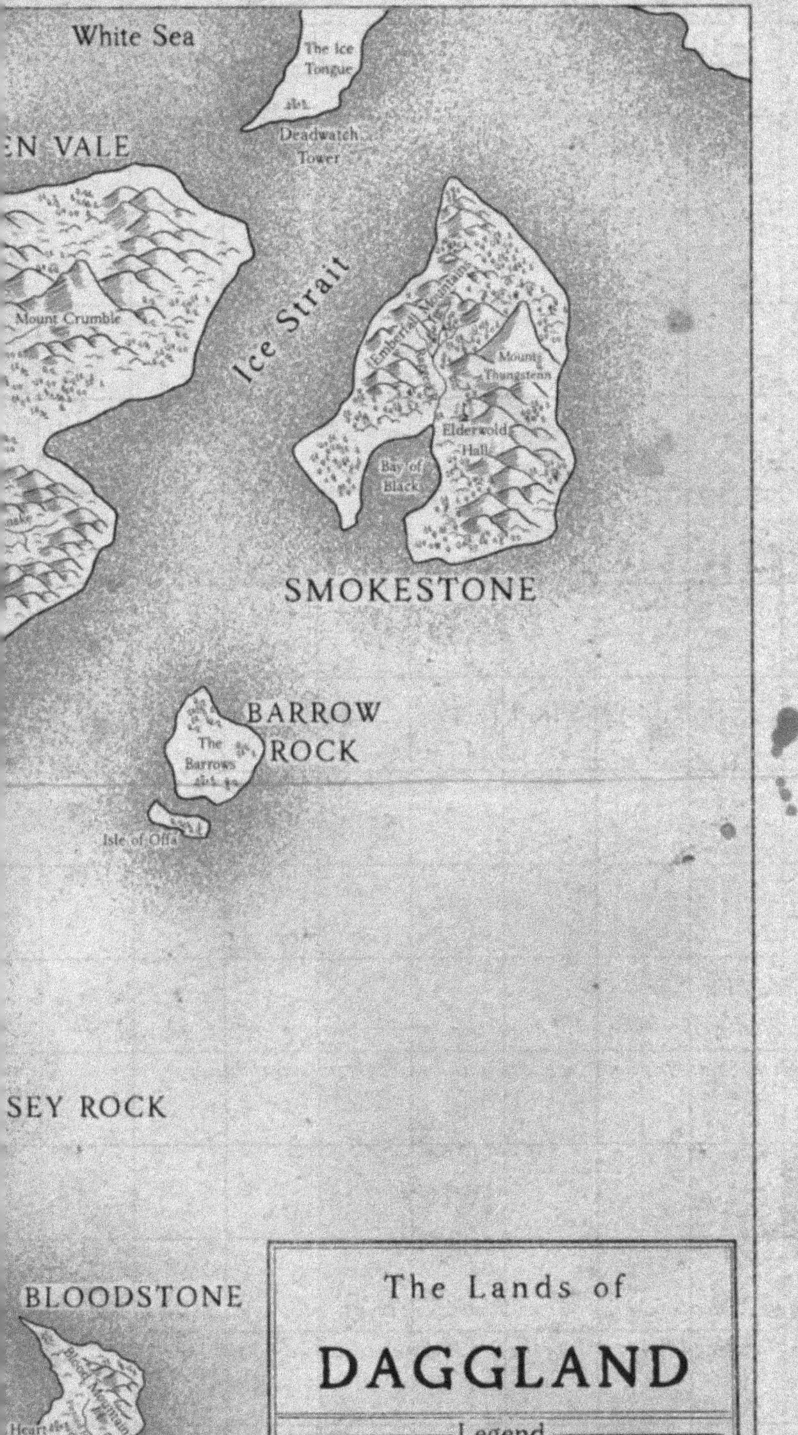

White Sea
The Ice Tongue
Deadwatch Tower
EN VALE
Mount Crumble
Ice Strait
Emberfall Mountains
Mount Thungstenn
Elderwold Hall
Bay of Black
SMOKESTONE
The Barrows
BARROW ROCK
Isle of Offa
SEY ROCK
BLOODSTONE
Heart
The Lands of
DAGGLAND
Legend
Hall
Village
Ruin

THE LAST BALLAD READING ORDER

THE TWO MAIN READING ORDERS ARE AS FOLLOWS:

Melodic:

This describes a thread of sound informed by two or more notes playing in tandem, capturing both expectation and suspense in its unfolding.

The Sound of Starfall

A Memory of Song

A Chorus of War

The Melodic reading order allows the reader to experience A Memory of Song informed by notes from the past, causing increased tension.

Volatile:

This describes something that is liable to change rapidly, making the music's mood or direction mysterious and hard to predict.

A Memory of Song
The Sound of Starfall
A Chorus of War

The Volatile reading order allows the reader to experience A Memory of Song deaf to any previous influence. This will generate the most impact from the twists and turns of the story.

THE SONG SO FAR...

THIS SECTION HAS SPOILERS for THE SOUND OF STARFALL and A MEMORY OF SONG. This is meant as a brief recap for people who want to catch themselves up before starting A Chorus of War. I strongly suggest you read BOTH of the previous books in the Last Ballad Series before starting this one!

THE SONG SO FAR...

THE SOUND OF STARFALL

Three thousand years before the events of *A Memory of Song*, a cataclysm known as **the Starfall** befell the Known World and destroyed the world-dominating force known as **the Yehvenki Empire**. It was from the ashes left behind that the Order of Warlocks, still known in present day as the **Ailaryan Order**, was born.

The Yehvenki Empire ruled the world with their magics—**Words** that, when sung, could manipulate the world in any way they saw fit. The Yehvenki called themselves the Usurpers of Nature.

The Warlocks inherited their empire and their magics from the **Creators**, whose entire race vanished over the course of one single night. They were believed to have Ascended to join the level of their god—**Karaat**. The more worship Karaat receives, the stronger his Words become.

The Yehvenki had conquered all of the Known World and indoctrinated nearly the entire globe with the teachings of Karaat. His prayer was echoed from the Sheed Mountains to the Mongrel Hills.

The Yehvenki took their power too far—they abused it—and the death cult known as **the Abori** came to stop them. The Abori used their magics and a **mage** to bring a star down on Yehven to destroy the Warlocks and their Words. The Abori **dream eaters** sent dreams to the Warlocks—dreams that showed the Warlocks being slaughtered along with all of their guards and servants. They showed the city of Ailar burning, and **the star falling**. They showed the Warlocks' own deaths—for one hundred years, the Warlocks had dreams of the Abori's coming, so when they finally came, the Warlocks were terrified.

With a looming comet burning up the sky and the Abori death-cult approaching, a Warlock in self-imposed exile, named **Adeqor**, and his wife Sera betray their former allegiance to the New Order and join the Ailaryan Order and their radical leader **Eralis** in **the tunnels** instead.

Adeqor travels into the burning, riotous city of Ailar to locate his old partner, **Insa Rolin**, hoping to learn if Insa had finished their long-time work of gaining Ascension. After some trouble in the city, Adeqor takes the mysterious book written by Insa, called Necro, which contains multiple spells, including one to extend life.

Adeqor finds his way back to Sera amidst danger. Their servant, Mose, who is also Adeqor's half-brother, shows up just in time and leads them to apparent safety in the tunnels. There, Mose kills both Adeqor and Sera, takes Adeqor's purple robe and the book of Necro, and makes his way to the safety of the tunnels where he poses as his old master, Adeqor.

The Ailaryan Order doesn't question Mose when he claims to be Adeqor. Mose learns they are plotting a new world to write after the Starfall. One where they are looked up to as gods and live eternally.

Chaos unfolds in the city and betrayals boil over. The Abori attack, and the comet impacts, but the tunnels hold, and the Ailaryan Order survives. Mose, now Adeqor, claims that his song will be the last ballad to ring out for eternity.

A MEMORY OF SONG

In the immediate aftermath of the Starfall, the surviving Warlocks of the **Ailaryan Order** delved into the dark magics that **Adeqor** gifted them through **Insa Rolin's book**. They traded their ability to love for long life and set into action their plan to Ascend to godhead, just as the Creators had before them.

Three thousand years after the Starfall, the Ailaryan Order still holds sway over the rulers of **Ardura**, though the Order has become riven and sundered, and their reign has all but slipped through their fingers.

In **Ayeland**, the Banshee **Ellorin** has recently helped **King Calen Alder**, the Ruler of Solace and King of Ayeland, conquer the northern kingdoms of **Mal Hallow** and **the Fells**. Some of the former Mal rulers bent their knee and swore allegiance to Alder, earning them their lives. Others, like **James Culdaine's** family, refused to accept the Ayelish as their overlords and died fighting.

When the **Lord of Kallahorn, Baleth Longsongs**, a former Mal king who bent the knee, declares himself a king and sacrifices his Ayelish-born partner, **Annie of Morland**, to summon dark magics, Ellorin convinces King Calen Alder to attack Baleth.

Alder and Ellorin succeed at taking Kallahorn. They hang Baleth, and they find that his daughter, **Fiora Longsongs**, and his heartbound Annie, have escaped. They also find out that Baleth has been singing songs of Old **Yehven**—the Words of **Karaat**. And not only that, but the Words are spreading throughout the continent, surfacing as if from a long slumber. Karaat's power is still weak enough that the threat can be quelled, but to prevent the magics spreading any further and pulling the world into oblivion, Ellorin invokes the Ailaryan Order's "failsafe" and commands **the Mother of Nature** to close the **Gateway to the Otherworld**, blocking the **spirits** of fire, earth, wind, and water from entering the main world.

Drought and darkness infect the world as the elements refuse to live. Fires won't burn, the rain won't fall, and no wind will blow. The earth sits stagnant and bloated without the ability to eat its refuse. And now, King Calen Alder of Ayeland has summoned an army of sellswords and brigands, bigger than Mal Hallow has ever seen, to re-conquer the north and to join him in Kallahorn.

James Culdaine's parents, the rightful king and queen of **Mal Hallow**, died fighting Calen Alder and the Ayelish. Afterwards, James abandoned his duty as heir and ran into the mountains of the Fells, where he joined a clan of Feldarra led by the fearless kihl'dor, **Wulfee**. He lived ten years as part of Wulfee's clan, and in that time, he met and fell in love with **Maggie**, a melancholic mage who had spent most of her life being abandoned by those afraid of her. His love for Maggie came to define him.

Soon after the elements stopped working, Wulfee's clan was attacked by a horde of Hawka, bipedal beasts that roam the northern hills, separating James from Maggie and the rest of the clan.

James is hunted by the Hawka for an entire day, from sun-up to sunfell, until he finally finds refuge in a small cave. There, nearly freezing to death, the **souls of the dead** come to him and give him life. A quirky transporter from the **Raven's Guild** named Eurick arrives and claims to be searching for James. Soon after, the dead crowd in the cave and sing out to James, saying "Help us."

When Eurick realizes James clearly sees something he doesn't, the raven becomes intrigued, calls James a **seer**, and tells him that he has been sent to retrieve James by the wizard, Adeqor. If James comes with Eurick, **Adeqor** can explain to James why the elements died.

Along the way, James runs into a band of **Rangers** led by **Haro**, who wants to kill James in vengeance. Before Haro can seek his revenge, they are attacked by a horde of Hawka and are forced to fight with each other instead of against.

James's **monster** comes out and he kills many on both sides of the battle. **He eats dead souls to heal himself.** He is the only one who sees them. He is a **Druid** of the Old Blood of the Mal, capable of walking between the worlds of life and death, and not only seeing the dead, but gaining life from them by breathing in their ghost bodies. James and Eurick leave an injured Haro for dead.

Eurick and James finally find Adeqor. The wizard takes James and Eurick to a cave and explains that the spirits of earth, fire, air, and water have a cycle that flows from the **Other-world** to the above world and back again. If the **Gateway** is closed, the spirits cannot flow through.

Adeqor takes James to **Lindis**, where James pulls the great sword called **Essikah**, crafted by the ancient wizard **Bazal**, from the ground, where it was growing like a tree.

Travelling past the great Standing Stones of Fever, James and Eurick see Adeqor's true nature when he brutally kills a village of stragglers. They learn that **Ellorin**, the Banshee, is hunting them. Adeqor is terrified.

Travelling through the Wick Arbor on a detour, James, Eurick, and Adeqor are captured by another group of Rangers led by **Florence**, and are brought to Ockam to be sold to **Lord Derudin**.

In Ockam, **Lord Derudin and the Blood Company** greet the party by cutting off Adeqor's right hand and the fingers on his left. Derudin then bids James, Eurick, and Adeqor to travel with him to **Dawning** with the intention of bragging to **Lord Brinley**.

Derudin's son, Eridan, arrives, and James recognizes him from when they were young. Their dads fought together against the Ayelish. As the group is leaving, James meets **the bard, Itchy**, and **the Lovasi scholar, Mineera**.

Travelling to Dawning, the Blood Company is attacked by Hawka, and Adeqor escapes. James's monster comes out again, and this time it really disgusts him.

The other survivors regroup at Dawning, where Brinley tells them about the coming war. An **army of sellswords** from Mal Hallow, led by **the Wolf**, has joined a mass host of soldiers in Ayeland. Together they are marching. They have already taken Tusk and Ockam.

In Dawning, James learns that Maggie has been captured by Rangers and is being held close by as a hostage. Before a funeral is held for those he killed, James slips away from Ockam to find Maggie. As he leaves, Adeqor finds him and captures him with magics.

James awakens to find that Adeqor has brought him to **the Hermit's hole**, also known as an **Earth Faerie**'s hole, in the Hallow Hills. Knowing that it is time for him to finally face his demons, James enters the Hermit's lair to finish what he started as a child. There, the Hermit helps James visit the Otherworld and talk to the gods.

In the Otherworld, James talks to **the Old Gods** and learns how he can harness his power, known as **the Ways**, to defeat the evil of the world and bring back the elements. The Old Gods also tell James that a powerful Warlock named Bazal has escaped, and that he is a danger. If any black magics were to be used in the Otherworld, then the elements could die forever, and the world could become a grey wasteland.

When James rises up from the Otherworld and escapes the trap set for him by the Hermit, James is reunited with Maggie, but she is badly sick. She was hurt in the Hawka attacks and her face is scarred, but not only that, it seems that she is dying because the world is dying.

James sets out to face Ellorin, the Banshee, and her hordes of Hawka with the new found use for his power. He raises an army of dead and uses them to spook the Hawka. He kills Ellorin in one-on-one combat. After defeating her, he eats her soul, gaining many of her memories. The remaining Hawka, who were fighting beside Ellorin, charge away, disbanding the Glennish army led by **Lord Richard Brynmor**.

In **Rosen**, the last blood of the Mal assembles to make a last stand. James and a small party leave to travel to **the Mountains of the Mother** at Kallahorn.

Along the way to Kallahorn, Ellorin's memories begin to attack James. He learns that Adeqor had lost his ability to use the Words from a curse inflicted on him by the Mother. In an attempt to reverse the curse, Adeqor broke into the Otherworld and freed Bazal, then taught Baleth Longsongs to use the Words of Old Yehven, which attracted Ellorin. Adeqor had hoped all along that Ellorin would rush in and close the Gateway to kill the elements. When she did, it allowed Adeqor to recruit James, get him to Essikah, and make his way back to the Gateway to re-open it. Adeqor had hoped to convince James to kill the Mother by telling him he was saving the world, because if James kills the Mother, Adeqor could reverse the spell she holds over him and regain his powers.

James's party arrives at **the Mother's Shrine**, and with Adeqor's help, they enter **the Mother of Nature's** abode. Eurick leaves. Calen Alder, carved with **Blood Words**, is waiting for James, bloated and infected with magics. James is nearly killed in combat with Calen Alder. Maggie finally lets loose some of her power and kills Calen Alder.

The Mother sends James through trials that make him face his childhood traumas. He learns that the Warlocks want to send the world into darkness, where they will survive in tunnels and "restart" human civilization. Just as the Warlocks did after the Starfall. The Mother tries to convince James not to kill her, and to let the world die. The alternative is to watch the world become infected with the Words of Karaat, and that would be much, much worse.

James kills the Mother of Nature, and the elements return to the world.

Adeqor begins to chant strange Words, and seemingly gains his powers back from the Mother of Nature after James kills her. A mysterious red mist swallows Adeqor and he disappears. As the mist approaches James and Maggie, they find that they are trapped. Just in time, Eurick arrives to save them.

As winter fast approaches, James and Maggie, along with the other rulers of the Hallow, gather as many folks from the north as they can and make a stand at the Lovasi Castle in Kallahorn, where James has strange encounters with dead gods.

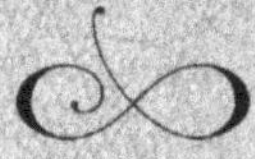

Wulfee, a kihl'dor of **the Fells**, has spent the last ten years hunting her ex-heart, **Sweyne**. Sweyne started to go mad near the end of his and Wulfee's relationship. He wore a **wolf mask** that was cursed by old magics, and it drove him into debauched madness. Sweyne got their youngest son, **Tarek**, killed by forcing him to fight in single combat at a young age. That, amongst other things, drove Wulfee to hate Sweyne.

One night, Wulfee left Sweyne, and she took two thirds of his army and their son, **Braden**, with her. She rode all through the night to get Braden somewhere safe—the village of Barley, in the Fells—where she could leave him to keep him away from the war she was about to have with Sweyne. Her son cried and begged her not to leave, but she had to do what was best to save him from violence.

Now, ten years later, Wulfee is still searching for Sweyne, and she has not seen her son in all that time. The only family she has is her clan. It is an old northern belief that a person's soul cannot go to the sky halls—a place for warriors and elders to spend their afterlife in glory—if they have vengeance in their heart. Wulfee believes the only place she'll ever see her dead son again is in the sky halls. It means the world to her to track down Sweyne and gain her revenge so her soul can rest easy.

Shortly after the elements die, a horde of Hawka attack Wulfee's clan of about fifty folk. Many of the clan are killed or separated, and Wulfee manages to escape with only three others, **Pike**, **Gen**, **and Maggie**, who are very injured from

Hawka scratches. Even after the Hawka attack, Wulfee insists they keep hunting Sweyne instead of looking for potential survivors of the Hawka attack.

Wulfee, Pike, Gen, and Maggie travel to the small village of Lorne, where Pike was born. They meet **the Widow of the White**, a strange prophet who tells the crew there is a person calling themselves **the Wolf**, who has just passed through Tusk heading south, causing a lot of trouble. Wulfee is convinced that it is Sweyne. She and her crew head south towards Tusk.

Travelling along the White River, Wulfee and her crew stop at the village of Barley. Wulfee fears seeing her son here, she fears he will hate her. In Barley, Wulfee doesn't find Braden, but instead, finds his heart and his son, **Tara and little Sweyne**. A healer named **Benn** helps Pike try to heal Maggie. He tells them of a shaman named **Shaqqa Ro** who lives close by in the Dark Arbor and will be able to help Maggie. The crew spends a night and then heads for the shaman.

Wulfee and her crew arrive at the shaman's hut. The crew and the shaman make a deal to leave Maggie with the shaman for seven days. There, they meet a mysterious **Ranger** named **Haro**, who offers to help the crew get to Tusk. Wulfee reluctantly accepts the help.

At Tusk, the Ranger waits for the crew outside of the city at the Standing Stones of Tell. Wulfee, Pike, and Gen, go into the city and split up to try and find information on who the Wolf is.

They learn that the Wolf is a sellsword from Mal Hallow who was purchased by Calen Alder to bring an army of Mal mercenaries south to meet up with a larger host of Ayelish soldiers. The Wolf and his army would then turn around and move north again to sweep Mal Hallow. Wulfee decides to seek the Ranger's help in learning more about the Wolf. She wants definitive proof that the Wolf is Sweyne before she commits herself to this war.

Haro allows Wulfee to use an old Lovasi tool, the Eye of Olan, which allows her to see far distances. On a hill, overlooking the Wolf's garrison, Wulfee spots enough proof to convince her that this Wolf character is Sweyne, her ex-heart.

She returns to Tusk and tells her crew. When the crew tries to leave for Maggie, they find that the guards of Tusk have closed the gates, and everyone inside is trapped. The Wolf and his army are coming, and they need every person they can get to defend the town and Castle.

The Wolf attacks, and the people of Tusk are slaughtered. Before the Wolf breaches the gate and captures Mammoth's Head castle, Wulfee and her crew manage to overwhelm the guards and escape. They meet Haro outside of the city and ride away to get Maggie.

Wulfee finds that Shaqqa has sold Maggie to the Rangers. Wulfee questions Haro, but Haro swears he isn't involved. Instead, he offers to help. Haro leads them into **the Hallow Hills** to find Maggie.

In the Hallow Hills, Haro leads Wulfee and her crew into a trap, wherein he imprisons them in an old Druid barrow. Haro recognized Wulfee and Maggie, and he plans on using them as hostages to attract James Culdaine, so Haro can kill him for revenge. Fearing Gen would be a liability, Haro scares away Gen and sends him off into the Hills alone.

After some time in the barrow, Haro comes down to inform the crew that they will be leaving, as James Culdaine is dead.

After travelling for some time with the Rangers, they are attacked by a pack of Giy'er. Gen is with them. He is injured. Pike and Maggie have a chance to escape and run to Foulds to join the wizard. Wulfee chooses instead to stay with the injured Gen, and the two of them are captured by the Rangers once again.

The Rangers are in distress—their leader Haro has been killed and they don't have a plan. Wulfee convinces the Rangers to travel to Pool, where Kihl'dor Odhran will accept them. Pike knows this is a lie and confronts Wulfee. The two argue. Pike reminds Wulfee that his daughter lives in Pool and believes him to be a murderer, and they aren't welcomed. Wulfee drives them towards Pool anyways, saying it will all be okay.

Being pursued by the Wolf and his army, Wulfee and the crew are backed up against the Fell River, where their only choice is to fight a losing fight or risk drowning by crossing the great river. Gen can't swim; he is ready to fight. Wulfee accepts that she will die rather than abandon Gen to die by himself. Pike stays with her, and the three face death heroically. Wulfee makes Gen a karl in a makeshift ceremony.

At the last moment, Gen pushes Wulfee and Pike into the river, saving them, and he stays to fight. It takes twenty folk to bring him down, but eventually they do, the Wolf giving the final blow. Wulfee vows to find the Wolf and kill him if it's the last thing she does.

On the other side of the Fell River, Kihl'dor Odhran Ironfist takes Wulfee and Pike as prisoners to **the island of Pool**. Pike challenges Odhran to single combat, which he accepts. Pike narrowly wins the battle and earns himself and Wulfee freedom. The two of them leave Pool and head for **Rosen**.

At Rosen, Wulfee leads an army of misfits to a great victory over the Wolf and the army of sellswords and Ayelish. Wulfee finds the Wolf on the battlefield. The two fight, and Wulfee injures him badly. Before she kills him, she removes the Wolf mask and finds that it is her son Braden. He looks at Wulfee with hate in his eyes and tries to deliver a fatal blow to her once more. Wulfee kills him. She realizes that he wanted to kill her for his own revenge—for his own place in the sky halls.

Wulfee walks away into the mountains, alone.

Months later, Wulfee is with a small group of survivors in the mountains, who call themselves **si'darra**, or people of peace. Her grandson, **young Swey**, is playing. Tara and Benn are sitting around the fire with her. Wulfee has become unrecognizable after so much hardship and having her hair shorn. When asked her name, Wulfee hesitates. Being Wulfee is too painful for her, so she decides to be someone else—she decides to hide. Finally, she tells Benn and Tara who she is. **Etta**.

Now begins the second verse of the Last Ballad, A Chorus of War.

A
Chorus
Of
War

PART ONE

"Like the generations of leaves, the lives of mortal men. Now the wind scatters the old leaves across the earth, now the living timber bursts with the new buds and spring comes round again."

Homer

STOLEN DEATH

"Tell me the story, Etta!" Little Swey's feet crunched in the snow as he ran towards her, red-cheeked and leaky-nosed. His breath smoked in the cold as he screamed it this time. "Tell me the story! Please!"

Etta couldn't help but laugh. They had been walking for three days straight through the cold snow. The Fell Mountains were overwhelmingly large around them. Sentinels and pines stood tall like soldiers guarding the foothills. Only stopping for late lunch and sleep. Only smelling woodsmoke and ice. *The boy should be exhausted*. But he didn't stop running. Ever.

"Alright, Swey, come here so I don't have to yell," said Etta. The boy had taken to being called Swey. It was a boyhood affinity to have a nickname, but Etta didn't complain. Saying his full name still gave her the chills and brought back unkind memories of the man whose name he shared.

Swey walked beside her. And their boots crunched through the icy snow in unison. Four of the mountainfolk walked in front of them, carrying the stretcher that held Benn. Four others were mounted on the crew's only horses, their saddlebags fat with foodstuffs and tools. Benn was still passed out and soaked in cold sweat from the large dose of ander, but he was breathing. He had come down with a strange sickness over the winter, and it had only gotten worse. It was an easy vote when Etta bid they carry him to a shaman to fix him. "This is a long story, Swey," Etta said.

"We've still got a ways to go yet," Tara said. "The shaman lives deep in this river valley. It will take us another moon to get there, at least, and if a storm hits..." She had grown fond of Etta's stories, too. When Etta had first arrived, Tara was prone to long bouts of melancholy, but as of late, she seemed to be coming out of it, wearing a smile more and more, wearing it like a warrior wears their braids—as proof she'd made it through. *Will you ever smile again?*

"What story?" Holden asked. His big nose pointed up to the sky with his chin up high. Holden was a tall young man and a fine warrior. He wore chainmail and boiled leather, and was adept with the axe—a karl of the Fells. He had earned three braids in his time before arriving in the mountains, and he still wore them proudly. *As he should.* But he was still a boy at heart when Etta started with her stories.

"The story of the greatest karl that ever lived!" Swey shouted. He jumped around a bit, kicked some snow, then scooped up a snowball and threw it at nothing. "Gen the karl! You know he took on twenty armoured folk on horseback, and they still couldn't take him down." Swey was ecstatic.

Holden raised an eyebrow and nodded with intrigue. "Bare-fisted, eh?" Holden said. "Twenty, on horseback, damn, really?"

"The Giy'er have fists like rocks and skin like hard leather," Etta said.

"Just start at the beginning, would you?" said Tara.

There were fourteen of them who made the walk from their camp in the mountain river valley to carry Benn to the deathstealer. They stopped to set up camp and cooked a small dinner over the fire.

Later, each of them would lie down to go to sleep. Thirteen of them would find a nice deep rest beneath the stars. Etta would lie awake as she relived the last twenty years of her life. Going over everything, forcing herself to face her wrongdoings. But feeling the pain of it all made her feel lighter in the mornings. Even with less sleep, she felt lighter. She reckoned one day, if she kept fighting, the pain would get so light it may just float away from her. But for now the pain was heavy and wet and cold, and it hung over her like an icy fog. She was dripping in it—drowning.

For now, she had her stories, and folk who wanted to hear them. All thirteen of the crew crowded in around her to listen. "This is how Gen the karl saved my life," she started.

"WHAT'S WRONG WITH HIM?" Swey's mouth hung open in shock.

"Nothing's wrong, Swey, don't stare." Tara pulled the boy away, having a look at the man herself. Etta had no mother to tell her not to stare, so she had a good look at the naked man crawling in the mud. His skin seemed to be stretched too tight over his frail and bony body, and his spine looked like it might slice through it.

"Skhlrrroosss," the man hissed, and the four carrying Benn nearly dropped him. It sent a chill up Etta's spine, and she was glad to see Tara pull Swey closer as they walked by.

Etta caught the man's gaze as she passed.

"No help." The man wiped mud from his face with a filthy, crooked hand. He was crouched like a fiend.

"What?" Etta took a step closer.

The man was sickly pale beneath the mud stains. His eyes were bloodshot red and shaking in their sockets. "No help." The man leaped forward on all fours; Etta saw Braden's face on the man and she couldn't move—Etta froze to the spot and closed her eyes. But the man stopped and started cackling. "There's no help, the gods are being killed." The man fell back down in the mud, seemingly in pain. He pulled out handfuls of his hair as he screamed at something unseen. He rolled on the ground. He ran off.

By the gods... what can become of us? Etta turned and caught up with the group.

"What was wrong with him, Etta?" Holden asked.

Etta had seen eyes like that before. *Faerie magics—stuff of the deep earth.* "I don't know, Holden," she said. She didn't want to talk about magics. "Lotta hard times have befallen folk. Hardship does strange things to us."

It was a rough road they followed, built a decade or more ago but not maintained. Someone had marched north with an army and hadn't come back. Etta could only guess wearily at who might have done it. *Sweyne.* The thought stung at her like bees. *Sweyne.* Always hovering, always piercing. *Still alive.*

"How much farther?" Swey whined. The boy was tired.

"A ways still yet." Tara looked at Etta like she might tell Tara differently, but the truth was Etta didn't know. Little Swey moaned, and the man called Calum, a traveller who hailed from the Isle of Scales, picked the boy up and threw him on the front of his saddle.

"View of the mountains is a bit better from up here, eh?" Calum winked at Etta. Etta tried to smile but her face only contorted into a crooked grimace, but Little Swey laughed from the horse and so Etta felt as though things were alright. This crew had kept looking to her for answers, and she had none to give. When Benn's fever had come five days on, Benn himself had turned to Etta for help.

"Lead them to the deathstealer," Benn had choked out in so many gasps one night from his cot as Etta washed his brow with cool water, and steam rose out of his skin like smoke from a smouldering coal. "You know the way. Please. I have no other choice but death."

Etta remembered a woman with a different name who had once been kihl'dor to thousands. She led that number and more to their deaths without glory and without remorse, and the lot of them cheered behind her as she led them into the fog that was war without even an ounce of fear. And that fearlessness spread like the bloody pox amongst those who followed. But Etta was not that woman, not anymore, and she had no desire to lead.

Still, thirteen twisted shadows stretched out beside that ragged crew on the old road like the crooked branches of long dead trees, and the black shape that was Etta was out in front.

An hour up the road, the crew came to a small hamlet—four sod-roofed cabins surrounding a blazing clanfire. The black plume rising up to the sky made Etta think of James. *He did that...* Etta had been thinking back to the wither year often, that's what folk had come to call it, and she didn't like what she saw there. Part of her wished the world *had* died. Everything was different now. Folks lost faith in the gods—they lost hope all together. The very air she breathed felt wrong—infected. As if the rot of the world came loose like a broken dam and flooded the souls of all alive. Her food was bland, the colours she saw were dull and putrid. Only Swey and Tara gave her warmth in the darkness.

"Where is everybody?" Swey held his hand to his brow and surveyed the area from atop Calum's horse. He had become quite the little wayfinder.

"I don't know." Etta looked around, wondering. To Holden, she said, "Go check the houses."

Holden blew snot out of one side of his nose and was off.

The young lad Aris pulled out his axe. Etta only had to shake her head, and Aris sheathed it again.

The blazing clanfire was crackling fiercely as Etta approached. The thick, black smoke stuck to the back of her throat and burned her nostrils. She hadn't seen a fire that big since—*oh gods.*

Shrill screams pierced the smoky air.

"They're in here." Holden was standing apprehensively outside of the house as the screams poured out from within.

Etta could now make out the black charcoal figure of the pyre and the person tied to it through the flames and smoke. They stood upright instead of lying down. That meant one thing in the north. *Sacrifice.*

"Get out. Go!" a deep voice bellowed, and Holden backed up a few steps. The door slammed shut behind him.

Etta couldn't take her gaze off of the pyre. Holden had tripped over something backing up and fell to the ground. The horses whinnied and nearly threw their riders off. The four holding Benn let the stretcher fall to the dirty snow as they stumbled. Swey was trying to get mixed up in it all, but Tara held him back. "No, Swey," she said, "run *from* trouble, not to it."

Etta didn't think the boy should have even come on this journey, but Tara insisted on him being there. She said it was no good for a boy to go without adventure. *When the arrows start flying, the adventure will really begin, eh?* Etta took a deep breath to calm herself. She supposed she did the same thing with Tarek and Braden. Taking them here and there as she and Sweyne traipsed through the north. *What do you know about being a mother? How can you judge any one?*

The folk of the hamlet gathered in their doorways and glared out at her with bloated eyes still stained with the residue of seen horrors, and Etta felt more than ever like she would vomit.

"What are you doing here?" A woman in hard leather stood by one of the houses. A sheep *baahed* from somewhere unseen.

"We're only passing through. We're in search of the deathstealer who lives near here. Our friend has a sickness," Tara said as Etta gagged. Her stomach had been betraying her much as of late. *Weak insides—torn up and broken.*

The woman let her eyes slip between the lot of them, saying nothing.

Etta glared at the woman. "Can you point us in the right direction?" She felt the need to fill the silence.

"There." The woman held a thick finger to the north. "But it's nearing dark. It's not a journey I'd make at night."

"We have horses to guide us," said Calum from his mount.

"Aye, but it's not the dark I'd fear for. It's the spirits that have been birthed here today. They will be on the loose."

Etta looked around at the hamlet. Each of the doors were shut and no light flickered in their windows. Only the crackling clanfire blazed on.

"What happened here?" Etta took a few steps closer to Swey, who was standing tight to his mom.

The woman in leather made no expression. "We did what we had to do. He couldn't stay here any longer."

"Who couldn't stay here?"

"Dallen. The earth was taking him. The faerie magics took his mind. He killed Yallia."

What? Etta remembered the man they saw on their way in. *By the Gods...* "What happened to him?"

"We sent him back to the earth. He couldn't stay here." The woman wrung her hands shakily.

"What do you mean back to the earth?" Etta felt a sting in her gut. *Magics...*

"We buried him. He was turning into... something. I don't know. The spell required sacrifice. Ren had gone mad when Yallia died, anyway. He was mad, anyway, you see? We'll be better for it. We'll all be better for it."

Etta thought of the naked man. *He was not buried. Not anymore. They buried him alive...*

The woman looked around nervously. Then at the blazing fire. "Everyone will be okay when the burning stops. It's the sight of it we can't bear. It will all be okay. It's been burning all night and all morning. It won't stop burning."

The crew had already started to move northward out of the hamlet. Only Etta remained, transfixed on the flames—on the life so recently extinguished. *Why is flesh so fickle?* She could see the pine tar stains around the outside of the pit. It would burn for hours more still if the pyre was lathered in tar.

"For life there must be death." The woman had tears in her eyes and held a distant stare. "We had to make the trade to ensure the earth took Dallen. We had to. Surely you understand." Etta understood full well. The world had turned its people mad when the fires went out. These were just more of its victims.

"Aye," Etta said. "Aye, I understand." *It's easier to believe the stories we tell ourselves than to face the fact they aren't true.* She lingered for a moment longer before leaving to catch up with the crew.

"What the fuck was that back there?" Holden said to Etta as she fell in beside him. *Answers. They're always looking to me for answers.*

"Just some folks doing what they believe to be right." Etta scratched at her burned hand. "Who are we to know different?"

Calum the traveller dismounted his horse. "I know whatever I saw back there was twisted."

"The world's gone twisted," said Etta. "So, do we set up camp or keep going?"

"I'll ride ahead," Calum said. "Scout the road so we know how long of a walk we can expect."

From the stretcher, Benn groaned as if to answer. Etta couldn't bear to see him in pain. The old man had saved her life twice in the short time they'd been together. He asked her for help, and by the gods she was going to do her best to help him.

"Then we camp. We could all use the extra rest." Etta knelt down to pick up a few loose sticks. "Let's get the fire going, eh?"

Soon the iron cookpot bubbled over the fire as Cullen, the cook, threw in chopped wild onions and garlic, and then a salted venison leg. "This," Cullen said, sniffing at the pot, "this will cure what ails us, lemme tell ya."

The smoke rose into the sky, grey and skinny, and as Cullen served the stew, Etta tried not to think of the charred figure she saw in the clanfire.

"**I**T'S HERE," HOLDEN SAID. The warrior had the loudest voice of the lot, and he loved nothing more than to use it. "The deathstealer is waiting."

Before them was a wooden hut on fowl-stilted legs. As Etta watched the purple fools' fire dance in the windows, she remembered carrying Braden to a similar hut once. *And the deathstealer saved him. This is not Shaqqa Ro. They are not all bad.* Etta still couldn't bring herself to look at the shaman when she became visible, standing on the balcony, waiting for them.

Calum the traveller spoke up. "When I came here yesterday to tell her of our arrival, she was standing there in the same way." He twiddled his fingers, and Etta saw the sweat on the back of his neck. "She just stands there all the time, I reckon, waiting for something."

"Or someone." Etta deflected Calum's anxious gaze.

The hut sat in the throat of two hoary old pines, whose branches hung like drapes over the shaman's abode. The rocky hills behind swelled into mountains, crowned with a golden sun that melted into blue sky. The reek of mouldering loam rose out of the ground like humid air. Dirty slush piles clung to the trunks of trees.

"It's warmer here." Swey held his arms out, basking in the air.

"A hotspring," Etta said, sniffing the air. "It's sulphurous."

Then, a voice from above: "There need only be one other." The shaman cried out to them from her balcony. "The rest will sleep down there—make camp."

The whole crew looked to Etta at once.

The shaman clacked her long yellow nails on the worn wooden railing. She clicked her dirty, brown tongue and glared at Etta with sorcerous eyes. *The magics are strong in this one. She will heal him.*

"Help me get him on my shoulders," Etta said.

"Surely she'll allow us to carry him up," Aris said. Etta could see the lad was eager to have a part in this.

"When a shaman says a thing, they mean a thing." Etta removed her heavy fur and handed it to Tara. "She'll only allow one of us."

Aris sighed, but the lad easily unstrapped Benn from the stretcher, and with the help of Cullen, they lifted Benn onto Etta's shoulders. She climbed the steep, rattail-shaped stairs one at a time. Before reaching the top, Etta glanced back at her crew. Calum was already stretching out canvas and pulling out a hammer and pegs to make their tent, and Cullen had pulled out his butcher knife and chopping block and begun slicing strips of smoked hare and dicing the wild carrots he had stooped to gather along their travels. Tara had got a fire going and sent Swey, Young Courtney, and Aris to the river with buckets for water.

The shaman greeted Etta with a warm smile and a touch that lingered far too long.

"Come in. Yes, hurry." The shaman quickly shut the wicker door behind them, and Etta was hit with a wave of incense. Herbs hung from the ceiling like so many green bats. Chicory and fresco. Mint and ginseng. Lavender and rosemary and thyme and burgess. Tyne of lily and wisp of etta and blue leaves of ander. Harrisene and pically and hollygreen. The smells assaulted Etta's nose. "What ails this one?" Etta heard a voice but she could only remember the smells. Her mom had picked these herbs. She lived with these herbs her whole childhood. *In young Etta's world—a world that was so safe.* "Eh?" said the deathstealer. "Never mind, put him down."

Etta let Benn slide off her back to the wicker cot lined with birch bark. He was pale white, almost blue, and his nose was crusted with yellow-green snot that had leaked into his beard. His chest rattled with every breath.

"He's come down with a sickness." Etta knelt beside him and became aware of the sour smell of him. *He's gone unwashed for weeks.* "He doesn't breathe well. He's been in and out of wakefulness." Etta brushed the hair off his forehead. Her hands were dirty and cracked. *So have you...*

Just then Benn stirred awake as if Etta spoke words of sorcery.

"What... where am I?" Benn groaned. His eyes found Etta, and he desperately reached for her. "Where?"

"It's okay, now, Benn. It will be okay." Etta held his thick, clammy hand.

"Help," Benn rattled, and closed his eyes slowly. He squeezed Etta's hand, and she held onto it like it was the only thing she could do—because it was. "Water."

"Get him water!" Etta spoke loudly.

The shaman produced a piece of bark with water pooled in it and held it bowl-like in her hands. Then she dumped the water down Benn's throat. She opened jars big and small and took from some but only sniffed at others, and mixed all that she had gathered in a stone mortar and ground it down with her pestle, and each movement was precise.

She gave Benn more water. She picked herbs and ground them between her hands and rubbed them on Benn's skin and in his hair. She soaked a rag in a black iron cauldron hanging next to the fire, and she used it to wipe clean his nose and his beard. She sang, and Etta felt the song move inside of her and come alive like an animal or an insect fluttering, and soon the shaman began to dance and stomp her feet in rhythm with the song. Purple flame flickered, and the deathstealer sang notes older than trees as the sun fell behind the mountains, and the wolves picked up the chorus along with the crickets.

Etta felt the stars above moving with the moon, and the shaman sang as she picked things from jars and put them in Benn's mouth. She stripped him naked and washed him down and stood over him as she sang, and covered his chest with something that burned Etta's eyes like mint and vinegar. The shaman covered Benn's nose in it and his ears, and she sang and Etta found that she could not sleep. The deathstealer put the cauldron over the fire and let the steam fill the hut. Moisture dripped from the ceilings and sucked dirt off the walls as the hut sweated.

"Breathe, you fool!" the shaman cursed at Benn, and even chanted it. The chant accompanied the sun rising, and when Benn groaned and sat up, Etta saw life in his eyes that wasn't there the night previous. "Two more nights," the shaman whispered.

Etta looked at the wicker door.

The shaman shook her head. "You leave together or not at all."

The deathstealer worked at making various medicines through the day, and as the sun set that night, she covered Benn in the medicines and sat by her purple fires and spoke.

"The Old Gods are dying, you know?" The shaman threw white powder on the fire, and the flame changed to blue. "They are being killed. The gods war with each other for no end. New gods, old." The shaman rolled four human toe bones carved with runes and studied the way they landed. Etta leaned in, always curious by a reading of the runes, and felt a pit open in her stomach when the shaman shuddered and scooped the runes up with disgust.

"What did you see?" Etta couldn't help but ask.

The shaman's eyes were of the deepest green—almost black—and they pierced into Etta in a way that reminded her of drowning. How they took her breath away. "It's the same thing I've been seeing since the fires came back. I see the sky falling."

Etta woke with the sun on the third morning, and Benn woke soon after to cough chunks of yellow phlegm into a bucket beside his cot. The shaman walloped his back with the sole of an old, raggedy boot and laughed like a madwoman, then seemed to talk to the phlegm. "Out of it. Go now, git. Come on!"

After many hours of lying in steam and clearing his lungs, Benn sat up in his bed and Etta moved beside him and rubbed his back.

"I can damn well breathe again," the old man smiled, and coughed.

The shaman left the hut with the chamber pots for many hours, and when she came back, she held a defeathered duck by the neck in one hand and the empty chamber pots in the other. She butchered the duck and cleaned it with water from the cauldron, then cooked the breasts and cut the rest into strips that she hung over the fire on an iron grate. The shaman put wet rushes on the fire and smoked the meat, and Benn began to cough. The shaman poked at the fire to dwell the smoke and then pulled bushels of herbs down and one by one tossed them in the fire. The smoke filled the cabin, and Etta's eyes grew heavy.

"Breathe, haha, breathe it." The shaman danced over to an array of bottles and selected three of them. She unplugged their wax stoppers and dumped the bottles onto the fire, and the smell was like sweet honey and balsam needles. "Breathe!"

That night as Benn slept, the shaman spoke into her flames, either to Etta or to the fire she didn't know, but Etta listened anyway.

"The Old Gods have been killed," the deathstealer whispered. "Yes, but the prophet lives. The Reaper walks amongst us, and the gods live within him. It will be him that does it, then? Him or the woman? Both."

The Reaper?

"Who is the Reaper?" Etta seemed to snap the shaman out of a trance.

"What?"

"The Reaper. What do you mean?"

The shaman smiled. "The prophet of the dead. He lives. What that means for us the runes have yet to tell me. He will either save us or bury us."

James. Etta dared not speak his name to let on that she knew this Reaper. Deathstealers are wary of omens. But Etta had dreamed of James of late, too. She couldn't escape the guilt she felt. *You knew... the wizard told you he was...* Etta couldn't forget her visit with the soothsayers either. *They told you he and Maggie were godkillers. They told you to get rid of them...*

The shaman left the hut with buckets and returned with fresh water. She made a sweet tea of bramble leaves and mint with stevval leaves and corium, and before long, Etta was waking up to the sunrise and the sound of the deathstealer chanting. Benn was sitting on the bed, taking deep breaths, holding his face over a bowl of something steaming and pungent.

"You smell that? What do you smell, tell me?" The shaman pulled one of Benn's ears and looked inside.

"I smell nettle and dandelions." Benn flinched as the shaman tugged his ear harder.

"Yes. Good, and what smell is lacking?"

Benn inhaled deeply.

"Thyme?"

"No, no. Your sickness has passed and so the smell of death has passed. There is no smell of death." The shaman opened the latch on a window shutter and pushed it open to let the pink light of morning spill in. Suddenly, the shaman's face sank, and she held her hand to her mouth.

"What is it?' Etta looked past the shaman to the red sun that streaked the sky like blood.

"Nothing. You must go." The deathstealer rushed past Etta. In a dark corner of the room, the shaman crouched and rolled her runes. Etta couldn't stop herself from standing over the deathstealer and looking at how the runes landed, though they meant nothing to her. The shaman shook her head and quickly scooped the runes into a hempen pouch.

"What is it?" Etta couldn't stop herself from asking. Benn was standing beside her now, too, mouth wide open. The shaman looked out the window again, and Etta followed her gaze. The sun was a gaping red wound in the sky.

"The world, lass, it bleeds." The deathstealer flicked her hand at Etta. "Go." The deathstealer's face turned sour. "Get out. Go now. My work is done." She stabbed Benn with her eyes. "Your sickness is defeated, now go!"

Benn scrambled to his feet. Glass jars and stone mortars fell to the ground in his wake. "What do I owe you?" he choked out as he picked up the fallen equipment.

"Owe me?" The deathstealer scowled. "If I wanted a damn thing from you, I would have taken it while you slept. Owe me? You know nothing of the world."

Benn backed up, turned and left, and Etta followed him, stumbling out of the wicker door. Dried herbs crumbled in Etta's hair and all around them. She started sneezing.

The fresh morning air hit Etta like a plunge in the river on a hot day, she breathed it in; behind them, the deathstealer slammed the wicker door shut. From behind the thin wall, Etta could hear strange songs being cooed.

Below, the crew eyed them wearily.

As Etta approached their camp, she saw only sullen faces and startled eyes.

"We can't linger," said Calum. "Folks are being slaughtered in these mountains."

"Slaughtered?" Etta didn't understand. Tara held Swey close to her chest. Holden clutched his axe in hand. Aris and Young Courtney sat huddled by the fire with their arms wrapped around their knees.

"We heard it last night and the night before. Somehow they missed us. Maybe they avoided the deathstealer on purpose. But folk are being killed."

"What?" Etta found herself reaching to her belt for an axe that wasn't there.

"It's not the killing that worries us, there's always death in the Fells," said Holden. "It's who's doing it that got our tails up."

With a severed human arm in one hand, Calum stepped forth into the fire light. The arm was charred and crisp brown. Calum held the arm high over the fire so all could see. Etta thought she saw bite marks in it. Calum took a deep breath and sighed. "Cannibals."

THE DEEP PLACES

BLOOD ON ITS OWN had never made Halda hurt before, but the screams of her people were enough to turn her bones into flaming coals. Screaming was just pain leaving the body, her Aunt Thora had said, and blood was life draining from it. Life, like pain, is temporary.

Halda's hands were shaking with adrenaline. The thrill of the sacrifice was still with her. The darkness of it stained her, and as she gazed out to the blood-streaked sea, she could feel the voice of Offa riveting through her. *It is coming...*

Halda rushed below decks to ease her bones and escape the screams. She tried not to slip where blood had soaked the wooden steps. *Goddess Mother, Offa, please stop screaming. Please accept our sacrifice.* Halda might have whispered a prayer to the stars, but she knew it would take the gods time to recognize her sacrifice—three hundred gutted on the stake and bled into the sea. Enough to wake the Blood God's monsters from their slumber and cause a storm eye to brew in the sea. *Enough to signal Offa we have come—we have heard Her. Enough to receive more answers. It has to be...*

Halda had waited many long years for the Dead God, Offa, to appear in her runes and in her fires. When the fires went out last year, Halda thought she had lost Offa forever, but she was wrong. And Halda would not fail Her now that She had finally come back.

And now that blood was in the water and screams were in the air, the krakens would come. *They're on their way up from the deep places now, and when they rise, the Children of Daggland will truly rule the seas, just as they once had in the days of Sig Arfa. This is Ox'olin. This is the end.*

It was only six weeks past since Halda saw in her runes what she had only ever read in old grimoires. The Comet of Thungstenn Ton and the pale blade and skull. Halda knew what that meant. *Aunt Thora taught you that much, at least...* The comet had meant the sky was going to fall, and the Earth Mother, Offa, would rise up to meet it. The seas of the Blood God will drain as the Earth Mother fills her veins with it once more. The pale blade and skull meant the Reaper had risen from the Otherworld. He had brought with him the fires and rain. He brought with him the winds. And he would bring with him the death of the world. *Godkiller,* they called him in the old rune tongue. He let a darkness into the Otherworld that can never be reversed. But if Offa would rise, then Daggland must rise, too.

"Bring them all to Whale Rock." Halda had told Rakkar Hegglund of Ash River "You are the only one I can trust to do it."

"Whale Rock?" Hegglund gasped. "Is it really time? Is it really happening?"

Halda had touched the old rakkar's hand. He had been through much in losing his sons and daughters during that wither year, and she knew this would nearly break him. "It is happening, Hegglund. It is happening, but we are ready," Halda had said, and Hegglund nodded. He and his rakkarren set sail down the Ash River and into the Black Strait. Halda never saw him again.

Halda set sail towards Farrock Bay with her own rakkarren, Harald, son of Bannen, at the helm. It took every bit of energy she had in convincing Harald to disembark.

"You haven't been here," he had said. And Halda couldn't even argue. She had neglected her rakkarren more than any ruler had the right to. They were her own small army, a full ship of trained pirates and warriors waiting for adventure, and she kept them docked at Massey Bay while she sat in her rock and watched fires for years on end. *For Offa—it's for Offa, the Dead God,* she told herself. And she was right. *Weren't you?* The end was coming, and she had learned of it before any other. It was a prophecy written in the sagas, and it was becoming truth—reality. All of Daggland must rise. All of Daggland must sail.

Three weeks later, twenty-seven rulers and all of their people arrived on the coast of Farrock Bay, at the jagged cove island known as Whale Rock. Halda still didn't see Hegglund there. *He at least spread the word before he abandoned you.*

The rakkars of Daggland lit candles and made sacrifices and held feasts for seven days as they debated leaving. Then, the winds returned and the fires burned, and as the clouds grew ripe with rain, all knew that Halda, dawter of Hemon and Harla, the Knower of the Witch Den, had seen it true. Her runes had told her of the end and the end would come.

But the Reaper offered redemption, and Halda urged the rulers of Daggland to breed hope and not fear. Sorrow would not fuel the Earth Mother, they must keep hope and heed the Reaper's call. These were the times that would be written into history. The dead rulers of Daggland had risen to fight with this Reaper, and so shall the living. The Dead God would be fed. *We will calm you. We will make it right. You are the Dead God no longer. You will live once more.*

Halda could make anyone listen to her words when she needed to. But Halda wanted the power the Reaper could give her—the power to communicate with gods more freely. She wanted to water the land with blood and feed the Dead God's desire. And when the Dead God rose, all of

Daggland would fight with the Reaper at their side. But she knew she must hurry. The krakens were coming, and the shores of Ardura were in sight.

Halda squeaked open her cabin door and entered the small dark room. She lit a lumpy tallow candle with her flint and found her wares. In the orange, glowing light, she held her knucklebone runes and rattled them in her hands. Gently, she rolled them into a wooden dish. She watched desperately for the sign she hoped to see. But still, the runes would not reveal their secrets to her. *How many more must I sacrifice?* She prayed for the answer, but the answer was never delivered to her. Offa screamed all night beneath the weight of the moon. *More.* Offa called to her. *More and more.* Only blood can soothe the coldness of the Dead God's prison. Only blood can soothe loneliness.

Halda could use her words for anything. When she spoke, folk listened. She was of the old blood of Sig Arfa, and she had magics on her tongue. All knew this. She was a niece to Thora Witchheart—the Knower. So when she stood in front of all of Daggland at Farrock Bay and gathered all of the folk too old to fight onto the ships, none argued or fought against her. When she sacrificed those same folk and loosed their lifeblood into the Sea of Stars to feed the Blood God, the others onboard chanted and prayed alongside her. *They gave their blood willingly to the sea for such a cause. They are braver than I'll ever be.*

The screams from above deck slowly faded as the elder men and women bled out. She could feel the darkness, hear the corruption in the water lapping against the hull of the galley. It was a dark spell to penetrate the deep places; it was an even darker one to wake the obsidian beasts that lurk there. The krakens rule the seas, and Daggland rules the krakens.

Halda rolled her runes one more time. The knucklebones clicked and rattled in the wooden dish. When they came to a stop, Halda nearly flipped the dish.

"Fuck!" She scooped up the runes and put them away in her neat leather pouch with the yellow lace that she had dyed herself with dandelion paste.

No answers. Again, no answers... She put the lace around her neck, and let the pouch rest at her chest. *Where it's safe.*

She hurried back up to the deck. The answers would soon reveal themselves. *Be patient. This is a new age for us. A new age for you.* The runes had gotten her this far, and she had to trust that they would show her more. *Get to the Reaper. I know that much. Get to the Reaper and then?* The runes refused to show her.

The sky was black and starless, and Halda's breath smoked against the dark. The deck was slick and sticky with blood. Halda found her captain Harald leaning over the bulwark, watching the trail of blood streak the water behind them like crimson oil.

"They are waking," Halda said proudly. "I feel them."

"And so is Daggland," Harald said, and held his chin high. "It's been many years since I've felt so alive. Not since Kari was still with me."

"Kari would be proud to see it," Halda said, looking out to the dark sea, lit by moonlight and blood. In the waters around them sailed the armadas of countless rakkars, big and small. Thrice times thirty Daggland galleys filled with blooded killers ripped through the waves, sails fat and full with cold wind. Rakkar Erik of Smokestone, Rakkar Sara of Farrock, Rakkar Gunnar of Oldstone, Rakkar Toren of Morden Vale. And countless other rakkars from smaller lands and islands. All of Daggland had sailed. Ten thousand hardened reavers. All of Daggland had risen. All of them knew the prophecy of Ox'olin. The Dead God would rise.

Thick blood poured off each stern in a steady stream. The flag of Massey Rock, a black kraken on a sea of blue, waved above while ruddy oarsmen sweated below. It was the first time since Sig Arfa that Daggland sailed beneath one flag, and they sailed beneath that same flag now. *Sig Arfa's kraken.* Halda reckoned things were just about as they should be. Their hulls were bloated with smoked hams and bacon, pickled herrings and salt cod, so much salt cod, and applesauce and mead.

"Land-ho!" shouts from the folk in the crow's nest echoed. They were in Ardura. Halda looked to the stars and the moon. They would reach the Standing Stones known as Grave by Springtide.

Her runes had not lied. *They couldn't. Offa wouldn't...*

The Daggs made port without worry of a bay. Off the Isle of Darra, they sailed into the channel, which the Daggs called Deadvoice Channel, for the wind that whistled there was believed to be old dead Dagglandic mariners singing. Halda barked an order, and the message spread like fire.

Each of the oarsfolk withdrew their paddles, and through the oar-holes came thick beams of wood. *Daggland spruce, and nothing less would suffice.* The crew worked frantically upon the deck, hooting to each other and shouting orders down a chain like ants. They worked in near perfect tandem to lower large wooden buoys, which looked like arms of some great wooden god, over the side of the ship, lengthwise. Others attached the arms widthwise to the many wooden beams that stuck out of the oar-holes by swinging them into place so that the beams penetrated the grooved holes of the arm. The ship had transformed into a massive winged beast that stood as sturdy as a mountain upon the waves of the Old Sea.

Once the ship was steady, Halda watched the smaller boats lower from the decks and make berth. She smiled as the crew loaded each boat to the throat full of supplies. *We could make war for ten years with all of this food.*

The mariners loaded hundreds of barrels full of fermenting barley malt and goat milk and pine syrup. Kegs of smoked sprat and spiced herring and candied tadpoles. They loaded hundreds of planks, six feet long and half as wide, with salted cod and haddock and whitefish and sturgeon. They loaded chests full of smoked frog's legs and pike and trout's eggs, all wrapped and separated by parchment. There were jars of honey beyond count. *We are Daggland, our bees buzz mightier and shit sweeter than anywhere in the world.* Barrels of fermenting honeycomb and kegs of new and aged mead. The Daggland warriors filled their small boats and paddled out towards shore, bay or no bay. Once berthed, the long oar-boats lowered their arms much the same as the massive ones attached to the ships. *The waves couldn't bring us down if they were ten feet tall,* Halda thought. Somewhere, many thousands of feet below, the krakens would soon catch hold of the smell of blood. *That much blood could wake all of them.*

Harald came up from below. His feet creaked on the wooden deck.

"We'll stay moored for as long as it takes to see the chosen folk get to shore." Harald gripped the bulwark like it was alive and he was wringing its neck. "The rest of us will remain with the ships and harrow the coasts."

"This is Ox'olin—*the end*," Halda said, "Don't forget our message. Remain strong here."

"You think I could forget our message?" Harald snapped. His brow was covered in sweat. *This scares him. He is terrified of what we've done—what he has to do.* Halda smiled. *But he will do it. Oh yes, he will. That is the root of his anger. He hears the Dead God screaming just like the rest of us. And there was no denying the fires were dead.* "You're gone," said Harald. "You're always gone, and it's just us here on *Red Morning.* It will be no different now. But I will serve because I have made oaths to do so."

Halda bit her lip. She deserved that. She had been no rakkar. *You're a witch, you have always fancied yourself as your Aunt Thora, Witchheart... A Knower.* Halda had left most things behind in exchange for her fires and runes. *Olrick...* She had loved once—still did if she was honest—and she had let it go. *Let it die so the Watch Fire would not.* Olrick wanted sons, daughters. Olrick wanted more than the oar, more than the hoe, he wanted a life bursting with love. Halda couldn't give it to him—wouldn't give it to him—and he found it elsewhere. She thought of him often on those dark, wet nights in the Witch Den. He would have made those nights warmer. She thought of the kids that never were. They would have made the darkness brighter. But she never let her thoughts linger long. There was no point in stabbing her soul with her own razor-sharp thoughts.

Harald raised his chin. *He's proud you have nothing to say to that. He knows it stung you. He knows he's right. You are no rakkar.*

Halda watched as the Dagglandic warriors leaked out from the armada on hundreds upon hundreds of smaller boats, like a colony of god-crazed bees seeking blood in place of nectar.

"The Dead God will not forgive the dismissal of Her word," Halda stated. *He needs to be reminded that I have no choice. The runes do not lie.*

"We will not dismiss it, then. You really think you can find the Reaper? They call him a Half-God. A World Walker." Harald's eyes were drunk with battle lust. He dreamed of raiding southern castles like Sig Arfa and having brown-skinned southern babies, and those dreams were enough to help him choke down his fear. *Daggland will live in paradise in the last days before Ox'olin; we will all have whatever our dreams can conjure, so long as our hearts pump warm blood. We will have it all.*

"I know I can," Halda lied. "I have seen it true. The Reaper waits for me." Her hand fell to the leather pouch that hung from her neck where her runes lived. The runes had not told her where to find the Reaper or what to do if she did. They had told her little, but it was enough for her to discern. *They will only ever show you just enough. The Standing Stones of Grave. Springtide. The Reaper. It was enough.*

The end was coming, and of that Halda had no doubt. She had used the flames and the stars to ask other types of questions and got many different kinds of answers, and with those answers and her readings of the runes, she could tell a great deal of things. *But sometimes you're wrong.* She ignored herself. Daggland needed a good prophet to keep them strong during these times of crisis, and she had no choice but to be that person. *But you're not your Aunt Thora. No. Not even Thora is herself anymore. The fires drove her mad...*

"You should go, Daggland works fast. The warriors will be ready to march come sunrise," Harald said.

"Aye." Halda smiled out to the blood-stained sea. "They are eager to please the Dead God. They are as scared as you and I."

Winter's End

"I T'S DYING," JAMES WHISPERED.

"Light another one," Mineera answered.

James lit up the second torch as the first one started to fade. He had misjudged the distance to the rune door. The Maw God had been plaguing him, and the thought of meandering in the darkness bit into him. James felt like he hadn't slept more than a couple of hours at a time since he'd killed the Mother of Nature. And now he was hearing voices from below, muttering in strange, babbling tongues that made his spine freeze. He couldn't bring himself to walk down there alone after last time. *I have to leave this place. Mineera will think you a damn fool, but let her. Something's not right here.*

James held the torch up to his face. "If we don't turn back, we will have to return some of the way in the darkness. I don't know my way without the light."

Mineera held up a piece of parchment with a maze of lines cut into it. "I've been mapping the way. I can feel the way back even in the dark."

James hadn't noticed Mineera writing with a needle, stabbing into a parchment and marking their way with small dots.

"Let's go." Mineera twirled the knife in her hand. "I need to see this door."

I do too, but I'm afraid of what it means. James nodded. Since he had opened the Gateway to the Otherworld and brought back the elements, he had been haunted by his dreams. Ellorin's memories still latched onto his own, and he found himself having strange visions of things he had never done. Rune doors and rituals and dark Words whispered.

"*Help us.*" Dead voices called out to him from the black as he went deeper. James didn't have to watch Mineera's face to know she hadn't heard the whispers. *Only you. These are whispers of the long dead... this is your curse and no one else's.* Brushing his fingertips along the smooth surface of the tunnels, he walked in the shallow, red glow of torchlight and followed the voices. *How many have died down here?*

The depths of Kallahorn were a cobweb of tunnels. They wound through the dark, black rock of the Mountains of the Mother and opened up into dozens upon dozens of massive caverns with vaulted ceilings that stretched up until they disappeared in darkness. Small bones and old, dusty clumps of petrified debris cracked and snapped beneath his feet as he walked. Small animals scurried off into unseen corners and disappeared. And the scratch of Mineera's needle to parchment echoed like a ripping wind in those dank halls. *You could get lost down here forever.* And James thought that not all the bones he treaded upon were animal.

The torchlight flickered and nearly went out as James slowly climbed down a steep staircase.

"It was deep down," James whispered.

"The door?" Mineera leaned her head closer to James's face.

"Yes. It's far below."

"It would need to be."

"Why?"

"Protection from above." Mineera poked another hole into her parchment. James didn't even want to ask any more about what she meant.

The stairs went down and down, and the cold stone seeped must and hoary dust. The veiled voices of the dead echoed off the narrow walls and buzzed around in James's head like dying flies.

"*You cannot do this,*" a snarl from the cracks. "*Your curse will eat you in the end...*" James batted his eyelids and shook his head.

"You alright?" Mineera gazed at him curiously.

"Aye." *How many died down here...* James glared at Mineera, at the fading torchlight. *She doesn't hear them. She doesn't know. Oceans of them. Lifeless oceans.*

The smell of the Maw was like dead leaves and wet fur, and it bit into James's nose and made his eyes water. When the ground levelled out and James felt a large expanse open up around him, he knew *it* was there. Somewhere in the darkness. The Lupin. The Outcast. The Maw. Thrice gifted and thrice cursed. It had been watching him. A ghost of a god.

Still running his hand along the wall, James kept forward.

"*The gods are dying, seer. What does that mean for you?*" The Maw's voice burned his ears like hot water. James jerked his head like he was trying to shake something loose. Mineera stared at him. Her eyes held more worry than curiosity now.

They kept on. The Maw slinked on behind him, the ghost of a beast long misunderstood.

"*You'll only mess this up more than you already have.*" The Maw showed James its twisted, bleeding snout and its wicked, yellow teeth as it spoke. "*Leave this place. You don't have what's necessary.*"

It was only twenty steps until James's hand ran across the smooth indentations of the first rune door. He held the torch up to it, and his eyes widened. He let them soak in the strange beauty of it. Tracing his fingers along the runes gave him an odd sensation that made it feel wrong somehow. If he kept on down the hall, he would find hundreds of doors like this one. As sure as he was of the tunnel up to this point, he wasn't confident to go any further. The voices were echoing from the dark. They were deeper. *And the Maw is not alone. How many gods are dead? Who killed them? Adeqor...* He couldn't stop himself from thinking about it. *Adeqor killed them... you let that monster in the Otherworld, and he is wreaking havoc. You were warned of this. You were warned...*

"*Come deeper. You don't need the light,*" the voices said as if they were in his head, listening. Suddenly James felt the urge to grab *Essikah.* "*Stay with us.*"

"Did you see enough yet?" James said.

Mineera was tracing the symbols she saw on the door onto a fresh piece of parchment. "Almost. Another minute."

The shadows in the tunnel beyond James's sight seemed to pull at him. *Come further.* They said, *help us.* He gripped the torch tighter when he realized he was about to drop it. James turned and traced his hand along the rune door once more.

"Does it mean something to you?" Mineera asked.

"To me?" James was surprised by the question. He should be asking *her* what it meant. James figured this meant she didn't know either.

"The door. The runes. Is there something in your cycles?" Mineera held the torch up to the rounded door. White with green runes. Preserved by thousands of years of darkness.

"The cycles speak of the Starfall," James said, "but they speak nothing of this... *place.* In their refuge in the mountains, the Feldarra rescued what Mal lived through the Starfall. Perhaps this..."

"Ah," Mineera said. "Yes, that is the story I've heard too. But I don't think the Feldarra could have done this."

"Can we go?" James said.

"Nothing more to see here, not yet," Mineera said.

Not ten minutes later, the torch light died and the darkness swallowed James. The voices attacked.

"Are you alright?" Mineera guided him up and up the stairs with her needle map.

"Aye," James said. "Don't like the dark."

"Stay close," Mineera said.

The stairs wound up and up like a cooper's bore of stone. The twisted stairs carried them, wanderers from the darkness, back into the light. The voices of the dead sang to James the myths of lifeless gods and blood magics. Songs of Sorcerers and sky fall. Their cries cut like swords and burned his mind like hot coals. His ears leaked blood that wasn't there, and James bore the burden of all of it like a crown—the King of the Dead, the Reaper. And Mineera guided him out of the darkness. The scholar stood on the same precipice as gods with her understanding of the world, and James followed her blindly, his only defence against the voices.

"Stay close," Mineera said again.

"Aye," said James.

And she led him up and out. *Without her, I would have been lost down there. Lost to madness... the dead will pull you down...*

James closed his eyes and breathed in the day as he and Mineera emerged into the lower halls of Kallahorn, where the sun lit up the cold stone with long golden beams piercing through the tall windows. Small fires burned between small huddles of people in the courtyards, and the halls were filled with their smoke. James felt a hand on his back.

"You don't have to keep going down there," Mineera said. "I can find the way on my own now."

James took another deep breath and opened his eyes. "It's not a choice. Something waits for me down there."

Mineera opened her mouth to say something and then stopped. She studied James curiously before walking away. *She thinks you're a bloody monster. She's not wrong, is she? Prove her wrong...*

The people watched James as he walked through the courtyards. They watched him like a dog guarding food scraps, and their gazes cut into him like cold. He had pushed himself farther than he ever thought possible, and still most folk didn't see the King of the Hallow, they saw the prophet of the dead—the one who talks to ghosts. Some folk had started calling him *Reaper* behind his back. *Godkiller,* he heard them say it. If he hadn't heard it from the people's mouths, Eurick would have told him. The raven somehow knew everything that was happening around the castle at all times.

James treaded through the mud in front of the stables and turned to go pet the horses, and then one in particular.

"Hey, buddy. Sweet boy." James rubbed Bren's muzzle and patted his withers. James had found his old horse drinking water from a stream in the sparse arbors around Kallahorn while hunting this winter. He almost couldn't believe it when Bren came trotting over to him.

"Naaay," Bren whinnied. *"Buh huhuhuhuh."* Bren leapt up and down.

"Easy there, boy," James laughed. The other horses were riled. The Mal had amassed hundreds of them from the scattered Ayelish army. They lived amongst the filth of so many horses and people together, and they were happy for it. With the horses, they could get away.

The horses nuzzled James, and he tried to give each one of them love. Bren snorted, grunted, nickered.

"Hey, man," a voice from behind. Then James felt hands on his shoulders. "Man, what are you doing here?" Eurick was catching his breath. "The lords have gathered. They're waiting for you."

"Where are they?"

"Throne room." Eurick put his hands on his knees, puffing. "You go, man. I've got mead to drink, anyway."

Claydon and Brinley have hardly left that throne room all winter.

James walked towards the King's Tower, the massive steep-roofed hall that pondered over the central courtyard of Kallahorn with drooping windows for eyes. The glass was stained in shades of blue and green and yellow, and two spiralling black stone spires grew like fungus on the front corners. Kelson the Conqueror had built this hall into the spires that previously stood here. Mineera had told James that she believed the walls and spires of Kallahorn were here long before the Starfall. Whoever built them vanished without a trace. This monstrosity was all they left. *And who built the tunnels below? Was it them, too?*

James ignored the gaze of a small child who sat alone, holding a bunched-up woollen tunic in his arms. There were hundreds of orphaned children clinging to the cracks and alleyways of Kallahorn. If James acknowledged all of them, the weight of his own uselessness would be enough to crush him dead.

He could do nothing but watch as the Hallow folk's food stores depleted, and the rulers argued about whose land to take back first when the snows ceased. *You're supposed to lead these people. They're looking to you for hope.* James thought of Wulfee. She could instill hope in the worst of times. He thought of his dad, and how he could instill a passion to fight. *Are you going to be your dad's son? Or are you going to let this beat you?*

James could do nothing but watch as everything slowly crumbled. He hadn't slept in months—his nights were full of taunting voices from Ellorin and the Maw and long wanderings with his spiralling thoughts about Adeqor. And the sleep he did get was filled with nightmares. The only bright spot in his infinite darkness lay beside him each night—Maggie. She was the reason he went on.

James climbed the stairs to the large wooden doors of the hall. The oakwood doors were carved with Lovasi runes and words and treated with old Yehvenki magics of unbreaking. Kelson had gained ultimate knowledge of the known world and used it to build his own majestic fortress on top of Kallahorn. A menagerie of stone works and glass and twisted metal. *What did Kelson know about the runes below? What about this place drove him mad?* James figured the answers were ones he didn't care to know. *But you need to know, don't you? The Maw won't ever let you forget.*

James turned around, and the courtyard stretched out before him. The cold, white snow had completely crusted the black stone of Kallahorn, and the yellow-gold sun made it shine like diamonds. Cold winds blew in the window holes from the mountains, and sheets of snow drifted and piled in corners and against walls. The sun marked the ice-crusted calendar dial at the twenty-fourth Wayk of winter. Springtide was only two moons away. They would need to leave this place soon, or they would all die here. If Ayeland attacked, they would be sieged in and starved out in mere months. *That and the bloody place is full to the arse with ill omens and ghosts...*

The rulers of Mal Hallow sat around the rounded trestle table next to the gaping firepit in Kallahorn's throne room, and James took a seat with them.

To James's left sat Maggie, draped in white bear furs. All of the rulers were adorned in jewellery they had found in Kallahorn's vault and then split amongst themselves. Gold torcs and rings and silver earrings and Daggland steel knives. Sorcerer's armbands and bracelets.

"Let's go get those bastards." Brinley slammed a ruby-ringed fist on the table. "We cannot linger here any longer. The new year is already a moon-cycle gone, and still, we sit here in this wretched place as our food dwindles. I want my lands back. Sessely and I need to bury our daughter's bones!"

"None of us want to linger, but we need to stay organized!" James stood tall. "We've only enough food to provision one march, and if we try to move before the snows break, we will all die out there. We need to have folk worrying about finding good farmland and sowing crops. We need to have folk looking for survivors in the north and uniting all we can. We can't split up and go off to fight different wars. If we do that, the Hallow will die out by Springtide."

James had been taking advice all winter and trying to decide which was good and which wasn't. He hated words, and now he was forced to say so many. *Why a king, dad? Why couldn't you have been a quiet smith?*

Everyone had a different opinion, and when it came down to making a decision, James needed to make the one that would save the most lives. *That's what Wulfee would do. That's what your dad would do.* The snow fell, a ghostly curtain draping the sky, and it kept falling.

"We can attack Rosen from the frozen river. The ice breaks along the river bed will allow us good cover. From there, the rest of Mal Hallow is ours," Ruwen said. "Our folk are hungry enough to take it."

"The Ayelish will have surely spoiled the food stores there. If we march all the way to Rosen and the granaries are empty, we will all die," James said.

"We need the favour of the stars," Claydon said. "We should march to the Standing Stones and not turn our back on the Springtide ceremony of our ancestors."

"Sacrifice?" Ruwen seemed disgusted.

"Aye." Claydon stood tall.

"We've sacrificed enough." Brinley slammed his fist on the table again. "I won't stand for it."

James could only look out at the white sheet drifting down from the clouds. He saw Adeqor's face in it, laughing.

"No sacrifice," James said. He didn't know how to fight wars—he never learned that from Bren—he paid no attention. His dad told James to fight, and he fought. If he put too much thought into why, it would break him. *Why is he making me kill...* James despised the art of war.

The rulers were silent. Just then the door burst open, and Eridan staggered in.

"Is it not time for breakfast?" Eridan hiccuped. Brinley's face went red.

"We're discussing war, you child," the dragon slayer spat the words. He clutched at the dragon-tooth necklace around his neck, as if to offload his rage into it.

"We need to fight for our lands," Ruwen spoke calmly. "Rosen will have stores enough for us to feed the army. They were stocked to the brim when we left at the start of last winter. It would take a larger force to drain them than any petty rulers that would have survived breaking off from the Wolf. And even if the granaries are spoiled, our farm lands are plenty and far, and we could have a good crop this year. We can feed all the Hallow if we just take Rosen back."

James wasn't convinced. He had a better plan. "If there isn't grain—"

"There will be." Ruwen put her hand on James's shoulder, and her eyes met his with fervour that mirrored Wulfee's. "There will be."

Eridan stood tall when all else had sat. "We can't go to war without making things right with the gods—or whatever gods still live." His voice echoed coldly off the black stone. "You expect any favour to come our way after what darkness we've been witness to." His voice smoked in the cold air as he walked closer to gaping windows. "Our souls need to be cleansed, folks, our hearts mended. We must pay our respects to our ancestors and visit the Standing Stones of Grave, where Hendurinn himself was sent off by oak and thorn and ash. My dad spoke of doing it for years but never ended up going. Look how that ended for him."

"You can't blame the death of Derudin Deadmaker on lack of respect for the gods," James said. "It was the wizard killed him, not the gods."

Eridan was still looking out the window, flakes of snow salting his black hair for a brief moment before melting into darkness.

"You can't blame the boy for wanting to make it right with the gods," Claydon said.

"Nobody is blaming anybody for a goddamned thing." Brinley slammed his fist on the table again. James had suspected the drayke's teeth around his neck had filled him with rage all winter. Even his heart, Sessely, had come to James worried about a new sort of intense rage that burned in Brinley.

"Just seeing the stones would be enough to boost the morale of our people," Ruwen said. "It would be enough for us to take Rosen back. From there we can take the Hallow. Surely, Ayeland won't march until summer. We have time if we leave *now*."

Brinley sighed. "We will be fighting small groups of brigands broken off from the Wolf's main force or petty Ayelish rulers hoping to make easy names for themselves," he said. "They will be winter-sore and void of purpose. If we are organized and we remain disciplined, we can beat them. But we will need everyone. All in. We can't have folk wandering and farming. This is all we have left. We need to hit them like a fist." Brinley slammed his fist again. "And I will not participate in the vile acts of our ancestors. I have grandchildren who will rule in my place one day, and I don't want to pass on the ways of Old—the ways that broke the Hallow. I want to give them a name—land. I want to move forward. We can get better, you know?"

"Like the bloody Ayelish?" James said. "Like they have names for themselves? Are they any better than us?"

"So we can *defend* against the bloody Ayelish!" Brinley yelled. "So we can stand up to them as equals! So we don't have to run like prey every ten years when the Ayelish march over our borders to take our land. And I will not see any of our own people sacrificed like deer."

James could remember being in the shadow of many different Standing Stones and looking up at them with the same awe that the nytewoods inspired. He remembered Adeqor bringing them to life with glowing magics at Fever. *Perhaps you can find answers there. Perhaps you can find* him. James hated himself for allowing the thought to grow in his mind, but he couldn't stop thinking that he actually *missed* Adeqor. Without him, James was completely lost. *Essikah* hung on his back like a curse, slowly eating his soul, but every time he put it down, it called to him to pick it back up. It called to him but even if it didn't, James would go back and hold it because he had come to *need* it. It was the only thing that understood the dead like he did. And it wanted to feed on the souls that would be trapped in the stones.

"We will march to the Standing Stones. In three days' time," James announced. The room was silent. "If we're to make it there by Springtide, we will need to leave now. The snow is still heavy."

"I never doubted you for a minute," Eridan said, and took a bite of a shrivelled apple he had seemingly produced out of nowhere. "When you want to find where you're going, you need to look at where you've already been. My dad had always said. Our ancestors will guide us."

"Aye," said Claydon.

"Aye, we should have left two weeks ago," Eridan said.

"This is folly." Brinley crossed his thick arms.

"We march to the stones." Ruwen stood tall. "And then we take Rosen?"

James traced the crude grout crusted between the flagstone floor with his eyes. He had a mad idea forming in his mind. "No," James said. *This curse will eat you.* The Maw knew nothing of James Culdaine. The *gods* knew nothing of him—not truly. The rulers of the Hallow doubted James's every word, but they didn't know him either. He was the King of Mal Hallow—the King of the Dead. His was the blood of Hendurinn. His father had told him that he was destined to be written into history, and now he was doing it. *So what songs will they sing of you? Oh, Reaper, the seer of the dead.* "Rosen is too much of a risk. We march to the Grave Stones and pray to our ancestors." James watched the hard faces of the rulers of Mal Hallow as they studied him. "And then we sail to Pool."

"**C**OME ON." JAMES AWOKE to Maggie shaking him.

"We march in the morning," James croaked.

"Let's go. The moon is golden-silver and the stars are alive." Maggie hummed. She kept shaking him. She was fully clothed in thick white bear furs and wool, and James laughed with her as she helped him dress in the same. He was half asleep and tried to coax her into bed, but she wouldn't have it. "You won't want to miss this." She pulled him out through the dark halls and past the twisted spires and old walls of Kallahorn, and out towards the Mountains of the Mother. The snow fell, and James followed in Maggie's small footsteps and felt his nostrils stick together from the cold air and his lungs fill with winter.

They walked below the moon and the stars, and there was nothing but the two of them and nature. *Tell her. Tell her now.* But James was terrified she would not understand. It was *his* nightmare, even if she was in it, and it wasn't fair to make her suffer too. They walked as the moon shone, glittering silver on the fresh white snow, and James said nothing.

In the foothills of the Fells, James watched Maggie dance through the snow like she was born in it. They followed the tracks of hares and squirrels and let the pines brush against them as they hove deeper into the arbor and further from Kallahorn. The owls and the ravens wove through the bare branches and perched upon their high boughs as James passed beneath them.

Maggie tackled him, and they rolled in the snow, and James felt the cold powder drift down his shirt and pants and fill his boots, but the warmth of Maggie made it okay. The pines and the cold and Maggie were the only smells, balsam and peonies and honey in the winter. There was the wetness of her lips and the cold taste of her tongue, and the twisted spires and mammoth black walls of Kallahorn brooding in the distance.

The further they were away from the castle, the more James felt like maybe he could just stay away. Turn away from this duty. But when Maggie smiled, he knew he could never run again. He was the Hallow King, and folk looked to him to save them. He was a legend from the cycles—he was Hendurinn. *But what happened to Hendurinn* after *the wither year?* The cycles didn't tell that part. Only that he was sent off in death at the Grave Stones many years later.

"We have to go back," James said.

"Why?" Maggie gazed at him. "We could leave now and they'd never find us. We could go to the lake. You remember the one? We could live there."

"Folk are looking to us to lead."

"Folk are looking for a way out. Someone to put in front of them in case things go wrong."

"It's more than that, Mag, it's in my blood—Culdaine. Folk need to believe in something bigger than themselves. They need to believe that their own time is just as meaningful as the past."

Maggie smiled and turned away. "Time is different in nature, you know? The past and the future are the same. Things just keep going round. Why don't we just go straight through? You and I?" Maggie looked like she was going to say more but stopped herself.

"What do you mean?" James grabbed Maggie's hands. Maggie pulled them away.

"Nothing," she said. "We should go back. We leave in the morning."

"No, what do you mean straight through?"

Maggie shook her head. "Like, instead of waiting for everyone else to realize the patterns... I don't even know. We should go back to the castle." She grabbed James's hands and her eyes met his, and those said more than her words ever could.

I love you, I'm scared, too. James's stomach fluttered. It started to snow and James pulled Maggie in close to him. Her head nestled below his chin, and he brushed her hair behind her ear. He breathed her in.

"One day we'll turn away from all of this and leave. We don't have to tell anyone at all. We'll just go," he said. Maggie didn't say a word, but James felt her emotion. She wouldn't leave without him. But James knew Maggie had had enough of playing queen. "But for now, we need to stay. Whatever happened last year is not over. I feel it in my bones and see it in my dreams. We need to do something."

"What?" Maggie said.

James didn't know. *The wizard would know.* "We'll find out," he said, and that was good enough for Maggie, for she didn't say any more.

James and Maggie walked back to the ancient fortress that was Kallahorn, and the hard snow crunched beneath their feet with each step while fresh powder fell and covered them like a blanket. The white in Maggie's hair made her look older, and James imagined their future. He saw a child in his nightmares. *Their* child. *Tell her.* But he couldn't. *Don't dream for what you can't dream to lose.*

"I think we should pay respect to our ancestors," Maggie said.

"What?" James's mind was lost somewhere warmer, and he hadn't quite heard what Maggie said.

"We need to pay respect, or the gods will surely leave us to die. I'm scared, James. I've heard voices... things, in my dreams. I think the gods have gone mad." Maggie was serious, and James had rarely seen her this scared.

"So—"

"Sacrifice." Maggie grabbed James's hands. "We have to. Please."

STORIES

The black of night mocked Etta with its silence. Every shape she saw in the dim darkness cursed her as a kinkiller.

"If we stop, they'll surely find us." Calum, the traveller, hadn't slept in two nights to ensure the crew stayed on the right track.

"Aye," said Etta, though it had become hard to care about anything but the pain in her lower back, and the thousand thousand Bradens that harassed her every thought. The weight of Swey in her arms kept her mind from slipping too far into the darkness, though. Each of the crew had taken turns carrying the boy through the night as he slept to keep moving.

A wolf howled somewhere in the shadow of night. It had been following them.

They rode on into the dark, following the little star of firelight upon Benn's torch, and when they came to the crossroads, Etta's jaw dropped at the sight of the jagged outlines of heads on posts, stark black against the silver moon. *No… no the Wolf's dead, it can't be.*

As they rode up, Etta dismounted to see the carnage. The heads had no eyes or tongues, and the males had their members nailed onto their chins. Black blood crusted the poles they were skewered on, and Etta reckoned she'd never seen something so vile. The bones of the dead remained, piled up neatly below the heads. They had been chewed up and eaten. *Before or after they were stacked in neat little piles...*

"What the fuck happened here?" was all Etta could say. *It can't be him. It can't be Sweyne... yes. It can.*

Cullen's eyes were gaping.

Calum said, "I'd rather keep riding and not fucking find out."

They all nodded. Swey woke and looked upon those heads with wide eyes. Tara tried to cover his head and Etta sang *Your Name Upon the Moon,* and Swey calmed as they plodded on into the night.

"They won't get us," Swey said. "We won't let them."

"Aye." Etta looked between Swey and Tara, smiling. "Never."

Benn was happy to lead. When Cullen began to sing *Cook Me up a Rabbit, Cook Me up a Hare,* all joined in, and below a blanket of stars, they lit up the mountains with song.

In the morning, they packed up and rode on and no one was singing. *Dreams will do that...*

After many hours of trekking, a black plume of smoke became visible. Then the hamlet that birthed that plume. It was bloated and ashy and reeked of tar and flesh.

"By the gods..." Holden gripped his axe so tight Etta could see the whites of his knuckles. "They burned it..."

"None live," Calum said as he trotted back towards them on horseback from the small hamlet. The wooden owl atop the hamlet's totem pole seemed to be drowning in black smoke. *Who is doing this?*

The hamlet was spared but it had seen many sacrifices on this day, and Etta shivered as she saw ash-crusted limbs poking out of the bloated fire.

"It must be the Ayelish," Benn said. "The mountain clans would never commit such atrocities above the eyes of the gods. There is a code as old as the cycles. This... this is beyond that."

"Why would the Ayelish come this far into the mountains? There is nothing here for them." Calum dismounted and brushed his horse. "This is something else. Something... dark."

"It makes no sense," Tara said. "These mountains used to be peaceful, I was raised in these mountains... it makes no sense."

"Nothing does," said Etta. "Things are changing. Slipping away like water in your hands."

"Unless these Ayelish ain't welcome back home, either..." Holden slapped the back of his axe into his palm.

"Several bands of soldiers broke off from the army when they knew they were going to lose the Battle of Rosen. They were displaced and scattered," Benn said. "It could be any one of them or many banded together. Strange things happen to folk during long hungry winters. It's best we get back to camp and head further into the mountains now that winter is chased. We're too close to the rivers..."

"We were fools to think we'd find peace here," Tara said. "I'm a fool to think I could come home."

Etta frowned at the face Swey made at his mom's words. *The same face Braden gave you when you told him we wouldn't be safe in the north—that we'd have to leave...*

"We will find peace, the lot of us," Etta said, and Swey's face brightened with what Etta thought looked like hope. "We just first need to get back to camp so we can all go together. We are stronger together."

"They won't get us," said Swey. Etta knew the boy needed to believe it.

"They won't get us," Etta echoed.

"Aye," Holden said.

"Aye," said Benn.

"Aye," resonated the rest, and not one of them spoke again until it was time to camp.

They lay beneath the stars that night to try to sleep. As Etta glared up, each golden dot in the black sky had Braden's face carved into it. *You're a child killer. You're a bloody wretch, and death deserves to catch you.* Etta closed her eyes but no sleep came. Gen's laughter echoed in her mind; Maggie's smile lingered. *And James.* She saw him in every lick of fire, heard his voice in every crackle. *You'll never be Etta. Etta hadn't turned her back on love. Etta hadn't killed all the good in herself yet. She was pure and innocent. You are rotten and stained.*

Etta remembered her mother and father and the day she fell in the frozen river. *That was the day Etta died, and you should have died with her.* Every day of winter was like a fresh knife blade to her stomach. She told herself she was Etta now. Etta was happy. Etta felt no pain. But lies couldn't fix a shattered soul.

The stars were a thousand thousand golden fuck yous, and when Etta closed her eyes, the darkness held a single face, blood dripping out of his mouth through cracked teeth, a scar on his left cheek. The same scar as... She could still see the look on his face when he meant to kill her. *It was Sweyne inside of him boiling up.* She saw her baby boy, clung to her breast in the cold halls of Kallahorn. *One day you will join them all again... Tarek, Braden, Gen... and you can pray to the gods that all others you have loved will outlive you... no more. No more death. Please gods, only mine. Only mine.*

Etta tried to lie to herself, but she couldn't believe her lies anymore. *You're sick. You're a vile, rotten thing.* The gods would keep her alive and make her suffer for what she'd done. Father Tree was in no hurry to see her. She had already been judged. *Guilty of child slaying. A murderer.*

Etta watched Tara. Little Swey was tucked under her arms and snoring. *I need to stay here a while longer yet. For him. For her. I need to make sure they're okay. Tara is strong, but she needs protection, too—we all do.*

Somewhere in the night, a wolf howled. Etta waited for an answer to the call, but one never came. It was a lone wolf that followed them, and Etta thought of the big grey wolf that followed her up the White last year. *Where are you, sweet Grey? Is that you again?*

Etta slept a dreamless sleep, and when she opened her eyes, it was morning.

On the cookfire, Cullen roasted chestnuts and boiled pine tea in an iron pot. When Holden and Young Courtney came back with three red squirrels on a stick, Cullen had skinned and roasted those up, too. After they had all eaten and warmed themselves with hot drinks, Swey asked Etta to tell him more stories.

"You've heard all of my stories, Swey. Why not listen to Benn tell one?

Swey sighed. "I've heard all of his stories, too, but yours are *better*."

Tara smiled. "The river gurgles up a better tale than old Benn." That got a laugh out of the lot of them. Benn looked embarrassed.

"I've been telling my stories for years. Ain't no one complained until now," Benn coughed.

"To your face," Calum said cheekily under his breath. And even Benn laughed at that one.

"Tell the one about the cook," Swey said.

"Yeah, you know, just leave out all of the secret parts about cooks," said Cullen, and they laughed.

Stories were one of the few things that made Etta feel like herself, and so she told Swey and the whole lot of them about the cook of Kallahorn who had risen up and became a great karl. She told them about *the Axe of the Moon* and of Korin Ironeye's victories over the Ayelish at Oster. And she pretended to be Etta. *Wretched thing…*

The stories were a welcome reprieve, for that day they walked through arbor and stream and up the base of the mountain, where they stopped and fished trout out of the streams and cooked them over small fires. They saw no sign of people, but that only meant that people didn't come *this* way. Etta knew from the clear sky that folk would be riding today. And Etta knew that many paths led to the same place.

At midday, they reached a high ridge next to a waterfall that overlooked the valley where the free folk had their camp. Nobody said out loud a single thing about the murders of ravens circling the valley. The waterfall was like thunder coming down, and it soaked Etta gently as she marched behind Benn down the steep ridgeway.

By night, Etta saw the ruddy light from the clanfires burning red in the dark arbor, and the shadows of the trees looked like twenty-foot guards. When Gwynn and Ryatt rode out to meet them with axes drawn, Etta knew that all wasn't as it was when they had left. *Something has happened here.*

"Come, hurry," Gwynn said when he was sure who he was talking to. He clutched Benn and pulled him in. "Good to see you well, B. I wasn't sure if... deathstealers, you know..."

"You don't trust 'em." Benn patted Gwynn's back. "And neither did I. But I saw little choice, and here I am. The mud in my lungs is gone."

"We thought you were all dead." Ryatt looked at Holden and quickly looked away. "It's nearly been two moon's turns."

"It's a long way," said Swey.

"Come, we must go." Gwynn hurried them along.

"What's gone on here?" Benn said. Etta would have asked the same question if she was Wulfee, but Etta didn't really want to know the answer. *Peace... you really thought you'd find peace in these mountains.*

"It's not as you left, guys," Gwynn said. "We were attacked and had to abandon our food stores. Three haunches of boar. Six racks of smoked venison. It's all gone. All of it. And... "

"They killed Kara," Ryatt said. "She was set to watch over the food. She was only looking out for bears, Benn. Not arrows..."

"What is this?" Etta felt a ping in her temple that said *Sweyne did it*, and her eye twitched.

"Spring has come hard and fast," Gwynn said. "A hundred hundred brigands sprung up like flowers. The broken pieces of the Wolf's army that survived the winter. And they're hungry."

"It was a long winter..." said Etta, remembering the human bite marks in that cooked Human arm.

"Aye," said Gwynn. "Come. The elders are telling stories."

The clanfire blazed like the sun, and like many Earths, these great elders of the Fells surrounded it. Ruddy flamelight danced on their hard, wrinkled faces like waves lapping. They all sat around the clanfire, and from one grey-haired, stone-faced woman came a deep voice that was their only focus. One voice. One story. Heard through a thousand thousand ears over a hundred hundred years.

As they got closer, Etta could make out what story she was telling. It was the tale of Timmon Two-face, the Ranger who became a Kihl'dor of the Fells. Etta took joy in seeing Swey's face light up at the sound of the elders' voices. *Etta loved these stories, too, almost more than anything.*

Swey grabbed for Etta's hand, and she recoiled on instinct. When she saw the look on the boy's face, she quickly reached for his hand.

"I'm sorry, Swey, sometimes I get scared." Etta gave the boy's hand a squeeze.

"Me too," he said. "And my dad said that's what makes us brave."

Braden... by the gods. "Those are good words," Etta said. She took a seat on a log around the fire and listened. *Wulfee would have been made to tell first story. The kihl'dor always tells first story.*

The story of Timmon was a peculiar one. Timmon was killed and his soul entered the body of a wolf. As the wolf, Timmon stalked his wife and protected her from other wolves and certain dangers. He howled every night to let her know it was him, but she never noticed. Finally, one night, Timmon was howling to the full moon and saw his wife coming. He ran to her, howling all the while, but soon took an arrow to his eye and shortly after, died. His wife killed him in his wolf body because she thought he was a wild beast coming to attack her.

Etta listened to the story for so long she fell into a waking sleep, and for a moment, some part of her believed Swey was young Braden. Panic struck as she scanned the fire for Tarek. Then a dagger of pain stabbed her heart when she realized she was old and alone, and the boy beside her was somebody else's child. *Your grandchild. He's your grandchild.* But Etta didn't have children and Etta had no grandchildren. *If you're to truly let it go, you need to forget... All of it...*

She watched Tara raise her arm and Swey snuggle beneath it. Etta took two long pulls off the chuff pipe when it came to her and coughed. Little Swey woke up from the coughing, and Tara smiled and carried him off to their bedrolls. Etta drank and smoked with the elders and bathed in the moonlight as the clanfire seeped through her bones and warmed the coldness inside of her. When a lone wolf howled, she thought of Timmon. *Poor bastard.* And had another drink, then stumbled away from the fire feeling like if she never woke up that'd be okay.

Etta found her bedroll much as she had left it, despite the destruction of everything else. She nestled under the big oak and closed her eyes. When she opened them hours later, there was vomit on her shirt and she had to piss. She thought a small oak tree was Gen. When she realized it wasn't, she wept silently to herself until the pink sun broke the darkness.

From the east, the sun rose salmon-red and swollen above the blue-white mountains, and in that morning light, Etta saw folk marching towards them and chanting war cries with axes drawn beneath haggard white-red flags.

Two Ways to Die

T HE FROZEN GRASS BROKE like shards of glass below the hooves of Bren. James rubbed the big brown mustang's neck and lowered his mouth to his ear.

"Take me there, sweet boy. I won't let harm come to you."

Two dozen carts and a hundred times that number of folk rode behind him. Maggie and Eurick rode beside him, and they led the party day after day as the days grew longer.

It was bittersweet leaving Kallahorn behind, and many of the Hallow folk clung to the halls and chamber rooms as everyone else left. Days and even weeks later, James kept getting word that new bands of stragglers had caught up to the baggage train behind. *People aren't meant to live in that castle, and they are especially not meant to be alone there.*

Mineera begged James for him to stay for another few weeks; she felt like she was close to understanding more about Kallahorn, but James couldn't oblige—his people had made up their minds to leave, and he needed to lead them. He needed to act, or one of the rulers would act for him. If the Ayelish had attacked them there at Kallahorn, the Hallow would be wiped out in one blow. They had hidden themselves in a dark corner all winter and didn't want to get caught with no place to go. The last time James had seen Mineera, she was on her way down into the tunnels again. He didn't know if he'd ever see her again. She said she was going to find her way back to Edura to publish her findings at the Great Library of Vasanti. James hardly understood what that meant but he hoped the best for that strange, kind woman.

"There's another one ahead." Maggie was disgusted.

"By the gods, man. Did they burn every one of them?" Eurick was breathing heavily.

James reared up his horse as they approached yet another charred farm field with a motte of frozen bones.

James dismounted. "Salt." He let the cold, grey dirt sift through his fingers as he studied it. "It's bloody salt again. As if burning it wasn't enough."

"Where did they get so much salt, man?" Eurick was sifting the chalky dust through his fingers now, too. "Did they drain the bloody sea?"

"The sea will never drain. It will flood us away before it drains." Maggie was still mounted and she took a drink from her flask and belched, and James had not seen a more fitting queen of Mal Hallow since Nara of Oster had reigned.

"These Ayelish know secrets of warfare that go back and back into books that were written during the time of Kelson." James kicked the dust and remembered what Mineera had told him. "They will try to beat us in ways we can never imagine. They will try to make this war the last. They've burned and salted these fields so they will not sow for us. Our people cannot live here."

"We keep going. The stones are still weeks out. We will find something." Eurick mounted and glared back at the sea of folk behind them. "Gods, there is no other choice, man. We must keep hope alive."

"The folk that did this can't be far off," Maggie said. "Their smell lingers on the wind. Sour, like bog mire. Unwashed."

They rode south through the countryside and came across another burned field full of scarecrows.

"Oh, gods, man." Eurick turned his head away, and James soon realized why. The scarecrows were dead folk impaled like straw cadavers. An Ayelish flag hung from one of the bodies and whipped in the wind. On the flag, the words *Reaper King* were written in blood. And below that was *Alder Remembers*. James dismounted and pulled the flag down, and the whole rotting body came down with it. Cold and soggy flesh smacked the ground. *Rest easy...* James glared at the other scarecrows, staggered throughout the hundred-acre field. *These are Hallow folk. Folk you couldn't save.*

"Why are there so many?" James asked. "I thought most had come to Kallahorn. I had no idea that many of our country folk still lived."

"Many of the barons protecting these hamlets came to Kallahorn. These folk either weren't told or refused to come along," Eurick said. "Not all were keen to join. Some took their chances of survival in their own hands."

"They're stubborn here in the Hallow," Maggie said. "My second parents were that kind of stubborn."

These are your lands being burned. Your people being killed. This is yours to protect, and you've hid all winter long. James remembered the swollen and bloated body of Calen Alder before Maggie killed him. The Blood Words had turned him into some kind of demon—a berserker from Hell. *That was the new queen's dad...*

James tore another body down from a stake, then another. He hadn't even realized he was crying until a hand touched his shoulder, and he turned to see Maggie standing there and his tears fell like rain.

"I can't do this," James sobbed. "I can't do it." And in his mind the Maw God laughed like a mad squirrel, and James beat the ground with his fists.

"You can," said a voice that sounded like Maggie. "You have to."

Hands gripped him from beneath his arms and pulled him up. "We'll do it together, man," Eurick said.

Minutes later, James sat against a stone as Eurick and Maggie tore the corpses down from their stakes. Soon the other lords came up the road and saw the scarecrows. James saw Brinley's jaw drop, and it seemed like the dragon slayer was unable to pick it up again.

"What happened here?" Eridan dismounted and sat beside James.

"The Ayelish," James spat the words.

"Reckon they think they can keep these lands if they can get us off them." Eridan pulled out a wineskin and took a long chug. "Even these stragglers are making an effort to destroy us. Reckon they think they can do it, too."

Eridan offered the skin to James, and James took a long drink of the sun-warm shine. "Aye."

"Wood!" Brinley screamed. "Gather as much as you can find. Aione, take twelve folk and fell an oak tree. Let's give these folk the funeral they deserve. Of oak and thorn and ash. A pyre to the gods."

"We should set up camp for the night." Ruwen looked at James to give the order.

"Right," James said, and stood up. "Let's set up camp and give these folk the funeral they deserve. We ride on in the morning."

Horses were lined up and cared for, canvas tents were unpacked and pitched, and fires started to spark up the night sky like burn bugs. Before long, songs were being sung and the pyre was being constructed in the middle of the burned field.

"It's almost here." Maggie was looking up at the sky.

"Springtide?"

"Well, yes."

James lay down on the ground beside her. The charred ground was still warm, and the dead pods of corn seed crunched beneath his back and popped like knots of wood in a fire. Maggie rested her head on his chest, and he stroked her hair as they watched the stars.

"You weren't talking of Springtide?" James felt a warmth coming off Maggie's skin.

"Springtide will be lovely."

"What do you see up there?"

Maggie turned her head so her eyes pierced into his, one green and one blue. "I see the Starfall."

They were silent then as they lay, but from many of the tents, James heard wet coughing.

T HERE WAS SOMETHING IN Maggie that *burned* James. She was so alive, something in her radiated with life, and he was so... *dead.* James feared Maggie felt it too. That underneath their passion that burned like the sun lay a secret repulsion. Both of them knew it but neither said; James figured it had to be that way. *Even the hottest flame will die once it's burned up everything.* Still, a voice inside whispered *this shouldn't be. This shouldn't ever be. For the love of the gods, can't you see that the two of you will destroy the world?* But James couldn't help it. He breathed Maggie like air. He needed her like water. She said the same of him and together they were whole, whereas apart, they were only a piece of something better. *So what is this darkness that circles us like carrion? Why won't it let us be?*

"Are you awake?" Maggie stirred. "Hold me."

James did, and his skin on hers and the crackling and spitting of burning wood, and the dancing flame that cast one shadow with two heads on the canvas was all there was.

After they had their love, Maggie quickly fell back to sleep. James lay awake listening to her breathing and the fire and the cicadas singing. He hadn't slept more than a couple of hours at a time since they'd set out from Kallahorn. He had hoped it was the castle causing his nightmares and that nature would cure him. He couldn't have been more wrong. It was like without the dark walls, there was nothing to protect him. *Ellorin. Adeqor. The Maw. The Lupin. The Outcast God. Help. Please.*

Every nightmare was the same. Ellorin appeared and James begged.

"What happened to Hendurinn after he opened the spirit world? Please, tell me," James pleaded.

"Alder should have killed you. You should not be here." Ellorin spewed hate-laced words.

If it wasn't Ellorin, it was Adeqor. If not the wizard, then it was the Maw. Drooling blood, blackened saliva and snorting robustly; breath smoked in the cold black of James's mind.

"What happened after? What happened to him? To Hendurinn?" James begged all of them. *"What do I do now? Is it over? Why doesn't it feel over?"*

"You shouldn't be here," they all said. *"This is over for you. There is no place for you in this. Not anymore."*

Each time James slept, he awoke shivering and soaking in sweat, grasping desperately for *Essikah*. He usually forgot where he was. He was usually sick or dizzy or both. But Maggie was there. Every night and every morning, she was there. Smooth and naked and *alive*. More so than he ever could be.

The fire danced, and Maggie breathed in long, slow breaths like the lapping of a wave, and James saw Maggie, twenty years her elder, standing in front of a small lake holding a child. The babe was crying, and Maggie soothed her with a calm word and a gentle caress. *Yes, it's a baby girl.* Her strawberry blonde curls and her small smile turned James's insides to mush. *Ai'mair Darra, baby girl, forever.*

James hadn't even noticed he had been sleeping until Maggie woke him.

"You slept, baby," she said. "It's nice out there." Maggie opened their tent and stood naked before the blue day. She took a deep breath and seemed to pull the light of the sun into the murky night of their tent. "It's going to be a beautiful Springtide. Ai'mair Darra, my love."

James sat up and watched Maggie dress. "Ai'mair Darra." The thought of Springtide made him sick. Most of the rulers had agreed with Maggie to give a sacrifice to the Druid souls of Old at the Standing Stones when the sun reached Springtide. James had promised Brinley and Eurick he wouldn't go through with it. *Tell her. It was a baby girl. She was beautiful. So god damn beautiful.*

But James said nothing as he dressed himself, and nothing as he and Maggie emerged from their cave of stick and canvas and joined the rest of the camp. The Hallow rulers were already gathered, and Eridan was yelling about something.

"Ah, here's someone who will understand," Eridan said as James approached. "You won't believe this."

"What is this?" James's head throbbed.

Brinley raised his finger to Eridan. "This one is as mad as his dad was!"

Eridan charged at Brinley, but Ruwen held him back by the cuff of his neck.

Eurick held Brinley by both elbows from behind. Eurick said, "This sacrifice, man. It ain't right." The raven looked like he might have been crying.

"Twenty more and counting died last night from sickness," Ruwen spoke calmly, still holding Eridan with one hand. "It's the bloody lung. Seen it before as a wee lass. This flux will get worse before it gets better."

James still wasn't following. His head throbbed with thoughts of a small child, *his* small child, and he clutched onto that peace as tightly as he could.

"And these fools think we can just sacrifice the dead and dying, sick with the bloody lung. As if the gods wouldn't know," Eridan spat. "A tainted sacrifice is like harrisene in wine. Poison."

"Nonsense!" Brinley stood tall, his dragon's tooth necklace clicking as if in anger. "It would be a mercy. To all of us."

"Eridan's right," Maggie said, her bear-fur coat glistening white in the morning sun. "The gods require a meaningful sacrifice. We must be heard." Maggie looked up to the sky as if she was waiting for it to answer. There was not a word amongst the rulers.

Eridan coughed to fill the silence, then said, "Right then. So, who will it be?"

The rulers dismissed without answering Eridan. He ogled James as if to prod him, but James turned away and helped Maggie with the horses.

Hours. Everything took hours upon hours and days upon days.

"They're stuck, man." Eurick pointed to the wheels of one of the wayns.

"Unstick them." James closed his eyes and rubbed his temples. They were just outside of a small hamlet, and their carts were stuck in the mud again. Groves of nytewood stumps lined the road, lumps of black wood and moss and mushrooms told the story of an empire that thought they were bigger than nature—Lovas. When Kelson came through Ardura and conquered its people, he killed his fair share of nature too, drilling road-ways through the entire continent. And now the road was sinking into the mud and the dead roots below as if to prove the road never belonged here.

"This road stretches from Kallahorn to Sareen, man, uninterrupted." Eurick said. "It's amazing."

"If it wasn't for the ancient Feldarra smuggling my ancestors away to the mountains, our bloodline would be completely wiped out because of Kelson," James said. He had never thought too much about how much he actually hated the bastard.

"Well thank fuck for the Feldarra then, eh?" Itchy rode close by, strumming his woodharp and humming songs in bleak tones. "It's just a little mud. Nothing to stop the Reaper, am I right?" Itchy laughed but James didn't find the humour. He hadn't liked the new moniker he had adopted. *I reaped my own parents, too, how about that? Want to sing about that, Itchy?*

A steady pounding drummed inside of James's head, and he could hardly open his eyes, for the light hurt them so. He rode ahead, alone.

"Where you going, man?" Eurick called out to him. James knew the raven had been worried, but he had no way to calm him. James felt like his head might burst like a dropped squash.

"To take a shit." James rode Bren at a trot into the hamlet. He saw, but only briefly acknowledged, soggy dead bodies hanging from the branches of oak trees. And in the cottonwoods, they were hanging fifty feet up or more like rotten wraiths trapped in the skeletal canopy. The cold wind whistled and turned the air into impalpable ice, and James rode Bren through the streets and suddenly he couldn't breathe. Bare bones, and barrels of bones, and bones protruding from half-rotten bodies silently begging to thaw so they can finish nature's job and decay.

James dismounted and walked into one of the abandoned hovels. He didn't even know what he was looking for. Inside was damp from the storms, and the rushes were mouldy and it reeked of loam. James rubbed at his temples and sat down on the haybeds, and rats scurried out from under him.

"Ah, fuck!" He flailed. Sat up and took a deep breath. *Dad, I don't know what to do. This war cannot be won.*

"*A leader is only as good as his army. Make sure you do whatever you can to please them,*" Bren Culdaine had told a young James. "*Know how to treat people. Listen closely, so you can respond in a way that will make them feel heard.*"

James had been running his plan through his mind to go to Pool for weeks. He didn't know how in the hell he was going to pull it off with this lot. Tired, lost, and now sick. But James had fought at Rosen, and he knew damn well that they had no chance to take the fort with what they had. The bridge would be impossible. Without the clans of Pool, they would be slaughtered. But the clans had enough power to slaughter them, too, if they chose to fight rather than join him.

James had to choose between two ways to die. *You should be at Kallahorn.* He couldn't resist the thought, but he didn't know why. *You're fighting the wrong fight. It's Adeqor you should be thinking about,* a voice inside of him said, but he ignored it. James knew that Queen Ianna and the Ayelish were set on destroying him and his country. He knew that to win this war, he would need something more than what the Hallow ever had.

He would need Maggie.

By the time the carts were unstuck and the convoy was rolling through the hamlet, James was still sitting in the hovel. It had been two weeks since they left, and they had been plagued by sickness the whole time. Many were too weak and fever-stricken to walk and so others carried them, who in turn got sick. James felt like he had killed those people himself. *Would the sickness have come to Kallahorn, too? Or something worse?*

Maggie came and sat by him for a time and held his arm without saying a word. Then the two of them got up and mounted their horses.

The people who once lived in this place had been butchered like dogs, left to rot. By the smell of their corpses, they were only a few days to a week dead. Young and old lay in the muddy clay streets with dead eyes and sunken faces in pools of clotted blood. An Ayelish flag lay beneath a post, crumpled in the dirt where the wind had blown it down, as if the Earth rebelled against the Ayelish, too. *"Alder Remembers."* The words were written in the northern language in big block letters to maximize the chance of James seeing it. He doubted very much Ianna herself had come through these parts yet. *She must have sent a herald to instruct the Ayelish that still remained.* Another thought crept into James's mind. *Or another Warlock came in the winter. Probably barefoot, casting spells and eating souls to stay warm.* James shivered as he remembered Adeqor melting bodies at the Fever Stones.

"I reckon they scourged all the Hallow," Ruwen said.

"And here we thought they wanted to settle these lands," Brinley said. "They want naught but to destroy us completely."

"Let them try," said James, and clenched his fists. He looked at Maggie and bit his lip. *She could kill every living thing and stand alone on this earth which is surely hers.*

And they passed a dozen or more hamlets like that, ripped open like bloodied scabs that will leave a scar on the land. Some burned to blackened char and others left barren. All bore the message *Alder Remembers*. They passed bodies and more bodies, cold, blue, stinking dead, and their souls wept a haunting serenade to the trees and to the streams.

Where are you? James asked the night sometimes when he was taking a piss in the arbor. *Help me.* But most of the dead had gone. Left him like most else. He only saw the dead on rare occasions outside of arbors now, as frequently as he had when he was a boy. He hated that he missed them. *You're a demon.*

Day after day and night after night, they hove on, and two weeks turned to three to four. James watched the moon through a whole cycle and a half. And he watched as each night the rulers sat by their own separate fires surrounded by their own people. Each night they grew further apart. All of them looking up at the moon, watching it wax and wane its way through to the end of winter.

"Springtide is only a half-moon away," Brinley said.

"We won't make it in time," Claydon complained.

"We have to," James said.

Then it was a quarter moon, and they rode on, and the coughing was like a chorus, and more folk dropped dead each day, and each night they burned them on pyres of oak and thorn and ash, and prayed to the gods, who James was certain had forgotten them.

Two days before Springtide, through the dim fog of the morning, James saw stones in the sky. Too smooth to be a mountain and too tall to be anything but the Grave Stones.

He rode with Eurick to the cliff, an hour's ride to their east, so they could get a better view.

Below, surrounding the Standing Stones, were hundreds upon hundreds of fires burning. Black flags cracking madly in the wind all around.

"Whose is it?" James asked.

"Oh gods, man. It can't be. There's no way."

"Who?" James looked closer and saw a black kraken on blue. He knew that flag. *But what is it?* His mind was blank. "All of those under the same flag?"

"Oh shite, man."

"Whose is it?" James yelled this time.

"Daggland, man. The bloody Daggs."

THE BODYSNATCHER

Haro's world exploded into dullness as he took the woman's body, and all the colour faded away from his vision. The woman bucked like a wild horse and fell to the ground wincing and screaming in pain. And Haro felt it, too, punching at her lungs and trying to crack her spine in two. *This is what it's like to take another's body. You had forgotten the horror of it.* A blue jay fluttered around her ear and pecked at her cheeks, and she swatted it away. He wrestled with her conscious mind and, after a great struggle, subdued it to a far recess somewhere inside.

Now that she had finally stopped resisting him, he took his first steps using her feet.

She poked out of her dark corner and held him down occasionally as she tried to steal her body back, but she was weak, and Haro had almost completely shaken her after only a few moments of walking with her body. He moved towards the trickling stream, shining silver in the moonlight, and his blue jay chittered alongside him like it was trying to tell him something.

"What is it, bird?" he said with the woman's mouth. The bird chittered.

He had taken a body, but his memory was still lost somewhere.

Why did you do this? Who are you?

He remembered his childhood, snail stew and bramble berries, fresh trout from the stream. Wind flowing through her red hair. Her mothers gentle kiss on her forehead. *No, no these are not your memories.*

The woman's soul fought to stay alive within her body. And she was draining Haro of his strength to keep her at bay.

HELP! she shrieked.

He watched the water trickle freely. He studied brown and green buds emerging through a blanket of thin white snow. He saw a blue jay chittering at him. *This bloody bird...*

"Haro." It seemed to twitter in some tongue he might have known once. "Haro."

He remembered giving birth to her first child, the pain and the rapture of love that poured forth with the blood, and the quick sure hand of her husband, Grig, to stem the bleeding amidst such chaos. He remembered her mother, red-haired and warm. He remembered—

No, these are not yours. These are not you.

"Haro," the blue jay twittered.

He remembered his wife. The smell of her neck, the taste of her lips. *Ifanie.* He saw her blue eyes and heard her voice. He remembered a child.

Yes. These are yours.

He remembered his son, his laughter, his smile. *Owen...* He remembered him crying in pain, dying. He saw Ifanie in a red-poppy dress and heard her voice. *"Ai'mair Darra."* He remembered the taste of her tongue and the smell of her. *Sunflower and thyme.* He sniffed the air and smelled only fish and worms on the damp day.

He remembered James Culdaine.

Yes.

And still, a soul fought within his frail body. *She's dying, this one, you'll need to find another. She's sick,* Haro thought. And the sick woman's soul seemed to scream out, but Haro held her tongue. The sickness was in her bones; he felt it there like a nose full of snot. It weighed her down, made her slow.

This body will serve for now, but you'll need to find another.

The sun had begun its fall towards night. The woman was hungry. With the woman's eyes, Haro scanned the treetops looking for a plume of smoke. There was one close by and another farther off. *Is this your house, woman? Do you live alone?* With the woman's legs, Haro walked up the river towards the smoke.

He drifted like a vagabond upon the stream, whipping in the wind and letting it guide him. He remembered dying at the hand of that mountain warrior called Pike. His soul slipping away and the Maw God laughing at him as he floated, bodiless. Haro's bird had given him its body without question. He offered it up to Haro with joy. He and the bird were one.

When Haro was asked the bird's name, he laughed. *Haro is his name, don't you see? He is me.* But the longer he spent in that small body, the more of his mind slipped away. *"I'm not done with you yet,"* the Maw God had snorted to him as his soul found its way into his bird.

It was two weeks after he died before Haro had found the hunter in the cabin. He had taken the man's body without remorse and used it and his cabin to live out the winter.

It was your fault we lost him. His body was good, strong. Haro cursed himself. He had cut part of his hand off chopping wood and ended up catching the rot. He spent his last days in the hunter's body drinking malt and eating the haunch off a great smoked moose and singing songs of Ossian and Aonis and Hagen the Great. It was only in the Wayk of winter when he was sure the man would not see out another week that his blue jay came from the arbor, and together, they flew away from the place where the man's lifeless body spent his last winter.

That was weeks ago... a month maybe... Haro looked up at the sky. It was nearly Springtide. He'd been in the bird for nearly half a season and part of him still felt the effects. His world felt grey and freezing cold. As a bird, he saw colours as bright as the sun and ate little and slept less. Now he was so exhausted it was all he could do to force this sick body to move.

Tucked into the woods, nestling itself gently beside a trickling stream of silver-clear mountain water, Haro saw a pale wooden shack with a ruddy warm glow coming from within. A shadow danced along the walls as its caster moved from one side of the shack to the other. A flickering of firelight erupted, and a thud came from whatever the caster had placed in the fire.

Then the other soul inside of him made an assault. It had been lurching, idle for too long, and Haro knew this was coming so he braced himself. She attacked fiercely. Haro fell to the ground inside of the woman's body, and all went black when her fingers stabbed knuckle-deep into her eye sockets. She grabbed hold of one eyeball between two fingers and commenced ripping it from her own skull. Haro spat blood and screamed and fought her arm away. She bit and tore at the skin of her arms and ran a hand through the dirt to find a rock and bludgeoned herself with it. She fell to the ground, and Haro felt warmness trickling into her ear and down her neck.

Haro fought and regained control, and when he opened the woman's eyes, still blurred and spotty and sticky with blood, he saw a man running from the pale shack with an axe drawn. *Grig, it's Grig.* But when the man saw Haro, or the woman he had become, his eyes gaped open like black pits in rocky hills, and he screamed some kind of sound that Haro hadn't heard before.

"Dalla!" his voice curdled.

When Haro stood, he felt the woman's eye swinging loose from the socket, dangling by a bloody red tendon and slapping against his cheek. And then he saw it with his other eye. Blood dripped from his fingers as if it were rain, and he was drenched in it.

The woman inside of him had left, gone on to her next life, and she left Haro with a dying husk of a thing with her dying strength. Haro's skin was torn to shreds. His nails were torn off and broken and bloody and lodged in his arms and face. His eye was loose, hair torn out in patches, which he saw blowing around in tufts on the ground. His tongue had been chewed off, and most of his lower lip was missing. His ears were full of blood, and his eyes were sticky with it. *She was strong. Stronger than any you've taken before.*

The man ran to Haro. "By the gods, Dalla, what have you done? By the gods, what have you done?" He crumpled to his knees in front of him. He *will not be so strong.* Grig's eyes were bloodshot, and Haro saw the madness frothing up.

With e'daru's gift, Haro reached out and assaulted the man's soul and slipped inside of him like he was putting on a fitted tunic. The man was weak, scared, and when Haro made the jump, the man's soul scurried away like a mouse to the corner of his own mind. Haro settled into his body in an instant without resistance.

Haro held a pink and scarred hand to the sky and admired it. *Not so bad a scar as I've seen.* It was a burn scar that covered his right hand up to his elbow, and when Haro made a fist, it stretched and pulled like he had run out of skin and his hand wouldn't quite ball up. It was pink and shrivelled and nasty looking. *This man was brave. These were good hands. This body is worthy.*

The woman lay desolate on the ground, a shamble of torn human flesh and hair. *She fought hard, that one. She could have been the end of me.*

Haro picked up the woman's corpse. His new body was strong. He carried the corpse to the weather-worn shack of wood and dropped her down on the muddy grass in front. Haro pulled open the deer hide door, and the smell of fresh herbs assaulted him. They hung from the rafters in every assortment of green and brushed Haro's head as he walked in and sprinkled dryly around him.

A pot sat boiling on the fire in the grey stone hearth; the brown stew inside bubbled and spat and smelled like it was on its last possible boil of many. Smooth rocks smeared with blue paste or red or orange were scattered across the oakwood table and down on the pine bench, and all over the golden rushes on the floor next to small stone bowls of amber coloured oils. Haro smelled each one. *Sunflower and lemon balm and eucalyptus and carnisa.* And there were many more he didn't know—pastes and liquids he had never seen or smelled. Some he could make out as a complicated mess of things. *Lavender and sweet-currant and bayroot and dogplant. This woman was sicker than hell.* Haro had never seen so many medicines. *Who were these people?*

Haro saw a small shelf in the corner of the hut, lined with scrolls neatly rolled and placed deliberately. He unrolled them manically. Each was scrawled with a strange script and pictures of different leaves and seeds. *Medicine folk. These are deathstealer magics.* He let the scrolls fall from his hands and land where they would, upon the rushes or wooden plank bed or the shelf on which he found them. He touched many of the things he saw and many of the things he didn't touch at all. He went outside.

In the back, by a small garden infested with the green chutes of garlic and onion, Haro found a small wooden shovel, and in the shack, a flayed hemp rope. He tied a fallen branch of a nytewood to the shovel with the rope—and dug. He wanted a hole big enough and respectably deep enough for the woman called Dalla, and then he buried her in it. He prayed the Crow to honour her death.

That night Haro fell asleep in the shack face down from exhaustion. He woke on the floor in the middle of the night to a rat scurrying away and to strange whining squeals that sounded like many animals being killed violently. He scrambled outside and heard only crickets and saw only burn bugs flashing like make-believe stars. A drunkenness had seized his body. Like the man had fought back while Haro slept and had taken back part of his mind. Everything was a haze.

Who am I? Why am I here. Dalla. Save Dalla. Yes. No.

A nytewood gleamed golden in the moonlight, and Haro fell to his knees beneath it.

"Why?" he cried out to no one.

"To find him," the tree seemed to answer. Haro screamed, and he didn't know if it was the man screaming in pain or himself in fear. Only the

crickets answered and an owl hooted and fluttered off, its wings beating the night air.

Haro must have fallen asleep, for he dreamed of the Maw. *"I'm not done with you,"* the Maw barked at him. He dreamed of e'daru and of his Ifanie. He dreamed of his Owen. He dreamed of James. *You have to find him.* He dreamed of Aonis, the hero with a thousand faces.

When he awoke, the shack was on fire. A blazing effigy of Dalla and the man's former life. Haro sat beneath the nytewood and watched the shack burn. *The pot. That damned rank stew...* He sang to himself the songs of Ossian and of Timmon. He remembered quotes from wizards and Warlocks. He remembered being killed and being reborn. *How many times? How many bodies? I can't die. I won't. How old are you, really?*

"I'm not truly mad. Not truly," he said aloud. "Not yet. Not yet."

The skitters buzzed in his ear, and the trees seemed to sway and pulse with spring. Haro noted the moon. *It's nearly Springtide.*

In the wood he saw a shape—a moving silhouette. It stopped and swayed in the night between the dark trees, and it sang out to him in a harmony so sweet he didn't even realize he was moving towards it. It neighed and sneezed and made itself visible. A black horse with locks long and smooth as the night sky; and it shimmered like the stars, too. It purred at him with a strange calmness, and Haro reached out his dirty, bloody hand and touched it. Its eyes were gaping black holes filled with the night sky. *E'daru.* Haro got lost in those eyes.

And then e'daru became him, and he became it.

Haro watched the man called Grig from the eyes of e'daru. He watched the man admire his burned hand in the same way Haro had. He watched the man smell the trees and swallow deep of the fresh air. He watched through the eyes of the e'daru as the man gazed back at him and smiled. The man lay down in the grass and felt it with his bare skin and feet, and Haro made a strange neighing sound from his horse's mouth and watched. E'daru used the man's body, and he sniffed at the moon and howled into the night.

Then, Haro was himself again. He looked back at the e'daru with a strange emptiness in his gaze. Grig, the man who was once hiding in the corner of his own mind, had completely vanished. *E'daru took him. E'daru ate Grig's soul.* Haro felt like he was inside of an empty stone castle in the dark, alone.

The e'daru walked back into the deep arbor, and Haro followed it. He was barefoot and covered in soot and sweat, and his stomach roared at him and his thighs and forearms were on fire, but he had to keep pace with the e'daru.

Through the dark wood, the e'daru led him down a trail. Soon Haro saw the blushing light of a fire through the spring-bloated wood. He heard voices.

The e'daru nudged him forward with its nose, and Haro turned around to see it was gone. Haro sat on his haunches and listened to the voices from afar. Men and women. They spoke of food and lack of it and where to go in the morning. They spoke of a cousin of the Lord of the Glenn travelling by cart down a road through the Wick.

"The Wick and all in it are ours," another said.

It didn't take long for Haro to identify them. He stood and walked towards them, broken and bloody and not at all himself. When they saw him coming out of the black night, they all stood.

"Who is it?" a voice said.

"I am Haro."

"By the gods, he lives."

Whispers of "Haro" and "Thrice blessed" fluttered around like moths. There was a shuffling as the three who sat around the fire stood and bowed. The firelight made the folks' greenhoods shimmer in the night like some distant Orantine sea. "We're yours, Haro."

A Gift from Daggland

T HE SUN PEEKED RED and orange from the flat of the land, and the stones stood tall like hardened trees placed by folk and not gods. Maggie chewed on pine nuts and picked mushrooms in the sparse arbor next to their camp. The dew kissed her toes, and she filled her lungs with the moist morning air. Snow clung to the shadows of trees in dirty clumps. Maggie felt bad for the snow, that it had to waste away in such obscurity. Leaves, at least, changed their colours and danced to the ground when it was time for them to die.

Why won't you talk to me when I'm awake? Do I scare you so? Maggie ate one of the mushrooms, the earthy sponginess of it slid down her throat. The blades of grass slid beneath her bare feet and seemed to *lift* her. The dew held many faces, and to those, Maggie spoke.

Sometimes I think I might fall into the sky, or the other way around.

"And in the sky, one is free. In the sky one can be," the mist told her, but Maggie had learned not to trust the mist, just as she should not trust the

fires. Both liked to linger and fill space. Spirits were shrouded in cloudiness, and she was still unravelling their mysteries. The earth spoke untruths if you took what it said literally in the Human tongue, and Maggie hated to work out the riddles it left for her. *You must go east to go west.* It made little sense.

The spring moths found her as the sun started to warm the air, and its rays struck the dew like golden slanted trees, and the moths, green and yellow and red, fluttered around her in the sunlight. Spring chicory and doraine blossomed in blue and purple and bathed in the morning's mist. Maggie knelt down and cupped a doraine bud in one hand. *She wants things, this bud; water, warmth, friends with a face like hers who don't want to trample her. She's like me.*

The birds sang and Maggie dug her toes into the soil. She felt the *life* below her. Crawling, burrowing, being; Maggie could touch their souls with her mind. *Little bit. Just a little bit.* Maggie dug down with her magics and felt around. She stole the life from the worms, and the ants and the grubs and the woodlice. All of it. She drained the soil grey and watched it dull to dead grit below her feet. The soggy clumps of half-decomposed leaves dried and turned to dust, and when Maggie whispered to the wind, it blew the dust about her like rain. She held the life she had stolen in her chest between her teeth; it slipped out her nose and ears. She let it roll off her fingers, and the dancing dust around her feet came alive with all of the colours she had ever known and more. Maggie's eyes rolled back and she felt a calmness. She took a deep breath, and she filled her lungs with the morning, then let the energy slip out of her and back into the grey earth. The soil blackened, and the smell of rot hit the back of Maggie's throat. She dug her toes in the cold, black earth and held her arms to the sky. With her magics, she could feel the small bodies of insects and small rodents lying dead below the soil.

Tell me where to go, please. Talk to me in the waking world. Gods, I'm so afraid. Maggie spoke to the voices she heard in her dreams, but they would never talk back. She talked to anything that might hear her but nothing did.

She was a child born into the wrong body. Her kin were the trees and the rocks, and they spoke a language far older than she knew. *But you did know it, you have just forgotten. You have only forgotten.*

Maggie waited every day for an answer to her dreams but nothing ever came. *The gods have left you. They will not help you in this.* The more she told herself, the more she could believe it. *Alone but for James. He is all you have.* She had to stop waiting for her prayers to be answered. Whatever spoke to her in her dreams demanded to be answered. Maggie knew she could not go on like this—she couldn't stop herself from being *her*. She couldn't stop whatever ate her up and demanded *life*. *And the sky will fall like a blanket and suffocate the world and you'll be smiling, and not because you're happy but because you have gone mad.*

"Mag," James's voice came from behind her. "I was worried when I woke and you were gone."

He fears one day you will *leave.*

"The morning mist was so friendly this morning, I needed to walk amongst her," Maggie said. James smiled at her and she grabbed his hands. Out in the valley, over his shoulder and towards the stones, Maggie watched as a waving white flag above mounted folk came closer and closer. James turned to look.

"I'm going to talk to them. The rulers voted that you and I should go alone," James said.

"Talk?" Maggie thought she was about to kill the rider.

"The white flag... They want peace," James said.

"They're Daggs. Nothing but pirates," Maggie said.

James cocked his head sideways. "Who told you that?"

"It's known."

"The Daggs have magics," James said. "They are more than pirates. They are fierce. Not to be on the wrong side of. They may be carved with Blood Words like Calen Alder was."

Maggie felt indirectly insulted. James had become openly paranoid about magics since the Mountains of the Mother. He feared it was in the veins of the earth and would bleed out from unsuspected wounds. He hated his own powers and thought of them as a curse. Maggie told him he was wrong and tried to comfort him, but she feared he was right. Her own magics had grown to bursting. It was all she could do to keep herself from killing all around her. By getting it out in short bursts, she eased the itch, but only slightly.

"If they have magics, let them kill us. Our story will end together." Maggie gripped James's calloused hand and watched his grim lips curl into a grin. She reached into him and felt his heart with hers; she danced to the thumping of it in her mind. Once Maggie had only felt love like the leaves, forever changing and evolving with the seasons—growing and dying over and again. Now, with James, she felt love like it was the burning rock at the centre of the earth—never moving, forever aflame. *Forever dancing.* And it was so alive with magics that it would outlive them both, forever. *Ai'mair Darra.*

"Let's see what they want." Maggie let James help her mount Bren.

"I should make a truce. Invite them for a feast. Treat them as family. It's what my dad would have done."

He doesn't consider that his dad might not have always done the right thing. "Let's see what they want."

They rode out towards the waving white peace banner.

"SPRAT?" MAGGIE QUESTIONED THE jar of small fish handed to James. She didn't like the smell of it.

"Aye. Smoked sprat in cod oil that is. They'll help ya see in the dark, those.' The Dagglander who called herself Halda was almost elegant in the way she thrust the jar at James. "I insist."

James took it. He poked at it with a finger. "Nothing says peace like small fishes, eh?"

"Don't eat it," Maggie whispered. She didn't trust the sea in the way she trusted earth.

"Ah, here." Halda dug her dirty fingers into the jar of small fish and came out clutching a few of them, and then shoved them into her mouth. "Seriously. Good stuff and will help you put some colour back in that face of yours, they will."

James put the lid on the sprat, and Maggie took them and tucked them away into their bags.

"Lots more where that came from. And shine and mead to go with it." Halda seemed proud of what she had to offer. That made Maggie wary. *Hoarders are proud. Greed and pride are sisters.* "So, what do you say? Bring your whole lot to our camp. What other choice do you have? Springtide is only days away. The sun has told it true. With us, you've got nothing to worry about."

Maggie grabbed James's hand and squeezed it. She wanted to pull the life from this woman and chew on it. James squeezed back. Maggie knew they had no other choice. They couldn't beat this lot in a battle. Not the way it was now.

"We'll come." James said. "But judgement must be spared. You are foreigners on this land and what we do on Springtide when times are bleak is our own business. I will have enough judgement from Father Tree and I don't need it from you."

He sounds paranoid...

"Aye. And we'd expect the same courtesy." Halda chewed loudly. "Our god is loud. She is suffering. We have only come to ease Her pain and help all those who walk on Her."

"Your god is the earth?" Maggie had heard these stories, twists of what was believed and widely told about the Dagglanders and their strange gods.

"Aye. Earth Mother . The Dead God."

"She is dead?"

"She sacrificed Her body to create the earth when Father Sky flew up to the heavens to create the sun and the moon and the stars. Her blood is the sea—drained of Her when She gave birth to a son, Her and Father Sky's only child. She called him Oade and declared him the Blood God. She bid him to rule the seas in Her name. That's why we're here, lass, the Dead God is about to come alive. Father Sky is falling, and She will rise up to meet Him—but only if we can give Her enough strength."

Maggie glared at Halda suspiciously. *These people are mad. I can smell it on them. Woodsmoke and sea salt and madness...*

"Don't take my word for it." Halda held her hand out. "Come. Come with me to our camp."

Around the base of the stones, fires blazed in such quantity that Maggie thought the Dagglanders meant to burn down the great nytewood that bloomed in the centre of the stone ring. The stones were hugged by a grove of charred, dead nytewoods on one side and the mountains of the Fells on another. Fur-clad men and women mingled and ate and drank and sang songs while children of every age hopped, wrestled, and ran about. Iron pots bubbled and stewed over cracking fires.

One man, his golden-brown beard as thick as the foliage in the Fell of summer, shuffled in a strange assortment of steps that Maggie almost thought looked like a dance. When more of the Dagglanders joined in with him and a bard started to strum and sing in time to his steps, Maggie knew he wasn't *just* drunk and it *was* a dance.

But drunk they were—they reeked of mead and sour shine and smoked meat, and the air was clouded with chuff. And they were filthy. So many had dried blood or other grime smeared on their faces that Maggie almost thought it was some kind of crude warpaint custom. Even the dirtiest of the Mal splashed water on their faces from time to time and rinsed off the sweet spots.

"It was a long ship ride down here. We faced heavy storms," Halda said.

"I'm sorry for your losses," James said. Maggie blushed. *He's able to be respectful when all you want to do is kill everyone here and take their ships to Edura.*

"Losses?"

"From the storms."

"There were no losses. Only sacrifices," Halda said. Maggie thought James might say something then, but he was silent.

The Standing Stones of Grave were dressed in old grey-green lichen that looked like a sash of ceremony placed there by these brutes in fashion. The spirits were loud, screaming out to Maggie from the fires. They were being abused and misused for purposes beyond what they were born to do.

"We are preparing ourselves for Springtide. You spoke of judgement, well, Offa is fond of justice and will cast judgement upon the blight that has befallen us. We are prepared to offer a great gift in exchange," Halda said.

Maggie's eyes flicked open. *Offa?* She had heard songs of Offa in her dreams. *Mother?*

"Why did you come all this way?" James asked.

"Are more ships coming?" Maggie blurted.

Halda laughed. "Our ships are sailing the coast. All that remain." The fierce Dagglander glared at Maggie with leather eyes. "Why did we come? I told you, our god is hungry," Halda spat.

"So how will you feed Her?" Maggie said.

Halda laughed. "Blood," she said. "Sacrifice. But come, it's better if I show you. Come meet the Rakkar of Morden Vale."

"Rakkar?" The word sounded familiar but it was lost on Maggie.

"Ruler, king, queen," Halda said.

Maggie nodded to James for luck, and he nodded back. They hadn't come this far into the Dagglanders' camp to turn around.

The rakkar's pavilion was erected from two sails and was braced with mast-heads so the tent looked like a mutated ship that struck upon the land badly and beached there. Dozens of armed folk with black steel axes and black chain armour stood in rows lining the entrance to the rakkar's chambers. Maggie knew Daggland steel when she saw it, and it fascinated her to no end. She remembered the stories from the clanfires, that the Dagglanders forgot how to make the stuff after their empire went mad.

Maggie figured they had so much Daggland steel stockpiled that the loss of the skill didn't matter. Seeing each of the warriors armed with black steel made her shiver. Their dented chestplates were carved with krakens, and no two looked the same. Some depicted krakens with their tentacles spread out like tree branches. Others showed the great beasts swallowing ships or the moon. Some showed the krakens as they charged, curled up like tadpoles. Maggie grabbed James's hand as they walked through the gauntlet, and one of the Dagglanders opened the tent flap for them.

Halda led them inside, and the smell of fish smacked into Maggie's nose. A warrior of a man with snow-white skin, warming his hands over a blazing hearth fire, stood naked with his back facing the door. The man's shoulders looked carved of rock. He turned around slowly and exposed a great golden-brown bush around his member.

"Rakkar Toren of Morden Vale," Halda introduced the naked man standing before them with an odd casualness.

"Why do you disturb me, Halda?" The man's beard looked like the point of a shovel. Maggie was surprised at how little shame he had.

"You think I would disturb you for no good reason?" Halda spat, and rubbed a small leather sack that hung around her neck. "This is the King and Queen of Mal Hallow. They wish to make an alliance."

"Alliance." The naked man said the word like it tasted good on his tongue. "Is this true?" He looked at James. James looked at Maggie.

"Aye, it's true," Maggie said. The man smiled a crooked smile. Maggie could see some sorcery in his eyes. *What were you watching in those fires?* Maggie didn't like the smell of him.

Toren smiled. "I'm glad to hear it! We're here for one reason and one reason only—to make war. Either you're with us or against us."

Maggie hated this man's confidence. He hadn't even made a move to cover himself yet.

"I worry about my people," James said. "War follows me, I need to protect them."

So fuck you, Dagglander, go home, Maggie thought. She didn't like intruders. In Maggie's life, meeting new people only meant meeting more people who would abandon her or try to kill her one day. *They will find out about you. And then what? This is too many people to be around. You can't escape from that many people.*

Toren pointed to the flap of his tent. "You see those people out there?" he said. "Three thousand of them followed me here. There are another seven thousand here that followed the other leaders of Daggland. All of us followed her." Toren pointed at Halda now. "The Knower of Massey Rock." Toren reached for a robe and draped it over his bare shoulders, and tied it at the front with a frayed rope. "You worry about your people? There is no safer place to be than right here at our camp, lad."

"We're with you," James said. "The Hallow needs as many allies as will fight for her."

Maggie's eyes widened.

"We don't fight for you, we fight for Offa," Halda said.

Maggie noticed Halda coveting the leather pouch around her neck and watching James. Halda caught Maggie watching her, and Maggie didn't look away. *What do you really want, witch?* Maggie could smell the woman's anxiousness seeping out of her skin. Maggie had heard stories of Dagglandic witches, ones where they lure unsuspecting victims to feasts and boil them alive in black steel pots. The water boils twice as hot in those Dagglandic things, Maggie had heard. Bloody useless though—a normal boil was enough. Halda still hadn't looked away, and Maggie held her gaze.

Finally, Halda looked back at Toren who said, "So, you'll stay and honour our god with us to thank Her for safe travels? We were just preparing, surely you saw the pyre." *Pyre? Is that what that palisade was? It's the size of a bloody fort wall.*

"Aye," James said. "But me and my heart will need a drink."

Rakkar Toren smiled. He snapped his fingers, and a boy came from somewhere in the shadows. *Where the fuck...* the boy gathered brass cups and filled them with an amber liquid from a tapped keg in the pavilion. He gave one to James, and Maggie snatched the other one and sniffed at it. The life of fermentation made her happy. *This drink is alive.* She drank it in two sips. The pavilion was full of steam, and Maggie soon found the source of the fish smell in the stew pot boiling on one side of the hearth.

"And a bite to eat?" she said.

"Aye," said Toren.

The malt had made Maggie's head swim, and she found herself feeling childish, wanting samples of everything that the rakkar had lying around. Cod stewed with leeks and onion and herbs with thick hunks of barley bread, blood sausage and liver oats, boiled cabbage with garlic and honey, raw salmon eggs, and candied clams with onions.

"Rakkar Erik hates this stuff," Toren said, shovelling red, raw salmon eggs into his mouth. "You've met him, right?"

Maggie shook her head no.

Toren waved his hand. "The fat bastard is hard to miss! You'll see him soon enough. Here." Toren handed Maggie a spoonful of salmon egg. She took the spoon and let the eggs pop on the roof of her mouth, and the savoury juice ran down the back of her throat. "You'll meet the whole lot, surely."

At the behest of the serving boy, folk began to shuffle into the tent one by one, each holding some various comforts. Cushions and goblets and cutlery. Over Toren, a woman draped a fine black robe of black wool with kraken scales at the elbows. *The bastard went from no robes to two.*

A bard holding a woodharp came in and plucked her strings and turned the little wooden pegs and nodded approvingly before she started to sing a song that Maggie had never heard. Something about the woman reminded her of Itchy. The bard had been growing ever closer to James, and for some reason, it made Maggie uncomfortable. *Like he should only have me. Me and no one else.* She knew that was ridiculous but the thought lingered. She didn't want to share him.

Maggie drank warm mead and ate fishy stew, and Halda sang an old Dagglandic song about Mal Hallow to honour their hosts and show respect.

"Ah! Maggie, James, you must meet my rakkarren," Toren said. A group of ragged individuals strolled over. Brightly coloured bandanas of pink and yellow and sky blue held long hair off their sun-worn faces. Maggie knew them for sailors just by the look of their leathery skin, but these sailors wore armour. Black steel armour carved with krakens and other various sea beasts, seals and walruses, leviathans and cycloptic sharks, El'vie and the carpies.

"This is Haron, and Samuel, and Dirk"—they nodded in turn—"and Rora, and Kaley, and Barth."

Toren's rakkarren danced and sang seemingly harder and louder than anyone else in that entire camp. Maggie was shocked at how much they all sang and drank and ate. Many times she shared a smile with James as *more* food came from somewhere. And that night the Rakkar of Morden Vale's pavilion was as alive as spring.

"So." Toren slammed an empty goblet down on the pine table. "What do you say?"

Maggie looked at James. He was smiling. Rakkar Erik of Smokestone was snoring in the chair across from Maggie, his chin resting drunkenly in his chest. He was a large man, just as Toren had promised, three hundred pounds of flesh, and Maggie reckoned a great deal of muscle, too. The man looked like a boar.

But before the boar passed out, he had agreed to an alliance. Rakkar Halda of Massey Rock had agreed, too, and so had the rakkars of Oldstone and Farrock, and so it was settled. Maggie had learned that each of the Dagglandic rulers had a rakkarren that served as their personal guard, but more than that too. Halda, Erik, and Toren had all three asked their rakkarren to *vote* on whether or not to ally. The rakkar's gave all the power of decisions over to the group.

These people fascinated Maggie, but she didn't trust the Knower, the witch called Halda. She felt a strange energy coming from her. *She's unsure, that one. Unsure of me, of James... unsure what she's to do next. She's too much like me.*

James stuck out his hand and Toren grinned and shook it.

Something in the fire whined like a bat, and Maggie's stomach turned. *This will either be the death of us or the very thing that saves us from death.* When Toren passed her the wineskin, she took it and drained it.

"THEY'RE AYELISH, MOST OF them"—Toren took a drink from his wineskin—"and sellswords and mercenaries from Mal Hallow and the Fells."

Out of a teetering wooden structure marched three sullen-looking folk, naked but for their breeches and their chains. Black steel-clad Dagglanders marched alongside them, prodding at them with spears if they trailed behind.

"What do you mean to do with them?" asked James. Maggie couldn't help but wonder how many of them were in that building. She reached out through the ground and felt them there. *There are hundreds more of them in there. By the gods, what are these people doing?* She could feel the prisoners' energy cooped up. Being drained.

"We mean to give their lives to the Dead God come Springtide," Toren said proudly. "My people fought and won these folk by the rights of conquest after we landed here in Ardura, and in the eyes of the gods, they are ours to do with what we please."

The three folk that the Dagglanders had chosen to bring forth were all men. Two with black beards walked ahead, and one with a long grey beard trailed behind. He was covered in black and yellow bruises and wore a latticework of scars around his chest and back.

The greybeard looked up, and Maggie held his gaze. His eyes were as green as a forest in the Wayk of summer, and they sang out to Maggie in sombre notes. *The Bluebird Twins have not been kind to this one.* His life was weak, barely there. When the greybeard saw James, his eyes widened but he didn't speak. Maggie saw recognition there.

Maggie grabbed James's hand. "Do you know that man?" She pointed at the greybeard. The two younger men had hopeful looks on their faces that she may as well have pointed at them.

James studied the man, and Maggie studied James. "I don't know him," James said. The man looked like he would talk if he wasn't in chains with a spear at his back.

To Toren, Maggie said, "Who is that man?"

Toren looked at Maggie, then yelled at the grey-bearded man. "That is the Queen of Mal Hallow speaking. You best answer her. Who are you?" Maggie felt the greybeard's life blossom inside of him. *Hope. He's found hope.*

"Bryn—" he coughed wetly. "Brynmor. Richard Brynmor, m'lady." He bowed.

"Brynmor?" James clenched a fist. Maggie didn't know names but she knew souls. This one was good—warm.

"Aye." Brynmor rattled his chains. "Not so much my old self at the moment, though."

"Brynmor of the Glenn?" James said. "They called you the Hammer."

"Aye, lad. Not doing much hammering anymore." Brynmor's mouth twisted into something like a smile. "You look good, Culdaine. That sword suits you."

"How do you find yourself in chains this far north?" James said. Maggie felt Brynmor's heart thumping. She felt his blood thickening.

"It was a long winter, lad. Is it true you killed *her?*" Brynmor said. "Alone, without an army? Ellorin?" Brynmor held a shaky hand out to touch James, and James backed away. Brynmor hung his head. "She haunts me... that Warlock... Ellorin."

Toren said, "We found him already chained in the cells of a crumbled stone fort near the coast off the Isle of Darra." Toren scratched his armpit. "He was imprisoned with these two and three others. What we saw there... the lot that had these folks cooped up... let's just say Offa was happy to receive their blood." Toren looked over at the rickety shack that held the other prisoners. "They had these folk chained there not as prisoners but as chattel. Feed. They had completely lost their minds—eating Human flesh will do that to you." Toren spat and took a drink of his wineskin. "We're giving these folk here mercy, at the very least."

Brynmor swayed, like a strong breeze might blow him over.

"This man is a prisoner of Mal Hallow," Maggie said. "He led an army to sack five of Mal Hallow's forts."

Toren smiled. "Take him, then!" he said, "We've got more! And what a lovely gift to seal our alliance!"

Brynmor fell to his knees and gazed at the clouds. "By the gods, Hare, thank you for your mercy."

"Get up," James said, and Brynmor stood. "Let's go. We've been gone long enough."

"Surely you'll stay for the celebration?" Halda said. "We mean to give these men to the Dead God as thanks for our safe arrival in Ardura and our new alliance. Daggland and Mal Hallow have a long and intimate history. It is an honour to uphold that tradition."

Maggie had heard stories of Daggland her whole life. She had always dreamed of meeting the black steel-clad warriors and hearing their songs of krakens and great white whales and battles won and lost.

"We can't stay." James was anxious to leave, and Maggie thought she knew why. He had made an alliance pact without talking with any of the other lords first. He feared their judgement. He didn't trust his own. *This was an easy choice. If we chose to fight, we would have been destroyed.*

Maggie and James left the stones, dragging Richard Brynmor on a leather lead attached to his thick Daggland-steel manacles. The lord was barefoot, bruised, and bloody and didn't complain a word of it.

"You had no choice but to make that pact." Maggie hoped her words could heal James as they had so many times before. "You had no choice." She took his hand that wasn't holding the lead. James's eyes fell on her with a strange distance in them. He arched his back like *Essikah* burned him, but he tried to hide the pain.

"There's always a choice." James's words sent a chill down Maggie's spine.

She had heard those very words in her dreams—nightmares. *"Come,"* the voice had said.

"I can't. It's not my choice. It's not my choice." Maggie cried.

"There's always a choice." The dream nymphs taunted her. *"And you're making the wrong ones."*

All Maggie heard was her boots whispering in the grass as she and James walked back towards their ragged people with their gift from Daggland, the Lord of the Glenn, leashed at their heels.

A Reading of the Runes

"**T**ELL ME TRUE, OFFA." Halda rolled her bones on the dirt. They showed her nothing. But she didn't need her runes to tell her that something was strange about the woman who had come to their camp. *The queen...* Because of her, Halda couldn't be certain that the Reaper would be so easily manipulated.

Halda knew nothing of this land and trusted less. A land with trees like monsters is no land to trust. She had already come to miss her den—the wet rocks and the salty fog.

Halda gathered her runes and put them in her leather pouch, and hung the pouch around her neck from the string. *The woman...* Halda walked out from the bower she had been working beneath and through the camp, towards the pyre. She could see the silhouette of the three victims standing on a raised wooden platform high above the crowd, who had gathered to watch their deaths. It would be a clean and quick death. Nothing more than to feed the soil with blood and to show their thanks. The Speaker of the Gods stood upon a stool so that she was higher than the victims, and she began reciting the story of Offa.

"Great Offa, we give thanks. We, Your children, are forever in Your service." Halda erupted in cheer with her people. Black paint streaked down from the Speaker of the Gods' eyes like daggers, and her lips were black as coal. She was dressed in a robe of black wool with kraken bones dangling from her arms. Real or some kind of imitation, Halda hadn't a clue. They had hoards of kraken bones back at Massey Rock, the emerald and brimstone island where Halda had spent most of her life. She could still smell the salt and the brimstone rock and sulphur of the springs there. *And soon the krakens will swim again, and I will be with them.*

"Great Offa, when You rise up," the Speaker of the Gods continued, "we will be ready to give our lives to You. We are ready for Ox'olin and we will do our part to ensure Your strength."

Halda felt hot spit land on her chin from her own mouth as she screamed along with her people. These folk had each been raised with the stories of Ox'olin, and each of them was ready for it. They would drink and feast until the moon was at high now, and Halda would allow herself the indulgence.

The Speaker of the Gods raised her arms. "Out of Offa's dead body, the world was born and us with it. Her hair became the trees, flowers, and herbs. Her skin made the grasses and flowers. Her eyes produced the wells and springs and small caverns of the world. From Her mouth poured forth the great rivers and canyons. From Her nose came valleys and mountain ridges. Her blood was cut from her veins when She died, and She became the seas. She then placed Her son, the Blood God called Oade, in the sea to protect them. From Father Sky came the sun and the moon, and all the stars and clouds. But Father Sky has not always been kind to us, and so our Earth Mother stripped Him of His name to prevent His powers ever surpassing Her own." The Speaker yelped like a seagull, and all of Daggland yelped with her. "A time will come when Father Sky descends once again, and the Dead God will scream for life and rise up to meet Him. When that happens, the Dead God will swallow all of Her children, the seas will drain to fill Her veins, and all of Her body will be whole again to wander with the stars. That time of destruction is called Ox'olin."

"Ox'olin!" Halda screamed along with thousands.

The Speaker held a finger to her mouth, and all were silent. "That time is here," she said, and all stayed silent. "Our very own Prophet of Offa, Halda, the Witch Heart, the Knower's niece, has seen it true in her fires. We all saw it true during the wither year. And so the Witch Heart has united us here to serve our own mythological prophecies. And we *will* serve. You've heard Offa screaming in your dreams—you are not alone." The Speaker put her hands on her ears. "You hear Her screaming with your own ears, I know you have because I have, too. She is hungry. We must feed her with lifeblood. We are Daggland and when the Dead God rises, She will see that Her children have heard Her call and done their work to make way for Her."

And the cacophony well and truly erupted. None yelled like Daggland yelled, and they proved that now. Halda tried to break the wind with her howl. Sig Arfa's army had broken a mountain with theirs.

She had heard the Dead God screaming loud and clear. Never before had Halda heard such madness as that. For weeks, the Dead God moaned, sending winds from the sea that destroyed one in four of their ships in harbour. *And then the fires went out. And no one could deny it any longer. The Dead God needed to be fed. Ox'olin had come.*

When Halda had lit the beacon fire atop Mount Thungstenn to signal Ox'olin, she had ended three hundred years of civil wars with the lowering of a single torch. The rakkars of Daggland all united at Massey Rock—thrice times thirty-three ships and thirty-three more. More than any Dagglandic port had ever seen.

"Not since Kelson has there been such strength in this world." Halda had boasted at the feast that evening. *But Kelson didn't have to sail the Sea of Stars in winter.* They had run into strange polar winds that froze their sails into bricks, and not a person could go above decks. And when the Lights of Crytun rippled in the sky, they weren't their usual greenish pink but rather a strange purple and brownish hue that made Halda sick. *Karaat has pissed all over this world.* Daggland lost a third of their fleet coming south, but even a third of what had assembled was an army big enough to do whatever was needed in the name of the Dead God.

Halda turned down a wineskin that was thrust into her chest and instead filled her hand with a torch. She went to her tent and gathered tallow candles and wooden holders, tucked them into her cloak, then made her way back to where she could be alone.

Under a cluster of small pines, Halda sat upon the brown needles. With her hand, she cleared the needles away from a small spot. With the torch, she lit her candles placed gently around her. Carefully and precisely, she removed the leather pouch from her neck and removed the runes from the pouch. She held the bones in her hand and kissed her knuckles.

"Tell me true, Offa." She rolled the runes, but they bounced strangely on this foreign soil, and one went outside of the area she had cleared and lit and landed on the dark needles.

Halda rubbed her eyes—and blinked. She saw a skull and a flower. The runes were telling her something about the Queen of Mal Hallow. Halda gathered the runes and held them in her hands and kissed her knuckles again. "Is it *her* You want? *Then* will You tell me where to go? What to do? When You are coming?"

Halda rolled the runes again. They clinked softly, and when they stopped rolling Halda smiled. *The runes don't lie. They never lie. The blood of a queen is twice as sweet.* She saw two skulls and a flower. Death and death and life. The Dead God wanted both—king and queen.

As the sun descended, the nightfires erupted across the land with flames ten feet or higher. Great haunches of fresh game turned on spits over pits of hot coals that were shovelled from the great fires. Charred meat and smoke filled Halda's nose, and she salivated.

She found Toren playing his harp and dancing nimbly, barefooted and bare-chested, sweating before one of the fires. Around him, men and women and children sang with their arms around each other, some so drunk the only thing keeping them from falling over was the person next to them. They told stories from the sagas and stories from their families, and when the meat was cooked, they tore it off in great chunks with their hands and ate it while the grease dripped off of their chins and caked their cheeks and hands.

When the moon was high, the lot of them were so drunk they howled at it along with the distant wolves. The victims on the pyre looked down at the drunken crowd that had re-gathered around them. Halda thought that the prisoners looked brave up there, serving Offa like this. *Braver than you.*

The Speaker of the Gods didn't even make a speech this time. When she held her scythe high and stood over the victims, who were now hogtied with rope and lying on the ground on their stomachs, the Dagglanders howled and hooted like the night they had gathered at Massey Hall for the unity feast. As the Speaker of the Gods slit the victims' throats one after another in quick succession, the crowd only got louder. *This is Ox'olin. We have gone mad—mad with obedience to Offa.*

The victims' blood drained from their necks in a great rush at first, and then a trickle, and then nothing. The Speaker lifted the dead husks by the hair and then let them drop, and they slapped into the bloody mud and lay there silent in the moonlight. It made Halda think of the Queen of Mal Hallow. Two skulls and a flower... to kill a queen and a king.

A queen's blood is twice as sweet. I could kill the queen, too. A king and queen's life for the truth is a trade I'm willing to make. Halda looked up to the stars—to the Mother's face. *Tell me where to go. Please. Let this sacrifice be enough. Show me what to do.*

The stones vibrated as the Dagglanders stomped and shouted and lit the night on fire with their song. Halda knew she would not sleep that night, and not from the noise of celebration but from the twisted face she saw in those runes. *Two skulls and a flower... but what if Offa means for me to join them?* It was the second skull that Halda didn't like. *It's just not clear.* Halda hated second guessing herself.

As she lay on the ground beneath the stars and listened to the revelry slowly fade to sleep around her, she watched the stars and talked to Offa.

"Tell me. What do I do?" Halda took her runes from the pouch and kissed her knuckles. *Do I kill these two or join them? Who is the woman? Are they important?* Somehow Halda felt they were important. She had come all this way to the Standing Stones of Grave and *found* them here. She had to trust Offa. She saw no reason to kill them. *Two skulls and a flower—it's just not clear.*

Halda rolled the runes and watched them with great intensity. When they stopped, a great rush filled her body, and she almost looked away as if in disbelief. They had given her a reading she could understand clearly. She studied the runes again and smiled. *Yes. Yes, of course.* Her mind drifted to Aunt Thora's stories. Halda let her eyes fall into the stars again. *Of course... mage...* Aunt Thora had told her that two skulls and a flower meant mage.

"And you know what the mage is a sign of, yes?" Aunt Thora had said, stooping over the great fire in the den. *"It means nature wants to show you a truth you can't find."*

"And where do I find nature's truths?" Halda had asked. She expected her Aunt Thora to tell her to find them in the trickling of a stream or to hear them in the wind. Instead, she had said: *"Soothsayers."*

Aunt Thora had stooped so close to the fire then that her hair began to curl and singe. *"No one knows their true names."*

Halda kept a rosewood chest in Toren's pavilion, which held all her possessions in this world. A blanket of brown lambswool her Aunt Thora had made for her. A brass eye she had found in a shipwreck. Various gems and stones and hundreds of rolls of parchment. Halda ran her finger along the rolls and unrolled the one she selected. *Mage.* Her finger landed on another word. *Soothsayers.* "Of course."

Toren stirred and so did the two men beside him. "What are you doing Halda?"

"Offa has told me true, Toren."

"Right," he mumbled, and stretched. "So is it the king we're killing or the queen? I'd also still be happy with both."

"Neither yet. They may both serve a purpose in this," Halda said. "The prophecy of Ox'olin holds many intricacies, but I have seen one word written in every translation I have ever read, and I've never known what it meant." Halda beheld the scroll once again beneath the torchlight. "Tonight, the symbol for that word appeared in my runes, thrice."

Toren's face was drooping with shock. "What? What word?"

"Mage."

Toren shook his head. "It can't be. Those stories are not all real."

Halda felt sick that she may have misread the signs before. Mage was the Dead God's prophet. Offa's daughter. *If we mistreat her...* the thought of disappointing the Earth Mother made Halda sulk. "Sometimes those old stories turn out to be real," Halda said.

"So what will we do?" Toren said.

"I need answers," Halda said. "Instruct the folk not to harm any of the Mal until I return."

"You're leaving?" Toren looked shocked.

"Aye."

"How will you get answers? Your runes?"

"No." Halda nervously touched her runes as if worried she might offend them. "The soothsayers."

THE DEMHONI

*W*AKE UP OLD BROAD, *you're dreaming...* Etta stood as still and unmoving as rock. A swarm of dull figures moved towards her, their shadows stretched out before them like black spears. Many were mounted, but many more were not.

Etta stood, stuck to one spot like mud had swallowed her boots, unable to take her gaze off the mass. Her eyes darted about, looking for a wolf's mask perhaps, she didn't know. The thing inside of her bones that lit up like a clanfire at the sight of enemies had burned out when she killed Braden. *Like so many other things.* She could only gaze as the dull figures became men and women and children, haggard in their appearance like feral animals, and they began to run and snort and snarl like them, too. Above them rose a tattered banner of dirty white with a red smear that resembled the red eagle of Ayeland.

There was a buzzing in her ear that rose to a rumble. People moved about her—Holden, naked but for his breeches, held an axe in each hand, Cullen held a small iron pot and a flaying knife.

A heavy hand on Etta's shoulder made her jump. "Who?"

"Come." Benn was standing with Swey. The boy held an axe in both hands. Tara was close behind him, also bearing an axe. Etta followed them, floating along like a wraith as the rumble in her ears rose to many piercing screams.

"By the gods," Benn mumbled. Tara screamed like her neck was being rung out. Etta kept checking to make sure it wasn't. *The boy is terrified.* He stood blank-faced, weary-looking.

"Where are we going?" A voice came out of Etta that she thought might be her own.

"This way." Benn was breathing heavily. "Into the arbor."

The ground below Etta's feet rumbled. The air stank of blood and death, and behind her, Etta heard the clashing of iron and screaming. *The horns... they forgot to blow the horns to warn our people... the horns...*

She saw the boy. "Swey," Etta blurted. She needed to taste his name.

"Where's Mom?" Swey blurted back. Etta didn't know. *That is your daughterbound...*

"Hurry," Benn answered.

The arbor grew thick around her, and she ran with her arms in front of her face trying to block as best she could the branches as they ran up a rocky hill through a bony wood. Etta tasted blood in her mouth, and her eyes never left Swey.

"Come on now." Etta pulled Swey up the hill. "We won't let them get us."

"My mom." Swey looked back.

"We'll find her," Etta said. *By the gods.* She hoped she wasn't lying.

When Benn crashed through a bramble patch and threw himself into it, Etta followed, pulling Swey along.

"Jump, Swey," Etta said.

"Are you serious?" Swey's eyes welled up.

The boy is terrified. "There is no other way. Pain won't last, Swey, it can't last." Etta grabbed Swey like a bear and jumped into the patch. She landed hard on her back with Swey still in her arms. The bramble bit into her like a thousand teethed skitters and kept biting, but she was less damaged than if she had walked in. Benn was covered in small cuts and bleeding all over. Swey's grey eyes held her own like he was afraid to look away, but he was largely uncut thanks to Etta holding him. Etta reached her bloody hand out and held his small pale one. The bramble stabbed like tiny arrows, and the pain in the boy's eyes made Etta sick.

"It will be okay." She tried to believe her own words. His eyes never left hers. *He fears the answers to his questions... Tara, where did you go?*

They lay in the bramble, and nothing moved about them for many minutes. In Etta's mind, she heard horns bellowing and the screaming... *always the screaming...* She held Swey's hand and slowly realized where she was lying and why.

"What happened?" Etta feared Benn wouldn't answer because he had gone so still.

"Those cannibals..." Benn held a finger to his mouth to keep her from talking further.

After many more minutes, Etta heard footsteps. By the look in Benn's eyes, he heard them too. Swey was crying softly, and Benn held his big, dirty hand over the boy's mouth as Etta held the boy's hand.

"It will be okay," she mouthed. The boy never looked away as the footsteps got closer and closer. *There are many of them. Three, four maybe...* When the footsteps stopped right in front of the bramble where Etta lay, she took one long look at Swey. Benn had one hand over the boy's mouth and the other gripped his axe. Etta would never touch a weapon again. Not even now—she'd rather die.

Etta heard voices. Two men and a woman. "Who's in there?" said the woman.

"Just there, look," a voice growled. *Is that?*

Benn's snarling lip fell into a small smile. "Calum, you sum a bitch, that you?"

"Aye. Benn? Best hurry," Calum growled.

When Benn stood up, Etta followed. She picked up Swey and carried him out of the bramble, bloody and red-faced as a newborn. Calum, Young Courtney, and Cullen stood before them. Cullen had his right arm, which looked like smashed meat, in a sling made of his shirt.

Etta stood silent before them, holding Swey's bloody hand.

"Do any live?" Benn asked. "We must go back."

Calum shook his head. "You don't want to go back there."

"Do any live?" Benn asked again.

"You don't want to go back," Calum repeated. "Those aren't just cannibals, they've turned Demhoni."

Benn ran off towards the camp, axe in hand. None followed.

"Benn, please don't leave. Please." Swey was blubbering. "Please don't." But Benn didn't turn around.

"We have to go after him," Calum said, but he didn't move.

"Demhoni?" Etta said.

"I saw it in their eyes." Calum walked in the opposite direction of Benn. Etta followed. Swey's eyes never left her.

"We have to find my mom," Swey said.

"Benn will find her," Etta said, and prayed to the Hare to not make her a liar.

E TTA SAT BY A stream on a rock and watched as the clear water gurgled over the pebbles, and she thought of James. *He did that...* Many nights Etta had lay awake since she'd killed Braden, and many nights James had seeped into her thoughts. *What will come of him?* And when the stars danced like embers in the night, she thought of Maggie. *Some say you're a*

danger... What are you, Maggie. Who *are you?* Etta had never asked her. She had only assumed that she already knew. *You know nothing. Not even yourself.*

Swey had fallen asleep by her side after eating a bite of the rainbow trout Cullen had pulled from the stream. Cullen still worked at a small fire now, cooking the bones into a broth in his small pot. Even with one arm in a sling he was a better cook than anyone else in this lot.

"You better hurry with that." Young Courtney dipped her hands into the stream and took a drink. Her hair was braided in two buns. "I'm hungry," she said. All she had done since Etta met her was eat. Even now, her and Cullen were thinking of food.

Cullen smacked his lips. "Bone broth," he said. "Mmh mmh."

"It's possible they're not tracking us..." Calum was sitting on another rock beside Etta. He looked at Swey cautiously. "Benn may have distracted them enough. He may have saved us."

"How many still live?" Etta said bluntly. Calum glared at Etta as if she had accused him of murder.

"All of them," Calum said just as bluntly.

"My mom?" Swey said.

"All?" Etta stood up.

"They're Demhoni, Etta," Cullen said. "They eat the flesh of Humans to absorb their life. It's a curse from the race of Old Gods—a fungus that grows on their brains. A great spite from Father Tree. They were tying up the elders and—they keep them alive, Etta."

"If it wasn't for Holden, they would have tied us up, too." Young Courtney came up from the stream, chewing something. "And where were you?" She looked at Etta.

Demhoni... "You really think it's a curse?" Etta couldn't help but think of the wolf mask. *It came from Hell, Sweyne had said.*

Cullen knelt to pick some herbs and tucked them away into his leather pouch. "A curse or a sickness. Once one starts eating Human meat and performing those Oldarborian rituals, it spreads to the others. There are stories in the cycles."

"I heard very few of them," Etta said. She only remembered hearing those stories from Sweyne. Never from her parents or the elders.

"Maybe your elders were hiding something," Young Courtney said, the end of a honeysuckle dangling out of her mouth.

Etta said nothing and looked at Swey. *Nothing matters but him. Nothing.*

"The stories ain't nice." Calum sat down beside Etta. "Probably for the best they didn't tell you."

"Did you see Tara?" Etta asked. "The boy's mom?"

Calum shook his head. "The crew did a good job at scattering like rats."

When Cullen brought his pot of broth over, Etta took a small sip and woke the boy and made him eat.

When they had finished and stamped the fire out, they kept walking. Swey walked out in front with Calum, pointing at things and asking questions. *Our little wayfinder... he wants to find his mom. He believes he can. Do you?* Etta didn't know.

"Where are we headed, you reckon?" Cullen asked.

"I hope if we keep upriver, we'll find another clan," Calum said.

"Mom would have run upriver. I know it," Swey said.

"What then?" Young Courtney asked, slurping up the last of Cullen's broth.

Calum shrugged.

"The El'vie live by the river in these parts," Etta said.

"What's worse than folk who eat other folk?" Calum said, and Etta saw some fear in those eyes like he'd seen something that had been burned into him. "I'll take my chance with the El'vie."

They walked on.

It was a long hard winter for the lot Etta had joined. They called themselves the *si'otha*. The peaceful folk. They had dreamt of making a safe place to live, free from war. Each of them had been hurt in some way and had nowhere else to be. But all they did was kill. Animals to eat. Animals they couldn't afford to feed. Sick folk, dying folk, and crazed folk that came out of the snow with blackened limbs and distended bellies like bloated wights. They killed them all.

Etta had sat by the clanfire and watched her grandson play as she told her stories. *He needs some kind of normal childhood,* she thought. *Yeah, just like yours. Full of blood and iron. All he's seen is violence and fear.*

When the sicknesses rolled through camp, Etta didn't care if the cold caught her lungs and killed her. Some nights when she lay awake, she wished it would. *You deserve it, old broad. Son killer. You're a kin killer and a coward, and all you have left is a lie.* She would wake in the night and reach for Tarek, for Braden, but she was alone and shivering. She would stare at young Swey in the night. *For him. Stay alive for him.*

And all winter the wolves had followed the *si'otha*—one in particular, howling at the moon each night only metres away from their camp, as if it was letting them know it was there, watching. *Is that you Big Grey?* Etta hoped it was.

And each night, the elders sat around the clanfire and told their stories, twisting their many braids and smoking chuff out of long-stemmed wooden pipes. Some of the stories Etta had heard but many more she hadn't. There were ten elders when Etta had first arrived. And over their travels, ten more had joined them. Some long-grey-bearded old men and some crusty-eyed old women and one, Yesa, who claimed to be neither man nor woman but a child of the stars. When Yesa told the story about the wyrms of Kallahorn, they stood on top of the log or stone they were sat upon and wiggled their arms about as if they had channelled the dance of the wyrms through the fire and the stars.

"The wyrms died," Yesa told them with the firelight blinking on their leather face, "long before Lindis burned. But when that great fortress burned amongst the great northern arbors of Mal Hallow, they awoke something worse than the wyrms." Yesa would stick their chin out and blink one eye towards the fire as if it had hexed them in the past. "The hissing of the flames is the Old One's song, you know?"

When they stopped that evening in a small grove of oak trees and started a small fire as the sun fell into a black meridian, Etta couldn't help but hear the flames hissing louder than she'd ever heard. *The Old One's song...*

Cullen came crunching through the wood towards them.

"What'd you find?" Swey asked, hopeful.

Cullen shook his head. "The game had as hard a winter as us without their autumn hoarding. There's naught moving out there but the wind."

"Well, we best put this fire out then." Calum kicked the fire out and sat down against a tree.

Etta sat in the dark and listened to the stream gurgle and bubble as she brushed Swey's hair with her ragged fingers.

"Is my mom dead?" Swey asked.

"No," Etta said as if she believed it. "Benn will have found her." *You should have found her. You should have gone with him—Wulfee would have.*

"I need to find her." Swey looked older than any seven-year-old had the right to. "She would come find me if I was lost. I need to—"

"Benn will have found her."

"Are you sure?"

No. "Yes." Etta brushed the boy's hair and felt his body shudder as he began to cry again.

"If she dies, I will die, too, right?" he said. "Without anyone to take care of me?"

"She won't die. *You* won't die," Etta said. *Not for a long time.*

"Those people will *eat* her," Swey said, and Etta knew that realization scared him fiercely by the trembling in his voice.

"Benn will have found her." Etta felt sick to her stomach remembering the bite marks on that charred arm. *They were Human teeth. You knew what they were then but couldn't admit it. Human... What can become of a person? What evil lurks in the light that can snatch a folk's soul and own it?*

"They'll eat us, too, if they catch us, the Demhoni. My dad told us stories of Demhoni from the cycles. They eat the life from people to gain their strength." Swey was fighting back tears in the dark, and Etta held him to her chest.

"Your dad shouldn't have told those stories," Etta said. Speaking of Braden grinded her shattered heart to dust. "They'll never catch us, okay? You hear me? I'll keep you safe." Etta kissed his forehead. "They won't."

Etta saw the whites of Cullen's eyes slip off her like oil. "Where do we go, Etta?" Cullen said. He was scared, too. They all were. *But why do they always turn to me?*

"We keep heading north up the river. We hope to get far enough ahead of these Demhoni to lose them," Etta said. Nobody said a word. "Have I told you about Pike the Karl and how he won single combat against the Kihl'dor of Pool beneath the nihr'el with only his shield?"

"Yes," Young Courtney said from the dark, chewing. "But I'd love to hear it told again."

"Me too." Swey cuddled into her arms.

"Aye," Cullen and Calum echoed. "Me too." Cullen sniffed at his pot. "Tell it then."

THE ORACLE

IT WAS A HELLISH hot sky, and the sandy earth was much the same as it picked up in gusts and sliced at Julien's face like so many small diamonds. The sun held court and burned all for the heresy of daring to stand below her. But Julien and his rabble kept on. He would find the Oracle, or he would die in the searching.

"Water?" a voice came from below, but Julien hadn't the energy to bow his head to look. He pulled his shawl tighter to his face and stepped over the dying man. He had made an awful mistake by dragging this many people here, but he couldn't turn back now. He had made promises to his people, and he intended to keep them.

The sand shifted beneath with each step so that walking became an effort far beyond any Julien had imagined, and he had long been cursing his decision not to trade his Lavesheen leather boots for open-toed sandals to the flat-nosed merchant in Saltsan. *"I'm a man of Talent,"* he had told the merchant. *"I wouldn't be caught dead without my boots."* Lavesh held many strange customs that Julien had picked up in his years there—having boots made by a well-known craftsperson was one of the more obscure ones. Julien's boots, crafted by Tiago Dilario of fine Lavesheen bull leather and fitted with phosphor bronze laces, whined in the sand like they were cursing him for bringing them along to such a wretched place.

The sun beat down on Julien and his rabble harder than any enemy. It burned their skin raw and flaking, and sucked the water right out of them until folk were falling over dry and as dead as a tumbleweed. It beat them morning afternoon and evening until the night beat them with windstorms that sent the sand up in gusts sharp and swift enough to burn and cut and blind. The flat, purple sky flashed with lightning like glowing silk spider webs.

"We need to turn back, sir," those with good sense begged Julien.

"No." Julien had seen when and where he was going to die, and it wasn't here, and it wasn't now. He was born to fulfil a long line of prophecy in his family. Destiny had chosen him to bring an empire back to life. "We keep going."

Twelve days of war with the sun and the sand and the mind, and on the thirteenth night, Julien sat under the hot moon and removed his shawl. It was black with dust and grime, and Julien rinsed it with water and wrung it out and let the water drop and bead in the sand. It disappeared into the earth as the sand drank it up almost as fast as it fell.

Around him, men and women lay dying from thirst, from heat exhaustion, from infections and fevers, begging for water. And here he rinsed his shawl with it. These folk had fought so many battles with him; they had killed so many by his word to get to this desert. These folk served Julien at Odessa and at Talent, and twice at Boretta.

Julien dragged them to fight for whatever Magister paid more. The rulers of Lavesh called him traitor and turncloak and most of all *fool*. They doubted him and they hated him, but he didn't care about the rulers. He cared about his family name and the people who tried to erase it. He cared about his crew, his *rabble*, and now Julien had led them across the Ayelish channel to a place that made Hell look good. *But Karaat has told you true. You have seen your future. You have to believe.*

Julien dumped more water over his forehead and down his pants. He chugged his water flask dry. He was Human and would be lying to himself if he didn't fear death out there, but he needed to lead, and he could not show an ounce of weakness.

When Julien stood before his crew, they looked at him and listened. He had crawled his way up from the blood-soaked mud of the bottom ranks of sellswords into leadership, and each of these folk respected his strength. He earned the right to lead by proving there was no one alive that was better for the job. His name meant nothing to these folk, but his words meant everything.

"One more day," he lied, hoping he hadn't, "and we will drink from the Oracle's teat."

Julien's rabble erupted in a raucous cheer. The men and women who had followed Julien were red and raw, and they complained that their tongues were as dry as wood. But the rabble cheered and yelped into the night sky. They screamed and hollered into a dark plain where the stars and an endless sheet of hellish earth called sand was all there was in any direction for days and days. These folk were vagabonds and drifters, bastards and orphans, and they had all found each other and made a career out of killing. And in Julien's experience, nothing formed a bond like spilling blood.

"Esterbraun!" they chanted wildly like mad pack animals and belted out to the moon, and shook the ground with their callings. They were Julien's rabble, and they would follow him to Hell itself if he told them that was what they needed to do. He had made them all rich, given them lands, made them powerful. The Magisters could exile him from Lavesh, but they couldn't stop him from taking a third of the sellswords in all of Lavesh with h im.

Julien had landed a thousand soldiers on the coast of Esher, south of Saltsan. "The Oracle will make us gods!" Julien had said, and the soldiers bellowed out a cheer. He was the god of mercenaries. A brigand prophet who had talked to God, and his crew would follow him anywhere. He was going to find the Oracle.

The next morning, just as the golden sun began its ascent, Canri knelt in front of Julien, holding an ornately carved chest of nytewood.

"Open it." Julien had seen his treasure just hours ago, but his eyes still craved to feast on it.

Canri opened the chest, and Julien beheld the large, bleached, yellow bone that sat inside atop a black cushion. Julien's gold-ringed finger reached out and stroked the bone. Canri stared wide-eyed, waiting. *Every time he thinks the curse will catch up with me. Every time he is wrong. I am of Old Blood. I am Draku—immune.*

Julien stood and closed the chest. The lightning storms had lit the sky with glowing silver webs all night and hadn't stopped. *Rain is coming.*

"Karaat has told me that today we find water. And on the next night, we find the Oracle." Julien raised his hands, and his crew went wild. It was only them who would be mad enough to yelp into that hellish sky with so much thirst on their tongues and in their throats. And it was only them mad enough to walk into that desert knowing less than half would come out. And it was only them who knew whoever *did* leave that desert would become immortal through song and story when Julien met his destiny. *Karaat will see it true. The Draku live.*

"Your ancestors were born out of these sands." Julien raised a fistful of sand and let it drain through his fingers. The crew gathered round and sat on their calves and listened. "Long ago, a great lightning storm attacked these lands and turned pieces of this desert into many shining clear crystals. Those crystals sat in the desert here for a thousand thousand years and more, studying every creature and every sunrise—learning the land as a god knows it. When finally the great lightning storm had returned from its many year slumber, it attacked the sands once more, but this time the crystals rose up to defend it, and the lightning struck them instead. But you know what happened?" Julien tossed the remaining sand in his hand in the air, and it scattered in a dust cloud that caused his crew to explode with revelry.

"We fucking rose up!" they screamed. "For Esher!"

"That's right." Julien paced through the ranks of his people. "The crystals shattered and fell to the earth as blackened husks. But the crystals were only cages to you! You cracked through the burning blackened husks that were aflame with lightning fire and walked upon these sands for the first time. From that day forth, the Esheri have been here. And from time to time, the place needs cleansing of the filth that tries to live here!" Julien let his people celebrate their own origin. They cheered and chanted his name, but he knew what they really wanted—a place to call home and a leader strong enough to take one for them. "And when the Draku came to these lands with fire, the Esheri fought alongside them because they remembered their birth—fire made them stronger. They were the fiercest army this world has ever seen! They ruled from the White River to the Bone Islands and even further south, too. We are here to obtain that glory once again, my friends—family. That and more. When the Draku rise again, Esher will be on their backs!"

The rabble found water that day, and they all knelt and dipped their faces into the oasis and drank and slept under the trees. They woke and drank some more and spent the night sleeping on the cool damp sand. In the morning, they drank as much as they could and filled their waterskins and soaked their clothing, and Julien led them on into the hot day. Still, the sky screamed with lightning, and Julien knew a storm was coming.

The sun chewed them up that day, even after all that water, perhaps because of all that water, and when folk started to fall and the crew stopped to help them, Julien had to give the order that no person stop on any account to help others. If they did that, none of them would make it through the desert. They carried on, and Julien couldn't bring himself to turn around when he heard folk crying out for him to save them.

They spent the night huddled together, protecting each other from the sandstorm.

"It is Karaat's test. That is all." Julien spoke these words, and they were enough to give hope to the people who were thirsty and starving before him. The sand cut their skin and ripped their lungs. It burned their eyes and left them begging for its mercy. "We will shine through," Julien said. "I've seen my future and it does not end here. Yours does not either." And as Julien spoke these words, the sky lit up in streaks of purple and pink and green from the heat bolts. The stars danced on a midnight rainbow, and the sand and wind cut and suffocated the only witnesses.

They found more water the next day, a small pool in the bottom of a dried-up lake that the Esheri call arroyo. Julien was so exhausted from the heat that he couldn't trust that the water wasn't an illusion until he fell into it and soaked his whole body. Soon all of them were wading in the ankle-deep water. Drinking and resting. Above, the lightning danced, and Julien passed the last bottle of rum back and forth with Canri.

"Do you ever doubt yourself?" Canri asked. The massive man looked up to Julien like a big brother, and Julien would never lie to him.

"No. I don't." Julien took a long swig. "When you have seen tomorrow, today is just a game."

Canri stared back in amazement and nodded.

"That's a storm coming. We can't stay here," Julien slurred. The rum hit him hard with an empty stomach.

Canri studied him with questioning eyes. "I can't much walk," he said. Julien could hear his crew singing songs of Kelson and of Pennifer, and they lay in the pool and drank the water.

Soon Julien passed out.

He awoke with his mouth full of sand, and his ears were ripping with wind. His people were shuffling around in a panic, struggling to get some sort of canvas structure to protect them from the cutting sand. The sky was purple and webbed with silver lightning. Julien tasted moisture in the air.

"We have to go!" he screamed, but no one heard him over the wind. He felt a drop on his nose. *Fuck.* Then all at once it was pouring. The water fell from the sky like a river had burst open in the clouds and bled into the earth. Water flowed over the cracked and parched earth of the arroyo and pooled in pockets. The pockets filled and flooded, and when they burst, the water rushed angrily out of them.

The wave swept Julien's feet out from under him. He was riding the current towards the centre of the pool when he felt Canri's big hand clutch his tunic and yank him to his feet.

The whirlpools picked up as the rain fell, and people were getting carried into the pool, pulled underwater, and weren't surfacing. The rain beat off the ground like a million wet hammers and drummed Julien's skull as he tried to bark orders to deaf ears.

"Go!" he screamed. "Walk, don't swim." But folk were getting swept away and drowning, and Julien waded through the whirlpools to pull men and women to their feet.

"Come on." Canri pulled at Julien. Even a man of his size was struggling to stay on his feet. "Out of this arroyo."

"I won't let my people die while I watch." Julien didn't have to tell Canri that this wasn't the place he would die. Canri had been beside Julien and had heard the gully-witch of Boretta speak the words for himself. Canri knew when and where Julien would die.

In the wickedness of the torrent, Julien plucked his people from its grasp and soon hundreds were on the banks of the dried lake chanting his name.

"Esterbraun," they cheered. "He'll never die. Karaat says he'll never die!"

It rained for two days as they huddled together like mice on the shore of the lake, and the sky was on fire with silver flame as the lightning danced. When the storm was over, they fished thirty bodies out of the arroyo that was now a lake.

They buried each of them shallow in the sand and said a prayer to Karaat, and then they were off. Not at all the ceremony they deserved, but it was the best they could manage.

The Oracle never made herself visible, though Julien was sure he had travelled far enough. *You missed it. You've passed it and you've gone too far.*

He pulled out a small steel circle, which held a red needle. The needle spun wobbly before settling in one direction. Julien looked behind him to where the needle pointed. He had purchased the tool off a peddler-witch in Odessa. She said it was from the old world, and a Sorcerer whose soul was trapped inside told it how to always find north. And Julien remembered Karaat's words in his dreams. *"Go north,"* the voice of Karaat had told him on the night he showed Julien his death. *"Don't stop."*

Julien put the small steel circle away and continued walking. *North. Don't stop.* Most folk Julien knew would be terrified to have witnessed their own death. *But they don't choose to see the positives. I'm invincible until that day.*

When the Oracle's temple became visible in the murky desert, Julien was sure it was an illusion. Curved red-brick walls rose from the golden sand, and a worn brown onion-shaped dome crowned it. A white stone statue of Kassius stood as tall as the red walls. Years of sand had scorned and sanded the face of Kassius away. *Perhaps Kassius the Deceiver would have liked that.*

"Do you see that Canri?" Julien said. "Or have I gone mad?"

"I see it. I see. Is it..." Canri stammered.

"The Oracle," Julien stated.

"What is that statue?"

"That is Kassius, Canri. The Draku King. My ancestor..."

"In songs, they call him Kassius the Deceiver," Canri said. Whispers of *Kassius* floated around the rabble like unwanted flies.

Julien faced his people and pointed at the statue. "You see that?" he yelled.

His rabble yelled back. "We see it!"

"You know who that is?" Julien shouted.

There was a great looming silence for a moment before someone yelled, "The Deceiver!"

"The Deceiver," Julien said, "and you know why they call him that?" Silence again.

"Kassius was the first Draku king of Esher, chosen by the Oracle after hundreds of years of turning down others who had made the journey to see her." Julien stood tall now, his rabble loved stories of victory. "Thousands upon thousands of folk had braved the desert waste and turned up at the Oracle only to be denied entry. Before Kassius, the people of Esher knew a hundred different kings and queens. Every town had their own ruler, and Esher was far from peaceful. These rulers were corrupt, poisoned in their minds by darkness. War and murder were everything, and the Esheri people were subjugated in their own lands.

"Then Kassius the Deceiver held a grand party at Red Sky Rock in Sareen to celebrate the birth of his new dragon called *Ermegal*. The Esheri rulers were all eager to align with him for their own purposes so most, if not all of them, arrived in Sareen. Kassius had a grand feast served, prepared by the finest cooks, and the finest drink and smoke in all of Ardura. All was readily available to Kassius. There were singers and fools and jugglers and plays took place in the streets that lasted for twelve hours or more.

"Soon, the drunken kings and queens started to demand they see the dragon. Kassius had hoped they would ask. His guards sealed the doors of his grand hall shut. They pulled the large, red rug that lined the middle of the hall, revealing a massive stone trap door. Kassius himself snapped the locks with his sword *Ladyfinger*, and from below the guest of honour burst forth. *Ermegal* killed all of them in a flaming slaughter, and in one night, Kassius became the Draku King of Esher. In one night, he became the Deceiver.

"But Kassius still needed the Oracle's blessing for the Esheri to fully accept him. At the time, the Oracle was the Esheri's only god and her word was fact. But she was known to hate the Draku, so Kassius deceived her with his charm. He was the first Draku to impress her—the first to earn her respect. And after only three weeks of visiting, the Oracle declared Kassius King of Ardura." The rabble cheered and hollered. They celebrated their victory. "And now I am here to do the same!"

But what will she think of you? Are you worthy?

"And who cares what some desert hag thinks?" Julien had said to his father, Damen, as a boy.

"The Oracle is from the blood of Sorcerers, boy. She is older than time. Her judgement is knowledge. Knowledge is power. Never forget that, son," Damen had told him.

Kassius's fame had become legend. It is told that he ruled Esher for three hundred years after his visit with the Oracle and helped to fight against the invading Warlocks. *But he didn't succeed.* The Warlocks laid a curse on the Draku so they, and their dragons, would never rise again. Anyone who even touched the bone of a dragon would shrivel into a charred corpse. It was an old curse sung into the rhythms of the earth—as true as the rising of the sun, the song continues.

But the curse didn't affect all Draku. Some were immune, and so the Lovasi Warlocks and the Draku went to one last war. Kassius fought against the Warlocks, who had all of the might of Yehven behind them, and still, he nearly won. In the end, the Deceiver was deceived by one of his own and murdered. The war ended, and the Draku faded into nothingness under Lovasi rule. Many years later, Kelson was born in Lovas and conquered all of what Kassius had created here in Ardura. He built his monstrous castles of stone and dead trees and mortar and the memories of the Draku and their dragons were buried deep beneath them.

When the Oracle sees who you are, she will bow down. You are twice the man Kassius was. If she really sees all truths, she will see that. She will have to grant you questions. She will have to...

Julien spat on the statue of Kassius as they trailed by. When he approached the door, his rabble knew to stay behind. This was not their part. None of them were near mad enough to do what Julien had come to do. None would risk the Oracle's judgement unless willing to die. *Only you. But I know I'm mad so I can't* truly *have gone completely crooked.*

A stone stairway led down below the sand to a white door with green runes carved into it. There was an inscription carved in the same runes on the doorway leading down to the stairs. Julien's mother had taught him how to read old Yehvenki to prepare him for this very day, and so Julien read the inscription out loud to savour the taste of the words.

Irill tur sa'illes. Speak true and enter.

"You must know yourself, son. Never forget. Knowledge is power." Damen's words rang true in Julien's mind since the day they were first spoken to him.

"Irill tur sa'illes," Julien said aloud. By speaking those words, he shared breath with Kassius. *Kassius spoke these very words in this very spot. The name Esterbraun has been laughed at for long enough.*

When Julien received that dream from Karaat, he knew that his destiny had come. When the fires went out and the wind and rain died, Julien knew it was the sign he needed to act on what he had been shown. The dream had told him that he was Draku, and that his father and grandfather weren't mad. It had told him where to find dragonbone. And it showed him where he would die so he would not be afraid to do the things he was born to do.

Julien descended the stairs. At the bottom, he touched the white door with his ringed fingers. The door glowed and shimmered, green lights danced throughout the runes that were of a language far more ancient than Yehvenki. He pulled out a small silver-white stone rippled with ice-blue veins.

With knowledge you can bash truth over the head and watch it bleed out. Speak true and enter... Julien touched the stone to the door, and the door swung open. Julien's body rushed with warmth, and his heart leapt from his chest. *The truth is that no words will open this door. It's a door that has been locked, and how else to open a lock but with a key?* The stone was another gift he had taken from the peddler-witch along with his north needle, or rather, the stone was the true reason he had gone to that witch in the first place. Julien had heard the story about the Sorcerer's key to the Oracle's den his whole life. Most people don't think it's true. Most people want nothing to do with the Oracle after the wither year. The folk of Esher have started to believe that she caused it with her sorcery. But Julien had grasped onto that story and followed every thread of it that he found. It led him to the peddler-witch in Odessa. He never thought she would have actually had the stone, but there it was, on display in the crude hut she called a home. Julien had never felt more alive than the day he first held that stone. *Until now.*

"Canri," Julien called up the stairs. The albino appeared at the top with an unlit torch on top of Julien's ornate chest. Canri looked at the open door, at Julien, and his mouth gaped as he continued to look back and forth. "Bring that chest down here, would you?" Canri ducked and followed Julien into the Oracle's den.

Black mould crusted the corners of the vaulted ceiling above. The wet, grey stones that made up the stairs, walls, and ceiling seemed out of place amongst the sandy desert—like they had been dragged here from some far-off place to construct this temple. And like any true Yehvenki temple, the true marvel was what they could build on the inside, not without.

Julien lit the torch and followed a long hallway. He almost couldn't believe what he saw—the beauty of it took his breath. The walls were carved with art pieces. Julien saw depictions of battles where folk from one side were throwing stars and folk on the other side were holding trees by their root systems and batting the stars away. He saw pyramids and great skinny towers, and above them, a falling star. He saw dead horses and dead folk riding them. The crude art went on and on in ornate detail. *Kassius walked these very steps and saw these very carvings. What did he think of them? He was an artist, like you are. He would have appreciated these immensely.*

At the end of the hall, Julien opened a door that seemed to be made of brass. The hinges squealed and a horde of bats flocked up from some unseen pit. Julien felt his stomach turn sour, and he nearly vomited but forgot all about that when he heard the voice.

"You've made it."

"Yes," Julien said. It was silent for a time, but Julien had been instructed by the gully-witch to always wait for the Oracle to respond.

"And what have you brought for me, Esterbraun?" the Oracle sucked her lips. She wore a dirty, ragged old shawl of stained white over her frail body. She looked like an elderly beggar.

She knows your name. She knows you. Julien snapped his fingers, and Canri came forth holding the chest. It was of black nytewood and rimmed with golden braces and clasps. The Oracle's eyes widened. She clicked her tongue. "I've brought you a legend as great as your own. A living Draku."

The Oracle stuck a thumb in her ear and glared at Canri. "Him?"

Julien shook his head. "Open the chest, Canri."

The albino opened the chest, and the dragonbone shone dully in the dim den. The Oracle stood, her knees cracking like knots in a fire, and studied the bone with accusing eyes. "It's fake."

Julien reached into the chest and picked up the bone. He clutched it firmly and held it up so the Oracle could see. It was as strong as steel and lighter than wood. "Dragonbone of Old."

The Oracle clucked at him. "It's not real. Leave here."

"Take it, Canri." Julien thrust the bone at his friend.

Canri stared dumbfounded. "What?"

"The bone. Take it." Julien thrust the bone one more time. He held Canri's eyes. *You think I would lie to you? It's a ploy. Go along with it. Like we always do,* Julien said without saying. His friend seemed to understand. They had been through hundreds of plots together before and came out most of them on top. Canri smiled.

"Of course," he said with a smug smile on his face. And Julien knew that Canri thought he had been duped this whole time they had been together, and the bone had been fake all along. The big man took the bone. He held it, and Julien saw all the nerve melt out of him when nothing happened. The albino relaxed his shoulders in visible relief.

The Oracle glared. She held her bony hand towards the door. "Go." Julien noticed the gold ring on her finger covered in carvings.

"Ah," Canri gasped loudly. "AH." Then he screamed. His arm began to blacken like coal. "Help," he screamed louder now. "I can't let go." His hand clutched the bone like a vice, his fingers crooked around into an impossible shape. His arm was black to the shoulder now, and the charcoal rash started to creep up his neck. Soon he was screaming like an animal being butchered. His char-blistered skin smoked and stank of frying flesh.

The Oracle backed up and pressed herself against the wall. She looked back and forth at Julien and the man who was seemingly burning alive. After many minutes, Canri stopped screaming. *That was your best friend, there.* Julien sighed. He knew that in a dying world wrought with war and ruin, even friendship could turn cold or rot.

Julien had heard Canri plotting one night while he thought Julien to be asleep. *He plotted to kill you this eve if you made it out of this den alive. He didn't believe the gully-witch's prophecy, or else he thought he was above it. He would sell the dragonbone and start his own company of sellswords. He thinks the time has come for him to rule suzerain over these parts. The folk have begun to lose faith in me, but I am about to bring it back for them.* Canri's blackened hand turned to ash in Julien's fingers as he pried the dragonbone from it.

The Oracle studied Julien from the shadows and slowly came towards him.

"Come," she said, "sit by my fires. I am going to tell you everything you seek to know."

The flames crackled and danced, and the Oracle sat before him like a blacksmith at a forge. The Oracle was known to work visions of the flame better than any deathstealer or witch. And the Oracle didn't just see the truths of tomorrow, she spoke them into existence. Some called her a Maker. Julien's dad had called her a false prophet—some kind of abomination Hellsent. There were other small groups throughout the south that shared Damen Esterbraun's beliefs, but they were nothing but tiny cults in the shadow of belief. The Oracle was the closest thing to a god that walked this earth. She spoke directly for Karaat.

"Is it fortune and fame you seek? Do you want all of Esher? Say the word and it is yours."

"I seek more than fortune and fame. I seek to take back the empire that belongs to me—that belongs to Karaat."

"What would you want to know, then?"

Julien had rehearsed this answer over and over in his head through the years in exile and the long weeks in the desert. He could ask anything and have it made reality, but his dad had warned him of the way the Oracle's words can be twisted and misunderstood. He had to consider his questions carefully. Julien had no interest in Esher—his family had ruled and lost Esher thrice already throughout history. *Esher is stale and sandy.* Julien's ambitions were higher. He was a prophet of Karaat, he was Draku, and he swore by the mercy the Creator had blessed upon him that he would bring back his people's former empire.

"I want Hest. I want to rule Ardura as Kelson did—as Kassius did," Julien said. "I want to bring peace to the world and reunite my people."

The Oracle glared at Julien, and her eyes shone like stars. "Hest?" She spoke with the same condescension the Esterbrauns had been greeted with for generations. Julien stood by as folk degraded his grandfather and his father anytime they mentioned their blood. Anytime they mentioned Draku, they were laughed at. They had no way to prove their blood, and so folk only doubted them.

"Tell me, if I attack Hest, what will happen?" Julien asked.

"If you attack Hest..." The Oracle seemed to consider her next words carefully. Her eyes slipped away from the dragonbone and she studied the flames as if she was reading a book. "If you attack Hest, a great empire will fall."

Yes... Julien was silent for a time as he became entranced by the flames. They drew him in with the dancing of their energy.

"What else would you know, child?" The Oracle's aura had turned dark. Julien traced the rigid fracture lines in the dragonbone with his eyes. He could almost see the eldritch darkness leaking out of the cracks.

"I want to know what knowledge lives in the libraries of Hest. My grandfather used to speak of a book. A book that would bring the Draku culture back—our book of creation."

"Your grandfather was mad," the Oracle said in dismissal. "What else would you know?" *Karaat has told me all I need to know anyway. What I need is a catalyst to my own ascension.*

"Are you afraid of death?" Julien spat on the flames, and they hissed.

The Oracle looked at him like he was a bug. "Do you know what I am, child?"

"You're a remnant of a dead world. Your very existence gives credence to legend." Julien was deep in his own mind now, remembering the nights and days he'd spent with Benecio, and Audacio, and Phosphone. "If it were up to me, I would burn everything and everyone that Yehven produced. Right down to the wick of its existence and burn that too. Especially you. False Prophet. Sorcerer. Your people and the Warlocks, you killed my ancestors and my parents, and before you kill me, I am going to take back what is rightfully mine by the word of Karaat. I'm going to take back our existence and make the Draku known once more. Unbury my culture from the sands of time."

The Oracle was about to harm him in some way, Julien saw the violence in her eyes. Without a thought, Julien clubbed her over the head with the dragonbone.

"Filth!" she snarled, holding a hand to her face. Julien again noted the ring on her finger. It looked almost identical to his own but for the carvings. *Did they inject simple items with magics?* The look of terror in the Oracle's eyes was enough to let Julien know the truth even before her skin became char-rashed—that she was no god, she was simply of an ancient race of semi-mortal beings. When the blackness took over her skin, Julien smiled. The sound of the Oracle's scream as she died was deafening.

Julien hoped they heard it all the way in Hest.

ANSWERS

"M MRRHMM," THE PRISONER MURMURED through the gag in his mouth from the back of Aldred's horse.

"I don't like this any more than you do, okay?" Aldred said. He was well and truly sick of his twisted prick of an uncle. "When you're on that table, just tell him what he wants to bloody hear. You don't need to die today, okay?"

"Mrrmhmm," said the scout.

Aldred thumbed the letter in his chest pocket. A raven had brought in a delivery of messages from Hest, and Aldred had found one with his name on it. *And in her handwriting...* "You ever been in love, scout?"

"Mrrhmm," the scout said.

Has love ever done a single thing other than break your heart? Are you like me, scout?

The Hester camp seemed haunted, void of anything warm. The moon was a cold grey that lit the camp an even colder blue. Soldiers were slumped over around fires burning down to the coals. Usually, the night before battle, chuff smoke, sweat, and stories left half told lingered around the fires. But now, the only sound other than the horse's hooves was the odd cough from one of the tents. The army was still on winter rations, and food was in short supply. *The entire country is bleeding and hungry but still we fight to conquer more land...*

Aldred rode through the encampment to Sir Brooton's tent and hitched his horse out front.

Dustey, the boneman, parted the tent flaps and came out to meet him. He looked at the body and shook his head in disbelief.

"You found one? Brooton was right. Prick's always right," said Dustey, and untied the Esheri scout from his horse. The scout was dressed in loose fitting garb and wore cloth around his face and head.

"Didn't even try to hide. I found him walking on the Sunroad, singing," said Aldred.

"Mmmrh," said the scout before Dustey dropped an elbow into the side of his head. Dustey never hesitated to hit a person when they couldn't hit back.

Aldred helped Dustey carry the captured scout into Brooton's tent. The captain of the King's Army had a heavy oaken table rusted with bloodstains set up in the middle. The table came with the army on every tour. It needed its own team of horses to pull it, along with all of Brooton's other luxuries. *"It gets answers,"* Brooton would tell the king when the king would complain about the extra cost of the work horses. *"Answers win battles."*

And my father, the king, is a fool who believes every word his older brother Brooton says.

So the Hesterland army pulled an obscurely large oaken table through three kingdoms and a hundred towns. Brooton tied people to the table, and the people gave Brooton the answers he wanted. *Benecio said: understand thy enemy.* Brooton took that and fucking ran with it. He got inside of the enemy's head and looked through their eyes. He pulled truths out from the inner souls of folk who didn't know those truths were there.

Eight summers Aldred had spent tying people to that table and spreading fear of the Lion. This year, he'd even wintered with the army in Behru and spent all four seasons committing war. With his Uncle Brooton's army, Aldred sieged and butchered and starved an enemy people who were already beaten by the elements. And now, the Hesters held forts they had no hope of keeping in a country that had nothing left.

But Natt Floyd just had to have Red Sky Rock, and he convinced the king to give it to him. A bloody big up jump from Friars. Lord Natt Floyd of Friars waited five weeks for Brooton's army to take Sareen by siege before he arrived with his own army just in time to sit the throne.

"Sorry I was late," Natt had said to Aldred. Some of the corpses were still smoking on the sandstone cobbles around them. *"We got held up in leaving! Looks like you didn't much need us, anyway."*

Aldred clenched his fists thinking of it—thinking of his dad and that fucking Warlock who gave the coward Natt Floyd power. *They shit on you and give people like Natt Floyd a palace in paradise.*

"Mmmmmrh," said the scout as Dustey secured the last belt around his left ankle. Aldred took the gag out of the scout's mouth.

"You will both die tonight," the scout choked out.

Aldred put the gag back in. He wasn't in the mood to see more dying, but he knew very well that this scout wasn't going to tell Brooton what he would want to hear.

Dustey grinded something with a mortar and pestle. He was more than just Brooton's headsman. He was a boneman—a witch-priest of the Dead Isles of far southern Sothura with knowledge of the secrets that fester in those wet jungles. Brooton had found Dustey ten years or so ago in the Bone Islands, wandering alone and delirious. He claimed to have dreams of dragons, and Brooton loved those stories.

Brooton took Dustey in and nurtured him back to health, and the boneman had been around ever since. Aldred had known Dustey near half of his life and had never gotten to the point where he was completely comfortable around him. The boneman *knew* things, things that he saw in his fires. He was the blood of Old, Draku; Aldred had heard folk talk about him, and he was dangerous.

Dustey's skin was stained the colour of clotted blood, and his dread-locked hair was the colour of bones. His leaf-green eyes bulged beneath bushy, white eyebrows.

Aldred watched the boneman grind his mortar and pestle and pour and mix and stir things that Aldred couldn't identify. He had set up his tinkering station in Brooton's tent, an array of tools and glass bottles full of brightly coloured salves and liquids for getting answers out of people. What kind of sorcery Dustey mixed up, Aldred didn't want to know.

Aldred thumbed his letter again. *Praise Eralis, Eshlynn, I miss you.* It had been a long and dark winter with the boneman and Brooton as the Hester fyrd besieged the Esheri cities along the Sunroad. Battles that will be written about in books as glorious victories, but Aldred knew the truth. He knew how easy it was to author lies.

The siege of Soren, then Lysess, Behru, Saray, and lastly, the Cherry of Esher, Sareen, where, when they arrived, the pink cherry trees of lore were brown and dead, and black wasps swarmed the rotten cherries below. Aldred couldn't wait to see the Lovasi Castle of Red Sky Rock. When he finally did, he pissed on the outside of it and left. It was a monstrously beautiful hunk of stone, and it made Aldred feel ill.

Aldred had helped his uncle sack towns and cities with little to no resistance. They installed their own Hesterland rulers in place when the fighting was over. It was all a success. *That would be torn apart by rebellion within a year.* In a single year of darkness, the Hesterlands had grown its territory more than a third in size. *And you killed starving people to sack broken towns. It's going to take years to get Esher back to its former state, and now that is your burden to bear.*

Aldred had watched Brooton slay Caris Serahnon of Soren, and then watched Brooton slay Caris's son, Trist, in Behru, though Aldred could have sworn that it wasn't actually Trist they killed. It was an old trick Aldred had read about in the stories of Phosphone—dress a sacrificial lamb in the lion's clothing and let the lion live to plot revenge. *But someone needs to die right? As long as the people* believe *he's dead—that's all that matters, really.* Aldred was sure that even Brooton knew it wasn't really Trist he was killing. But the show and the throne were all that really mattered.

Bullies. The Lions of Hester are no better than the big, bad cat from the fables of Phosphone—the one where a lone wildcat starts fighting and chasing off all of the other animals around them until the wildcat had so much territory that it could roam and roam for days without seeing a single other animal. Then, one day, all the animals that the wildcat had chased off appeared on the horizon in a mob—they chased the wildcat down for years and finally killed it horribly. One by one, the animals re-settled the land the wildcat stole from them.

In Lysses, Aldred and Brooton had found the prophet of Odius. Odius and his descendants had overlooked the shrine there in the foothills of the Hills of Soma for a thousand years. They grow yellow-gold and purple mushrooms there and use them to talk to the gods. Brooton hung the Prophet from a eucalyptus tree and trampled the mushrooms and got rid of them in other ways.

"The Lion is god in these parts now," Brooton had said one night as he stood in front of a blazing fire, his eyes bulging from his skull; his mind was so ravaged with mushrooms. "No need to talk to the gods when the folks can pray to us."

They spent three weeks in Lysses. Brooton burned the ancient eucalyptus grove there, and he and his closest hundred devoured mushrooms until they were sick and vomiting black. They vomited and ate more and continued like that. Aldred could hear the group of them up all night, chanting and dancing around the burning eucalyptus trees, blabbering aberrant things in crude tongues.

Pissing all over it... Aldred had thought as he crept through the fitzroya and dragonsblood bushes one evening to witness the depth of madness his uncle had fallen to. *We're pissing all over this country and its traditions.*

After that evening, Aldred heard Brooton praying in strange tongues every full moon.

Aldred had later found scrolls that stated the eucalyptus groves had been there since before the Starfall and were sacred to the people that lived there. *What can become of a man?*

The territory belonged to the Esheri for a generation and had been ruled under their own kin by the names of Marwen and Serhanon, and before them, Yuri and Maku, now called Jonathon Rose of Timpany the Lord of Soren, and Katelyn Merris of Bralter the Lady of Lysses. *They rule in nothing but name. These people don't respect us. They would kill us in our sleep if they had a chance.*

All of Esher trembled in the wake of the Lion. And they cursed the Lion to death.

When Natt Floyd of Friars finally arrived at Sareen, he and his army found the castle of Red Sky Rock abandoned. The matriarch of House Marwen, Queen Taya, had abandoned her Lovasi Castle and secretly fled, leaving the city to be sacked. *Because there is nothing left here, or else they've squirrelled it all away into the Hills of Soma through their wormholes.*

Dustey scooped the contents of the mortar with his bare hand, a dull red and sulphurous paste, then wiped it all over the scout's eyes.

"Mmmmrhhppph," the scout said, struggling to get loose. "Mmmmrrppphhh!" Agony hung thick in the air.

"What'd you do?" Aldred had a foul taste in his mouth.

"Blinded him," Dustey said, and smiled a bone-yellow grin. His emerald green eyes pierced through his dark face.

"Why?" Aldred's mouth hung open. The scout flailed his torso, and the leather straps stretched and moaned. Dustey shrugged, then went to his station to tinker. *This is madness...*

Dustey pulled away from his workbench, holding a goblet carefully with both hands.

"What's that?" said Aldred. Dustey took a sip from the goblet.

"This is for me," he said, and swallowed, wiping his lips with the back of his shirtsleeve. "Fire water." Dustey took another sip from his goblet, swished the liquid around in his mouth, and spit it out onto a pile of dry logs on the fire pit.

"Dagdora!" he sang, as if he was chanting some sort of spell. Nothing happened. "Damn!" He wiped the dried paste off of the scout's face with a rag.

Aldred found a drink of his own, from Brooton's private stock. A bottle of red from Timpany that was set out alongside dozens of others on top of a cederwood chest. Aldred drank straight from the bottle. He was thirsty and drank deep.

The scout had calmed considerably, and Dustey removed the gag.

"Who the fuck are you?" Dustey usually got right to the point. He produced an iron rod from under the table. The boneman held the rod over the scout's head and *whooshed* it through the air. Dustey wanted him to hear it.

"I'm no one," said the scout. "A humble messenger."

"Message? What message?" Dustey's left eye twitched. They did that when he got bloodthirsty, Aldred noticed.

"The message is for one person and one person alone," the scout said calmly.

"We will pass it on to him," Aldred said. He was tired and truly just wanted this to be over with. He wanted to read his letter from Eshlynn, alone. *I'll be home soon, my star, please wait for me...*

"The message is for him and him alone." The scout had no fear in his voice, and that made Aldred angry. He nudged Dustey to do something.

"Do you want to die?" The witch-king put the steel spike into the tip of the guard's ear.

"I would happily die for the messiah," the scout said. "It would be nothing less than a privilege for you to kill me."

Aldred didn't like that answer. *These Esheri would do anything for their Karaat.* Aldred didn't like people who believed in something, like this person did. So adamant in their cause, so certain in their path. Those were the type of folk that kept getting up, the ones that kept coming. *Dare you say... you're jealous? Because your god is so meaningless to you?* Audacio wrote that a person is only as strong as what they believe in. That a person will rise to meet any occasion, however improbable, if their belief supersedes sense. *This man believes more than you could ever hope to.*

Dustey cracked the iron bar over the scout's shinbone. The scout winced, but held in a scream. He composed himself quickly. So quickly that it was unsettling.

"My orders were to make sure *he* was here," said the Esheri, gesturing his head towards a wall where no one was standing. Aldred looked at Dustey sideways and raised an eyebrow.

"Who?" Aldred's stomach twisted. He felt nauseous.

"You. Prince Aldred. The messiah wants *you.*"

Aldred scoffed. "Messiah?" Aldred spit into the fire, and the pit hissed. "Who are you speaking of, scout?" Aldred had been waiting for some kind of trick to appear. He couldn't shake the sense that all of Esher had roused them—let them take their country as part of some kind of trap. The Hester fyrd had gone too far south and left their flank exposed. The Esheri could close in and trap them. *And now they have...* Aldred felt his blood boiling. *I told Brooton this would happen. I told him.* "You can tell your messiah he'll need a bigger army if he wants to take *me* out." Aldred paced.

"He doesn't want to take you out, Aldred, he wants to take you in," the scout said. Aldred studied him, his mad smile, and a smile crept onto Aldred's own face.

"What?" He laughed. "Take me *in?*"

Dustey smacked the scout somewhere with the spike, and the Esheri couldn't hold back a scream that time.

"Is this a jest? What is the message?" Aldred finally said.

"We are the Army of Truth. We have been given a message from Roqeda to pass on to you. When you meet us in battle at tomorrow's sunrise, look for the Priest of Truth. He will be dressed in elaborate garb and wearing the message of our god on his chest."

"What is this?" Aldred said. "Tell me this message now, I'm not playing games."

The scout smiled. "It cannot come from these lips. It would have no meaning. You must find the priest and hear his message. The Army of Truth is waiting for you at Soren."

"At Soren?" Aldred barked. *They've trapped you. They've flanked you and trapped you in this country...* "This is nonsense. Tell him to come forth. I can't guarantee my people won't kill him when we march through." To the Boneman, Aldred said, "Make him say yes."

"Tell them not to kill the priest," the scout said, as if it was that simple to control wild, bloodthirsty killers in the heat of battle. "He will be clear enough to you. Tell your people not to kill him, or if they do, find his body and read his message yourself. The boneman has the eyes for it."

Dustey spat on the scout's face. "What do you know of my eyes?"

"I heard you speak those Words of fire. You can read the priest's message with the same eyes that interpreted those Words."

"I will piss on your priest," the boneman said.

"You do not know who you're fighting," the scout said, short of breath. "Our messiah, the priest Miri, is not a brigand or a late member of a dying dynasty. He is not a prince or a king. The messiah told us he'd make the wind die and the rain stop when he left. He said that he would resurrect the Reaper from the Otherworld to snub the eternal flame and leave the world in darkness without fire. We laughed when Miri went north, but months later, when the fires refused to burn and the earth went thirsty, we knew the hands of the gods had touched him." The scout said, a smile crept onto his face. A look of pure bliss and profound happiness followed.

Aldred had heard of divine intervention. It seemed a mad thought to him when he first read of it in the Book of Eralis. But seeing the Esheri smile after being blinded and broken and tied to a table convinced Aldred that this man had some sort of a god *inside* of him. *A god or a demon?* Aldred squinted. *You can write your own path. You can be your own author—god or demon, or in between, it's your choice.* Audacio had said that, and it was a line that Aldred had never forgotten—and he still heard it said in his mother's voice.

Dustey took a gulp of the firewater from the wineskin, then blew it all over the dry wood.

"Dagdora!" This time the logs burst into flame.

"The belief is strong in you." The boneman gazed at the scout with what was surely amazement in those green eyes. The Esheri laughed under his breath. "Karaat lives on this day. The Army of Truth is waiting for you at Soren. Go."

"It's never worked before," the boneman said, gazing in amazement at the small flame. "Never."

"*Akovha Liet Neia,*" the scout whispered.

Aldred thought it kind of sounded like ancient Yehvenki.

Dustey glared at Aldred and held a finger to his lips to signal silence. The scout was saying the same thing in the ancient tongue, over and over, louder now. "*Akovha Liet Neia!*"

Aldred was entranced by it. The words held a beauty in the way they flowed together. Each syllable bounced and was gently caught by the next one. Each word gently caressed the one before it. He had read much about the Yehvenki and their dark empire before the Lovasi conquered them, but he didn't think anyone still spoke the language. Aldred watched the words flowing over the scout's cracked lips, watched his tongue move, slurring dark words.

Then the scout's head fell heavy to the ground. Dustey stood behind, holding his headsman's sword, three feet of black Daggland steel carved with purple runes of fire.

A moment passed before a steady flow of blood leaked from the spot where the Esheri's head used to be. Dustey set aside his sword and put a wooden bucket under the main flow of blood as calmly as he would have put a bucket under a leak in the roof. The Esheri's head was on the ground, in the rushes by Aldred's boots. The scout was looking at Aldred with open and mangled eyes, as if he could suddenly see again in death.

"Explain all of this to Brooton." Aldred left the tent.

He felt a sickness in his stomach, one that came often. He hated his family. He hated his place in it. This life was not for him. *Books, I just want my books and Eshlynn. I want to have a family, farm the land...*

Aldred walked outside of camp and sat by himself beneath an old, budding beech tree. He leaned against a flat rock of slate and rested his head back. He took the letter out of his pocket and ran his fingers over the writing. *Aldred Hester,* it read. *Eshlynn...* He had thought of her every day since he left. He had sent her letters at every chance. Part of him was starting to think she hadn't received them. *But she did. She has read your words. She knows how you feel.*

Aldred opened the letter and started reading.

He wished he hadn't.

ALDRED ROSE WITH THE sun the next morning. His sleep was usually just bursts of closing his eyes then waking up in a cold sweat from visions of the withered and starved corpses strewn in the streets of Soren and Lysses, and Behru. He was lucky last night, though, and dreamt of Eshlynn. He could still feel her lingering in his memory as he woke. The smell of her and the touch of her skin kept him sleeping through the night. Then his stomach twisted into knots as he remembered the letter. *You've been gone too long, Aldred, it was dark here during the wither year, lonely. We worried we wouldn't see tomorrow. I've found a lover.*

He opened the flap of his tent and walked outside to feel the bite of the morning air. He had come to appreciate the weather of Esher, and especially that of Behru, which hugged so closely the great, blue vein called the Esheri Rush. The mornings were the most beautiful of all, when the fog of heat had yet to gather and when the birds sang loud and clear. The sun left a dull orange stain on the world as it sat oblong and ugly in the morning sky.

Four thousand ninety. He didn't know why he still counted the days. It was a habit he picked up after the accident to help him deal with some of the pain. *Time heals all wounds. Angelico wrote that.* And Aldred believed the ancient philosopher when he first read him. His faith had been dwindling as the number got higher and higher, though. Four thousand and ninety sunrises since the day he'd killed his mom. *Eleven years, two months, two weeks, one day.* No one would ever let him forget, so he reminded himself. Four thousand and ninety wasn't enough time to heal that wound. *How much longer, Angelico?*

Aldred felt a strange calm in his body and whispered to the morning sun, "Karaat, please, give me the power to bring back what was lost." He felt strange afterwards, worried someone might have heard him praying to the wrong god, but somehow, he felt that his prayer was heard, and that scared him most of all.

Aldred walked through the camp towards Brooton's tent. A few folk were out in front of their tents. Sharpening knives and swords, taking a morning piss, poking at fresh wood in charred pits longingly, likely savouring the flames after last year. These were the lower ranks. Farmers plucked from their fields and given the king's standard issue gear: a chain shirt with a silver lion on the chest, a thick hunk of wood shaped like a shield, a rusty steel sword, and a mouldy scabbard. The fyrd, the great Lion, Gavyn Hester used to call it, and so it is still called today. The word meant fight in the old Ayelish tongue of Hearthill, where the Lion roamed. The fyrd was the closest Aldred's family's dynasty had to a standing army.

Aldred heard interspersed shouts of agony behind the thick canvas as he got closer to Brooton's pavilion. He didn't have to go inside to know it was Dustey screaming. Aldred had only been tied to the table once, that was enough for him to learn not to question his uncle Brooton. The boneman didn't learn so fast, though. *He knew better than to kill that scout and he did it anyway. Even if I did tell him to do it. He deserves what he gets.* Aldred tried to tell himself, but he was sick of making excuses for his uncle and himself.

"Hey, nephew. Good morning, ain't it?" Brooton said. He was shirtless and sweating, holding a pair of bloody shears. Dustey was tied face down on the table, his bone-white hair pulled off his back. His threadbare shirt had soaked through with sweat. He was gasping for breath.

"Heard you two offed that scout without me last night," Brooton said, panting. "Dustey here told me everything. I took another finger off him. That's three now. Might have to cut him loose from this world soon, nephew." Brooton picked up a piece of a bloody ear from the table. He held it up for Aldred to get a good look. It was half of Dustey's ear. "Maybe he'll learn to listen a little closer with only one ear. I told him to never kill a prisoner without giving me my time with them. I need that quality time, Aldred, to help ease my bones." Brooton threw the ear aside and dropped the shears, then wiped his hands on a rag.

On the floor beside the table were stacks of books. Brooton bent down and found *Benecio's Strategy of War* and placed it flat on Dustey's back. He opened it up. Those soggy, yellow pages pressed between two pieces of rotting leather contained more knowledge than the average person knew what to do with. A book written in a time when things were better, when people were wiser. The old Lovasi Empire had salvaged knowledge from the ancient annals of Yehven. This book contained knowledge to keep an army two steps up on any other. Aldred had nearly memorized the whole thing.

The book rose and fell with the boneman's breath. Blood flowed from where his ear used to be; it pooled onto the table and *drip, dripped* slowly onto the dirt by Aldred's boots. Aldred would cauterize it momentarily, probably to the boneman's delight, as everything fire made him oddly gleeful.

"Think there's a page in here on how to kill a priest of Karaat, nephew? I want that fucking book."

CHOICES

THE GREENHOODS WERE VISIBLE from a hundred yards away; they hadn't tried to hide themselves. James couldn't help but think of Haro. His history with greenhoods wasn't great. There were four of them by James's count, and each looked as haggard as the next. Their green hoods and tunics were torn and filthy, nothing more than rags, in true Ranger custom, and they reeked as they got close. *No Haro.* James thanked the Bluebirds.

"Hey there, traveller," one of the Rangers said as they walked by. His eyes were wide, and he wore a sardonic grin upon his thick lips. His arm was one big pink scar from elbow to hand, and the man didn't try to cover it at all, and James nearly winced at the sight of the shrivelled pink thing.

"What is it you seek here?" James said bluntly. In truth he just hoped they weren't against him.

"Most likely the same as you. Food, friends, answers to all of this," the greenhood said.

The Ranger studied Brynmor for so long that James felt anger boiling up inside of him. "The Rangers all gathered in the Wick after the Battle of Rosen," James said.

"Oh yeah?" The Ranger held his gaze upon Brynmor. Slowly his companions walked away and slowly the Ranger's eyes slipped from Brynmor to follow them. Something about the Ranger must have made Brynmor think he had an opportunity. The old man lunged suddenly, and the lead slipped from James's hands.

"Help!" Brynmor shouted. He slipped to the ground when he tried to run. The Ranger with the scarred arm knelt down and helped Brynmor up.

"Help," Brynmor said feebly as James approached, his sword throbbing with the want for souls.

The Rangers stared for a moment so James waved *Essikah*, and the Rangers turned away from Brynmor and kept walking. The greenhood knelt down and picked something out of the mud. *What-*

James heard footsteps. He turned to see Brynmor running at him with fists drawn. James dropped *Essikah* to the ground and laid his fist into Brynmor's soft cheek as the old man came for him. He heard a hollow crack as some of Brynmor's teeth popped loose. James shook his hand out as if it would stem the stinging pain.

Maggie was glaring at him in a way that made him hate himself. *She feels the darkness in you. She's going to run from you. Get yourself together. You're a Culdaine, like your dad. Why can't you be like him? And your mom? She believed in you right until the end. She may have been the only person other than Maggie who ever truly loved you.* James thought he might be sick, looking at what he'd done to Brynmor. *You're a goddamned monster. A kin-reaping Hellspawn.*

"You need to hear me, James, it wasn't my fault." Brynmor had fallen to his hands and knees, and was spitting gobs of blood out of his mouth. "The Banshee came to my home and threatened the lives of all I held dear if I didn't join them." The cracks between Brynmor's teeth leaked blood, and his eyes were so bloodshot they seemed to bleed, too. "You would have done the same, and so would your dad. I had no choice."

"There's always a choice." James thought of his own choices and spat.

"Hear what he has to say, James. Give him that much," Maggie said.

Brynmor coughed. "Thank y—"

"Speak, then." James took a deep breath to cool his blood.

"I took the Banshee th-through," Brynmor stammered, "through the Wick and the Hallow Hills on false routes and conspired hoaxes to give you and the Hallow as much time as I could. I had hoped I would find a solution in the field but none came. I sent my daughter back to Elurra to keep her safe and assure my people I hadn't gone mad. That's why I helped Eridan escape. I had hoped he would tell you my cause. I hoped he would understand."

"You *helped* Eridan?" James had heard a much different story from Eridan. *You weren't listening to the story. All you cared about was Maggie.*

"Didn't he tell you?" Brynmor's eyes widened. James saw hope in there. *He is a hopeful man. It will kill him.*

"Eridan hasn't mentioned it," James said. "You took his home. His father was murdered by a Warlock of the same order that you had allied with."

"Eridan can't see past what you did. He cares little for what you meant," Maggie said, and with her words, the look of hope drained from Brynmor's gnarled face.

"I will pay for what I've done. Just send word to my daughter, my people, that I lived through the winter. Send my bones back home. Give me that much."

"I will give you fair judgement before the gods." James pointed to the black outline of a nytewood twisting up to the grey sky. "And I will allow my people the right of choice. I rule the Hallow as a fist—many small fingers bound together to make something bigger. That's what the bull moose stands for. You see that banner?"

Brynmor nodded in understanding. He seemed to find comfort in the gods. Even so, James wasn't immune to the rumours he'd heard circulating that the gods no longer answered—that they had been killed.

James had no use for prayer when, every evening, the Maw visited him in his dreams. *"I'm not done with you,"* it growled at him in mournful tones. Sometimes, the Outcast just stood over him watching, its bipedal legs thick with greasy hair and bulging with veiny muscle, dripping sticky, hot saliva out of its blood-stained jaw. Its red-veined eyes burned into him like venom, and its chortled breath smelled like rot and vomit. James couldn't speak and he couldn't move, but he knew looking at it that the Maw was dead. He sensed it when it approached him in the deep places below Kallahorn in the waking world. The ghosts whispered it to him in dead tongues he couldn't recognize. He wasn't seeing a god but a ghost of one, and it only spoke to *him. "Who killed you?"* James had wanted to ask, but the words wouldn't leave his mouth. The Maw would come and go, but it always spoke one phrase to him. *"I'm not done with you."*

When James and Maggie came within shouting distance of the camp, James heard the cheers. *They think I've brought some sort of victory with this prisoner. They think I've brought hope.* In truth, James had no idea how he was going to help all these people survive. He hadn't any idea at all on how to lead them, and what was worse was that he truly worried the folk at Pool would fight them rather than accept their alliance.

James looked at Lord Richard Brynmor. *He bent the knee to Alder, to Ellorin. He sacked Ockam. He is a symbol of our people's hardship. I need them to know I see their suffering. He will be judged as guilty, but he at least needs the appearance of a trial.*

Eurick was the first to ask. "Who is it, man?"

"People of the Hallow. I bring you Richard Brynmor. The former Lord of the Glenn. Once known as the Hammer." James kicked the frail man forward, and he stumbled and fell flat on his face, his arms too weak to brace his fall.

Itchy strummed his harp and sang *The Dead King Rises,* and the Mal people erupted in cheer. James heard whispers of "Ockam" and "Derudin" start spreading amongst the folk. Brinley and his heart Sessely shoved their way to the front with Aione and Brigid, and the small child who clung to Brigid's leg. All five wore smiles.

Ruwen glared at James and said, "Bastard! Where'd you find him? We thought you had gone to make pacts without us."

"The Daggs had taken him prisoner." James ignored the second part.

"And what of the Daggs?" Ruwen asked. James looked back to the stones and the mass of people that had swarmed them. "Will they be leaving?"

"They're bloody mad," James said, "But they have asked for an alliance."

"And?"

"What choice do we have?" Maggie said. Ruwen tilted her neck and squinted.

"I don't trust Daggs," the She-Bear said.

"I don't trust anyone anymore," Maggie said, and James was happy to stay silent.

When Eridan came forth, he was shirtless and sweating and reeking of malt. He wore a scowl upon his face that James thought would scare away a crow.

Brynmor knelt, panting. "Forgive me, sweet son. I'm so sorry."

Without saying a word, Eridan cranked his boot and struck Brynmor in the face with the toe of it. There was a loud smacking pop, and Brynmor keeled over to one side and landed hard on the dirt. He didn't get up. The crowd of Mal began to cheer.

"This man sacked Ockam!" Eridan screamed, and James felt the raucous energy building. He reached out for Maggie's hand. "Is this our Springtide sacrifice, good King?" Eridan said mockingly. James glared at him.

"This man will be given trial before the gods. We are Mal, not wildfolk. We need to establish order if we are to rebuild." James spoke as loudly and deeply as he could.

"This is our enemy!" Eridan's eyes were wide and glowing white in the dim sun. *He's full of madness, this one.* James glared at Eridan. *The man is not the boy.*

"He helped you escape," James asserted. "He deserves a trial."

Eridan scorned Brynmor with his eyes. "He helped me with *nothing!*" Eridan spat on the old lord who was still unmoving on the ground. A yellow-white gob trailed down Brynmor's cheek slowly.

"He will have a trial tonight by the nytewood," James addressed the crowd. "You are welcome to come. We speak as one voice in the Hallow. Together, our voices will be loud enough for the gods to hear us."

"The gods are dead," someone shouted, and then more shouting, and soon folk were pushing and yelling at one another.

James studied his people. Few paid any attention to him or the unconscious lord on the ground before him. *They're starving. They're scared. They don't care about justice. They need hope.*

"Is it sacrifice you want?" James yelled, and that got the attention of some. *If they want this man dead, I will kill him. I will sacrifice him to the gods if that's what it takes.*

Maggie grabbed his hand. "James—"

The folk began to revel. Eridan urged them on. Brinley and Sessely had huddled together with their two daughters and Brigid's small son and scoured James with their eyes. *Don't you dare,* their eyes said to him.

"Then we'll kill him," James asserted, and the world was alive with the voice of the Mal as they erupted in cheer. James looked around and thought of his dad's army. *They waited on every word he said. He ruled with justice and order. He did the right thing. And you killed him. Killed him dead. And mom... you're the true enemy of this country. You're the enemy...*

James had led nearly three thousand people from Kallahorn. Now, just a little more than two thousand six hundred sat brooding on a cold remote plain in the north, clinging to a frozen sliver of joy bred from a small taste of revenge. They were plagued with coughing-sickness and bloody-lung and exhaustion, and all were hungry. Along the journey, many of the old had just disappeared into the arbors to die in peace. James had little hope to offer and less justice to serve. He had led his people to their deaths, and he was losing them. And to make it worse, Brinley's scouts had all confirmed that the Ayelish were gathering at Mammoth's Head Castle, probably preparing to march on the north.

Ianna and Ayeland would come for them, and when she did they had to be ready. This was his only chance to give his people something to look forward to. *Kill the man who sacked Ockam and show your people there is hope of victory. We will take our home back, one murdered lord at a time. The Hallow will be one. The Hallow will be ours again.*

By sunset, Brynmor was chained naked and bleeding in an iron gibbet, swinging gently from the nytewood's lower branches, at which James had promised him trial.

"Ain't this some kind of world, man?" Eurick put his hand on James's shoulder. "One victory leads to another war, forever."

James glared at the gibbet like it was mocking his dad and what Bren Culdaine stood for—like it was mocking the whole damn Hallow. *Your mom and dad died for peace, and in their honour, you bring war. These are not your people. They belong to the land, not you. They only called you king when you could save them. What is a ruler who can't offer rule? What is a ruler who doesn't sleep?*

James tried his best to hide his night terrors, but he knew by now the rumours had spread. *The Reaper cries at night. That, and awakens screaming.* He talked to ghosts that no one could see, and so the rumours that he was mad and spoke to himself started to arise, too.

"How many more victories do we have, Eurick? How many?" James sighed.

"Hey, man." Eurick grabbed James by the shoulders and with his big fist, pounded James on the left side of his chest. "We have as many as there are in here. As many as we need for peace."

"You believe in peace?"

"I believe we'll all find our own little bit of happiness somewhere if we keep searching, and in that happiness, there is peace. And I believe in your heart, James. I believe it's big enough to save the world." Eurick looked up to the sky, and James looked up there with him. The clouds were black and the sky was grey, but the sun poked through in places. The rain was coming, and with it the mud.

"We should get moving before the rains come down too hard."

"Aye, just one thing?"

"What is it?"

"Can I have some of that fish you've got in that jar there? Been eyeing it since you came back."

James laughed. He had forgotten he was carrying it. "Smoked sprats."

"What?" Eurick looked wildly confused.

"The fish. That's what they're called."

Eurick looked at the jar lovingly. "Ah! We called them something else on the Ryne. I call them salty. Had them little fishes at the Guild on Ryne all my life. Little bit of home I thought I'd never get back, this." The transporter tucked the jar of smoked sprats beneath his arm and trotted off whistling.

The pack horses were being fed and tended, the wayns were loaded and strapped, and folk were filing into order. Two thousand and more souls of Mal Hallow moving for the stones. In them, James saw moms, dads, brothers, sisters, smiths, cooks, warriors, shamans, and they all looked alike in that moment. They wore furs and chainmail, they wore leather and wool. Some towed grain wayns and some herded the cattle and sheep. Some just hobbled along solemnly with their arms around eachother.

They were Mal Hallow. Broken and limping but still alive. Still moving forward. Still fighting, with dull axes and rusted armour. *I won't let Ayeland take this land, Dad. Not while I live.*

Toren had claimed he had food for all of them, as much as they wanted, and that all would be welcomed with a Springtide feast. Rakkar Toren, Rakkar Erik, and Rakkar Halda had gifted a promise—that they would honour the gods to give thanks. James had no idea what kind of twisted ritual to expect, but he knew this was what his people wanted, this is what they needed.

"When Springtide fades," Brinley Scareye shouted so all could hear, "we need to make our attack. That is when we take the Hallow back.' He had his maps scrolled and tucked under his arm like he couldn't wait to make battle plans.

"They will be ready for an attack no matter when we move, Brin," Claydon said. "Moving slowly would be to our advantage. We don't want them to feel threatened and march from Mammoth's Head before they mean to. We need as much time as we can manage." Macts and Aron stood by Claydon's side and together, James thought they looked like three heads of the same person. Aron and Macts had grown thick golden beards like their father. Their hearts and children had all tagged along, too, and Aron's three kids and Macts's two seemed to share the same look, only missing the beard. All of them had a rough winter and spent much of it berating James to give them more of the food stores.

"We've been moving slowly for nearly two moons," Ruwen said and spat. "I'm with the dragonslayer. We need to make our Springtide sacrifice and be on. I don't want to mingle too long with these Daggs."

"What do they intend to do here, anyway?" Aione pegged James with accusing eyes. "You talked with them, right? What did they say?"

"They intend to find peace. Same as us," James lied. *They intend to kill all they can and feed the soil with blood.*

"They should never have come here." Brinley scratched at his scarred eye like there was something buried under it. "Nothing's as it should be."

Sessely held his arm. "Patience, Brin," she whispered to him. James's mom had always called Sessely of Dawning Brinley Scareye's unboiled half. She was calm water where Brinley was boiling over.

"We'd be out of food if they hadn't come," Maggie said. "We still may run out."

"Maybe it's time the lot of us went our separate ways," Ruwen said. "It'd make more sense to spread out."

"No," James blurted. "We stay together. We are the Hallow and this is war. We will take our homes back together or they will slaughter us all."

Ruwen spat.

Macts and Aron looked at their dad like they had the same plan of leaving, and the two of them expected him to speak up then but nothing was said.

"This is nonsense." Brigid emerged beside Brinley. The youngest crow of Dawning had grown fierce since her eldest sister was killed, and her two sons were growing to be much the same. But now, she spoke with a calmness James envied. "This is Springtide. Our king is right, we are stronger together. Everyone just needs to stop whining and get on with it. We have made a plan. We will make a Springtide sacrifice, then we take Pool and gather the strength of the mountain clans that took refuge there under Kihl'dor Tess. From there we take Rosen. Our king has told us this. We just need to be patient. My dad has it all on his maps. It will work if we are patient and stay together."

"Well said, dear." Brinley scratched the black scar of his eye. "And as long as the Ayelish *don't* march from Mammoth's Head anytime too soon," Brinley added.

"Aye, and that," Brigid said.

"They will march come the Wayk of spring, when the snows are fully clear and the rains calm," James said. "That has always been when the Ayelish come, when the mud dries."

"Aye, but they're angry now, they know we're weak," Brigid said. Her words started an uproar of arguments. "They may attack sooner. Maybe later. We won't know until it happens."

Claydon banged forward with Macts and Aron. "We do not want to risk our own people to attack Rosen. After Springtide, we will be marching to Tusk, with or without the lot of you."

"You will be slaughtered!" James blurted.

"We believe them to be weak and out of sorts," Aron said. "I just want a place where my wife and children can live in peace."

"And same for mine," Macts agreed.

"You're out of sorts to think you can win!" Eridan had come back, fully armoured in chainmail. He pulled his axe and pointed it at Claydon. "You don't mean to take Tusk. The lot of you mean to go back to Kallahorn. I heard these two boasting about it." Eridan pointed the axe blade back and forth between Aron and Macts. "They fancy themselves the ruling lords of Kallahorn. Have their kids rule one day, they fancy."

James looked at Claydon. The lord had backed away, and his face was sunken in and red as an apple. "Is this true?" James said flatly.

"I—this is—whatever he says is a damned lie!" Claydon seemed to choke on his own words. "Liar!" he barked at Eridan.

"It's true, King." Eridan sheathed his axe. "Too many snakes in this mound, King. Best to keep your eyes open." With a strut, the rightful heir to Ockam walked off alone towards the Standing Stones. Soon, James had no choice but to follow.

"We move on to the Standing Stones of Grave. We will be welcomed with a feast. It's the best I can do for you at this time," James said, and he and Maggie led their people into the sea of Daggs behind Lord Eridan of Ockam.

The Hammer of the Glenn gripped the bars of his gibbet and glared at James with ghost eyes. *He's already dead inside...* "Let me tell you something before you shut me up." Brynmor held his arms up in defence.

James glared at him. "I'm not going to save your life, Brynmor."

"That's okay. I owe you this, at least."

"Owe me? Owe me what?"

"I've been chained up and heard these Daggs talking for a month or more now. They mean to kill you and Maggie. They've been searching for you all this time. The Reaper and mage, they call you. They're going to butcher you."

THE EL'VIE

"**I** 'M HUNGRY." SWEY WAS dragging along, but Etta didn't have the strength to carry him any longer, and both Calum and Cullen had said the same.

"We'll stop and find something soon, Swey, but we can't stop this close to the river." Etta told him as calmly as she could manage.

"Then why do we keep following the river? Can't we just stay where we can rest?" Swey's innocence tore at Etta's chest.

"The river will lead us to people. But many folk travel the river, including some we wouldn't want finding us, so we can't stop here," Calum explained. Etta had seen many tracks of things in the mud by the shore, Human and non-Human, and she knew they had strayed far enough north that the El'vie would be roaming the streams for trout and frogs and turtles, and they hated nothing more than poachers.

They stopped for a moment as Calum knelt over one of the Non-Human tracks and poked at it with his finger. "What is it?"

"The El'vie roam these rivers and streams and live in the mud and mire of their banks," Etta said.

"Are those the things that live in Pool?" Swey asked, his eyes ever wide and curious. Etta could see him connecting the dots inside of his mind, his world growing bigger.

"There are many stories of the El'vie. The ones who live in the Lake of Pool are an old and sacred tribe, but their people stretch far and wide throughout the mountains of the Fells. They are seldom seen though, unless encroached upon."

Calum spat, "Scum."

"There was a time they helped the Feldarra." Etta had heard that story around the fires.

"That song has been long forgotten," said Cullen. He was picking the small buds of honeysuckle and nettle leaves from the ground around them and gathering them in his shirt. Swey was watching him, and when Cullen had filled his shirt, he packed the buds and the leaves into a pouch and handed the pouch to Swey. The boy snatched it up with his small hands and coveted it against his chest. "We'll make a mighty fine stew later, boy, with a trout and some pine nuts. You hold on to that." Swey nodded, and they kept walking through the mud.

It was midday when Etta first saw the fire smoke twisting up towards the white clouds of the blue sky.

"Who is it?" Cullen asked.

"I don't know," Calum answered.

"Is it Mom?" Swey's eyes welled with tears.

Etta took a good long look at the fire. It looked like a clanfire the way the smoke billowed. "We'll see."

They approached cautiously, Young Courtney, Cullen, and Calum all with their weapons drawn. When the folk around the fire stood and two of them walked out to meet them, Etta knew them for who they were and smiled.

"By the gods it's Benn and Gwynn," Calum said with palpable relief.

The big grey-bearded warrior Gwynn made big old Benn look small. Etta knew he would be one to follow the moment he came into the *si'otha* with his stone-like stature and confidence. *It's just too bad he isn't capable of leading us anywhere special...*

"By the gods," Gwynn bellowed. "It's good to see you alive. Come here, come." He gestured them forward with his big hands, waving. They went to him, and Benn gave Etta a big, warm hug that she needed more than she knew.

He squeezed her and she squeezed back, and Etta looked at him and said, "You fucking lived."

Benn's face was straight. "And I pulled these two from the spit." He gestured towards two elders sitting cross legged around the fire, shrouded in their woollen grey robes like mounds of dead earth. "These folk, Etta, the Demhoni... you wouldn't believe..."

Etta took a look around the fire. Holden sat naked but for his breeches, bloody and muddy by the fire with his head in his hands. Aris lay on his side with bloody strips of cloth strewed about him and a gaping wound in his side, which he seemed to be airing out. There were a few others, too. Tana, Relia, and Caden sat between the elders, sullen and stiff-looking like they'd been shocked so bad they couldn't move.

One of the elders Etta recognized as the child of star and sky, Yessa. *Tara isn't here.* The boy stood beside Etta. She grabbed his hand.

"She's not here." He didn't even cry this time. Etta reckoned a part of him already accepted the worst. *He's Braden's boy. He's strong inside and out. He's Wulfee's grandson. Wulfee, not you. Who are you? Wretched thing...*

Etta pulled him close to her. "Listen, Swey," Etta said. "We're going to find her, okay? Okay?"

Swey's jaw hardened into a look of determination. "Yea, okay." He stood tall. "We'll find her. *I'll* find her."

Gwynn heard the boy and knelt down to his level. "I have seen tracks in the mud, and we have borne witness as well. The El'vie have been roaming this river. Two of the creatures approached our camp from the river last night. We screamed at them and the elders sang old curses from the cycles, but the beasts never spoke back and they never moved. They just stood there, staring with eyes like white diamonds in the night. Like the brightest stars I've seen."

Swey stared at Gwynn like he was speaking to him in a language he didn't understand.

"Your mom wasn't taken by the cannibals, boy. She's still out there. It could be the El'vie that took her. The elders say the El'vie used to help the Feldarra at one time."

"There will be plenty of time for stories," Calum raised his voice. "Tell me, what are we doing? What is happening here?"

"This is war, Calum. It's caught up to us even in our hiding," Gwynn said. "These Demhoni are Ayelish folk that fell from the Wolf's army or came from somewhere else, but they used to be Ayelish folk, that much is clear from their banners and armour. Whatever curse has befallen them over this dark winter... by the gods, whatever it is, I just hope we can avoid it."

"So what are they doing? Why are they killing us?" Calum had his hands balled into fists.

"They've gone sick." Benn's eyes were black-rimmed, and he pouted as he spoke. "A madness is in them, one that lies in all of us, but it won out in these folk. The Demhoni are an ancient horde of cannibals who ate the blood and flesh of their victims and believed to be taking their life force by doing it. The Demhoni believe they are growing stronger with each victim."

"What possessed them with the curse?" Calum asked.

"Their own cursed hearts," Benn said. "Too much time and not enough food or love. Some believe it's a mind fungus that spreads its spores through story. It only takes one. One, and then it spreads like the pox—like bloody spores."

"You've seen this before?" Etta said, more a statement than a question.

Benn turned his head away.

"We heard them chanting prayers to Karaat," Yessa said. Their voice sucked Etta's attention like water through a broken dam. "Prayers of blood and stars," Yessa continued. "And one led them in their prayer. She called herself Heath of Ilbury. Her teeth were filed into daggers, and her eyes had turned as red as blood. She... she drank blood. Cup-fulls of it, and laughed. Said she was drinking souls. She was the first—it spread from her."

"You escaped them?" Young Courtney popped a pine nut into her mouth.

"Because of Benn." Gwynn nodded at the old man, and Benn smiled.

"Emmer would have done more." Benn looked up to the sky.

Etta helped Benn as he tended to the wounds of his folk. She cleaned the axe bite on Holden's leg, which had begun to fester; she made a poultice of mud and tarrowroot and hollygreen for Aris and held it fast as Benn tied it tight around Aris's body. Relia and Caden had come back from their search for ander empty-handed. *Pike would have found it.*

"It's okay," Etta said.

"We'll use the tarrowroot and hollygreen, and this is nice good black mud here, rich stuff," said Benn as he tied a poultice on one of the elders' thighs.

They rested as long as they felt safe, but Gwynn had opted not to have a fire and to walk through the night single file by the light of a single torch.

By the third day in the mountains, something had caught their trail.

"How close?" Benn asked.

Cullen sniffed at the air. "Too close."

Through the bony hills, they crawled along, exhausted and hungry and scared as they heard the footsteps close in on them from behind.

The ground flattened out, and the arbor cleared around them in a near perfect circle, and Etta stopped dead in her tracks. Covering the clearing were many stakes with the rotting heads of folk weeks dead. Flies assaulted the air with their piercing buzz. The folk had their guts hanging out, and most of their eyeballs had been picked out by birds and hung by gory red threads from black sockets. In their mouths, Etta saw fish bones stabbing through their cheeks and tongues.

In the very middle of the clearing sat a deep, blacked pit with charcoal and ash surrounding it. The dead still wore most of their armour, but chestplates and hauberks were strewn about in the mud amidst a scattering of rusted iron gauntlets and sun-bleached leather gloves. Etta kicked a chestplate over and saw the red eagle of Ayeland staring back at her.

"These are Ayelishfolk." Calum sounded like he couldn't believe his own words.

"By the gods..." Cullen touched one of the dead, and the body slunk down from the stake and tore apart like wet paper. Its bloated entrails ripped, and rotten fish slid out.

"It's the El'vie done this." Etta remembered the stories. *If you over fish these waters, the El'vie will come for you. They'll snatch you up and fill your mouth with fish until you choke on it.* She thought it was just a story to scare the children and to keep poachers in good conscience.

"We can't go any farther north." Gwynn's voice was gravelly and unsure. "This is a warning."

"We can't turn around south. We can't fight those Demhoni, not alone. They number in the many hundreds now, and more wander in each day. Their rituals, Etta... they claim they'll live forever," Benn said. Swey was crying and Etta held him close.

"East," Gwynn said. "We'll go east into the mountains."

"To fucking where?" Calum held his arms up.

Etta said, "We can live there. In pea—"

"There is no fucking peace," Calum said. "And there are no valleys to the east or west. We can't live off of mountain rams and nettles. Not with this small of a group. We need... fuck I don't know what we need." Calum was pacing.

You need to be organized and trained in combat, armed and ready for an ambush and well fed. You need a leader. You need a kihl'dor.

In a trough of stagnant water, Etta saw her underself glaring back at her. *Why did you run? Why did you leave your people?* her underself asked through cold, blue lips. Etta had never missed Pike more. Or Maggie or James or Gen. *But those were Wulfee's people, not mine. Etta has no one and Etta is stronger for it. Etta is innocent and she can start over. Etta didn't kill her son—she has no sons. Etta is free of that burden.*

Her underself gurgled at her. *You have a grandson. No matter who you are.*

Etta looked at Swey, and her heart lit up like dawn. *He is not yours... he is not Etta's.* But her heart couldn't lie like her tongue so Etta walked over to the boy and kept Swey close to her.

They had no fire, but Yessa told stories just the same. Their grey hood tight around their face, grey braids snaked out and clung to their shoulders like roots. "The El'vie," they said, and licked their lips, "are not of nature, though they have surely fought for that right." Yessa looked at the stars as if they had talked badly to them. "They were created in the name of Karaat, long ago. They came to Ardura like an invasive species in the time of Draku and spread through the rivers and lakes. Long have the Mal and Feldarra fought with them, and after many hundreds of years, they were forced into obscurity and a strange sort of vanity at Pool. They are not of nature, though they worship Her. The El'vie are of old magics, unnatural, and they should be feared," Yessa said. "Though I worry, it's already too late. I smell them nearby. They watch us." Yessa sniffed.

Etta lay awake that night and heard many of the others shuffling about, too. *How do you sleep after a tale like that. El'vie. Demhoni. How do you get yourself into this shite?*

In the morning, they carried on walking north. "We have to hope it will be better," Gwynn said. "We can't go back. We can't." Gwynn had been the first to head off and all else followed. He was hardly a kihl'dor, and wouldn't claim to be, but he was the best leader they had. *Not a kin-killer. Not so wretched as you.* "We have to keep an ember of hope," he said, and

Etta tried to believe him—she had to. *Etta believes in hope. You have to believe it can be better.*

THE SHELL OF THE crawfish cracked like shattered bone as Etta bit into it. The juicy, sweet flesh below was so good she was filled with excitement at the prospect of having more.

"They were everywhere, under every damn rock I tell ya. A bloody gold mine," Cullen said as he *kerplunked* another batch of raw crawfish into his boiling pot.

A large stream trickled and bubbled through the hilly arbor at the low end of the mountain valley, and the *si'otha* sat by it and ate. Etta watched Swey smile as he shoved a second crawfish in his mouth. The spring sun sat fat and yellow at its noon summit, and Etta tried to position herself to catch the breeze from the stream on the back of her neck.

"Careful to chew the shell right good," Etta said. "I knew a guy, Colrig the Rock, he near damn choked on a crawfish shell that got lodged in his throat. If it wasn't for big old Gen slapping his back, he surely would have died."

"For a meek lady, you seem to know a lot of karls," Benn said. The old man was all kindness most of the time, but he had become suspicious of Etta as of late. *And rightfully so. He watched as you stood still instead of warning everyone that those cannibals were coming. And surely, he thought us all to be cowards for not following him back to save the others.*

"What's that matter a goddamned thing?" Etta said.

"I just think we should be true to ourselves and each other if we're to really be *si'otha*," Benn said. "There should be no falsehoods or lies amongst us."

Etta was about to stand up and say something when a loud splash came from the stream behind them.

"The fuck was that." Calum stood up and grabbed his axe.

All looked out to the river, but Etta looked to Swey. She grabbed the boy and pulled him close.

The elders whispered curses; axes were being drawn and the *si'otha* were all standing.

You're all looking the same way. Fan out. Protect your flank. Shield wall—paladin style, just like Emmer by the gods... Etta thought. "Swey," she said.

"Yes."

"Don't let go of me."

"Okay."

Etta turned back towards the cookfire and held her breath. Her chest seized, and the sound of warhorns from twenty years, ten, seven, two years ago echoed in her mind. *Grab an axe.* But Etta couldn't. Wouldn't.

The El'vie were squishing through dead leaves and mud, slippery slow-like towards them dressed in sealskin leather that looked like dried fish skin and with bright red gills on their throats that looked like gaping vertical knife wounds. They held sharpened stones and whips of woven bladderwort, and their eyes glowed blue as a river stream. Etta scooped Swey into her arms, and her legs were moving on their own towards the river. Benn was the first to notice Etta running.

"Behind!" he screamed. Etta couldn't bear to look at him and see the disappointment in him that she was running again. Swey was breathing hard against her chest. Behind her, flesh collided with rock and iron as the si'otha fought, and the bludgeoning sound of it made her sick.

She fell to her knees and vomited, letting Swey fall to the mud of the riverbank. When Etta heard squishing footsteps come up from the river, she tried to reach for her axe but it wasn't there. Benn had tried to make her carry one on her belt, but she couldn't. *Etta is not a killer. It was Wulfee did it. It was Wulfee. If you kill again, how can you deny it? How can you deny what you did? What Wulfee did. You...*

Etta pulled Swey close as the El'vie approached. "It was Wulfee!" she screamed at the wicked blue thing standing before her. Its bloody red gills flexed and writhed as the thing gurgled in air. *Unhuman. Unnatural.* "It was Wulfee," she said softly.

More of the El'vie came out of the river, their eyes blue as the sky and flesh like sealskin. They stood and swayed together, watching, studying. There were three of them now, one taller than the other two, and that one pointed at Swey. Etta held him close to her. "It was Wulfee!" she yelled again though she knew these creatures couldn't understand. Then the tall one pointed to Etta, and the other two came to her. She couldn't move. *Wulfee would have killed all of you. All of you.*

When one of the El'vie smashed a rock into Etta's skull, she felt nothing at all before her world went black.

SPRINGTIDE MOON

"THE OLD GROVE, THEY call it." Eurick's stories always made Maggie happy. She walked side by side with James as the raven led them and a small group through a maze of charred nytewood stumps. It was the day of Springtide, and the entire Dagglandic encampment was as raucous as a storm. *Day and night will be the same length on this day.* Maggie had asked James to come with her, away from all the noise for a few hours to ease the thumping in her head, and James asked Eurick, too. Soon, Itchy was trailing along and singing Maggie's favourite songs. "This was the largest grove of nytewoods in all of the Hallow, bigger than what's in the Wick by two," Eurick continued.

"What happened to it?" Maggie knew the story well but she wanted to hear it told by another. *Sometimes I just need to hear waking voices.*

Eurick smiled, his grin as wide as his face. "There's an old song about this here wood. A song with your name."

Maggie of Old Grove. Maggie had heard it a thousand thousand times and more. Her third mother would sing it to her all day and night. *Seven. I was seven when she left me.* After her third mother and father had forgotten her in the Dark Arbor, Maggie sang the song of Old Grove over and over until exhaustion took her and she crawled down into the barrows of Oldwood.

"Maggie of Old Grove," Itchy the Bard said. "I know it well."

"Old Maggie had buried her husband here in this grove beneath one of the nytewoods," Eurick said. "She visited his grave tree each night and waited until the moon reached its highest point, at which time the ghost of her husband, Loren, rose up to dance a single dance with her beneath the stars. The folk of the small hamlet that was once here by that stream, called Ol'ikn, which means sapling in the old rune tongue of the Mal, had cursed Maggie for being a witch and a spirit-talker. They banished her from their commune. But all of the folk knew she hadn't strayed far, for they heard her haunting ballads from the grove each night. When the Ayelish attacked and burned the nearby hamlet, they too heard the witch-songs from the wood and burned the grove down in fear. Old Maggie was never heard again. Now the Old Grove is haunted by *two* ghosts, and many have witnessed Maggie and Loren still dancing here, between the charred stumps beneath the stars and the brightness of the silver moon."

Maggie had goosebumps thinking about that story. It made her think of losing James and also made her miss the families that had left her.

Then Itchy started to sing:

"And Maggie stayed forever
For one last dance.
Through years and weather,
For one more chance,
To tell her Loren she loved him.
And Maggie stayed forever,
But Loren never came,
Maggie cried for her lover,

All was silent but flame.
And Maggie stayed forever
For one more chance.
Till in death they were together
And in death they finally danced."

Amidst the charred stumps, Maggie let the song carry her away as she wandered. Tiptoed and barefoot, she walked through the loam and the mud. She liked to feel the earth on her skin—between her toes. There was so much *life* in it.

Soon she heard the same voices that swam in her dreams. Spirits of black light slithered through the dead wood and hummed. Maggie stood and followed them.

"Come to us," they said.

She was terrified. "Who are you?"

"Maggie?" James's voice echoed from somewhere. "Where are you going?"

Maggie didn't want to drag James into this yet. She ran ahead.

The voices from the wood were singing. *"The gods are dead."*

"Why are you telling me this?" Maggie hadn't realized she was crying until she spoke, and her voice quivered. At the sound of her voice, the small shapes ceased to move.

"Maggie!" James was yelling from behind.

Maggie couldn't take her eyes off the small shapes. *Nymphs...* Maggie had seen them before, as a child. *With your second mother and big sister—Flora. I looked up to her so much...*

The nymphs took a Human form and stood before Maggie. Three naked women, covered in loam and mud, sang a song so haunting Maggie couldn't help but sob.

Soon leaves and small twigs wove themselves around the bodies of the nymphs and they fluttered before Maggie as gods of Nature.

They left me. They all leave me. I am alone. Alone but for James, she thought. *When Flora saw me making the dust dance and glow, her eyes flashed with putrid hate. I wanted to die. She told her mom and dad,* our mom and dad, *what she saw and two days later I was alone and singing Maggie of Old Grove again.* "Mage." Maggie had heard her second mom and dad talking with Flora the night before they left her. *"By the gods, she's mage..."* And Flora cried so hard it broke Maggie's soul. *She was broken in turn, to find out you were a monster.*

"Come to us," the nymphs sang to Maggie. *"Come home."*

"How?" Maggie fell to her knees. She wanted so badly to go to them, to whoever had been trying to talk to her in her dreams.

"Find the Abori."

Abori... "Who are you?" Maggie was sobbing. The nymphs had made her feel so safe and warm that she couldn't help but let her tears out.

"I am Na'reen. I will save you, girl, but you must find us. With that, I cannot help or the magics will be weakened." The voice turned to gravel, and Maggie heard crunching in the grove behind her. When she turned back, the nymphs had gone. *"Find us."*

"Maggie?" James was out of breath. Maggie stood up and fell into him. "I was worried—"

Maggie put her finger over James's lips and fell into his eyes. "I need to leave here, James."

James stared at the spot where the nymphs were, but Maggie knew he would see nothing. "What did you see in here?"

The nymphs are your curse and yours alone, just as the dead are his... "Nothing." Maggie threw her arms around James's hips.

James hadn't taken his eyes off of the arbor beyond the charred wood grove. "Do you want to go?" he said.

"Mmhmm." Maggie hated keeping things from James, but there were things she just didn't know how to say. When they were together in Wulfee's camp, Maggie had told James everything. *Everything.* But it was the first time in her life she felt like someone cared about her and was actually listening to her. Maggie had told James every detail about her past life—her three families, her sister Flora, her mentor Hagel, and how they all abandoned her to die—and James had told her everything about his life, and she truly believed that he had.

But something had changed between them since the Mother of Nature's Shrine. Maggie had felt an awakening to her power that she never had before. Where before it was always humming sweetly in the back of her mind, now it crashed and thundered like a violent storm in her foremind. *Nature has come alive and She is reaching out through you…* and James had become afraid of magics—of *their* magics. He was terrified of becoming what Calen Alder was.

Itchy was playing *The Flowers Burn Blue for Dixie,* and Eurick was singing along when Maggie and James returned to them. Eurick took a long swig from his wineskin and, with a warm smile, offered it to Maggie. She took it and the taste of the shine almost made her gag. *Just get it in ya.* Wulfee had always told her, and so she did. She never used to like drink or smoke, she had always preferred to dabble in her magics for the thrill. But now she wanted both.

Maggie sat beside James, who had sulked down on a log. It was black and charred, with small black and yellow nytewood chutes growing from the branch stumps and small brown mushrooms crawling all over it.

"I haven't stopped thinking about what Brynmor told me. That the Daggs mean to kill us." Maggie was still dizzy from whatever she just saw, but that thought was swollen and throbbing.

"Me neither," James said. He was sullen. *He feels useless again…* "But I don't know how much I can trust Brynmor's word. He would say anything to save himself."

Maggie thought about that a moment and realized she didn't trust him either. *A warm soul lies just as fiercely as a cold one. The only difference is intention.* "We could leave, you know. Just you and I."

James sighed. *He wants to. Deep down he wants to.* "I should confront her, that witch, Halda," James said to Maggie. "Find out what it is she really wants. I don't like the way she looks at you."

Nor I the way she looks at you. "It's Springtide. The gods mean for us to rest on this day."

Eurick had overheard Maggie and James talking, and they walked over to him. Propping his leg on the log, Eurick said, "The Daggland witch speaks of prophecy and magics. She may be worth hearing."

"She speaks about the same things that my father spoke of. End times and gods rising." James kicked the dirt.

"Tell me, Eurick," James continued. "What happened to Hendurinn after the wither year—after Bazal? The cycles left that part out."

The raven sighed. "You know, I've been thinking about this. I don't think I've ever heard a story about what happened *after.* Things got better when the elements came back, I suppose, and then one day he died of old age... probably."

Itchy plucked a sour note. "The bards only write songs wearing the sweet summer dress of poetry. Rarely will you hear a song of an ugly whore, though I met one once in the town of Glavelin that was surely worth a song." Itchy plucked another note. "If only she was from Morland. The Whore of Morland has a better ring to it."

"Just speak plainly, man, don't talk to us in your riddles and rhymes," Eurick said. James still had his head hanging.

"If there is no song about it, it must not have been pretty." Itchy stood and slung his woodharp on his back like a weapon. "Best you ask that witch what she knows. The witches of the world tend to know what the songs forgot."

"Then I'll do it. I'll ask her what she knows and why she's *really* here. She may have convinced her people that she is here for their god, but I'm not so sure," James said.

"Aye," Eurick said. "And I'll come with you when you do."

"We should head back." Itchy's eyes shifted throughout the charred grove.

"You scared of ghosts?" Maggie asked him.

His eyes met hers with a dead stare. "Yes," he said, and walked away. The rest followed.

Maggie breathed deeply of the fresh air. She could smell, beneath the charred and dead wood, new life—small shrubs and insects and worms, flowers and herbs and grasses. It was all there; beneath the scorched surface, life prevailed. The spirits of earth lived. *And something lives in me, too, something full of life below my scarred and useless body. It has lived there my whole life. If it hadn't lived there, maybe I would still be with my first mom or my third—with Flora or Hagel. If I could kill this mage, maybe I could live with James. We could have a child... maybe...*

The words that the nymphs had spoken to Maggie burned into her like hot coals, smoking up her mind. *The Abori... but where are they? Across the sea? North and east?*

James was mumbling to himself as he walked when Maggie came up beside him. She could sense his anger and frustration. She put her hand on his back, and he jumped. *He was so deep in his own head he hadn't even noticed me.*

"I won't be taken advantage of," James said, gripping Maggie's hand. "It's all I have left, to protect my people. To protect you. It's all I have left and I won't fail."

Maggie wished she had more to say, but her tongue had become mush in her mouth. *How can you support him when you can't support yourself?* The sword on James's back glowed like a dying moon. *It's eating him, even now.* But Maggie didn't know what to do.

T HE HALLOW FOLK AND the Dagglanders had blended with ease, and the camp had become one living, breathing thing. It was easy to be friendly when you were hungry and folk were feeding you. Maggie had never seen so many people in one place. The noise of it disgusted her. She could barely hear the wind most times or the birds. The grass was trampled and muddy, and it all smelled like shit and piss and sweat. The Springtide moon was hiding somewhere below the horizon. The sun was fat and hot in the sky, and all awaited what was to come. Maggie saw Halda and Toren whispering and pointing at her and James as they came back.

"They're staring at us," James growled. When he looked at Maggie, she saw fear in his eyes. James unbuckled *Essikah* and drew her in one long motion. To Halda and Toren, he yelled, "If you mean to kill us, do it now!"

So much for subtlety... Maggie grabbed James by the arm. "James—" He shook her off. Many of the folk around had gone silent. All were staring. A few Daggs pulled axes of sharp, black steel. Halda and Toren stood speechless, gazing at James like he was a rare animal. "Try it!" Spittle flew from James's mouth.

The pressure of being king is too much for him... It's all become too much and everyone can see it.

"James," Halda said. She looked between James and Maggie. "If we meant to kill you, we would have done it *before* we fed you, not after. Or at least *during*, like the red dinner that Hanrad the Hard hosted for Illen of Smokestone and his rakkar."

"We are not so stupid to waste so much good food." Toren chewed on a boar bone as if to prove the point. James heard Erik snoring from his pavilion. It was hardly a coup at this point. And if it was, Maggie suspected Halda was in on it alone.

James started to look around, bewildered. *He's embarrassed.* Maggie held his arm and helped him to lower *Essikah*. His muscles were fully flexed from the weight of the great sword.

"These are dark times, and with the dark comes many fears." Halda held up both hands in a gesture of peace. "There is no need to doubt us, King. You are safe here. Together, we will take your kingdom back from these Ayelish, just like in the days of Old. Daggs and Mal, shedding blood side by side." Halda stepped forward and James stepped back. Maggie remembered the clanfire stories about the time when the Daggs and the Mal *stopped* shedding the blood of others and started shedding the blood of each other. James glared at Maggie like he was drowning and her eyes were the only thing keeping him afloat. *The sword eats at his soul, I can feel it every time he holds it. Even strapped to his back it's a demon.*

More of the Daggs had started to close in around them, but Maggie saw Toren make a gesture to them, and they all parted and continued their celebrations as if nothing had happened. James buckled *Essikah* back onto his back.

"There is no need for this, James," Toren said.

"Come." Halda took another step forward, and Maggie stepped in front of her. Halda stared Maggie up and down and smiled. "Queen. Allow me the honour to host you and the king in my tent. Let me show you what I've seen. Let me ease your suspicions." Halda looked over Maggie's shoulder to James. "We all know something bigger is happening here. No need to hide it from each other. This is a prophecy."

Prophecy. Maggie hated that word. There were no good prophecies of mage.

"We can talk here, if you mean to talk," James said. Eurick pushed his chest out, and Itchy slipped off into the dark somewhere like a shadow.

Halda grinned sardonically. "Of course." The Dagglander clutched a leather sack at her neck. She glared at James. "Reaper. It's you I seek. It is an old prophecy that when the sky falls and Ox'olin is upon us, the Children of Daggland must follow the Reaper, the King of the Dead, to our last days. When I heard the King of Mal Hallow was being called the Reaper for his deeds and skills, I almost couldn't believe it. But now..." Halda eyed Maggie up and down. "I don't know what to think. I thought that when I found you, the signs would be clear of what we are supposed to do. But they are not. I've only been given one sign."

"What is it?" Maggie asked.

"Soothsayers."

"Soothsayers?" James said it like Halda was a child. "The soothsayers abandoned their hermitage in the Wick years ago. They all hide in the mountains on the Isle of Ryne now. We have seen them with our own eyes. They studied Maggie when Wulfee brought her to them. They are not what you think they are. They are beasts of another time."

Soothsayers... Maggie hated that word. She hated those... *things*. She hated what they said about her. They made her sound so... *monstrous...*

"This is prophecy. You're all a part of it," Halda said.

"My dad believed in prophecy. What happened to Hendurinn after the wither year? What happened? What am I supposed to do?"

"Things have been shown to me," Halda said. "My god speaks to me through my runes and in the flames. I need answers to what She has revealed—interpretations. I need to seek the soothsayers. I feel there is more that my god is trying to tell me. About why the gods are dying. About how to stop it."

"How? How can you get answers?" James sounded desperate. *He is truly lost. The wizard, at least, gave us answers. Now we are drowning in an ocean of ancient magics and lies.*

"In the morning when we march on Pool, I will go my separate way. I will seek answers from the soothsayers."

"The soothsayers don't talk to anyone. I saw them and they said not a word," James said.

"You saw only their eyes, James, their shapes," Maggie said. She remembered those things. She had seen them—their bodies. Crooked, hoary old things full of grumbling magics. *Like fermented Human.* They *judged* her in ways that made her hate their very name.

"They may hear me," Halda said, "I know their language—the language of runes. And I know their *names*. But I know not the way."

Their names... Maggie didn't like the sound of that. There was great sorcery in the names of creatures like those.

"I will take you." Eurick stepped forward.

"The Ryne is where the Raven's Guild is, are you sure?" James said. "You don't have to go, Eurick. Surely the Guild will find you."

"They won't." Eurick shook his head. "The last place they will be looking for me is right under their noses. They tend to stay in and around the Guild. And, Halda said it herself, she knows not the way. I know all the ways to all the places, man," Eurick said. "This is what I left the Guild for. This is my chance to help. This is where *I* come into this story. Let me take her there, man. Let us find the answers. What Hendurinn did after. I want to do that for you."

"A raven of the Transporter's Guild? I saw your cloak but didn't think it could be real," Halda said. "Or at the very least, you had stolen it."

"Aye, it's real, man. I'm the only living raven to have never failed a job, you know?" Eurick stuck out his hand. Halda looked at his hand like it was a turd.

"So why are you here, then?" Halda asked.

Eurick's face fell flat and he pulled his hand away. "Chose to leave the Guild on my own accord."

"So you're a deserter, and the Guild will be after you." Halda glared at James. "You think yourself clever to stick this man with me? You want to be rid of us both?"

James clenched a fist. "That is the best person I have in my whole army. You should be bloody honoured to have Eurick as a companion."

Halda grinned. Toren seemed like he couldn't wait to join the revelry around them.

Eurick stepped forward. "I will take you to these soothsayers safely. Ain't nobody else here that can say that for true."

Halda grinned. "Right then. Tomorrow morning, after our celebrations, the lot of you will march to Pool to gain allies, and Eurick and myself to Ryne to find the soothsayers."

Maggie, James, and Eurick walked away from the Daggs and towards their own people. James's forehead was soaked in sweat, and Maggie could smell the saltiness of it soaking his whole body. *What other than that sword eats at you, my love?*

Eurick dissolved into the crowd but Maggie stayed by James, and they headed for the rulers of the Hallow and their children by one of the clanfires. Brinley had his maps laid out on the ground with coloured stones all over them, and the dragonslayer himself was sprawled out pointing at various spots.

"You go. I can't hear all this talk anymore," Maggie said. James held her gaze with his, and Maggie saw sadness in his eyes. *He would rather go with you but he has duties. He doesn't want to fail...* "Find me before moonrise," Maggie said. James smiled and nodded.

MAGGIE LAY UNDER A small maple and watched the stars for a while and thought about the Abori and the stories she'd heard. *They live north of east. They eat dreams and birth them, too. They have children with bears and wolves and owls.*

After some time, she couldn't handle her own thoughts and got up to wander in the night and to smell the moon-growth and whisper things to the spirits. She found herself drawn to the rusted iron gibbet that held Richard Brynmor. The old lord saw her coming and stood and bowed.

"Queen," he scraped out in a broken voice.

"I'm no queen just as you're no prisoner. But here we both are wearing names like ill-fitting garbs," Maggie said.

Brynmor fell back on his arse and leaned against the bars. His face was sagging with defeat.

"Tell me, what happened to you, Brynmor?"

The lord's eyes lit up at the chance to speak his truth. "Ellorin happened." He straightened his posture. "She arrived at Castle Stone Tree with those beasts, the Hawka. They were swaying like drunks and moved at her every command. She had some kind of magics that made the other Warlocks we'd had at court seem like mere children. She stood before me and my wife, and my daughter and two grandsons, and threatened to release her hold on those beasts and kill us all right there. She said all I had to do was sack Ockam. I knew Derudin had left, I had received his message, so I said I would do it. I figured he'd have a meagre force there that I could talk to and make some kind of a deal. And I did. We only killed twenty people at Ockam. I helped Eridan escape when the Banshee had taken off to hunt James. I thought I could find a way out of it, but when James killed her, and the Hawka broke free from her hold, they slaughtered us. I ran and somehow escaped but it was rough. I had made it out with one other soldier, a woman—a mother of two. She had been bitten by a Hawka and died in my arms two days later. I survived three weeks in the cold and snow before a group of Ayelish folk found me. Blood-crazed out of their minds from the wars and all of the killing they'd been forced into. They would have eaten me if I didn't prove so helpful in navigating. The soldiers were mostly sellswords and couldn't read the maps. They wanted to find the coast. So I led them there. When we got there, they chained me up with the others they'd caught along the way. I had watched them eat plenty of other folk on the journey so I had an idea of what they planned on doing with me and those others in chains. It was weeks in that prison with those folk. All of us were starving. I watched a woman in chains with me eat her own fingers, right down to the knuckle. When the Dagglanders arrived... they were right, when they arrived, it was a mercy to us. We'd rather have our throats slit than be eaten slowly." Brynmor was crying now. Maggie couldn't believe what she was hearing—what this country had become. "I just want my wife and my kids to know I made it. That I didn't let them eat me."

"We will tell them. We will give you an honourable death," Maggie said.

Brynmor stared at her and blubbered something that sounded like "Thank you."

"Who were these Ayelish? Where did they come from?"

"They came from Kallahorn. They were King Alder's people. James let them leave with their lives, and they terrorized the Hallow all winter.

They couldn't return to Ayeland because they had abandoned their king, so instead they went wild, claiming themselves to be an ancient order called Demhoni. A fungus attacked their minds and made them hungry for Human flesh. James should have killed them—Calen Alder's army. He should have killed them..." Brynmor hung his head. He took a deep breath. Maggie admired the strength of this man. "They all follow someone named Heath," Brynmor continued. "They're in bands spread all over the north now. They're only getting bigger, and soon they will converge in the mountains. They talk of a place called Elwyd—a place they think will help them live forever. Some of the misplaced Mal have joined them, too, no doubt." Brynmor seemed full of energy now. He got up and held the bars. "You can stop them. Go back to Kallahorn. Protect it."

Maggie didn't care about protecting anything. She was ready to leave this entire continent. She was ready to finally *belong*. "We'll give you an honourable death, Hammer, and make sure your wife and children know that you died with honour."

Brynmor opened his mouth, but soon closed it again without saying anything. Maggie felt the energy seep out of him. She walked away and heard him sobbing behind her.

Maggie walked back to where the Hallowfolk had set up their camp. Hundreds of tattered tents leeched onto the stones and the fires, and the charred grove of dead nytewoods brooded over all.

James stood with the lords by the central clanfire. They were shouting at each other and arguing about something Maggie cared little about. She had tried to play queen, but found it was all an act. *An act for James. We're both putting on acts and it's false. Our true selves long to be together, but can't.*

When James saw Maggie walking by, his eyes slipped away from his argument with Brinley and stuck to her like honey. She smiled at him and shook her head. Her heart beat faster. He was the most beautiful thing she had ever known. More beautiful than the flower buds blooming in early spring, and more beautiful even than the sunrise igniting the red and yellow and orange leaves of the trees in the Fell of autumn.

James smiled and went back to his argument, and when his eyes left her, Maggie felt a longing stronger than her need for another breath for his eyes to behold her once more. Maggie knew she couldn't pull him away from where he was. *He wants to do right by his parents. He wants to rule this land and guide them. He wants the best for them.* If he left any of these council meetings, he would lose his respect as king. He was barely holding it together, but Maggie was incredibly impressed by how he managed to do it. *No matter how loose his reign, he holds on.*

Maggie lay on the soft grass beneath a small maple tree and watched the clouds drift. She lay for quite some time as the sun began its slow descent and the moon became visible in the pale pink sky. The celebrations had begun and folk had started to gather by the pyres.

James found her beneath the tree and together, they went to watch the sacrifice. When they got up close, Maggie realized the pyre wasn't burning just for one. Troughs of stone snaked down the side of it and conjoined to a stone bowl three feet wide and just as deep. A line of prisoners in black chains marched solemnly towards the pyre, Brynmor amongst them with his chin high. *He looks strong—he looks like a Hammer on this eve.*

"This is what our people want." James's voice was tense. Maggie touched his hand to calm him. *This will please the gods. This will silence the voices in my dreams.*

Maggie was expecting some prayer, some word to the god, but there was none of that. The Springtide moon was fat and brimming silver-white in the purple sky. Maggie drank in its energy.

"Do you feel that, James?"

"Feel what?"

"The moon." Maggie closed her eyes and breathed deeply of the night. The damp and cold and young green life filled her nostrils and her soul with life. At that moment, she knew that she and James would have a child. Something had come alive in the earth, and it was alive in *her. Springtide. All is reborn. All is new. Winter is over. You can be new. You can leave this and find them. The Abori... but James. I can't leave him. I can't.*

James looked saddened by the fact that he couldn't understand Maggie. "No," he said, "I don't feel it." And he turned his attention back to the pyre and the madness about it. "Maggie, Brinley's outriders have spotted the Ayelish gathering at Mammoth's Head. He said there could be ten thousand of them, maybe more."

"Ten thousand?" The number was so large Maggie couldn't even imagine.

"Aye. Queen Ianna leads them. They want my head on a stake." James gripped her hands, and by the way he did, Maggie knew that number was bad. Maggie held James's hand, and together, they watched one of the slaves climb the pyre. By the way James watched, Maggie knew he had put a lot of faith in this sacrifice to garner the gods' favours. For some reason, that terrified her.

The Speaker of the Gods, still dressed in black wool with kraken bones dangling, directed them where to lay their head, and without a word or prayer or gesture to anything greater than herself, the Speaker hooked her black steel blade under the victim's chin and slit their throat to the wick. The victim gurgled some last words that went unheard as blood bubbled and frothed from their neck and ran down the twisted pyre in a scarlet trickle. Maggie listened to the spirits as they danced in the wind and in the flames of the many fires. *Death.* They sang. *Dying.*

One by one, in a mad procession, the folk had the blood spilled from their throats like boars. The crimson waterfall shone a crude red in that near full moon, and the bowl of blood was as black as the darkest night. Soon the bowl was overflowing, and the Dagglanders howled like maddened wolves at a moon that seemed to howl back at them.

Maggie beheld the stars, and in them, found the faces of all she'd ever loved. Mothers, sisters, Wulfee, James. She saw all she was and ever would be—eternal. *"You are the stars. You are bigger than living, can't you see that?"* the voice in her dreams had told her. *"The moon and sun are your children and all the world bows to you. They stare up at you in wonder and will never understand you. But I understand you. Come to me, my nature-child. Cross the sea and come. You will be a mother. There is always a choice.*"

A familiar hand on her shoulder made her jump. She was so deep in remembrance it scared her badly.

"We don't have to watch this." James slid his hands from her shoulders down her to her waist and pulled her close. She let her body shape to his, and the smell of his breath made her skin prickle.

"I want to," she said, and watched the shaman wearing a bearskin, the head of the bear over her head as a hood, with black streaks running from her eyes, take up the bowl of blood and raise it to the sky. Red gore slopped all over the shaman's hands and arms.

"Ox'olin!" she shouted. The Dagglanders screamed so loud the ground shook. The Speaker of the Gods seemed to be in some kind of trance upon the pyre as blood squirted from the neck of one of the victims and showered all below. "Ox'olin," the crowd chanted. They were so many and so loud that Maggie thought they might shake a star loose. She hoped they would.

"We should go." James pulled her arm.

"No." She got closer so that some of the blood misted her face. She drank the energy around her like a horse coming to water after a long ride. She drank and was full. And in that dark of night with blood misting and stars shining, Maggie felt more at home than she could remember.

PART TWO

"History is a nightmare from which I am trying to awake".

James Joyce

A TRADE

J ULIEN DRAGGED THE ORACLE's corpse behind him through the sand. The smell of the sea had never been sweeter. Julien breathed it in, almost couldn't believe he'd made it. He looked behind him at his withered crew. Less than five hundred had made it to the Oracle and back with him. *But these folk, these folk will never leave.* They were the start of something great, but he needed more. He needed an army if he was to take Hest.

The old, gold dome of Saltsan's Temple twinkled in the sun like a star. *And you'll have that star and all the others.* The bulbous rooftops and onion-shaped towers were mostly sunken and deformed, patched over with rotting wood chinking. The town was built in the style of Old Yehven, erected by Kelson to honour the Creator. Julien found that incredible, considering the town itself felt ancient. They had been making salt and selling slaves here for centuries before Kelson came and built the town and its now crumbled walls. Even before the Starfall, they made salt here, if some of the books Julien had read at Odessa were to be believed. The walls and streets were made of sandstone brick. The towers and shops and hovels of the old Lovasi town were all made of sandstone brick, but many more crude buildings erected of red clay brick and canvas clung to the ancient town like parasites. It was a city of bricks, and it didn't discriminate which bricks it took on. The town had one road that wound between the many salt flats dug into the sand, which gave Saltsan its name.

The banners of House Orlen were plastered on every corner marker and every well. Julien recognized the grey sword on a field of salt-white from his studies of heraldry at the Palace of Odessa under the employment of Magister Libby. Old Libby was so paranoid he had forced Julien and every attendant to his court to know every potential enemy. Julien also recognized the Hester flag, the golden lion on purple. Saltsan was usually heavily occupied by a Hester military force, but Julien only saw folk of House Orlen. He assumed with the wars going on, the Hesters couldn't spare the people.

Few merchants shouted wares here, and even fewer farmers looked for seeds and grain. Saltsan was full of sun-baked slaves that shovelled salt twelve months a year until they died. The town had been ruled by the Orlen family for nearly two decades, and they were loyal to the lions of Hester all that time. Julien knew all this from studying with Libby at Odessa.

Julien tightened his hands around the ropes that he used to drag the Oracle's body through the desert. He summoned his strength and pulled again. The Oracle's body was a tattered mess at this point, torn ragged from the cutting sand. He had been exhausted for hours, but he dared not ask for help. He had killed the Oracle, and he would drag her body back to Saltsan alone, just as Kassius had done with the prophet of Odom, from Lysses to Behru.

By the time Julien and his remaining crew had reached the outskirts of the town, a small crowd had come out and gathered around him. Whispers of "Oracle" were being passed around, and Julien's crew raised their chins in the air like the royalty they now were.

By the time he reached the dusty sandstone streets, the crowd had grown to half the city. Julien figured that would be a good enough audience and dropped the rope he had used to drag the Oracle through the desert. He spread his arms and shouted, "I am destiny come." He pounded his leather chestplate. "I have killed the Oracle and stolen her powers. I know the future!"

The people murmured to each other and pointed at Julien, and he knew he would need to do more. He held his hand out showing the Oracle's ring. The gold glinted in the sun, and Julien heard more gasps. *They believe it.* Julien had carved his own gold rings with the same markings he saw on the Oracle's ring. The real ring was in his pocket.

He knelt down and grabbed the Oracle's hair to lift her head up. Her face was black and crusted with dragon-ash and covered in blood and sand. She looked like something at the bottom of an old fire pit, and Julien held her head by the hair so all could see, and her body dangled limply below. "She told me I would be the king of all Ardura. I will start by capturing this town."

"Until the Hesters come back," a voice from the crowd rose above the snickers and giggles.

They laugh at you... "The Hesters do not scare me, friend. They did not scare my father or his father. I spit on the Hesters." Julien stepped over the crumbled sandstone walls that once stood around Saltsan and towards the palace at the town's centre. A palace in a Yehvenki city was always marked by an onion-shaped dome and circular main hall shouldered by four towers crowned with spiralling minarets topped with devils, so Julien found it easily. The crowd followed him and his army, and Julien saw more than one armed town guard slink away into buildings or alleyways to avoid them.

"What is this?" a drunken voice boomed. A twig-skinny man wearing a dark red cloak with nothing beneath staggered out into the sandy streets from a caravanserai. Flute and harp music and smoke burst out of the door behind him. His leather thong sandals slapped on the brick. Julien knew by the white-salt crown he wore on his head that it was Lord Lyle of House Orlen. "Who are you?" Lyle said.

Julien stayed silent.

"He says he's Esterbraun," a voice from the crowd sang.

"Esterbraun?" The skinny man traced Julien with his eyes and laughed. He had six armed guards with him, three on either side, holding steel swords. "I've never heard that name. What do you want in Esher? There is nothing here for you."

"There is everything here for me. My entire life has led up to this moment so that I would be ready." Julien stepped aside so that Lord Orlen could see the dead Oracle.

Lord Orlen looked at the dead body and at Julien. "Are you fucked, man? You drag a dead body into my town through the desert and start speaking nonsense and inciting crowds?" The lord looked to his retainers, and Julien could tell Orlen was deciding whether or not he should start a fight. Surely, he could rally enough people from the town to outnumber Julien, but Julien's folk were here now and ready with swords drawn.

"This is the Oracle." Julien remained calm.

"The Oracle?" Lyle said. "You expect me to believe that this thing is the Oracle?"

"Look at her," Julien said. "Look at this." He offered Lord Orlen the fake gold ring.

The lord snatched it up. He inspected it and touched the carvings. He looked up at Julien. His face was puffy and his nose was red, and his eyes were bloodshot and he said, "Why did you do this? Are you completely mad? A fool?"

"I am destiny come," Julien said without hesitation. He could see the terror in Lord Orlen's eyes, and Julien knew that he had him now. "Me and my folk are just going to the harbour. Tell me, whose ship is that I see docked? That is no merchant ship."

"That's Bones's ship. He's a crook, but he's my crook. You'll find him down at the harbour. At a pleasure house or inn. Can't miss him, he has one eye. Don't you go causing trouble down there."

"There is no need to cause trouble. We'll be gone by morning. You can keep that ring."

Lyle pocketed the ring and licked his lips. "Be gone by morning," he said. The lord's retainers looked at him with disgust. *These folk hate him.* Julien could see that the retainers were all staring at the ring with the same hunger. *They all want to be in his place.* The lord turned around and went back into the caravanserai and left them. Julien and his rabble carried on unprovoked.

"T EN SHIPS," JULIEN SAID. The Epithosian sailor gawked at him with one big eye. Julien wondered what kind of brawl this fellow got into that caused him to lose an eye. *It seems so small a target, an eye. Bad luck, that. He's down a leg and an eye, and I still fear the man.*

"You want ten ships?" the sailor laughed the words out. "This is Saltsan, fellow. The only ships you'll find for hire here are merchant's vessels to carry your salt."

"I saw your big beautiful ship in the harbour. With oars and a scorpion on the bow." Julien was taking a shot that this man was Bones just by looking at him.

"I have one ship. That one, and it ain't for hire."

"Surely a man that has a ship like that can get nine more. Come on, Bones." Julien knew that by naming him, he had shocked the sailor.

The sailor squinted his eyes, and Julien could tell that the man was thinking carefully about what to do. "And where would you take these ships?" Bones looked beyond Julien to his rabble of followers. He chose not to ask how Julien knew his name. "That's not enough folk to operate ten ships.

Julien smiled. "I'm going to take them home, my friend. To Sareen, where I was born. And of course it's not enough, I need you to supply the people, too. Soldiers preferably, for aesthetics, but it doesn't really matter."

The man wasn't impressed. He clearly couldn't make out if Julien was jesting or not. "What'd you say your name was?"

"Esterbraun. Julien Esterbraun."

"Esterbraun? That's an old name. Name like that could get you into trouble round here."

At least he knows who you are. "Well that's just the thing, friend, I'm looking for trouble."

Now the Epithosian sailor understood, and his grin showed Julien that he had this man's attention now. Julien pulled out his necklace, which held a wooden emblem of the eye of Karaat. The man made the sign of the eye over his chest.

"Praise, Karaat," he said. "Those Hesterland bastards destroyed the temple of the graces in Sareen. The Warlock Adora renamed the new construction built in its place after herself."

"So, I heard," Julien said. He *hadn't* heard that before now, but he needed this sailor to believe he was all-knowing. "And my plan is to burn the Hesterlander ruler who dares sit the throne in Sareen over the ashes of the temple." He whistled, and Ashan brought forth Julien's carved chest. Ashan was another of Julien's rabble, only two-thirds the height of Canri, but what he lacked in height, he made up for in complexion. His skin was dark and his hair was darker, thick and long and curly.

Julien knelt down, and without any ceremony, opened the chest. The dragonbone lay there, ancient and beautiful. It looked like no rock or bone on earth but like something from another world. *The moon, maybe.* Julien looked up at the blue sky and envied the moon in its perfect concealment. *If I could hide like you, moon, I would slip right into Hest and take the city—the Jewel of Ardura—like it was nothing.*

"Praise Karaat, is that..." The sailor gawked at the bone, and Julien knew that the man was probably thinking of how many coins he could get for it.

"Dragonbone," Julien finished.

The sailor made the sign of the eye over his body and continued to gawk at the bone. Julien waved his hand, and Ashan closed the chest and locked it. "Who are you?" Bones said, and Julien could sense fear in him now.

"I am Old Blood. I am Draku, and I've come back from the grave of my ancestors to kill the Warlocks and spread the Word of Karaat. I have come to take my place as Emperor of Ardura. Call me shadow walker or night lurker or simply *Satanaga,* which means living-dead in the old tongue of my people. I know you are not a sailor but a sellsword. I know sailors' hands and I know the hands of warriors. I have touched the hands of peasants and lepers, queens and kings, and I know by looking at your hands that you are a man of the sword just as much as you are one of the sails."

"I should kill you for talking this sorcery." Bones looked scared.

"Kill me? I was about to make you the offer of a lifetime, Bones. An offer to change your life forever. I want to make you the new Lord of Saltsan." The sailor was still angry, but Julien knew how greedy most sailors were internally. Their possessions came and went like the tides, and they were always hungry for more cargo and especially for promises of land where they could store and protect their plunder, and so the sailor tilted his chin up to hear more. "If you help me take Sareen, I will give you the throne here in Saltsan."

Bones looked at Julien like he was mad, and maybe he was. "The Hesters will come back. They will kill both of us. You're a bloody fool."

"I'm not afraid of the Hesters."

"You should be," Bones said.

"Are you going to help me or not?" Julien scratched his crotch.

"What do you get out of it? Other than the ships?"

"I get to laugh back at everyone who's ever laughed at my family name."

"By dying?" Bones said, and thought he was rather funny by the way he laughed.

Julien didn't dignify Bones with an answer and instead just showed one of his fake Oracle's rings again. "This ring is what the Oracle used to tell futures," Julien lied. "And I've seen yours. A lord. That's why I came to you. You cannot fail. This town is rightfully yours."

Bones looked at the ring and at the dead body of the Oracle behind Julien. Julien could sense that Bones had thought of himself as the Lord of Saltsan before and had imagined all the gold he would make by controlling the salt pits and the wharfs here. It was worth a thousand thousand times what ten ships cost. "You're mad, right, a bloody fool?" he said. "Surely, you're mad."

"Completely." Julien grinned. Bones grinned back.

"Get me the crown of Saltsan, and I'll get you ships. But if you think you're getting ten, you really are mad. I can give you three ships. That will be enough to carry your army," Bones said. "It will take two weeks to get the ships and the folk to row them."

Julien was in no place to bargain; he knew he was already pushing his luck. Three ships were more than he even hoped for. "Three?" he said, feigning contemplation. "Okay. Three it is."

Bones stuck his thick calloused hand out, and Julien shook it. "Tell me, Esterbraun," Bones said, "how do you plan to take a city as grand as Sareen with three ships?"

"It wouldn't be destiny if everyone knew, Bones. You're going to have to extend me your trust and accept the crown of Saltsan as payment enough." Bones glared at Julien and Julien smiled. "But trust isn't earned, of course, it's bought!" Julien tossed one of the fake Oracle's rings to Bones. The sailor snatched it out of the air and looked at it closely. "Take that as a sign of my goodwill. The next thing I give you will be a crown."

Bones hesitated, for he wasn't a man who took orders often, but soon he calmed and nodded. "Two weeks," he said. "I leave tomorrow." He pocketed the ring.

"Then tonight I will make you lord," Julien said.

THAT NIGHT, JULIEN AND his rabble covered the body of the Oracle in black tar and hoisted her stinking corpse onto one of the flag poles beside the golden lion of Hester and the grey sword of Orlen, then Julien shot it with a flaming arrow.

"In the name of Karaat, I give you the soul of the Oracle." Julien spoke from atop a barrel and pointed to the flaming effigy. "You don't look to her for your future anymore, you look to me." The people cheered and many were dancing and praying to the flames, and Julien knew Karaat was strong here.

The moon was bright, and before long, half the town had gathered. The slaves could walk freely in the night hours, and they walked freely to gather round Julien. The folk spoke of how their lord betrayed them and how the hungry summer would come again when the Hesters come back and take all of the harvest Lord Orlen had promised them. They spoke of the old ways of Esher, before the Hesters came, and they sang long-forgotten songs, and Julien sang with them and listened to their woes and promised them things would get better. That *he* would make them better. He washed the brows of the sick folk lying in the streets and he listened.

Julien's family had been exiled from Esher when he was just a boy. As a man, Julien had been exiled from Lavesh. He had been unwanted and laughed at his whole life, but now, finally, he was someone. *And Karaat made it so. Karaat has told it true.*

Folk were sharpening blades and fastening belts and tying hair in knots. They were battle drunk, sick with the fever of change.

"I will give you a new lord on this evening. A man of Karaat. Someone who knows how to protect." Julien basked in the revelry that followed. *They hate Lord Orlen so much they would kill him themselves.*

Julien led his rabble towards the palace and the townsfolk followed. They held swords and axes and spears. They held cudgels and pitchforks and fish hooks. Torches pelted the night sky, thrusted by angry folk. They were going to kill their lord. "This is for your families," Julien said, and his people cheered. "This is for Karaat! This is for an empire of peace—a land without war!"

The lord's retainers were hammered drunk and unarmoured, and Julien himself slayed two of them with his rapier. The others were mauled by townsfolk.

When Julien kicked down the door to the palace, the lord was naked, dancing around a fire, hammered drunk and singing. Three naked men danced with him, and when the door burst open, they fell to the ground in fear. Lyle cowered as Julien walked him down. Julien kicked him in the ribs and stepped aside to let the people swarm in and kill their lord. They beat him and broke him alive until finally he succumbed beneath the hands of the people he was supposed to protect.

When Bones arrived with his hundred warriors to see what had happened, the battle was already won. The folk of Saltsan bowed to Bones, just as Julien had directed them to. Bones looked shocked; he gazed at Julien.

"Your new lord!" Julien pronounced, and the folk cheered. "Praise Karaat."

"Praise Karaat!" the people echoed.

"Two weeks," Bones said, "and I'll have your ships and the folk to sail them, too." The Lord of Saltsan removed the crown from Lyle's pulpy, caved-in skull and placed it on his own head. The folk cheered and celebrated. They tore down the banners of Orlen and of Hester. They burned the temples of Eralis and sang hymns of Karaat. When the moon rose fat and full of gold, the folk of Julien's rabble howled at it like jackals, and the whole town of Saltsan seemed to join.

And Julien hoped they heard it all the way in Hest.

THIRSTY

I T SEEMED A STRANGE thing to Aldred, war. A name for a reason to meet up in a field of mud and kill one another on behalf of someone else. War had been carried out for hundreds of years on the very stretch of land on which Aldred stood, ever since Kelson died.

The town of Soren was known by many as the Town of Blood. It has seen more conquest than any other known place. *Maybe only Darry has seen more.* Aldred hated Darry for its smell as much as for its people. It had only taken Brooton and the fyrd a week to march up the Sunroad from Behru. Aldred prayed every day for the journey to be over—his own thoughts drove him mad on the long days' travels. *I've found a lover.*

Aldred looked out at the empty field that would be strewn with corpses in a matter of hours, and across that field, the Army of Truth had assembled to meet him. It was laughable. *The Army of Truth is a joke...* Even a brigand wouldn't dare put together such a shambled, unimpressive army.

Army was too good a word. They looked no better than a clan of northerners. They wore leather armour and held sticks. Every soldier had chainmail armour and Esheri silks covering most of their face. They stood sullenly in the distance like a small, dying forest with their pikes raised.

Is this a joke? It must be some kind of trap. Aldred's young scout had returned panting for breath.

"How many?" Aldred asked him.

The boy put his hands on his knees. "Around two hundred, sir."

It's a trap. It has to be a trap... "Two hundred isn't enough," Aldred said. "Unless they are completely mad, there are more of them somewhere. Be aware."

The sound of war horns rang out as Aldred led the ranks to a halt on the frontline. The golden lion of Hester roared upon a field of purple above folk's heads as flag bearers hoisted their poles towards the red sky.

These people may have been farmers, but most of them had already spent years on a battlefield and grew tough skin for it. A fyrd could be just as tough as a trained army after enough years of combat. *And they fought for something purer—something bigger than glory or the thought of knightship. They fought for their homes.* Every winter on the front lines, they fought and held the borders.

The fyrd drew their swords and banged the hilts on their shield faces. They stood close and ready to get into formation. The fyrd chanted war songs while the drum bearers smashed the skins of their drums with as much vigor as they would smash an enemy's skull.

Across the field, the enemy marched. *It must be a trap.* Aldred gazed around the battlefield like a hawk. The enemy had no war horns. They had no flag. They had no shield wall. *Who the fuck is leading them? Something isn't right here.* The sound of heavy steps in unison echoed across the field. The Hesterfolk readied themselves. There was silence amongst the ranks.

"Form up!" Aldred yelled. And the fyrd moved together and locked their shields. Clashing and cracking as iron edges met hardwood. "Tighter than a beaver dam, folks, hold up!"

Aldred clopped *Yeller* back and forth in front of his folk.

"These people are going to try to stop you from going home," Aldred yelled. "Home to the land that feeds every son and daughter of our kingdom. The lands that you folk tend to personally," he said, and that got only a slight rumble from the fyrd.

"The king wanted to send the sheriffs. Thought that you couldn't handle the borders of his kingdom any longer." That got their attention. A few cheers bellowed from the middle ranks. "Well, I told the king to fuck right off and give me my farmers because you're tougher than any of the winter-fattened knights or nobles he'd muster. Give me my fyrd any day!"

"Fuck yeah!" said a solitary voice. Then cheers, louder than lightning.

Aldred revelled in it. *This is the only thing you're good at—talking.* "I said fuck the knights and the sheriffs!" Aldred shouted, and at the word *knights,* his voice squeaked. The folk still erupted in cries of elation. *Maybe you're better at crafting the words than actually saying them.*

The steady sound of the enemy marching droned in the backdrop. "Fuck all the nobles. Shit on them!" The fyrd blew their horns and banged their drums. They waved their flags harder to make up for the lack of wind. They clashed their shields together and screamed with everything in them. Most were damn near crying; they were so ready to defend their land. The men and women of the Hesterlands roared like lions before him. *Praise Eralis, it's hard not to be proud of the Lion.*

Aldred unsheathed his sword, *Phantom.* It was three feet of shimmering black Lovasi steel. "We're not about to let a single one of these bloody Esheri live through this," Aldred announced with his sword raised to the red sun above. *But for the priest. Lookout for the priest...*

As Aldred charged Yeller forward into battle in front of everyone, he felt a pit open in his stomach when he thought about the scout. Cries erupted and all charged forward. Lock step motion. Aldred let Yeller bolt out to make a good show for his army before falling in behind the shield wall. "Hold!" he shouted. "Tighter than a bloody dam!"

The Esheri smashed into the shield wall in a bloody splatter. Sticks thrust right through chain plates. Most of the Esheri folk who arrived first were impaled before they could even swing their sword. The second row fared little better, and the third row lost significant ground, having to jump over the line of bodies. Folk swung and stabbed, hammered and smashed at the enemy. Screams of agony and elation. Of fear and ecstasy. Limbs tore, guts spilled. The Esheri launched spears from the back, and one came especially close to Aldred's ear. He heard it cutting through the air. He let himself fall to the back, looking frantically for someone who may have been leading this attack from the other side. Anyone of minor importance. *The priest. Miri, they called you. Where are you?* But it was just a blanket of chain-clad and spear-holding Esheri fighting to no end. Their head-silks were a rainbow of colours—bright green and blue and orange, all stained red with blood. The Kingsfolk had sliced through most of them, and the battle had developed into bloody chaos. The enemy had fallen out of order, and the fyrd were at risk of doing the same.

"Break!" Aldred announced. "Pinch!" He screamed, and the fyrd obeyed. They broke the shield wall in a single motion, then spread out and surrounded the remaining Esheri.

Another spear appeared in Aldred's vision, and he moved chaotically to avoid it, and suddenly the ground punched him flat in the face.

His nose was numb, head ringing. He spit grainy dirt out of his mouth and forced himself to stand.

Dazed, he unsheathed his sword. He swung it in a circle and fell to his knees again.

A hand touched Aldred's shoulder and handed him a water skin. "Egan," Aldred said, "I thought I was dead for a moment." Aldred drank deep of the water skin.

Egan was holding Yeller by the collar. "If you died, then you've come back to life, sir." Egan offered Aldred the reins to Yeller, his lips curling into a smile.

Aldred mounted and kicked his heels, driving Yeller into the thick of it. He trampled two Esheri, eager to dismount him. Bones crunched, and a squeal followed. Then nothing.

Aldred raised *Phantom* and let it fall onto a man's neck as he rode by. His blade pierced flesh and sunk into the bone, crisp, like slicing an apple. The man fell fast and heavy beneath the blow. The fyrd surrounded the enemy and pinched in on them. They slaughtered them as they corralled them. The plan was to force the enemies to retreat into the hills, where Brooton was waiting to finish them off. But these folk stayed and fought to their bloody deaths. Aldred trampled or sliced as many as he could along the way. Swinging a sword mounted was as easy as pointing, as long as it had a good edge on it. *And Lovasi steel is the finest.*

Aldred was given *Phantom* by his father's Warlock, Adora. When she arrived at court, she came bearing gifts for all. *If I had known all else she would gift me were nightmares and pain, I would have turned Phantom's blade on her back then.* Aldred gritted his teeth thinking of that bloody Warlock and sliced into another enemy. *Enemies. That's all they are. That's all they are...*

The Esheri thrust their sad spears as Aldred splintered them. Both spear and soldier. His army was so superior that this wasn't a fight at all. It was simply a massacre.

The Esheri refused retreat, so the fyrd continued to slice them down. They bloodied their swords beneath the bloody sun. The field was covered in a red mud as the Hesterland farmers took the life from each and every one of their opponents. The last few didn't even beg for mercy as they were being sliced down in a line. Aldred had no part in that, didn't even watch as his folk did it. He'd had enough of killing.

He rode Yeller around the perimeter of his army. There were no Esheri left. No priest, either. *Who led these people here? Who are you, Miri?*

Aldred had a sick feeling in his stomach. He couldn't help but feel he'd been jested somehow. Angelico stated that when something is too good to be true, it probably is. *Where are you, Priest?*

Aldred looked out to the ridges that surrounded the bloody field. He couldn't help but feel that someone was staring back at him from one of the ledges.

"Ey!" Aldred raised *Phantom* to the dim red sky. The army cheered erratically. *There are fewer than fifty of ours dead. Benecio would be proud of this. He would be ecstatic.* Aldred saw his reflection in *Phantom's* blade. The half light made the blood splatter on his face look like crude freckles, and he couldn't help but imagine himself as Kelson. *How did you do it, Kelson? How did you deal with this pain of no one understanding you?*

Aldred looked around at the dead. Heads were missing necks, limbs missing torsos, guts missing a stomach to hold them. Directly below him, he saw two right legs that had both lost their owner and their boot. Hands stuck up from the bloody mud where Aldred had trampled folk down into the earth. Men and women, all with families and stories of their own that led them right here to this end, were circled overhead by black birds waiting to eat their corpses.

Aldred's stomach roiled, and he bent over to throw up. Three retches, and he was done with it. *How did you deal with this pain, Kelson...* Aldred had a lot to say, and he'd say it one day. For now, all he wanted was what he had already lost. *Let me bring back what was lost...* He hawked spit into the mud. *Pick your battles,* Benecio said.

Maybe it's time Brooton had an accident. Aldred knew the witch-priest, Dustey, might be willing to help him with that. He mounted Yeller.

"Loot and claim, people," Aldred announced. The farmers erupted in raucous celebration. The sand was ripped up from the battle and clouded the air so Aldred held his sleeve to his mouth to try and get a good breath. Then, there in the sand at Yeller's feet, Aldred saw a beautiful white-glass flower. *A lightning flower?*

He dismounted and crouched beside the little thing. It was shining as white as lightning, and when Aldred reached out to touch it, the flower shocked him. *Esh spoke of these... I have never seen one before. She said they grow when lightning strikes the sand, and some of the lightning still lives in the flower.* Aldred plucked the small glass stem and held it in his hand. *"It signifies change, Dre—a new beginning,"* Eshlynn had told him. It was as solid as a rock. He tucked it away in his boot. *For Esh. You can get her back.*

Aldred looked around at his people robbing the dead. He knew only a sick few got joy in taking life. And those few would drink the hardest, speak the loudest, and sleep the longest. The rest of them were Aldred's people. The ones who wake up in a cold sweat after seeing the people they killed face-to-face in a dark dream. The ones who have forgotten how to love and be loved because their demons had eaten the best parts of them. This world wasn't built for his people. The King of the Hesterlands liked to remind Aldred of that, always.

Towards the valley where the Soren River flowed through the cracked earth, Aldred rode to tell Brooton they'd won.

ALDRED WAS THIRSTY. As he smacked his dry lips to try and remember the taste of that Timpany red, he thought of Eshlynn. He missed her more than all things. More than his cotton sheets or the bloated feasts. Much more than the cellar of Timpany red. He missed her touch, and he craved her smell. He missed her presence. Just the feeling of her closeness. It wasn't just the fucking with her. It was something more. Something that made his tongue stop working if he tried to express it in words. She made it all better for the rare hours he got with her. *Angelico said, love is being.* He'd be with her all the time if he could.

I've taken a lover... the words burned into him like red hot arrows. Aldred had feared that more than dying in battle. Returning home to find his love had found another. *She promised you. She promised. You gave her your mother's stone, and she promised to keep it until you got back. She'll be thinking of you, the stone will remind her of you when she's with—whoever.*

You can save this. He remembered his prayer to Karaat. *Let me bring back what was lost.*

Atop a great hill, a black shadow in the red sky burned Aldred's eyes. A cindered wooden strut tower and piles of grey ash where the palisades once stood were all that was left of the town of Soren. The Soren River rolled far off in the valley where it flowed long and fierce into the Red River far beyond, misting the sky above, its roar was like droning thunder.

There were innocent people screaming here—the ghosts of their voices stains the sky. The smell of smoke hung dead in the air and gave Aldred chills. The town had stopped burning weeks ago, but the smells hung around like ghosts smoking in the ashes.

When Aldred had left Kelson's Keep last spring, there was a fire raging in the hearth in the King's Hall. The very same fire that the First Lion, Gavyn Hester, had lit with his own hands when he conquered Hest from the old Lovasi rulers. It had burned for nearly two hundred years, and each ruler of Hester was sworn to keep it burning. Not once was it extinguished by an enemy. *Did you keep the fire burning through the wither year, Father?* Aldred figured his father's pride would be hurt in a way he could hardly imagine. *What kind of madness will have taken over him now that he has broken tradition?* There was a time, long ago before his mother's death, that his father was warmer towards him, but those days were long gone.

Aldred rode Yeller at a trot down the hill and westwards from the dead town.

Brooton and his folk were positioned on the other side of a hill. The horses were hitched, and the soldiers were all sitting around, not looking particularly ready for battle.

The bastard never planned on fighting. He was always two steps up on Aldred, and it made him feel sick. No matter what Aldred did, Brooton got the credit. Adora, the king's Warlock, would throw parades in Brooton's honour, giving him a grand seating ceremony and dozens of lavish gifts like spears and shields and women. Aldred was given a seat by the salt with the fyrd.

Some people nodded to Aldred as he rode past. Most didn't. Brooton was sitting around a fire with Dustey and two other men.

"Nephew! You made it," said Brooton. He was drunk. He fumbled around his ankles and raised an empty bottle. "We were so certain of your victory, we celebrated for you."

Aldred dismounted. He smelled red tar smoke. As he hitched Yeller to a post beside Crusher and the other warhorses, Aldred saw cakes of red tar stacked up. In Esher, the two major houses, Serahnon and Marwen, produced red tar cakes of soma and made heaps of gold by getting their people hooked on it. The new rulers would be inheriting the trade it seemed.

Dustey scratched at a bloody cloth over his ear, then pierced Aldred with his bloodshot emerald eyes. "How was it? The battle?" Dustey asked. He was sweating.

Aldred stood tall. "It wasn't a battle. A slaughter, more like," he said, unconvinced by his own words.

Dustey scratched the place his ear used to be. The other two men grunted something drunk, then started to laugh with each other. "What of the priest?" Dustey pressed, "Miri. Miri, they called him?" The boneman stood up and reached for Aldred.

"Nothing yet," Aldred said, moving away. "Though my soldiers are looting as we speak. He may be amongst the dead."

"Well, nephew..." The whites of Brooton's eyes were crimson red and bulging. "We're all proud of you, eh? I lied before. We weren't sure you'd make it," said Brooton, and he put his arm around Dustey.

The boneman shrank below Brooton's arm. "Are they dead? All of them?" asked Dustey. "Was there anything said? Any sort of ritual? Chanting?" The boneman had beads of sweat pooling on his forehead. *He was afraid to face this Miri. He was just as sure it was a trap as I was and wouldn't face it. He would have left me for dead...*

"All of them," Aldred said. "Only fifty or so of ours."

"We need to go back for the priest," Dustey said. His eyes were distant, two red suns blazing. The red tar consumed a person's mind, and so Aldred knew that Dustey would be obsessed with nothing but this one thought until the high wore off. "Before someone else finds him. The book."

"I want that fucking book nephew." Brooton grinned a mad grin. "Oh, yes. I want it. Whatever it takes." He rubbed his hands together.

"What were the Words that the Esheri scout spoke of, Boneman?" Aldred asked. "The Words that you and this priest know?"

"Blood magic," Dustey croaked. "The scout said the priest would speak Words of blood magic that I would understand. Words of Old Yehven—of Karaat."

"This is what we've been waiting for, nephew. Let's go back and find the body of this priest." Brooton stood, stumbling a bit, and to his army, he said, "Ready, folk, we march in twenty minutes."

THE EARLY EVENING SKY began to blush in purple and pink as the sun descended. Jerith, Brooton's bishop, recited the rebirth prayer of the sun from the Book of Eralis in a drab, single-toned voice as they marched.

> *Return on the morrow*
> *To turn the sky blue*
> *To ease all our sorrow*
> *Of night and its dew*

Then the prayer of quarter moon, signifying that the Lord Eralis, once again, watcheth over a new week, and the hours of sin have come to an end. *Literally for some.* And no prayer of Eralis would be complete without condemning the devil named Bazal.

"Worst of all sinners!" Jerith pronounced, arms wide, to the group of soldiers as they marched. Aldred heard sighs from the people. "Murderer of Good Eralis, Bazal was, and we must start each day with a good helping of hate for him. It will keep your bones strong! Say curse the godkiller!"

"Curse the godkiller," the people repeated dryly.

Aldred rode up front with Brooton and the other few dozen folk on horse. One hundred and ninety of Brooton's personal guard on foot, and the mules and pack horses pulled supply carts behind them. With the burnt palisades and cindered tower of Soren still in sight in the far distance, they marched back into the Soren River Valley.

Aldred had no use for his usual prayer lately. *I've taken a lover...* The letter had torn him apart, and still he wasn't able to stop himself from reading it a half dozen more times. *You were gone too long.* Aldred's heart was on fire, his lungs crushed his rib cage as he struggled for breath. He looked to the clouds. *Karaat, let me bring back what was lost.*

He felt stained after he said the words. *You're praying to the wrong god.* But Eralis only took from Aldred and broke him, and Aldred began to wonder why any person would continue down a path that so badly wants to hurt them. *You have nothing. All you've ever loved is dead and gone.*

Aldred had lost all things good in his short life. When his mother died, so did the voice that brought every story in Hest's library to life. When his mother died, a hate was born inside of his father, a hate that was meant only for Aldred. Then his father let Adora into his bed. He and the Warlock had neglected Aldred, made him feel hated, sent him to war and pouted every time Aldred returned alive. *And Adora... always in your father's ear, she hates you more than anyone... She wants you dead.*

Eshlynn was the brightest spot he'd found since those old days of reading and laughter. *I've taken a lover...* Aldred felt like he might be sick.

Carrion birds swarmed in the sky and squawked over the battlefield. A dinner bell for the other birds. The smell was kept at bay from the cold of spring. The farmers moaned that they wouldn't be able to break ground, even if there was rain to water the crops. They moaned that they'd been gone too long—and they had.

Aldred knew well enough of the situation in Hest from his brother. William had sent ravens to Aldred *last year* with messages saying that the granaries were empty, and there was no harvest last Fell of autumn. William told him that he'd better win some battles *and* some grain. Another year without food would cause mass famine with such ill preparation. *Maybe even beyond the scale of the fall of Lovas.*

Brooton nibbled on a whole loaf of bread as if none of that was an issue to him. His long chin worked with his jaw as he chewed. His bony cheekbones and wide eyes made him look like a living skeleton at times. He was completely unbothered by what was happening to anyone but his own self. Brooton wasn't afraid of a little riot in the city. *And are you? Yes. I'm terrified...*

"The peasants could never breach Kelson's Keep." Aldred's father had liked to boast. And he was mostly right. Kelson's Keep was the greatest of all the Lovasi castles. Massive drum towers roofed with slate and walls of cut stone—a man-made mountain. A secret miracle.

Kelson's Keep and the city below, Hest, were positioned at the mouth of the Roaring Sea, allowing the Lions of Hester to rein suzerain over the most fertile land in Ardura for two hundred and one years and counting. The Lions owned the Roaring Sea and all of its shores. The harbours and wharfs of Hest were the fattest in all the land. All trade from the east flowed through the Lions' paws first.

King Gavyn Hester stole the castle from descendants of Kelson in conquest and put his name on the city, which was formerly called Rhosanti. But even the Great Lion, Gavyn, didn't dare deny the fear that the name Kelson instilled, and he refused to change the name of Kelson's Keep.

No matter how rough things got for the Hester dynasty, all they had to do was retreat to Kelson's Keep and thwart the lesser attackers until they gave up. And they always gave up. *Or starved trying.* Kelson's Keep was built on top of a massive catacomb of underground wells. They would never run out of fresh water. And the caverns down there were filled with granaries once stocked to the brim with grain. But now they were dryer than the Behruvian Desert.

Aldred rode through the field of corpses amidst thousands of folks looting, and he still felt alone. Most of the dead bodies were stripped of boots and vests. The people couldn't resist good leather. Aldred knew anything else of value in the pockets was gone too. *No point in leaving it on a dead person.*

Egan found Aldred and offered a waterskin. Aldred drank the sun-warmed water, pretending it was something sweeter and redder. He looked out at dead bodies strewn across the bloody field and up to the sky. Night was falling fast, and it was a blood moon. The blood moon held omens darker than the sun could ever dream of.

"May Eralis watch over all of these souls as they journey to their apex." Jerith, the bishop, said in his drab voice. "May Karaat not lay his burning hands upon you on your ascent."

Brooton turned to Aldred. "Have you ever met a necromancer, nephew?"

Aldred shook his head no. *Praise Eralis, what am I doing?*

"Me neither," Brooton snorted. "Dustey says these parts have a great history with necromancy. Some magics of the dead lurk in these dunes." To the army, he shouted, "Find me this priest! Ten cakes of red tar to whoever gets me that book he's wearing."

The lot of them scattered amongst the dead, searching.

I've taken a lover... Eshlynn had told Aldred that the blood moon in Esher wasn't named after the colour.

"*When Karaat takes half of the light and half of the heat from the world, it causes the cold things to stir,*" Eshlynn had whispered to Aldred one night as they lay together naked on her roughspun sheets. "*When the sun sleeps, it allows for the dark things to wake. When the moon bleeds, those cold dark things walk. I've seen it, Dre. I've seen it with my own eyes.*" They were dark words spilled between such sweet lips.

Aldred sat around a small fire with Brooton and his generals, but he wanted no part in the conversation. It was Eshlynn he wanted to fill his mind with. He *wanted* to hurt if it meant thinking of her. He wanted to wallow in memories of her and drown in them. Eshlynn told all sorts of dark tales that she had learned from her Lavesheen milkmothers. She was full of secrets and wonder. *Unforgettable.* Aldred looked away from the moon and felt a chill run through him. *Is she in the arms of that lover? Is he inside of her right now? Does he see your mother's stone around Eshlynn's neck, pressed against her tawny skin?*

A soldier approached Brooton. "We've found the body of a priest," he said. "He has a book strapped to his chest."

"The book!" Brooton was elated. "Right. Boneman, let's go." To Aldred, he said, "Are you coming nephew?"

Seeing is the beating heart of believing. Angelico had written that. Aldred nodded. "Of course." *I must see this.*

"The red tar you promised?" The soldier held his hand out.

Brooton's face turned sour, and Aldred hated that look in him—it was the look of his demon coming to life inside. "Yes, of course. You're not calling me a liar? I told you I would give a prize to whoever found the book, and I mean to." Brooton walked towards the soldier.

"No-no," the soldier stammered. "I—"

"Tick!" Brooton called out, and a lumbering fellow came forward from Brooton's personal guard. He was so pale his veins were visible through his skin, tinting his body a bluish-purple. He had no eyebrows, no hair on his face at all, and the hair on his head was all white. And because of his paleness, his beating red eyes shone like two suns in his skull.

"You want me to kill him?" Tick grumbled. He raised his hands to show that they were blood stained.

"No, nothing like that, Tick," Brooton said. "I want you to sit down with him and make him smoke ten cakes of red tar—it's his prize after all! All ten cakes. And don't let him leave until they are gone—all of them."

Tick looked confused. He looked at the soldier who was sweating now. "That much? Surely that will kill—"

"It was his prize, and I won't be called a liar," Brooton said.

Just then the soldier tried to run. Two of Brooton's guard tackled him to the ground. Tick dragged the screaming soldier by the heels into one of the tents close by.

Aldred watched the two guards who had tackled the man go to the pyramid of red tar and remove some cakes, probably ten, and walk into the tent behind Tick. *You could stop this,* Aldred told himself. He knew he *could* stop it, and equally knew he wouldn't. *You're no hero, are you?*

A circle of soldiers stood crowding over something when Aldred approached. When the soldiers saw Brooton coming, the circle parted to let them in. The messiah was lying half dead in the sandy dirt. He had a black beard tipped with white that went down to his belly, which was bare and full. He was barefoot and dressed in strange furs of bright orange from an animal Aldred didn't recognize. The messiah held out his hand, and it made Aldred jump. *He lives?* His brown skin was cracked and bleeding. *The hands of a labourer.* Aldred put out his hand and touched his palm.

"Are you Miri?" said Aldred. The priest smiled.

"I am Miri. But that is not important. I speak for Roqeda," he croaked, and pointed to the book on his chest.

The boneman's eyes flicked open. "Roqeda speaks to me, too. What does he tell you?"

The messiah croaked something incoherent and pointed to the book again. The boneman leaned in and put his ear to the dying man's mouth. Dustey's eyes turned flat and sullen.

"What did he say?" Aldred asked.

Brooton stood with his arms crossed. "Answer him!"

The boneman grinned falsely. "He said that he would give you the power to bring back what was lost."

Aldred felt sick. His heart tried to leap out of his chest. His first instinct was to turn and run from this. *He heard your prayer...* Aldred didn't believe, but Benecio said that seeing is the beating heart of believing, and in Dustey's green eyes, Aldred saw a great belief that this was all very real. The boneman unstrapped the book from the messiah's chest and began shuffling through it.

"What does it say, Boneman!" Brooton screamed.

The messiah called Miri croaked out more words and this time Aldred could hear him. "Karaat knows you didn't kill your mother, child, not truly."

It was only an accident. "Wha-Who are you? How do you know this?" Aldred squirmed.

"I know things, child. I see it true," said Miri. "I know it was an accident, and so does Karaat."

"I loved her," said Aldred, tears came from a deep well in his chest.

"I know." Miri suddenly seemed to gain energy from some unseen source. "And she loved you."

"What is this, nephew? Boneman?" Brooton was angrily prodding. He unsheathed his Daggland steel sword, *Nail.*

Dustey stood tall and with the book open in one hand, began to recite words Aldred had never heard before. "*Akovha Liet Neia.*" Dustey was out of breath somehow. "Yes," the boneman said, breathing heavily. "Oh, yes." He began repeating the strange words from the book again. "*Akovha Liet Neia.*"

"Now kill me, become me." The messiah offered Aldred a strange knife. It was rot-green and carved with golden runes of some ancient tongue. Aldred found himself accepting the knife with an odd intensity—like the knife was holding him as much as he was holding it. He had a strange sense that the knife would kill him.

The boneman's words were thumping like a drum in Aldred's chest. The messiah's eyes popped out of his head, glowing white things, and he whispered "Roqeda."

Aldred, terrified, stabbed the messiah through the heart with the knife, and something came alive inside of him. The messiah smiled as he died, and

Aldred felt a smile on his own mouth. He felt a tug on his hand where the messiah's had closed tightly around it.

The boneman had stopped reciting words and instead croaked out, "What the fuck?"

Around Aldred, corpses began to stir. Dirt shifted beneath their limp bodies as something compelled them to move.

And something compelled Aldred to move. Something beneath his skin. Crawling up his arm and into his chest. It started to know him, and Aldred invited it in. Through his legs and into his head. It knew him better than he knew himself, and he couldn't ignore the sensation he had. *Why not let it?* He was full of it. *What is it? Happiness?*

"No, child. That is power. To bring back what was lost."

Around him, the dead folk that he and his people had slaughtered earlier began to stand. They stood on crooked legs with cracked skulls. They stood with intestines dangling and eyeballs hanging. They stood around him, dead. And Aldred felt it. *Blood magic.* Whatever life was inside of the cold flesh, Aldred supplied it. *Is it me?*

"Yes, child. It is yours now," said the messiah from inside of Aldred's head.

"Where is it coming from?"

"From me. The Otherworld," the voice whispered. Aldred smiled. If it was really his smile or if it was the messiah's, he didn't know. Didn't care. But it wasn't the messiah inside him... *"No, Miri was but a vessel, child. Call me Roqeda. I am a god, or will be."*

The corpses rose and marched on the tents that Brooton and his people had set, and they tore the canvas with sharp steel, and with pieces of limb or bone, they killed whoever was inside.

Aldred heard the screams, but they sounded sweet to his ear. He heard cries of help and cries of twisted horror as the fresh dead rose, too. The farmers of the Hesterlands fought with bravery against these folk earlier, but now they crumbled to the ground before them like leaves in fall. The fyrd was broken. Aldred saw horses fleeing in the distant light of the blood moon and smiled.

"You can't run for long, Uncle," Aldred screamed. He had never felt so powerful. *He ran from you. Brooton ran from* you.

"From us," Roqeda whispered.

"Yes." Aldred smiled. "Yes, of course."

"It's him that's hurt you?" Roqeda asked in a way that told Aldred he already knew.

Him, and everyone, Aldred answered, and in his mind Adora taunted him. *"But I will hurt you more than all of them,"* she said.

Guttural bellows of horror and pain rang out in the night as the farmers continued to wake and step out of their tents into a nightmare.

The dead scratched, bludgeoned, and choked the Hester fyrd to death. The farmers who ran were chased. Folk Aldred had spent the last year with. Folk that had fought and died for him.

Why? Why am I doing this?

"To make things right—as they should be."

The blood in Aldred's veins felt warm, like he'd had a few too many bottles of red. He liked it, so it was hard for him to let it go, but finally he willed himself. He let the power drain from him like a piss he'd held too long. The dead bodies fell back to the dirt where they belonged. Some still twitched, fighting Aldred's will, but he was too much for them. He supplied the life and he cut it off, just the same. *Was it me?*

"Yes. Both of us."

Aldred walked through the carnage and found his tent. Dustey and Egan were inside, cowering to one side. Somehow Aldred knew they lived, because in some recess of his mind, he had bid the dead keep these two alive. *These two will be important to you.*

"You're an author now, child."

Like Angelico? Like Benecio, Iro and Phosphone?

"No, child. Better. You're the author of new history."

Aldred's head thumped. He was terrified. *I don't know if I want... this... whatever this is. Why me? What has happened to me?*

The voice that called itself Roqeda spoke in a deep and bellowing voice that made all of Aldred's head thump even harder. *"This is what you prayed for. Karaat has heard your prayer and sent me to help you bring back what was lost. There's a stain on this world that will spread and leave nothing but ash. I think you can help me stop it, Aldred. I need you to show me some of those old books your mother read to you. Have you seen one by Insa Rolin?"*

I've heard of it but never seen it. Mother told me never to open it. That it may not let me close it again.

"I'm not your mother, child, and that book has the power to save the world. It has the power to save you. *"*

Aldred glared at Dustey and Egan cowering in the tent but couldn't find words to say. *What do you say after that?*

Egan handed Aldred a waterskin. Aldred pushed it aside. He wasn't thirsty anymore. "Come on," Aldred said. "We're going home."

BIG GREY

T HE BOY WAS SITTING next to Etta when she opened her eyes.
"Swey," she called out to him. The boy looked up, sniffled, and came
closer. "Are you not tied up?"

"No." His eyes were red and puffy.

"Why didn't you run?" Etta said.

"I don't know where to go." Swey sniffled.

"A knife," Etta said. "Find one, quick."

"Where?" Swey said.

Etta looked around. She saw all of their gear piled up by the river.
"There," Etta said. "With haste, but be silent."

The boy went and Etta looked around. The three El'vie were slicing
Gwynn's stomach open and pulling his entrails out while his scream slowly,
so slowly, faded to nothing.

The boy came back holding a footlong seax. "Is this good?" He held it
up.

Etta smiled, "Aye, lad, c'mon."

Swey knelt and worked the seax's smooth single edge at the wet rope around Etta's wrists.

"It's too hard." Swey looked around nervously.

"You can do it," Etta murmured. "You can. You're strong." Benn was tied up near her, and his eyes found hers with desperation. "Hurry, Swey, you can do this."

"I can't!" Swey threw the seax down and threw his face into his hands. "I need a mom. I need my mom."

"Listen to me, Swey. I've never told you this, but I knew your dad once, okay. He was the bravest man I had ever seen. Braver than he even knew." Etta was crying now and only realized it when tears started to drip from her nose.

The boy's eyes were alight with hope. "You knew him?"

"Aye, I knew him. He was important to me, and so are you. So I won't let anything happen to you, okay? And when we find your mom, I'm going to keep her safe, too." Etta sobbed. Her heart was in flames.

Swey cried now, too, but he gripped the seax and worked it on the rope. Etta could see the blade sinking into the rope, the hempen fibres slowly curling, fraying. Once Swey had cut through one of the strands, the rest fell easy, and Etta ripped her hands free. Etta saw one merrmonster pull a live trout, squirming like a snake, from an iron bucket and force it down Gwynn's throat. Gwynn made a violent, choking sound and squirmed like the trout, but two merrmonsters held him fast to the muddy ground where his entrails lay beside him.

Etta grabbed Swey's small hand—the boy couldn't take his eyes away from Gwynn—and dragged him over to Benn.

"By the gods, Etta," he said. There were bloody red patches where his ears used to be. Etta cut him free. Benn's hands flung to the holes in his head.

"By the gods..." Etta muttered.

"The guy who took my ears had a necklace of them. Twenty or more ears, and some were brown and shrivelled like a pruned apple." Benn crawled around in the mud and found his axe. He found a smaller one, too, and gave it to Swey.

"You may need this, boy. Your mother sure knew how to use it," Benn said. *And your father, too, he knew it so well one ended up buried in his skull.*

Around them, merrmonsters were cutting the ears off of the elders. Etta slid her hand over Swey's eyes and had to turn away herself when she saw Relia hung by her feet, swinging from a low hanging tree with her skin peeled off like a rabbit.

"By the bloody gods..." Etta murmured.

"They're hungry. Same as us, and food is scarce up here. They fear us as poachers. This is their warning to others not to come here." Benn gestured towards the arbor at the base of the mountain foothills. "That's our only chance. Up and away from the rivers."

"Then what?" Etta asked.

Benn shrugged. "Pray to what gods still live."

She wondered what Wulfee would do, but Wulfee would have made different decisions long ago and would have found herself in a whole different kind of mess.

When they all stood, an El'vie took notice and walked towards them.

"Don't move." Etta stood completely still. She had heard a tale by the clanfires once that if you didn't move, the El'vie couldn't see you. When the merrmonster started to run in long, mantis-like strides towards them, Etta knew that story was bullshit. "Run! Swey!"

They ran.

Benn didn't move. He pulled his axe. Etta stopped and looked at him.

"Go. Save the boy." Benn sliced the air with his axe. Etta's eyes sunk into his, and she hoped he'd see her pain and that she wouldn't have to beg him to come, but he said nothing.

"Please," she said to Benn. "I'm begging you, don't leave me—us." The El'vie was moving like an insect towards them, and Etta knew she had to pull her own axe or run.

"Run, Wulfee. Become yourself again. That peace you're looking for, it's in your own heart—it can't truly die while you live." Benn turned to face the merrmonster and cried a guttural scream. Etta turned and ran, Swey was already far ahead, waiting for her, shuddering, panting.

How did Benn learn my name? Has he known all along? Behind her, Benn screamed for a moment before there was only silence.

Swey ran, brandishing his axe in hand. Etta followed. Neither turned around.

"WHAT HAPPENS WHEN YOU die?" Swey had finally chosen to speak. They had been walking in silence for hours.

Etta pointed at one of the nytewoods. "Your soul leaves your body and makes a pilgrimage to a nytewood, where it marries itself to the spirits."

"Then you become fire? Or earth or whatever?" Swey tapped his toe on the dirt as if to test if it was hot.

"Some do. Some become other spirits, like wind and rain or plant life and soil, some are reborn into the world as insect or bird or Human. Some, the greatest warriors, rest forever in the cloud halls, some go to the icy caverns below the earth called Hell, where the serpent Tulu lives and eats souls gone rotten, and some linger forever here and haunt the stones and woods—the bones of things." *You'll be having a date with Tulu, won't you?*

"Even *them?*" Swey had resorted to calling the El'vie *them*, like if he called them by their name, they would reappear.

"All things. We are all one." Etta remembered seeing the drayke uncaged and doubted very much that that beast had a soul of the same nature. Yessa, the elder, had said that the El'vie were Created outside of Nature, but Etta left that unsaid.

Etta watched Swey stare out into the deep arbor as they continued to walk uphill towards nothing. *He's looking for his mother out there. Noting landmarks, tracking, watching and learning... just like you did as a girl.* "Your mom isn't dead, Swey." Etta put her hand on the boy's shoulder. "I feel it. We'll find her."

"Gwynn said *they* probably found her." Swey's chin fell into his chest.

Etta knelt down to meet his eyes with hers. "There's only one thing keeps the fire in all of us burning. Every fire needs an ember, and hope is that ember, Swey. You have to keep it burning, you see? Never let that ember fade. The smallest ember can become the biggest fire."

There was a crack-snap in the arbor that made both Etta and Swey jump. From no more than twenty yards, a wolf cry pierced into Etta and made every hair on her body stand alert like soldiers ready for ambush.

"By the gods!" she screamed, as if that would scare off the primal fear blazing through her. The wolf trotted closer, snapping through the brush like it was at home there. Wulfee would have reached for her axe but Etta stood dumbfounded, and when the black snout of the wolf pierced through the brush in front of them, she held the wolf's eyes with her own.

It's that big bitch that followed you up the White. Human eyes... The big grey sniffed at the air, held Swey in its gaze, and then pierced Etta with its eyes again. Two yellow-green orbs with black slits looked like a pit where things went to die. The wolf howled so loud and fierce that Etta couldn't help but cry.

The wolf sauntered over and sniffed at Swey, and Etta couldn't move even as she saw the boy's trousers darken at his leg. *Wulfee would have killed this bitch, Wulfee would have... killed her own son.*

Almost as quickly as it came, the wolf turned and sauntered back into the arbor. When it reached the brush, it turned to look at Etta and pierced her with those two black pits in its skull. *It wants you to follow it...* Etta didn't know what spoke to her, but something seemed to pick at her thoughts like a fly buzzing around her ear. *Follow it. Grab the boy and follow it.*

Etta grabbed Swey's hand and walked with him into the dark wood behind the wolf.

By a small pool covered in slime-green moss with yellow and pink lilies in blossom upon the surface, the big grey wolf sat on her haunches burning Etta with her gaze, as if waiting. The pond was sitting stagnant in a small clearing where bramble and young green goldenrod grew knee high.

The wolf yelped, and from somewhere in the middle of all that green, a woman wearing a green hood appeared, standing. She walked towards the wolf, and when she drew near, the wolf assaulted her with its tongue.

"Who are you?" the woman asked.

"Etta."

"From where?" the woman questioned.

Etta thought for a moment. *The Fells. I am Feldarra.* "Nowhere."

"Aye," said the woman, "I'm familiar with nowhere. I got left there myself when Calen Alder butchered my father." Etta studied the woman. She still wasn't comfortable around the greenhoods. And she didn't recognize this person. The woman continued, "Thought I'd adopt this greenhood. I've been called one enough of my life that it only felt natural. I wove the hood of barkcloth from ficus and dyed it with grass and mint and lilacs. I did it just as the Rangers do."

"Who are you?" Etta wrung her own hands out. *That wolf has been following you since last year when the Hawka attacked, maybe even longer... they're going to kill you—Swey...*

The woman stood tall with one hand on the big bitch, and the two of them were more aligned than the stars on Springtide. "Fiora Longsongs. I'm the Princess of Kallahorn, though I've voluntarily given up my seat there since my father, Balen, was crucified by Calen Alder."

Etta had heard the name Longsongs, that Mad King Balen caused Alder to march last spring and started this whole thing, but it was Kallahorn that held her attention. "Kallahorn." The word seemed to slip out of her lips.

"Are we going to Kallahorn?" Swey tugged on Etta's arm. "Can we, please?" *The boy longs for safety probably more than I do. At least I have tasted it. He's never even sniffed it.*

"Kallahorn is many miles east, Swey, and through the mountains. We won't be going there."

Fiora laughed. "If we're lucky, we won't ever go back there, boy." The woman knelt down, and Etta stepped in front of Swey to block him. Fiora stood back up. "Easy there. If I meant you harm, I could have committed it upon you more times than stars exist." The wolf rose, and the fur on its hackles stood to attention. It bared its teeth and rumbled. "Don't you recognize this wolf? She's been with you for many seasons now. Watching over you."

"Why would I need watching over?"

"There are still people in this world who care about you, Wulfee. There are people who want you safe."

Etta's eyes fell to the ground. "Don't call me that. My name is Etta." *She knows you. They all know you. They know what you did...*

"Etta. Whatever your name, it doesn't matter, you are cared for more than you know.

"All who loved me are dead."

"Not all."

"Who?"

"Baerd. Maken. Havel. You may know him by a different name. He has worn many names since I have known him."

Swey's eyes pierced into her. "*Please,*" they said without words. *The boy needs to feel safe.* Etta had never felt safer than with that eighty-pound wolf next to her.

"Where?"

"North and north up this river valley, chiselled through the mountains. Almost to the coast. There are thousands upon thousands gathered now. The si'darra we are called."

"The Feldarra," Etta blurted.

"Si'darra. The shield people—more than just the Fells and Mal Hallow needs us now. The stars have told it true, and I've heard their reading. The sky will fall unless our work is complete."

"What work?"

"The Reaper's Lullaby."

"What?"

"Come, I have a small camp I have not returned to for many months. My friends are waiting; they will explain much more than I can. I have spent far too long being schooled in great houses and made-up gods, and far too little being schooled in the bones of the earth and her voice." The wolf howled, as if to second what Fiora had said.

"We need rest." Etta's back and legs were on fire.

"There isn't time. The El'vie and worse, the monstrous Humans of Ayeland are buzzing around like an angry bee hive. I've been praying to the Hare that you make it this far so I can finally contact you safely and alone." Fiora looked at Swey. "Alone-ish."

"We need food. *He* needs food," Etta said.

"The wolf will hunt for us," Fiora said, and saliva fell from the wolf's tongue in long, goopy strands.

Etta disliked dogs—they reminded her of Sweyne. She didn't want to place her trust in one. She watched the sun setting behind Fiora, and the frogs had begun to sing their deep croaking song in the pond, and the whippoorwills and the mourning doves carried the high notes. The night would bring the stars, and the stars were a million Bradens burning into her with a fire so bright it would outlive her and a thousand of her children's children. A flaming judgement for her to live beneath as long as she dared to draw breath in this world.

Etta felt Fiora watching her, and when Etta met her gaze, Fiora smiled and walked northwards with the big grey wolf at her heels.

"Can you walk?" Etta asked Swey.

"Aye, I can walk," he said, holding a flinty glare to the arbor ahead.

And they did.

"Let me tell you the story of how Gen once got his head stuck in a beehive," Etta said.

Swey laughed. "I like that one."

The wolf howled.

THE BONE WAYN

THE ONLY THING HARO could remember about his old self was the hate. *James.* He hardly remembered where it came from or what started it. *James. Culdaine.* Haro remembered the name. *But what does it mean? You've had too many bodies. Too many minds.* Haro's blue jay fluttered down on his shoulder. *But you have been here. You have always been here. What's it all for?* The blue jay twittered nothing that made sense.

Haro sat around a small fire with his new companions, and they ate squirrel meat and snake. *Thank you, Maw, for this meal. Thank you, Maw, for my hood.*

These folk had helped Haro cut fine strips of wood from elm and ficus and mulberry trees and then helped him soak them in fire-hot water. They helped him tear those strips into fine threads, which they ran through a heavy green paste of grass and mint and lilac, and they helped Haro hang each of those green threads to dry and stiffen. From there, they let Haro do the rest because it would be dishonourable for any Ranger not to weave their own hood. Haro wandered in the arbors until he found the antler shed of a great bull moose. He cracked the antler bone with a rock and pulled a boneshard off. With his knife, he carved the boneshard into a spindle. With that spindle he, one by one, wove the green threads into a hood—a Ranger's hood.

"The other Ranger bands have spread out after the battle of Rosen," Haro said, "Timmon and Rend and Elley took their bands into the Wick and the Hills. We can try and catch up with one of them," Haro said. He had been flying weekly over the other Rangers with his bird to mark their progressions. He had been searching for Coal and his former band, hoping upon hope that they survived. It had been months now, and his hope of finding them had nearly faded completely.

"We had something else in mind," Kat said, "that we would rob the Glennish wayn cart traipsing through this land. Just like the Rangers of Old, protecting the hills, roads, and arbors of Mal Hallow."

"We've had enough fighting for a while, if we can help it," Uma said.

"I'm telling you"—Grady poked at the fire with a stick, and Haro watched the embers dance up to the darkening sky—"these Glennish nobles, they don't travel light. I'm telling you."

"The Glennish are occupying Mal Hallow now, from Fever all the way to Dawning," Kat said. "They've been poking around a lot. Bout time we let them know that the arbors and hills still belong to the Rangers before they get too comfortable. Before you came, Haro, we were watching these Glennish come and go. Fat wayns full of riches they ride."

"The Rangers of Old were master thieves," Haro said. "Aonis stole from the rich and gave to the poor."

"How much you think they're packing on that thing—the Glennish?" Uma ripped a piece of squirrel meat with her teeth and chewed loudly.

"There's naught in there but bones," said Kat.

Uma scoffed. "And what makes you say that? You Glennish? How would you know?"

"They came to gather the bones of their fallen," Kat said. "We saw them picking through those dead folk two weeks ago. How many more bones you think they found in that time?" Kat pointed vaguely at a hypothetical wayn cart. "There's bones and more bones in there."

Grady spat in the fire, and the fire hissed back at him. "I bet we'd get something for those nobles though. Some kinda ransom."

Ransom... "Those bones are more valuable than gold," Haro said. *Yes, of course...* He flexed the fingers on his burned hand. He couldn't quite get used to the restricting feeling of it. "And their cloaks..."

Kat flipped her greenhood up over her red locks. "We don't need cloaks." She stuffed a wad of sweetbud in her mouth and spat green. The smell of the bud made Haro want some for himself, and so he asked Kat for a wad.

"Their cloaks have the grey owl brooch of House Brynmor. Those will give us access to the Fort of Dawning, which the Glennish occupy at the moment. The wayn is carrying the bones of ancestors that are in want of burial. We will be admitted with open arms. We can have an audience with Queen Grace of Elurra. I'm sure she will be leading her army in place of Brynmor." Haro spat green and felt a lightheaded sensation through his whole body.

"Why would we want an audience with a queen? We're bloody greenhoods. And what makes you think she's in Dawning?" Grady said.

"Because." Haro stood up and held Grady's eyes with his. "That man, the prisoner who begged us for help back there was Lord Richard Brynmor. I believe the Glennish will pay us whatever price we name to bring them back here and track that old man prisoner. Why do I think she's at Dawning? Because those folk wore a copper brooch, not just any stitched cloak. Those were folk of the queen's own ilk, probably sent by her own orders to find the bones and body of her father." Haro pulled the silver ring from his pocket. "And this." He held it to the sky. "Brynmor's own ring—proof. They will believe every word we say. It's carved with his full name and his heart's. This was from a heartbound ritual. Instead of knives, rings were given—that's the Glennish tradition."

Haro had seen the old man Brynmor holding something in his hand when they walked by. Culdaine was too busy eyeing down the Rangers, but Haro had seen the old man staring at him. Brynmor had dropped something on the ground and stomped it into the dirt.

Haro had knelt down and picked it up right there in front of all of them and no one noticed. It was Brynmor's ring.

"There is no way that old man was Brynmor," Kat said. "Brynmor was a proud man. Strong and sturdy as a rock."

"Even strong folk fall down," said Haro. "Even the young get old."

Haro rubbed his eyes. The sweetbud had worn off and made him sleepy. The Maw had tortured his dreams again last night, and he wasn't looking forward to facing them again.

"*What do you want? Leave me,*" Haro had screamed.

"*I'm not done with you,*" the Maw whispered.

Haro's time inside of the bird had brought back primal memories. Memories of past lives—more than Haro could count. They were all around him, like stars in the night sky. And he lived so many of them. *So many... but why? There must be a purpose. Why do I still live? Revenge? Can it be so simple as that?*

"I say we rob 'em," Grady said. "Take their coats and their wayn, and go to Dawning. Give the queen that ring."

Uma scoffed. "Why don't you go and tell Haro what happened last time *you* tried to rob someone."

"Hey, shut up about that." Grady threw a stick at Uma, and she dodged it cooly.

Haro laughed. "Of course we're going to rob them." He picked up the stick Grady threw and snapped it over his knee. "And kill them."

"Woah." Kat grinned. "Just like that, eh? Alright, you convinced me."

"We will tell the queen that Culdaine killed them," Haro said. "That we saw it with our own eyes and we, as Rangers, are just doing our duty of the arbor to report it and bring them back safely."

Uma loaded more sweetbud into her mouth. "Then what? Gold?" Uma offered the sweetbud to Haro, but he brushed it away with his hand this time. Haro heard Uma's bear grunt from somewhere unseen.

"Gold, sure. But most importantly, we will strike even the balance of things. Wrongs will be righted," Haro said.

"What good is gold to a Ranger." Kat pointed to her lynx lying in the shade, bathing itself with its tongue. "What do you think she would do with gold? Eat it? Shit it out again?"

"We do it because the Rangers of Old would have done the same thing." Haro made a fist with his scarred hand and held it up to the sky. "The Rangers of Old took from these petty rulers and gave back to the small folk of the hills—the folk of the arbors. It's in the green book, the woodlore. We are going to help the starving and lost folk of the Hallow, Kat. We can give the gold to the people."

"Ah, okay, like Timmon," Grady said. "Real original. But original is good." His squirrel chittered from the trees.

"I like that," said Kat, and her lynx yawned. "I really do."

"So how are we going to go about it, then?" said Uma.

Haro grinned. His head was still clouded with past lives, some of which he wasn't sure were even his, but despite all of that, the woodlore remained clear. *It is carved into me as if I were a tree. The scar of the woodlore will always be there.* "You've heard of woodlore?"

"Heard of it." Uma spat green. "Believe in it? Not so much."

"And what's so hard to believe?" Haro asked. "That some Rangers long ago translated the secrets of nature into stories? That knowing them will give you the power to lead, to make a difference in the world?"

"What makes it hard to believe," Kat said, "is the fact that the Rangers haven't been feared for generations. Our bands fight each other for territory and do nothing close to the deeds written of in the woodlore. Timmon is long dead, Aonis is long dead, and Hagen the Great is even deader than both," Kat said. "Even in the presence of you, the thrice blessed, the woodlore seems more fable than truth."

Haro flipped his axe around in the air and snagged the handle, then tossed it into a tree with precision. "But have you heard of Ossian?"

"Ossian?" Grady said the name slowly.

"They say he never died," Uma said.

"Oh, he died alright, but it was only time that could kill him. He was known for cheating death, always finding a way around it. He could see the future."

"What does any of this have to do with hijacking that wayn?" Kat said.

"Nothing at all," said Haro.

"So, we're *not* going to rob them?" Grady seemed disappointed.

"Can any of you shoot this bow?" Haro picked one up from their packstuffs.

Grady smiled and snatched the bow out of Haro's hands. "Finally, you're making sense to me. We all know our way around one o' these."

A MERCHANT'S WAYN ROLLED up the Northroad like a thunderstorm. Three horses pulled thrice their weight in bones, stacked ten feet high. It was a full day's ride ahead of the Glennish host Haro, and his new band had been stalking.

Haro spread his wings and let the air fill them as he swooped over the Fell River. He looked in awe at the Lovasi Bridge of Rosen glinting in the sun. The red eagle flags of Ayeland rippled from the wooden palisades of Fort Rosen, and as the merchant's wayn approached the bridge, Ayelish soldiers in white gambesons and polished helms rode out on warhorses to meet them.

Haro glided down and landed on the branch of a twisted old willow. He watched the merchant give the Ayelish something out of a pouch. *Gold*. It seemed. The merchant put the pouch away, and the Ayelish rode back to the Fort, and the merchant crossed the bridge without trouble. *They're collecting tolls.*

Haro flew from tree to tree and for a short while; he watched carts and wayns roll past the fort. Each time they paid a toll, and each time they passed unharassed.

Haro dipped out of a fat oak and swooped below it and ate the fermented acorns off the dirt. Then he hopped along the roots and into the arbor and dug up hazelnuts with his beak and ate them until he couldn't eat anymore. He fell asleep in the shade on the branch of an ash tree, and when he woke he flew back to himself.

When he dipped out of the sky, he could see Haro crouched by a log beside a fire with other people around him. He landed on the log next to him and reached.

When he opened his eyes, the blue jay was twittering. *It holds you longer and longer each time. It has a small part of you after such a long winter.*

"So?" Grady was poking at the fire with a stick. "What did you see?"

Haro peered at him through hazy vision. He blinked and took a deep breath. "We have to pay a toll."

"What?" Uma said as if she had never heard the word before.

"A toll. There are Ayelish soldiers at Rosen. Not many, but enough. They are extracting gold from all who pass."

"Where are we to find gold in this economy?" Kat said.

"I saw three or four wayns go by just today. Folk are preparing for war and things are moving. We'll have to rob the Glennish *before* they reach that bridge or we won't make it across ourselves," Haro said.

"They would charge Rangers of the Wick a toll? What has this world come to?" Uma said.

"They fly Ayelish flags, but they are more likely acting under a petty ruler, broken off from the defeated army last fall," Haro said. "They are not acting with the nobility of the Ayelish.

"Okay, well, are we going to do this thing, or what?" Kat grinned.

"Aye." Haro winked.

Haro and Grady stood on one side of the road while Kat and Uma took the other. All held bows with five arrows stuck in the dirt in front of them. When the thundering sound of the wagon echoed through the arbor, all of the animals scurried off and the birds took flight. Haro nodded to Grady who nocked an arrow. *This is it. If this goes wrong, you'll be back in your blue jay.*

The smell of the horses was on the breeze now and Haro whistled, telling Kat to send her lynx to the road. Seconds after the whistle left Haro's mouth, a silver-white lynx strolled cooly onto the road, big as a mountain wolf. The horses made strange sounds and slowed down to a stop. The wagon kept its momentum and the harnesses buckled behind them, and the horses were thrown forward. In a mess of iron and leather, the horses whined. When they stood and realized their harnesses had snapped, they scampered off in all directions in the arbor.

"Fuck!" came a loud voice from the wagon. Bones had spilled all over the dirt and were being crushed to splinters below the wagon wheels. The Glennish poured out of the wagon in their owl-stitched gambesons and shouted at the lynx and waved spears at it.

Another whistle from Haro and arrows began piercing the Glennish—through neck and through face. Haro watched as his own arrow skewered a person's cheeks, and blood misted out of the hole. Haro ripped one of the arrows from the dirt in front of him and loosed.

In just a few moments, seven Glennishfolk lay dead and bleeding on the Northroad.

"Let's be quick about this, eh? I don't want to answer to anyone who comes along," Haro said. The Rangers stripped the folk of their blood-stained white gambesons, stitched with the grey owl of House Brynmor, their chain shirts, and their iron helms, also carved with the Brynmor owl.

Haro and his new band unloaded a big section of bones from the cart and filled it with the corpses they had just created together, then covered them with the bones again.

"Think they'll stay fresh all the way to Dawning?" Grady was sniffing at the bones.

"No," Haro said. "No, I don't think they will."

"How well does a squirrel smell, Grady?" Kat asked. "My lynx will be keeping her distance."

"By the gods, Kat." Grady puffed his cheeks. "I could smell a bad nut from a mile away."

The Fell River roared above the clattering of the wagon and the clanking of bones. Haro could smell the mist in the air, and he breathed it in. In his hand, he held a worn leather pouch full of Glennish gold—coins pressed and stamped with the owl of Brynmor. Coins were of little use in Mal Hallow and were better used to buy sharper weapons if you were headed further north than that. But Haro had learned that the further south he went, the more they craved the shining yellow rock.

"How much is in there, you reckon?" Grady asked.

"At least enough to get us over this bridge," said Uma, "and enough in my boot to buy a barrel of shine when I find one for sale." She smiled cooly to herself.

The Ayelish flags whipped in the wind on top of all four corners of Fort Rosen. The wooden walls looked to have been repaired, and the keep had fresh thatch on the roof. Just as Haro had guessed, the Ayelish soldiers rode out to meet them atop three big white destriers. Each of the soldiers held a six-foot spear, and the iron edge glinted in the sun. Haro didn't dare look past them at the bridge, shining white.

"What business do you have here?" one of the Ayelish soldiers said. He was fifty or older, grey-haired and reeking of man. The other two soldiers were younger men. Haro knew by their bloodshot eyes that they were hammered. *These are less than petty rulers. These are outright squatters...*

where is Ayeland? Why have they not marched yet? Are they just going to let the north slaughter itself?

"We are crossing back to Dawning with our fallen. We mean to bury them with their kin," Haro said. His Glennish accent came out flawless. He calmly touched the owl on his gambeson.

"We're of Brynmor's ilk," Grady spat out. His squirrel chittered and ran up his leg and body and perched on his shoulder. The older soldier studied him.

"Brynmor, eh," the man said, eyeing the squirrel on Grady's shoulder intensely. "You been hanging around Rangers up in those hills?"

Uma was glaring at Grady with so much intensity Haro thought Grady might just fall over dead.

Grady waved his hands in dismissal. "Rangers? No—" His squirrel scurried away.

Haro held out the leather pouch full of gold. "I apologize. We mean to pay our toll and be on."

The older soldier took the pouch and looked inside. He passed it back to the other two soldiers who both looked inside too. One of them removed a coin and bit it. Haro didn't know why. *These fuckers would eat the stuff they like it so much.*

The older soldier studied Haro, studied the bones. "That's a lot of bones," he said.

"A lot of dead folk," Uma grunted.

At the gate of the fort, another host of Ayelish stood armed and armoured. On the towers, Haro saw archers. *That could be every single one of them, or there could be hundreds more inside.* The soldier studied the bones and glared at Haro.

"Who are you?" he said.

"Come on, Arthyr, let these morbid fuckers go. They paid more than enough," said one of the younger soldiers. The old man turned, looked back at Haro and at the others.

"I know that scarred arm, and I know that face," the soldier called Arthyr said. "And I don't know these three."

Haro felt his skin boil up. He could have his axe drawn quicker than the old man could blink. But Arthyr just smiled, as if he was proud of himself for knowing what he knew. *Whatever it is he thinks he knows.* "Listen, I understand, sometimes you've gotta do things to get by." The soldier gestured at Fort Rosen, still glaring at Haro's burned arm. "We're all just trying to survive, ain't we?"

Haro said nothing.

"You tell the queen at Dawning that Rosen sends their love and wishes her the best of luck in the wars to come. We'll all need it. Praise the Stag..." The old man turned and his war horse neighed loudly.

Haro and his band rode on and crossed the bridge of Rosen. Their bone wayn rattled like bare trees in the winter wind, and the dead buried below them were silent.

Pool

THE DAGGS MADE OAR-BOATS from planks hewn from raw pine and birch and oars hewn of nytewood branches. The folk of their ranks cut and shaped and smoothed the planks with the diligence of masters, and when James stood on the banks of Pool and watched them, he was in complete awe.

"You'll ride with me, King Reaper," Toren said, and James and Maggie followed him to a long oar-boat that had been crafted, shaped, and carved with the head and tentacles of a kraken on one end, all in less time than one sun cycle.

"You folk can build," Maggie said.

"Aye," said Toren. "Ships we can build. Fortresses, not so much anymore." Toren packed a bowl of chuff and lit it from a torch. James saw the tips of his moustache searing when the Dagglander pulled the torch away. There were other folk in the boat who James had recognized. "You've met my people, right? A rakkar of Daggland keeps with him a party of their closest, strongest folk. We call it our rakkarren."

The rakkarren were clearly different from the other Daggland warriors. They were wearing kraken bones through their ears, and black ink smeared beneath their eyes. They wore brightly coloured bandanas and wisps of smiles on their faces.

"Everyone of us would die for each other," Toren said.

"Aye," a man with a long red beard shouted.

"Aye, Haron!" Toren said.

The rest of the folk joined him. "Aye!"

Toren jumped up on the bulwarks. "Aye, Mantha, and Dirk. Aye, Rora, and Kali, and Jax!"

"Aye!" The Dagglanders echoed.

"My rakkarren would die for me and I for them. You ride to Pool in good company."

"I don't want to kill anyone if we don't have to," James stated. "We need these folk to be our allies, we are only trying to be intimidating."

"That will not be a problem," Toren said, and howled like a dog. His rakkarren joined in, and James slid closer to Maggie.

James watched the folk of the Hallow assemble on the banks of the Lake of Pool. They were beat down and haggard looking. Half-starved and crippled from sickness. *My people.* He thought and shivered. *This is what you've led them to. We've naught but a small sliver of hope.* Hordes of wild dogs had clung onto the Hallowfolk like parasites, and James could hear them barking and snarling at the edges of the surrounding arbor. Still, with their mangy furs, wet leathers, and rusted iron, the Hallowfolk marched under the brown bull moose on yellow.

The men and women of Daggland wore black steel chainmail and held black steel axes as they marched below banners stitched with a black kraken on blue, and they filled the boats they had crafted. *One flag for all of Daggland...* He had seen Toren's sigil of the serpent eating its tail carved into many of his things: knife, goblet, chests, but he still only flew the flag of Daggland. *They really are committed to this.*

"Our ancestors," Toren said, "were captains of one of the greatest empires to ever grace the Remembered Lands. They carved themselves with the Blood Words and sold their souls to a debt that ultimately came due and killed them, King Reaper." Toren held his black steel axe up to the clouds. "They left us with their scraps, their ships, their weapons, and even these scraps are enough to take Ardura."

On the shore of Lake of Pool, Brinley, Sessely and their Crows of Dawning gathered beneath the black crow on gold. Ruwen and her pack of burly warriors gathered beneath the black bear on blue. Claydon Coldfoot and his two sons Aron and Macts, and their small families, stood in front of the remaining Tuskan army below the grey mammoth on green. Eridan stood in front of a small but vicious group that flew dozens of white flags with bloody red hands. Each of the blooded folk in Eridan's ranks held their own flag with a bloody hand print made from the blood of their first kill—the Blood Company. Behind him, he heard shouts of "Mal Hallow!" as Eurick hoisted the banner of Culdaine, the brown bull moose on yellow. *But only one flag for all of Daggland.* James remembered his dad leading the Mal under a single flag.

"Culdaine!" folk shouted from the ranks. *They still respect the name. They respect the history of this country, and with that you can win them back... you have not failed yet...*

James stood on the bench in his boat, and from the shore he shouted to his people. By the gods he wasn't good with words, but he would need to find some now.

"This flag has flown on this land for as far back as we remember. Hendurinn flew this flag and Kooullen the Great flew this flag." James pounded his fist on his chest. And the Hallow folk pounded theirs. "My family has died beneath this flag, and new generations have been conceived and born beneath this flag. We are gathered here today to ensure this banner keeps soaring!" The folk were elated, and James drank it in like water. *Okay, enough about flags now...* "We do not want to kill these folk of the Fells. These are our kin-folk—family. We are simply here to remind them of their oaths. To bid them fight with us and help us take our land back. The ancient oaths should not be forgotten. We have paid our due to the old gods and now so must they."

The Hallow folk lit the banks of Lake Pool on fire with their voices as they bellowed out cheers and sang songs of Old. *The Dead King Rises,* and *The Hand and the Heart,* and *The Bells of the Fells.* The words of those songs seemed to carry James's boat forward, through the strange, murky green waters of Pool, as they sailed in mass to the island of Pool at the Lake's heart. They sailed so close together that the folk passed skins of shine and tossed sacks of barley flour back and forth from boat to boat on their way over. The songs grew ever louder as the shores grew more distant, and soon James couldn't see land anywhere. Only the songs and the oars carried any sound, and James's thoughts slipped into darkness.

"I'm not done with you." The Maw had visited him every night since the sacrifice and still gave the same message. *Then tell me what to do!* James screamed into the silence of his mind. *Tell me what to do and leave me!* But the Maw refused to answer him. It only stepped aside and showed him the mutilated ghost of the Stag. The God of War's eyes were bleeding, and when the Stag opened its mouth, roots poured out like worms. *"Helphelphelp,"* the Stag moaned in agony. *"Help,"* it said. James thought of Adeqor—the Words he sang as the mountains came alive and swallowed him up.

But even the dead had stopped asking James for things, and he struggled to know his place. He saw them sitting by the banks of rivers or on the stumps of dead trees, but they ignored him now, as they always had before. *They only cared about you when you could help them. The dead are no different from the living. Did they treat Hendurinn the same way? Did they stop loving him when the wither year ended? It's Essikah—they're afraid of it. It will eat them.*

James was pulled from the darkness of his mind by a soft hand on the back of his.

"It's beautiful, James, the fog and mist love it out here," Maggie said. James pulled her in and tried to see the beauty that she did. When he failed, he beheld Maggie instead. *One green eye and one blue.* He breathed her in and lived in the smell of her for a moment. *You're no king. But you are heartbound. That I can handle... that I can do.*

James had seen other things than the Maw and the Stag in his dreams, too. As if beams of light stabbed into the dark from somewhere better, James watched Maggie and a child—*our child*—dancing in the rain in front of a lake. And they *knew* him. *"Dada!"* the small voice said, and she had one green eye and one blue. *"Come play with me, dada!"*

"We're here," a voice like waves crashing pulled James from Maggie's embrace. Toren was standing on the front of the boat as nimble as a cat, taking each wave as it came by moving and thrusting his hips as if he was born to ride them. He stretched his finger out towards the grey line of land in the distance. "There are no boats."

James wondered how Toren knew that. James had to squint to see a blurry outline of land. When the World Tree became visible through the thick fog, James lost his breath. *By the gods...* he had never seen the nihr'el, he had only ever heard Gran's stories about it. *Most* folk hadn't seen it up close. *It's thrice the size of the other nytewoods.* Maggie squeezed James's hand in excitement.

"That is what gods look like," Maggie said. "That is Nature screaming *'Yes, look at me.'"*

"It's greater than any castle and any bridge." Rora, one of Toren's rakkarren, held a finger to the sky. "Offa is truly above all."

"When the Dead God lives once more, time itself will stop to gaze at Her beauty when She rises up." Haron raised his finger, and the other rakkarren joined.

Toren, still balancing on the front of the boat like a bird, raised his finger higher than all. "And may She *rise!*" His voice crashed above the waves, and James vibrated from the shouting that erupted around him.

As the boat struck land and the Dagglanders poured over the bulwarks like the water they were birthed from, James prayed to the Crow that no death would come from this.

The El'vie lay stagnant on the banks, bathing themselves and paying no mind. James ran up the bank and past them without waiting for anyone else. He felt an urge to go onwards.

The wildflowers and the yarrow and the chicory were bushy and green in the Wayk of spring, and James saw no flattened paths. Black flies and horseflies and dragonflies buzzed in James's ears and slapped at his face and tried to nest in his hair and beard and tear at his flesh. He hadn't shaved or groomed himself in any way for many weeks, and it became more obvious to him now as he swatted and picked at the bugs. *You're a wildman, dirty and mad. Hungry and witless. Had Hendurrin fallen in the same way?*

He carried on through the tall grass, and the rabbits and the mice scurried at his feet, and deer pranced off in the distance towards the arbor, and James felt like all the natural world would clear a path for him if he kept running.

The nihr'el's knowing face loomed through the fog, and the land the great tree shadowed was adorned with a gathering of broken-down hovels. Wet mats of brown thatch sat like rotting hair on top of collapsed piles of grey and weather-worn wood. Ravens and blood vultures squawked and flapped away heavily from between the wreckage, and James could smell the bodies those birds had been eating. *By the gods... what happened here? There is no one left...* James shivered and couldn't shake the feeling that he'd caused this somehow.

James could hear the other rulers of the Hallow shouting as their boats landed on the shores of Pool, but he could only keep moving towards the nihr'el. Winding through the broken-down shacks, stepping over cracked pottery and broken tools and dead bodies, James was drawn to the sound of a faint voice quivering beneath an apple tree that had sprouted out from the dead village. He could see the dark green leaves and the pink and white apple blossoms poking out above all.

"Down and down and back again." The voice was singing—the words of the old song from the cycles about the Starfall. "Oh, how I miss the light. Down and down and back again, to an all-eternal night." Chains clanked in rhythm with the singing and echoed through the empty streets. From the alleys and the dark corners, the dead souls came to greet James, and together they hove on.

Under the apple tree, James saw a black steel gibbet with a man inside, naked but for his breeches. A large group of dead folk crowded around the cage and sang in tune with the man, seemingly unknown to him. Young and old and butchered and fine, the ghosts of the Hallow came to live beneath the shade of the nihr'el like stars come to the night sky.

"Who are you?" James called out.

The man was unkempt and looked like an untended garden. His wiry beard sank into his chest, and his grease-ridden hair was falling out in clumps, made obvious by the patches of baldness on his flaky scalp. "I am nobody." The man was startled by James's voice. An overturned wayn cart lay beside the gibbet with small, neatly stacked piles of tack within reach. The man saw James looking at the food and made a growling noise. "That's all they left me with, just kill me if you take it."

The dead were singing loudly; James was frightened at the feeling that was growing inside of him, that he had missed these ghosts. "I'm not going to take your food."

The Hallowfolk and Dagglanders that had made the crossing were all making their way towards the voices now, fast approaching.

"Who did this?" James cared more about that than this man, but the strange look on the man's face made James want to kill him.

"Demhoni..." The man said, and his lips quivered. He buried his chin in his chest and whimpered. "She called herself Heath... She said she was Demhoni... a flesh-eater."

James's eyes flicked open as Gran's stories throbbed in his memory. *The Demhoni prey on Humans, eat the life out of them, and take their lifeforce—flesh and all... a fungus eats at them from inside.* "She must be mad. The Demhoni are an old gran's tale."

"Mad?" The man's eyes bled with pain, "You want to know mad? She made me watch! She made me watch. She made me..." The man rattled the bars of his gibbet.

Demhoni—they come from Hell and get inside a person's mind and bid them eat life. Gran's words rang in James's mind. "Watch what?"

"Mad isn't mad enough a word to describe her..." The man was trembling.

"Watch what?"

"My son!" The man shouted. "She ate him and she made me watch. She ate him..."

"Why did she leave you alive?" James had unbuckled *Essikah,* almost by instinct.

The man's eyes were bloodshot and veiny. It seemed like he had suddenly remembered things long forgotten. "To tell..."

"Tell?"

"Aye. She was locked up in that castle forged of Hell magics, called Kallahorn, while Calen Alder carved himself with the Words of ancient lore. She watched him go mad and it leaked into her. Spread like a fungus. If her former king gave her the madness, the winter flared it up." The man's eyes slid up and down *Essikah.* "I know that sword. I've heard stories about the person who carries that sword."

"What stories?" James growled.

"I heard it was you. It was you who let the Ayelish folk cooped up in Kallahorn free with their lives. I heard the other rulers of the Hallow begged you to kill them and you wouldn't."

James clenched his fists. "The Ayelish begged me to live, the Mal begged me to kill them..."

"After you let them go, they became Demhoni... they did a hell of a job to this country. Left it raw and bloody. This woman, Heath, this *Demhoni,* she's the type that shoulda been killed a long time—"

James thrust *Essikah* through the bars to pierce the man's rib cage. He actually enjoyed the weight of that sword in his hands now. The man's eyes were vacant and blood dripped from his dead mouth. *Essikah* had a way of killing instantly. As the man's soul left, James drank it in through the sword. The coldness seeped into his bones, and his breath fogged for a moment as the soul became him. James felt his mind open up, his legs unstiffen and the aches in his back had gone. He stifled the thought that he actually missed this feeling. *They call you Reaper, now... the King of the Dead.*

When Toren and his rakkarren arrived, James was sitting atop the overturned wayn, twisting an apple blossom in his fingers.

"There's no one bloody here, King Reaper, you thought wrong," Toren said.

Brinley wasn't far behind. He studied the dead man and scratched at his scar eye. "What did he say?" The dragon slayer asked. Sessely, Aione, and Brigid stood firm beside him, pecking at James with their eyes.

"He said nothing." James found Maggie's eyes and held them with his own. *She will know the monster ate him, she'll smell the soul on me.*

"Why did you kill him?" Aione kneeled down beside the gibbet, touching the fresh blood with a finger. James was impressed that the smell seemed to faze her not at all.

"End his misery." James dropped the apple blossom he had been twisting and jumped down from the wayn. "He'd been here alone for too long."

"Things ain't what you thought they'd be, are they?" Eridan emerged from the gathering crowd. "Who did this to him? Surely he told you."

"He said nothing." James wasn't ready to let everyone know that *he'd* caused this. *Demhoni...* He couldn't even bear to let the thought take root.

"Never in a thousand thousand years has the World Tree sat unguarded," Sessely said, "The Feldarra should be here..." She wandered through the debris. "Emmer herself guarded this island. It's a disgrace to leave."

"Piss on the Feldarra," Eridan said. "They only showed up at the last minute at the Battle of Rosen."

"Aye, but they came," James said. *What happened, Pike? Are you out there somewhere?* James craved to hear the old warrior's voice tell him everything was okay, just like he used to all those years ago in Wulfee's clan.

"And now they're gone. Probably hiding in the mountains they love so dear." Eridan pulled a dripping piece of hardtack out of a goblet and chomped into it.

Bluebirds, let Wulfee and Pike have found each other out there in those mountains.

"So if there is nothing here, what then?" Toren seemed disappointed. "My folk need blood." The Dagglanders seemed to be salivating.

James watched the clouds rolling and brooded. Ruwen was glaring at him and nodding with a hungry smile on her face. *What would you do, Dad?* "We take Rosen back," James said. "If it's just us then so be it. If we can hold the bridge there, we can protect all of the Fells. We can rebuild. The Northroad north of the Fell River will be ours. It's not much, but it's enough to get started. I had hoped we'd have the Feldarra at our back, but we can still do this."

"Now you're talking like a king." Ruwen spouted as she raised her axe to the sky. The warriors of the black bear roared along with their leader. "You hear that, people? We're going home!"

"But the Ayelish haven't even marched yet," Aione boomed. "My father has dozens of scouts that claim they have not left Tusk."

"All the better," Ruwen said.

"It's not *all the better*. It means we could have stayed at Kallahorn. We've been wasting time, energy, food. All of this has been a damned waste."

"We've done what we thought was right," James said weakly. *They despise you...*

"Would be a shame to come all this way and leave so soon," Toren said. "Look at her, she's beautiful." He was gazing at the nihr'el. "Let us camp here this night and make sacrifice to the Dead God."

"Our people do not spill blood beneath a nytewood, especially the World Tree," James said.

"And yet blood is spilled beneath those black branches all the same." Toren's eyes were stuck on the World Tree in the distance. "Let us at least see it up close, touch it. We have stories of this great tree in our sagas, and I would love to give my rakkarren the gift of praying to it."

"It's been so long since I've been here," Maggie said. "I was just a little girl the first and only time I touched her, the nihr'el." Maggie looked as excited as a small child, and James thought of Gen. *He always dreamed of coming here—of becoming a karl.*

"We may gain favour with the Old Gods if we pay respect to the nihr'el," Brigid said. "Though I have stopped hearing them when I pray... maybe they are still there, somewhere."

James turned and admired the folk who had followed him here. *They've followed you through the whole damn country, and what have you given them?* There were thousands of them. James had never gotten a straight answer from Halda or Toren when he had asked how many Dagglanders had landed, but looking at them now, it was clear that their warriors alone outnumbered the Hallowfolk by three to one. *They could turn on you and take this country for themselves in an instant...*

"Let us march on and camp on this isle tonight, King Reaper, let my people see the World Tree." Toren grinned. His stout chin and healthy young beard made James nervous. He hadn't felt old until that very moment. *He would crush you in single combat if you had no dead souls to save you.*

Maggie squeezed his hand.

"Aye," said James. "We sail back to the mainland upon sunrise tomorrow." James stabbed Toren with his eyes. "But no sacrifice. Not here. And by the gods, I mean it."

RED MORNING

"THIS WAY, MAN." THE transporter held one hand out to help Halda up a steep hill while his other grasped a thin tree. Halda accepted the help. They had been seven days gone from camp, and every day of it was something new with this raven. He ceased to stop talking about the land and its different landmarks and who put them there or what. Stories of Druids, wizards, and of beasts only known to history. He spoke of faerie magics and of the dead rising. *Does he not know what task is at our hands? This is Ox'olin. We must be focused. He is completely ignorant.*

One night, by the fire, Halda told the story of Sig Arfa and his renowned victories against the Lovasi, and Eurick had the gall to try and question the sagas, claiming that he had heard *different* stories of Sig Arfa. Stories of Blood Words and cannibalism.

"Those are but small parts of a greater story. Sig Arfa was larger than life." Halda had told Eurick. "His deeds are as countless as the stars. It wasn't until he was killed that his army carved themselves. They thought it was their only chance to fight the next wave of Lovasi without Sig."

"That ain't what I heard..." Eurick muttered, and the two of them agreed to disagree.

Now they walked in a kind of awkward silence for long stretches at a time.

"Look it over there, man," Eurick said. "We can almost just start to see the lighttower that lies at the foot of the Fell River. It's only half the size of her sister at Tide, but only because she toppled. At one point, Kelson would have known this lighttower as the tallest in all of Ardura. It's still taller than any lighthouses *we're* able to build." The transporter pointed his big, grubby finger through some trees down the hill, and Halda squinted and just barely made out a black shadow that made the maple trees and the poplars look like toothpicks. "Another wonder of the Lovasi, man. They used to sail ships right up this river, the lighttower marked the way. The Lovasi brought supplies up the river and docked their great barges at Rosen and crossed on the bridge there and brought everything up to Kallahorn for Kelson. Only the gods know what he was doing up at that castle. Something about that place doesn't feel right—like, when we were there, we were living in some insect nest that wasn't made for us or by us. Only the gods know what that place truly is, man."

"You know I'm a woman, right?" Halda glared at Eurick, and the raven looked embarrassed. "You keep calling me, man, and I'm very close to shoving my axe up your arse."

"Ah, I'm *so* sorry about that. Oh, boy. I know you're a woman, of course. Pluck the Crow. Just a habit of speech, you know?" Eurick's face was redder than a berry. "Oh gods, I really am very sorry, I didn't mean any, you know, offence or nothing."

Halda spoke as little as she needed to with her mouth. She preferred to have her battle of wits with the spirits of fire or wind in the privacy of her own Den. And she always preferred the answers her runes gave her than any answers that spouted out from Human mouths.

"It's beautiful though, innit?" Eurick took a deep breath and smiled like he was resting next to a hearthfire with a warm meal. "When we get there, we can make sail for Ryne. A small fishing hamlet has festered around the old ruins of the lighttower. There's something about those old creations that make folk believe in the gods.

If the krakens haven't gotten them all yet. "I can't see shit," Halda said. "Get me closer, raven. My rakkarren will be sailing up and down the coast there, surely we will find them."

Halda followed Eurick down the hill and through a long and narrow valley where Eurick killed a squirrel with a slingshot, tied it up, and let its little body hang from his belt; they continued on.

Night fell before the lighttower came back into view, and Eurick started a fire below a nytewood and cooked the squirrel over a small spit, and split it with Halda. The meat was warm and greasy, and she felt it give her body the sustenance it craved.

"Can I get you a blanket from my pack, man—er, Halda?"

"No," Halda said. "I like the cold of night."

The raven lay in silence, but Halda was sure he didn't sleep, just as she didn't. The nytewood hummed strange silences that Halda couldn't quite pick up on—like a sneeze that fades before blowing—she would hear it, then it would die. *The tree is speaking in a language you know nothing of, even if you* could *hear it. It's full of magics, this.*

When the moon was bright and white, Halda rolled her runes and squinted to see them in the pale, lunar light. Still, they told her nothing of the Reaper. Nothing of the Mage. *The soothsayers... What will* they *tell me? What do they know?* A large part of her feared her task greatly. *But the fires and the runes don't lie. They led you to the Reaper at those stones on Springtide. What are the odds of that? You must trust this is right. You must trust your path.*

When she did finally sleep that night below that wicked, black tree, she dreamed that she was in a prison cell like the one below Massey Rock: cold stone below her, no sea in sight. She tried to find her runes but they were gone. Only her thoughts and the darkness kept her company. And in that lonely dark, the Dead God spoke to her.

"What's in a name, Halda? What's in a name?" Offa asked.

"Names are the bones of things. Names give meaning."

"Names tell secret histories." Offa's voice was ambrosial. *"Now listen carefully. These names are cornerstones of our history. The soothsayers, they are of a substance as old as time—akin to Nature. But even they have names. Demi, they are called, Torcan, Lan, they are called, and Oswe. They don't see futures but remember old pasts. They have watched all of history and mark it on a wheel in the heavens. They look at the wheel and can mark what has been and what is to come."*

Halda awoke in a cold sweat. For a moment she thought the nytewood had a face and that it was scowling at her, then all at once the face was gone. It was still dark outside, but she could hear the birds starting to sing. *Offa, I have heard your message. Demi, Torcan, they are called, Lan, and Oswe.* It was so rare that she got a message from Offa with so much clarity. *Aunt Thora mentioned their names. She said no one knew them...*

Halda took a deep breath and couldn't control her excitement. She rubbed her hands together; she clenched her fists and waved them in the sky. *Offa, oh, sweet Offa, thank you. Thank you. I won't take this message for granted.*

By the time the skies had risen orange and pink above the sun, Eurick was packed and leading Halda over streams and through small arbors and glens. They passed crumbled stone towers overgrown with moss and mushrooms, around broken bridges and through thick, primordial forests. The raven made strange marks on trees and tasted various things from the landscape and put his ear against rocks and whispered to them, and he was never lost.

"This is a ruin of your own ilk's kind." Eurick pointed to a crumbled tower. One side stood tall amidst the rubble as if the stone was giving Halda the middle finger.

A fuck you from my ancestors. Why did you destroy our empire? Why did you wreck it all? the tower seemed to say to her.

"The Daggs that built this would have been here even before the Starfall, man. It's really—"

Before they went mad with Blood Words... "Sickening?" Halda said.

"Amazing. I was going to say. They were wise enough to survive the Starfall and were still strong enough to defeat Kelson all those thousands of years later. I think it's one of the greatest songs our world has ever known."

Halda rolled her eyes. *And what do you know of destroying good things, transporter? What do you know of having a past that could never live up to your present?* "The ancient Daggland Sayers that built mountains with songs and birthed the Krakens—they first used the Blood Words. They were able to survive the Starfall with their magics. After the Starfall, the Sayers became mad—cult-like. They abused their ancestors' power and, like the Yehvenki, destroyed themselves. They fell under the grim spell of the Words and destroyed everything. We live in the scarred flesh of land they left us. We live amongst stories and deeds that none of my ilk could ever live up to. We live in the shadow of a greatness that was so awful it destroyed itself. When my ancestors carved themselves with Blood Words, they crippled their children for generations to come. In Daggland we do not celebrate these creations." Halda pointed at the ruins, pretending her finger was a dagger. "We celebrate Sig Arfa, who beat Kelson, and then that bastard Thungstenn Ton who first carved himself. Sig Arfa was fighting his own blood-carved empire that turned against him when he died. They thought it was the only way to beat the next wave of Lovasi invasions. Maybe they were right. But before Sig did, he sent the krakens back to their deep places so they would be there if we ever needed them again. He kept Daggland alive. Enough so that Lovas never came back, and we eventually fought down our own demons and lived even longer, in his honour. This—" Halda spat towards the crumbled old tower. "This is a black scar that I can only hope my people forget in time. That is why we have stayed away from this land for all this time. That is why the sea and its islands and inlets are our home now. The land holds scars that the sea smooths over, but only after enough time has passed."

Eurick's mouth hung open like he couldn't figure out what he'd said to make Halda react this way. "I didn't mean any offence, ma—"

"Offence? No, you didn't offend me. Do you know what I, Halda, dawter of Hemon and Harla, have accomplished? For a thousand years and more, since the attack of Kelson, Daggland has been at war with itself, fighting to reclaim a former glory that will never return. Sending ourselves further and further away from what we chased with each year, with each war. When those fires re-ignited and the winds howled once more, I ended a thousand years of war with the lighting of a single torch. Offence? You want to remind me of ancestors that nearly extinct me? Ancestors that made the life of me and mine much harder because we were stuck in the dark shadow they left, buried deep in the scars they provided? And now my people are forced on this pilgrimage of murder to appease a god that those ancestors angered."

Eurick looked like he was about to cry. "I'm sorry, I didn't know—"

"Nobody knows. That is why Daggland sailed. That is why blood will be spilled. So the world remembers that when the sky falls again, Daggland will still be here, clinging to the shreds of earth that remain. Daggland will rise again amidst the darkness and chaos." Halda gazed up to the sky longingly as if to seek the approval of her parents. *Father would have been proud of those words you just spoke. Olrick would have been down right rowdy.* "Now take me to these soothsayers, raven. There are things brewing that are bigger than any history known to you or I. Things that need to be riddled out."

"Aye. I'll get you there. If I can promise you one thing, it's that I'll get you there," Eurick said. "I'm the only living raven to have never failed a job, you know? Well, guess I'm not really a raven anymore, at least not one of the Guild's."

Halda prayed to the Dead God silently in her mind, and Eurick's boasting slowly became background noise as they trekked through the small hamlets and villages that had been decimated first, by the rebel Ayelish armies, and then by Halda's own Daggs on their way to the Grave Stones.

"Is it true," Eurick started, "that the Daggs were born out of the sea?"

"Aye," said Halda. "Aye, 'tis true. We went to sleep in the sea when the Earth Mother Offa rose up to meet the Sky Father. After many millennia of the sea bending us, we floated to the top, crusted in salt, and when the sun warmed our blood, we woke and were washed ashore. We gained our souls from the first trees that our soulless salt bodies cut down. And our ships have souls, too, transferred from the very wood they're hewn from. Those souls keep us safe on the sea, and if any of us dies, our souls join the ship's soul to be held safe until we return to land. When we build ships from the trees our Earth Mother gifts us, we master the seas that once bent us beneath its will." Halda eyed the sea like it had scorned her. "But the Dead God has called us back to land. Back to feed Her."

"Feed Her?"

Halda ignored the raven, the sight of a dead raven on the road had caught her attention. She walked closer and saw the beady black eyes of the bird staring back at her. Black beak, black feathers, black tongue. "Dead ravens are a bad omen." Halda wiped her forehead, she had all of a sudden felt hot.

"From who?"

"Offa," Halda said. Eurick gulped.

Halda could sense he wanted to ask what the omen meant, but Eurick kept his mouth shut. Perhaps he didn't want to know the answer. *Ravens are a symbol of sight in the old Dagg sagas. A dead raven means blindness. Perhaps Offa is telling you that She will show you no more...* Halda felt sick. If she couldn't interpret this message—if she led all of Daggland here for nothing... *no, no, no. That won't happen. It can't... It won't, it won't. Keep going. Keep searching... the soothsayers will know.*

It only took another two days to reach the rocky coast. Halda smelled the sea first, then heard the waves crashing at the shore and smiled. A thick, salty fog hung over them like the sky had dropped its clouds. *I have been away from you for too long.* Black ash shifted like sand beneath Halda's boots as she walked through the remains of a fishing hamlet. Small boats were moored at a gnarled old wharf, tucked into a small inlet, and unburnt.

"We burned this place to the ground after we had fed Offa." Halda knelt down and picked up a handful of ash, then let it sift through her fingers. "There was a group here when we first landed in Ardura, Demhoni they called themselves, but truly, they were cannibals—driven mad by this harsh world. That, and a head fungus. They were Ayelish folk once, family people, probably. We slaughtered them and bled them like pigs in the name of Offa." Halda smiled. "We took their prisoners as our own. One of them turned out to be a lord of the Glenn." Halda stared out to the sea. She breathed deeply of the damp, salty air.

"That's all well and good, man—er, Halda." Eurick pointed his thick finger to the wharfs. "But those little ships won't be enough to take us all the way to Ryne. Those are small fishing vessels, not meant for crossing no channel."

"Offa is working at her great loom, weaving our lives one thread at a time. She is guiding us, writing our future as we live out the present. Unweaving her mysteries takes more than plain sight, Eurick."

Eurick looked confused. He looked around.

Halda stabbed him with her eyes. "I wouldn't sail in one of those if I was drowning in the middle of the Sea of Stars. We wait for my rakkarren. They will be here."

"How do you know?" Eurick looked anxious. "There are no good maps of the sea, you know, just floating at the will of the wind. Ravens aren't seabirds."

"They will come. They were sailing up and down this coast, and it will only be a matter of days before we see their sails," Halda said. She *had* to believe it was true. *All I have is prophecy—all I have is the promise of answers that no one else can find. A thousand years of war ended with the lighting of a single torch. I will not fuck this up. The Dead God has chosen me, and only me for this task. My rakkarren will be here because they have to be. Offa will see it true.*

On the banks of the Channel of Darra, Halda tied her Dagglandic banner, the black kraken on blue, to a branch and buried one side of the branch in the sand. The kraken banner snapped and cracked in the sea wind. For hours she sat on her arse in the sand and watched that flag dance. She ran her fingers through the salty sand and breathed deeply of the sea fog that had shrouded her. *If you're wrong in this... if Ox'olin doesn't come, you've destroyed an empire.*

After some time, Halda walked to the water's edge, dipped her swollen hands into the seawater and closed her eyes. *Offa I'm home. I'm home.* When she opened them again, she saw blue sails flapping on the horizon. A black kraken swam on those blue sails, and they carried Halda's people. *Red Morning* burst gloriously into full view, and Halda could already hear the ruckus picking up on board as someone from the crow's nest surely spotted her.

The ship anchored some thirty yards off shore, and two smaller boats were lowered into the water from the deck. They paddled towards Halda.

"This is the most we've seen you in years," Harald said, standing with one foot on the bulwark of the small boat. The rakkarren helped Halda and Eurick into the boat and began to paddle back out to sea.

"Okay, man, just take it easy there, eh?" Eurick was gripping the thwart with white knuckles. The Dagglanders assaulted the water with their paddles, and the violence of it seemed to make the raven uncomfortable.

"You'll be okay, raven," Halda said, "once we get to *Red Morning*."

The raven was green in the face. "Right," he gasped softly.

To Harald, Halda said, "Have you seen any krakens yet?"

Harald smiled so wide Halda thought his lips might slide right out of his cheeks. "Aye," he said.

Halda's chest fluttered. *It worked.* "And?"

Harald's eyes were lit up like the sun. "They're fucking brilliant."

A NEW FELLOWSHIP

"I**T'S ABSOLUTE HELL OUT** here." Fiora stood with her hands on her hips, shaking her head. Her brindled locks, mottled brown and grey, stirred in the breeze.

"Aye," said Etta.

They stood on a ridge looking over the White River carving its way through the Fell Mountains. A hundred miles or so directly to her south, Etta would find the derelict town of Fever. *You're well and truly north now...* Etta remembered hearing stories about this river valley that ran through the mountains. That this is where the Feldarra were first born—they fell onto these banks from the mountains.

Chalky grey plumes of smoke swirled up into the rainy day. The El'vie, or the petty rulers, or both, were burning what looked like every small hamlet along the river. The White River had many smaller vassals that fed her from the mountains, and along every one of those were settled mountainfolk, many were warring tribes but mostly fisherfolk, and what was happening was pure slaughter.

"Reckon the whole world is being slaughtered right now," Fiora said. "And the gods have gone, too."

"You can't know that," Etta said, though she was starting to believe it, too. She had prayed to the Crow to keep death away from Benn and to the Stag to give her strength, and neither had come true. She was weak and haggard, and her back felt twisted like tree roots.

And how did Benn know I was Wulfee? My red curls have grown back but... She had prayed to the Swan most of all. First, to remain ugly and hidden with her short hair, but her hair grew nonetheless, and it gave her a comfort she didn't know she needed. It gave her something familiar. But her most important prayer was to beg the Swan to protect Swey. *By the virtue of your nature, protect him. By the gods I can't do it all alone.*

"Baerd knows many things. The Old One speaks to him. He said the gods are dying," Fiora said. Her wolf howled to re-enforce her point. "I got the message from Rat who got it from Baerd. He told me that I had to move in and make contact with you. That it was time to bring you to them at Elwyd."

"Elwyd?" Etta hawked spit. "Is this some kind of joke?" She moved closer to Swey. *The daughter of Lord Baleth Longsongs? By the gods... how do I keep getting sucked into this shite?*

Fiora laughed. "By the gods, I wish it were all a joke." Baleth Longsongs's daughter walked away, and her wolf followed. "Elwyd is our home, where the si'otha have gathered. You won't believe it until you see it. Come on," she said. "My camp isn't far. The quicker we get there, the more rest we'll have for tomorrow. We've got a long journey ahead. To Elwyd."

The fuck? Etta hated the idea that there was a place she knew nothing of in the mountains that Wulfee had spent her life living beside. She followed Fiora but said nothing. *Wulfee would have fought this. She would have caused trouble.*

After a few minutes, she was walking next to Swey and telling the story of Gen the Karl. A part of Etta felt lighter, like she was making progress somehow. Progress on what she didn't know, but something felt different. She was alive. Swey was alive. Maybe there was something bigger happening. *And who is this Baerd.* He could have been someone from her past. Her brother, Lars, still lived, as far as she knew. He was fourteen years her elder and he hardly knew her, but Etta understood that he lived in the mountains and fought amongst the folk-of-the-furs at one point. *Pike, is that you?* She thought it was most likely him. *It has to be him... He's convinced Kihl'dor Sera and the low mountain clans of Pool to seek refuge further north. A force of their size could really make a difference up here.* But this wolf had been following her much longer than she had been away from Pike, and so she thought it had to be her brother or a former clan member.

"Did I tell you my mother still lives? Annie Longsongs of Kallahorn, the rightful queen."

"Woah, really?" Swey was excited. "A queen?"

Etta gritted her teeth. Everyone believed King Baleth Longsongs had killed his wife, an Ayelish born Florhen of Leveny. Their very marriage was a scandal in the first place, Baleth being known to have skinchanger blood. Her death was what started this most recent war. *Now this girl is telling you it was all for show?* "What do you mean she lives?" Etta said.

Fiora held out her hands. Her wolf growled. "Easy there. Before you go saying that my dad started a war. Alder was coming back to Kallahorn anyway. His tour through Mal Hallow was just to plot the easiest route back to Kallahorn. He told my dad as much when he visited a year prior. He visited all the fiefs and demanded respect from the petty rulers who sat on false thrones. My dad had read the histories and knew it was an old Alder trick to kill one of their own and blame it on the husband or wife of the slain as a way of cutting ties with that family. It was my dad's idea to get ahead of Alder, and before Alder could frame him for the death of his own wife, he killed her himself."

"All this for Kallahorn?" Etta hated that black pit of a place. "That seems like an awful fucking idea."

"No, can't you see? It was to push a boulder down the hill. One that had been stuck for millennia. It was to start this—all of this—to awaken the evil of the world so we can kill it once and for all. The prophecies—it's all coming alive right now, we are a part of it. We're going to destroy the dissonance in this world once and for all."

"I'm sick of the fucking prophecies." Etta covered Swey's ears. "You're mad," she said. "You know that, right?"

"Not mad. Though, it all seems mad, doesn't it? But we will take Kallahorn before the year is out. Kallahorn is where this started, and it's where this will end."

"The year is half over already. It will never happen," Etta said. She had seen this game played a dozen times. Ruler takes Kallahorn. Ruler loses Kallahorn. Ruler plots to take Kallahorn back. She played the game herself with Sweyne, the senior. They had lived a life of luxury and without want. Then it was stripped away by ill-timed defeats and misplaced wits.

"Aye, our leader plans to take it back. If not this year, then next. The si'darra have been forming an army. A big one," Fiora said. "And this is about more than just war."

"It's always about war," Etta said. "It always comes back to war."

"My dad said this could be the war to end wars," Fiora said.

"Your dad was known for telling stories."

Fiora studied the ground. "I know what folks say about my dad. They call him Longsongs out of jest, not out of respect." Fiora stroked her wolf. "But he had the old blood of Rangers, and he talked to the spirits. That same blood runs in me, and my wolf proves that his tales of being half-breed were more than just long songs. And he read so many books and scrolls that his eyes stopped working and so, near the end, it was I who read them aloud to him. What I learned in those books and scrolls made me question why people were calling my dad mad when it was clearly the entire world that had gone mad. There are so many things that we have forgotten. A past as rich and as tragic as anything you could ever imagine. And the deeper my dad read, the further back he went into all those old scrolls in Kallahorn, the more was revealed to us. We live in a world that was designed to make us slaves to those above—the Warlocks, the gods, it's all a game. These prophecies keep arising. Wars are fought over and over again, caused by the same things. History is a song with a chorus of war and many, many verses of tragedy. But the prophecies tell of a world where the song is silenced. A Reaper's Lullaby. The burden of silencing it has been passed to us." Fiora's passion was burning inside of her like a forge, and Etta felt the heat coming off of her. Fiora really believed this. *She believes more fiercely than you ever have.*

Etta watched Swey as he threw rocks into the arbor, ignoring all that was being said. *Go with her, for Swey. Go and learn what she speaks of.* Etta took notice of the sun. "We better get going then, eh? How far is this camp?" she said.

Fiora smiled. "Few miles. Come on, we'll stay away from the rivers."

A STAINED SHEET OF canvas stretched between two elm trees, and a fire below crackled and smoked. Three trout hung gutted on a drying rack out front. Two women and a rather small man sat around the fire. The man poked at it with a stick.

"Ah hah! I told you she wasn't dead!" the man said when he saw Fiora come out of the arbor. He glared at Etta and Swey, and his mouth went flat. His two front teeth hung over his lower lip like a rat's.

"Oh shut your trap, Rat, none of us truly thought she was dead," said the younger woman. "We were only worried was all."

"I'm fine, though I can't say the same of our country folk. Times are lean," said Fiora.

"By the gods." The older woman's eyes were all white. She stood and felt for Fiora and pulled her in for a loving embrace. Etta took this to be Annie Longsongs, the Queen of Kallahorn. "It's good to have you back, my dear." The former queen looked past Fiora with her all-white eyes to Etta and Swey, and though Etta knew she could not see her, she felt the woman's stare just the same. "And you two. Come. Sit. Welcome."

Fiora held her arm out. "That's Rat with the greenhood. Young one is Nettle. Old one is my mom, Annie."

Annie had stepped forward to greet Etta with a hand on her shoulder. "Come. Sit," she said.

Nettle held out a ladle with steaming liquid in it. "We're making soup," she said. "With nettles." She smiled.

"Where is Owyn?" Fiora asked.

"He's looking for you. He's been gone two days," said Annie. "Lot's going on, Fi, we were worried about you."

"So you sent Owyn out and risked his life?" Fiora pointed at Etta. "I told you it would take time to find her. Will you never trust me?"

"There are wars on every front, Fi, even up here in the mountains," said Rat. "One gets squelched and another pops up."

"Bazal calls on us, my dear," Annie said, "We could not risk losing you. Owyn insisted on going. If you were captured by the El'vie or one of these Ayelish—"

"But I wasn't captured," Fiora said. "And now we must linger in waiting for Owyn to return."

Swey tugged on Etta's arm. "Does she mean the Bazal from the story of Hendurinn?"

Fiora and Annie still argued.

"Bazal?" Etta had hardly noticed that Annie had said that. It pissed her off how little she knew. "No," she said, "it can't be." Though now the question burned in her as well. To Annie, she said, "You speak of Bazal?" Fiora and Annie stopped arguing, and both of their heads bobbed towards Etta.

Annie glared at Etta with her white eyes. "There is much and more you don't know, Kihl'dor," Annie turned to Fiora. "And that is why this time to wait for Owyn will be beneficial. So we can fill our new friend in."

Etta shivered. "I'm no kihl'dor," she said.

"You're the greatest kihl'dor the Fells has ever known," Annie said. "At least since Emmer."

She knows you... Etta was silent.

"You are more than what your name is, Etta. It does not matter what you call yourself. I know who you are."

"You don't know shit!" Etta barked, and felt immediately awful.

"That's a queen you're talking to." Nettle stood and cocked the ladle as if she'd use it as a weapon.

"It's okay, Nettle," said Annie. "The kihl'dor is on a journey we know nothing of. Let her find her way. Her true self awaits her at the end of this road."

Etta was ready to bark off with more curses like *"Fuck you, you old, blind bitch!"* but held her tongue. She was through with hurting people with words and weapons.

Luckily, young Swey filled the silence before Etta could change her mind. "Why are your eyes all white?" he asked as only a child would.

Annie laughed. "The coloured parts of my eyes were eaten by hungry crows on my way through the Otherworld upon my birth. Father Tree had no time to give them back to me, so I was born without." Annie said it with so much conviction that Swey just nodded his head with his mouth gaping. Etta knew that probably wasn't true, but she had stopped trying to question the gods long ago. Things just were as they were, and Etta couldn't do anything to change it. *But maybe you can...* Etta ignored the voice inside of her.

"Can we have a clanfire tonight, Etta?" Swey had seemingly been satisfied with Annie's answer and had moved on. Clanfires were the Feldarra's way of showing the gods their thanks. To show that they had survived another day. Etta hadn't said thanks in far too long. She had felt like the gods had cursed her by sending Braden that wolf mask. By getting him caught up in all of that shite. By getting *her* caught up in the same shite. *But it wasn't the gods' fault, it was yours. You chased that bastard Sweyne for ten years and found nothing. He disappeared—as good as dead. You should have left it. You didn't need to find him. You never needed to leave your children in the first place. This is your fault, and no one else's. You brought yourself to this point in your life. No one is going to bring you back but you. Us.*

"Aye," said Etta. She would say thanks tonight. "I reckon we can."

Etta found a good spot and gathered some kindling, then placed small sticks in a cone shape over the kindling and leaned bigger logs over the top of them. With a flintstone she sparked a flame, then huffed on the small flame to make it bigger until it took hold of the wood. She remembered a time that Gen held flint in his big hand and wondered why it wouldn't light. *Another life. Another you...*

"We have a fine fire here," Nettle said, pointing at the cookfire with her ladle. "Don't see the point in starting another, other than wasting wood."

"That is a cookfire. The smoke is being blocked by the pot." Etta pointed. "A clanfire must be visible by the gods."

"Ooh, a proper clanfire?" Rat smiled with his big front teeth gleaming in the ruddy light. "Like from the cycles? This is proper, innit?"

"A clanfire will be great fun," said Annie.

"We shan't linger." Fiora crossed her arms and huffed. "I'm telling you. You haven't been out there. Those Demhoni are bloodthirsty—flesh-hungry."

"Oh, calm yourself, you're scaring the boy," Annie said.

"Can you tell stories, Etta?" Swey was rubbing his eyes. The sun was setting, and Etta could feel a rain coming.

"I'm all out of stories, Swey," she said.

"I've got stories," said Rat. He was poking at the fire with a stick. When finally it was truly ablaze, they all sat around it. Swey sat close to Etta, and she put her arm around him. He tucked his head into her arm and she felt a warm tingle in her stomach, and she was reminded of Tarek and Braden.

"Tell me of Bazal. How is it you speak to him?"

Annie laughed. "He has come back, Etta, from his place of imprisonment in the Otherworld. He lives now with the si'darra, in the woods and caves of mountain valleys. But it is not me who speaks with him. It is Baerd."

Baerd, Baerd, Baerd. Who the fuck is this guy...

"He was bodiless," said Rat, "Bazal was. Just a spirit when he came to us."

"So you talk to spirits in the woods?" Etta was trying to hide her excitement to know more.

"He has taken a body," Annie said.

"A body?" Etta questioned. "What folk live in the woods of the mountain valleys? The Feldarra I know are at Pool."

"The Feldarra spread far and wide, Etta, you should know this," said Annie.

Etta didn't like the way Annie made her feel stupid. "Why is that something I should know? And what body? What kind of shite are you folk doing up there in the mountains?"

Annie pressed her fingers into her eyes like the question wasn't even worth answering.

Fiora spat into the fire and said, "He took the body of a dying old man. And had he known, Oris would have gladly given his body to Bazal."

"Baerd told you this? Bazal took the body of an old man?" Etta was confused. This all sounded like a bunch of shite.

Annie pursed her lips.

"I don't like this story," said Swey.

"Neither do I," said Etta. "If I wanted to be caught up in prophecy and horse shite, I would have followed James into the mountains."

"Your time to follow James will come, Etta," said Annie. "He will play a part in this, too."

Etta didn't like how much this blind bitch thought she knew, and she especially didn't like that this whole lot was treating Etta like she knew nothing. "Are you going to tell me what's going on here? It's not too late for me and the boy to leave."

Swey squeezed Etta as if to say he didn't want to leave, and Etta didn't either but she couldn't be dragged along.

Nettle waved her ladle. "This is about what happened last summer. The Warlocks and the gods and the spirits. Great big shite."

Etta knew all about what happened last summer. By the gods, she had held Rosen Bridge against the Ayelish to give James the opportunity to close the Gateway. It was gods and prophecies that drove everything. *That was Wulfee, the killer—the son murderer. That was you. You did that. You can't hide from this forever.*

"Bazal escaped the prison that the Warlocks had locked him in." Annie said. "He sought the si'darra, the shield people, for they had helped him in his first fight against the Warlocks. Baerd and his scouting partner Hagen found him.

"When Bazal arrived, it took a while for them to interpret what he was saying. He spoke in old languages, but after a short time, he learned to communicate. He said the sky was falling. He said the end was here. He knew how to stop it but he needed *us*. The si'darra. And Baerd said he couldn't do it without *you*. So here we are."

"So you just said yes?" Etta said. "You believe everything this Baerd says?"

"Baerd has no reason to lie about this," Rat said. "Our life is peaceful in the mountains."

"He knows much and more of the wither year, and he helped us through that time," Annie said. "He is well respected amongst the si'darra. He is clearly some kind of magician. And we have oaths, Etta, ancient oaths carved into the mountain shrines, written in the cycles, sung by the elders. They are so grand and so repetitive that they cannot be ignored. The si'darra still say them in our rituals, though they have been lost amongst most of the Feldarra. These oaths speak of the end time—of the Starfall. They speak of time and the Wheel of Udransil, which we are all stuck to like grass to the earth as it spins through eternity. These things have happened before, Etta, and they will happen again after us. But Baerd claims that Bazal knows how to end this. End it forever."

"How?" Etta blurted.

Swey was on the edge of the log. He was eating it up. "Magics?" he uttered, as if afraid of the word.

Annie laughed. "Tell him, Fi."

Fiora smiled. "He speaks of three stones—keys to open an ancient door below Kallahorn. A magic sword. A song of silence. Gods. He speaks of magics and more, but when you hear him tell it, you will believe, for it is the truth—a truth that is written in the bones of the earth, waiting for us at this very moment to read it. Baerd will take us to Bazal once he has you."

"There is no door below Kallahorn, I lived there for three years. All that is down there are tunnels and more tunnels."

"He says there are doors. And he says there are keys," Annie said.

Etta scoffed. In truth she hadn't ventured very far into those tunnels. There could be dragons down there and she wouldn't know it. "So why do you need me?" Etta truly wondered. *You're nothing. A wretched thing. No. No you're not. You were beautiful once. A wisp of etta. That was long ago...*

"Because our army needs a kihl'dor." Annie's white eyes reflected the fire. Etta felt that fire spreading into her.

A crack in the woods made her jump. Five figures came out of the night holding a single torch.

"Owyn?" Annie stood, and held her hands out to the night. "I smell him," she said.

"Aye," he said. The other figures became visible beside him.

"Mom!" Swey screamed. Etta held him back when he tried to run. She couldn't trust shadow figures.

"By the gods!" Tara crumpled to the ground. "My baby. Oh, my baby." Etta let go of Swey, and he ran to her and they cried together in a weeping ball.

"My baby," Tara screamed. "By the gods, my baby."

Cullen was there, and Calum the traveller. Silently stalking behind them were two elders.

"By the gods," Calum said. He looked pale as snow. "Etta, you made it. Bloody hell."

"Aye," Etta said. She glared out into the night behind the new arrivals, expecting Hawka to burst out of the woods to kill them all. "We all made it," she said, and something in the woods cracked in response. *Hawka.* Etta remembered the wild, carnivore stench of them. *No, you would smell that. You would smell that... it's just a wolverine or a snowy owl.*

The elders had found their way to the clanfire like moths. They warmed their hands by it as if the heat would save their lives even in the warm spring evening. Nettle was serving some of her nettle soup to Calum and Cullen. Etta saw Cullen point to the soup and ask Nettle something about it, then ate more with a satisfied look on his face. Owyn and Annie were discussing something.

"Thank you." Tara sobbed. She was holding Swey in her arms. "Thank you," she said again to make sure Etta heard her.

"It's the way of things," Etta said, referring to the northern tradition of caring for orphans. But in her heart, she felt pride that went beyond traditions. For the first time since Etta had killed her son, she found her new purpose through Swey. She wouldn't let anything happen to him. She would fight to make a better world for him, and for his mother. *Your daughterbound.*

Somewhere in the deep darkness of Etta's own soul, she began to search for someone familiar. Someone that would help her get through the aching bloody pain of getting through this.

She was looking for Wulfee.

SELLSWORDS

T HE SOUTHERN COAST OF Esher was a rocky, barren place. The only green came from small, grubby succulents that clung to old rocks and dry sand, and skinny cypress trees that sprouted from the sandy soil along with brown and yellow tufts of thistle. Julien walked above decks aboard the ship her captain called *Saltspray* to try and ease his churning stomach, but the sight of the coast didn't help. *To shipwreck here would be a cruel torture.*

"Are you sick?" the captain asked.

Julien shook his head. "Not sick, just entirely overcome by nausea."

The captain of the *Saltspray* was a squat old woman with sun-brown skin like leather and salt-white hair like straw. Her face was rugged with lines, and her cheek bones were like crags that held up her sunken eyes. Her name was Hild, and she snickered at Julien like he was a child. "Greensick."

"At this rate we'll be in Sareen before winter," Julien said, and Hild laughed at him.

"You know nothing of the sea. To skip across the Bay of Bones would be the death of us. We must hug the coast this time of year. Not to mention there have been kraken sightings in the north." Hild gripped the bulwark and closed her eyes and breathed in the sea. She was right, Julien knew nothing of the sea other than that he was always getting exiled across it, and that it was usually difficult to cross.

"How long until we make port at Jakaray?" Julien looked up at the sun. It was already spring and he knew all of the best sellsword companies would be sold already, but if they made it there in good time, he could surely find one. *There must at least be one...*

"You wanna know how long, boy? How long does it take for the sea to know ye? What language does the wind speak, and the tides? You wanna know how long till Jakaray? Long enough for you to calm yourself and relax those nerves. You're a twitchy one."

Julien regretted asking.

"If you look at the sea long enough, boy, the sea will look back. I'll get ye to Sareen by way of Jakaray, and we'll get there when it's time. It ain't up to ye or me, it's up to the sea," Hild said before she walked away.

Julien said nothing. He and his rabble had had a hard enough time trying to fit in with the crew on the *Saltspray,* and Julien had sensed that Hild and her crew distrusted and disliked him. He would have been wiser to have struck a deal with Bones to come along, but Julien knew that was never going to happen.

The Epithosian sailor had left many ships and a strange, skinny-nosed person called Shapireo to look after Bones's new salt empire while Bones himself crossed the Old Sea to get more ships and more people from Epithos to protect his new kingdom. It would take a deal sweeter than anything Julien could conjure up again to top that. *But you have won your ships, now you just need to hope they are all mad enough to listen to you.*

They had been a week at sea, and Julien had yet to gain his sea legs. He hated the bloody sea, all it ever did was drown folk and produce fish, and he hated fish. Growing up in Sareen, it was always fish this and fish that.

Everything of life came from the river in Sareen—the Esheri Rush. Many outlets of the river ran directly through the city of Sareen in canals and a hundred hundred bridges ran across those canals. The great Lovasi Castle, Red Sky Rock, sat at the city's centre and shone like a ruby in the sun, glinting across all of Esher. *I will pluck that ruby like an apple.*

Julien loved the Esheri Rush, and he missed the sound of her waters running. At least the river could be tamed to a degree. The river was predictable, but the sea was cruel. The river guided one gently along and allowed one to drink her waters. The sea tossed one about, and her waters were poisonous. *Yes, and Sareen has been poisoned, too, and I have come to cure her illness.*

Julien looked out at the blue-green water and the sun reflecting in it, and in that moment, he had never missed his home more. He was nine when John Hester and his Warlock exiled Julien's family to Lavesh. They were suspected of being Old Blood, and instead of killing them, John said he would give them mercy and send them to Lavesh.

Julien heard boots shuffling on deck, and Ashan came up beside him. "Morning," the warrior said.

"Morning," Julien answered, and together they watched the sea and smoked soma from Ashan's long wooden pipe.

"I don't trust that knight," Ashan said after a long silence. Julien wondered how long he'd been contemplating that. The sea was alive with radical colour. The soma brightened Julien's world.

"The Lion Knight?" Julien could see the rays of the sun throbbing.

"Him."

"Ah, he's probably the safest of this lot. In my experience, traitors usually hate the enemy more than you do."

"The knight calls himself Rolan. Whether that was the name his parents gave him or he stole it for himself, I can't be sure. Rolan was the name of a Warlock who fought against the Draku."

"And Julien was the name of a devil from beneath the earth," Julien said. "The Warlocks and Draku both praise the same god: Karaat. We are not different. What you fear in that knight, he should also fear in me. For all he knows I could end him with but a Word. Karaat is strong today." Julien felt a fire at the back of his throat and wanted to spew it all over Rolan. The knight was a part of Hild's crew, and Bones had told Julien that Rolan was the best leader amongst the lot. He was a member of House Wence, related to House Hester from a line of lesser cousins. But Bones was a strong leader and had told these folk that Julien was their general now, and they listened to Bones without question. But Julien still needed to earn these folks' respect, and Rolan would be the key to that.

"You should not doubt a name like Rolan." Ashan was seemingly deep in thought about the knight and the story he stole his name from.

"And Rolan should not doubt a name like Esterbraun."

Ashan shook his head as if he disagreed. He had crossed a desert with Julien and watched him kill the Oracle, and still Ashan doubted him.

Since Canri had died, Julien had confided his trust in Ashan—what little of his trust he was willing to extend. As a sellsword and an orphan, he had become used to not having true friends or family. Everyone wanted his place as leader, and they would kill him or betray him at any opportunity. Julien's true genius as a general was staying alive for as long as he did. *But when you fight for what is right, folk will follow.*

Julien had been fighting for an everlasting peace his whole life. First in Lavesh, now in Esher, and soon throughout the whole continent of Ardura. *And they have doubted you since day one. Soon they will know your family's name. Soon the whole world will remember the Draku.*

"Do you remember what happened to my people here ten years ago?" Julien asked. Ashan shook his head no.

"I don't know many stories," Ashan said, and Julien knew that was a lie. Every soldier knew stories. All they had was stories and scars and dreams.

"Some stories are sweeter than others, Ashan. And not all are worth knowing." Julien ran a hand through his hair. It was hard and crusty from days at sea. He looked at the captain still making her rounds and shivered at the thought of his hair turning into that white straw. "The

Hesters had torn the country apart to find folk with ties to the Old Blood in their lineage. King John and his Warlock Adora had felt threatened by an old prophecy the Ailaryan Order had found that said a Draku would rise up and take the Lion Chair one day. So John Hester gathered all of the suspected Draku from throughout Esher at Sareen. He raided homes and netted Humans like animals. Then he corralled us all onto boats and told us that we were to sail to Lavesh. We sailed up the Esheri Rush and around the Bone Coast, and when we reached this very bay, we saw more ships on the horizon. 'Pirates!' I shouted. My father said, 'No, not pirates,' and he looked worried. Then my mother looked worried so I was scared. Soon a whole fleet of ships appeared on the water in front of us. They had come from Jakaray and Sima, and they flew the banners of House Love and of House Marwen and above those, they flew purple flags with a golden lion."

"Hesters..." Ashan spat.

"Bang on, friend. Hesters, and a lot of them with Warlocks aboard whispering at the winds and conjuring mists from the water. They sailed up on us, shrouded in one such mist, and all feared that we had been tricked into thinking we had received peace and that the ships were there to sink us.

"Their sails got bigger and bigger and their hulls were made of cedar wood, and they were massive in the water that day. They got closer and closer and they got so close that I was sure they weren't going to attack, that they were just going to keep sailing, but just as soon as that thought had made itself comfortable in my mind, I saw archers appear from below decks. They lined up in neat rows, and just as folk realized what was happening, the arrows came. They pierced bodies and they stabbed in the planks and the masts, and blood spilled all over the deck, and the planks were slippery-wet and full of arrows. The Hesters didn't want to sink the ships so they pulled up next to us, and folk with swords and knives hopped from one ship to the other and started to cut down everyone who had escaped the arrows.

"My dad was busy sawing the window of our cabin wider while my brothers and I stood guarding the door of our cabin with pieces of jagged wood in our hands. My mother was screaming and holding my crying baby sister. We all escaped the ship, but the sea is another beast. Only me, my youngest brother, and my father made it out of this sea. We drifted for weeks and finally landed in Talent where fisherfolk took us in and gave us work to live by. In the following years, we went from selling fish to selling our swords. Praise Karaat, how I hate fish. The smell, the taste, the look of the damn things... but more than the fish, I hate the Warlocks. I hate every single one of them for what they've done. And they have no idea that I lived, that Esterbraun can't die. That I am Draku and have three thousand years' worth of bad blood in my veins pumping hate for the Warlocks of Old Yehven. Later, my father died from a bad belly, and my brother died from the same. Poisoned, no doubt, for uttering the word Draku to the wrong folk, but they told me that I could not die—that I *would not*. Our legacy lives inside of me, and I was meant to spread it."

Ashan was gazing at Julien, and Julien knew that he had touched the soldier in some way with his words. It was only the clink-thump of steel boots on wood that drew Ashan's gaze away from Julien. The steps came heavy and suddenly. The turncloak knight Rolan had come above decks.

Rolan looked like a court jester in full steel armour upon a ship, but he seemed not to care. He, unlike Julien, didn't seem to mind what others thought of him. The armour was a signal to Julien that Rolan did not trust him. Rolan saw Julien and smiled as he walked towards him.

"Am I supposed to call you general?" Rolan said. His voice sounded like gravel shifting.

"You'll go straight to the bottom wearing that, eh?" Julien jested. Rolan didn't even smile. Julien said, "You can call me whatever you want as long as you listen to me when the fighting starts."

"Hah, fighting." Rolan touched the hilt of his sword as if in prayer. "You can point me in the right direction and release me, but once I pull *Lady,* not you or anyone can tell me what to do."

Julien grinned. It seemed very irresponsible of a knight to pull a sword and to stop listening to orders, but he grinned anyway on account of the knight's naivety. *He probably said oaths in front of some alter and believes they mean something.*

"You don't actually think you can do this, do you?" Rolan said. "Surely you know this will fail. The Hesters have ruled for two hundred years, and nothing can change that. Not you or anything."

"I know I can do this. I have seen it happen in dreams," Julien said. And Julien believed in something more than gods and oaths. He believed in legacy. "Surely you know the Legend of Draku from the Kelson Chronicles."

"I know many stories," Rolan said. And Julien knew he was at least more honest than Ashan. *Which isn't saying much.*

"I have been told my whole life that the Draku were nothing but a failed test. A fucked-up experiment by the old Warlocks to see what kind of strange things they could create. Well, I am more than that. I am Draku, and I feel as you feel. I want to prove to the world our Creation was worthwhile. I want to make a world where things like Warlocks don't exist. A place of peace. Karaat has told me that it can be true. He has shown me when and where I would die, and it's not here and it's not now. The Oracle told me that if I attacked Hest, a great empire would fall. The world is mine."

Rolan looked at Julien like he was mad. He opened his mouth then closed it again. "You have three ships. Three... And if you lead these folk into a losing fight, they will leave you. They will evaporate like a morning fog."

"I'm a sellsword, you don't think I know that?"

"Then what do you think you're going to do with these ships? Sareen has three concentric fifty-foot walls and a moat filled with sewage and garbage. Red Sky Rock is surrounded by another two walls and is in the middle of a river outlet. Only a fool would assault that great city from the river."

"We're not going to assault it from the river. We're just going to get close enough that whoever is occupying the city will come out to meet us. There are palaces on the banks of that river. Three ships are enough to get their attention, surely, and someone will come."

"Then what?" Rolan raised an eyebrow.

"They'll invite me to dinner."

"To dinner?"

"Of course. It's been so long since I've had good Esheri food. But you're right, we need more than three ships. We'll need to buy some sellswords in Jakaray."

Rolan smiled. "Sellswords? You have gold hidden somewhere?"

"I have all of the gold of Sareen to buy them with."

"Praise Karaat. You're mad. Bones has sold me to a madman."

"Just wait," Julien said. He was confident that the things he had been seeing in his dreams and the messages he had received from Karaat were true. *The Oracle proved them true...*

It was about half a year ago now that the first message came. In the Rise of winter, when the fires had returned. Julien was sitting by the fresh, crackling flame and staring into it in awe. He hadn't known if he would ever see it again, so he soaked in every second of that moment, and as he watched the flames, a voice spoke to him.

He looked up and saw no one around him. He thought he *was* mad, then, at that moment. But the voice spoke again. It spoke backwards, but Julien had played at reading backwards when he would get bored in the libraries at Odessa, and so he could make it out. "*Taarak,*" it said to him. "*Ukard Lliw Esir,*" the voice told Julien. *Draku will rise.*

Every night Karaat visited him, and every night Julien became more and more sure that what his family died for was worth fighting for. He was sure of it.

Julien's father and grandfather had long spoken of a dragonbone in Lavesh and they were thought mad for talking of it. Then Julien found that bone from the peddler witch in Odessa and used it to kill the Oracle. Nobody doubted the existence of *her*.

His grandfather also spoke of a book in Hest. A book that held the spells that created the Warlocks. Spells that granted everlasting life and souls beyond bodies. A book that held the secrets behind the creation of Draku written by the Creator, Insa. Julien meant to find that book, too, and he meant to use it to put an end to the Warlocks and the Order of Ailar. He meant to use it to build a new empire under the Draku banners, and to resurrect the soulkin of his people. Because, as well as the book in Hest, his grandfather spoke of something else there, too. He spoke of a dragon husk, dying but never dead, that lay beneath Kelson's Keep in Hest, resembling a stone of the earth.

JAKARAY WAS STEAMING IN the heat. The coastline was a cesspit. Year-old carcasses littered the beaches, and the crocs had bred and made themselves dens in and amongst the rotting dead to gorge. The green scaly things were fat, and Julien figured they had been gorging for nine months without much contention other than the vipers. Tallow reeds and sugar canes grew from the shallow water like tall grass. They slid through murky green waters slowly along the filthy coast towards the harbour.

When Hild's ship moored, no one came to greet them or charge them tolls. Julien simply disembarked and walked into the stinking town.

"You think I'm going to let you go off without me and make plans to kill me with some sellsword in a whorehouse?" Rolan had appeared without his steel armour this time, and Julien couldn't believe how big he still was. His arms looked like tree trunks beneath his leather jerkin.

"If I was going to kill you, I would have done it already," Julien sneered.

"If you were going to kill me, I would kill you first," Rolan said.

Julien smiled at him. "I'm going to find a sellsword captain, but not in a whorehouse."

"Well, let's go then," Rolan said.

The docks were brimming with a strange assortment of folk. One-eyed sailors and sailors with skin as black as charcoal and sailors that spoke languages that sounded like birds dying. Whores and mongers and folk looking for work upon the ships shouted and begged and tugged on Julien's clothes, but he slipped past them and into the sandstone streets of Jakaray.

Banners of light blue emblazoned with two golden suns hung from balconies and from well posts. *Banners of Marwen.* Soldiers wearing chainmail and leather marched the streets with light blue cloaks trailing behind them. Most of them held spears instead of swords. Julien felt hot just looking at them.

The houses were made of wood and canvas, and some of the older ones still had sandstone bases that newer builders had hammered wooden struts into and stretched canvas over. Jakaray was another one of Kelson's cities, and because of that, the streets were straight and wide and lined with cypress trees and date palms, and Julien didn't have to worry about getting lost.

"Sellswords?" he said to a merchant, and she pointed down an alleyway.

The alleyway smelled of shit and stale piss, and rats scurried away underfoot. Julien followed the sound of hammer strikes around a dogleg in the alley to a blacksmith's forge.

She pounded the anvil and spat when Julien stopped in front of her. "What d'ya want? I've got naught but chains for anchorage here, no weapons."

"I'm looking to buy sellswords," Julien said.

"Well you should have gone to Sareen," the smith said, and struck her hammer so hard it made Julien's ears ring.

"We were told we could find them down this alley. Point us in the right direction," Rolan said. "Please."

The smith stopped her work and studied Julien. "Who are you?" she said.

"Esterbraun. Julien Esterbraun." He put his hands on his hips. "This is Sir Rolan of House Wence."

"Esterbraun..." The smith seemed to ponder that. "Listen, they ain't quite sellswords, but there's some folk in that brick building round the corner to your left who might know where to find them. Don't go causing trouble now, though."

"Why would you think that I would?" Julien smiled.

The smith looked at him but didn't smile. "You're a fool to go around using that name, you know that? How many people you told that name to?"

"So you've heard the stories of my family?" Julien asked. "Have you heard I killed the Oracle?"

The smith studied Julien up and down as if she was looking for some mark of the Draku, but she said nothing. "Just don't cause any trouble here. We've had enough of it."

"There will be no trouble," Rolan said, "I swear on my honour."

The smith spat, and Julien didn't know if that was her opinion on Rolan's honour or a gesture of how much she believed there would be no trouble.

Julien found the brick building, patched with wooden struts and canvas where the bricks had crumbled. The door was a canvas sheet stretched across a gaping hole in the wall. Julien moved the canvas aside with his hand and stepped in.

"Anyone home?"

Julien was met with glaring eyes. Folk huddled around a gnarled table of old cypress and drank from clay cups, grunting beneath thick beards and sitting in wicker chairs. There was shuffling in the corner, then a baby whined and Julien saw four women in the corner holding children. Two were babes in arms, and two clutched at their mother's legs.

"I was told I could find sellswords here. Where is your captain?" Julien spoke the words but didn't much expect an answer.

"And what would *you* want with sellswords?" One of the men slid his eyes up and down Julien. Julien knew he didn't look much like a captain at the moment. He was in the same clothes he had worn for the entire boat ride in which he vomited and sweated, and he hadn't had the time or resources to polish his boots properly. His appearance garnered doubt, but he was okay with that. *Passion will eat doubt every time. Ignite passion in them and you will have them.*

"I want to kill Hesters and burn Warlocks," Julien said, and watched the folks' faces lift from the table to study him.

One of them took the hood of his roughspun off his head and stood. "Well, you're in luck," he said, "because thanks to the lions, this country is chock full of sellswords. They've gone and turned the whole damn country into a cesspit."

"And that's why I've come, you see, to pull this country out of that pit."

"Lots of folk have said that. Many have even tried." The man slipped the roughspun from his shoulders and revealed leather armour beneath, inlaid with a red scorpion in the chest. An old iron sword was sheathed at his hip. He brushed his long black hair out of his face. "What'd you say your name was?"

"I didn't say," Julien said, and Rolan scoffed.

"My friend here doesn't mean to be rude," Rolan said. "My name is Rolan."

The man laughed. He stuck out a calloused hand, the hand of a warrior, Julien noted. "My name is Trist." Julien shook his hand, and Trist pointed to his companions at the table. "This is Lexa and Cleo, big one at the end is Aldin."

Julien nodded to all of them. "Esterbraun," he said, and none of them reacted. The name seemingly meant nothing to them. And theirs meant nothing to him.

He was horrible with names, he had known so many. Sellswords came and went and died, and in his travels, all of the names blended together. He would have an easier time remembering the folk by monikers. Lexa is *lazy eye* and Cleo is *chewed ear*. The big one could just be *big one*.

"When the wither year came to Esher, the Hesters came with it. They must have thought the chaos and disorder of it all would be enough to topple our governments, and they were right. Folk fled the cities, the two major armies of Serahnon and Marwen diminished, and the Hesters took everything along the Sunroad. If we tried to fight a true war, the Hesters would have ravaged the countryside and caused mass famine across the whole country. It was easier for the lords and the brigands to leave and disperse amongst our many towns and cities. The Marwens went one way, the Serahnons another. So when you talk about killing Hesters, I'm ready to listen. If I *did* have sellswords, what would you do with them?" Trist said.

"I'm going to conquer Hest," Julien said.

Trist laughed, leaned back in his carved-oak chair and crossed his arms as if waiting for a better answer.

"Not all at once, of course," Julien said. "But I have seen it in my dreams. I have heard it from the lips of the Oracle. Hest will fall, and I will be the one who topples it. But first, friend, I want Sareen and Red Sky Rock. The ruby-jewel of Esher. It was my home once, and it has been poisoned. I want to free my people from the lion's claws and the spells of Warlocks. I want to put the rightful ruler back on the throne."

"And that is?" Trist asked, and Julien knew Trist was testing his loyalty.

"An Esheri," Julien said vaguely. "The blood of sand and stars. The blood of Kassius."

Trist's face lit up with joy, and Julien knew that the mention of Kassius had been enough. "In the name of Karaat and in honour of Kassius, I will help you take Sareen," he said. "If the price is right."

Julien smiled. "I will give you the throne."

Trist's face twisted. "Throne of what?"

"Sareen," Julien said.

"You don't want it for yourself?"

"I told you, I want Hest. Sareen is a stop along the way. I only hope I can make some kind of alliance with the Lord of Sareen," Julien said, and he could see in Trist's face that he liked the sound of *lord*.

"So how many folk do you have? Brooton Hester came with three thousand and just barely beat us," Trist said.

"I have five hundred."

"Ships?"

"People. I have three ships."

"*Three?*" Trist seemed to be second guessing himself. "It would seem to me that in fact I am the one with the army, and you would merely be the one helping me, not the other way around," Trist said.

"You can word it however you'd like. The outcome is the same. You, Lord of Sareen."

"You're a damn fool, you know that?"

Julien snickered. He had been mistaken for a fool his whole life, and it didn't bother him none at this point. It made it all the sweeter when he inevitably proved them wrong.

"Show me," Trist said.

Cleo produced a map from under the table and slammed it down. Trist pointed at Sareen. The map was finely detailed, and Julien could see the three layers of walls and all of the gates and streets and canals, and most importantly, he saw Red Sky Rock.

Julien repositioned the Oracle's golden ring on his finger and touched the keystone in his pocket. He could hear Karaat's followers singing, their midday prayer echoing in the streets. *It's time.* He didn't need logic when he had eldritch knowledge. *Knowledge is power.* He had seen the place where he was going to die, and it wasn't here or now. He had seen himself sitting the lion's chair in Hest, and he had heard the voice of the dragon husk calling to him from the dark of his dreams. *Say the Words, child. Say them. Dagdora. Make fire with your breath. Dagdora.* "Tell me, friends, do you believe in magics?" Julien said.

Cleo rubbed her hands together. Trist grinned. "We all lived through the wither year. I'd be as big a fool as you are if I didn't believe in magics."

"Good," Julien said, "let me teach you an old song of fire."

HOMECOMING

ALDRED BURST OUT OF a deep sleep and sat up in a cold sweat. *You've been gone too long. I've taken a lover.*

He was in the back of a cart, and the jostling made him feel sick. His head was booming, and the creaking wheels and thumping hooves made his eyes hurt. He felt a chill run down his spine and realized he was very cold. The pissing rain pelted the canvas over his head, and the air was damp and smelled of worms.

"You're alive..." said Dustey, with a strange bit of relief in his voice. Aldred coughed. Egan looked ecstatic.

"Shouldn't I be?" Aldred didn't want to know the answer. He'd dreamed some dark shit. *Of graveyards and thrones...*

"I'm not entirely sure if any of us should be," said the boneman. Aldred leaned his hand back into a pile of something white and coarse. He was in a salt merchant's cart. *What happened?* The last thing he remembered was standing around the fire with Brooton and his folk.

"You know what happened. You liked it," a voice came from inside Aldred.

"I'm afraid we've run out of water, sir," said Egan. Aldred looked through him, still confused. The patting of the rain fogged his mind even further.

The boneman sat next to him and had a strange smile on his face. "What did he say?" the boneman asked.

"What?"

"The messiah. You spoke to him. What did he say?" Aldred racked his thoughts. He couldn't recall what happened before... the sensation.

"Not much," Aldred said, rubbing at his temples and closed his eyes. "How long has it been?"

"Three days. You've been sleeping for two straight," Dustey said. "You missed Springtide."

Two straight days? "What?"

"You were chosen by Roqeda," Dustey said. "It was written in magics and sealed with blood. I saw it with my own eyes."

He seemed erratic, and Aldred didn't much feel like dealing with him. He felt like shit. *Four thousand ninety-four. Four, zero, nine, four.* Suddenly he felt safe—grounded.

"Surely he said something?" the boneman pressed. He held an old book in his hands. "I saw you kill him. The ritual was complete. You raised a field of the dead. They slaughtered everyone. Everyone. This book. The Words..."

"He did something to me," Aldred said. "It was like he was inside of me. My head. My thoughts."

Egan looked terrified.

Dustey grinned. "Yes. inside. Yes, okay." He sat back and pondered something. He mumbled to himself.

The cart bounced on, over the Hester Fields where the bounty of the country was held in soil. Aldred remembered the lush canopies of vine and tree and fruit-bearing plants of all kinds that filled the spring and summer and autumn months with sweet aromas and beautiful sights. There were none of those things now, even in the Rise of spring there was nothing. Just stunted sprouts in a grey field. *All the farmers are dead. The fyrd is fertilising the fields of Soren.*

Aldred bounced towards the towering city of Hest and Kelson's Keep looming behind it. It had been Aldred's home all of his life. The biggest and most fortified city in all of Ardura. Kelson built it as his home when he conquered these lands, and his family ruled there for eight hundred years until the Ayelish King Gavyn Hester, the Lion from Heart Hill, conquered the lands for his own two hundred years ago. He renamed the lands from Rhosanti, their Lovasi name, to the Hesterlands, and claimed independence from the heritage of Lovas. Other kings emerged, and the once great empire was divided into warring kingdoms.

The Hesters emulated Kelson in every way they could, with the exception of conquest. They were happy with their lands and made their focus on keeping them. *Until now. Until your dad John Hester got greedy when the world died one summer. He thought he could reach for that sun.* Phosphone wrote the fable of Eno, the eagle who claimed he would touch the sun to make up for the fact that he had smaller wings than the others. Eno flew so far and so high that the sun burned him up, and his ashes sprinkled back to the earth.

The Hesterlands are considered the most fertile and the wealthiest kingdom in all of Ardura, and have been the target of conquest since the Lion claimed the lands two hundred years ago. Esheri rulers from the south and Ayelish rulers from the northwest have had their eye on the prize of Kelson's Keep for centuries.

But the Hester dynasty had never fallen. Aldred looked at those far off walls and thought that that was probably the safest place to be in all of Ardura. Nobody gets in who isn't wanted. *You hate it here yet there is nowhere else for you to go...*

He had left in the Wayk of spring last year, more than one year ago, and could tell from the surrounding area that things had gotten as bad as he had feared. They were into spring now, and still the fields sat fallow and unsown.

The roads were still lined with kingsfolk, all of whom poked their dirty faces in the back of the salt truck to have a look at what was coming into their land. No one in the right mind would turn away a salt merchant in times like these. Aldred's countryfolk looked tired. Unkempt and haggard with dirty cheeks and noses. It had been a long winter, and it was shaping up to be an even longer spring.

None of the city folk seemed to recognize him, though, and he didn't really know how that made him feel. *They forgot you... or have you changed so much?* He looked at his hands, his skin was milk-white and he could see blue lines running through them. *What happened?*

"Who knows what Brooton told them," said Dustey, picking at the scab he had in place of his ear.

The massive granite walls of Hest grew larger as they approached.

"The king does not like stories that don't involve victory," said Aldred. "Maybe Brooton said nothing." Dustey laughed out loud.

"You really don't remember, do you?" The boneman gave Aldred a haunting look. "You don't see what we saw and say nothing, man. Bards make songs about stories like this."

Egan shivered visibly. "It was very memorable, sir," he said.

Aldred felt weighed down. Cold and heavy. He found holes in his mind where logic should be. *Angelico wrote nothing of this.* He spat. *Benecio and Phosphone wrote nothing...* Aldred had spent his life maintaining order. He always read one page at a time, left to right. There were no shortcuts.

"So, what then? What now, Boneman?" he asked. Dustey shook his head.

"I'm not the one who knows the answers. The messiah will guide you, I'd recommend you follow," he said. Aldred felt a curdle of anger in his belly. He started to remember the power. He remembered the feeling of life flowing through him. *Or was it death?*

"What is all this, Boneman!" Aldred pointed to his sickly face, rubbed at his sunken eyes. "Tell me what happened." He remembered Dustey speaking words from a book. He remembered a knife that glowed green with death. He remembered something inside of him. *Something powerful.*

The merchant driving the cart turned around curiously. The salt merchant and his rabble of three were more heavily armed than any one of Aldred's fyrd had been.

Dustey laughed, as if to ease the tension. "I know as much as you, sir Prince. We saw what you did. I must find the old books of Yehven down in the apothecary basements of the Keep to know more. What you should be worried about now is what your uncle has said to the king about you."

Aldred considered that. His father's Warlock, Adora, had devoted her time at Kelson's Keep to making sure that Aldred would stay hurt and pining. She was the first person to ever call him kinslayer after Aldred's mom died. Adora knew the death was an accident, but she still called him kinslayer as if he did it in cold blood, and she spread those rumours through the whole kingdom. To the world, Aldred was a kinslayer, a cold-blooded killer and warrior.

"Good for nothing but war, that one," the High Bishop Sparo had said during Aldred's trial. "This one isn't even worthy of death. Let him live with the pain of knowing what he's done."

They probably think you don't feel pain... Aldred clenched his fists. *You've been gone too long. I've taken a lover.* Aldred had felt more pain than was right. Far more of it than love or joy.

"*No more, child,*" the voice came from within Aldred's chest. "*No more,*"

"Don't betray me, Boneman," Aldred said.

"My name is Dustey."

The cart creaked to a halt at the front gates of Hest. Purple banners snapped and cracked in the wind, and the golden lion upon them seemed to roar with the fierceness of the element that brought them to life. The gates were held by a massive granite barbican with two round watchtowers on either side. The stone was veined with purple streaks. Kingsfolk in leather tunics draped in chainmail and holding bows eyed them from the turrets. A group of city guards, armed and armoured with the golden lion on their chestplates and a purple cloak over their shoulders, spread out around the cart. Each one of them was studying something different.

There were many laws on the Kingsroad. Cart axles had to be six feet apart, no more, no less, to ensure the ruts in the road stayed uniform. Cargo had to be taxed by weight. Merchants had to have proof of purchase. Any deviation would result in fine and confiscation. They didn't take kindly to theft on the Kingsroad. There was no rule against carrying passengers, but it was always a point of great interest for the guards to know who was coming in the front door. Aldred could tell he was recognised right away.

"It's the prince," the guard said, unbelieving. Aldred shied away.

The guard smacked the guard beside him who was inspecting the axles. "It's bloody Prince Aldred," he said. The other guard looked at Aldred with the same disbelief.

"Why are you transporting Prince Aldred?" one of the guards asked the merchant driver.

The merchant dangled a bag of coins in his fingers. "Paid me."

"You're thought dead, you know?" the guard told Aldred. "You look like shite."

"Your uncle has gone bloody mad after the battle of Soren River," said another guard. "Your father threw him in the dungeons."

"Dungeons?" Alreded said below his breath. He almost couldn't believe that Brooton was gone, just like that.

"It's that easy, child," the voice from within said. *"But you need to trust me."*

"It's Prince Aldred!" The rest of the people at the gates were starting to catch on. A small commotion followed, and Dustey nudged Aldred to get out of the cart. Cityfolk gathered in swarms to the front gates. Hoping for any news that wasn't bad news.

"He's alive!" someone proclaimed in a gloriously loud shout. "Prince Aldred lives! He's the Undead Prince!"

Aldred was overwhelmed by the swarm around him. Hands touching him, voices being thrown this way and that. He was like some kind of... *messiah*.

Faces. Hands. Voices. It was too much for him. Aldred put his hands to his ears and crouched over.

"Someone get this man a horse! The prince can't ride to the keep in the back of a bloody salt cart," Egan yelled. "And for the sake of Eralis, would someone please get him a damn waterskin."

"Go to court, child, tell your father you lived," Roqeda said.

Aldred smiled. He couldn't deny that he'd been longing to hear the voice again. Even if it *was* just to prove he hadn't gone mad. He mounted the magnificent white mustang that was provided for him and rode through the streets of Hest.

"The Undead Prince! He lives again!" a voice from the crowd shouted.

"Undead Prince!" the crowd repeated in staggered waves. They reached up and touched his legs and his horse, and they were crying and it really felt like they loved him.

A wry smile crept onto Aldred's face. It was jagged and wrong, and wasn't his, but he wore it just the same as he rode up towards Kelson's Keep through crowds of starving cityfolk that were chanting his name.

Aldred rode through the thick barbicans of the keep and through the courtyard. The magnificent Lion's Oak centred the courtyard and was a warm, bright green, and seeing it really made Aldred feel at home again. The chant from the city had carried its way up to the castle, and the people in the courtyard chanted "The Undead Prince!"

The towers and structures of the keep towered around him like a forest of granite nytewoods. Throne room and cathedral, feast hall and library all stood more than a hundred feet tall, their sloping slate roofs stretched towards the grey sky at impossible angles as if reaching for their place with the gods. Drum towers as wide and tall as nytewoods guarded each corner, and skinnier towers grew out of the sides of those like granite mushrooms.

The purple flags with the golden lion of Hester flapped in the wind, as if they were waving Aldred hello.

Aldred rode up the chipped granite staircase, worn in the middle from so many years of use, to the grand throne room. Massive marble statues of the Warlocks of the Ailaryan Order stood on either side of the steps. Adeqor was at the top wearing a brooding scowl. They were built by Kelson as a reminder that there were powers above himself—that even he was owned by someone.

Gavyn the Lion kept them as a reminder of how fragile Humans are. He said that if the Empire of Lovas hadn't tried to control nature, maybe they wouldn't have fallen. Aldred used to respect those statues of the Warlocks, but he looked at them now and scowled. He wondered if any of them had raised the dead. *Probably not.*

Long purple banners with the golden Lion of Hester blanketed either side of the entrance and covered up most of the imperial eagle of Lovas that was carved deep into the thick stones beneath. Guards swung the eight-foot thick Daggland-cedar doors open as Aldred approached.

The throne room had vaulted ceilings that stretched fifty feet above Aldred's head, painted with chipped and flaking murals of some battle that happened two thousand years ago, fought by folk in open-legged bronze and copper armour. Dusty, stained banners of places that no longer existed hung along the walls between stuffed lion's heads and a single dragon's head that, Aldred suspected from some reading, may actually be something called *wyrmgator,* from the Bone Islands. Dominating all, on the left wing of the hall, was the grand statue of Eralis, erected in pure blue diamond. On the right wing, in brilliant opposition to the blue-diamond Eralis, a statue of Bazal was erected in pure jet. It was tainted somehow, erroneous and twisted. It's like Bazal's statue was laced with the hate of a thousand years of anti-prayer.

The long, grand hall was occupied by its usual patrons, and they all swung to look at Aldred as he dismounted.

King John Hester, or as Aldred called him, Dad, sat in the Lion's Throne holding a goblet as smug as ever. His grey hair was still peppered with black, and his beard had been freshly trimmed. He wore slippers, and an opened silk purple robe revealed a muscular and grey-hairy chest.

Aldred's brother William was on his right in his armour and purple cloak, and Bishop Sparo on the left holding his ridiculous staff. The other members of the King's court stared just as glaringly. There was High Wise One, his cousin Gavyn Hester; his other cousin, the Commander of the City Watch, Rober Hester; the Master of Coin, Vinsent Carlin; and brooding over all, Adora, the Warlock. *The venomous woman still lurks...* She looked like she herself was a statue to rival Eralis and Bazal, carved of the most brilliant white marble with eyes of sparkling amethyst.

"You lived?" William scoffed, his brown eyes glaring. He wore full armour, his black hair and beard made him look like their father probably did twenty years ago. "You show up *here?*"

"I missed you, too, brother," said Aldred.

The king stood up and almost didn't find his legs. He had clearly had a few too many goblets full of red. "You live?" he said. "Brooton said that he saw you slain? He said you were dead." The king gritted his teeth.

Aldred noticed the hearth still blazing. *He re-lit it. Praise Eralis, he had to kneel and re-light the damned thing.* "I live, Father. Brooton rode away before the battle was finished."

"He's lying!" William blurted. "He was probably hiding the whole time. Or else he's a bloody traitor. Is it only you that returns?"

"Silence!" The king backhanded William and stumbled down the steps of the dais towards Aldred. Adora pierced him with her sharp eyes. She looked displeased, and so did his dad—like he did when Aldred was a boy. He stood up straight, puffing his chest. It was something that Brooton hated. He called him a peacock. Aldred always admired his dad's kingliness, if he couldn't admire a damn thing else.

"What we know is that you have conquered five major fortresses in Esher and one of them is in ashes. We know that as of last week, our fyrd was nearly three thousand strong, and as of today, still fewer than two hundred have returned. So, tell me, son, what happened? More importantly, answer me this. Who is going to sow our fields? You?" The king drank deeply of his goblet. Aldred knew better than to look his dad in the eye and say a single word that wasn't the truth.

"We were attacked in the night, unawares. All of our folk were slaughtered in their sleep. I don't know how many there were. They came and went so quickly. Brooton rode off before the battle had finished. He seemed spooked. He let us down. People were calling his name as they died. I will sow the fields myself if I have to, if that's what it takes," said Aldred.

The king glared at him with Hester blue eyes. "And why didn't they kill *you*?" he said.

"I didn't let them," Aldred said, still not lying.

William scoffed in disgust. "Lock him up for treason! He's obviously given the enemy information," he said. "He's allied with them."

The king threw his goblet at William, spilling red wine across the dais steps before covering William's pants. The goblet clinked on the stone floor behind the dais.

"You think I like putting my family in the cells?" he spit in William's direction, but it landed on the front of his own chin. He approached Aldred and grabbed the back of his neck with a sweaty palm. He looked like he had more to say, more to question. He was trying to find the words, then all of a sudden didn't care.

Then Bishop Sparo stood up, burned Aldred with his all-white eyes, and spoke in a drab voice. *For a man who can't see, he sees an awful lot.* "We need to hurry along the building of the Temple of Eralis," said Bishop Sparo. "Our faith must lie with God now."

"Triple the workforce. Double the taxes to pay for it," the king said.

The coinmaster Vinsent Carlin raised an eyebrow. "We're trying to take water from a stone here, Your Grace. The people have no money to pay taxes with. There are no crops, no farmers to do anything about that. We should be calling in our allies and pooling supplies. Spending what money we do have on grain from Neira."

"Get the coin," said the king. "Tax the whore house, the ale houses. Do what you must."

Vinsent nodded. "Okay, Your Grace."

"We've got bigger problems than coin," said the Bishop Sparo. "Our Grand General Brooton has gone mad. Rambling about unholy things such as the dead rising and nonsense of black magics and Blood Words. We have famine to worry about. Riots and rebellions to control. Heathen factions growing within these very walls. This city cannot last through the year without food reserves being restocked. We have floods in half the kingdom and drought in the other half. Krakens have returned and are clogging our trade routes through the Roaring Sea and across the Old Sea. Queen Ianna Alder will surely use this as an opportunity to try and seize more Hester land for Ayeland. That bastard Calen Alder was obsessed with it and his daughter is no better. They are looming in the north and west. We just lost nearly three thousand folk in the fields of Esher, and the towns we conquered there sit barren of food and full of fighting folk no use to us. The kinslayer must take Brooton's place of Grand General to ensure our armies keep moving to find *and* take any food that's out there. We're losing this kingdom, and not even Eralis can save us." Sparo scratched his head and took a deep breath. "It just ain't right." He made the sign of the star on his chest.

The king grimaced and let go of Aldred's neck. "You heard the bishop. You can come stand in here and take Brooton's place, or get the fuck out of my court."

Aldred took his place beside Adora. She had said not a word since Aldred had entered the court. The Warlock glared at him, and in her purple-white eyes, Aldred could see the truth of what she knew staring back at him. *Roqeda lives inside of you. He lives there and I see.*

A Broken Oath

S UNFELL CAME AND LIT the sky with a fool's fire of pink and purple and orange. James slid his fingers through Maggie's brown hair as she rested on his lap.

"I could feel the tree watching us while we made love," Maggie said. James didn't know how that made him feel. "It's alive, James. It lives with the souls of everything that has ever died." Maggie waved her arms as she spoke, as if weaving her very own existence with invisible string. "Our lives will never burn out, James, they only smoulder for a time before they ignite once again. We live in the *trees*—in the roots. I feel them, the others."

James could feel the others, too, but the dead, to him, only felt cold and lonely—like they were missing life. They never seemed overly content to be out of life. *They begged me to free them. The lingering was torture. They were only smouldering and needed to be ignited...*

"We should just stay here tonight," James said. "Away from everyone." The cold grass felt good on his bare skin. He and Maggie were in a small clearing in the brush of an arbor close by to the nihr'el. James could still hear the echoes of the Dagglandic songs in the dusk air as they made their camps and lit their fires.

"The other lords will be making plans for the morrow." Maggie sat up, and James devoured her with his eyes. Her bare skin, milk-white in the dusk light, was like a steaming meal if James was starved. "Our folk are tired of moving around. They want rest. I've heard many groups talking together about leaving to settle somewhere in the Fells. You can't miss another council with the rulers."

"What is this game we are playing, Mag?" James knew of the issues he faced, still, he only cared about Maggie. "Why do I still play at king? I have fallen so short of what my dad was. There isn't even a point. What is this for, if not for us to be together? We could leave. Like you said. We could go."

Maggie pushed herself close to him, and James pulled her in. "You play at king because for every person who wants to leave, there are five who look to you to save them. The Ayelish rulers are gathering under Ianna's red eagle at Mammoth's Head, they will sweep this entire country if we don't stand up to them. We need to protect our home, and most of these people still look to you and no one else." Maggie's head sank into her chest. "I have dreams, James. Dreams of death and fire and the sky falling, but you know what I see when the flames clear?" Maggie's eyes lit up with a magic James had only seen in his own dreams. "I see *you*. I see *us*. When the sky rises again and the fires burn out, you and me and our child are alive."

"I have the same dream, Maggie. Our *child*..."

"But it's false, James. I have other dreams, true dreams, and the nymphs of Nature that speak to me in them have no kind words to say about you or I. They say that what I see is only a riddle to be worked out. That the *you* I see in my dreams isn't you, but Mal Hallow. I'm not *me*, but a representation of Nature. Our child is our people. You see James, we are more than just the two of us. There is more to this than you or I know. Old Druid blood still runs in our veins. I feel like the Mal have a place in this, beside Her—Nature."

"I can't understand it, Maggie. At least with the wizard, we had answers..." *Mineera. Mineera was searching for—*

"The Hills," Maggie said. "The Hills hold answers to ancient questions."

"Huh?"

"Earth magics are strong there. They were *born* there," Maggie said. "They whisper to me, the spirits."

"It will take us the summer to get there. That's *if* we are able to take Rosen back." James didn't even want to mention how long it would take and how many wouldn't make it if the food ran out.

"What other choice do we have? Something is calling me there. Some force." Maggie brushed a strand of hair from her eyes.

"Halda, the Dagglander. She knew things... we could wait for her to return from Ryne and—"

"We need to do this ourselves. For the Hallow. For *us.*"

James couldn't unstick his eyes from Maggie. "Do you remember the first time we lay together?"

Maggie smiled. "It was raining and the grass was cold, green all around. The maple tree that shaded us still smelled of sweet sap. You had butter on your chin, and I wiped it off with my finger and licked it."

"That drove me bloody mad for you. It was shortly after Springtide." James breathed in the smell of Maggie and the grass and the budding trees. He appreciated nature more when he was with Maggie. "I had never felt love before you, Mag. Not like this. I thought I had, but you lit me on fire with it. I have been burning alive for eleven years with lust for you. Before the world died, you were all I could see. Now that it lives again, you are still the only thing I look for each morning. I have killed so many people, I see them in my dreams and they haunt me, Mag, and so do you. You tell me it's bigger than just you and me, but I am incapable of looking past you. I have lost you once and I won't lose you again. I killed my own family, Maggie. The monster ate them as it ate so many others. But you tame that thing inside of me. I just want it to end. I want the memories I have to be grown over by new ones. If leading our people to the Hills is the only way to make that happen, I will do whatever it takes. I will fight with everything I have to give our people peace if it means I get a single moment of it with you."

Maggie's eyes were alive with passion, and when she kissed James, he could feel her soul touching his—stroking it and whispering *"I feel you—I know who you are."*

"I'd kill the whole world for you, James." Maggie's breath was hot in his ear as she whispered to him. She kissed his neck, his chest. "I'd kill them all so you and I can live."

Together, James and Maggie dressed and went to council with the rulers of the Hallow as the moon rose fat and yellow in the purple sky above.

"**W**E WILL NOT SPILL blood beneath this tree." James jabbed his finger towards Eridan.

Eridan waved his hands defensively. "It's what the Daggs want, not me. They're getting restless—they say they need blood to calm the screaming of their Dead God. These fuckers are gnarly when they're restless."

"We will burn their sacrifices on a pyre like the Mal of Old and the Feldarra have done beneath this tree since its existence. Oak and thorn and ash," Maggie said. Most went silent when Maggie spoke. James figured that none were quite sure what she really was—whether she was Human or God—and neither was he. *She is life and you are death.*

Finally, Eridan spoke. "Alive."

"What?" Brigid coughed. Ruwen's eyes flicked open like she'd been stabbed.

"Surely you don't mean the sacrifices?" James said.

Eridan's eyes were the colour of the sea when it's angry. "This is what they will want. I'm trying to save us from the Crow's talons. Death is at our feet, and we may step in it if we're not careful. The Daggs could revolt and kill us all in an instant if we don't keep them happy."

James ground his teeth. He knew Eridan was right and it made him sick. *You did this. You brought these brutes from another world to your ancestors' most sacred place.*

"If we spill blood beneath this tree, we are no different than the damned Ayelish," Brinley said.

"Those who do are thrice cursed," Aione said.

"It's been told in the cycles, since the beginning of time." Brigid seemingly couldn't let her sister get in a word without having her own opinion heard.

"Look at what happened to Calen Alder," Sessely said. James didn't need reminding of what happened to Calen Alder.

By the nihr'el, great plumes of grey-black smoke rose up to the sky from fires thrice as tall as James. The pounding of the Dagglanders' deep singing voices echoed across the crumbled village and thumped in James's ears. "If we challenge their sacrifice and they turn to fight us, all of Mal Hallow would be extinguished in one night of slaughter. Claydon is the only ruler of old blood not here, and I don't think it would be long before he bends his knee to these folks."

"You mean to go through with this?" Brinley spat.

"What other choice do we have?" James spouted. "Let's save our fighting for the folk who took what's ours, not those trying to help us get it back."

"There are traditions, ancient oaths, and curses," Brigid said. "You don't understand, James, spilling blood in sacrifice beneath the nihr'el would mean death for all of us. The gods and spirits would curse our souls."

James shivered at the word "souls". He had met the gods, and he agreed that they seemed pretty judgy. *The Maw would mock you forever.*

"We're going to have to start new traditions if we mean to live out another year," Maggie spoke softly but her words stabbed like knives. "I've heard these Dagglanders at prayer and I've felt their souls. They are fed by a different fuel than you or I. If we went against them, we would be extinguished. The Hallow would die."

"By the gods." Brinley threw his arms up. To his heart, Sessely, he said, "They mean to go through with this."

Eridan laughed. "It won't be so bad, old dragon slayer. Not half as bad as seeing my dad strung up in Foulds, eh? What a treat that is to remember every evening." Eridan walked towards the nihr'el and the Daggs. "I'll tell our new friends here there will be no objections to their blood sacrifice. Oh, and I'm going to get bloody hammered with them, too."

Brinley scratched his scarred eye and scowled. "You've bloody cursed us all, King Reaper. The blood of these people is on your hands."

"And who made Eridan the middle man between us and the Daggs?" Sessely asked. She wore a glare that could cut steel. James wondered the same thing. No one answered her.

When the rulers had parted and dissolved into the crowd, James and Maggie went back to their own place to be alone.

"Don't listen to them, James. You're keeping us all alive," Maggie said.

These are the decisions a king makes—the ones no one else cares to. "My dad would have done better."

Maggie smiled. "Aye, but you forget he's dead. He may have done better but he was older. You have time to get there. Keep working through this. For *us*."

James didn't say anything but just enjoyed the feel of Maggie by his side. Their footsteps cracked and snapped through the arbor as they sauntered back to the ring of grass they had lay in just hours before.

"It remembers us, James, the grass," Maggie whispered, and James closed his eyes and let her voice fill his mind with its sweet song. "I love to lie with you beneath the stars, James. Our child will be born beneath them one day, I know it." Maggie touched her belly and smiled.

"Do you really think the sky will fall?" James brushed Maggie's hair with his cold hands. The dead hummed songs from the cycles in the arbor, and Maggie closed her eyes as if the ghosts' song was a phantom lullaby.

"I know it." Maggie's eyes opened in an explosion of colour. *The earth and the sky. Green and blue.* "I have dreams, James. Dreams where I'm told things, taught things."

"By who?"

"Dream nymphs. Abori, they call themselves. *Na'reen* comes most often. They visit me—since the Mother..."

"They told you the sky would fall?"

Maggie trembled. She leaned in and touched her lips to his ear. "They told me it would fall." Maggie put her hand on James's. "But I think Na'reen means for *me* to stop it."

Maggie nestled her head into James's chest and he held her there, saying nothing. *Tell her about the voices you hear. Tell her about the Maw.* But James couldn't bear to say the name aloud.

"We'll stop it then," James said.

"In time," Maggie said. "You have a kingdom to lead to safety."

"Aye," James said. *And they don't want to follow me, and I don't know where to go.*

"There must be magics in the crickets' song that puts us to sleep," Maggie said, and James stroked her back and thought about how the end of the world lay wrapped in his arms.

When sleep took James that night, the Maw mocked him.

"I'm not done with you," it said. *"Kallahorn will swallow you."*

"Kallahorn is cursed." James tried to shout, but his voice was only a faint whisper in the presence of the barking Maw.

"Cursed by you. You're but an ilk of that crop. A shadow of what once was," the Maw growled. *"Darker than Druid, boychild. Darker than moonshadow."*

"What happened to, Hendurinn? Did you kill him too?"

The Outcast God's mouth gaped, foaming saliva dripped from yellow fangs, and its breath smelled like rotting flesh. *"You'll find out."*

"Then be done with me!" James tried to unbuckle *Essikah* and found that it wasn't there. Instead he held just a small twig from a nytewood.

"That's not your choice. The gods are dying, Reaper. You, and only you can speak to them now. You can stop this."

From behind the Maw, the Stag staggered forth, bleeding from the eyes. Its antlers were cracked and jagged, growing stunted black leaf buds.

"Stop what?" James screamed.

The Stag, eyes frothing blood, opened its mouth to speak, and from its rotten muzzle, roots dangled wormlike and dripped black mud. *" Not what, Reaper, who..."*

James shot awake, coughing and drenched in sweat. He thought of Adeqor, his bare feet slapping the loam of the forest floor. He smelled the bodies melting and saw Adeqor's eyes burning with passion.

Maggie was shaking him. "Hurry. They're leaving."

James and Maggie fell in with the other rulers. Brinley, Sessely, and their daughters refused to even look at James. *The sacrifice must have gone over last night.* James figured if it hadn't, either Toren would be fighting him or Brinley would be talking to him.

"You've cursed us, Reaper," Ruwen spat the words. Black bags hung beneath her eyes like puffy shadows. James opened his mouth to speak but the She-Bear had already turned her back on him.

The boat ride across the Lake of Pool seemed longer going back than it did coming. Toren droned on about how he thought he would have seen more of the El'vie bathing in the lake like in the sagas and was disappointed he didn't get to kill one. Brigid explained that many of the El'vie abandoned Pool and went north into the rivers for the winter, and that some may not have made it back, or something else kept them from getting here, or they were just simply hiding.

Toren's rakkarren roared at the sky and sang songs, trading verses with one another so that all of their voices could be heard by the Dead God in solitary.

"What have I done, Maggie?" James murmured.

Maggie kissed his forehead. "You've won us an army of Daggs to take Rosen," she said. "From Rosen we might be able to hold the Ayelish again. It is our only chance."

"I thought the clans would still be there." James had hoped to find people he understood. *People like Wulfee, and Pike, and Gen...*

"They weren't, and so we carry on," Maggie said.

As they approached the mainland shore, James saw folk scrambling and carrying on about something. "What is going on?"

Maggie shrugged. When the boat was close enough that James could hear Brinley's screams, he started to make it out.

"By the gods," James said.

"What?" Maggie grabbed his arm.

"Claydon is gone."

Before his boat had even hit land, James jumped into the shallows and traipsed ankle-deep through the water to dry land.

Brinley was burning him with his eyes. The dragon slayer held a thick finger up to James accusingly. "You," he said. "You've cursed us." Sessely held Brinley's arm down.

"Where did he go?" James looked to the Hallowfolk, and they all ducked their heads. "Where did he go!" Spittle flew from James's mouth as he shouted.

"To Kallahorn." Eridan came up from behind James. "Where do you think?"

"He took three hundred folk and three quarters of the Dagglanders' food stores," Logan of Wick said. Logan was a big, red-bearded warrior who James had always respected.

"Erik and his ilk of Smokestone were supposed to be protecting it!" Toren was shirtless and had drawn his axe. "He went with them? I'll gut the fat bastard."

"They all went with Claydon," a woman came forward with a cloak of green stitched with a grey mammoth. "He promised them rulerships and blood. He convinced them there was a great wealth on that isle that the lot of you went to get without them."

"James," Maggie called to him, but he was already on his way to mount.

Toren and a few hundred Dagglanders took to mount as well, and soon James was leading them toward the Northroad. There were only two paths through from Pool capable of supporting the supply carts and baggage wayns that Claydon stole, and both led to the Northroad. James knew that if he didn't guess correctly on which way Claydon took, he could find Claydon further up the Northroad. *He thinks you are weak—that this cause is lost.* The thundering of their horses' hooves shook the ground as James led Toren and a wild group of Dagglandic warriors up and down the hills of the Fells. *How many are behind me? Three hundred? Five?*

It was only an hour of riding before James saw the bloated train of Claydon Coldfoot. He had raised his mammoth banners. James had bet that the bastard would take the more difficult path, thinking if anyone followed him, they would take the easy way. *Nothing about you is easy, Claydon.*

Claydon's train scrambled into a hundred little colonies as soon as James, Toren, and the Dagglandic host became visible upon the hillock overlooking the moors. It was clear they thought they would have more time to escape.

James pulled *Essikah,* and the full weight of it was enough to skew Bren to one side while charging. When James and Toren smashed into Claydon's host, the people of Tusk crumbled beneath James and his Dagglandic allies like flowers beneath boots.

James rode Bren up and down the flattened bodies, slicing down any who tried to fight against him. He dismounted and fought beside the Daggs like the Mal of Old. *Like Hendurinn and Gared and Ryatt.*

"Stop this!" James pleaded with the warriors, scanning the field for Claydon so he could tell him to call this off. "We are all folk of the Hallow, why are you fighting me?" James screamed violently, his soul on fire for having to slaughter his own. "Why!" he pleaded as folk tried to kill him, and he cut them down.

When James found Claydon, he was cowering behind a dying horse, the animal's chest rising and falling rapidly as it struggled to breathe. James walked towards him slowly. "You're a fucking beast of a thing, Claydon, to turn our own against each other. A fucking animal."

"Come on, Culdaine, this is ridiculous." Claydon stood and held his hands together in a begging motion. "Someone has to rule Kallahorn. We can't just *let* the Ayelish or these Daggs take it, that is an atrocity. Kallahorn is the crown jewel of the Fells."

"Kallahorn is cursed." James held *Essikah* in both hands and longed for the dead to ease the weight of it. "Mal Hallow is our home. We needed to stay together, you bastard. We can't win it back without all of us. If one of us thinks to be better than the other, our country will crumble beneath the weight of that person."

Claydon reached for an axe that was on the ground in front of him, and James sliced his hands off.

"Ahh!" Claydon held bloody limbs up in the air and glared at them.

"Where are your sons?" James held the blade of *Essikah* to Claydon's neck.

"You think I'd tell *you?*" Claydon spat, and James cut his head off at the neck. Blood squirted from Claydon's neck hole, and the head made a hollow thump when it landed, and then bounced a few times as it rolled away. When James picked it up, Claydon's bloody face was crusted with dirt and loam, and his hair was sticky and red.

Blood still dripped from Claydon's head as James tied it to his saddle. Bren nayed as if to say he disapproved of adorning heads, but James just rubbed the horse's chin and whispered softly in her ear, *"It's okay, boy,"* and the horse calmed.

"You done here?" Toren was shirtless and bloody, holding an axe in each hand. His blond hair was tied in a knot on top of his head and it, too, was blood-drenched.

"Claydon's sons and Rakkar Erik of Smokestone retreated to Kalla-horn," James said. "I'm sure of it."

"Let them go. I'll get that bastard Erik. I'll get him. He broke this Dag-glandic alliance, and I'm worried it's going to be hard to keep it together now. Especially with Halda done run off."

James didn't have the time or resources to chase Aron and Macts, and he especially didn't have the energy to fight a Dagglandic rakkar along with them. He needed to keep the bull moose flying. "Aye." James mounted Bren. "Let them keep Kallahorn warm."

"We're going to stay a bit." Toren wiped his nose with his forearm. Behind him, Daggs were slinging the dead up in trees by their ankles and slitting their throats so the blood rained down upon the soil. "Sacrifice."

"Aye," James said as he rode away. *By the gods...* "I'll send more folk back for the food wayns."

"Now you're starting to sound like a king, Reaper. We'll take many heads on our way to Rosen with you." Toren's voice had never sounded so good to James.

A Whisper from Another Life

"**I**'M TELLING YOU, THAT'S moose shite," Rat explained, pointing at a pile of dung.

"Moose don't come this deep into the mountains, Rat, it can't be," said Nettle.

"Well, I'm telling you it is," Rat insisted. "I know my shite."

Etta had seen enough shite to know that Rat had got it right. "What would drive it into the mountain valleys?" Etta looked around at the barren landscape for answers.

"There is no food left. Even the foraging animals can't find it. So many plants died last year and so few have grown back this spring," Annie said.

"That bastard, Calen Alder," Fiora muttered. "Never have I been more glad that a person is dead. Never did a bastard deserve it more."

Etta had heard all sorts of stories of Calen Alder. She hated the bastard herself just for getting Braden caught up in his shite. But any bloke who thinks they're bigger than the world is one Etta would like to see fall. There had been rumours about Calen Alder carried by some of the late comers to the si'otha, Cullen being one of them. "I heard it that Alder carved himself with Blood Words," Etta said.

Fiora sighed. "Aye," she said, "we heard the same shite." Etta knew the story of the Blood Words from the cycles. The old Dagglandic Empire carved themselves with Words of magics and turned berserk to defend their islands against Kelson and the Lovasi. It worked to help them defeat the Lovasi invasion. They are the only country that wasn't conquered—the only country with pure blood back to the start of time—but they ended up causing the entire Dagglandic Empire to go mad and kill themselves with dark civil wars that lasted ninety-nine years—thrice times thirty-three.

Fiora and Calum led the group through a valley of wildflowers. Etta's feet glided through blue and pink and yellow and orange, and still it all seemed dull and grey to her. The elders walked behind with grey hoods up and said nothing. Annie walked with them, as if absorbing knowledge through their very presence. Tara and Swey walked with Etta. The boy, even with his mother here, didn't want to be far from Etta.

"Why did Alder do this?" Tara asked. "All we wanted to know was why. None of it makes sense."

"Aye," said Rat, "none of it makes sense. No truer words have ever been spoken."

"It makes sense to those who have the sense to know it," Fiora said.

"Ah!" Annie proclaimed. "Your dad always said that. The sweetheart, I miss him."

"Aye," said Fiora. "I miss him, too, Ma. And he knew Alder would attack Kallahorn. There is a level between us and gods, and on that level, the Warlocks play games invisible to our eyes. Spirits, and souls, and magics make the world go round, and those who understand those things can shape the world to their liking. Bazal will explain this to you in a language that makes sense to your ears when Baerd takes us to him. But the reason

Calen Alder attacked Kallahorn is because the world is going to end, and he wanted his family to survive that."

"End?" Swey said, gripping Etta's hand along with his mom's.

"But the fires burn again. It's raining," Etta said. "The world is not ending anymore."

Annie chuckled.

"Oh, the soup's not even begun to boil," Nettle said, waving her ladle as if she'd fight off the boil with it.

"The gods are dying, Etta," Fiora said bluntly. "All but one, Karaat, and He is growing stronger every day."

Etta wanted to argue, but she had felt the absence of the gods and couldn't help but believe it. *The gods have left you to rot on this earth alone for what you've done. You'll never see the cloud halls. You'll linger.* "Why? Why kill the elements? Why Kallahorn?" Etta asked.

"These are things we do not know. These are questions for Bazal. But first we must regroup with Baerd. Come," said Fiora, and Etta followed.

For hours, they walked through spring-bloated woods, stiff with growth, and over crags and glens, wide with girth, and Fiora led them deftly to a small river that cut through a sprightly valley in the mountain. Through the mountain pass, they came to a long lake that reflected the sun.

"Just there, beyond that crag," Fiora said. "Baerd may be out hunting. I don't hear the dogs."

Etta hated having dogs around. They reminded her of Sweyne. "Probably for the best," she said. "I'm damned hungry." *By the gods, Young Courtney was always hungry... another you couldn't save...* "Is Baerd here alone?"

"No, not alone," said Fiora.

"He and Owyn came down from the si'darra last spring to help Fiora and me escape from Kallahorn," Annie said. "They came with others—a whole crew. Cook, smith, Ranger. And more and more keep coming. They stayed to wait. They said Bazal sent them."

"Right." Etta liked this less and less.

The camp was nestled at the bottom of a grassy hill framed by the mountains. A stream gurgled down the hill and through the camp, and made its way through the crags and valleys of the mountains out to the Fell River. A long mudhall roofed with moldy thatch bellowed with woodsmoke and sat squat and lonely beneath the hill. Twenty or thirty people sat out front or stood doing various tasks. Etta counted three sheep in a small pen beside the mud hut, and a drying rack beside a pile of cut logs held many fish. A forge throbbed redness into the grey sky from the west corner of the camp, where someone hammered iron on an anvil. And a dog pen was erected there beside the forge. Etta knew the dogs liked to be near the forge for its warmth. Sweyne always had them cooped up there.

"It's not much, but it's where we spent most of this past year," said Fiora. "I started to think Bazal would never summon the Feldarra to come. It was a long wait here."

"He summoned all Feldarra?" Etta seemed surprised. She thought of Pike.

"Aye," said Fiora, "through dreams—chimeric earth magics. I had the dreams myself... we saw the Feldarra marching from Pool months ago as soon as the snow broke."

You're not Feldarra anymore. That was Wulfee. That was... Etta was having a hard time forgetting herself. The dog that was Wulfee refused to lie down inside of her. *Because you can't hide from this. You can't hide from what you've done. One day you will have to face it.*

"At Bazal's camp, they work magics in their forges and make steel that won't break," said Rat, chin up. "They make green fire, and they make balls of mud filled with black powder that burst open walls when they are lit." Rat waved his arms around, illustrating what the weapons would do.

"And at this camp," Nettle said, "we work pots of stew and soup. We work a spit. And we chop wood."

"And we wait," said Owyn in a sombre voice. His eyes were grey-clouded and sunken. *This one is tired. This one doesn't trust you—not yet.*

"Wait for what?" Etta hated prophecy.

"For you…" Annie said in a soft voice.

A chill ran up Etta's spine and all through her body. *For fuck…*

"The great battle is coming," chomped Rat.

"Aye," said Fiora. "It is. And we'll be ready for it."

"Baerd is out hunting. He should be back before moonfall. He rarely stays out all night," one of the folk standing said.

"Not like Fiora," Annie chided.

Fiora scoffed. "I run with the wolves at night. It's a freedom you'll never know."

"Ah, that's where you're wrong my dear, because each night I dream with the birds and the dolphins and the horses. Where you can only run, I fly, swim, and run faster and longer and with more grace," Annie said.

Etta noted many weapons on a rack. Maces, and axes, and cudgels, and spears and dozens of shields with the symbol of the nihr'el carved into them. All pieces she knew well and knew how to use. All pieces she would never touch again. She looked at her hands. *These hands killed your son…* A pain fired off in her chest but it was good pain. *Deserved pain.* She needed to face the truth. She couldn't hide inside of Etta forever. Wulfee was in there somewhere, cowering, waiting to come out, but Etta would need to coax her. She studied her hands again. *These hands killed your son…*

Tara and Sweyne were sitting together eating soup from shallow wooden bowls. Etta went and sat with them, and Nettle brought her a bowl of soup.

"Fresh garlic in there. That'll wash out all the bad in you," Nettle said.

"What is happening here, Etta?" Tara asked. "Are we welcome to stay?"

Etta looked at Annie, who must have been listening, and nodded as if to say yes. Etta noticed that Annie seemed to hear most things that were said. *She can't see, but she knows more than those who can.* "We're going north. To join these si'darra," Etta said.

"It's not far from here," said Fiora. "Two days of riding at most. Our garrons are well rested. I can't believe I'm finally going back, and with you, the person we set out for more than a year ago."

Etta still couldn't believe these people were following her all this time. It irked her to no end. "You just followed me all this time and watched me suffer? You just stalked me like goddamned prey?"

Fiora tilted her head as if she wasn't expecting Etta to react that way. "You wouldn't have come if we had tried to take you earlier. You would have attacked us and you know it. Baerd told us to wait until—"

"Until everyone I loved died around me? Until I was alone and helpless?" Etta wanted to scream. *You waited until I was weak. Until I was dead inside.* "Baerd, Baerd, Baerd. *Fuck* Baerd. Baerd's a cunt."

"Etta," Annie said. "Baerd told us to wait until he had answers to the questions you would ask. He knew you'd be stubborn."

"Stubborn?" Etta took a step forward. *Wulfee would have shown you stubbornness with an axe to your face.*

"He wanted to make sure," Annie continued. "All this time we have been deciphering some ancient mystery. It's only now Baerd understands what Bazal is trying to tell him. It's only now we are ready to strike. And until we were ready, we couldn't approach you. Fiora kept a close eye on you with her wolf and even helped you a few times when you were in danger."

Etta pointed to Tara and Sweyne and to Calum and Cullen. "We are looking for peace. My days of fighting are over. We've come this far with you because we had no choice. But I won't fight."

Annie held out her hand. "Etta—"

"I won't fight."

"You have to understand, Etta," Annie said, "this isn't about fighting for your country or as part of your oaths to the Feldara. This is about—"

"I have no oaths! My oaths are piss in the wind, and I'm telling you I won't fight. Don't tell me to understand. You'll *never* understand me or what I've been through. Don't for a second think you or this fucking Baerd cunt can ever tell me to understand. You don't think I fucking understand?"

Annie pursed her lips. Fiora was silent.

Then the arbor lit up with war cries.

"By the gods." Owyn grabbed his sword—rubied at the hilt. "They followed us."

"Oh, no. Please, no." Tara sighed, grabbed Swey, and wrapped him in her arms. "Crow, please don't take my baby. Please don't take my baby."

"Let me fight, Mom!" Swey shook loose and pulled out his axe.

"Sweyne!" Tara yelped.

The war cries from the arbor were louder, closer.

Etta knew from the wickedness that it was the Demhoni. *Fungal dark—mycelium minds.*

Baerd's folk cleared the weapons rack and began to scream their own cries. They all took up their shields, carved with the tree of Feldarra, and pounded their weapons on them and clanked them together.

"Wall!" Owyn shouted. "Wall!" And they formed up and knelt down, and their shields made a wall. Owyn turned and pointed at Etta, his grey-clouded eyes lit with battle fire. "Behind!"

Etta grabbed Tara by an arm and dragged her, but she resisted. "No, please, no. Swey."

"Come on!" Etta screamed. "It is safest behind the shield wall." Etta gripped Tara's arm tighter and dragged harder, and finally Tara gave in and came. But Swey didn't move. "Swey!" Etta screamed, and the boy gritted his teeth. Etta picked him up as she had scooped up Braden and Tarek once and ran with him to the shield wall.

The boy resisted. "Let me fight!" he screamed. He twisted.

"I won't let you die while I hide," Etta said, and yanked Swey into Tara's arms.

The boy dropped his axe and started to cry. "You don't know me!" Swey said. "You know nothing of me! You think you do because you met my dad once." Swey picked up his axe again, moved back beside his mom. "I'm nothing like him. I *fight* for my family. I won't leave her! I won't let them take us!" The tears in Swey's eyes and the pain in his voice cut Etta worse than axes.

She was short of breath. The thought of Braden was too much for her right now. *Too much.* Horns were bellowing in her head. *Who's blowing them? No one? You're mad.* "I won't let you die here," Etta said. It was all she had.

Etta inspected the arbor and saw folk in fresh cut furs and leather freshly boiled, and they no longer wore chainmail or waved the banner of the red eagle for Ayeland. These folk had become truly wild in their endeavours. They held sticks crowned with human skulls and each paraded one of those macabre idols as they burst through the arbor towards Etta.

Etta collapsed behind the shield wall. Tara, Swey, the two elders, and Annie Florhen crouched there with them. The elders held cudgels in their pale, bony hands. Etta counted at least twenty folk in the shield wall as she lay in the dirt. She watched Swey as he and Tara held each other and cried. Tara whispered things to him, and they smiled and laughed a bit through their tears every once and awhile. The ground was shaking.

"By the gods," Etta heard Calum say, and a few others echoed his curse. Etta prayed to the Bluebirds for luck. She promised the Crow a hearty sacrifice if she would keep death away for one more day. *At least for the boy.*

She hated being helpless. *Wulfee wasn't helpless. No, but Wulfee was a murderer. A freak.* Etta gazed at the weapons rack and regretted not taking an axe just for good measure. She always used to prefer an axe for it could slice through mail with ease. To break mail with a sword, she would need to lunge, and she fucking hated lunging. *Wulfee loved weapons. A grim thing, she was.*

"Tighten up, you buggers, here they are!" Owyn shouted, and the wild-folk were running and shouting mad chants, and the ground shook. The shield wall tightened up, shield clanking on shield, and the next second, there was a blinding crash as iron thumped into wood. And then iron on i ron.

"Tighten up you buggers!" Owyn hollered.

Death cries mingled with war cries as the shield wall broke, and the wildfolk surrounded them. Etta could see full well now that these were the same cannibals that attacked her si'otha. *The Demhoni...* their clothing was filthy now, they weren't even recognizable as Ayelish—half human. *The earth has reclaimed these...*

The elders were swinging their cudgels. Swey tried to run, but Etta grabbed his arm and wouldn't let him. He scowled at her.

Around Etta, folk screamed and cried, and in her head, the warhorns sounded. Bellowing out a rumbling echo that shook her skull. She put her hands over her ears and cowered on the ground and shook her head from side to side, but the horns wouldn't stop. She saw the Red Valley. She saw Kallahorn. She saw Braden—always Braden. She saw his dead face and she screamed, "It wasn't me!" She wasn't sure if it was out loud or in her head. "It was Wulfee!" And around her, iron struck iron and wood and flesh, and all broke beneath it. *Nononononono.* She saw Braden's dead face. *Twisted jowl, bleeding, flesh slit like leather, couldn't hold it together, couldn't save—his face, wanted to kill you, hated you, Hell.*

Then Etta was holding young Braden. He felt so real in her arms that she had to look at his face, and when she did, she realized it was Swey that she was holding, and that she was going mad. "I'm mad," she said, and Tara was crying and Swey was screaming. The boy wiggled free. The boy swung his axe at a fiend that tried to kill him. He struck flesh. Twice, thrice. Bloody whips flew from his axe blade.

Etta glared at a cudgel that lay on the mud in front of her. She glared at the elder dead beside it. Then saw a wild woman glaring at her. The Demhoni who was once Ayelish licked her chapped lips and danced her fingers around her axe hilt, then ran at Etta.

Swey was screaming at her to pick up the cudgel, and Etta glared at it like it was the worst kind of poison, and Tara screamed, and someone died and thumped down beside Etta, which made her jump away. The horns bellowed. Piercing, piercing, walloping ear drums.

She looked up to see the wild woman still running at her. She could smell the stench of her and saw the hungry look in her eye, and Etta smiled. *I'll linger with Tulu if I have to. Crow, save the boy, please save the boy.*

Then an axe exploded into the wild woman's cheek, and she fell over, hard and dead. Etta saw the person who threw the axe turning away to fight. She thought it was Sweyne the senior, but she was half-mad at the moment so instead she lay in the mud.

"He's back." Tara was cowering beside her. "Thank the gods he's back."

"Are we winning?" Etta gasped, her head was ringing with war horns and thumping like a drum.

"Aye," said little Swey, breathing heavily, smiling, blood-soaked. "We are now."

Around her, dogs howled and barked madly. Ripping, tearing, bloody jaws and teeth. Wicked howls.

Etta heard the dying folk whispering things that weren't quite words. Her dad had called that the song of the sleepers, and so that's still how she heard it—as a lullaby. Etta closed her eyes and imagined a time when she knew who she was and smiled. *Wulfee used to smile. She used to love. So much love it burst her heart open.*

Soon Tara was shaking her, and Swey was jumping up and down. "It's over, Etta. We're okay."

"It was a small group that attacked—they thought they could take us." Owyn looked like a pale bloody ghost. "Bastards thought wrong."

Etta stood and looked around at the dead. Cullen and Calum still lived and that made her happy. "Etta, eh?" A man parted the crowd. His voice was like ice, and it immediately silenced the war horns in her head. She looked at him and blinked.

The man stuck his hand out. "Etta, I'm Baerd. We knew each other by different names, once."

Etta stared at the man, and when a fire ignited inside her, she knew who he was. She didn't know if she should scream, or cry, or bite, or find an axe to sink into this man's head.

Baerd laughed awkwardly with his hand still outstretched. Around them, people were dead and dying. They had just been attacked by a horde of Demhoni. Etta felt half-mad. *You could be dreaming this. It could not be him, just as Braden was not really him...*

"Can I start by saying I'm sorry?" Baerd's voice sank into Etta's skin like oil. It left her feeling slimy.

She gritted her teeth. "You don't get to be sorry," she choked out. Her chest felt like it would tear open if she moved too suddenly.

Baerd put his outstretched hand to the back of his head.

Etta wanted to spit in his face.

It was Sweyne.

A RIVERSIDE DINNER

T HE ROCKY, BARREN COASTS of the Bay of Bones slowly faded into sandy beaches sloping into turquoise waters. The skinny cypress and tufts of brown thistle had turned into lemon trees and loquats, eucalyptus and suber. The coast brimmed in green and yellow and brown and orange, and it smelled like paradise. *Like home.* Julien breathed it in. Dolphins swam and played and laughed in the blue-green waters around *Saltspray* while packs of ibex watched from the shores.

"The Esheri Rush is moving white and hard this summer," Hild said. "This will be a pleasure to sail." The old sailor seemed to appreciate a challenge. She gripped the bulwarks and breathed in the sea, and Julien smiled at how happy she seemed. *One day, when I sit the throne in Hest and folk no longer laugh but bow to my name, I'll be that happy.*

After three weeks at sea, Julien and his rabble had actually started to find their sea legs. Ashan was taking a turn at the masthead, which he had absolutely refused to do when they first boarded. "Only a bloody fool would climb a thing that high," he had said. And now he was playing the fool and calling out when he saw rocks. Rolan had learned to dead reckon and read the stars from Hild, and Julien had asked her to teach him, too.

"*I can teach ye, but it won't be easy,*" Hild had said, and she was right. It wasn't easy, but Julien was starting to get the hang of it. He knew the wolf star, which was the northernmost star in the sky and didn't move. He knew how to trace the different constellations in his mind and learn their relative positions to each other. He knew all the stars and what they were called, he knew how to find the bouncing bear formation and Kassius's bow. He knew of the boar and the snake, the bearded tree, Karaat's eye, and the Giy'er's belt.

Every night Julien worked at it, and every day he recited the Words he had memorised from Libby's books in Odessa. "Dagdora," he said. *Fire.* His grandfather had shown him the Word at a young age, and his father had continued to show him. One time Julien had watched as his father used the Word while removing a knife from his mother's belly when his baby sister was born. The Word sealed the wound with fire. In an instant it was done. As soon as the Word had left his father's lips.

"*The Words of Karaat are not all bad, son, you see?*" his father had told him. "*Where the Warlocks went wrong was trying to use them to control everything. They wanted to control all of the elements and more. Draku only needed one Word. They only wanted mastery over one element, and that is why they never lost control of the magics.*"

Dagdora, Julien sang, and a small flame ignited in front of him, hanging in the air. The Words have to be sung in the exact right way, in the exact right note. The flame extinguished into a puff of smoke. *Karaat is getting stronger.* Julien almost couldn't believe it when he saw the flame appear for the first time a few weeks ago.

In Jakaray, he had heard that his deeds in Saltsan had started to spread. That folk had heard the Oracle was dead and that a prophet of Karaat had killed her. *His worship is growing, and His Words are gaining power.* When

Julien had whispered a Word and made fire dance in the sky, Trist and his rabble shook Julien's hand immediately. *I am Draku.*

Bootsteps behind him snapped Julien out of his deep thoughts. He recognized Rolan's heavy armoured boots immediately. "Rolan! One of my most mediocre friends," Julien said, though Rolan didn't smile.

"Don't underestimate this," Rolan said. "Sareen is heavily guarded, and King John gave the city and the castle of Red Sky Rock at its heart to Natt Floyd of Friars. I fought beside Natt in the Battle of Blackshire. He's one of the fiercest warriors in all of Ardura. The finest with a sword I've ever seen, and when it comes to leading folk, well, they listen to him. Let me tell you. Hell, I listened to him," Rolan said.

"I'll be sure to kill him first then," Julien said.

Rolan took off his helm and slammed it down on the planks of the deck. "Stop being a god-damned fool, guy! You'll never take that city. Not from Floyd. Not from the Hesters."

"This is not where I die, Rolan. I have seen my death, and yours, too." Julien lied, but Rolan was paying full attention now. "Karaat has spoken to me. He has told me that now is the time. I am Draku, Rolan, and I will bring peace to this dead world. I will resurrect it from the darkness and bring fire and light to those who lost their way. We cannot fail, Rolan, and I cannot die. Karaat has told me true."

"Praise Karaat," Rolan said. "You're—"

"Mad? I know," Julien said. "Though Angelico said one who is truly mad doesn't believe they are. So I can't be too far gone, not yet."

Hild shouted at the deckhands and Ashan shouted from the masthead, and the sailors all shouted at one another as *Saltspray* readied to make the turn into the Esheri Rush. They had faced harsh weather and rains for most of the trip, and Hild wanted to hurry up and get into the Rush before they were hit with a storm coming off the Bone Islands or Sothurra.

As they sailed up the Esheri, the winds were flat and calm, and Hild ordered the oarsfolk to start rowing. Trist was nowhere to be seen, and that was perfect—just as planned. Hild sailed directly up the gullet of the Esheri, and soon, Ashan was shouting down from the masthead that there was another ship approaching.

"It's Natt Floyd," said Rolan, and made the sign of the eye on his chest.

Floyd's banner was a round, brown shield on a field of grey.

"Why the shield?" Julien said. "That looks like a northerner's shield."

"The House of Floyd originally comes from the north side of the Hesterlands. Up near the Gorge at Watchtower Keep. Their family fought with Gavyn the Lion when he came down and conquered Hest from the Lovasi. The Floyds were given Friars and have prospered ever since."

The ship approached, and Julien could see the hull of red cedar, and he could tell that that ship had sailed a long way to have been made of wood like that. It pulled up along *Saltspray* and Julien could see Hild and the captain talking, and then the two shook hands and the captain from the other ship threw a rope bridge across, which Hild caught and secured to the bulwark of *Saltspray*.

Then a man surfaced from below decks surrounded by armoured soldiers. The man wore a stiff leather jerkin and a grey cloak with a golden shield brooch fastened at his neck. His blonde hair was trim and short, almost as if to accentuate his stiff jaw. His face looked to be carved of stone.

Julien approached him as he would any commoner. "Welcome aboard, Lord Floyd, it's a fine afternoon!" Julien held his arms wide.

Lord Floyd's face held its stone demeanour. "Why are you here?"

"I thought you might invite me for dinner?" Julien said, but Lord Floyd didn't budge.

"You're lucky I didn't sink this ship and drown you in the Esheri," Lord Floyd said, "Tell me why you're sailing a ship full of sellswords up my river without a flag to show your allegiance?"

"My allegiance is only to Karaat, Lord. My folk are armed and trained, yes, but we only fight in the name of Karaat. I came to offer my services to you to act as a city guard of sorts."

Natt Floyd lifted an eyebrow, and that was enough to make Julien think he was getting somewhere.

"What makes you think I don't already have a city guard?"

"The fact that you personally sailed out here to greet us. I would never allow you to do that. This is the job of a good city guard, you see. And Lord, I'm the best there is."

"Who are you?" Lord Floyd said. "I've never seen you."

"Esterbraun. Julien Esterbraun."

"Esterbraun?" Lord Floyd let some poison drip into his words.

"My father was Damen and my grandfather was Elario. My mother was Iris, and she was the true master of all three of us. I had two brothers and a baby sister. Their names were Lucien, Darian, and Kalila, and they have all been killed by my enemy. We trace our blood back to Kassius the Deceiver."

Natt looked back to his guards and studied Julien. He looked to Rolan. "Does he always speak like this?"

Rolan shrugged. "I just met him."

"You say you want to come to dinner? Come, I have already been feasting upon the banks of the Esheri in celebration of my hard-earned victory while my folk are cleaning up the city. Eat with me, drink with me. Tell me a story that is sweet enough to convince me not to kill you and sink this ship. Then I'll bring you back here, and you can be on your merry way," Natt said. Julien realized he was trapped now. If he refused, Natt would kill him. And in truth, Julien had no good reason to be here other than to kill Natt, and Julien hadn't thought this through to the end. *But you've got time. Time is all you need. Trist will be here. He will.*

"I thought you'd never ask."

THE WIND WHISTLED THROUGH the great marble arches of Natt Floyd's newly acquired riverside palace. Julien was thankful for the wind because the whole place was filled with smoke. The palace was just down the river from Sareen, built in the old Yehvenki style, with a flat roof and pillars instead of walls. It was designed to keep cool on hot days and summer nights. The rulers of Old would have lounged inside while slaves and servants cooked for them outside and brought the food in for them. Julien even saw some of the old stone stoves as he was coming in. But House Floyd still observed some of the ways of the north, so Natt had ordered four massive bonfires be started in each of the palace's corners. Servants were turning spits of goat and cattle, and cooks were boiling water and cooking stews on the coals, and the smoke gathered at the flat ceiling and swamped the place.

"Come, sit." Natt brought Julien to a table of yew and they sat down, and soon Julien had a cup of sweet red wine in front of him. "Tell me, are you the biggest fool I've ever met in my life or do you have some plan here?"

"That would be very difficult to answer without comparing myself to the other fools you've met."

Natt pulled out a fillet knife and placed it on the table in front of him. "I left all of my patience on the battlefield."

Julien noted that there were at least three hundred soldiers here, and he didn't want to get himself killed. "What I told you was true. I came to fight for Karaat. For the memory of my people."

"Your people?" Natt asked.

"The Draku."

"You're bloody mad. The Hesters rule here now, and with them comes Eralis. We will burn the temples to Karaat in the coming months and kill all those who worship Him. Simple things that every ruler knows. But first things first." Natt held up his pewter goblet and tipped it down his throat. "Another," he barked out, "you want another?"

Julien downed the rest of his goblet and shrugged. "Why not!"

"Two more!" Natt yelled, and in a moment, Julien had a full glass of red wine. "Listen. I've had enough of killing for this year. It's time to spend the rest of summer and the harvest drunk off my arse and happy. Enjoying this." Natt spread his arms as if he was showing off a view, but the smoke was so thick in the palace that Julien couldn't see a lick of the sea or sky or even a single tree. "I'm going to take you back to your ship, and you're going to turn around and go somewhere else. You've amused me, and I think the world needs interesting people like you. Most fools are so dull, you see. Enjoy this meal, and then get the fuck out of my city."

Julien drank and looked through the smoke and hoped Trist didn't abandon him. He had never put so much faith into a sellsword, and he hated it. *This one was different though. This one had quality. And the look in his eyes when you spoke fire into existence spoke volumes.*

The meal was of the finest food the Esheri landscape had to offer. To start, Natt's servants brought steaming flatbreads of wheat, pastries filled with honey and creamed goat-cheese, porridge flavoured with dates, fermented yogurt, and cracked wheat, and an array of fine cheeses with creamy hummus. And soups of red lentil and chickpea stewed with garlic and olive oil and onions and cumin spice. Julien would have asked for another bowl of the soup if the servants hadn't appeared in the smoky, cavernous room carrying the main dishes on their shoulders. Pigeons stuffed with rice and cracked wheat, succulent goat stuffed with rice, nuts, dried apricot and dates, and a green, slimy stew in which the spoon was served standing straight up like a tree.

"What is this one?" Julien asked the servant who plopped it down.

"Molo, made of jute leaves and garlic, served with—"

"Yes, served with rice." Julien noticed that everything was served with rice, and he wasn't complaining. At Least it wasn't fish.

Finally, the Esheri served the spit-roast goat.

Julien used a piece of flatbread as a trencher and filled it with chunks of steaming goat from the spit and smothered it with drippings. When he was done with that, he even ate his bowl of green slime and couldn't believe how good it tasted.

"It will help with your indigestion, that," Natt said.

Julien laughed, then suddenly he realized that Natt had distracted him with food this whole time and they had hardly spoken two words to each other the entire meal. *Maybe it's for the best, you can't give anything away if you say nothing at all.*

When naught was left but grease on the table, the Esheri bards started to play their lutes and the smoke cleared, and finally Julien could see out into the hills. Many of the folk were good and drunk, and Julien knew that as long as Trist didn't abandon him, he would arrive at nightfall to this palace, so Julien had to act now. "Have you heard the stories of Letharr, the demon Draku, and his rabble, the Letharri?"

"Demon Draku?" Folk murmured and gathered round. There was nothing drunk folk liked more than a story, especially of a place they knew little of.

"The Letharri came in the night with a thousand flaming bats to kill unbelievers. Demons from Hell that were sent by Karaat to kill folk that dared question Him." More and more folk gathered round now, good and drunk, and ready for a story. Julien continued. "They say he couldn't die, Letharr, that he walked right up to the gates of Sareen and unlocked them with his bare hands and walked in to capture it back from the Warlocks, who stole it from him."

"He had the eye of Karaat on his chest!" Natt joined in on the fun. "It glowed red, they say." He narrowed his eyes at Julien, probing. *Are you testing me, Esterbraun?* Natt seemed to say with his glare. "And what other stories have you got, Esterbraun?"

Julien smiled. He told stories of Yesham and of Torold the Fine. He told the story of Lexium and the fall of the sand wyrms. He had a hundred stories and more. And he told the story of Draku.

"They were killed off and their memory buried," Julien said, and folk listened. Julien was now almost certain that Trist wasn't going to come. *He fooled you, the fool.* Julien knew he hadn't much hope of doing anything other than what Natt Floyd had laid out for him. He would get in *Saltspray* and sail away. *Back to nothing. Back to obscurity...* The moon was high. Most of the folk were passed out drunk. Even the bards had stopped singing.

"Karaat is dead, along with the other gods," Natt said. "Whoever told you those stories is just as mad as you are."

"Karaat lives," Julien said in argument.

Natt just laughed. "Whatever you need to tell yourself."

Finally, Julien saw a flicker of light in the night. Then many hundreds more.

"*Dagdora,*" Julien sang, and a ball of fire appeared in the air in front of him. With a tilt of his neck, the fire flew across the palace room, and the table of yew ignited into flames. "Karaat lives. And now you've angered him. The Letharri come. Look." Julien pointed. Natt Floyd looked out into the night, and his stone face turned flaccid.

"*Eralis...*" Natt swore. Soon folk were pointing, panicking. Some started to yell and more and more woke up and yelled along with them. The redness in the west came closer and closer like a thousand glowing embers dancing in the night. Folk were starting to run out into the desert and into the river, and Julien knew many of them would starve or drown.

The flames came closer, hundreds of red dots. Trist had instructed his soldiers well, and it seemed to Julien that not one of those torches had gone out. He cut them to the exact right length and dipped them in tar and lit them at the exact right moment for them to get here, just as Julien had planned. By the time folk realized the demon lights were soldiers on horseback, too many of them had already left. Julien cut Natt down with one clean strike to his shoulder into his neck. The lord's eyes were gaping wide as he croaked his last breath. *He's terrified. Terrified that Letharr had truly come.*

Trist's company, alongside his son's, slammed into the palace at full speed on horseback. It was an easy slaughter for them against folk who were so scared and so few. When they were done, they burned the palace with their torches.

Julien had made sure that Trist had instructed his folk to leave one alive. *One alive to tell the tale.* And Trist, with his sunken eyes, told the boy that *he* was Letharr and these were *his* demons, and that they had come to burn the world in the name of Karaat and the Draku.

When Trist had finished speaking, the boy ran off and Julien had no doubt that the strong young man would make it to Sareen and tell the tale. And Julien had no doubt that the boy would be well and truly terrified to the bone while telling it.

"The soldiers want to attack Sareen tonight. They are bloodthirsty," Trist said. He was covered in blood and smiling. That told Julien a lot about this man. It told him that he could do more than just talk and wasn't afraid to show that.

"We have to be patient now. Let the tale spread. Let it take root. Then let them doubt it a bit, let it start to fade. Then we will arrive. Demons in the night. Then I will get you your crown."

Trist smiled. "You mean I will take it myself?"

"Word it however you like," Julien said. "When we are both kings, you on your throne at Sareen and me atop the Lion's Chair in Hest, it will not matter."

Trist raised a goblet of wine and Julien raised one with him. "To victory."

"To victory," Julien said. "I only wish we'd spared the cook. That woman did things with rice that I'll never forget."

"War's a shame, ain't it?"

"War's a shame," Julien agreed. "Now, I've got to find my way back to my ship. Old Hild is probably worried sick about me." Julien stood and his head spun from the wine, so he spun around and sat again.

"In the morning?" Trist said.

"In the morning," Julien agreed, and Trist filled his goblet, and the two of them sat on the banks of the Esheri Rush and watched the riverside temple burn to ashes beneath a great sky of stars.

COLD

K ELSON'S KEEP WAS COLD. The stone held winter like a puddle held water long after the storm was over.

Aldred looked out into the cold night from his chamber and sighed. He had bathed himself using cold water—the warm wouldn't clean him.

Egan had returned to him and brought him plates of cheese, salted venison, and pickles. He ate while he drank two goblets of the finest Hesterland red. All of it cold. He sat on a bed lined with purple Ni'Anese silk and ran his hands across the cool smoothness.

He hadn't been home in a year, and his family hadn't missed him. Eshlynn hadn't missed him. *I've taken a lover...* He had nothing. He expected more than *nothing*. He expected, at the very least, warmth. *How long after I left, Eshlynn? Did you even miss me for a minute?* Aldred feared so badly that she hadn't. The thought of it hurt, like touching a flame, even getting close to it burned him.

It was cold and lonely the first weeks back, even with Egan in the room with him, and Aldred found his thoughts wandering to the night of the blood moon. *It didn't really happen. It couldn't have happened.*

Aldred remembered the cold blood running through his veins, the power surging like a thunderbolt. *And then that thunder became life. Life for the new dead.* Aldred wished it scared him more, but he hadn't been able to stop thinking about it. Like the first time he had sex, he just craved to have that feeling again. *And I could do it better next time, too.* He had wished to get rid of Brooton for a decade, and only a couple of days after the messiah's promise, Aldred took his place in court. It just didn't seem like it was reality. *Seeing is believing. But you were blacked out for two straight days. What took place inside of your mind during that time? What happened that night the dead rose around you? You saw, you were there, and you still don't believe it.*

Aldred tried to shake the thoughts loose. He looked at his hands, at himself in the mirror. He looked sickly. Pale and cold skin stood out against his auburn hair. He saw something in himself that wasn't there before. *But what is it?* "It's a cold world out there, Egan, it'll beat you down, let me tell you."

"That's the hard truth of it, sir, no matter your station. You and I are going to the same place one day, ain't we?" Egan said. He was clever, and Aldred both loved and hated that about him.

"To the worms." Aldred ran his hands through his hair. Whatever was inside of him, he wanted it gone. Out of him. He could feel a dark stain in his heart, on his lungs with every breath, and he wasn't ready for the worms yet. *Angelico wrote nothing of this.* Aldred felt sick.

Books had always told Aldred everything. They were his comfort, and the Hesters had inherited the biggest library in all of the known world. Though there were rumours that Kelson took many of the books from Hest and brought them to Kallahorn. Aldred knew that still nothing could surpass Hest's shelves. They were hauntingly large—like the bones of dead mammoths lined up row by row in the dark. Aldred had spent most of his childhood there, his mom reading to him from different works while William played with swords in the courtyard.

It was then that Aldred fell in love with the classics. The Lovasi scholars of Old. Angelico wrote of every living thing he came across and every situation living beings found themselves in. *But he wrote nothing of this. Nothing of blood magics.*

"Not him, but others..." a voice in Aldred's mind spoke.

Aldred hadn't considered that. *But who?* The Lovasi had mapped the entire world. They named every plant and animal. Angelico Corronidis wrote of it all. He wrote of everything there was to be written of, and more. His apprentice, Benecio Mori, wrote everything known of strategy in war, and life. He wrote of the inner workings of the brain, and how to predict actions to a fairly accurate degree. Phosphone wrote fables and epics.

But blood magics were old. Older than the Lovasi, and the Lovasi scholars buried the knowledge of it. They didn't want it to be known that they were stealing ancient doctrine and passing it off as their own—that perhaps, they weren't the greatest civilization that this world had seen—that they had just inherited it all, and they were doing a piss poor job at managing it. That's what Aldred's mom had taught him. And he believed her.

Could some of it still exist? Those ancient texts? Then another thought connected in Aldred's mind. *The boneman can read Yehvenki.* Aldred smiled. *Yes. Yes he does, could there be an ancient text in the library? One that Dustey could read?* The Lovasi kept the parts of history they liked and buried the rest. They tried to control Nature. They fell. When the Priests of Eralis rose up in the Hesterlands in the wake of Gavyn Hester's conquest, they buried the ancient knowledge further.

Aldred knew this from books. He had learned on his military expeditions across Ardura that this was not common knowledge. Nobody knew a thing anymore. The past seemed like a fable to most. *The apothecary...* Aldred remembered. *The apothecary...*

In the basements, an old apothecary still operated. A witch-doctor and his thralls crafted salves and lotions to cure various ailments. Aldred had been there before to obtain burn lotion for Eshlynn's small cousin. The witch-doctor had Yehvenki scrolls stacked up on shelves.

Maybe Angelico or Benecio didn't write of it, but someone did. Aldred stood up, knocked the mirror and the pale bastard in it to the ground. It was good Lavesheen glass and didn't break, but made a sharp ting when it landed.

"Woah, are you okay, sir?" Egan rushed to pick up the mirror.

"Fine," Aldred said. *You're going mad. It isn't real. You're going to end up in those cells with Brooton.* Aldred took a deep drink from the golden goblet Egan had given him. "I just think it's time I start writing my own story, you know, Egan?"

Egan nodded.

It was at least worth seeing what the boneman would find in those scrolls. *He's wise, the boneman, perhaps that's why you like him so much. Perhaps that's why you fear him so much.*

Aldred dressed and plucked from his boot the tiny white lightning flower.

ALDRED'S FOOT SLIPPED FROM the slick ledge and the sole of his boot landed in some cold sewer water.

"Oh, Eralis—" He shook his foot out. His lantern light was flickering wildly, threatening to extinguish as the oil sloshed back and forth over the wick. He gagged and dry heaved from the smell. *Not covered in it, at least. Praise fucking Eralis.* He didn't enjoy slithering underground like some kind of bug. But the city of Hest had grown into a festering mess since Aldred had left. The winter had seen a division of what supplies remained, and Aldred's father had decided that there was nothing he could do about it. Theft and murder had become common nighttime activities amidst a lawless backdrop. After the riots started in the lower slums, a place that the people of Hest called Rattrap, King John demanded that every guard in the city spend the evenings in the safety of the guardhouse outside of Kelson's Keep. And so, with the guards removed from the streets, Hest became lawless in the night.

Aldred's dad had decided that the best way to deal with starving cityfolk was to not deal with them at all. *And how is this working out for you, King Father? How is this going to end? Will the riots spread?*

Aldred knew that people would do anything when they were hungry, especially the ones with kids. It's a sad truth about the human condition that he had a hard time accepting. It didn't take long for a whole population to starve out and die. He'd done it to the Esheri during the siege of Soren, and Lysses, of Saray, Behru, and Sareen. He'd done it to them again and again, and now he had to live with the visions of the wreckage. *One year, thousands starved. But not you.*

Aldred promised himself he would be a better king were he ever given the chance. *But you won't be, and Adora will make sure of that.* Now, he couldn't be sure that there wasn't someone in the streets who would kill him, hoping Aldred had a few coins on him.

The people of Hest gave you a warm reception when you arrived. They still love you. But Aldred knew that those folk had only cheered because they had hope that Aldred would return with food—spoils of war. He had nothing, and those folk probably looked to the south for days hoping for a wagon laden with food to come bouncing up the Kingsroad behind Aldred. *The Undead Prince, they call you now. They think you're a monster. What will Eshlynn think?*

The cityfolk turned colder under the moonlight. Aldred had been told by Rober that gangs of thieves and murderers ran the streets in the slums of Rattrap now, and they needed to eat. *They will get braver and braver.* A brick of cheese would be three times the silver it was last month, and it had already doubled. These were desperate times. *Angelico said desperation is the key to creation.* Aldred didn't think anyone around here would be creating anything but bastards and dead bodies.

He climbed an old Daggland steel ladder up to street level. He was below a stone fountain, crafted into the shape of Kelson. Angelico said that during the city's golden age, these fountains had water flowing through them, day and night. Kelson's brides danced under the moon amidst the misting waters of these golden fountains. Aldred couldn't see how it could be true but stopped wondering about it years ago. *Even the most amazing thing can become mundane after enough time.*

He came out of a trap door beside the fountain base, extinguished his lantern, and left it by the trap door. Most folk avoided the labyrinth of tunnels below the city because of how easy it was to get lost down there and never surface. But Aldred had maps from the library, and so he could use them with confidence.

Kelson's statue stood ten feet tall over him, missing his nose and one hand. He was in a small alleyway that may once have been a courtyard. Now daub and wattle three-story houses loomed over him like crumbly, rotten clay and wooden monsters. A wooden sign with a hammer painted on it swung from the rafters on shining iron chains, marking Eshlynn's forge. *Other shops let their chains rust. Esh polishes hers clean every week.*

Aldred knocked. *I've taken a lover.* There was no answer so he knocked again. *Is the lover here now? Am I a complete fool for coming here? Our love is dead.*

"*No, child. You're not a fool. What was dead can live again.*"

"Who's there?" Eshlynn called from inside. Her voice sounded far away.

Esh. "It's me, Esh. It's Aldred."

Eshlynn opened the door. She saw him and smiled. The kind of smile to pull a person out of darkness. "Dre! I thought you were dead." Eshlynn's sweet voice made him melt. She hugged him so tight he struggled for breath. *I would gladly be smothered here.* Her long, brown hair rested on smooth, brown shoulders. She wore nothing but a soot-stained cotton shirt that draped down to her lower thigh. Green eyes melted him like spring ice. "Come in, please, come in," she said.

Aldred feared there would be someone else inside. *Is he here now?* Aldred gazed around the room cautiously. The room was warm, and the air was thick with coal smoke. Chains of iron hung from pegs in the wall. Drawers filled with various dirt-cladded rocks scattered everywhere. *But those dirty rocks, when polished, are so incredibly beautiful. Their gemstone shine is only hidden beneath a rough exterior.* Eshlynn's forge cast a ruddy warm glow. Aldred didn't see anyone.

"You've been gone a year," she said. "I thought you'd be back last autumn. Folk have been saying you're dead."

Aldred pulled out her letter. Eshlynn held her hand to her mouth. "God, Dre, I wasn't sure if you'd received it. When I started to hear the rumours of your death, God, Dre, I just hoped you didn't receive it—that it wasn't one of the last things you saw."

"So it's not true?" Aldred hated how desperate he sounded.

"Dre..." Eshlynn looked down. "It is true, Dre, but God, I didn't wish you dead."

"They doubt me," Aldred said. "All of them." He so hated how desperate he sounded. Flashes of dead bodies filled with life invaded his mind. "It's just been a lot." He had to fight back tears. Part of him still believed it didn't really happen.

"They've always doubted you, Dre. And that hasn't stopped you yet."

Aldred hated that he was crying now. "What's their name? Your lover?"

"Dre, don't do this to yourself." Eshlynn took a step back, and to Aldred, that spoke volumes. "You know there are two things you can't choose—love and death, Dre. *You* told me that."

"I won't stay long. I just wanted to tell you that I've missed you. That I lived. That I may not have if not for thinking of seeing you once more," he blurted. He felt like a fool but then saw that Eshlynn had pulled his mother's necklace out from below the neckline of her dress.

"I kept this safe, Aldred." Eshlynn took the necklace off and offered it to Aldred.

"Please," Aldred said, "keep it. Please, just tell me we weren't nothing. That it wasn't nothing."

Eshlynn's eyes glazed over with sympathy. She held the necklace to her chest. Aldred could see that she didn't like hurting him. "We weren't nothing, Dre. We weren't nothing. I'll keep it."

"I love you, Eshlynn," he said.

"I missed you," she said. "You left a massive hole in me, Aldred. I was cold without you here, I needed warmth, Dre, you have to understand. He, Sebastian, it's not his fault either, we just found each other, Dre, like death finds people, love found us. It's getting tough around here to keep food in our stomachs. I'm selling gemstones and jewels for less than a wheel of cheese at this point." Eshlynn laughed sadly.

Aldred's upper lip twitched a bit.

"He talks to me like you did, though," she said. "He makes me feel like I'm more than enough. I can talk to him about places close and far and in between. I talk to him about Lavesh and Esher."

"I find Lavesh a fascinating place," Aldred said. "Benecio—" Eshlynn put her finger on his lips.

"Lived there, yes. I've heard all of your stories from books. Tell me of *real* things. Where have you been all this time?" Her green eyes were wide and sparkling. Aldred dove into them and was lost for a moment. "You at least owe me that."

Aldred didn't want to think about where he'd been. He had spent the whole time waiting to get back *here*. "I found this for you." He held in his hand the lightning flower.

Eshlynn's eyes lit up. "You found a reibloom!" Eshlynn took the small flower from Aldred's hand and twirled the stem, and the flower sparkled like a diamond from the light in Eshlynn's eyes. *Reibloom.* "It's beautiful," she said as she gave it back, "but reiblooms are not to give. A lightning flower represents change—in the person who found it. A spiritual awakening. This is yours, Dre, I can't take it from you." Eshlynn put the flower in

Aldred's hand and closed his fingers around it. "I found my reibloom long ago. It changed my life forever."

Aldred looked at the flower. *Change. A lot of change, and none of it good.* "I've been leading the king's army." He thought of Brooton in the cold cells and felt oddly safe. He put the reibloom back in his boot.

"I heard there was food in the south," Eshlynn said. "So much they could never eat it all. Did you go south? To Esher? To Lavesh? East to Lovas?" she said, and Aldred could see that she was imagining each place in her head as she said it.

Aldred shook his head. "There's no food," he said. "We sacked three towns and found nothing but starving folk. They all thought we had brought *them* food." Flashes of bony, gaunt faces gasping for air as they crawled on their knees flooded Aldred's memory. *"Help us,"* the dying folk had begged him as he and the fyrd sliced them down. *That was no fight. That was no battle at all.*

"It really is all going to shit, ain't it?" she said.

Aldred nodded. "I could take you away, Eshlynn," he said. "You don't have to be here anymore. You could be a princess of Hest." Aldred didn't even care how desperate he sounded now.

"Hah!" she laughed. "And what makes you think I *want* to be a princess now? I didn't before you left, why now?" She sat up, intrigued.

"I just thought..." he said, really feeling like a royal idiot now. "It was something people dreamed of..."

"And tell me, how would you know what my dreams are?" Eshlynn leaned in. "You've asked me to be your princess how many times now? Haven't you learned by now that I don't care about your coin or that Lovasi monstrosity you call home? It's like, because everyone in your life has used you and manipulated you, you want me to do the same. You *want* me to take things from you. You *want* me to gain from you. I think you'd be better off without the Hester name. Without the coin and the castle and the army. You'd be better off if you could just be you—stripped of it all." Eshlynn walked to an open barrel of water and dipped her coal blackened hands in it and washed them as she spoke. "I like to hear stories and tell them. I like the feel of hot steel beneath my hammer. I like to get shit-faced drunk and laugh. I *love* to dream, Aldred. How much dreaming does a princess do?" Eshylnn said. Aldred was worried he'd gone too far again. "I'm not a bloody princess. I'm a blacksmith. My mom was a blacksmith, and so was hers. Sebastian understands that—he understands *me*... you could never understand me, Dre, because you don't understand yourself."

Sebastian... "I thought you would want to get out of Rattrap, out of this rotten city," Aldred said. "What if the riots get worse? Where will you go? These walls won't protect you. You should want something better for yourself than what your mom and her mom had. You deserve it," Aldred frowned. "Will *he* protect you?"

"Dre, don't go there, okay. Don't bring Sebastian into this. You're trying to tell me what I should want when you don't even know what you want for your own damn self. You think you want *me*, but you haven't seen me in more than a year. I've only been an idea in your mind all this time, a still picture of who I was before you left. You didn't imagine me changing, you didn't imagine *us* changing together. You wanted a dream you had conjured from your books—a still-life fairy tale that you can read over and over. What do you really want, Aldred Hester? Is it love? Find it within yourself first. Angelico said you must find what's within before you can find what you're without," said Eshlynn. Aldred smiled.

"You read that far?"

"I've been reading. I remember most of what you taught me, though some of the Lovasi words don't make sense to me," she said. Aldred felt his love for her swell up.

"You could save this. You can bring her love back just as you brought back the dead." Roqeda's voice echoed from different corners of Aldred's mind.

"I could move you both into a house," Aldred said, "up on the hill side of the city. You and him both. That way, if the riots start—" Eshlynn put her finger on his lips.

"Dre, honey. I'm not going anywhere. It wouldn't be the same *me* hidden away in that house on the hillside," she said.

"I understand," Aldred said. At least, he was trying to. *She doesn't love you. She doesn't want you. She wouldn't care if you died.*

Aldred lowered his head. *Bring back what was lost...* He could revive this love just as he'd revived the corpses on that field. *But how?*

"How else?" Roqeda said. *"For something to truly come back to life, it must first truly die."*

A wicked glare crept onto Aldred's face.

"Are you okay?" she said, and put her warm hand on Aldred's arm.

That strange, eldritch trance wouldn't leave him. "I'm okay."

"Take care of yourself, Dre," Eshlynn said, guiding him gently towards the door.

"You too," Aldred forced himself to say, before dipping out of Eshlynn's shop back out into the cold night. He glanced at her polished sign once more. *Sebastian...*

From somewhere in the city, Aldred heard screaming. And then he saw flames.

FORT ROSEN

"*D*EATH MY DEAR, GIVE *them death,*" the wind whispered to Maggie. The red eagle flags of Ayeland rippled in that wind, like cloth-bound waves atop the wooden palisades of Fort Rosen, and the Lovasi bridge sparkled white beneath the sun behind it.

"How many?" James asked.

"Hard to say," Ruwen answered. The rulers had gathered by a shallow stream, and Brinley had stretched his maps out on the grass there. Maggie listened to the conversations of the birds and the squirrels and the spiders. *They are all just looking for home... They are all just trying to eat and to live and to love.*

"If we attack them head on with everything we have, they will never expect it." Brinley slammed his finger down on his map where Fort Rosen was drawn. "With the folk we have and the Daggs behind us, we can crush them. We can scale the walls and take the fort with minimal loss."

"If they have archers in those towers, we will lose many hundreds," James said.

"Hundreds we have," Brinley said. "This bridge is everything to us. It is the key to winning back the Hallow and defending ourselves against the coming wave of Ayelish."

"We can hold anyone or anything there," Ruwen said. "This man slayed a drayke upon that land just last autumn-moon." The She-Bear raised her arms to the sky and her people roared. "We will tear those walls down to get in. We have built them up before and we can do it again!" And the folk of Rosen slammed their fists into their chests and shields, and roared in unison.

The noise of it all had spooked the critters, and Maggie didn't have a chance to tell them thank you for letting her listen to them and for making her feel welcome here. *Give them death...* The words the wind spoke to her still fluttered in her ear. Wind was always the most violent of the spirits. Gentle fire would but flicker and fan if not for the viciousness of the winds, the seas couldn't send forth waves taller than castle walls, the trees would rarely fall. But the poor birds would be so tired should the wind cease its violence, so Maggie learned to live with its savagery.

The Dagglanders were draining pine sap and boiling it into tar. Black smoke clogged the sky, and the sight of it made Maggie sick.

The rulers carried on in conversation as Maggie walked in the stream barefoot away from them. She felt James's eyes burning her back, but she knew it was only because he longed to come with her and not because he was upset she was leaving.

When she was alone, she slid her mind underground. She felt the soil and the bugs crawling within it. She felt the roots and the mycelium that had become heartbound to each other, and she touched their lives with her own.

Slowly, she knew the ground and the trees and the animals, and she drew their lives into her lungs like a breath. Small bodies fell from trees—birds and squirrels and crickets and cicadas fell lifeless onto the dead grey soil on the bank of the stream. Crawfish and bass minnows and brook trout floated to the top of the water and flowed past Maggie's ankles. She closed her eyes and breathed deeply and felt the pain in her soul dissolve into the wind. Leaves fell and small twigs cracked and broke off from the trees, and when Maggie exhaled, the trees moaned with life and the soil blackened with sustenance. The small animals awoke, as if resurrected, and scurried off, and the birds flapped off into the trees or upstream as if they had only dreamt a brief glimpse of death.

James's voice echoed up the stream as Maggie made her way back. *Give them death.* Maggie knew she could save hundreds of lives by simply taking hundreds more. *It's as easy as that, right?* She had never felt more confident in herself. If she could get close enough to the walls to feel the lives of all those inside, she could simply steal it from them as easy as breathing. *The quicker you find peace, the quicker you and James can be away from this.*

Maggie touched her stomach. She had prayed to the dream nymphs for a child and since their night at the nihr'el, Maggie felt one growing inside her. She and James had never had a seed take before, there was no reason other than Maggie's dreams to believe it would work now. *But the world is different now. Old songs have been remembered and magics linger on the winds and in the fires, rain, and earth.* But what scared Maggie most was her overwhelming want to *feed* the growing seed. Feed it with the life of others.

Maggie stood in the stream, and when the rulers had finished, James came to talk to her.

"Queen Ianna is coming, Mag. Ten thousand or more are gathered at Tusk now. They have to march any day now if they mean to attack."

"Let them come," Maggie said recklessly. *I'll kill them all with a breath.* She had grown hungry to use her powers, and especially on those who caused so much pain to *her.*

James seemed untroubled by her statement. He just smiled. "It's nice out here," he said. "It reminds me of Oster."

Maggie was happy to hear James speak of home. She always wondered why he didn't more often. If she had a home, she would speak of it always. *Your home is with us, child.* Memories of the dream nymphs fluttered in Maggie's mind like butterflies. *Come home to us.*

"Are we attacking tomorrow?" Maggie watched the water flow through her toes and form ten white lines where it went between them. *Five mothers. Five fathers. You've had as many parents as toes,* she thought.

"Aye," James said. "It's going to be bloody. A proper battle. Fort Rosen is made of treated Daggland cedar. Even the Daggs admit the only way in is to scale it."

"It's not the only way." Maggie gazed at James. He was like a beautiful black rose in a field of red ones. He looked at her like he knew what she was thinking. *We share a mind, don't we, my love? You already know what I'm thinking.*

"I will keep you safe," he said. "The Daggs are crafting turtle shell mantlets of boiled leather and pine tar for protection. Walk right up to the wall beneath it, they said. I will make sure no harm comes to you, as if you need me for that."

"I know you will," Maggie said, "but you can't be anywhere close to me."

James hung his head. Maggie knew that James understood what would happen if Maggie used her powers to take the lives of all in Rosen. She would take the lives of any who stood equal distance behind her. "Brinley wants to send a small host in to test their defences and then smash them with a fist of us. You could go in with the first group."

And kill them all. "I will do it for the Hallow. For *us.*" *They would all die, anyway...*

"Does it hurt you?" James asked.

"No," Maggie said, and just thinking of the feeling made her bubble with excitement—to play with that many lives. "I absolutely love it."

MAGGIE WORE HER FAVOURITE green dress over a jacket of iron ringmail, strapped at her waist with her sister Flora's old belt. She needed to feel powerful. She needed to feel brave. The Mal folk around her sang songs of death from the cycles. Folk from Oster and Foulds and Tide. Folk from Wick and Fever and Lorne. Folk scattered and missing home—a home that was no longer there. *These folk are you and you them. These folk are grown from the nourishment of the same streams and the same fruits. The same fields and the same game in the same arbors.*

The warrior folk of the Hallow wore iron helmets with crow-beak visors and in the shape of bear heads, and with wooden moose horns fitted into them. The blooded folk of Eridan wore no helms at all and painted their faces with mud. They held axes forged in fires, fuelled by charcoal made from oak and hickory hewn from Mal arbors with forged iron mined from the Fell Mountains or the Hallow Hills. *They are folk of this land just as you. And their families love them—not like you.*

Maggie thought about telling her old mentor, Hagel, that she was wearing full armour and about to assault a walled fort. *He would tell you that you were mad, as he always did.* Hagel was the first person who ever encouraged Maggie to use her power—to try and control it. He encouraged her in many ways, and in many ways, Maggie missed him. *But you killed him. The only person who didn't run from your powers was killed by them...* Part of Maggie's heart still broke every time she thought of it. His limp body smacking the ground. His blue face. *By the gods...* she had pushed too far that day.

The Dagglandic warriors sang in their deep, bellowing voices. They held black steel axes and adorned themselves in black steel on their chests and heads. *A wall of metal, them, both inside and out.*

War horns bellowed out from atop the towers and walls of Fort Rosen. And there were archers. *So many archers.* The Ayelish flag waved madly from the towers. Stragglers from the Wolf's army.

"How close do you need to get?" James had asked Maggie.

"Twenty yards or so," she said, but she knew she needed to be closer to take the life of every person in Rosen.

"Let's take the piss out of em, eh!" Logan of Wick screamed, his red beard looked like the end of a shovel, and the rest of the folk screamed, too. "The queen is here with us, let's show her what her people are made of!"

"Those arrows would argue you're made of flesh," Maggie said.

"Ah, but my flesh is like tree bark!" Logan laughed. "So, Queen, what kind of sorcery are we about to see?" Logan whispered to her. His grin was shite-eating wide.

This one is mad for glory. "What makes you think sorcery is afoot?" Maggie asked.

"Why else would *you* be frontline?" Logan leaned in closer. "I can't bloody wait, Maggie. I can't bloody wait." Logan had been a good chosen leader and was always looking for glory. *James chose well to send him—he will do anything to avoid looking foolish. He will make the right moves.* Maggie was happy to be under the same shell as he.

Behind them, the Hallow army and the Daggs hid amongst the moors, out of sight. The vanguard marched closer to the walls, and when they reached a certain point, Logan instructed them to hoist the turtle shell over their heads. A hardened shell of leather caked in tar, then another layer of leather and tar, and so on. Some had twenty or more layers and weighed as much as a bull moose. Most arrows never even pierced half way into it. And it wasn't long before Maggie heard the iron rain pelting the shell.

Seven human-propelled turtles crawled towards the walls of Fort Rosen and screamed like Banshees with Logan out in front.

"Ayeee!" they screamed. "For the Hallow!"

The iron rain continued to fall, and soon folk were taking shafts to their lower thighs and ankles.

Attacking Rosen from the south meant crossing the bridge, but from the north, it meant facing the fort.

"Get up!" Logan shouted, and Maggie hoisted a woman beneath her arms and pulled an arrow shaft from her leg. Maggie cut the woman's trouser leg with her knife and wrapped it tightly around the wound.

"Thank you, Queen." The woman sighed in relief. *Don't thank me. That only makes killing you harder for me.*

"Aye," Maggie said, and the turtle carried on. Soon Maggie could hear the shouts of the Ayelish folk on the walls and knew she was close. The arrows fell and the Hallow folk continued to fall, and when the first turtle shell dropped, Maggie knew it wouldn't be the last. Then an arrow took the same woman who Maggie had just patched up. She fell over and blood bubbled from her mouth.

"Keep moving!" Logan shouted "We—" He gargled strangely and when he fell over, Maggie knew that he had taken a shaft to the lung. *None at all*, Maggie thought to Logan's question of how much sorcery he would see tonight.

When two more of her crew went down, the turtle shell fell and smothered Maggie under its weight.

Her world was black, and with all her strength, she could only manage to move very slowly. Muffled voices and the sound of her own breathing were all there was. Maggie dug her fingers into the dirt and pulled herself towards the small crack of light until finally she came free of the turtle shell.

When she saw blood dripping from her arm, she knew she'd only been shot. Around her, fallen turtles that looked like porcupines stretched out flat and dead on the dirt. Two turtles still stood, but they weren't moving. Maggie stood and ran for them, sharp pain shooting up her leg with each step. Something had twisted when the turtle fell on her.

More arrows pierced the dirt all around her as she ran, and when one hit the iron of her chainmail, she dove into the dirt and crawled towards the turtle where a big man with a bear helmet pulled her under.

"It's gone to shite," said the man. And Maggie could already hear the rest of the army charging in from the moors in support.

"No!" Maggie shouted. She closed her eyes and reached out with her mind. She felt something but it was too big, too obscure to hold. If she couldn't do this fast, the rest of the army would sweep in and Maggie would kill them all. *All.*

"We're going to fucking die out here," one woman said.

Maggie could feel the souls of the Ayelishfolk marching, assembling in the courtyard, ready for a breach. *There are hundreds of them there. They would bloody slaughter us.* Archers filled every inch of wall, and the arrows were still falling like rain.

Maggie felt the spirits all around her, and she could hear them singing to her. *Use me,* the spirits sang to her.

She reached, and her mind exploded with the lives all around her. She felt them squirming in and out of hallways and doorways and stairways like worms crawling through the dirt below. She could feel folk on the wall and felt the passion brewing in them from their killing, bubbling in a stew from a fear of dying. Maggie felt the souls that were leaving this earth and felt the ones that were being drawn into it. Then the lives of the Hallowfolk and Dagglandic peoples flooded in too, and she was overwhelmed.

"Ahhhhh!" she belted, and the woman looked at her like she was a rabid beast. "Ahhhh!" Maggie felt foam at her mouth and blood on her tongue and a thousand lives hanging on a thread tied to the tip of her finger. *Pull it. Pull it!*

Two rocks seemed to crush her head from either side, and her eyes were flooded with tears. "NO!" she cried, but wasn't sure if she spoke or just thought it. The sea of souls began to swallow her, and her physical body was bleeding and crying, she was exhausted.

The ground shook from the charge behind her, thundering closer, and the smell of the Ayelishfolk stung the back of her throat as she breathed them in. The turtle shell was thrown to one side and the folk around her charged again for the gate, and Maggie felt them all. *Death my dear, give them death.*

And with a single breath, Maggie stole the life of all around her. The earth turned cold and grey, and even the sky seemed to dim and flicker. Maggie was flying. Her feet still touched the ground, but her mind was soaring with the memories of hundreds of different lives.

She felt all of their joys—child birth, love, pleasure, family—and all of their sorrows, too. She loved and lost and lived a thousand times over in a thousand different places. She grew old and grew young and knew the names of a thousand thousand sons and daughters and grandchildren.

The sun warmed Maggie's skin as she lay on the dead ground. She sang *Maggie of Old Grove* softly. She knew that she lay in the middle of a circle of death. She could hear the silent whisperings of the newly dead leaving this place in troves. *The song of the sleepers, Hagel had called it.* Their fear hung in the air like fog and shrouded Maggie like a blanket. She could feel the lives of the Mal and Daggs behind her.

But it was warm. It was so warm. *And the birds, they're silent, too.* There was no iron rain and no shouts, and the ground did not rumble or shake. *You killed everyone. You killed James.* She wanted to die.

But when Maggie saw James's black hair draped over his shoulders and saw home in his brown eyes, she thought she had died too and that she and James could finally be safe. When she felt James's callused hands slide beneath the pits of her legs and around her shoulders, she *knew* she was dead.

"I've got you, baby." James's breath was hot in Maggie's ear.

"Are we dead, James? Are we finally dead?"

"We live Maggie. I've got you. You did it."

"What happened?"

"Fort Rosen is ours."

When Maggie closed her eyes, she smelled peonies and honey, and soon the dream nymphs were calling to her.

THE DRAUGR

HALDA HAD ALWAYS LOVED the feeling of an oar in her hand. Smooth wood against her rough skin—each made that way by the other. The soft splashing of the paddle into the blue moving water, the misting of the sea across her hands and face and body, and the taste of salt on her tongue and in her nose. The deck beneath her was nothing but a vessel, her true carrier was below—the sea. Her rakkarren by her side, Harald at the helm.

"You know." Eurick pointed his finger. "They say the coastline used to be hundreds of miles into the sea, maybe where we're riding now may have been land once."

"Who says these things?" Halda had heard the same thing sung about in the sagas, but the raven was always coming up with obscure sources for his knowledge and it fascinated Halda beyond all else. But on the sea, there was nothing better than stories to pass the time and to help the mind wander. The sea had a way of calming her, even to Eurick's ramblings.

"Oh, it's an old favourite of the ravens. Can't go a year in the Guild without hearing that song." Eurick fidgeted with his pack, touching things to make sure they still were where they were ten minutes previous.

After some time, the winds in the Channel of Krakens proved girthy enough for Harald to raise a sail and allow the crew to come above decks. The captain was guiding them close enough to shore that Halda could hear the seagulls squawking and could see the seals and the walruses bathing on rocks or frothing about in big, white foaming circles of sea as they fed in frenzy on the minnows. The boat creaked and moaned and to Halda, those sounds were home.

"The Channel will whip us around this isle in no time." Harald gripped the bulwark and breathed in the salt air.

"Aye," Halda said. *You'll be in front of the soothsayers in no time. But what will the soothsayers tell you? You may not like it...*

Halda was a prophet of the Dead God, and that came with certain responsibilities. If she saw something in her fires or in the reading of her runes, then she acted upon them, for they were direct messages from Her. But if she misinterpreted the messages, she could be outcast or killed. The rakkars of Daggland had decided to exile Halda's very own Aunt Thora to the Isle of Offa. They called her mad.

"These are the mouths and ears and eyes of Offa, child." Halda remembered the teachings of her rune-mother, Aunt Thora, as she gave Halda her first set of runes by a crackling fire. *"And when Offa speaks to you, you do not deny Her voice. This will make you wise beyond all folk. This will make them bow to you as a prophet."*

And they did.

Erik of Oldstone was the first to proclaim Halda a prophet when he heeded her warning after she predicted a great storm. That same storm ended up sinking Freya's fleet from Smokestone and winning the war decisively for Oldstone. When she predicted the explosion of Mount Crumble even before the people of Morden Vale had any inkling of it, many folk called her mad, but Erik of Oldstone sang her praises. Finally, the people of Morden Vale evacuated the mountain base, and mere days later, their small hamlets and villages were swallowed by the molten rock, and black, sulphurous smoke that spewed from the mountain.

After Aunt Thora left and Halda had access to all of her potions and tools, Halda began to host council with any and all who wanted answers. *Don't you forget why Thora left—not left, sent away. Don't you forget the fires turned her mad.*

"Serve Offa, Halda," Aunt Thora had said before she left. *"When She calls, heed it. Do not let me down, Halda. These teachings have been passed down from generation to generation. Use them to help, sure, but do not forget why we gaze into the fires in the first place.*

Halda told folk of their past loved ones' fates beyond the veil of life, spoke magics and committed acts of sorcery that would kill tumors, breathe life back into folk who had drowned, and bring infants killed in birth back to life with a touch. She helped all she could.

But it's all a lie... all of her magics were tricks that could be learned. Tricks she learned from her Aunt Thora and promised never to tell. *But they all believe you, and there is power in wisdom—a power beyond any.*

"They must believe you when Ox'olin comes. You must make them believe you, Halda. Do not fail this task." Aunt Thora had begun repeating herself more and more near the end. *"Do not fail this, Halda. Ox'olin will come. It is coming..."*

"I won't," Halda had told her, and she meant it. She was only a girl then.

It was only a few short years after Aunt Thora had left that the Speakers of the Gods, one from each isle of Daggland, conspired on the Isle of Offa, off the coast of Barrow Rock. When they returned from a five-month long meeting in which they communicated with various gods and entities, Halda was given her spot in the Witch Den upon Massey Rock. She was fifteen.

Perched high on the Cape of Krakens, the Witch Den was a grand stone tower made of strange green stone and chipped with ancient markings that were put there by the first Dagglanders to rise from the sea. In the sagas, there are songs of great Dagglandic heroes dragging rocks up from the bottom of the sea left by a race of Sorcerers—the same ones that the Dead God rose up against in the first battle. Other stories say the tower was already there when the Dagglanders rose, and they simply moved in.

In the Witch Den, Halda's skills grew rapidly. Soon she could predict storms and droughts alike by the temperature of the sea and the taste of the wind. She could predict deaths of rulers and births of rulers' children by making visits to them and studying their skin and their movements and looking into their eyes. *That was the most adventure your rakkarren got. Traipsing from one island to the next, waiting for you to poke and prod the other rakkars and their families.*

For twenty years, Halda had been known as the Prophet of Offa, or the Knower of Massey Rock. For twenty years she honed her skills so that when she heard the voice in her fires that told her the world would die, she knew it was Offa telling her true.

She lit the torch and all of Daggland came. And the world died. She had never wanted to be wrong more in her life. But now Offa had directed her somewhere she didn't trust, on a land that was far and foreign. Now she lived in fear that the voices she heard were just tricks of her own kind being used against her. *Don't lead me astray, Offa, not now, not after all these years.*

"What is it that you think those soothsayers can tell you, anyway, eh?" Eurick was chewing on smoked sprat. "Folk say all they give out is riddles, and their riddles cause madness. Their answers are laced with poison that eats the truth and leaves a pit of lies."

"Those," said Halda, "sound just like the type of folk I need to talk to."

Eurick scrunched his face at her. "I just don't like riddles, man, it's like, just speak to me plainly. Bards are the worst for that, you know. I knew one called Itchy, and I swear—"

"I don't need you to understand the answers they give, transporter, I only need you to take me there. The rest is in the hands of Offa."

"Offa, eh?" Eurick looked up to the sky. "You know, there's so many gods, and all of them real. There's so much more to it than we all know, eh?" The transporter mumbled to himself as he walked away.

Halda leaned over the bulwark and breathed in the sea, yet again. She took the salt water on her tongue as she did when she was a girl. And Harald guided *Red Morning* carefully through the Channel of Krakens and into the dark waters of the River Blackstone on Ryne.

"Gotta moor her up before we reach Ardeen, man." Eurick had circled back around and was talking to Harald as if Harald would listen. "Ardeen is a raven's town, built up there over hundreds of years to service the Guild. There's old blood there, and ravens everywhere. Even I would get found out there, no doubt."

The ship heaved through the river at a pace that only a Daggland-made ship could reach. *Harald does not know this river an inch, he has never sailed it, yet Oade guides him. Not all the small gods are dead, not yet.* Halda squinted at the green waters and the strange white trees on the shore. She felt a weight in the air, like a clear mist that made breathing heavy but didn't impair vision. *There has been great sorrow here. This island holds secrets...*

"We've gotta stop this ship, Halda," Eurick said. "The captain won't hear me."

Halda hadn't even realized she'd stopped listening. "Land-ho!" Halda screamed, and her rakkarren moved with fury, scrambling like ants below decks to their oars.

"Land-ho!" they echoed. Ria scaled the mast and untied the sail while Denn and Barret reeled it in and rolled it and tied the sail up and away.

Harald had the ship moored in an outlet by a small sandy beach on the west side of the Blackstone. Halda and her rakkarren lowered their ships and rowed.

"Ardeen is on the east bank, better stick north and west, eh." Eurick held his hand to his face to block the sun from his eyes. "Don't worry, I'll get us there. This is just another job, man, never failed one. I don't think it's a stretch to say I'm one of the greatest ravens to have ever lived."

They camped that night upon the beach, and Barret and Haron cooked a boar over a fat spit and they all sang songs from the sagas late into the night.

The raven even joined in and sang along with them despite much protest at first. "Okay, fine, I'll join in for a few songs. We shouldn't sing too loud though, eh?"

When they sat around the fire, Eurick told a story. "The draugr, man, that's what they call it here." The raven held his arms up above his head to imitate antlers. "It has horns like a stag and walks on two legs. It has the body of a wraith, and its purple eyes haunt the darkness of Ryne."

"What is it?" Barret asked.

"It's a curse of the old gods, man. Their race once roamed all of Ardura before the nytewoods bore the race of Mal, and the Druids killed them all. The draugr is a curse, a sign that things went wrong."

"I'll kill it when it shows itself!" the warrior named Den raised his axe in the air, and the rakkarren cheered.

"You won't," Eurick said. "Nobody has. Just leave a sacrifice by your camp each night and it will leave you alone—a hare, a boar... something. It needs lifeblood."

"You're kidding, right?" Harald asked.

Of course he is...

"Not kidding, man. The draugr could kill us all in an evening and we'd never even know. We'd just go to sleep and not wake up again."

This is the sorcery spoken of in the sagas. This is the work of the Creator gods...

Harald stared at Eurick like he was a wart on his nose. He opened his mouth to speak but closed it again. Soon the rakkarren's bard Sigrid Windharp was singing again, and there were no more stories of the draugr.

"The less the better, when it comes to travelling." Eurick put his hand on Halda's shoulder. She could smell the shine on his breath, and the seriousness in his face almost made Halda laugh aloud. "We can't take this whole crew. The ravens will find us. I've told you about—"

"Yes, you've told me." Halda smiled. "It will just be me coming with you."

"Better that way, safer."

Halda woke with the sounds of strange birds. This far up the river, it was hardly brackish, and she longed for the smell of salt. *I am far from Massey Rock. Far from my safe place in my den.*

The raven had his bags packed and as the sun rose, Halda and Eurick left.

"Take care of the ship. I will be back. If I am different when I return, pray to Offa for my old self," Halda said, and Harald grinned his grim smile and nodded. She shook the captain's hand and he grunted something, then pulled her in for a hug.

"Don't leave us here, Halda, please. You promised us we could sail the coasts," Harald said. "Don't you leave us here. Don't be gone too long."

It was only minutes into walking when Halda knew this island was cursed. She could feel it in the air, in the strange blue-green grass beneath her feet. *This island is old, and its secrets dark.* Halda recognized the oaks and the maples and the many pines and birch between them, all brimming green with summer's bounty. She could see the great golden canopies of nytewoods kissing the clouds, and the pink sedge, and turtleshead and milkweed growing around the fat, blue streams, but a strange, snow-white tree grew on Ryne that made her uneasy. It grew thin fern-like leaves as white as its trunk.

"Strange, ain't they?" Eurick said as if he had seen Halda staring at the trees.

"I have heard no songs about these trees," Halda said.

"Ah, no songs to be sung, there are more and more every year. They're called winterwood. Not even the ravens know where they come from or when they started to grow here. But they grow thin and tall and stay white as snow all year." The raven stopped in front of a cluster of the white trees and laid his hand on the trunk of one of them. "And they are as cold as ice, man—er, Halda."

Halda touched one, and a shiver seemed to jump out of the tree and crawl through her skin then down her spine. "They are the ghosts of trees." Halda didn't know where the thought came from, it seemed to leap from her mouth. The raven gave her a curious gaze and studied the trees himself as if pondering the thought.

"Best we keep moving." Eurick pulled his attention from the trees and glanced around nervously. "Ravens could be watching these parts."

Eurick led Halda over crags of blackstone that jutted from moors of heather and wildflowers, and to Halda, the island looked like a rainbow had fallen out of the sky and landed here. They crossed gurgling streams of clear, blue mountain water and they stooped and drank from it deeply. They ate smoked sprat out of small jars and when the sun began to fall, Eurick set two traps, and by the time he had the fire blazing, one of the traps had caught a hare.

"This one for draugr," he said, and tied a small lead around the hare's neck and legs and tied the other end to a tree away from their fire. When the second trap went off, Halda could tell by the sound that it was much smaller than a hare.

Eurick went to check the trap and came back with a red squirrel. He cleaned it and cooked it on a spit.

"Why not leave the squirrel for draugr?" Halda asked.

"You have to give it more than you take," Eurick said.

"How will it know?"

"It knows." Eurick took down the squirrel and cut it up into steaming, greasy pieces and handed half of them to Halda. She gladly ate what little there was, and when Eurick offered her a wineskin, she gladly drank deep of the shine that filled it.

Drums pounded in Halda's head when she awoke. *Sweet, Offa... too much shine.* She wiped a spot of drool from her cheek and pulled herself up.

The raven was snoring loudly off to one side. Halda cracked her neck and stretched her arms into the air and almost shat herself at what she saw. *Oh, sweet Offa. I must still be drunk.*

She got up and paced towards the bloody mess she saw on the grass. A small skull with bits of pink cartilage hanging from it lay in the carnage like a bony apple. *It's the hare... the draugr...* Halda knelt and picked up a small white twig—a bone, picked clean. The hare's small ribs were cracked and sucked dry of marrow. And in the soil, Halda saw footprints. They looked like those of a man walking on tip-toes in bare feet. She followed them and saw a pair of forceps, pieces of parchment scattered, glass jars broken and discarded. She smelled sprat and cod oil. The raven's pack was torn into shreds, and their food stores were gone.

"By the gods, man." Eurick's deep voice made Halda jump. "We better leave something bigger tomorrow night."

THE BLUE KNIGHT

"**I** WOULDN'T LIE TO you." Haro held his palms out and grinned. In front of him stood a half dozen knights mounted on Glennish warhorses with a host of armed soldiers behind them.

"You saw it happen?" one of the knights removed his helm to get a closer look at the corpses. He had identified himself as Don Ryatt. The Glennish called their knights Don instead of Sir or Sal. Haro rather liked that, he had always thought it foolish to try and divide the world down the middle between men and women when there was just so much in between.

"With my own eyes." Haro flexed his burned hand. Grady opened his mouth but closed it when Uma smacked him. Two of the knights rode over to the wagon of bones and glared at them, then at Haro. "I'm just trying to do good by you and yours. The same man that killed these folk has Lord Brynmor tied up as a prisoner. Your lord is long of beard and nail and is in a bad way. He needs help."

"And what help would you bring, Ranger?" Don Ryatt said.

"Revenge," Haro said. "Me and the Queen of the Glenn share the same cause. The same person that killed these folk and had Lord Brynmor captive killed my family as well." Haro smelled sunflowers and rain, and Owen's sweet face was smiling at him in a faraway place inside of his head. The memories felt strangely distant.

Don Ryatt laughed. "The queen is dead." He looked up at the young sun rising. "Her funeral is in less than two hours. Thought you were part of that with all these bones."

Dead... The other knights studied Haro, and one of them gazed at Haro's burned arm like it was the most disgusting thing she had seen on a person and wouldn't stop staring. "Why is her funeral being held here? Why wouldn't she want to go home to Elurra?"

"In the Glenn it is our custom to be burned wherever the soul leaves the body. It allows the soul to carry its former life with it on its journey through the nytewoods and into the Otherworld." Don Ryatt beheld one of the nytewoods on the horizon. "Her ashes will be carried back to Elurra and the Brynmor Barrow at Stone Tree after the ceremony."

"Princess Gwen is our queen now," a young knight said.

"Is she here?" Haro asked.

"No," Don Ryatt said. "It's the Blue Knight who leads us in Dawning. But not for too much longer. We are giving the Mal forts and villages back to the Ayelish and going home after the funeral."

"Blue Knight?" Haro was lost. He had spent too long in his bird over the winter and lost track of the schemes of kings and queens. He didn't know who sat what throne. The Blue Knight though, he had heard songs of.

"Aye, she's here to bless the dead."

"Please," Haro said, "allow me an audience with her. Allow me to tell the same story I told you."

Don Ryatt eyed Haro and the bones some more than the other knight and said, "Aye. Let him come."

"Aye," said another. "I would love to hear what Ossian says about all them bones."

"Well, let's go then." Don Ryatt turned his massive warhorse around and rode off. *Ossian?* Haro snapped the reins and bid his team follow. Behind them, the bones clanked as they had the whole way.

The green fields of Dawning were infested with crows. Haro's blue jay hated the black winged bastards. *It's death and more death.* The funeral drums were thumping, the birds were cawing, and the sun was hot.

"How did she die?" Haro asked. "The queen?"

Don Ryatt laughed. "Her Grace died after a long few months of fighting the winter sickness. We honour her in the way any queen of the Glenn would have wanted to be honoured."

A crow cawed as if in disagreement and flapped overhead, forcing Haro to duck.

"Praise Eralis, those black-winged bastards love the corn," Don Ryatt said.

"Why so much corn?" Grady snatched a cob from a wayward stalk. "I thought these fields were famous for their barley? I've seen these golden fields myself. I've drank of the ale."

"Corn is more efficient. The queen wanted corn," Don Ryatt barked. "Here, slow that thing down, come this way."

The knight directed Haro and his band right into line with a funeral procession. The funeral procession marched through the chest-high corn fields to a large clearing. They carried the body of the lord's mother on a plank of oak wood. Her hands and feet and neck were tied with thorns and a crown of them sat upon her brow. The wide, doe-skin drums beat in unison with each step the procession took.

"Knights from all over the Glenn have gathered to honour the lady mother. The finest from each province and their retinues. Don Gordyn of Beauty, Don Kenzy of Maple, Don Martyn of Till. And even the finest of them all has donned us with her grace."

The line of shimmering knights was led by a knight in blue armour. She stood out amongst the plumage and the shining steel of the other Glennish knights like a single star in an otherwise starless sky. Light blue hair draped the shoulders of her midnight blue armour. In her gauntleted hands, she held a black sword that seemed to have stolen the light from around her.

"Her hair is blue?" Haro had seen many things, but he had never seen a person with blue hair.

"Indigo." Don Ryatt laughed. "She dyes her hair with woad. She makes the journey through the Flats each year to fetch the woad and prove her worth of the blue armour. It is the old ritual of—"

"Of Ossian," Haro said. "To tap water from a stone and pluck woad from the puca's garden." *Ossian only used the dye to mark his face and arms and dye his beard though.* When Haro had heard the name, he just thought it was someone who used the name for optics. *But no... this person* lives *the name.* He had to see her.

Don Ryatt smiled. "Of Ossian, aye. The Blue Knight. Ossian of Green Grove."

"She's really here?" Haro couldn't believe it.

"Aye," Don Ryatt said, "she speaks with the queen's voice on this night. Ossian will be more than happy to avenge these bones and bring Brynmor back to Stone Tree, I'm sure. The line of Brynmor has only one now, a daughter, and she is back safe at Stone Tree." Don Ryatt smiled. "You didn't think you would get the glory, did you?"

"No," Haro said. *I don't need glory. I need vengeance...* Haro spat. Something about his own thoughts felt wrong.

As Haro rode the wagon up, he was directed towards the pyre. A woman in a patched cotton dress held her hands up for him to stop, and so he did. He and the band got off the wagon. Haro looked around for the Blue Knight, then saw her on horseback riding away.

The Glennish folk wore woollen gambesons, or chain, or plate armour of iron. And the knights represented all of the Glenn by waving their flags alongside the white owl of Brynmor. Don Gordyn of Beauty with his white horse on green, Don Kenzy of Maple with her orange maple leaf on brown, and Don Martyn of Till with their silver chevron on blue centred by the black sword of Baynard. The smallfolk hustled here and there with thatch of dried barley and thorn and logs of oak. *Oak and thorn and ash.* Haro was reminded of the Hallow funeral tradition.

But this was a Glennish funeral on Mal Hallow soil, and along with the thorn and thatch and oak, they started to add the bones from the wagon. They added rushes of thyme and of madder and sumac cones.

A man, naked but for a leaf over his crotch hung by a hempen thread, sang a song of mourning that Haro hadn't heard before. He thanked Eralis for taking the queen's soul. He had owl wings attached to his back with some kind of glue that stank like vinegar, and his face was painted white with chalk.

"The ghosts of the Glenn walk with us on this night, soldier," the man said. When he began to recite more jargon to others, Haro realized he was some kind of priest. "They were strong, these, I feel them in my leaf. The horses will gain much strength from them."

"The Blue Knight." Haro grabbed the arm of a passerby. "Where did she go?"

The person shrugged. Then the priest said, "What is the problem?"

"These people." Haro pointed to the pile of bones. "They were slaughtered by a madman. The same madman who's holding Lord Richard Brynmor captive."

The priest's eyes flicked open. "Brynmor, you say?" He looked at the bones, then back at Haro. *How many folk are going to do that?*

"Aye," said Haro. He saw the man staring at his burned hand, so he held it up and flexed it.

"You'll find her here at the funeral later. Until then, she may have gone to the pond," the priest said.

"What pond?" Uma asked. Her voice was like a thunderbolt after being silent for so long.

"She doesn't like visitors. She said—"

"She said, what pond?" said Grady. He was always more confident after someone else had already established dominance.

"The old Mill Pond," the priest said. "She says she talks to nymphs there."

"Will you take us there?" said Kat, pouncing in for the kill.

"I have to prepare—"

"Take us there and leave us. That is all," said Haro.

"She doesn't like visitors. If you die—"

"That will be our problem to worry about," said Haro.

"Oh, by the gods, we'll need mounts," the priest said, and they mounted and rode on.

The priest led Haro and his band out of the cornfield and past the Fort of Dawning to the stretch of arbor that sheltered the old Mill Pond. The Fort of Dawning looked in decent repair, like the Glennish had sacked it lightly.

"They took Brinley and his crows unawares in the night," the priest said. "Scaled the walls and had the town in hours. The way I've heard it told is that Brynmor let Brinley and his ilk go with their lives. There was hardly a fight. And he gave the same mercy to Ockam."

Old wooden struts sat half-rotting in the mud where buildings once stood. Bones lay like sun-bleached sticks, and Haro could almost hear the laughter that once lived here.

"Those bones say there was at least some kind of fight," said Haro. No one argued with him.

At the edge of the worn path where the road disappeared into the Wick Arbor, the priest refused to go any farther. "Just there yonder, you'll find an old busted mill and a pond. She'll be there. Bring the mounts back when you're done here."

"You afraid of the nymphs, priest?" Grady chittered.

The priest pierced him with fierce eyes. "Yes," he said, and turned and rode off.

Nymphs, Haro knew, were nothing to take lightly. If they had chosen to reveal themselves to a person, then that person was in need of some dire warning and most likely in great danger.

The arbor welcomed Haro and his band like a cool woody hug. The burn bugs sparkled, and the skitters drank his blood and filled their bellies with his life for their young, and Haro was happy to provide it. The branches of trees touched him, and the mouldering leaves and loam beneath him sang sweet whispers with each step.

Haro and his band dipped into the forest like it was a lake, and none of them talked as they swam through it, and soon the wheel of the collapsed mill became visible through the branches like a rotten wood sun.

Behind the mill, the Blue Knight sat in her blue armour on a green log and her blue hair looked like a mat of tangled flowers. A cold metallic scraping echoed across the small pond as the knight drew her whetstone across a long black blade that sat on her lap. The pond had a green scum coating it, and dragonflies and water spiders danced upon it as if it were grass.

"What is it, Rangers?" the Blue Knight said. "You are brave to come here. Surely someone would have warned you that I don't like visitors?"

His three companions stopped dead in their tracks, but Haro took a few more steps forward. "I know where Brynmor is," he said.

The scraping sound stopped. The Blue Knight looked up, then turned around. "There are many folk claiming to know Brynmors at the funeral," she said without emotion.

"Lord Richard," Haro said. "The Old Owl himself. He's with the remaining Mal army. He's being held a prisoner in despicable conditions. He needs the help of his people."

"His people..." The knight stood and smiled. She sheathed her black sword and walked towards Haro. "He has put his people through Hell." She clenched a blue-gauntleted fist. "Still. We miss him, he was a great war leader. We could use him in the wars to come."

Haro began, "They are forty miles north of here—"

"Calm, Ranger," the Blue Knight said. "I don't even know who you are or if you're telling the truth."

Haro smiled and produced Brynmor's golden ring. He held it out for the knight to take and she did. Holding the ring in her leather-gloved hand, she peered at it with squinted eyes. "How did you get this?"

"When Brynmor saw me looking at him, he dropped this and stamped it into the mud," Haro said.

The Blue Knight studied Haro, then the ring again. "I will need to discuss this. Weigh the options. We are too far along in our cause to make rash decisions right now. We have a funeral to think of in the meantime. A queen is dead."

"Right," said Haro. "And you can call me Haro."

The Blue Knight said. "Call me Ossian."

"Is that your real name?" Haro asked.

"Does it matter?" Ossian pierced him with cool blue eyes.

"Don Ryatt said you and the Glennish are leaving these lands?" Haro said.

"Not by choice but by necessity. Eldinian has turned Ayeland into a hellscape since Queen Ianna mysteriously died."

"Died?" Haro said. He really was aghast at how little he knew of the throne games and how many and often they died.

"Killed, more like. Or run. I spoke to a man who saw the execution with his own eyes, and he swears to me that it wasn't Ianna that Eldinian killed. But that's the story, anyway, and people believe it. The major rulers that moved in to claim the Alder throne, King Garrish of Leveny and Queen Florhen of Severn, have been killed, too. The other rulers have all bent their knee to Eldinian. The Ayelish are gathering a mass army at Mammoth's Head for only Eralis knows what. And at home, in the Glenn, our new Warlock Aelia has summoned all the priests of Eralis to Stone Tree for Midsummer."

"That could be a sign of unity," said Haro.

"Eldinian just hung every priest of Eralis in Ayeland on Springtide eve," the Blue Knight said. "He's murdered the Alders and all who tried to oppose their murder. That country is fighting itself now. I don't think it's a coincidence the other Warlocks are summoning the priests, too. The Warlocks talk, you know. They are killing the gods to make way for their Creator—that's what I think. We need all of us to be home. Every last sword we have."

"Karaat?" Haro knew well of the Creator God and the dark Words He birthed.

"Aye, and His Words. The Warlocks seek power again. Eralis stands in the way of that. Ellorin started it with her shit. I was there to watch her poison Brynmor's mind with my own eyes. The poor bastard had no choice but to side with her. She was the catalyst in all this. She had Calen Alder wrapped around her finger. Now the Warlocks are making bigger moves. They whisper in the ears of kings and queens. Wherever there is power, they are whispering."

"You're saying it's the Warlocks who cause these ongoing wars?"

"I'm saying they're whispering in the ears of rulers, and the rulers listen to them."

"But how can they kill a god?"

"If a god can be born, a god can be killed. Eralis was only a Warlock, once. The Old Gods were some beasts that ruled these lands before the Druids were born from the trees. And a new god has been born. A new god in service of Karaat, and it is killing the others."

"How do you know all of this?" Haro watched a frog jump beneath the green slime.

Ossian laughed a sad kind of chuckle. "Because my gift is my curse. The woad gives answers you want and many you don't. The yew and its ramblings have shown me many futures, all of which are godless. And in those godless realms, I have spoken to the spirits, and they have told me of the downfall. I have seen the before and after, and none of it rings like the present." Ossian picked up a handful of dirt and dead leaves, and let it slide through her leather gloves. "We are doomed to die with Nature if we cannot save her."

Haro felt oddly emotional, like that sentiment struck him deeply. "Then let's save her."

"You wouldn't know how," Ossian said.

Haro smiled. "No, but we can start by heaping glory upon you. The person who has Richard Brynmor is the King of Mal Hallow. The Reaper."

The Blue Knight's gaze was trance-like. Her deep blue eyes suffocated him as she stared into him. *She is trying to see if you're lying. I wonder if she sees my whole body is a lie.*

"You speak true, Ranger?"

"His name is Haro," Kat said. "He is thrice blessed by e'daru, a living legend. There are no truer words than his, for he speaks with the tongue of e'daru."

Ossian still stared at Haro for an answer.

"I speak true."

"How do you know he's the Reaper?"

"His sword."

"*Essikah,*" Ossian whispered. It seemed to Haro the Blue Knight liked the taste of the word. She knew her prophecies. "I tried to pull it from the ground once. It didn't move for me. For the best, probably. It was a wicked-looking thing. A wicked soil that it grew in—Lindis."

"Aye," Haro said, "and the Reaper is a wicked man."

The Blue Knight smiled in satisfaction. "You four will attend the queen's funeral? Afterwards, we speak of this Reaper and how we'll kill him. I have waited for the right quest to present itself, one worthy enough to earn me my song. To kill the man who slayed Mother Nature and learn his secrets, and to save a king while doing it—now that's a song."

T HE QUEEN OF THE Glenn was laid atop a bed of roses, and two golden coins stamped with the face of Eralis on one and the owl of Brynmor on the other were placed over her eyes. Her hands and feet were tied with thorns, and she wore a crown of them atop her head. Her skin was blue-white and her nails were yellow. Owl flags waved above. The Knights of the Glenn held the banners themselves to show the respect of their kingdoms to the House Brynmor. To show that they all recognized this house as their rulers. Bards and children that the priests called a choir were singing high-pitched songs that made Haro cringe. They sounded like many chipmunks dying.

The priest appeared and was wearing more than just a leaf now. A white robe was draped over his shoulders, and he held a book in one hand. Books were rare in Mal Hallow so Haro knew it must have said something important, and by the way the priest held it, Haro could see that it was valuable, too. The priest opened the book and began to recite from it, but Haro could only think of the dream he had woken from the night before.

He had seen Ifanie and Owen laughing in that dream. Their smiles lit up the dark and lonely world that he had fallen into. Sweet Ifanie's smooth hair and the smell of her... Owen, *my son,* and his laughter, his shaggy hair. *He looks nothing like you...* Haro saw them and his heart melted. *I miss you so much. So much...* But when he approached them, they didn't know who he was.

Terror leaked from Ifanie's scream as he walked closer. She held Owen and he whimpered, and she stood and ran, and Haro ran after them but that only made the fear he sensed in her grow. *Come back!* he wanted to shout, but in that dream world, he had no tongue. *Who are you?* Ifanie screamed at him. *I'm Haro. I'm Haro. But where does Haro start and all of the lives you have stolen end? Where?*

A burst of flames snapped Haro back into reality. The priest had finished droning and the pyre was aflame behind the queen. Glennish servants worked their way around the outside of the pyre, lighting it in many more spots, and soon it was ablaze higher than the surrounding trees. Only the nytewoods touched higher.

On the pyre they burned a boar and a goat and one unlucky servant. The bodies of the slain and the bones from Haro's wagon were on there, too, and the black smoke that poured from them was sulphurous. After a few moments, Glennish soldiers approached the flames with pitchforks in their hands and collectively pulled the smoking husks of the boar and the goat and the prisoner out of the fire. They let their bodies smoke and sizzle on the grasses as the smell of it choked the breath out of Haro so that he had to turn away.

And while the flames licked the sky, the Glennish lowered their queen into a hole that had been dug in front of the pyre. The bards sang morose songs that Haro didn't know, and they plucked lightly on their harps, and the music, the dead queen, and probably the smoking husks of dead things, had moved some folk into crying.

When Queen Grace and the platform of roses she lay on thumped at the bottom, the servants retrieved shovels and began to pile dirt on top of her dead, cold body. *What a sad and lonely way to rot, with the worms and the grubs...* When the hole was filled, the Glennish danced on top of it to flatten the earth, and the choirs sang with the bards, and the fire roared. When the wineskins started going around, Haro drank long and deep of the shine and danced along with the Glennish. *Who are you?* He thought, and his memories stirred, and memories that weren't his stirred, too, and he didn't know which were which anymore. *James. You need to find James. To kill him? Yes?* But in truth Haro was terrified that he'd made a mistake somewhere. It was too much, too much. *To change bodies—I'm getting too old for this.* But was he?

How old is a soul?

"Make way!" Shouts from behind caused a stir. The heavy *neighs* of warhorses pierced Haro's ears. The ground shook beneath the weight of their trot. *By the gods... Glennish warhorses...*

With leads of raw leather, Glennish soldiers guided the hellaciously large destriers up to the smoking dead husks. The beasts started to buck and bray when they got close, as if the smell had driven them mad. Their jagged, yellow teeth were the most unnatural thing Haro had ever seen. *E'daru, praise your beauty.* They chomped and *neighed* and drooled ice-white saliva as thick as mud.

When the soldiers of the Glenn let the warhorses go, they swarmed the charred and smoking remains of the bodies, and began to tear them apart with their mouths. They ripped and shredded and ate, and Haro couldn't watch. *This is not Nature. This is something else.* He had a horrible vision of some dark magics working into the blood of the horses and *turning* them into... these.

Flashes of the Maw flickered in his mind. *"There is a purpose to this—to you. Nature calls you. Nature needs you. Look. Find your purpose."*

Ossian cheered and drank, and Haro admired her for the mysteriousness she wore like a dress, out in the open for all to see but none could truly know the thread it was bound from. And the people of the Glenn drank and danced solemnly with each other on the ground above their dead queen as the moon rose in the black-blue sky. *The sky is the colour of Ossian's armour.* Haro hated how much the knight intrigued him. He wanted to *know* her. To learn her ways.

Grady was hammered. He was telling stories and singing songs around the fire. Uma was boasting of her many kills and holding her numbers up against the Glennish Knights, who all seemed to be afraid of her and also hadn't killed nearly as many. Kat had slunk off into the nearby Wick, and Haro did the same.

He lay on the cold soil beneath a tree and looked up at the stars through the black canopy. He lay thinking of Dalla. Missing her. If he hadn't been the very one that killed her, he would hunt and kill the person that had. *It was you.* Part of Grig still lived. And Grig hated Haro to pieces.

Haro flexed his scarred hand. *This hand has killed before. It would have killed you for killing Dalla. It is a strong hand.*

She was his Dalla. *I loved her.* She was dead now. He watched her die and he missed her. *Who are you?*

AKU'MAR

"THERE'S A LOT TO this, Etta," Baerd said. Etta spit in his face. She couldn't hold it. She came forward and he didn't move. He didn't wipe the spit, he just stared at her with his fucking all- knowing eyes and saw *everything* inside of her in an instant, just as he always had. *Because he* knows *you. He knows you like no other.* And she saw hurting in his eyes, and she pounded on his chest and she spit in his face again, and he let her do these things, and then when she broke down into tears, he hugged her and she hugged him back.

"I'm going to kill you," she said, and she truly meant it.

"I know," he said, and he hugged her again. "But just wait until we hear from Bazal."

Baerd wiped the spit from his face with the back of his sleeve and Etta turned away. Her head was exploding. She had spent ten years wanting nothing but to end this man's life, and now all she wanted to do was talk to him. Hear his voice tell her that they were going to be okay. Just as he always had. *We can have a family name,* he had said, *Wulfee, a future, a place of our own.*

There were bodies strewn across the ground. Blood and guts and limbs and lives, all to be forgotten. Etta stepped over them. She looked out into the arbor. *What the fuck are you doing? Where are you going? What is this? Who are you? Are you Etta? You're not truly, are you? You're Wulfee. You killed your son. If you can't live with that, then you need to die. You need to kill this man for what he's put you through. You owe that to Wulfee. You owe that to Braden...* Etta looked at the axes strewn in the mud. At the swords and cudgels. She turned and saw young Swey talking to Baerd. *He has no idea that man is his grandfather, and he is named after him.* It struck Etta then at how odd it was that she hadn't told young Swey that she was his grandma. *You have been Etta this whole time and forgotten the good parts of Wulfee.* She heard footsteps behind her but didn't turn.

"We have a bit of a ride to Bazal's camp." It was Baerd. "I understand if you don't want to, but I'd love to talk to you along the way, if you're up for it."

Etta said nothing and turned so her back was more directly facing him. She hated herself and what she had become. She wished she had the strength to turn and kill him right now, but she had nothing. Baerd walked away.

The folk that had survived dug a large pit while others gathered the dead and stripped them of their valuables and piled them in the pit. They had many fires going now, and they took hot coals and poured them on the bodies, and piled wood atop the glowing coals so they were set aflame. The smoke was thick and black and putrid with the reek of flesh. Etta sat at a small fire next to Swey and Tara.

"That wasn't all of them by half," Owyn said. He and Baerd stood by the fire next to theirs.

"Then we should leave before nightfall," Baerd said, and Owyn nodded. Soon Baerd was shouting orders for the lot of them to pack up and get ready for their two-week march. "We won't be stopping," Baerd said, and

Etta hated how his voice made her stomach tingle. She hated how it made her feel safe. She hated herself more than ever because she had become too weak to kill him. *You owe that to Wulfee. You owe that to Braden...*

"Come on," Etta said to Swey. "Have I told you the story of how Gen tried to feed trout to a donkey?"

THE BLOOMING GOLDEN LEAVES of a massive nytewood sparkled through the misty morning like a thousand thousand tiny suns.

"It's near as big as the nihr'el," Etta said.

Annie laughed. "To me, every nytewood with a face is a nihr'el, you know," she said. "And to the Feldarra of these northern parts, every nytewood is a World Tree. It was the flat land Feldarra that claimed there was only one nihr'el."

"It was an ancient order of Druids that wanted to make Pool a holy place. They carved the face into the tree and crafted cult-like stories and traditions to enforce their rule to the Feldarra and those factions are probably where your ancestors hail from," Fiora said. "My dad sang the song often. The same order that Emmer the Great was a part of."

Etta spat. She'd fought folk for disrespecting Emmer's name in the past. "Everyone sings the same songs with different words."

"She speaks true, Etta," Baerd said. "There is much and more you don't know, about the Druids of Old. They were here a long time before Kelson conquered and their blood was diluted. They... they weren't good, Etta."

Etta still couldn't stand to hear Baerd's voice. She hated herself for being too weak to kill him. *All those years you waited, and now he's right there... right there. Sweyne. Sweyne. Your name isn't fucking Baerd, you god-damned piece of—*

They had travelled three weeks now when Baerd claimed it would only take two. But the Ranger guide, Uni, took them on a route to avoid another attack from the Demhoni, so it had taken them longer. They made camp most nights, and Etta lay awake listening to the bugs chirrup and the fire crackle, and watched the moon and the stars and the burn bugs.

One night, an axe mocked her, blade down in an old stump near-by. *Kill him*, the axe said, but Etta couldn't. The axe had become a stain—a dirty rotten apple smeared on the floor of her life. *The axe killed Braden. And Wulfee held the axe. You. You held the axe that killed your son.* How could she pick up the axe to now kill the father of her son? *Can you solve death with death?*

Etta's ancestors lived and died by blood feuds for as far back as they can trace. A soul stained with vengeance won't go to the cloud halls. But Etta's soul had been torn out and ripped to pieces—far beyond staining. Whatever she had left inside of her held no feuds—it barely held the small ember of life she had kept going. And she knew in her heart that she wasn't going to the cloud halls now, anyway. She was so far beyond honour now that it was laughable. *There is no place up there for kinslayers. No place for abandoners. No place for liars.* Her soul was destined to linger now or go down. *All the way to Hell is where you'll go. With the ice dragons and the Warlocks of Old Yehven.*

Now, finally, they had come to the end of a slim mountain pass that opened up into a vast green valley. A river snaked through the middle of it that tumbled down from the east mountains and disappeared somewhere in the western range. A massive nytewood shaded a third of the diameter of the whole valley, and many other smaller ones sprouted up below. A face, grand and wise and knowing, was carved into the tree, and watched over all with sage eyes.

"Ah," Baerd said. "We've made it."

Plumes of smoke rising like trees to the mist marked the point of camp. "There's a hundred forges down there." Etta noted the mine openings in the mountain sides.

"Two hundred and thirty," Baerd said. "More than all of the north."

Rat whistled. "And that's that good stuff, too. None of that bent iron shite the Mal use. Iron and steel, woven like rope. Not too hard, not too soft."

"What would you know of the good stuff, Rat?" Nettle laughed. "I've literally seen you eat bugs from under a log."

"What does that have to do with anything?" Rat pulled his greenhood tight around his face, he seemed confused, and Etta reckoned that just about proved Nettle's point.

They walked into the valley, and when they came to a charcoal pit, two warriors whose hair was laden with braids, wearing furs over their shoulders, stood guard.

"What be it?" one grunted, and her voice alone was enough to make Etta's hair stand.

"Aye, it's Baerd. I've got the Kihl'dor of the Fells with me." He gestured at Etta with an outstretched hand, and Etta wanted to smack him. *The real Kihl'dor of the Fells would kill me if they knew I'd claimed that title without single combat to prove it.* Etta thought of Pike and his daughter.

The warriors peered at Etta as if she were some kind of rare bird, and when Etta jumped forward a step, the warriors lunged backwards. Etta laughed and somewhere inside of her, Wulfee laughed, too. "Right, right, go on. Just watch yourself on this charcoal, eh? It hasn't rained in days, and this could really light up."

They walked carefully along the narrow road that wound through the charcoal pit and through a dead forest of stumped trees that went on for miles and miles. *How much charcoal are these bastards making?* Etta noted horses grazing in pasture, and cattle and sheep, too. They had fields of barley and wheat, and rye that were green and healthy beneath the Fell summer sun. This was a proper town deep in the mountains, not just a camp.

They walked, and folk were everywhere, and all of them moved about with tasks at hand. Cattle wayns full of barrels of flour and rolls of wool and ores and rocks rumbled along dirt roads that were neatly maintained.

"What is this?" Etta asked. She was completely in awe that this could have existed without her knowing. *All those years you lived a lie.* She wondered why her parents had never told about this place. *Did they even know? The world is bigger than what you've been told and what you've seen... you never thought to look for Sweyne in the mountains—you thought it wasn't like him to hide.*

In the centre of the valley grew a massive nytewood, and on that nytewood was carved a crude face. Not as deftly hewn as the one at Pool, but a face nonetheless.

"Bazal's camp. This is what I told you about. This is the resistance that will save the world from Karaat. With help, of course."

"Is he here? Bazal?" Etta asked.

"Of course he is." Baerd scratched the back of his head. "But you can't see him right now."

Etta wanted to smack him. She had come all this way, made to believe there was some grand wizard behind it all, and it had been Sweyne the whole time. *You should have known, you stupid—*

Baerd continued. "He sleeps for long periods of time. He says he communicates through dreams with other entities of the world. It is magics we know nothing of, and I shan't disturb it, and at the moment he is not awake. But I can show you where he lies."

Etta spat for answer.

"Whenever you're ready," Baerd said.

"I'm ready for you to be fucking dead."

"Just let me explain, Wulf—"

"I don't want to hear you—"

"It was the mask, Wulf." *The mask...* Baerd continued. "That cursed mask had a hold on me I couldn't shake. It brought out everything bad in me and amplified it so that it was so loud it tore me to pieces. I'm sorry, Wulf. I'm so fucking sorry I can't even begin to tell you."

The mask. The bloody mask. "You don't get to be sorry!" Etta screamed. "You hear me. You don't get to stand there and tell me one god-damned thing about sorry."

"What happened, Wulf? Tell me what happened. Why are you hiding away in the mountains calling yourself Etta?"

Etta cocked her fist and broke Baerd's nose bloody. He flinched and held his nose, and looked at the blood on his hand, then smiled at Etta. "I deserve that," he said. "No, *you* deserve that. I've done so much to wrong you, but let me tell you about that god damned mask."

Etta was walking away but stopped. That mask had haunted her for eleven years. Braden had been wearing it when she killed him. She wanted to know—she had to know about this mask. She turned around.

Baerd smiled, and Etta hated the way his cheeks dimpled and how straight his jaw was. "That wolf we took it from, you saw it, it came from Hell. It was a creature of an old time when the race of Old Gods walked these lands in great numbers. Wolves and stags, owls and crows, and even trees walked and talked and fought with eldritch earth magics. But when the Mal Druids were born from the nytewoods, they banished those creatures through many years of war. The strongest of them were allowed to remain as gods in the Otherworld as part of a peace offering, and those we call the Old Gods. Over time, their power has diminished as their prayers and worship rituals were slowly forgotten. But when the Druids fought wars, they summoned the beasts from the Otherworld with the intent to slaughter them and wear their skulls as masks to absorb their eldritch powers. Every now and then, one of the beasts they summoned got away. They still roam the arbors and the hills and the valleys and riverbanks. The beast we found and killed that day, that wolf, was one of them. The elders taught me all of this when I first came here. They even have a name for someone cursed by one of those old beasts. *Aku'mar.* Lost one. The power of those beasts is incredible. I was more alive than I had ever been while at the same time dying inside."

Etta clenched her fists. "Why did you give it to Braden?"

"Braden? Wulfee, I lost it in combat—" A flash of realization crept across Baerd's face. "What happened to Braden?"

Etta couldn't even stop herself from crumbling to her knees. It was as if her flowing tears weighed a thousand pounds and she wanted to lay her head down. Baerd stepped forward to help her, and she screamed. "You don't get to fucking touch me. You don't get to be kind. Listen to me. I'm going to fucking kill you."

Baerd's subtle look of calmness had slipped away. He looked worried now, as if he was afraid Etta had actually lost her mind. *And you have.*

"When I first came here, I had a lot of pain inside of me that needed healing. The first thing I did was re-recite my oaths in front of that nihr'el. I have never felt more alive than I did on that day. I reckon you should sit by the nihr'el awhile, Wulf. You can go see Bazal whenever you're ready. You don't need me for that. My part was just to get you here."

"Why?" Etta hated him. "Why did you bring me here?" *You should have killed me so I don't have to kill you. I would rather die than commit murder again.*

"I told you this already, Wulf. Look around. We're building an army for Nature. And someone needs to lead it."

"Is this a joke? You're going to kill me in my sleep or something."

"It's not a joke, Wulf. You are the greatest leader this country has ever seen. Curse Hell, but you might be the greatest leader this world has ever known. Your blood is the blood of Emmer. Kelson would cower in his fancy Lovasi boots at the sight of you behind a shield wall."

"I told you I won't fight."

"I know. At least do this. Say your oaths. Remember why you said them in the first place. Then talk to Bazal. If you want to leave this place after that, I won't follow you." Baerd slipped out of the tent and disappeared in the bustle of the village.

P INK HONEYSUCKLE, AND SNOW-WHITE yarrow, and goldenrod as bright yellow as the sun bloomed in bounty beneath the nihr'el. Finches and larks sang, and the air was sweet with honey. *Even when the world was dead, you lived.* Etta looked at the beauty of the nytewood and tears welled in her eyes and fell to the dirt. *James... you did it. You really did it.*

The last time she had seen a nihr'el—her nihr'el—it was infested with death. She was chained beneath it and crows sang in place of larks, and the world around her was dying. *That was a different life. Before you killed your son. You were strong then.* A face was carved into this nihr'el, and it reflected Etta's soul and was sombre-looking. She remembered the first time she had beheld the nihr'el at Pool. She was just a small girl, and she had made the trip with her mom and dad. They told her to pray and practice the oaths she would one day say for real. The face was smiling then. It smiled for years until she went back last summer and saw that it was frowning now. *No, it was angry...*

"Why does its face change? Does it feel?" Young Wulfee had asked.

"Aye," her dad had answered. *"It feels with the intensity of every life that has ever lived. It sees the past and future as clearly as it sees the present. It lives and feels and knows more than we ever could. It is the power of all powers, and that is why we pray to it."*

Etta could remember that first encounter with the nihr'el well. She was Etta then, too, and she had been practicing the oaths with her dad for months and months getting ready for that day.

"I'm so proud of you, dear," her dad had said. *"This is a proud moment for any Feldarra"*

When she had arrived at the nihr'el all those years ago, there were torches stuck in the ground burning with whale oil that the elders had acquired by trading furs with the folk of Tide. The oily, black trunk shimmered in the firelight. A low humming had come from the elders' songs, and Etta still remembered the chill that traced its way up her spine from their tone. She was terrified. *And you couldn't let anyone know, or your parents would see you as weak. As an unworthy Feldarran.*

Wearing black robes and the skull of a boar, a shaman had muttered words from the cycles and prayed to the Old Gods. Etta stood in front of her, and the oaths she had practiced so carefully and so repetitively for months and months rang out in her mind, and she knew every word to say but for some reason she couldn't say them. The songs of the elders mingled with the mutterings of the shaman, and Etta remembered the feeling of all of those folk of the Feldarra staring at her, standing there at the base of this great tree, and not saying the words she should be saying. The longer it went on, the worse the words seemed to stick to her tongue. But just as Etta had seen her dad approaching and scowling angrily at her, the words poured out in a steady stream.

"*I will fight and protect these lands, the Fells and Mal Hallow, with my life. I will stand tall in the face of death and never turn my back. I swear to fight to the very end.*"

When she had finished speaking and turned away from the tree, the elders were singing different songs and the shaman had stopped muttering, and the girl who was once Etta was dead and Wulfee the warrior was born. When Etta had said the oaths, it gave Wulfee permission to kill the innocent girl inside of her and become a woman—a leader.

Now you need to say the oaths and kill Etta again. Find Wulfee in there. Etta knew that she could find strength inside of herself again. Something had kept her alive through all of this. Some force that drove her from the inside that was bigger than her.

Now, Etta stood below that nihr'el that wasn't the same one her father had brought her to, and she felt false.

She turned away from the nihr'el. *I'm not ready.*

When she made her way back to camp; there was a bustle starting. Folk were rushing out of their mud hovels and leaving their forges and rushing towards the central part of the valley where craggy ridges offered a view of the river that rolled beyond.

Etta ran with them. "What is it?" she asked a woman wearing a grin as wide as the Old Sea, who only shrugged in response and kept running. When Etta got to the centre, she let herself flow with the crowd. She was being pushed this way and that, and finally she could see a black line of people marching along the ridge and into the valley. "Who is it?" Etta asked a shaggy haired man who smiled wanly.

"*Si'koro,*" he said. "People of the flat land."

"What?" Etta had never heard that term before.

"Some call them the Feldarra," he said. "From Pool."

Etta wanted to laugh but was already crying, so instead she did an odd cry-laugh and knelt over with her hands on her knees. The shaggy-haired man looked uncomfortable and started to walk away but stopped himself and turned around. "You okay?" he asked. The crowd moved all around, and the man could take two more steps and be lost in it.

Etta stood tall and smiled, her gaze still set on the stream of folk, armoured and axed, pouring off the ridge and into the valley. There were hundreds of them. A thousand maybe. "I'm better than okay," Etta said. "Those are my people."

RED SKY ROCK

"**W**AIT FOR IT. LET the story eat at them," Julien said.

"These soldiers are growing impatient. They want war while they feel the momentum is on their side," Trist said. "You don't want to let that battle lust fade, I'm telling you, getting it back won't be easy. And the enemy knows we're here now, they will be preparing for our attack. We should march tomorrow."

"Have you ever heard the story of the snail and the frog, friend?" Julien was polishing his Tiago Dilarios.

"Why are you speaking of children's fables?"

"The snail and the frog is more than a story for children, friend, it's a story of life. The snail won the race by patience and persistence. The frog hopped in headlong without paying attention to his surroundings and got himself eaten. If we attack Sareen now, we would be nothing but flies in the mouths of frogs to them. They would slaughter us. Let the story of Letharr and his demons spread. Let it take root. Let the soldiers wait on the battlements and wonder where we are. If the stories were true or not. Let doubt infect them. Then in the evening we attack. Don't lose sight of our goal."

"*Our* goal?" Trist was drunk and seemingly agitated. "It was my army that slaughtered Natt Floyd. My army allowed for this to happen. What part do you think you have in all of this? How is it you sit here calmly with so much at stake? How do you speak of children's fables and prophecies from ancient texts as if they are meaningful? Are you truly mad? Has your head been rattled too many times? Tell me!"

"Karaat has told me true," Julien said.

Trist threw his arms up. "Karaat," he spat. "You speak of this god Karaat, and I hear about Him in a thousand hallowed hovels across Esher and the Hesterlands but never has He made an appearance. His supporters are poor, lice-ridden fiends, and even the Warlocks ditched Him in favour of Eralis in an effort to quell His sorcerous Words from spreading. He is a dark and dangerous god, and I've had enough of you speaking about Him. The sooner you realize this world is godless, the better."

"He is the god of Draku, too, and my people never abused His words. They used them for good."

"And how could you possibly know that?"

"My grandfather told the tale. He had read it in a book once, a book inside the library at Hest. It's the same book I vow to hold in my hands one day. The book of our Creator. The Book of Insa."

"Books, prophecies, these things don't win wars. Let me tell you something about battle—it doesn't give a fuck what's written down in some book. It's raw. It's animalistic. You say you're going to take Hest, but I'm not convinced you could even take a single farm without the little mind games you play."

Julien knew that Trist had had enough of clever plans and words. He wanted proof, and Julien had proof. "*Dagdora,*" he sang, and a flaming ball appeared in front of him. It hovered, eating the air around it viciously, and if Julien didn't set it in motion, it would start moving on its own, so he flicked his head towards a shrub of dogwood and the bush ignited into flames.

The fire burned so hot and bright that Trist had to cover his eyes. Julien walked over to the shrub and held his hands in the fire. They blackened with soot but didn't burn. *This* trick he had learned when he was just a child—that his flesh didn't burn as others did—and his father and grandfather had always bid him keep it secret, for it was the mark of Draku and therefore folk would kill him for it. But now, more than ever, he needed that secret to be known. He wasn't a fool. He wasn't mad. *Maybe a little.* He was Draku. Still, his hands were in the fire, and Julien could see that the doubt in Trist's face had transformed into horror or awe or both.

Julien held his soot-blacked hand up and made a fist, just as Kassius had done when he took his throne at Red Sky Rock. "With the Words of my maker's god, I will take back the kingdom that was lost to me long ago. It is not the planning of one season or even ten. I am destiny come, a prophecy that has been in the making for a thousand winters. When the Warlocks traded their souls to Karaat for long life, Karaat promised them that he would send a demon to claim them back one day. They didn't buy eternal life, they bought extended life. And I will give them what they are owed. I'm going to collect their debt." Julien walked slowly, and his freshly polished Tiago Dilarios whispered to the sand that they had grown to love. "So you wonder how I tell fables and sit patiently in a time like this? I've been patient my whole life. My father was patient and so was his."

"I understand," Trist said. "I'm fighting for my family's name, too. For a thousand years of history that could die with me if I don't succeed. We are the same, Julien Esterbraun, you and I. We are the same and also so very different. The world is a beautiful place, and life is a beautiful thing."

"Beautiful indeed," Julien said. "Now, we need to get Lord Floyd's head in a box. See that the box arrives safely at Red Sky Rock.

"And what of his body?"

"It will be a gift to Karaat," Julien said. "Now, one more thing. I saw your people flogging bats by the shore at night. Can they capture them alive instead? Put them in a cage?"

"Alive?" Trist said. "I don't see why not. What good will bats do you? Where I'm from, we go hawking, and it takes a great mind and a steady hand to master it. The hawks eat bats."

Julien laughed. "I'm not going hawking, friend. But I do know you're a betting man. Let's take wagers on how long a bat can fly while it's on fire."

THE SUN BAKED THE decks of the ship, and the bulwarks were so hot that Julien nearly burned his hand by touching one. *Saltspray* seemed to dance through the waves, sending seawater skyward with every dip, and with every splash Julien was reminded of how this ship got its name. The sea-sickness had left him now; it always left after a few days, and he was well and truly enjoying the sunshine. *Soon it will be dark winter, and I'll be cursing the cold.*

It had been five days since Trist's army had killed Natt Floyd, and no Hester had come up the Esheri to the riverside palace looking for him, which told Julien that whoever ruled in place of Natt had chosen to try and protect the city rather than meet an army in the field. This was exactly what Julien wanted. The more eyes he had watching him, the better.

His boots tapped smoothly on the wooden planks as he walked the decks. He was looking for any sign of traps. Whoever had taken charge in Sareen would surely be aware of a coming attack, and Julien had to be prepared for anything. Kassius had ruined a whole fleet of Epithosian warlords by laying spiked balls of steel in the river, floating two feet under, suspended by rope attached to moorings on either bank. The Epithosians had crossed the Old Sea to try and take what Kassius had, and they paid the price.

After Julien was satisfied that the deck crew was well aware of potential dangers and had somehow convinced Hild to slow the ship, he went below decks to his cabin.

Trist and his people had secured Julien a wire cage full of bats, hundreds upon hundreds of them, and he could hear them squawking madly as he neared his room. The smell of shit smacked him in the nose when he squeaked the door open and went in. The bats heard him there and went even wilder. They flapped madly and tried to fly from the cage, and the smacking sound they made was horrendous. His floor was covered in bat shit and urine, and the bats squealed.

"It's alright, sweeties, it's okay," Julien said. He put his hand flat on the outside of the cage. The bats calmed some, and then he whispered. "Praise Karaat for your beauty." And they calmed completely. Julien lay back in his cot and closed his eyes, and the bats made no sound. He imagined himself hanging upside down like a bat. *Karaat, come to me again. Guide me on this journey. Tell me I've done the right thing. Everyone doubts me. Though I cannot bear to doubt myself. Everyone but you.*

Julien remembered his father and his young brother. He remembered the day the Warlocks killed them. They had sailed north to fish cod. They could catch a load full of it and bring it back to Esher for cheap salting. They would make a fortune off the cut and dried strips of cod. Enough to get them closer to Hest. *Closer to the book of our ancestors.*

On their way back, they were stopped by a Hester ship that claimed they had fished the Crown's waters and the family's ship, *Windtalker,* was confiscated. They were given trial before King John but he was otherwise incapacitated, so his Warlock Adora held trial. The next day both of them were found dead from a bad belly. The Warlock sent their bodies back to Julien with a raven who told him everything that had happened. The raven said Julien's father and brother had claimed themselves as Draku before the court. He claimed them rambling mad and righteous with Karaat. Their bodies reeked worse than anything Julien had ever smelled from that poison. That was the day he joined a sellsword band, in fear that he'd be next. It felt safer to be surrounded by all those killers and all that steel.

But when Hest falls to a Draku and I hold Adora's head high for all of the Hesterlands to see, they will bow. Karaat will be proud.

Next thing Julien knew, he was startled awake by his door slamming open. And again, the bats were screeching.

"We're here, Esterbraun, the folk are gearing up," Rolan said. He was already armoured himself, of course, and Julien jumped up and followed behind him.

Nightfall had draped the Esheri Rush like a blanket. The waters were black, and now that the lamps on the wharfs and harbours of Sareen were visible, Julien almost couldn't believe what he was seeing. Around the outermost walls of Sareen, a thousand small fires burned. Their flames lit up the sandstone walls a beautiful orange and red and gold, and the flickering shadows of the fire danced upon them. *Karaat...* the fires were effigies to the Creator God, and it seemed as though his belief was spreading.

"They blamed their god Eralis for the wither year and for the Hesters invading," Rolan said. He was seemingly in shock, too. "They've come to worship Karaat in troves. I've never seen so many small fires."

And this is why the Words are working. This is why your magics are alive. With every believer, Karaat grows stronger, and you grow stronger.

Sareen's walls were tri-fold. One of yellow sandstone, one of clay brick, and another of red sandstone carved and dragged here from the Hills of Soma. Her gates were each facing the cardinal directions with a fifth to the northeast that served as a parade road. Julien hoped to get as close as he could to the southernmost gate, called the River Gate.

Hild had taken down her black sails and rigged up the bleached white ones of a merchant, and Julien had instructed everyone aboard to stay below decks. He didn't think that the Floyds would be fooled right up to the gate, but he just needed to fool them long enough to get close.

The *Saltspray* was being oared along by her crew below, and Julien had ordered Ashan to get the bats. The cage required two people to carry, so Rolan went with him.

Julien stood alone at the nose of the ship and let the seawater mist his face and run down his beard. *The Draku are of fire but water does not harm me. I am not natural. Not from the earth.* Julien had the thought before but it started to grow since his time at sea. *What are you, really? Is this a farce? Everyone thinks you are a fool. You were so certain they were wrong, but were they? You're going to try and take a city with a cage of bats? You killed the bloody Oracle...*

Julien shook his head. There was no time for doubting himself. No space for it. Sareen was big and beautiful in front of him. Above the walls, the Lovasi castle of Red Sky Rock towered in the crumbling city of Sareen. Three grand causeways connected three towers that were even grander. The towers sprouted out of a palace of marble pillars and white-veined pink-stone. Each of the towers was really three towers, one growing out of the other, with a palace at the roof of the one below, and terraces surrounding the balconies. They were made of the same red sandstone as the third layer of walls, and the towers were roofed with copper that had turned metallic green. *A Draku Lord would never let those roofs turn green. They would be polished daily.*

On the walls, Julien saw archers. The banner of House Floyd, a brown shield on grey, hung from the barbicans and each of the walltowers.

"House Floyd is still strong here," Rolan said. "Praise Karaat, you better have a plan."

"You will laugh one day at the fear you feel now."

The small fires seemed to grow in number the closer the *Saltspray* got. Julien counted up to thirty and stopped, but he didn't even count a fifth of the way down the wall. Then, the South Gate opened and a ship came through.

"They're going to try and sink us," Hild called out from the stern. "Ships in the yander. They're going to try and sink us, boy!"

"Keep steady," Julien said as two more ships slithered out of the south gate behind the first one. The ships had scorpion bows at the hull, and the decks were glinting with the armour of soldiers.

Hild gritted her teeth and spat, "I'm turning her around, boy. I'm not dying here today. Not for you."

"Stay on course!" Julien shouted. *Where the fuck is Ashan?* The ships were coming up the Esheri with great speed towards them. Julien could see scorpion crossbows on the stern of each ship.

"Praise Karaat, I took money from the wrong damn fool when I took this job." Hild spat again, and Julien wondered how she always had so much saliva. "I won't die for ye. Ye best believe that, boy."

Finally, Ashan and Rolan came up dragging the cage of bats. The animals screeched and smacked the cage with their wings and small bodies, and squealed in the night almost like hogs.

"These things are crooked, man! What's wrong with you?" Rolan was shielding his eyes and ears with a forearm.

"Incoming!" a voice came from the masthead, and then a loud thump into the hull of *Saltspray*. Then two more, one after the other.

"Water!" shouts from below. Then the folk streamed above decks, and Julien knew he couldn't hide anymore. "We're taking on water!" the crew was shouting. They had been hit by the scorpion bolts, and they had pierced the ship's hull below the water line.

"Well don't run around like bloody children, bail, you bastards, bail! Bail like ye never bloody bailed before!" Hild was screaming, and somehow her scream was heard above all others. "What are ye? Small children? Bail, for ye bloody lives!" Julien could see the ships loading their scorpions again. *You're not close enough. Not yet.* Hild was still shouting. "I'll go down with this ship, and it ain't going down today!"

The bats screeched, and Julien walked to them and put his hand on their cage. *They're beautiful. More so than any bird. Thank you so much for your sacrifice. Karaat will find the finest place in His hall for you. You can hang there and be free of this harsh world. You will live as the gods you deserve to be. Please, you sweet, beautiful creatures, forgive me for what I must do.*

A loud thump and then two more thumps made Julien jerk. The bats were hardly calm, even with his hand there and a prayer from Karaat.

"We're going down!" the crew was shouting. And now Julien saw archers on the Hester ships, and they held their bows to the sky in unison.

Fuck… Trist and his son's hosts were both in the fields beyond Sareen, on foot. Waiting and watching for the signal. Julien told him there would be a great fire on the beach at the south gate. A grand effigy in Karaat's honour.

"Take off your armour, Rolan," Julien blurted.

"What?"

"You will sink to the bottom. Take it off. We're going for a bit of a swim."

Rolan glared at Julien and shook his head. For a moment Julien thought he was going to argue, but he didn't. Rolan removed his armour, and the bats screeched and smacked. Then three more thumps into the ship. One bolt came up through the deck and impaled a woman to a mast.

The flames of the small fires ashore were close enough that Julien could see them dancing. *How long can a bat fly while on fire? Will it fly at all?* These were the questions he had been asking himself. He hoped the answer was that it could fly long enough to reach those small fires and the supporters of Karaat who stoked them.

Julien took his chain shirt off and his tunic below, and unsheathed his knife. He carved the eye of Karaat into his chest, just as Letharr had done. His flesh was dry and he bled like a pig, but he didn't scream. Rolan and Ashan looked at him like he was mad, and maybe he was.

Hild was screaming from atop the masthead now, "Bail, ye fuckers! Bail!"

And it was on that cue that Julien sang the Word. "*Dagdora,*" and a flaming ball appeared. It was hot and cracking, and Julien felt that it had more power than he had ever tried to control before. The flame danced, and the dance sucked him in so he was entranced and couldn't pull himself away. He watched it and almost reached out to touch it before Rolan snapped him out of it.

"Julien," the knight said, and touched his shoulder. Julien had told Rolan many times of the trance of Draku. The flames hold them, especially those of Karaat. But now the flame hovered big as a watermelon and hot as a forge. Julien moved it with his mind to the bat cage.

"The fuck are you doing, man?" Rolan said, one hand on the hilt of his sword. The ships grew closer, and the soldiers aboard had their arrows notched.

Julien opened the bat cage and let go of his hold on the fire, and the bats flew out of the cage in a frenzy and into the flames. They flew into the night sky squealing aflame, and some fell into the sea and some fell on the decks of the three ships, but many made it to the shores and their charred, dead bodies fell at the feet of the believers of Karaat. The fire scattered and caught the deck of the ship aflame, and soon the masts were burning, too.

And as the ships finally came nose-to-nose, they sailed right by each other, and Julien nodded to Rolan and Ashan, and together all three of them jumped. Then an onslaught of arrows came, and Julien heard them slamming into the masts and the bulwarks and into flesh. He heard folk dying and screaming. Then he hit the water, and when he surfaced, they were still screaming. The fresh cut eye in Julien's chest was stinging, but he swam and somehow avoided the ships and more arrows. He pulled himself ashore, shirtless and dripping, with the eye of Karaat cut into his left breast freshly pink and cleansed from the Esheri Rush.

The people of Karaat were chanting, celebrating the flaming bats and they stared at Julien suspiciously—expectantly, as he emerged up out of the water and walked onto the banks like a god. He showed the eye on his chest and said, "I am Letharr." The folk gasped. Julien sang, "*Dagdora,*" and the power of Karaat was almost unbelievable now. He flicked the flame towards the three Hester ships, not really believing anything would happen, but the ships' mastheads burst into flames. Julien said the Word two more times and now all three ships were in flames. *Praise Karaat...* Julien felt a chill, of excitement or fear, he didn't know.

A priest of Karaat stepped forward, holding the still smoking body of a bat in both palms. "Letharr," he said, and bowed on his knees. "Tell us. Tell us what you need."

Julien clenched a fist and held it to the sky. "Burn all who don't believe!" he shouted, and the many people on the south banks cheered and celebrated. "Give me this city! Take it for Karaat!"

"We have thousands more at each gate," someone shouted. And Julien knew he had increased the size of his army.

"Tell them their time has come. Karaat has answered their prayers." Julien said.

With the help of Rolan and Ashan and some other believers, Julien started a massive bonfire on the south banks of Sareen. They burned wayns and fences and pieces of hovels. They burned the wharfs and the harbour and the small ships. They burned the trees and the bushes. They burned anything they found. This would be the signal that Trist and his son were waiting for, and they would attack the east gate and surround the city. The people of Karaat were hollering and they lit torches from the many fires, and the three flaming ships sailed into the city through the water gates as they sank.

The people of Sareen would be horrified.

Julien walked in through the south gates, behind a rabble of rioting city folk. He walked across the sand-brick streets with his rapier drawn and laughed as he watched soldiers running from their posts. They had heard Letharr had come. Julien walked bare chested and bleeding, and behind him a rabble of believers bellowed out in a mad cry and burned buildings and stabbed and sliced folk to death in the streets. Innocent or not.

When Trist and his army broke through the east gate, they blazed through the city like a wildfire, and soon Julien saw the bright red scorpion of House Serahnon dancing in the wind on its black banners high in the towers of the city. *Serahnon?* Julien realized then that he'd been fooled by Trist. *He's no sellsword, he's a satanaga, just like you.*

By the time the sun was coming up the next morning, Julien was in the throne room. Trist was already sitting on the throne.

"You're welcome," Julien said. "Did you bring my bone?"

"You're a bloody madman," Trist said, smiling. "Yes, I brought your bone."

"Better give it over before House Serahnon comes to claim their throne," Julien twisted a grim smile.

"You know why I didn't tell you before? I don't trust you one bit. Not an ounce. I liked you thinking I was a sellsword. But you got me. I'm the rightful king of House Serahnon and King of Sareen."

Julien knew there was something different about this guy. "King, eh, that's a lofty title. It suits you much better than Lord. So, you've got money to pay me with?"

"I've got more than money, Julien. I'm going to help you get Hest."

"So you believe now?"

"No, but I believe that you will be a great menace to my enemies and watching you *try* will be the most entertaining thing I'll ever see. I never thought this would work, yet here I am, on my throne again and with hardly any casualties."

"It will take an army to cross the bridge at Darry. It is well defended," Julien said.

"An army we have, Esterbraun. And praise, Karaat, we even have someone crazy enough to lead them. You."

OLD BOOKS

ALDRED WAS SICK. HIS stomach felt like it was being wrung out. His throat was painfully dry. His head was a drum ceremony.

"Just relax, child." Roqeda's voice crashed like thunder. *"Trust me."*

"No!" Aldred screamed at the walls of his chamber. "No, I won't!" Aldred felt like a snake was trying to crawl up his nose, into his brain. Like he was being consumed from the inside.

"I just want to help you, Aldred. Help you to bring it all back," Roqeda spoke softly.

"I can't," Aldred moaned.

"Let me show you—"

"No." Aldred slammed his fist into his own chest. He licked his lips. His mouth felt like it was full of sand. *Where is Egan?* Aldred fumbled through his wares, looking for a bottle of *anything* to drink. He tossed aside all of his pointless belongings. Jewellery and looking glasses and strange Lovasi devices. Fine leather purses and pouches and packs from all over

Ardura. He threw it all into a heap in the centre of his chamber. There were a hundred knives in Aldred's armoury chest. They were decorated with rubies and sapphires and emeralds and diamonds, and he threw them in the pile. He hated all of this junk. The accumulation of a thief murderer. *That's what war has made you.* Finally, he found what he knew had been here somewhere—an unopened bottle of Timpany red. He opened it and drank the whole thing in a few gulps. He felt the warmth of the wine flowing through his blood and into his hands and feet. He felt his head swell with it.

He saw himself in the mirror and felt sickened at what was there. His hair was a mess, cheekbones sharply protruding through his gaunt skin, with blackened pools highlighting his eyes. Wine dripped from his chin, and there was a streak of it down the front of his purple tunic. Aldred unsheathed *Phantom. The sword can't help you against what's in your head. You're going bloody mad.* He needed the boneman more than he wished he did. He needed to find out what was inside of him. *Dustey will know by now, or else he will be close to finding out...*

"You already know what this is, don't you?" Roqeda whispered from inside. *"I can help you, Aldred. Help you get out of all this. Your prayers have been answered, child."*

Aldred swung *Phantom* at the head of the thing he saw in the mirror and was delighted at watching it shatter into a thousand pieces. *That is not you. That is not you. You wanted to be an author once, an author. Remember that?* Aldred fell to his knees, and there on the ground in front of him, he saw a letter scrawled in his own writing. He picked it up, trembling. It read: *Kill him. Kill him. Kill him.*

Aldred felt sick. He had no memory of writing this. He flipped it over and was even more disgusted. *Sebastian of Bell Street. Second son of bellmakers Trent and Lora. Twenty-two years old. Walks from Bell Street through Terring's Cross to Smith Way in Rattrap thrice a week to visit Eshlynn. Shame if something happened to him along the way.*

Aldred rolled the letter up and tipped it into the purple beeswax candle burning upon his oaken bedside table. He watched in horror as the thing burned up to a bit of grey ash. *What has befallen you?*

"Befallen?" Roqeda's voice roared like waves in a storm. *"I'm giving you the courage to do the things you've wanted to do all along. Can't you see I'm trying to help you? Your father, brother, that bloody Warlock. These people hate you. I will make them bow to you."*

Aldred burst out of his chamber and stumbled to the outer wall of Kelson's Keep. It was a two-hundred-foot drop from the chamber tower onto the rocky coastline below. "I'll get myself out of it. I don't need you," Aldred said out loud to himself. He leaned over the wall and had a good look down. He could fling himself down and never feel pain again. He could defeat Roqeda in an instant. *That is power... but Roqeda is not your enemy. Adora... the Warlock is your enemy.*

"You can bring it all back, Aldred," Roqeda roared. *"The love of your family. The love for your family. Control of the kingdom. Days of plenty in place of days of famine. Eshylnn. You can bring back your mother, Aldred. You can bring back all of it."*

"How?" Aldred was looking at the blue sky, but he spoke to Roqeda.

"The boneman. He has found a certain scroll. A copy of a book. Get me those books, Aldred. Get them for me and for yourself."

Down the spiralling chamber tower stairs, Aldred ran with his hand on the wall. When he reached the royal courtyard, the monstrosity that his father had beggared the city for was shining dully in the midday light. The Temple of Eralis had reached abysmal heights now. Aldred looked up and up at the spires and the stone towers and couldn't believe what his father was attempting. *It's going to bloody fall.* Aldred couldn't believe it hadn't already. It just went up and up without going out at the base. He wanted to pray, but he didn't know which god to send his prayer to, so instead he just prayed to the sun. *Help me bring light to my darkness.*

Aldred banged on the door to Dustey's chamber in the tower, and when there was no answer after the third time, he kicked down the door.

There was someone asleep in the boneman's bed. The sound of the door kicking open didn't wake him. He was a fat, bald man, snoring loudly. He wore a Wise One's grey robe. No one Aldred knew. He poked him in the neck, and the man awoke gargling and frightened.

"Glarrggh!" he said, fumbling around. He got caught in the sheets and fell on all fours. Aldred kicked him hard in the stomach. "Oof!" he rolled over on his back.

"Who are you?" Aldred unsheathed *Phantom* and held the tip at the fat man's neck. His eyes widened, breathing halted.

"Woah! Hey, woah." He took a deep breath. "Dustey sent me to wait here."

Aldred took the blade away from his neck.

"Who're you? Wait for what?" Aldred didn't allow room for the man to get up, not yet.

"Wait for *you*," he said, and Aldred nearly stabbed him. "Wise One Kirt is my name. Dustey wants me to take you to him. It's about Roqeda," he said. That name stabbed into Aldred's ears like knives.

"How did he know I'd come?"

Kirt shrugged. "He just knew."

"Keep talking."

"Dustey doesn't feel safe in the keep, with Brooton in the cells," he said. "The king will be looking for him soon, once they break down Brooton enough... then for you..."

"Is he threatening me?"

"Not a threat, just the truth. He has found the old Yehvenki scrolls you sent him for. They will help you to understand. Karaat. Roqeda. All of it. But they are deeply forbidden."

Aldred didn't like that the boneman went around telling people about all of this. "And what are you getting out of this?" Aldred finally allowed the Wise One to get up.

"I believe in something greater. I believe in order, just like you. I just want to see the world right again," said Kirt. "And I want to document it. For the Guild of the Wise Ones of course."

"And you believe what the boneman said? What he told you?" Aldred didn't know what Dustey had told him, but he figured it was enough if the Wise One knew Roqeda's name.

"I believe that he believes it. That's enough for me," Kirt said. Aldred nodded. "The Wise Ones are not swayed by any one belief. We take only facts into account. All other beliefs are useless."

"Right. Where is he?"

"This way." Kirt pointed to the door as if to ask Aldred's permission to leave.

Aldred sheathed *Phantom*. He followed Kirt through hidden passageways in the keep's walls, a honeycomb of small hallways, steep staircases, and tiny nooks and tinier holes peering into the different rooms of the keep. The Hesters used them rarely and mostly maliciously. The Wise Ones were the only folk who really used these tunnels with any regularity, and still, Kirt was seemingly lost, poking his head in every other room they passed. Every time Aldred poked his head into a room, he could only think, *Sebastian. Sebastian. Sebastian. If I saw them together, I would kill him.* Aldred lied to himself. *You wouldn't kill him if it would hurt her. You know you couldn't hurt her—you will make yourself suffer instead.*

"Say, Kirt"—Aldred tried to change his thoughts—"you ever bring your lover down to these tunnels?" Aldred laughed.

Most Wise Ones were quiet types, and so he didn't really expect an answer. They had a strange series of rituals they undertook as youths in training on their quest to shake off their grey robes for master's blue ones, and Aldred understood that those rituals left the adult Wise Ones sort of strange—and hairless, and still most never achieved the blue robe.

"Yes," Kirt said to Aldred's surprise. "My lover's bones are down here. Mery died when I was only twenty-two. About your age, actually."

Heavy... The torchlight reflected off Kirt's bald head, brighter than the sun. The bald heads, Aldred knew, were a result of one of those rituals. Every Wise One Aldred had ever seen was as bald as a baby.

"I didn't expect you to be so grim, Kirt," Aldred said.

Wise Ones spent their time reading and tinkering in their ancient labs. It was the life they assigned for themselves when taking the Wise Ones' oath and pledging themselves as apprentices to their new masters. It took, at least, twenty years of work under a master to earn the blue robe, and even then, for the few who managed it, there was no celebration, or congratulations, they just carried on with their work. Wise Ones preferred to move in silence and be unseen. They show themselves only in their art. Aldred's mother had told him all of this. She was very fond of the Guild the Wise Ones had established.

King Kyam Hester respected the Wise Ones and helped them to build a school—a place to store books and scrolls—and to study. The Lost-Wit King, Trent Hester, respected them less and burned that school. He banished the Wise Ones to the basements of the keep and made their black magics a crime. Though, he was never able to fully banish it. Wise Ones are like roaches. They got in the nooks and crannies and stayed there. For nearly a thousand years, they've moved through the walls and practiced their art in silence. Staying read in Lovasi literature and working to decipher the ancient Yehvenki Words, too. They studied how to make medicine from the natural world. The Warlocks kept close contact with them. The Words were considered extremely valuable, and anyone who could read them was of interest.

The first Wise Ones were used as advisors to Kelson and many rulers after him. After the fall of the Lovasi Empire, the written word faded. Pages lost their value amongst violent wars and decreasing living conditions. It was the sword that mattered, now. And a ruler who knew how to lead an army of people holding them. People had no time to appreciate or make art. They were too busy trying to survive the next attack. The Wise Ones lived in obscurity in those days, keeping their art aflame by carefully recruiting new members and passing the art forward.

In the dancing light of Kirt's torch, Aldred remembered what the Esheri scout had told him. That Roqeda wanted *him* in particular. *Why does he want me?*

Aldred had always been intrigued by the Book of Karaat. He'd read more than half of the book before he realized it said much the same thing as the Book of Eralis, just using different words. Any good scholar could see that. Aldred was well aware that both Angelico and Benecio were pagans and believed in many gods. Aldred didn't really know what *he* was, but he knew he probably wasn't worthy of an audience with any god. *So why me? Another question for the boneman.*

Aldred descended a steep and winding staircase behind Kirt. Then, they walked for a long while down a dark corridor that cut deep into the bedrock. Aldred had no clue the Keep went this deep into the earth, and it felt oddly disturbing. *More disturbing than raising the dead?* Aldred shivered, silently cursing what his life had come to.

"Here we are." Kirt started to ascend steep stone stairs.

"And where's here?" Aldred said. "It smells like shit?" He followed Kirt.

"Dustey's lab," said Kirt. He held his fist to a large, circular spruce-wood door carved with old runes and knocked in what seemed like a premeditated rhythm. The door swung open, and the boneman's red face was peering out at them, white dreads dangling. The room was lit with a haunting purple glow. Aldred smelled rotten eggs, burning hair, and melted flesh. Kirt entered and Aldred followed him into the cold, stone-bricked chamber. A cedarwood table, much like Brooton's, was in the middle of the room with a dead body on it. Three single-wick candles each burned with an ugly purple flame, crude and unnatural to the eye.

"What is that?" Aldred said, unable to look away from the purple fire.

"Yehvenki blaze, man. Witch fire," Dustey answered.

There was a pile of hay in one corner, and every inch of the walls, except for the door, was covered in bookshelves. The bookshelves were mostly filled, and books spilled out in piles around the room like the shelf had vomited literature. Witch things like twigs with sticky residue and glass jars filled with various odd things that Aldred couldn't name were scattered around in places where there weren't books. And jar upon jar of some black, crude oil substance sat open on the table. Dustey glared at Aldred.

"You look... better," he said, surprised.

"I feel so much worse," Aldred gasped.

Dustey shook his head. "No, no. You have the look of new life about you. An aura that you cannot see." The boneman came closer, looking into his eyes. Aldred strangely couldn't look away. "Yes. You have accepted him now. He has assimilated."

Aldred still felt sick to his stomach. *Accepted him? I didn't accept him, he burrowed his way in while I slept.* "What did you bring me here for?" Aldred said.

Dustey turned and found a book, and opened it to a certain page. "I found this. An old Yehenki scroll by the famous Insa Rolin called *Nekk-row*, translated into Lovasi by an unknown scholar. The scroll seems to have been injected with doctrine from the Book of Eralis, but in the bones of it, I found what we wanted," he said. "This page you must read." Dustey pressed the book into Aldred's hands. He took it. *Scholars were not unknown in Lovas. They were highly revered.* Aldred looked at the page, suspicious of its credibility. He read the title. *Soul Binding.*

Hmm. He kept reading, though some of the letters were old translations, Aldred could still make sense of it.

UndeƐ the crimson light of a blΦod moon:
Release the soul of a Human.
Let their blood soak the ground
Below the victim's feet.
While the blood is
still warm, say the woƐds:
- Akovha Liet Neia -
Let the magics bind, feel it in the depths of your

mind and body,
Stab the victim in the heart with a knife of Albalalsami,
Release your soul to the spell,
And let the second soul in.

Release? Aldred looked up from the page feeling sick.

"What is this nonsense?" He held the page with his thumb and flipped the book over to look at the cover. *Nekk-row.*

"It's how the world will be set right again. Death is only a new beginning. It's beautiful, really," said Dustey. "We could live forever, you know, the Warlocks have lived for thousands of years. It's all right here. Insa Rolin wrote the most powerful spells. But these are only copies of that text. The original isn't here. Some of the potency is lost."

"Kallahorn," Aldred said, in a daze. *Take the body...*

"What?" Dustey asked.

"Kallahorn," Aldred said, "that is where Kelson moved the books."

Dustey raised a wandering eye. "Yes," he said. "Yes, of course. Kallahorn..."

"Who is this messiah, Dustey? What aren't you telling me? Who is Roqeda and why did he choose me?"

"All questions I don't know the answers to. I'm telling you all I know. Roqeda is the messiah, Karaat is working through him to bring the end days. Roqeda says that one day he will be stronger than even Karaat, but for now he feeds on the prayers of Karaat like a parasite. He's just so hard to interpret. In my flames, he speaks to me backwards. I thought you'd be thrilled to know I at least found out *what* happened. Who did it or how to rid yourself of it is yet to be discovered."

Dustey walked over to the stinking dead corpse he had laid out on the table. It was a man no older than Aldred, with bare dirty feet and ripped trousers. His ribs poked through the skin of his torso. A common city man. The product of a cold winter, an even colder spring, and a stinking, rotten hot summer. Normally, he would have puked at the smell. At the sight of the rotting flesh. But not this time.

"You just killed this man, *tonight*..." Aldred looked at the boneman, who was smiling as if he had complimented him.

"I need bodies for my work," he said.

What a mad fuck. Aldred thought of what Eshlynn told him. *What do you really want, Aldred Hester?* He wanted to bring it all back. The old times. *Before Sebastian. Before Mom died. Before my family wished me dead.*

He looked at the dead body. Started to feel... something. A chill went through him, and he coughed as his lungs filled with coldness.

"Let it out, child. Let it fill the world," Roqeda said. *"Practice."*

No. I want to be rid of you.

"Don't say that child. Not yet. Just let me show you what you can be. What you truly want is to bring back what you've lost. Only I can help you with that now."

And the coldness crept into Aldred's fingertips, and with just a graze of one finger on the leg of the corpse, it quivered. The corpse stirred and sat up. It fell off the table into a heavy, contorted mess. *"Focus, child. You mustn't lose focus."* Aldred let the foreign thoughts spread over his mind like warm butter. He let them take over his own. And the corpse stood. It came towards Aldred and stood in front of him. *"You are a god, child. Do you understand?"*

"Yes," Aldred said out loud. Dustey looked at him bewildered and a little bit scared. Kirt, who had been pressed up against the wall, made a nervous retreat. He ran and clumsily slammed his shoulder into the door, falling back onto his arse when the door didn't open.

Aldred used the coldness in his hands to direct the corpse towards the Wise One.

"Hey, whoa!" Kirt pleaded. "Tell it to stop!" Aldred smiled. *Or was it Roqeda now?* The corpse fell on Kirt and began to bludgeon him with a rotting fist. It made crude sloshing noises as cartilage crunched beneath each blow. *Karashka Novo Leronnis.* Words started to flow through Aldred's mind. Words he didn't understand. Words that he wasn't thinking of. *Neco Toplata Erronis.*

And the corpse started to strangle Kirt. It squeezed something ghostly out of him, and it hung like a smoky aura. Kirt screamed weakly through lungs starved of air. The Wise One's body went limp, and the corpse stood tall. It craned its neck and loud popping sounds erupted. The dead man looked horribly alive. Crudely and disgustingly so.

Aldred turned towards Dustey. The boneman was wielding his sword of Daggland forged steel. The corpse launched at him, and with one clean blow to the dead things shoulder, the black steel of Dustey's sword cut down through its torso and into the corpse's waist. It fell over, releasing cold blood in a slow stream. Slower than was right. Aldred puked. Dustey laughed.

"You see? Spread the word of Karaat. Kill this holy kingdom of Eralis. Let it burn," Roqeda said. *"See what rises from the flames, child. You just wait and see."* A thought that felt distant in Aldred's mind escaped. He didn't hate it.

"Black magics…" said Dustey, shaking his head. "Wow."

Aldred was already craving that chill again. He knelt down and took the ring of keys from Kirt's waistline. All Wise Ones had keys to the apothecary and the books that were held there.

"Take this. Find the books you need to help me," Aldred said. It felt good to be assertive. He felt undeniably confident.

"I have other books here, as well. I will help you," Dustey said, and looked at the corpses with a tinge of disgust. "Whatever this is, I will help you discover it."

There were four more rotten books. Aldred collected those as well and glanced through the old pages. They were written in old Yehvenki.

"I can't read those books. They're of a crude translation. You'll have to take them to the library to decipher their true meaning. Don't let this beat you, Aldred," Dustey said. "See this through to the end."

Aldred gritted his teeth at the fact Dustey would doubt him, too. *They all doubt you.* "You don't understand what I've been through, boneman."

"I think you may find that I do," Dustey said, "I've only had the courage to challenge it, to let it all go."

Aldred collected the pile of old books that Dustey had picked out for him and left. He'd had enough. Roqeda's thoughts repeated in Aldred's mind as he made his way back to Kelson's Keep through the underground causeways. *Bring it back. Bring it all back.* His brother was the true heir to the throne. That's why they kept him safe at court while Aldred was sent to be killed in battles they shouldn't have won. *Mad Uncle Brooton got the glory heaped on him for victory when it was you who designed every tactic, every attack.* Straight from Benecio's work. Brooton and Aldred dominated the lords of the Hesterlands with worse equipment and lesser-trained folk. Because Aldred always kept them two steps up.

"Something could happen to both of them—William and Brooton. Things happen to people all the time." Roqeda's words struck like thunder. *"And Sebastian..."*

"No," Aldred said, and his single word echoed in the tunnels hauntingly. But the thought still tickled him. War and heartbreak had turned him fickle. The thought of murder didn't make him so squeamish.

William was nothing but a false lion, undeserving and ungrateful. And after all these years, he'd never let Aldred forget about their mother. He'd never stopped heaping guilt upon him.

"You could end all of this pain, child."

The sun was already rising by the time Aldred made it out of the tunnels. He took a deep breath. *The smell of autumn. Four thousand two hundred and forty.* The year had gone by so fast it made him feel sick. *What have you been doing?* Aldred took another deep breath thinking of his mother—hearing her voice. His left eye twitched. He looked at himself in the nearby well. His face was slimy with sweat, his skin was a greenish colour. His eyes were black with bags. *You should sleep.* But he knew he wasn't going to.

THE BREAKING OF THE HALLOW

"I**T'S A BLOODY WRECK** in here." Ruwen paced the great hall of Fort Rosen. James could hardly hear her over the squawking ravens outside. *Even in the rain, they feast.* He stepped over body after body, cold and grey and with their eyes wide open as if in shock. There wasn't a drop of blood.

A great fire pit still smouldered in the centre, hissing as the rain dripped in from small holes in the roof. Animal bones and rotting skins and Human feces were piled up against the walls, and as James went further into the hole, the buzzing of the flies became louder than the ravens.

"What did she do, Culdaine?" Ruwen asked, "What is she, truly?"

"What she did was take Rosen back," James said. "And she is a queen—my heartbound."

Ruwen squinted her eyes and studied James. "I ain't ever seen nothing like this before," she said.

"The Ayelish *still* haven't left Tusk." Brinley's voice boomed and captured all attention. "It would almost seem like they've abandoned this country." Brinley was holding his maps open and slamming Tusk with his finger. "They're just bloody sitting there!"

"They've probably struggled to make a foothold with all this rain." Brigid was holding a sleeping babe in one arm. "Food was scarce, and perhaps they couldn't march an army on such meagre rations."

Ruwen spat. "What does it matter? We can hold this bridge and this fort against anything. We've proven that much. We got here before the Ayelish army could reinforce it."

"How's Maggie?" Eridan asked, but James hated the smirk on his face.

"She's tired," he said, and didn't let his eyes leave Eridan.

"Rightfully so," Eridan said. James could tell he wanted to say more, but he just kept grinning. Nobody had wanted to talk about what Maggie had done. James wasn't even sure if every person knew *what* she had done, just that magics were performed, many died, and now Fort Rosen was theirs. *They're afraid of her. And they should be...*

James understood that with Rosen, they held all of the Fells. He could set up supply trains back and forth from Kallahorn once they took it back and set folk to work what fields they had left. They could raise cattle and sheep and grow barley and corn. With Rosen they had a chance. *But Brinley and Eridan will not be content with just Rosen. The Daggs will not be content to stay here and farm. You have started a war, and the wheels keep turning. But do we even stand a chance? After we take the Hallow back, how would we ever hold it unless we remain as one? You're leading these folk to their deaths if you leave Rosen.*

"Our work is not done," Eridan said, finally breaking free of James's gaze. "We should keep striking while the Ayelish are getting themselves organized. Only the gods know what chaos has birthed itself in their towns and cities. It was a wither year for all, remember. And the Warlocks meddle in those parts." Eridan produced a wineskin from somewhere in his breeches and took a long swig.

"Listen," Ruwen roared. "Whatever game you rulers play is no game of mine. Trying to take the Hallow for our own with this petty party of displaced folk would be folly. The Hallow's best chance of survival is to stay *here*. To rebuild. To heal. These people need to rest their bones and warm their loins for a season. They need to see crops in the field to know winter won't be as long and hard. We were lucky enough to have made it back to Rosen before the Ayelish. I commend you, King, for taking us here. You very well may have saved this country despite all the shite you've gotten into. But going any further would be complete foolishness. It's far too late in the season."

"We can't do that, Ruwen," Eridan said, "look at our folk. We are completely wrecked and broken. These people need their homes." Eridan crossed his arms. "We ain't waiting another winter."

"And what do you think would happen if somehow we did take the Hallow back?" Ruwen roared. "They will keep coming. They will keep torturing these folk as they have for a hundred years. You know what King Alder offered me and my folk when he came through with that Banshee last spring? He offered me a *name*. A name to pass down to my children—the children that later died fighting him. A name just like Culdaine, so I, too, could be remembered in songs and in cycles to come."

James stood dumbfounded before Ruwen. *Why is she talking of names?*

Ruwen stood tall. "We live in a world ruled by a past that is too large, too overwhelming to deny. But we need to break free. We've fought the Ayelish for too long. Let them have the Hallow. Let them do what they will, and we can live here in the Fells in peace. The Feldarra and the mountain clans seem to have abandoned it all, anyway. Give your people peace, Culdaine. Give them *names* and a future to look forward to. A future where folk can see small versions of themselves wearing the same name, living in the same home."

"The Daggs, the prophecies." James was mumbling. "I don't—"

"Let the Daggs fight the Ayelish if they will," Ruwen said. "Let them go. You stay here to lead. By the gods, lead us."

James only then realized that Ruwen, and the other rulers, were blind to what was really happening. *Do they think Adeqor just* left? James could feel him lingering, he still heard Ellorin's thoughts echoing in his mind, thoughts of starfall and death. So much death it would swallow the world and bloat the Otherworld to bursting. So much death that not even the gods would live.

Queen Ianna Alder and Ayeland were the immediate threat, but James knew he'd have to fight the darkness he let loose when he opened the Gateway and brought fire back to the world. *I'm not done with you, James.* The Maw god's voice still whined in James's ear. And James knew that whatever was meant by that wasn't going to be good.

"We have to keep going. We have to fight," James said.

"For what?" Ruwen said. Her eyes were hard, but James saw a sadness in them.

James truly didn't know for what. *For the memory of your family. For the memory of your people.* "To give these folk hope," James said. "To let them know their ancestors didn't die for nothing. To let them know that their lives have meaning."

Maggie said, "You speak of names, the names of our people are written in the land. They are the earth and the trees and the streams. This land is our name, our family, our whole existence."

Ruwen said, "The only way to keep that hope alive is to stay and meet the Ayelish, or whoever, here." Ruwen tied her long, tangled hair into a bun. "We have won here before and we can win again. We will not let them pass this bridge. We can rebuild, together, as your dad had imagined. We can be strong if we settle." Ruwen held out her hand and James shook it. "I've lost my children, they never had children of their own, so all I have now is to fight to give the people who followed me all these years something." Ruwen's face was like iron.

This was a different Ruwen than the one he'd gotten to know. She was home, she was lighter, but most of all, she had purpose and reason. It was more than James could say for himself. *Fight for home. Make your mom and dad's death mean something, right?* All their death was to James now was a stinging reminder of what a monster he was. *Kingkiller and a kinkiller. But you can fight for your country. You can fight for what your mom and dad believed in.*

"For now we stay," James said, "but it warrants a discussion with the other rulers."

"Of course," Ruwen said, "I wouldn't have it any other way."

By evening, the rain still fell and the cookfires burned solemnly beneath shelters. Folk in wet furs and wet leather sat huddled together close to them. Folk with red hair, yellow, hair, black hair and brown. Folk from Mal Hallow and the Fells and Daggland and some didn't know where they came from, truly. *Like Maggie.*

James walked through camp, a saddlebag hanging from one shoulder, hand in hand with Maggie, and sat at the various fires in turn for a short time and said hello and listened to the stories of his people. *It's important for a ruler to be known by their people,* James's dad had always said, and those words echoed in James's head now as the rain patted down and clinked against *Essikah.* And all of his folk were saying the same things.

"The gods are dying, King, they don't answer our prayers any longer," one muzzle-headed boy said. An iron pot of stew bubbled over a crackling fire. A group of young girls worked to shelter the firewood from the rain by stretching beaver furs over them like blankets. A bard blew the sweet notes of *Down and Down and Back Again* lightly on a wood flute. A woman draped in a white wolf fur fed her babe from breast and looked solemnly into the hissing flames.

"The gods live inside of us when we embody their virtues," James said. He had heard Gran say that once.

"Ain't you supposed to be able to talk to them? Can't you ask them why they don't answer us?" another sitting around the fire said.

James remembered the Maw's words. *I'm not done with you...* "They don't tell me much," James said. "Mostly they just ask for help."

"Do you help them?" The man looked up, hair dripping wet beneath his grey woollen hood.

"Aye," James said, handing the man a dry cloth from the saddlebag he carried. "I try." James reached into the bag and pulled out a jar of smoked sprat. He showed it to the group and placed it down by the man's legs. "This is for you. We will be through this hardship soon," James said. The folk looked at him with something that James thought might be respect. *Be your dad's son.*

At another fire several folk nursed open wounds, and Maggie helped to wrap them. "What is happening, King?" The question came in many ways across the many fires James and Maggie sat beside.

"I don't know," James told them. *By the gods I wish I knew.* "But if we remain strong, the darkness shall pass."

James ate with the folk, boiled mutton and tack, and he drank with them, barley ale and shine, and in their haggard, dirty faces, he saw himself staring back. Folk from Wick, Foulds, Lorne, Fever, and even folk from O ster.

"Your mom's gardens were beautiful, even just last year they bloomed in rainbows," a bright-eyed girl told James. "I can still smell the wisps of etta."

James and Maggie sang with the Hallow folk, songs from the cycles and songs that James had never heard. *The Rack of the Mal,* about Bren Culdaine, nearly brought James to tears. *They loved him here. He is a legend. Your mom is a legend. You are a monster...*

When James and Maggie tried to leave, the folk pulled them in. "Oh come on, King, Queen, just one more dance, eh?"

And so James and Maggie pounded the ground with their feet and filled the night with the echo of their lungs as they added their voices to the songs. The rain only fell harder as the night got darker, and the folk of the Mal danced more fiercely. *They are living as if they may not live again,* James thought, and it nearly broke him. *Give them hope. Fight for them.*

By the time the moon hung at its highest point, James and Maggie had made their rounds of the camp and sat and listened to hundreds of stories, all telling the same tale, that the gods were dead, that their country was dying, and that the Ayelish still weren't coming—and that seemed to scare the people just as much as if they were coming. *What are they doing?*

"Why haven't they marched, King?" the people asked. "Have they given up the war?"

James doubted very much they had given up the war. "Don't let it get to you—they want it to mess with our heads," James said. "They want us to be thinking of them, always."

When James and Maggie returned to the rulers' pavilion, only Brinley, Sessely, their daughters, and young grandchildren sat by the fire there.

"Where are the others?" James asked.

Brinley waved his hand dismissively. "Cursing the gods, most like," he slurred. He held a wineskin loosely in one hand, drooping on the log he sat upon like he could melt into the shape of anything. "Talking shite."

The children were playing stones and hopping between squares drawn into the dirt. James couldn't help but think of Maggie. Of getting through this. *The house by the lake. You were holding a child, Maggie. She was the most beautiful thing... by the gods...*

"The Daggs are readying another sacrifice," Brigid said, poking at the fire. "Eridan and his blooded are getting drunk with them. We need to keep an eye on these factions, or we're going to have rebellion on our hands."

Sessely said, "Ruwen and her folk have retreated into the broken fort and lain amongst the wreckage like mice."

"Rats, more like," Aione cursed. "Tilly hated those bear-brained bastards. Being here feels like spitting on her grave."

Brinley laughed drunkenly. "She hated them good, dint she?"

"The Daggs are giving sacrifice to honour the golden unicorn," Brigid said.

James and Maggie had laid and looked at the golden unicorn constellation every night since Springtide when it became more visible in the sky as the sun moved towards Autumnwane.

"It's beautiful," said Maggie. "The most beautiful connection of stars I've seen. It's like they're heartbound to each other."

"Aye, they're beautiful." Brigid walked to the edge of the pavilion and looked up at the black and starless sky as rain dripped down her face and off the ends of her hair. "It's sung of in the cycles that when the golden unicorn rides the night sky, it will drop a star upon us."

Maggie gripped James's hand tighter.

"I know the story," James said. His stomach was twisted into knots and he held vomit at the edge of his throat. *"It's coming..."* The Maw's words barked at him and stung his earlobes.

"Have another drink, Bridgey, don't be such a downer." Brinley held the wineskin towards his daughter. "Tilly always liked a bit of wine, eh?"

Brigid took the wineskin from her dad and drank deeply. "Corwin is putting the kids down tonight, why not?" The sour smell of the shine reminded James of Wulfee.

"Why haven't the Ayelish marched yet, Brin?" James said.

Brinley laughed, raised his wineskin and drank more. "I don't know. My scouts say everything looks normal. The only thing I can think of is that they fear an attack from *behind* them, from the south."

"From their own people?" James didn't understand. "That makes no sense."

"Unless someone challenged Ianna for the throne after Calen died," Sessely said. "A civil war that hasn't been fully realized yet."

"Can't you find out?" Maggie blurted. "Send your scouts."

"We can't get past Tusk and Mammoth's Head," Brinley said. "We're in the dark."

"We're lucky for this," Brigid said. "We're not ready for them, regardless."

"It's not luck to have no understanding of your enemy," Brinley said.

"So what are we going to do, King?" Aione said. "Wait for the sky to fall on us?"

James said, "We need time—"

"You'd fight for Ruwen to take her home and then leave the rest of us to live in her scraps? You wanted us to believe you were *our* king. Bren would never abandon us like this."

"I'm not my dad," James said, "I've learned that much, at least."

With that, James and Maggie left the fire and delved back into the rain. James hated himself for what he had forced himself into. He had said more words this year than he had in his entire life, and it was sucking him dry. *And every time I speak, there is someone who doesn't agree. Every decision I make only makes more people upset.*

"Don't lose hope, James," Maggie said. Her eyes filled him with everything he needed to live. "Not everyone is going to understand us. Not everyone can know what we know. When I took the life from those people at Rosen, James, it made me realize—we can have anything. *Anything.*"

"All I want is you. Peace. Time," James said. He wasn't sure how to feel about the way Maggie was talking. She had killed hundreds of people and only seemed to express joy about it. *And yet you are drawn to her more for it. You* love *her for it. Together you'll destroy the world.*

"For now, you have me," Maggie said.

That night James and Maggie fell asleep holding each other, and James dreamt of the Maw. He dreamt that he was sitting beneath a great nytewood, and the golden petals were falling all around him. He was sharpening *Essikah*, even though it never dulled, and he could smell peonies and honey. A baby cried from somewhere, and the Maw crawled out of a shadow.

"Do you understand yet?" the Maw snarled.

James shook his head. "What am I to understand?"

"Your purpose." The Maw sniffed at James, its snout was raw and red.

"My purpose is to lead this country to victory against the Ayelish. To give them peace."

"Imbecile." The Maw's claws dug into James's cheeks. He felt hot blood dripping from beneath the sharp points. *"You are a Half-god seer. A World Walker. Have you forgotten?"*

"The gods don't talk to me anymore. They have gone."

"They are dead, mostly. Father Tree remains hidden."

"How are they dead? What happened?"

"The Backwards God has come."

"What do I do? Why am I cursed with this power?" James shouted, but his voice made no sound. The Maw God only cackled loudly and howled at the black sky all around them.

"God backwards spells dog," the Maw continued to cackle.

"Help me!" James still made not a sound. "I need help. Tell me what to do. Please."

"Speak to the gods."

"You said they were dead."

"And you are the Reaper who speaks with the dead. Find them. I'm not done with you. I will need you in this fight, but you need to understand."

"Understand what?"

The Maw cackled and howled and pounded its chest. Drool hung from its twisted jaw and its eyes were red with madness. *"Riddles, child. Riddles on riddles. The Sorcerers made sure to hide their secrets well. My tongue can only clack riddles. Find the gods and be done with this body. It is your responsibility to fight him now. You and no one else."*

When James awoke, he was soaking wet in sweat. Outside, he heard war horns. *By the gods, what time of day is it?"* The sun was shining brightly as it only could after a long rain. James shook Maggie awake and the horns sounded again.

"What's going on?" she said. James shrugged and the two of them got dressed.

"I had dreams again, James. More vivid than ever," Maggie said. "I can't contain this anymore."

"I had dreams, too, Mag. I need to find the gods..."

Maggie's face flushed. "James. That was what I dreamed. The gods were calling me. I know where to find them. I have seen it a hundred times now. Across the Old Sea."

James traced the rigid lines of the maple they stood beside, contemplating what the Maw was really telling him. *Should I leave my people? Does being king of a dead country in a dying world even matter?* When the war horn blew again, James and Maggie rushed outside.

Toren was leading the Daggs in a drunken song and blowing his war horn on every eighth beat.

Sig Arfa was the all-time best,
Big of arm and strong in breast,
He drowned the krakens to the deep,
And coaxed the dragons into sleep.

Eridan stood atop a barrel and shouted, and the blooded folk all had weapons drawn and hooted along with Eridan's words.

Brinley and Sessely had surfaced from their tent, and soon Brigid and Aione emerged from theirs.

"What is this?" Brinley asked. James looked at him and shook his head.

"We're going to take this country back!" Eridan boasted, and hundreds bellowed back at him. White flags with bloody red hand prints waved proudly. And Toren's folk had raised their own flags, too, the white serpent eating its tail on a field of black. James felt sick looking at it. *By the gods, Daggland has broken.*

Soon all of the Hallow Folk and Dagglanders alike were gathered to see what was happening.

"Tomorrow morning, we will march and attack Ockam." Eridan was hammered drunk, wrapped in a flag of Ockam like a blanket. "We will take every Ayelish life we see along the way! We will take back what's ours! A hundred miles to Ockam, people!"

The blooded folk and the Daggs were celebrating like they had already won the battle. When Eridan saw James, he hopped off the barrel and walked towards him.

"King Reaper! You care to rally your ilk and join us in taking back your country from these filth?"

"We need to bide our time, Eridan. Make a plan. Attack like a hammer-fist. We don't have time to poke around. We don't know why the Ayelish mock us by standing still. We don't know why Ianna isn't coming. We are blind, hungry, and our people need hope—rest. We just need patience."

Eridan shook his head. "No, James. Time we've had. Nothing brings hope like vengeance. *Nothing.*" Eridan touched the hilt of his axe. "Words, words. Words and time won't win us back what was lost—no, what was *taken.* We need to strike now while the Ayelish are still slipping around in the mud."

"It's the Glennish that occupy Ockam, Eridan, not one of these petty rulers that are more akin to parasites than war heroes," James said. "It won't be an easy fight for you."

"And we don't want them in our *homes!*" Eridan gritted his teeth. "Don't you understand that my people want to go home?" The folk cheered behind Eridan, and the mass of it was maddening. *By the gods...*

James knew he had lost them. He knew the Hallow army was about to break in two. *Or more.*

"Toren and his Daggs are going to fight with me," Eridan said. "We have six hundred warriors. We are going home, King, are you coming with us? Or are you going to stay here and farm?" Eridan turned and rode away without waiting to hear James's answer.

James mounted Bren and rode on behind him. Maggie wasn't far behind.

HUNTED

Castle Blackstone rose from the lake horizon like a dark sun drooping.

"It still looks a ways off yet," Halda complained. *Who made this?* She had only ever heard songs of the Lovasi castles in the sagas, but seeing one, even this far away, was breathtaking. *It's a monstrosity. Sweet Offa, it's beautiful.*

"The Lake of Scales is a big lake. We still need to walk around the western point." Eurick pointed to a stretch of water that had no end to it. "Just that way. You'll see the shore soon enough. That's where we're headed, then beyond. The soothsayers live in the mountains—in the Gwendarian garden."

"We could have sailed across this lake in two or three days. My rakkarren would laugh at this lake."

"The ravens and the Niths, and the merlings see everything that happens on that lake. Your ship would be seized if you got too close, and I would be taken prisoner. What about your precious soothsayers then, eh?" Eurick studied some tracks that looked to Halda like the same ones she had seen before—a Human on tip-toes. "We've got to be careful. Stick to the shadows of the trees and blend in with the arbor and the animals."

"Why would you come here if it's so dangerous to you? Why would you risk your life for this?" Halda asked. She knew her own reasons for going through with this madness, *Aunt Thora, I won't let you down,* but she needed to know Eurick's.

Eurick hesitated a moment, staring off into the arbor. "Because when I gave up being a raven, I promised myself I would do something for this world. I want to help. Whatever it is that's going on here is way beyond me or anything I've been taught at the Guild. But I can feel it in my heart that I want to do the best I can to help."

Halda didn't respond. *What drives him is his heart? I would love to believe that, raven, but trust comes hard in Daggland.*

Later that day, Halda and Eurick stopped by the lake and made a small fire. Using a small stick and a spool of string that Eurick had given her, Halda pulled a long skinny pike out of the lake that looked like a silver eel, and it squirmed in the dirt before Halda knocked it out with a rock. These freshwater fish, as Eurick called them, looked strange to her. She caught three smaller fish, two bass, and a suckerfish. Eurick strung those up and set them aside. *For the draugr...*

They ate the fish and sat by some bramble that grew close by the lake and picked blackberries, and Eurick looked around in every direction all the while. When something snapped in the arbor, Eurick screeched.

"Maybe having a fire is a bad idea, man. Let's keep those to a minimum from now on, eh?"

They walked the rest of the day through the moors, and Halda's boots whispered through the pink-flowering thyme and the green heather. She heard the streams from the mountains trickling through the crags and the hummingbirds and sparrows. When night came, the world was alive with the song of creatures and insects, large and small, buzzing and squeaking and croaking. Eurick insisted on not having a fire, and the night grew cold.

Halda thought about her Witch Den and the bed of fresh whitebear furs she slept upon there. The thundering roll of the waves crashing against Massey Rock's craggy shoreline echoed sweetly in her mind. The ghost of her crackling hearthfire warmed her body as she remembered home. A smooth scraping sound brought her back to the present.

"I think they're onto us. I feel something watching us," Eurick said, sharpening his sword.

"What does that mean for us?" Halda pulled out her axe and reckoned she better sharpen that, too. *Offa, give me guidance.* Halda hadn't used an axe since she was a mere girl. *Knowledge is my weapon. Runes, answers...*

"Means we keep our eyes open and our wits up. Nothing we can do now but keep going."

Eurick took the three fish and tied them to a stick he had staked in the ground.

Halda thought that she wouldn't have a wink of sleep that night, not with the draugr about. But the soft coos and callings of the wood animals and the insects and the water creatures had a certain spell, and Halda fell deeply into their trance. The Rynish wind was cool and pleasant, perfect but for the lack of sea-smell on it, and it was only minutes before Halda was carried into sleep.

"H EY," A VOICE PULLED Halda from sleep, but she didn't open her eyes.

"Olrick?" Halda still heard his voice and smelled him from time to time in half-sleep.

"If that makes you feel better about all this, sure, I'll be your Olrick," the man laughed, and Halda heard the laughs of a dozen or so more behind him. She opened her eyes and saw a man with hard brown eyes and charcoal streaks on his cheeks glaring down at her. He wore chainmail beneath a black gambeson with the sea-green Merling King of House Nith on the breast—Halda recognized it from her scrolls. The man's hair was long and black and matted with grease and loam.

Outriders... Halda tried to sit up, but the blunt thud of the man's heel to her chest sent her back to the ground. *Sweet, Offa.* Halda hadn't been hit like that in years. She regretted not having her axe handy. She looked around and didn't see Eurick.

"Don't fail me, Halda." Aunt Thora's words stung her eyeballs. *The bastard has left me...*

"What brings you to Ryne, alone, witch?" said another of the outriders as they closed in. All had swords drawn. *Twelve Iron Blades of the Merling King.* Halda had heard that song, even in Daggland. The merlings disliked the Druids and the witches, and they had been known to work closely with Warlocks and ravens.

"I've come to find the soothsayers," Halda coughed.

Whispers rolled amongst the dozen, and the man squinted his eyes at her. "Soothsayers? How do you know of the soothsayers?"

Because Offa has told me their names... "From legend," Halda said. "I am from Daggland. I seek answers about the wither year. Answers about Ox'olin."

"Ox'olin?" the man seemed concerned. "What do you know of Ox'olin?" He knelt down and offered Halda his hand. She took it and stood.

"It's coming," she said, and the twelve folk sheathed their swords one after another and whispered amongst each other.

"We have great respect for Daggland and your sagas," the man said. "Our king would love to—" A small axe exploded into the side of his head, and Halda wiped drops of hot blood from her face as she stepped away in shock. Another axe took one of the other folk down, and then Eurick appeared, sword drawn, and started to slice down the outriders like they were tall grass.

A woman lunged at Halda with her sword, and Halda fell over, moving out of the way. She fumbled at her side for her axe and pulled it just in time to throw it at the woman who would have plunged the blade of her sword down into Halda's chest. The woman stopped and gurgled blood and fell over. Halda lay on the ground in shock and watched as the raven moved like a bird amongst the folk of House Nith. Cutting their calves and their hands—anywhere their chain and leather left exposed. They fell screaming, half dead, and as the raven moved amongst the bodies, they grabbed at his ankles, and he stomped on their heads to stop their clawing. Halda lay and couldn't move. *I have not seen battle in too long. I have sat in my den and rolled bones and stared into fires and have forgotten the smell and taste of battle. I have forgotten how to handle the fear of it...*

Eurick sheathed his sword at his hip and wiped his forehead with his bloody hand so that his face dripped sweat and blood. He knelt over with his hands on his knees. "Outriders," he said as calmly as if he was observing the weather. "King Nith will surely be on to us now. And the ravens too."

"Those folk were going to help us, you imbecile," Halda barked.

Eurick's eyes flicked open. "Imbecile? Whatever they told you was a lie. King Owin Nith is an evil man. Half bred with the darklings that inhabit the mountains. The kin of draugr and its ilk."

"They wanted to hear more of the sagas. More of the soothsayers."

"You told them of the soothsayers?" Eurick sat down and sighed. "They'll be waiting for us around every corner, now."

"They were going to help us!"

"They were not!" Eurick said, "Believe me, Halda, they were not being honest."

Halda didn't know what to believe. "Where were you, anyway? I didn't even hear them coming."

"I was checking on our sacrifice. Draugr didn't come last night. What that means, I don't know. You were fast asleep, I didn't want to wake you. This island has a way of making you dream. Making you sleep."

"Aye," Halda said. "Where did you learn to fight? I've never seen movements so fine. Dagglanders tend to just try and bludgeon everything."

"The Guild." Eurick looked away. "They gave me everything."

Halda squinted. "Why'd you leave, truly?"

Eurick fiddled with his hands, he scratched his beard. His brow furrowed as if he was deep in thought. "I saw something in James, in Maggie. I saw the magics that live in the earth and I can't forget it." Eurick gazed out onto the Lake of Scales. "When I was a boy, travelling the world with my mentors and learning the ways of things, I saw peace and I saw war. I saw happiness in some places and sorrow in others. I have always dreamt of bringing happiness to those in sorrow. I wanted everyone to just be happy, man. Everyone deserves at least that. What I saw on my way to the Mountains of the Mother with James and Maggie made me believe that we can do it, and I wanted to help make it happen."

"So you believe me? That I have talked to Offa? That I am a prophet?"

"I believe you care enough about your people that you would risk your life to save them. Whatever is driving you means little to me. I see good in your heart, Halda."

Halda didn't know how much merit that held coming from a man covered in other people's blood, but it made her feel good all the same.

Another day of walking had been enough to finally peel the blisters off Halda's heels. She could feel the warm blood sliding down her ankles and pooling in the heel of her boot. The raven took them through more difficult terrain now, down rocky crags and through thick arbor to stay out of sight of anyone who might have been looking for them.

Before the sun set, Halda convinced Eurick to stop by a small grove of winterwoods. The ground was clear there, for the winterwoods never shed their snow-white leaves, even now as summer died and autumn was thriving. Halda took the pouch from her neck and rolled her bones. *Who is this raven? Did you send him to me for sacrifice?* The bones told her nothing. They only showed a crow, a tree, and a star amongst other pointless symbols. Halda had grown to trust the raven, and that scared her beyond any reading of the runes.

In the middle of the night, as the raven lay snoring, Halda stood over him and contemplated dropping her axe on his head. *He is a danger to you. These folk are searching for him. Don't allow yourself to get involved with this.* But the truth was that she had no idea where to find these soothsayers, and if she was honest with herself, the Isle of Ryne scared her like no other place had. And this far away from her rakkarren, she was alone but for this transporter. *His fate has been woven to yours now by the great thread. Offa has seen it true.*

Soon, the lullabies of the Rynish wild sucked Halda into deep sleep.

T HE NEXT MORNING HALDA woke slowly. Her head was pounding from dreams she couldn't remember. She sat up and cracked her neck from side to side. The raven was still snoring, so she walked herself to the nearby stream and knelt to have a drink. She stood and looked out from the arbor at a host of hundreds of soldiers in the distance.

Sweet Offa. Halda dove behind a tree. She peered out at the host again. Black flags rippled in the wind, and the sea-green Merling King upon them seemed to scream *"Nith..."* The stories Eurick had told about the Niths being related to the draugrs' ilk chilled her to the bone. *And you thought Dagglandic history was dark.*

"Well, that's not good." Eurick appeared beside her.

"Why so many of them?"

"You said soothsayers. You should never have said their name," Eurick moaned.

Offa has told me their true names. Demi. Torcan. Lan. Oswe. "Names are the root of things. If I can't say their names, then who?"

"People don't say their names. You just sort of show up in front of them and they speak to you. It is told in the old lores of Yehven to never tell a person when you are going to see them. No one should know, man— er, ah... Halda."

Is it me who is meant to be sacrificed to these folk of Nith? Is this Offa's way of giving my life to them?

"How do you suggest we get out of this one, raven?"

"There are many ways through this land. I'll get us there. I promise you, I'll get us there. I've never failed."

"And back."

"What?" Eurick gazed at the lumpy ground. "Oh, yeah, there and back again. Of course."

Halda watched the soldiers of Nith and didn't like what she saw. They held swords instead of axes. In the sagas that had rarely turned out well for Daggland. Only once in history, when they defended their homeland against Kelson, did the Dagglanders wield swords. *And carve themselves with Blood Words that turned them completely mad, destroying the empire.* And these Niths were organized. That was the worst part.

Eurick licked his finger and held it to the wind. He picked moss off a tree and smelled it then threw it away. "This way," he said.

It was only ten minutes before Eurick dove to the ground and held his dirty finger to his lips. "Shhh, man, shhh."

Halda dove to the ground next to him. Eurick stabbed his finger back in the opposite direction and slowly turned around. He didn't move.

"Here they are," a deep voice boomed. "Got them!"

Halda turned to face the voice and saw guards. *One, two*—twelve of them. Eurick stood and pulled his sword.

"This ain't gonna be nice," he said solemnly.

The crowd of soldiers parted and through them stepped a woman in a long, black-feathered cloak. She pointed a long, thin sword at Eurick. Her crest of hair was tied in a bun, and her blue eyes pierced into Halda, then slipped off her and found Eurick again.

"Put your sword down, Eurick. This game of yours is over. Back to the Guild now."

"Fuck," said Eurick, dropping his sword in the dirt. His sad eyes found Halda. "It's over, Halda. I'm sorry. I'm so sorry."

Sweet Offa.

THE PURPLE DRAGON ON BLACK

"**D**RAGONS?"

"You heard me." Julien paced in front of the Prince of Saray.

"Are you a bloody fool? Dragons don't exist." Prince Leonil was tied up by his wrists and ankles and knelt on his knees in the hot sand. He was a cousin of the orange lion Hesters, Julien could tell by his banner that showed an orange lion on a golden field. But he could also tell by his hooked nose and weasel face. The Orange Hesters were known to be ugly. Ugly and rich and mean.

"Not now they don't," Julien said. "But dragons did exist once, and they may again. The world is always in flux like this, you see?" Julien turned to Ashan, who was holding Julien's black chest. Julien unfastened the brass locks and slid loose the steel clasps and opened the heavy nytewood chest. He removed the bleached yellow bone that was in there and held it firmly.

Prince Leonil Hester glared at it with bloodshot eyes. "What are you doing?" he stammered. "What is that?"

Julien had led the army Trist left for him beneath the flag of Serahnon, a red scorpion on a black field, into Saray in the middle of the night with torches burning, singing songs of Karaat to the moon and the golden unicorn in the sky. The small garrison that had come to hold the town with Prince Leonil abandoned their posts, and Julien himself scaled the walls with the others. Once inside they turned the Orange Hesters red.

Ashan had kept Prince Leonil up most of the night questioning him, and so he looked worn out and exhausted. Not a prince at all. "This is dragonbone," Julien answered his question to stop his mind from wandering. *Now at least he knows I mean to kill him.*

He stayed silent. Perhaps, Julien thought, he had finally accepted his fate with grace. Then he spat at Julien's freshly polished boots so Julien smacked him with an open palm.

"I am Draku, friend. Look closely because I will be the last person you ever see." Julien waved the bone in front of his face. "Let me tell you the story of my people before I kill you. When the ashes from the Starfall settled, my people lived and thrived. They spread and grew in population and achieved many great things. Dragons lived here. They weren't beasts then, but great wise things that the Draku sought for council. The Draku of Old would climb mountains or descend deep into caves to find them and earn their council. My people considered them greater than themselves. The Draku lived in peace for a thousand years, and then the Ailaryan Warlocks came with their Lovasi war toys. They were jealous of the Draku and their kinship with the all-powerful beasts that were dragons, and they made war on us. They used magics and trickery the likes of which the Draku had never seen or could even think of. They made war on the Draku, and the Warlocks defeated them. They did their best to extinct us, but they failed, friend. They failed. And I am the result of their failure."

"You're nothing but a fool," Prince Leonil said. "Your people were nothing, that is why they're gone." Prince Leonil must have sensed his death nearby and wanted to die brave.

Julien hit Leonil across the face with the dragonbone, hard enough to break his cheek. The prince squirmed. *"Dagdora,"* Julien sang. A flame appeared in front of him, and this time he grabbed it with his hand. He gripped it so that the flames poked through the cracks in his fingers like flaming tongues. He threw it into the sky where it faded to smoke. Leonil's cheek had just started to turn ashy black.

"You're not special. Anyone can speak the Words," Leonil said. Being a spoiled nobleman, Leonil would have spent a lot of time around a Warlock in court, and the Words had no novelty to him.

"You're not wrong. They have to be pronounced exactly right and be sung in the exact right note, but any fool could master that with practice. What is really astonishing is what one can do with the magics the Words conjure. *That* is what separates the oxides from the steel, friend. That is what makes a Draku. Not every fool who holds a sword can call themselves Kelson. Many will flounder in the streets with crooked magics, and many will die from it when they start to spread. Especially now, when folk realize the Words are actually gaining their power back. They won't know how to control it—how to use it. Not like I do. They will bow to me."

Leonil was clawing at his blackening face. As the ashy rash spread over his eyes, he screamed and reached around like he could no longer see. Soon, he toppled over and his skin looked like charcoal. Julien put the bone back in the case.

"Take this back to camp, Ashan. Keep it safe. This bone will win us an entire continent."

Ashan laughed, and without saying anything, took the chest away. Julien took the opal icestone out of his pocket, the Oracle's keystone, and he admired it. That stone meant more to him than the Oracle's ring, he knew it was special somehow. He was as sure of that as he was Draku.

"Let's be quick about this!" Rolan was barking orders to the soldiers. "And let's burn Leonil Hester as a sacrifice to Karaat!"

Julien looked over the town. He almost couldn't believe how easy it had been. Saray fell in two hours, and Julien didn't lose a single person. His people were gutting the town for anything of value, and then they would move on to Behru, then the Darry ford.

"They'll be ready to fight again next week," Rolan said. "They'll be ready for Behru." Rolan had the look of bloodthirst upon him—a look Julien knew well. Julien had made him Grand General and, as a natural soldier, he had taken very well to the position. He took the job very seriously. "I'll make sure they're ready. But tell me, do you really believe the dragons will come back?" Rolan's voice showed his nervousness.

"I've had dreams of a dragon," Julien said.

"So, you believe in your dreams?"

"I also had dreams that I captured Sareen and Red Sky Rock," Julien said.

Rolan shook his head in agreement. He said nothing.

"Times are strange," Julien said. He noticed the golden banner of the orange lion Hesters beneath his boot. He picked it up and used it to wipe the spit off his Tiago Dilario's. Suddenly an idea struck him. "When we attack Behru, I will do it under my own flag. The flag of House Esterbraun. The purple dragon on black."

B EHRU WAS A SMOKING ruin. Julien was almost in tears. His mother had loved this town. She had been so excited to take him and his brothers when they were boys. To see the bards sing and the merchants shout their wares, and to see the mummers' shows, and jugglers, and flame dancers. His parents had loved dancing in the streets and drinking and laughing. Damen and Iris Esterbraun weren't afraid to showcase their love like a trophy. *They had all called us mad for telling the merchants we were Draku. No one ever believed us.*

Now, Julien was there with the flag of Esterbraun waving above him and hardly a soul alive in the town to see his triumph. He had endured weeks on the road of non-stop travel. Rationing every bit of food they had for his ragged company of sellswords and weakened natives. Trist had given Julien an army of three thousand while he stayed behind in Sareen, and though they helped Julien take Saray with ease, the true battle had been keeping the army together and orderly.

The army camped outside the walls of Behru. The walls were short, just ten or twelve feet, but they were made of sandstone and did more to keep an enemy out than even a twenty-foot palisade. Julien rode his horse through the burned and broken gate of Behru and walked around looking at the smoking ruin.

"What do you think happened?" Julien asked one of the priests of Karaat who was kneeled over, inspecting the dirt. His black robes pooled all around him.

"An Army of Truth," the priest said, holding a symbol of the eye of Karaat he had found sifting through the dirt. "They rebelled against Eralis."

"They rebelled against their oppressors," Julien said.

"Same thing," the priest said. He pocketed the eye of Karaat and then got up and knelt in a different spot, sifting dirt and sand through his hands. "They cleansed this land of hate. These soils are fertile for Karaat. For love. The blood stains on these lands have been burned clean."

Julien made a fist. *It was Draku blood in these sands, on this dirt.*

Outside, Rolan was waiting for him. "Eralis has been strong in these parts for centuries."

"People change, Rolan. You should, too. You deny a god for too long, and the god will prove you ignorant," Julien said.

Rolan glared at Julien and clutched his star. "This is madness. The Warlocks are going to intervene. What will you do then? They serve the same god as you. You are strengthening them, as well."

"They're afraid of too much strength. Why do you think the Warlocks have gone through so much trouble to quell Karaat's Words? They created the religion of Eralis just to fight against Karaat—to keep Him from getting too strong. When that old King in the North started using the Words last year, the Warlocks triggered the wither year to kill him—to kill everyone. They're afraid, Rolan, and they have no idea I'm coming for them. They're afraid of too much strength, and I'm going to smother them in it. I will bring the Words to life in full colour and watch the world burn. And you know, Rolan, how much I love the flames."

Rolan's face lit up. Julien had become accustomed to watching Rolan's face meld into various forms of shock, but this, *this* was something different. He seemed outright appalled. "I've served you well because that is my duty as a sellsword and I know that if I, too, want to run a company of my own, I need to pay my dues and earn respect on my name. But I swear to fuck that I will stop you if you go too far with this."

Julien grinned. He remembered saying similar words to old Libby, and he remembered just as well making good on the promise when he caught Libby about to sacrifice his grandson to the flames in some kind of eldritch ritual. *Stopping that was worth exile a hundred times.* Rolan was more like Julien than Julien cared to admit, and that truth gnawed at him. Julien had killed Canri for plotting his downfall. *Do I have to do the same to you, Rolan? How dangerous are you? How much Hester is still in you? Have I been deceived this whole time?* "You're from Darry, aren't you?" Julien said.

Rolan was visibly thrown off by the abrupt change of subject. "I wasn't born there, but I lived most of my early life there. Darry was my father's home and my prison."

"So, you love it there?"

Rolan gritted his teeth. Julien knew damn well Rolan didn't love it there or he wouldn't be selling his sword across the country. "A small piece of it, sure."

"So tell me, Rolan, when you say you will stop me if I get too far with this, is it Darry you have in your heart to save?"

Rolan shook his head and smiled like a man who'd been caught stealing. "You've got all of Esher in your hand, so why not try to rebuild? You could take Sareen as your palace and rule and be rich and have everything. Darry is held by my kin, House Wence, a house that is subservient to the Hesters, and *that* is the easiest way to maintain peace. The Hesters will keep attacking you if you seize Darry. My people will be subjected to war after war." Rolan was sweating beneath his armour, Julien saw his chest pumping. "Why Hest? Why does it have to be Hest—such an impossible goal?"

Julien made a fist. "Because, Rolan," he said, "my mother, father, and grandfather spoke of a secret destiny at Hest, hidden below the great castle. Books from the past that can explain who I am... *what* I am. There are books that can explain the Draku—our origin, our maker. The Draku's Book of Creation—it's proof of the birth of our culture, proof we existed and that we were great. Our mythology is written there, our everything is there. And my dreams, Rolan. Karaat told me it had to be Hest. It *had* to be. That is where my destiny lies. And I will take it."

Rolan shook his head. "Darry is too strong."

"I will make you king, there, Rolan. You can have it all."

"At the price of my family's lives? That's madness. Just stop this Julien. Just sixty trained soldiers could hold the ford against a thousand. Easily. You will be fighting over a bridge and scaling thirty-feet walls. Thousands will die."

"But we will win. You know we will win."

Rolan grimaced. He rubbed the lion on his sword hilt. He said nothing.

"You say sixty trained soldiers could hold the ford," Julien said, "but I don't think they have sixty trained soldiers. I think they have a couple hundred farmers in a fyrd that would rather be home. I'm going to send them home, Rolan. I'm going to make you king there, in Darry."

Julien had been worried that Rolan truly didn't care about his abandoned home and that he would have no leverage over Rolan going into the next battle, but he saw a flicker of ambition in him now.

"If you attack the ford head on, you may win, but you will lose half this army," Rolan said. "You will be sending thousands of people to their deaths. Even then, if you win this battle, you won't win the war. You can't beat the Hesters at war. I've seen dozens of people try, warlords tougher than you and with bigger armies. I've watched them crush everyone and everything that has come for them. All the Lions do is fight and win wars, that is their reputation. That is what they've done since the Lion Gavyn Hester came south and killed the last Lovasi Queen, Tullia. That is why we bow."

"Why did you decide to sell your sword, Rolan, truly?" Julien was satisfied with the confused look on Rolan's face. Julien was taking him for a ride. "How did a fine born Wence like yourself come across a fella like Bones?"

Rolan squirmed. Julien knew Rolan's history was dark, that he was a problem child of some kind, and instead of killing him, his highborn family sent him away. They must have paid Bones to take him, and Bones probably agreed vehemently. "Bones took me in when no one else would. I had only *Lady* and this armour," he said.

"Do you want to lead this army across that ford? Take credit for the victory for yourself? Become known as the unwanted boy who came back and conquered. " Julien loved watching Rolan's face light up. *Ambition killed the cat, Rolan. Haven't you heard the fable? Kitty wants too much milk and drowns in it. Lions really are just big cats, aren't they?* "There is only one condition."

"What is it?" Rolan said, and Julien smiled, he had him now.

"Fly this." Julien gave Rolan a piece of black cloth folded neatly into a square.

Rolan unfolded it and inspected the purple dragon on its field of night black. He looked up at Julien. Without saying a word, he nodded his head yes, got up and left, still holding the flag of Draku in his hands.

The next morning Julien led his army out of Behru and marched north up the Sunroad. There were small Hester garrisons in both Lysess and Soren, but Julien made a point to just march right on past the towns, and if anyone dared to come out to meet him, he would just crush them. If they were smart, they would have abandoned all of their soldiers to defend Darry. Hest was the prize Julien wanted. Not petty towns along the way.

Without resistance, it only took Julien and his rabble twenty days to make north up the Sunroad, and on the morning of the twenty-first day, Julien and Rolan stood at the edge of a cliff looking out over the Red River and the Darry ford that bridged it. There were crossings at three other locations along the Red River, but Julien had learned the hard way in Odessa that getting your army stuck in the mud at a poor river crossing was a sure way to have them brutally slaughtered by the enemy.

So, Darry was the only real option that made any sense. That was exactly why the Wences had grown rich and exactly why the Lovasi walls they cowered behind were so well maintained and peopled. Julien knew that Rolan was right, that half this army would be killed assaulting that ford head-on as they planned to do. But Julien also knew where and when he would die, and it wasn't here and it wasn't now, so he felt no fear.

"We attack in the evening," Rolan said. "They won't expect us in the evening."

THE BELLS OF DARRY clanged to herald their coming. The thick stone walls of the old Lovasi fort stood twenty feet high, veined with green vines and crowned with battlements behind which archers stood, their shadows casting down on the battlefield like black towers. The walls stretched to the banks of the Red River, protecting the Lovasi bridge that fords the rushing water. Even in the Wayk of autumn, the Red River rushed.

The moon was fat and silver, and the stars were golden in the purple sky of midnight. Julien stood at the flank of an army of three thousand. Sellswords all, from Esher to Epithos, led by their own ambitions. Julien knew that, and that's why he had become a leader. He showed people their own ambitions in himself. He was more of a mirror than a captain, but he kept that to himself. He had handed captaincy over to Rolan, and now he got to play the part of observer.

So, at the flank he watched the archers grow larger on the walls and listened to the thumping rhythm of the march, and just like Kassius, Julien followed his own army into battle. They were all on foot because horses were useless in a siege. Rolan had been putting his folk to work at building siege towers, and he had actually managed to erect four of them to the height of Darry's walls.

"Our only hope," Rolan said, "is that we have more people than they do. Many, many more people. We have to overwhelm them, or we will all die."

"Nice," Julien said. "Nothing like only having one option, eh? Makes life easier. If you achieve this, there will be great glory thrust upon you. This is for everyone who was happy to see you exiled, Rolan. This is for all those fucks who didn't think you mattered. They will bow to you now." Rolan was gritting his teeth. Julien knew he had touched something deep. "What'd they do to you, Rolan? Why aren't you with them?"

"My mother was a smith. My father fell in love with her over the many times he visited her shop to get his battle sword prepared. When she was with child, my father promised to keep her safe, but he couldn't keep himself safe. He was the youngest sibling of the king's brother and was given no real special treatment on the battlefield. He fought and died with the frontlines. After he was killed in battle, my mother was forced out of the castle. I was taken and raised in the courtyard to become a soldier. I was still a Wence, but in the evenings I left the castle and slept at my mother's smithy upon a thatch bed at her side. It was so hot in there I lay awake most nights. When she died I was thirteen. I had had enough of Darry and the courtyard and the other knights who called me *bastard*. I took the skills they taught me and used them to sell my sword for coin."

Thump, thump, thump. The steady rhythm of boots marching in unison pounded in Julien's chest. *Thump, thump, thump.* "I say it's about time we put you on the throne of that place."

Arrows pierced the ground ten feet from the frontlines, three thousand folk poised and ready. When the next round of arrows came, they pierced the ground only a couple of feet from the frontlines, and Rolan shouted "Charge!" And Rolan's army charged, screaming beneath the banner of Draku.

Arrows came again, and this time folk fell as they died from puncture wounds. Lungs burst open and stomachs and throats from the arrows, and Rolan yelled "Charge!" and they kept charging. Clusters of large Giy'er-like women from the mountain town of Casai pushed the siege towers that Rolan had constructed, and inch by inch they moved closer to the walls of Darry.

Julien was pleased to see that the onslaught of arrows was slowing. They were either running out of arrows or they were tired, or both. Either way it meant his folk moved closer.

Priests of Karaat lit effigies of Him and hoisted them high on poles to both encourage their own and strike fear in the enemy.

Soon, Julien's rabble was assaulting the gate with a battering ram. The siege towers reached the walls, and the smiths hammered stakes through the tower into the wall, and they were secured as folk started to scale them. It was all going to plan—better than planned.

Then Julien saw the Darryites wheeling a large vat to the battlements above the gate. Smoke was rising from it as the folk upon the wall hoisted the vat over on its side, and burning black oil spilled out of it. The smoking, black liquid fell on the folk battering the gate like a scalding blanket, and the screams that came out of them were enough to make Julien dizzy.

Then, as he looked up, he saw that Darry seemed to vomit the black oil violently from the top of its walls. The siege towers burned from the heat of it, and the people trapped inside either died from the tower collapsing or from the flames. Julien wished for the first one. *Burning alive is no way to go.* People burned and screamed and fell dead, and then the arrows came back. They came faster than even before, like the archers were dogs and smelled the blood on the field.

The sellswords died. They died fast and many turned to run, and Rolan ordered those who ran to be killed. "Charge!" he yelled, and still, the rabble moved on. They tried to scale the walls with ropes, and the Darryites burned them with hot oil and shot the rabble. Rolan ordered folk to scale the burning siege towers and rope the walls from there, but the Darryites burned them with hot oil and shot the rabble there, too.

Folk battered the gate and were burned alive, and when they finished screaming, more folk came in to pick up the battering ram, and they too burned alive.

"Charge!" Rolan screamed. Julien knew that Rolan had gone too far now to turn back. He knew if he breached these walls, the battle was over. "Charge!" he screamed, and led hundreds upon hundreds to torturous deaths.

An hour had gone by, then two. "Charge!" Rolan yelled, and the sellswords charged. Perhaps, Julien thought, the soldiers had convinced themselves that they would see Karaat on this day, for he had never seen so many willing to die.

Folk were trying to dig under the walls, and the hole was filled with bodies. "Charge!" Rolan yelled, and Julien knew that Rolan had well and truly given himself over to the madness of ambition. Folk spread out along the wall and tried to scale it at every angle, and they died while other folk kept digging under the wall. Hundreds were dead, and then a thousand, and then more.

And at the third hour, the hole was finally deep enough and wide enough that a massive section of Darry's stone wall crumbled into the ground. The first folk through were met with more hot oil dumped from above, but it didn't take long for the rabble to pour in through the collapsed section. Once they were in, and kept coming in, there was nothing the Darryites could do.

Julien watched as his rabble tore down the purple lion banners.

"Spare us," Julien heard townsfolk begging. "Please." But Rolan ordered them all murdered. They weren't in Esher anymore. This was Hesterland soil. *All of them.* And soon Julien was watching in horror as Rolan made his way through the town and killed and took what he wanted. Julien had awoken a beast inside of Rolan his family had suppressed. It was then that Julien realized how dangerous Rolan really was.

"Enough, Rolan, it's over. Take your throne."

Rolan glared at Julien, and Julien saw a demon in his eyes. "It's over when I say it's over," Rolan said, and Julien walked away.

He smiled at Rolan's golden banners stitched with a purple lion, the inverse colours of the main branch Hesters. It was only the smallest of changes, but to the Wences, it meant everything—it meant independence. *Ambition killed the cat, Rolan.*

Julien watched the clouds roll into the blue sky, and he worried about nothing. Karaat had told him when and where he would die, and it was not here and it was not now.

THE TRUTH

"THE CATHEDRAL HAS COLLAPSED, Sir Prince." A knight of the city watch bowed so low Aldred thought he might fall over.

Good.

"That's a travesty," Aldred said. From the window of his chamber, high in Kelson's Keep, Aldred watched the riots break out. He'd seen a few riots in his twenty-two years, but nothing like this. Thousands of cityfolk filled the streets and swarmed the guard tower at the gates of Kelson's Keep. The entire west quarter of Hest was on fire, and the flames kissed the blue sky of midday and seemed to burn all the clouds away.

"I've been issued as your escort," the knight said.

"And what is your name? Or shall I call you escort?"

"Sir Kenney of Talonsford, sir."

"Well, Sir Kenney of Talonsford, what do you think of all this?"

"I think it's twisted. Praise Eralis that the light prevails." Sir Kenney coveted a five-pointed star that hung around his neck and made the sign of the star on his chest.

"Sometimes things need to get twisted to avoid going the same way for too long. You gotta see things from a different angle, you know?" Aldred said. He couldn't remember who wrote that. *Maybe it was you?*

Sir Kenney looked at Aldred like he was mad. *Perhaps I am, Sir Kenney...*

"Not mad, enlightened..." Roqeda said.

Aldred couldn't pull himself away from the window. *How far will this go?*

"Till Eralis falls..."

The walls that surrounded Kelson's Keep were twenty feet wide, built with quarried pieces of solid granite and basalt rock, cut and placed to absolute perfection. It was a feat that left builders of today completely dumbfounded. In places where the stone had crumbled slightly, crude wooden palisades and masonry works patched over them. But the cityfolk would never get through the gates. Aldred, at least, wouldn't have to worry about that. *But Esterbraun could...*

Fitted in his Daggland steel armour and escorted by Sir Kenney, Aldred headed for the throne room to his place in the king's court. The months he had spent there had not made the deed any easier. Being around the king and Adora every day was like walking on the edge of a cliff—Aldred never knew when they'd finally push him off.

Aldred's stomach was turning, and his head was pounding. He was growing used to being a member of the court, but he felt absolutely disgusted by his memories from that night in Dustey's lab. He didn't remember anything from the time he left the lab. He woke up the next morning in a cold sweat, hands covered in blood. He was sick of the whole thing. Even thinking about how he obtained his uncle's seat at court disgusted him. He hadn't earned it, not really. *And when Brooton gets out of those cells, what then?* There was a dark stain on it all, and he wanted it gone.

And where the hell is Egan? Egan usually brought him spiced wine and cheese for breakfast. Aldred's stomach growled. Egan usually had no problem finding his way back to him. He was a good squire. Aldred couldn't help but feel worried for the kid. *He wouldn't do well on those streets.*

A loud cracking somewhere in the city made Aldred jump as he walked along the keep's terrace. *Novelty magics...* Strange things had started to happen in the city over the past few weeks. Explosions and yellow-gold fires that could only be explained by magics. Cheap spells conjured with Words gone wrong. Witches were selling the Words to folk in alleyways and basements, teaching them how to pronounce phrases correctly and with the right tone of voice. Aldred had even heard of sailors at the docks selling old books and scrolls from across the Old Sea that they claimed held Words of power. *Copies of copies of copies.* The music of the magics was wreaking havoc on Hest.

And worse, he had seen Adora using Words of power to extract money and food stores out of visiting nobles offering alliances. She had thrown multiple nobles in the dungeons, too, and silenced them with magics of sorts. A prince from Hearthill, a knight from the Gorge, and two from Brey were thrown in the dungeons and tortured for merely suggesting an alliance that involved giving back all of Esher.

Aldred ran his hand through his hair, trying to take his mind back to more familiar things. *Benecio, Angelico, Phosphone.* Days of reading without a care or worry...

"Ah! Little brother. You look awful!" William said, holding his arms open. "Bad sleep? Was it the riots? They should burn out in a few days. They always do."

He doesn't know a thing about the riots. Aldred thought about the moment he walked through the gates of Soren after they had surrendered. The emaciated, starving people in the streets... they were skin and bone, and their voices had gone and they still tried to fight them as Brooton ordered to finish the folk off. *People will inherently fight for their lives. The more desperate they are, the more dangerous.*

"I slept fine." Aldred felt sick to his stomach. Something was stirring in him.

Aldred and William climbed the great marble stairs to the throne room. Statues of dead kings and the Warlocks of the Ailaryan Order lined the walls in hollows lit by torches. Purple-cloaked guards swung the great doors open as Aldred and William walked into the throne room together. A long, purple carpet etched with golden lions in the centre ran towards a grand throne upon a five-foot dais. Long trestle tables of white-oak spanned either side with high top chairs tucked under them. The hall was dusty, full of old things that long dead people had gathered. Treasures from a world long in the past that isn't theirs anymore.

The king was already drunk, two bottles of red in front of him, and strumming a lute. He produced a horrible racket, and Aldred squinted his eyes. His head started to pound again.

Then a bell clanged from the upper tower to tell the city it was noonday, and it shook the walls. The doors swung open behind them and members of court trickled in. As if they had all been standing outside until the moment it struck noonday. The Master of Coin, Vinsent Carlin, was dressed in his usual brightly coloured fine silks. His cousin, Rober Hester, came in with the purple cloak lined in gold, flowing behind him to signify his status as Commander of the City Watch. Bishop Sparo shuffled barefoot in his usual threadbare robe. Then Aldred felt a pit open up in his stomach. The High Wise One, Gavyn Hester, cousin to Aldred's grandpa, came in with his blue robe flowing.

Every time Aldred saw Gavyn now, he remembered Kirt. He remembered, vividly, supplying life to his corpse as he raised it up.

All four of them took a seat at the grand wooden table off to one side. King John sat at the head with Adora close beside him, and two dozen or more seats sat empty beside them. This was the grand court of the greatest dynasty in Ardura. Aldred almost found it laughable. He'd read that Kelson had a court of four dozen advisors and professionals. The great secret behind the empire was that it was actually a republic, where one person had a little bit more power than the rest. *Angelico said an emperor is only as good as his ears.*

The High Wise One spoke first. His white beard was thin and scraggly, and his words were soft and slow.

"This brigand called Esterbraun has risen in the south with a great force worthy of noting again. It stands to reason that he will take back all of what we've gained and could even threaten us here. He is staining the country with the doctrine of Karaat. There have been mass rises of support for the heathen god, even here in this very city," he said.

"The One God would not give victory to those heathens!" Bishop Sparo retorted.

Gavyn argued. "I'm implying that there is a very real chance—"

"It *can't* happen!"

"You are clearly a—"

"Enough!" King John asserted by slamming his rock fist into the table. You two are worse than bloody children." Adora whispered something in the king's ear. The king turned to Aldred. "How fast could you have an army in Talonsford?"

Aldred had a knot in his throat. "Talonsford? You need every last soldier *here*. To defend the city against this Esterbraun."

"The scouts are saying Esterbraun has sacked and abandoned Sareen, Saray, and Behru, and he's been spotted crossing the Red River at Darry," said Rober, straightening his purple cloak.

"We should send an army to Talonsford to rout him," said the king. Adora whispered in his ear again.

"If we don't restock our granaries soon, we'll die hiding behind these walls," said Adora. "We have enough in our stores to last through winter if we are strict with rationing. Salt venison and elk from last year's hunt. Moose, rabbit, and bear too. The birds don't keep for a damn. Nine and eighty stores of grain. Pickles, jams, and vinegars."

"What about wine?" asked the king.

"There's lots of it. That's most of our storeroom. That's why we're short on food now…" said William. The king looked relieved.

"This is all well and good," said Vinsent. "But even if we wanted to send an army south, we haven't the coin to do it. Everything we had stored went into that monstrosity of a cathedral. We've got nothing left to outfit an army. Aldred is right, we need to focus on defending this city. No one has breached these walls since the Lion himself came down."

"The cathedral killed more than a hundred people when it fell this morning," the High Wise One said. "Just seeing it fall is enough to make folk lose faith."

"You shut your mouth, you bloody heathen!" Bishop Sparo had to be physically held back by Vinsent and William.

"Enough of this," said King John. "Adora, what would you have us do? Just tell us. End this."

Adora smiled; she brushed a finger up the king's chest. "We'll call in the sovereigns and knights of the Hesterlands. They've all sworn their fealty," said the Warlock. "These putrid filth owe us their lives!" Adora held her arms wide. "They will come to us or we'll kill them."

"And they're all unreliable heathens!" said Bishop Sparo.

"Don't talk about my family that way! We're not heathens!" Vinsent Carlin spouted. "House Carlin will fight for the Hesters as they always have. They will be here."

"You're all just idiots. That's what it comes down to," said Gavyn. "We're not equipped to attack. We are barely equipped to defend, if not for this castle that our ancestors stole. We can't even claim it as our own. That's why no ruler of Hester has had the bones to change the Keep's name." The old Wise One beheld Aldred hauntingly.

"So, what do you suggest we do, Gavyn? Sit here and wait to die?" King John took another sip of his red. He looked at Adora, who gazed back at him. "You're a foolish old man, Gavyn, with nothing to offer but fear and condescension. We're sending an army to Talonsford to show our strength, and we will still defend this city because we are Lions! And we're calling in our sovereigns. House Carlin, House Rose of Timpany, and House Haren of Hammerstone will ride to assist House Norris in Talonsford. All of the cousins of Hester will ride—a rainbow of lions. Not like those traitors from the north in Hearthill who sent us filth—a prince and knights from their rundown towns carrying idiotic proposals."

"You should *not*," Wise One Gavyn said, "have thrown the Prince of Hearthill and his retinue in the dungeons, no matter what their proposal. You should have sent them home, at the very least."

King John roared. "Would you question a king's word?"

Adora stood, towering over all.

Wise One Gavyn looked up at her, over at King John. "The point of council is to raise questions for all." He stared at Adora, who was burning him with her eyes, and gulped. "But perhaps I'll hold my tongue next time," he said.

King John jumped up and pointed at the tapestry map of the Hesterlands hanging on the wall. "*This* is what this kingdom was formed for. Strong alliances. We have House Maris in Bralter. There are Hesters in Valence, Haven, and Blackshire. They owe me their lives and everything they have. They will come and fight for me. They have to."

And if they don't? Are you going to fight a civil war on five fronts?

"It will take time to get the word out, Your Grace," said Rober. "The sea routes are clogged with krakens and they are starting to get into the rivers, which is harming our fishing industry. Folk are sailing out and never returning. The countryfolk are reporting whole villages being brought down into the river depths with one swipe of a rotten, black tentacle. We can't risk sending what few ships we have up river as messengers."

"And it will take a lot of coin we don't have. I will have to make extensive exceptions in our budget," said Vinsent.

"Make it happen!" the king shouted. "Get the money from the Faith if you have to." Vinsent mumbled something silently to himself.

"I will lead them," said Aldred. "I know Esher better than any person here."

"No. I changed my mind," said the king. "Last time you were out there, our army was slaughtered and my brother went mad. He said things about you that make me not fully trust you on a battlefield," he said coldly. "For that exact reason, I'm taking Brooton out of the cells and putting *him* at the head of this army."

Aldred gulped. "You just said he had gone mad, and now you want to have him lead an army?"

King John stood up and smacked Aldred across the face. "Don't you question me, boy." He turned to Aldred. "Aldred, you will stay and help Rober fortify the keep and the city watch against these riots. I want you down in the city streets," said the king. "Right, court dismissed."

Down in the city streets where I'm most likely to be killed.

"I don't think it's advisable that we send an army out at this time, Your Grace," said High Wise One Gavyn, a last plea. "We need all of our force here to people the walls. We can't have a single weak point. You forget we risk attack from the north as well. Queen Ianna Alder does not give veiled threats."

"I second that," said Vinsent Carlin. "The Ayelish have been far too quiet all year. We have reports of a large gathering of them at Tusk and Mammoth's Head, but there is an even larger gathering at Solace. All of the Ayelish rulers have assembled at Solace for some occasion. Something isn't right over there, civil war is brewing, or a schism most likely, but it could be some kind of muster so they can move in on our land while we fight the south."

"We could approach cautiously," said Rober. "I don't think we should leave ourselves vulnerable to the Ayelish."

"We have nothing to worry about from Ayeland, at least in Solace. The Warlocks rule there now," Adora said.

"What?" Gavyn said. "What do you mean by rule?"

"Eldinian has taken the throne there. The situation had become dire when a fight broke out over Calen Alder's throne." Adora admired her nails. "I've had raven letters."

"Dire?" Gavyn sounded furious. "Letters? Did you not think to share this with the bloody council?" He raised his voice, and Adora smiled at him.

The king scoffed. "Keep your voice down, Gavyn. We have alliances sealed by marriage with the Ayelish to keep them back regardless of who rules. Like Vinsent said, we've spent a great deal of coin to ensure that was the case. Harbourtown and Morland are close friends of ours, as well as Ilbury."

"It's not foolproof." The High Wise One stood, hands clasped at his chest. "What if the Ayelish marriage partners convince our allies that the Ayelish cause is better for them?" said Gavyn. "You need to consider things from every angle. You need to—"

"Don't you tell me what I need to do." The king stood up, shooting his chair back, making it tumble over. "Adora says we don't need to worry, we don't worry. It's that simple."

Adora smiled at him, slid her eyes up and down him. "I wouldn't lead you into harm. Then how would I spend my nights?"

"Haha. You see, Wise One?" The king slid his hands around Adora's waist. "We are sending an army south to Talonsford with Brooton Hester at the helm to meet Esterbraun. I will not allow that brigand filth to march on Hest. I will not put these people through a siege. With the riots in the streets, a siege would mean the end of us. We will stop him before he even gets here. And if he does get here, our walls will crush him like a fly. A dragonfly. Haha!"

The court fell silent. The king had made his word final.

Or was it the Warlock's word?

"Well, lots of work to do then. Best get to it." Vinsent got up and left.

The rest of the court got up and started to leave, Aldred with them. Then the king's voice echoed off the high-vaulted ceilings, like he had shouted upwards.

"Aldred," he said. Aldred stood still. "You stay."

His brother William turned around and looked at him angrily, suspiciously even. *Fuck you, brother.*

The court cleared out, and the servants shut the big doors behind them. The king had poured himself a fresh goblet of wine and summoned Aldred to sit beside him on the dais.

"Drink?" King John held the bottle at a tilt. Aldred grabbed an empty goblet and let his father fill it. He drank.

"Tell me, son. Are you aware of the stories your uncle has told about the Battle at Soren River?" said King John. Adora rubbed at his shoulders, her purple eyes were piercing.

Aldred felt like those eyes would make him bleed. He shook his head no. "Brooton told me many stories," he said. "I've been thinking about them over the past weeks, through summer and now deep into autumn."

"Your uncle is an unwell man. But he speaks the truth, most times. He's said things about you, son. Dark things." The king drank deeply. "Are you some kind of Warlock? Have you used black magics? Is this why your mother hid you away in that library?"

Aldred shook his head. He forced himself to laugh. "No. That's nonsense, Your Grace," he said.

The king sighed. "Adora told me you'd lie. But so easily? You *must* be my son. We Hesters are filthy liars and rotten cheats. The Lion is a facade to make folk quiver while we cut holes in their pockets and make them work our fields. A true monarch is good at seeking out the liars—at out cheating the cheats," he said. *Staying two steps up on arrogant fools like you.* "You were always a cowardly little shit. Maybe that was *your* facade. Maybe you're just as much of a Lion as the rest of us. I'll keep you close, and watch you."

Aldred was silent.

"Your uncle refuses to see you. I thought about putting you two in the same cell to sort this out, but maybe this is better. You can take his place here, permanently. I'll decide for myself if there's something wrong with you. Something *in* you, as Brooton said. My own discernment cannot speak filthy lies like a Hester can. As for Brooton, I'll make sure someone kills him in the field. He's become too much of a liability. He's a little bit mad, you know?" The monarch of the Hesterlands leaned in, and his breath spewed wine. His eyebrows sank and his lip twisted into a scowl. "I've sent you out to battle after battle hoping you'd die, you know that? I've kept you unmarried hoping you'd father a bastard, so I could kill you for that. I hoped maybe you'd fall in love, so I could murder your lover—so you would know how it feels. But here you are, rising up." The king's face was only inches from Aldred's. "You killed my wife, Aldred. I have been looking for a good reason to kill you for a long time. I hope this is it," he said. "Now go, take the wine with you. And get a bath. You stink like a corpse. I expect you to be in court tomorrow and every day. And if I ask you to fight, you fight."

Aldred felt a great weight on his chest, and breathing became difficult. He didn't ask for Roqeda to choose him. None of this was his fault.

Aldred got up and walked out of the throne room, his steps echoed and bounced off the great walls. He didn't have to *listen* to the voice. *It's that easy.* If he didn't listen, then Roqeda had no control over him. He couldn't save Eshlynn if he was hung to death. *Sebastian. Sebastian. His name is Sebastian and he keeps her warm. She doesn't need you. Not anymore... so kill him. Kill him. Make her hurt like you hurt.*

Aldred flushed the thought as the guards opened the great doors and let him out. Then a new thought came to him. *You could kill Adora.*

"Now you're thinking, child," Roqeda said.

She's the one who whispers in your dad's ear—the one who first blamed you for killing your mother. She is the one who plans the parades and who writes the histories of battle and heaps glory on Brooton instead of you. She's the one who kept sending you to war, and if you didn't go to war, you may still have Eshlynn. Adora hates you. Despises you. But why?

"Because you read," Roqeda said. *"You are at risk of knowing."*

Knowing what?

"The truth."

What truth?

"Insa's truth. The truth of everything. That the Warlocks are false. That they stole their powers from old Yehven and a mad wizard," Roqeda said. And Aldred carried on talking with him.

He was alone in his chamber now, and he knew the guards outside would hear muffled voices all night. They would think Aldred had gone mad and was talking to himself, but he was past caring.

But how would I kill her? Adora? She's a Warlock. She's immortal.

"You couldn't with your hands. Not in a thousand thousand years. But she's not immortal, child—only to time is she immune. But she can still be killed."

Then how?

"The boneman."

Somewhere, in the city below, someone screamed horribly.

A Glennish Wake

Haro dreamt of the woodlore last night. He was walking through the grove of white pine alongside Aonis, and the carvings in the trees were so numerous he was drowning in all of the symbols and letters carved into the bark. It was hard to know where the true woodlore ended and where the copies of copies started. With every generation, the Keeper of the Lore would carve the woodlore anew, into a younger tree. This was to ensure that the woodlore was never lost. But the trees measure their generations differently, and soon the trees carved with copies of the woodlore were so numerous that no one truly knew the original. Each keeper would add their own flair, some even added their own laws before they were eventually crossed out by later generations.

Haro was taught all of this as a boy reading from the Green Book. *Was that boy truly you? Or a body you stole? Where did it start?* Haro knew finding the beginning of his own story would be just as difficult as finding the original white pine that the woodlore was carved into. *A white pine will grow for five hundred years, and when it falls, it takes five hundred more to rot away. Have you fallen?* Haro had the feeling that he fell long ago. Part of him felt so old that looking at the white pines made him feel a strange kinship—like he was their elder. He fell so long ago that he was coming to the end of his rot.

What has it been for? To kill James Culdaine? Haro was starting to think it was more than just that. His purpose wasn't in the flesh but in the bones of things—the rocks and the earth, the sea and the sky, the wood and the water. But now, Haro had to kill James to be sure. He felt that killing James would be the only way to reveal the true meaning of it all. The memory lingered—it had to be important.

At the very least it gave Haro something in common with Ossian. A common goal that would allow him to get closer to her. To learn from her. *Because that is truly what it means to be a Ranger, right? To learn all of Nature's secrets?*

The Blue Knight had learned some of Nature's secrets that Haro had only heard stories of. *The woad, the puca's garden...* these were things Haro thought were merely part of a story. *But all of life's stories are based on some kind of hard truth, aren't they? Stories hold more truths than statements.*

From the Wick, Haro fluttered back into Dawning as cool and easy as his blue jay. The sun was only just peeking up from behind the eastern palisade, and the drums had already begun. A Glennish funeral, Haro had learned, lasted twenty days and twenty nights.

The folk strewed about the courtyard, and in the alleyways, they were making their way towards the dining hall and Haro fell in with them. There were Knights of Beauty with white horses on their green cloaks, knights of Maple with orange maple leaves on their brown cloaks, and knights of Till with black swords stitched on their blue and silver cloaks that reminded Haro of James. Haro looked for cloaks of blue but saw none. *Does she ride alone?*

In the Dawning smithy, folks wearing no cloaks at all were boiling what smelled like pine tar in huge pots that Haro imagined were probably once used to feed an army. Stacks upon stacks of newly crafted shields were piled up beside them. *Looks like Queen Grace had been crafting equipment out of Mal Hallow wood.* The workers would smother the shields in tar to have a nice weatherproofing on them that added strength. *Shields to last through a northern winter, those.* He grinned, thinking of the lengths these rulers would go to to get ahead of the others. *That's the way of Nature, too, isn't it? Queen Grace took and took and so Nature took back and stopped her heart.* Haro knew that the Glennish themselves would think that some god somewhere killed her, but Haro knew the truth. *The gods leave the killing to Nature. They'd rather just bask in the worship.*

In the dining hall of Dawning. two trestle tables were crammed in where there very clearly only used to be one. The first table was worn with knicks and stains and had turned old brown, where the second table was made of fresh, pale-brown wood that still smelled of pine sap.

A large hearthfire crackled at one end of the hall and large maps, scrawled on caribou hide, hung from the walls. The maps showed various areas of Ardura. Esher and the Hesterlands. Lavesh and Ayeland. The Glenn. But Mal Hallow and the Fells were missing. Two discoloured squares on the wall, the size of the other maps, marked the place they may have hung once.

There were wars going on, Haro knew vaguely. Ayeland had tried to conquer Mal Hallow in the previous year and just narrowly failed. But the Ayelish still occupied most of the land that used to be called Mal Hallow with petty armies that were left behind after the Ayelish lost the battle of Rosen Bridge. And Haro knew they were gearing up for another bout. Esher and the Hesterlands were gearing up for quite the blow, too, and Haro knew those maps would be valuable. Someone had already taken the maps of Mal Hallow and the Fells. Looking at them made him realize how much world there was outside of the forests and hills he had spent much of his life in. *Or lives...*

Ossian had invited Haro to eat at the dais but Haro had said he would only eat with his band, and so now he made his way up the wooden stairs of the dais with Grady, Kat, and Uma in tow. He took his seat beside Don

Kenzy, who sat beside Don Martyn, who in turn sat beside Ossian. Uma, Kat, and Grady sat on the other side of Haro and noisily took their places. Grady nearly tripped over one of the stairs, and Haro laughed thinking of their argument before dinner.

"What's the proper etiquette for animals at the dinner table?" Grady had asked with his squirrel chattering on his shoulder.

"Please," Haro had told him and the rest of his band, *"leave the animals outside."* He knew that was easier said than done. The Rangers and their animals were nearly inseparable. Like a second layer of skin. *You wouldn't ask a Human to leave their skin outside, would you?* But Haro knew the Rangers' purpose played a bigger role than hiding in the forests so these were the kind of customs they would have to adhere to.

Ossian had risen to greet them, and the other knights as well. "Ah!" the Blue Knight said. "The Rangers who brought us the bones of our fallen along with the news of our faithful leader."

"Welcome," Don Kenzy said, and half bowed. She was wearing a leather jerkin and her brown cloak with a maple leaf brooch held at her neck. Her red hair held three braids, and Haro wondered at what kind of single combats this knight had found herself in.

"Thank you," Haro said. His bandmates said nothing. They were uneasy when it came to nobility. They were just looking to get their coin and get back to the arbor. Haro appreciated that but he needed answers. He was a leaf blowing in the wind, and he just wanted so badly to know where he was going and where he came from. If he was really lucky, in the silence, he would learn the name of the wind that had blown him.

Ossian had sat back down and continued to argue with Don Gordyn about the value of building more windmills in the Glennish Flats.

"Your braids," Haro said. "I thought that was a Mal Hallow thing?"

Don Kenzy stroked them as if she forgot they were there. "Aye," she said. "I was born in Mal Hallow, in the town of Oster. I fought in the wars against the Ayelish under Bren Culdaine before he died, and I was forced to run and hide in Maple to avoid the Ayelish. I got myself knighted there."

She smiled. "In the Glenn they don't fight each other. Perhaps it's the fear of fighting against those horses of theirs. Or perhaps it's just in their blood. But the Glenn was mostly at peace with itself. The three towns on the Flats are generally aligned with each other, and we all pay homage to our rulers in Elurra at Stone Tree. That is why we are here now. Representation of the three towns is very important. We are given great honours at these gatherings. Respect goes both ways, you know. I've actually grown to hate the Hallow. Those sniveling bastards can't see past their own feast tables."

A cheer erupted when the doors of the dining hall flung open, and the cooks walked in ushering a great roasted boar with an apple in its mouth. Behind them came more cooks carrying more platters. Potatoes mashed with cream and butter, turnips and squashes roasted with herbs and honey, boiled cabbage sprouts and cream of pumpkin soup, apple sauce and cranberry sauce and pear sauce spiced with clove and nutmeg, milky cheeses that hadn't had time to ripen to full flavour but still held sufficient curd, and fresh, fluffy bread in rolls and in loaves and in hollowed-out trenchers. The bread from the trenchers was made into a bread pudding with eggs and honey and cream, and thinly sliced apples stewed in cider brandy were glazed on top.

Don Kenzy tilted a bread trencher up, and Haro saw her throat working to drink down the pumpkin soup. When she pulled the trencher away, some of the soup was left on her chin. She took a big bite out of the trencher which had turned soft enough to chew. "So, I'm curious about the animals," she said chewing, and took another bite of her trencher. "You share your soul with an animal, right? So what happens if the animal dies?"

"We linger for a while, but if we can't find another animal, we die, too." Haro said, also chewing.

"Really?" Kenzy took another bite and wiped the soup from her chin with her sleeve. "That simple, eh? And the other way around, too?"

"Yes. Our soul is one. Opposites that keep each other afloat. If one falls, the other falls, too. Though it's not instant. It's a long, painful process, more like decay than flat-out death."

The food kept coming.

"This is what we call a Glennish feast. We will eat lunch until dinner and then eat again. After that, we drink and dance. Queen Grace will be celebrated with full honours here on the land of her death."

"Why is that such a great honour?" Haro asked.

"Because," Kenzy answered, "if we are able to hold such a celebration, it means we are in a place of peace. We hold this same kind of celebration for the fallen soldiers anytime we take land. To show our ancestors that they didn't die in vain, that the land they died on was conquered. That we danced and sang and feasted and drank upon it after they were gone."

"I like that," Grady said, and drank deeply from a wineskin. "I like that a lot." He took another sip. "And this."

"Of course you like it," Uma said. "It involves squirrelling away a bunch of supplies."

Haro drank and saw Ossian watching him. "Ah, Ranger," she said. "Are you enjoying the feast?"

"Aye," said Haro, "but I don't see how you can sit here for twenty days when you know your king is so close and in such a bad way."

Ossian's face turned from gleeful to baleful. "Let me tell you something, Ranger," she said. "Queen Grace came here to occupy Dawning so that she could have a good middle-ground base camp to look for her husband. She searched for him tirelessly while at the same time looking to enrich her people and her country. She had an entire section of the Wick deforested to craft weapons. Shields, spears, raw lumber for siege towers. She was getting ready for war. A war she knew she would need to fight with or without her heartbound. Now, she's dead, and Eralis demands that she have her honour. She would want nothing else. To ignore her funeral ceremonies would be to ignore Eralis. And the queen, or king, wouldn't dare do such a thing in even their most dire of states. If Brynmor has lived this long, he will live another few weeks, surely. If he knew we left his queen wife's funeral ceremonies behind to die in order to save him, he would be furious.

It would mean a cursed afterlife, and he wouldn't wish that on even the people that captured him. You can be sure of that."

"So what is your part in all of this then? What are *you* doing here?" Haro asked.

Ossian smiled. "I'm the Blue Knight, Haro," she said. "I'm writing my story. One deed at a time. I survived the wither year and led the funeral procession over the good Queen Grace. Next, I will rescue the king and bring him home. But all in good time, Ranger. One deed after the other. Steady is slow and slow is safe."

"Nothing wrong with slow," said Uma. A smile was plastered on her face as wide as Grady's. All three of the band were hammered already.

"And you don't fear war?" Haro continued to press Ossian. He himself was feeling a good buzz.

"The Glennish have their own war to fight. The Ayelish have been an eagle's talon in their side for generations. More and more they press their laws on us, and more and more we are forced to submit. Soon they will erase our culture completely. Death by a thousand cuts rather than one sharp blow," Ossian said. "So I fight for myself and I fight for my homeland. I have seen a thousand futures and one. One where the Glennish are free and happy. Only one. And I will fight for it. Deed by deed, my song will grow louder."

"So what then?"

"War is coming, Ranger, you said it yourself. A big war. And I will be there, leading the Glenn. And I will be there when the Glenn is still standing at the end of it." Ossian clinked her goblet on Haro's, which was sitting on the table in front of him. "Be sure of it."

After the feast, Haro and his band left Dawning and made their way back into the Wick Arbor, where they all slinked off to be alone. Each of them had praying to do and a connection to be upheld with their animals. Haro required his band members to follow the Green Book to the word, and that meant entering their animal at least once a day, but no more, to keep them at hand. To keep them under control. To be able to weaponize them if needed.

They made no camp, for Rangers slept beneath the stars and not even a fire was made on this night. Haro remembered fondly that he used to chew sweetbud at this time and watch the stars and trace the constellations but now, he couldn't stand the stuff. He had tried to like it, but this body wouldn't have it. He preferred straight water and silence, and he missed more than anything the feel of Dalla by his side. *She was never truly by your side. These are Grig's memories.* Still, Haro lingered in them, wanting to make them his own. They were his only comfort. He felt a pain inside of his heart that was worse than stabbing. He had nothing. He had everything. Really, he had his bird and his bird had him and that was all, truly. *Then why do you feel so alone? So lost?* At least he was confident. He knew that whatever came of this he would not fail. He *could* not.

Haro sat alone beneath a cottonwood and found his blue jay.

IT WAS TEN MORE days of celebrations. Ten long days, and after the final feast, Haro still couldn't convince Ossian to attack.

Haro and his band had spent most of their days in the arbor, and even Haro's arse had grown damp and splintery from hanging about.

"So what are we going to do?" Grady chittered.

"I don't want to stay here," Uma complained. "There are too many other bears in this area. Too little food."

"We could slink off into the Hills," Kat said. "Good eatin' in them hills."

"Aye, and come spring we can spend some of this gold," said Grady.

"You wouldn't know what to spend your gold on if it came and smacked you in the face," said Uma.

"I'll spend my gold just fine!" Grady said. "I plan on buying a sword."

"What are you going to do with a sword?" Uma said. "You can't hardly swing that axe for shite."

"I swing it fine enough," Grady said, though his voice betrayed his confidence.

Haro held his arms up as if to slow his band down. "There'll be plenty of time to spend our gold, friends. But Rangers finish things they start. I won't abandon this plan."

"And the plan is... what again?" Uma said.

Haro smirked at her. "To kill James Culdaine. To help Richard Brynmor find his way home."

"And what does that do for us again?" Uma said. "We've got the gold we came here for. Those feathery fools of the owl actually paid us for them bones. You pointed those Glennish bastards in the right direction. Let's slink on out of here like good greenhoods and move on."

Haro hated how right she was. Rangers didn't linger, but something in him told him that James Culdaine was a part of this. He was drawn to him for reasons unknown, and he was convinced that scratching that deep itch would present him with the answers to what it was all for. "Listen to me, Uma. When the elements died last year, that set something into motion in the world. Something bigger than any of us can understand. I have spoken to gods, and I have seen this world with the eyes of e'daru, and I'm telling you there is more to this than we all know. The Rangers will play a part, and I am trying to decipher what part that will be. Something inside of me burns at the name of James Culdaine. He's important somehow. And Richard Brynmor is important, too."

Uma studied Haro, and he knew that she was a tough believer—her world was rock and earth, wood and water and her belief in higher things extended only to the end of the highest tree branch she could see with her own eyes. But he also saw wonder in there. *She wants to believe you.*

"I can feel it," Kat said, "I can feel something has changed."

"Is it true then?" Uma said, she tipped her chin up and puffed her chest out. "Is it true that you have had a thousand thousand bodies? Are you really the reborn Aonis? Like the Rangers say?"

Grady watched with his mouth wide open.

Suddenly a memory leaped up at Haro from the deep darkness of a thousand buried minds. *Aonis. The hero from the woodlore fables. The hero with a thousand thousand faces. He brought all of the Rangers together to fight the darkness before the Starfall. He's fought a thousand wars.* "Is that what they say?" Haro said. "Aye, It's me." And only in that moment did he finally realize he was probably telling the truth.

His band looked at him and none said a word. Uma bowed first and then Grady, and Kat followed.

"Then we'll follow you to the end. Till the sky falls on us," Uma said. Grady was looking back and forth between Haro and Uma with his mouth still gaping.

"To the end," Kat said. "Or until a better opportunity arises!" She laughed.

"Oh, yes." Grady rubbed his hands together; he was smiling now. "This is proper, innit? This is proper." He grinned widely.

The sun set fast on that night, and when Haro's band went their separate ways in the arbor, Haro found a nice place beneath a nytewood. The roots were thick and writhing around him and below him, and the soil breathed, up and down, like a chest rising and falling as the nytewood worked and pulsed.

Haro closed his eyes and felt the life inside of the trunk, the wicked old age of the tree was like a fog hanging around him. It was thick and heavy with memory—it had seen things. *It knows. It knows all.* It was telling him to *reach.*

Haro's blue jay came to him and soon he was swooping beneath the great canopy slowly, for his night vision was not great in the arbor. He broke into the open air, and the wind hummed beneath his wings as he tasted the moon-smell through the overwhelming silver light sprinkled upon the world. Every sense worked as one, and he spread his wings to let the wind take him.

Over dykes and small streams and up the grassy knolls and into the rocky hills where the silver light faded to a shadowy grey. He closed his wings and fell down the backside of the hills and out into the valleys and glens. He saw other birds flying alone at night and thousands of bats that squeaked at him to move out of their way. He flew with his bird and felt as free as the wind. The bird was he, and he was the bird. If the bird died, it would break Haro worse than losing any Human body. If Haro dies, he lives on in his bird. The bird has always been there. *Always.* They were born together and they would die together, just as Nature had intended.

In the old Mal cycles, there were fables of blue jays. Haro hadn't remembered reading them, but the memories of the stories were there, vividly. The people of the Hallow believe that a blue jay sighting was a sign of hope and of union. It meant tomorrow would be better and lost loved ones would be found. A blue jay brought people together, and from that union, hope was bred. *So what will you bring? What will be your last ballad before you rot?*

Haro flew through the night and let his vision colour his other senses. He was not like other blue jays. He could smell colours. He could see sounds. He could reason. He was Human in all but body. *Not like the other birds.* He was superior. But he had spent too long in the bird this winter, and now it felt too much like home. *Too much.* It used to feel just uncomfortable enough that Haro would do what he needed to in the bird then get out. Now, he was enjoying himself. Now the bird *pulled* at him. Tried to hold him down and keep him there.

He found the old Lovasi road, carved with smooth stones that looked different from the hills and crags and the mountains. Haro flew above the road and watched the many cracks go by and pondered the unnatural flatness of it. Then he sensed Humans. Ahead, there were rumblings and echoes, and then Haro could see their weapons glinting and armour shining in the moon in vivid colour.

It's an army... there were folk in furs and chainmail and leather and iron. They smelled like rust and sweat and shit. Haro flew over them and looked at their faces—they were maddened warriors.

These folk flew flags of serpents and of bloody handprints. Haro kept flying, and trailing far behind, he saw a man and woman side by side on horseback. They flew no flag, but Haro knew James Culdaine right away. He knew his smell. *James.* He was riding with the army, and all of them were headed for Foulds. *Brynmor? Where is Brynmor?* Haro circled the army again and saw no sign of him—no sign of any prisoners. *And this is only half the army. Did they split up? Did they kill Brynmor?* Haro didn't like how this looked, but as he circled, he spotted James Culdaine again. *That is all that matters, truly... Ossian doesn't need to know the difference... We can ambush them at Foulds.*

Haro flew back to himself, and beneath the cottonwood tree, he opened his Human eyes.

He ran back to the Hall of Dawning, where Ossian and the Glennish had finished celebrating the life of Queen Grace in a drunken revelry and had carried on to celebrating the moon and its star children for the last three nights. The sound was all-embracing, and Haro was nearly drowned in the thumping of the drums. Ossian had removed her blue armour and stood swaying beside another knight in her cloth jerkin. She held her black sword high above her head.

"They're coming," Haro said, panic dripped into his voice.

"Coming? Who?" Ossian said. The other knight hiccupped.

"The Reaper. Brynmor. They're coming."

"Here?"

"To Foulds. We can hide in the hills and ambush them there."

"How do you know this?" the other knight said.

Ossian put her hand on the knight's shoulder. "Rangers, guy. They have eyes in the sky." To Haro, she said, "Was Brynmor with them? Alive?"

"Aye," lied Haro, and clenched his scarred fist around his axe. He knew he had finally broken through to her. Ossian smiled.

"Suit up. Get your weapons," Ossian shouted. "We're going to steal your king back!"

The Glennish erupted, and Haro could have sworn that the moon was shaking from their rumble. Their war horses chomped and neighed, and smoke poured out of their noses in the cool night air.

"We're going to smash into them like hammers!" Ossian pronounced. "Right out in the open."

As they rode off, armoured like steel curtains atop war hungry beasts, Haro heard the voice of the Maw. *"Find him,"* the Maw snarled. *"This time you will finally know."*

Know what? Haro thought. "Know what?" he said, but there was no answer.

There was something important about James. Something he seemed to forget. *This time you will finally know.* The Maw's voice felt like boiling water in Haro's ear, but the song it sang was so promising.

Are you truly Aonis? Killing James would show him his true purpose. *Because Ifanie, Owen.* Haro tried to remember them but it was so hard. *Sunflower and thyme.* He reminded himself, but he couldn't conjure her face. He couldn't see his son's smile or hear his laughter. The warmth of Ifanie was hypothetical. *What is wrong with me? Who am I, truly?* He missed Dalla's warm voice. Her soft touch. *Who are you?*

Killing James would show him who he truly was.

It has to. Please.

DANCING WITH DEATH

THE DAGGLAND REAVERS AND the Blood Company crushed Oster like an insect. James walked through the courtyard in the fort, in which he had spent so much of his youth, stepping over the dead bodies of Ayelish and looking up at the palisades that the Dagglanders had made such short work in scaling.

There was hardly anyone here... Eridan had split his blooded folk into four groups to surround the walls. The Ayelish couldn't defend them from that many angles and soon, Eridan scaled the wall on the south side and Toren and his rakkarren poured over after them, waving their serpent banners. James watched it all happen and didn't try to stop it. He had been cautious. Toren and Eridan were weary of Maggie and what they had seen her do. James himself was weary, and so he and Maggie agreed that she stay out of this one.

But James had assumed there would be large forces defending each of the forts. That each of them would require a great commitment and cost many lives to take back. But Rosen and now Oster had proved him wrong.

Have you waited too long? The town of Foulds would likely be abandoned, and from there they could make camp and regroup to assault Dawning.

You are too slow. Your dad would have acted on this. He would have been more sure. The Ayelish haven't moved all year. They've let pieces of their army go mad or starve in the Hallow. What is going on here?

James wanted to be a better king, but he found himself thinking of Adeqor and the Maw more than anything else. *"I'm not done with you…"*

Then what? What am I supposed to do? Somebody help me. Somebody tell me what to do? What happened to Hendurinn after?

"I can smell the gardens, James. Were they all your mom's?" Maggie said. She had appeared from the dark on horseback not too long after James had ridden off, and he was grateful she followed him. *I can't be too far from you, love, or else I am without half of myself.*

"Aye." He took a deep breath and only smelled death. "They were her pride." The wooden statues carved of the many Culdaines who had come before were gone. Probably burned up by the squatters. Or the Ayelish Lord Irren, who Alder had given Oster to.

But the gardens remained along the insides of the walls and in a large cluster near the piling bodies. *That spot had sunlight all year round.* Pumpkins and melons and squashes were growing in a tangled web of vines though the fruits were rotten, stunted, or unripe. *Mom would have them prim and proper, no leaf grew that wasn't needed, and every bit of space was used to yield sunlight.* James looked at the leaves of the trees. *We're into the Fell of autumn already, and harvest is right around the corner. This garden would have been swollen and throbbing with food.*

He remembered that his mom, Nara of Oster, was renowned in other villages and hamlets as the Garden Witch. She knew all of the remedies for any ailment. Vinegar and saliva for powdery white mildew, bonemeal for yellow-root, blood meal for brown-leaf. James used to help her make worm compost in the summers, in which she would mix worm shit with fermented food waste, and then boil it into a kind of stew and let that cool before dumping it at the plant's roots. Even without Nara here, the evidence of her labours was still there.

Maggie walked along the walls and picked flowers, and James walked towards the hall.

Toren and the Dagglanders were stacking the bodies of the slain Ayelish in the centre of the courtyard. They would drag them out to the fields beyond the fort, hang them all by their ankles, and slit their throats to feed the soil with their blood. James had seen them do it too many times already. They screamed at the sky in prayer to their god, Offa.

James studied the dead and saw that they were skinny and weak—half-starved. Their weapons were rusted and blunt. One man lay with a broken neck beside a crown of sorts. It was fashioned out of wood and carved with the words *"Holy Eralis, recognize my blood."* James knew those words. They were the words a ruler of Ayeland says when they are given their crown. His dad had told many stories of kings and queens from the other kingdoms. Mostly to explain how they were doing it all wrong.

James picked up the wooden crown. *Another petty king made from the Wolf's broken army. How many have sat in this fort and called it theirs since you killed your dad? How many?* Lord Irren, an Ayelish born ruler, was first given the seat by Alder in the same year James's family was killed hiding in the Wick.

James shivered at the shite he'd caused and felt like slamming his head against the wooden walls to make the many voices in there stop. Even the ghosts mocked him. There were more here than anywhere he'd been in months, as if to remind him of how badly he'd destroyed his own home. *It's shrouded in death.*

"Help us," the ghosts sang. *"The gods are dying."*

"And what am I supposed to do?" James barked at the ghosts, and his voice echoed loudly in the drafty fort. They didn't answer him. It seemed to James that they didn't know.

Then Eridan appeared. "Look at that, King Reaper." Eridan slapped James's back and looked out over the desolation. "An easy victory. You should never have doubted me. I imagine Dawning and Ockam will be this easy, too."

James said nothing. He knew that in Eridan's mind, Eridan had taken control of the army, and they were following *him* now. The mere presence of James made that not wholly true. Some would still follow James, and the civil squabble that would arise would keep Eridan from doing anything rash towards James. *I hope. That and his fear of Maggie.*

Toren appeared next. He was shirtless and held his axe in one hand. *You shouldn't be here. You should be with your people at Rosen. You followed this lot to stop them, and you can't stop them. You won't stop them. They are lost.*

A warm hand on James's arm was enough to give him strength. Without saying a word, Maggie raised him up.

"You can go back to the bridge and raise cattle, King, if that is what pleases your people." Toren pointed at the pile of dead. "That's what my people want. And we're going to carry on. The Dead God is hungry. This *is* Ox'olin, and blood will be made cold. Halda has run off to talk to witches, I should have known the Knower would leave us. I will praise my god. The rakkars Gunnar of Oldstone and Sara of Farrock are with me now, too. They've had enough of waiting."

James didn't know what to do. All of the Dagglanders had raised their own flags now, and he couldn't be certain that any of them stood with him. Toren of Morden Vale's white serpent eating its tail on a field of black, Sara of Farrock's single brown spear pointed downwards on a white field with a red border, and Gunnar of Oldstone's black hammer on a field of mountain grey. They were the colours of enemies; the kraken had swum away, and all that James saw now were killers.

Ruwen was in Rosen now and wasn't leaving. She had already made the plans to raise cattle and sheep and goats and to strike land on some fast-growing, hearty cold-weather crops like squashes and turnips and cabbages to ensure a harvest, however small, come the late Fell of autumn. Brinley, Sessely, and their daughters had stayed with her, and so now the Hallow was split with no common goal to bind them. And now most of the Dagglanders had left. Only Halda's lot from Massey Rock remained at Rosen, and James knew that many of them had already slipped away with other Dagglanders or into the arbors to get away.

And now this lot was in chaos. Eridan and Toren gave separate orders and weren't working together but rather as two separate wholes. Even now James watched groups of Dagglanders led by Gunnar of Oldstone and Sara of Farrock dissolve into the moors and valleys beyond Ockam in different directions, banners of brown spears on white and black hammers on grey, which proved they followed no one but themselves. *Only the gods know where they are going. You've lost them... you've set this mad rabble of Dagglanders loose on your own country.*

Eridan had promised Berra Coldblood the lordship of Dawning once they took it, so even she was barking orders and directing folk now, readying for an assault to take her new home.

James needed time to think, so he took Maggie to the places he loved as a child. Through a small wood, over a gurgling stream, to the place he'd first killed somebody. An Ayelish spy on horseback. James was seven. *And the monster was there then, too, wasn't it?* He had seen the man's chainmail catch the sun through the trees, and James shot an arrow at where he figured the man's head would be. He heard a gasp, a thump, a whinny, and then the horse was running through the woods. James followed its trail and found the man dead with an arrow through his neck. He told his dad, and Bren and Nara held a feast for him that evening in the hall at Ockam with Derudin. *Eridan was there. The two of us drank a skin of shine and threw darts all night with the army.*

James told Maggie all of this, and she listened with a sparkle in her eye. *She loves death... it fascinates her, where all I can think of is what it would mean to truly feel* alive.

They crossed a small crag that overlooked the Fell River and sat on the grass that grew there. Maggie took off her boots and James did too, and they lay there for a while with their feet in the grass.

"What do we do, Maggie? What's this all for?"

"I don't know," she said, and that hurt James's soul. *You're supposed to tell me it's okay. You've always known what to say.* "But I've been having more and more dreams, James."

Dreams... Can we trust a dream? "Do they still tell you to leave? We can leave, Mag. We can just abandon all of this. Let these people figure this out for themselves. Hell, they already are."

"Leave and do what?" Maggie looked concerned. "We still don't know a damned thing about what to do. Where to go."

"We can get answers to this. Answers to our dreams, our powers," James said.

Maggie frowned. "I fear we won't like the answers, James. We could stay. We could stay and fight for the Hallow."

"I fear we're fighting the wrong battle. The gods are dying, Mag. The people feel it. The ghosts tell me. I've *seen* the gods dead. What difference would it really make if we stood up to Ayeland and the sky still fell on us all?"

"You really think we can help?" Maggie's eyes were brighter than the stars.

"I don't know." James hated so much that he didn't know a damned thing. "But I know Adeqor feared us, or at least what we could become. He needed us and our power, and so we must be important. He used us and discarded us, but we can find out why." James pulled *Essikah* close to him, resting on the grass between him and Maggie. "This sword, Mag, it was made for something more than closing that Gateway. I think I'm supposed to do something bigger than fight the Ayelish as our people have done for centuries. People don't care what their home is called or who owns it on a map, they just want to be there. They just want to be safe, by the gods."

Maggie touched *Essikah* and the sword vibrated. James heard scratching and moaning, and soon he saw the ghosts of the dead crowding in. They climbed up the rocky walls of the crag and came from the moors below. Maggie pulled out her engagement knife, and both she and James watched in awe as the stone on the hilt glowed. James thought he saw Adeqor's face in it. *Dad gave you that stone. "Protect this, James. Keep it close," he had said. "This has been handed down from Culdaine to Culdaine since the skies were new."*

Maggie looked at James and touched his hand as if she felt the ghosts were there.

"Tell me what to do!" James screamed at the ghosts. And Maggie gripped his hand tighter. The souls wore dead faces. They were soldiers once, killed in battles and lost their way to the nytewoods and so were cursed to linger. They were torn apart, skin flapping, limbs hanging.

A woman missing her left cheek spoke. *"The hills,"* she said, and stuck her yellow tongue through a festering red hole in her cheek.

"What hills? The Hallow Hills?"

The ghost turned and walked away, and the rest followed.

"What hills?" James shouted.

"James." Maggie calmed him with a hand on his cheek. "James, I dreamt of the Hallow Hills last night. I dreamt that you and I made love under a maple tree there and that a nymph appeared. She told me where to go, but I couldn't hear her. She spoke backwards, I think."

"The Hallow Hills..." James had known since he emerged from the Hermit's hole that he would be drawn back there again.

"There are magics in those hills, James. We must go."

"So we stay with Toren and Eridan and march to Foulds on the morrow?"

"When we get there, we can leave them. As long as we're together, it will be okay."

James couldn't believe he was really going to do this. He was planning on abandoning the kingship of his country, the right that his ancestors had fought for and earned and that many in the Hallow still respected. *"I'm not done with you..."* The words mocked him. *Well, I'll be done with it then! I'll be done with* you.

Something inside of James knew the Maw would meet him there in the Hills. He knew Maggie was right. "Let's do it."

"I scratched an itch at Rosen that I don't know if I can control any longer." Maggie said. "These monsters inside of us have grown too big, James. This is our only choice."

"Aye," he said. "Our only choice." *The only one that will allow us to stay together, that is. There are always choices.* James prayed to Father Tree that this was the right one. He hoped that his prayers were heard. He didn't think that they would be.

I T WAS TWO HARD weeks up the Northroad, from Oster to Foulds. James found Mal Hallow scourged and broken. There was no sign at all of Ayelish occupation. The food supplies that Toren had brought with them were diminishing fast with so many hungry soldiers and so many long days travelling without anything to resupply with. Farm fields were charred and grey, and many were salted. Crofters' shacks and farms sat deserted, thatch rotted upon the roofs, and when they arrived in Foulds, it was no different.

James remembered Foulds as the place where he found Maggie again. The place he last saw Pike. The barn that Derudin had hung from stood sturdy, and a few sheep had made their home inside. When James walked in, they came out bleating from the corner. *By the gods.* The rope still hung from the rafters, green and frayed and rotting.

"There is nothing here," Toren announced. The Dagglanders were tearing doors off and kicking down the buildings that were worse for wear—looking for anything of value. Soon, James saw the smoke from small cook fires rising as the soldiers, realizing there would be no fight, began to trap critters and cook dinner.

"Burn it," Eridan said.

"There is no need," Toren said, "it would do nothing to please the Dead God."

"This is where my dad was hung and killed," Eridan said. "This place has nothing worth remembering."

"Then we'll burn it!" said Berra Coldblood. And the Blood Company erupted into revelry. James didn't even try to stop them.

"It makes no difference now, James. There is no one here." said Maggie as she and James sat watching the wood and thatch of Foulds melt away into black smoke.

From the hills James heard rumbling and shouting. "Do you hear that?" he said to Maggie. He knew by her face that she did.

"Ayelish?" Eridan had a smile on his face.

"I don't know," said Toren, also smiling.

Then the source of the sounds became visible. Soldiers. Rolling like an iron tide from the Hallow Hills upon horses bigger than Humans. Their armour glinted in the sun, and their horses shook the earth.

"By the gods," James said. "It's a bloody ambush." Toren and Eridan were already riling up their crew.

"We've got a fight, folks. Fresh blood!" Toren announced, and the Dagglanders hooted and shouted and waved axes and cudgels in the air. With no order or formation, they charged towards the hills. Eridan and the Blood Company were right behind them.

"Now, James. We could slip away." Maggie tugged on James's hand, but when James looked to the southwest, he saw more folk on horseback pouring out of the hills.

"They've surrounded us, Mag. We're going to have to fight."

Soon James could make out the banners. Brynmor's owl, and the leaf of Maple. Till's sword of Baynard, and the white horse of Beauty. A pit opened in his stomach. *I knew I should have fought to keep Brynmor alive...*

James unbuckled *Essikah* and stood ready. The Dagglanders made their shield wall, hooting and hollering as they took formation. Eridan and his blooded folk formed up alongside them. Daggland cedar and steel embossing smashed together as the warriors locked their blue shields together.

"You're about to dance with the Dead God, people! Let Her know we're coming!" Toren bellowed, and the Dagglanders were out of their minds. Spittle hanging from their mouth and beards as they hollered death cries. Folk with iron swords and iron-tipped spears took the front lines, and those with axes, most of them, took the flank to be ready for the brawl when the shield wall broke, and with those folk, James stood. Maggie at his side with axe in hand and armoured well in chainmail. He knew they would fight side by side until the end. No matter what, they would protect each other. As long as they stood side by side, neither would allow their monster to come forth.

The Glennish knights charged ahead of those on foot, and James took a breath. *That will break them... these knights are not used to fighting shield walls. They will be discouraged when it doesn't break so easily.* And James knew it wouldn't. The Dagglanders were out of their minds and beside themselves. Battle drunk and bent up, and ready to kill or be killed. They clashed their shields together and chanted war songs.

We welcome death
We'll dance with Her

Over and over, they chanted the words in a low drumming song as they clashed their shields and stomped their feet.

We welcome death
We'll dance with Her

The Glennish looked strong though. James saw at least two hundred on horse and another few hundred of those monstrous warhorses behind them, and as they approached, there was no slowing of their pace. The ground shook from the weight of those great warhorses, and James could see the strange red eyes of the destriers, and he felt a sickness rise up to his throat.

The Glennish chanted songs of their own, and out in front was a knight in blue armour with blue hair streaming behind her. She held a sword of black steel, shimmering blue in the moonlight, and James saw a smile on her face. *They're just as mad as these Dagglanders.* "For Brynmor!" they shouted, and waved grey owl banners. "For the Hammer!"

The Glennish narrowed their charge as they readied for impact and smashed into the shield wall like the rock from a catapult. They went directly through the centre, flattening all in their way. They pierced so far into the shield wall that James had to swing at a soldier as they came through. By the look on the rider's face, James didn't think she expected to pierce that far into the brawl either. The shield wall was flattened, but the Glennish pierced too deep and the Dagglanders took their flank.

James unhorsed a man and killed him with *Essikah* before he could stand. Then the horse came for him like a wolf. Its jagged, bloody teeth chomped the air in front of James's face as James moved back. He tripped over a body, and the horse snorted as it lunged at him—and James skewered it with *Essikah* as souls of the dead flowed through the bloody tip. Iron clunking into wood, and iron on iron, and the screams of the dying were all there was.

James got up, and he and Maggie locked eyes for a moment. Her face was splattered with blood, and her eyes were bloodshot. The scars on her face seemed to frame her beauty and make her lips glow. Then she was swinging her axe into flesh and screaming like a banshee.

It was complete chaos in the brawl, and the wide swings of *Essikah* were slowing James down. Glennish were all around him. And as the dead souls lit up *Essikah,* she became lighter—light as a bone.

James swooped from one side to the other. Slicing, chopping, his fingers dripping blood from the hilt of *Essikah.* James peered through blood-soaked sweat for Maggie, but she had gone.

"Maggie!" he howled, but she was lost in the brawl. *Control your monster, love, control it so I can control mine.* In truth he was terrified she'd kill them all.

James was knocked over. He thought the breath had only been knocked out of his lungs, but when he pushed himself up, his shirt was soaked with blood. *Help me. Come,* James called the dead.

He stood in time to parry a blow. A Ranger was before him, green-hood up and splattered with blood. James's arm was weak, and he barely managed to deter his opponent's axe blade. *This one can fight...* James was dizzy and his breath had left him. The Ranger attacked and James parried weakly. The man kept pushing, the madness in him seeped out of his bloodshot eyes, and finally James couldn't hold him off any longer, and the Ranger sunk his axe blade into James's chest. Black stars danced across his vision. *Maggie...*

James fell over and lay dying, gasping for breath, blood bubbling in his mouth. *Warm metal...* The greenhood appeared standing over him. He held another axe in a horribly scarred hand. He was ready to drop it on James's face.

James saw his eyes, something about them was oddly familiar. He could feel the hate burning in the greenhood's chest like a forge. *Who are you?* James could feel that the Ranger was asking himself the same question about James.

Maggie, where are you? In death we will be glorious, Mag. Fucking glorious.

Then, lurking over the Ranger's shoulder, James saw the phantom figure of the Maw God. It looked at James with its bloodshot—not bloodshot, bleeding—eyes and smiled a wicked grin. Its craggy teeth dripped ethereal drool. It cranked its jaw, and James could have sworn it *whispered* something to the Ranger.

The Ranger turned around, his axe still raised in mid-air above James's head. *He sees it—he sees the Maw...*

The dead came to James, and in an instant, he breathed them in and let their lingering lives heal his body. He kicked the Ranger in the shins and got up. When James stood, the Maw was gone, and the greenhood was gawking at him with horror. With *Essikah* throbbing in his hands and as light as bone, James swung at the greenhood and watched the fear swell in the Ranger's eyes as he parried the blows weakly with his axe.

"What are you, James Culdaine?" the Ranger asked, and James's whole body shook with goosebumps. *He knows you...* James was shaking. The Ranger had asked him a question he couldn't answer. "Are you truly a godkiller?" the greenhood said.

"Is that what the Maw told you?" James asked, trying not to sound afraid.

The Ranger looked confused. The Maw appeared behind the Ranger again, snarling, and as the greenhood raised his axe, James took the Ranger's pink, burn-scarred arm off at the wrist. The Ranger screamed. James kicked him in the chest and bowled him over. The Maw God took off at a trot into the Wick Arbor "What did the Maw say to you?" James stood over the Ranger, snarling like a beast. He held *Essikah* at the Ranger's neck. "The Maw, what did he say?" James was shouting.

The Ranger spit blood at James and said, "Fuck you, Culdaine."

James took the man's severed wrist and dug it into the dirt.

"Ahrrg!" the Ranger screamed, and James did it again. The bloody stump was crusted with dirt and twigs, and even a pinecone. James kicked his rib cage and felt a crunch beneath his boot. He stepped over the Ranger and ran after the Maw. "Where are you going?" James shouted to the Maw. "What did you say to him? Is that what I'm destined for? To be a godkiller?" James yelled at the night.

The dead were all around James now, and he fed on them to heal himself—he was worn ragged. He ignored their pleas for help. He ignored them but to heal. *These were people. These are souls. Not fodder for you.* But James quickly moved onto thoughts of Maggie. *Where?*

And the fight still carried on around him. There was no order, and that was what the monster thrived on. The battle was a brawl. *Where is Maggie?* James howled and swung *Essikah* with both hands, and folk collapsed beneath it. *Like grass you trample them.*

The Glennish lay bloody and dying beneath their chimeric warhorses. James stepped over them, screaming hoarsely, "Mag!" But couldn't even hear himself over the sound of metal on metal on wood.

James killed all he saw—everything that moved. The Glennish chainmail crumpled and snapped and failed to protect the flesh when *Essikah* touched them, and they fell and kept falling as James slaughtered them.

The bloody Daggs were earning their name, and the Blood Company of the Mal were killing as if in competition with the Daggs, and together they had made an equal fight where there should have been none—they should have been crushed by the Glennish warhorses. James knew their reputation. *Why did they attack us so rashly? This ambush made little sense. The horses were spooked by the dead in these arbors—they're of a different darkness than the souls that lurk in the Glenn Arbor.*

Sweat soaked James's brow and dripped into his eyes, but he dared not take a hand off *Essikah* to wipe it, for Glennish came and kept coming. To kill was only to welcome another in their place. James was stabbed and prodded and beaten. The dead danced with him, fought with him fallaciously, filled his lungs and repaired his flesh, and he could not be stopped.

"Culdaine," a voice came from behind James. He turned, and a sword was coming at him. He had no time to parry, so he moved to take the blow to his chest to avoid losing any limbs. The blade rattled his ribcage as it sank into his flesh.

"Ahrghh!" James screamed. "For fuck!" He fell to his knees and somehow parried another blow coming at him.

"He's not here, is he? Is he still alive?" A woman in blue armour stood before him, her black sword was dripping with James's own blood.

"Who?" The dead souls flowed through James as he breathed them in. His whole body was ice—his breath iced and his eyes frosted over. He stood, rigidly, frigidly, and lifted *Essikah*.

The woman in blue gritted her teeth. "Brynmor. The Hammer."

James smiled. His mouth was dry, and his teeth were wicked and yellow. "I killed him," James said. He held *Essikah* with one hand now, and it glowed hauntingly in the night. His cut had healed over and only dried blood covered his chest. He was dizzy as all hell. "And I'll kill you," he said.

The woman in blue squinted her eyes. She looked at the place where she had sunk her blade just moments before, completely healed. "You really do dance with death, eh? Reaper?" she said.

"Yes," James said. Suddenly the Blue Knight slinked off into the battle, and James was surrounded by it again.

In the madness of it, he found himself. *Maggie. Find her. Stop this.* He blinked and found that he was removing the head of a Glennish knight. He was soaked in blood, his hands were slimy with it, and he was cold.

There were so many souls dancing around him and singing songs of the Crow that he couldn't tell them from the living. The dead chanted and praised James and healed him where his flesh had been torn, and kept breath in his lungs. *But why?*

The brawl was still carrying on. Hundreds lay dead as hundreds more fought on top of their bodies. Neither side was willing to retreat, and none had yet grown sick of slaughter.

"Maggie!" James screamed. But she was gone. *He* was gone, he had drifted a mile or more from where the shield wall once stood and the battle had begun. "Maggie!" There was nothing. He ran and heard voices behind him.

"The king flees!" folk said. "He's mad!" But they knew nothing. He wasn't mad, only madly in love—more than anyone could understand. He knew that Toren and Eridan would go on and sack Dawning with what folk remained, and then to Ockam. But James cared only for Maggie.

He scanned the bodies, praying to the Crow not to take her yet. *Don't you dare. Don't you bloody dare, Crow.*

He swayed his head from side to side like a rabid dog. Looking, sniffing. "Mag!" *Don't you dare, Crow. Don't you do it. Don't you fucking take her.*

James saw Maggie's chain shirt and helm discarded in the mud. He ran to them and picked the armour up. Coveted it against his chest. It had the moose head of Culdaine etched into them with her own hand and a flower, too. "Mag!" He scanned the horizon. *The arbor.* His legs were already moving towards it. *She's there. She's there. The Hills, she's there.*

"Victory!" he could hear the Daggs shouting. "Victory!" But a Glennish defeat meant nothing but victory for the Ayelish. *This, this is what the Ayelish wanted. For us to fight and destroy ourselves.* But James cared nothing about this, he couldn't care. He could smell peonies and honey wafting from the arbor, and he ran to it like a hungry dog to dinner.

PART THREE

*"He who fights with monsters should look to it that he himself
does not become a monster."*

Friedrich Nietzsche

NIGHT MOVES

"BY THE GODS, WULF." Pike opened his arms for a hug, and Etta broke down into tears as she accepted it. Pike's hair had grown back, and his grey locks hung over his cheeks; he hadn't re-braided them. "You live." He smiled and hugged her again. "Somehow, I knew you would be here. How is it you always live amidst so much death?"

"Some days I wish I hadn't lived, Pike."

Pike's face went straight. "I'm sorry, Wulf, I didn't mean—"

"I know." Etta noticed Calum and Tara looking at her. She was going to have to explain why this man, who she had clearly known for a long time, was calling her Wulf, but there would be time for that later.

The Feldarra were still pouring in through the thin mountain pass and trickling down into the valley. Sun glinted off spear point and axe blade, chainmail, and iron helm. They were a glistening trail of killers blanketed in mottled furs and leather. They were Etta's people. Folk she had once commanded in battle and in life. She had once run a clan of a thousand

Feldarra that slowly melted away into nothing. Most of those folk were dead now, but the ones who weren't had gone to fight for Odhran Ironfist, and now they were here.

You can't hide from yourself any longer. These people will know you. Baerd was greeting them all and pointing his finger at different green spaces in the valley of Elwyd, directing them to settle. There were many more children arriving as well, and the lot of them were all running around together. Etta remembered the joy of making new friends as a girl. The feeling of her world opening up just that little bit more. Now all she wanted to do was shut herself off from the world and be nothing. *Everyone you befriend dies. The si'otha, the Rangers, all of them...*

Pike was staring at her like he wanted to ask something but didn't know how. And Etta knew just what he wanted to ask.

"I'm okay, Pike," she said, and the old warrior's eyes lit up. "The gods know I've been lost, but slowly, I'm finding myself again." Etta pounded her chest. "I know Wulfee is in there somewhere."

Pike nodded, the old northern sign for luck, and pounded his shield with a fist. "And I'll be in front of you with my shield."

Etta pouted. "I'm not staying here, Pike," she said, and felt a sting in her gut as the old warrior's face crumbled.

"What do you mean? This is the Feldarra's great battle, Wulf. Like in the cycles. Don't you think it's some kind of fate that we both ended up here? That we *all* ended up here? We need all. We need *you.*"

"I want to leave, Pike. I have no purpose here." Etta looked at young Swey, bobbing up and down as he leaped from stone to stone. "He is safe here now. Safer than he would ever be with me. I am nothing but a danger. Look at what pain I have brought to all of my children." *Gen... Braden...* though she dared not say their names aloud. Benn and the si'otha—every life she touched turned to death.

"Braden wasn't the same boy you raised, Wulf. He was sick with the battle fever. Lesser folk have been cursed by it. It's not your fault."

Etta couldn't hear a thing Pike had said, for she had only seen Braden's face plastered onto Pike's, and she only heard Sweyne senior's voice. *The mask was poison, Wulf. It ate the best parts of me.* She reckoned it did the same to Braden. *If you had just taken the mask off... if you hadn't killed him, he could have changed. Like Sweyne has changed.*

Etta absolutely hated to admit to herself that Sweyne had changed, but he had. He felt warmer. There was none of the harshness to him that had developed but only a kind of easy strength. And she hated it. *How dare he change. How dare he.* "I don't expect you to understand, Pike. I'm not the same person you last saw. That person has gone away from me, and most days I'm certain she won't ever come back."

Pike just peered at her, his blue eyes wide. "They whisper your name throughout the Fells, you know? They whisper Gen, too." Pike looked at his shield as if it told a story. And it told many. "The Battle of Rosen Bridge. The kihl'dor that saved the world. The Giy'er who became a karl and single-handedly fought a hundred folk at the Fell River. Folk feared the Wolf more than—"

"It was the mask, Pike. The mask," Etta blurted, and Pike stared at her like she was mad. "The wolf mask was cursed. It poisoned his mind. It poisoned Sweyne's mind. He told me." *By the gods.* There was so much Pike didn't know. Etta didn't have the energy to tell him all. She could barely keep up with herself; it was all happening so fast. She could still hear Benn's last words ringing in her mind. *Find yourself, Wulf.* "It's too much, Pike."

"Aye, aye," he said. Etta knew that the old warrior wanted to know more about the mask and especially about Sweyne, but he wouldn't press Etta, so instead he just looked around. "Aye," he said again. Etta could see Tara and Swey going down to the stream. Pike saw her looking. "You go ahead, Wulf. I don't want to keep you. If you leave, just do me a favour, eh?"

"Of course," Etta said. She loved Pike like a brother and a friend, and she would truly do anything to honour a favour to him.

"Say goodbye before you go," he smiled, and Etta nodded, and he returned the old northern gesture.

The stream was gently hushing and in the grey, autumn day, Etta could imagine the gods whispering songs to her. Her dad used to tell her the sound of a calm stream was what the gods' language sounded like. It was one long, gentle song with a thousand thousand variations of background voice. The croak of a frog, the buzzing of dragonflies, and splashing of the trout eating the flies.

The smacking of a heron's thick wings took Etta's focus from Swey. It was landing to drink from the stream. The bird was big and blue, and Etta hadn't seen one that close in ages. It stood tall on grey, bony legs and spread sky-blue wings so that its shadow looked four times the size of its body. A trout jumped from the stream, and the heron snatched it in a cool motion and held the flopping brown fish in its massive orange beak and ogled Etta with glaring orange eyes that were cut deep into its white head. Etta glared back, and the bird smacked its wings at the sky, and after four or five smacks, it finally took flight and was gone.

Young Swey was pointing at the heron flying away and laughing with his mom. "Did you see it, Etta?" He jumped up and down. Tara frowned. She had heard Pike calling her Wulf, and Etta could sense her suspiciousness.

"Aye, I saw it," Etta said. "A blue heron is a good omen in the north. It means luck is with us. The Bluebird Gods live inside of the blue heron. One in each wing."

Swey nodded and thought about that, then smiled and ran off to skip rocks.

"That was a great story, *Wulf*," Tara said.

"I was going to tell you," Etta said.

"When? What else have you lied about?" Tara looked at Swey, who was in the stream now. "Be careful!"

"I will!" Swey screamed back. He was dripping wet already.

"I was going to tell you when I believed it," Etta said. She reckoned that was the best answer she could give. "I used to be Wulf. But not now."

"We've had enough liars come and go in our lives." Tara nodded towards Swey. "I haven't minded you getting close with him, he appreciates your good words and your stories, but I don't want his head filled with lies. I don't want him to think you're going to be there for him, and then you just leave. I had that enough in my own life, and I don't need it for Swey."

You're daughterbound to me. Swey is my grandson, Etta wanted to say. *I killed my son and I will never leave you,* she would have said, too. But she couldn't. She had to be Etta. She had to find peace in her heart. "I only lied about my name. But in truth it's not a lie. I don't think of myself by that name anymore. I'm not, Wulfee. Wulfee died at the Battle of Rosen Bridge. I'm Etta now. I want peace. I want it to be over."

"What? What do you want to be over?"

"*This.* Running. Chasing. It's been one or the other for me my whole life. I'm tired. I'm lonely. I want an end."

Tara put her hand on Etta's. It was soft, despite the scratches, and only then did Etta realize how rough and scarred her own hands were. "I feel it in my heart you're a good person, Etta. Benn felt it, too. Things will get better."

"Aye," was all Etta could say. *Things will get better...* Wulfee used to say that to her children—to her army. *They only get worse... they only get worse. More will die.*

She watched Swey play for a while, and he was sopping wet from the river and covered in sand and dirt. He threw rocks and fought other kids with sticks, and together they jumped on moss-covered rocks and tried not to slip, but all of them did.

Soon, Etta was back in the midst of the valley and felt the energy building with all of the people. They moved around her, going in every direction. Cattle wayns trotted by, loaded with ander and cottonweed and milk-tongue, and other herbs she didn't know but were probably for healing also. The wayns carried rods of iron and darker-coloured metals. They carried trunks of pine and aspen and birch, and Etta saw folk carrying massive saws together in a chain.

Smoke from the forges was so thick that Etta coughed at times, especially in the most crowded spots, and folk hammered at those forges all day.

Someone offered her a small sour apple, and she snatched it and ate it in fear of not finding anything else with all these people about. *Sweyne probably has a plan. He always has a plan.* There were granaries that looked like stunted nytewoods standing at one side of the valley. Etta reckoned those were full to the brim. She made her way to the kitchens and found that Cullen had appointed himself as head of kitchen, and no one had tried to stop him. He was rolling dough, and when Etta waved at him, he only nodded, refusing to take his hands off the dough.

"Good flour here, Etta, hardly any flies," he said. "Mighty fine loaf this will make. Mighty fine."

Calum was sitting around a budding clanfire with a few dozen grey-bearded elders, and Etta joined them to smoke some chuff. They tugged on their braids and told stories of wars long past, and Calum told his stories of travel, too, and the elders listened and coughed.

"And this," one of the elders said with smoke billowing out of their mouth, "is the kihl'dor who saved the world. The kihl'dor who defeated ten thousand Ayelish at Rosen Bridge." The elders all stared at Etta, and she smiled awkwardly and took a big puff off the chuff pipe and tried to hide her face in the smoke.

It was five thousand, six at most. She slipped away from the clanfire and saw that Baerd was standing on top of a barrel giving a speech in his booming voice, but Etta dared not listen.

"You want to sleep by us?" a voice said, and Etta knew it was Rat. "We've got a good spot by the stream. Might be able to cook up some trout tonight," he said.

"The herons have eaten all the trout," Etta said, and smiled.

"What are you talking about, lady?" Nettle shook her ladle at Etta. "I could catch a trout in the middle of a field."

"Come," Rat insisted. "Fiora and Annie made you a spot."

It was then that Etta realized they had come looking for her. It made her feel okay. She had many people here who cared for her, and that was a feeling she hadn't felt in a long time. A security that was palpable. The clanking of steel hammers at the forges made her even more safe.

The place that was made for Etta was nothing more than a hempen sack spread on the dirt and a wool blanket that sparsely covered her body, but she had rarely ever been so thankful for something in all her life. *You should be dead, old broad. You should be dead so many times it's not even funny. But you live. You're not done here, yet.*

She fell asleep, exhausted, to the sound of Annie and Fiora singing songs from the cycles.

THEY CAME IN THE night.

Etta was dreaming of Braden when she heard the first screams. She burst from beneath her woollen blanket to find others standing, looking around in terror and confusion.

"What's going on?" Etta screamed. She looked out to the camp and saw no torches. No light. Then she heard more screams. This was a surprise attack, and they weren't here to fight or they would have come in a shield wall. Etta made her way to the crowd of folk in the centre valley where the nihr'el grew.

"What happened?" she screamed, and no one had answers for her. Folk were looking around and pointing in different directions, but there didn't seem to be any fighting happening. Then Etta saw Pike pushing his way towards the trunk of the tree. "What happened?" Etta asked him, and his eyes turned wet.

"By the gods, Wulf," he said, and tried to hug her.

Etta pushed him away. "What's going on?" Folk were crying out now. Gasps of despair and heartbreak. People died and folk were just finding out. "By the gods, Pike, if you know bloody well, tell me."

"The Demhoni, Wulf, they slipped into our camp and took people. Took them alive. Only the gods know what for, but they were in and out and didn't kill anyone. They came up the stream and out of the arbor."

The stream... Tara and Swey had slept by the stream. Etta's feet were moving before she finished the thought.

"Wulfee!" Pike's voice was barely heard over her footsteps. As she got closer to the stream, she saw folk out front of tents sobbing and crawling in the dirt with grief. She saw folk holding weapons, axes and swords and spears, pounding on shields, and brooding as they stood over their grieving loved ones.

It's the middle of the night... The Feldarra had been guarding the mountain pass against any possible attack, but this wasn't an attack, they just trickled in from the mountainsides and the arbors and up the stream, taking people and leaving again. *A hundred needles rather than a single fist.*

The stream seemed to make no sound as Etta came to it. Her chest thumped, and her stomach sank into her arse looking at a stretch of empty dirt blossomed with footprints. *Gone.*

"Swey!" Etta screamed. "Tara!" *By the gods. Blood.* There was blood in the dirt. She ran up the stream until the arbor closed in around her and the sounds of the valley muffled. "Swey!" Her eyes burned as if her tears were boiling water. And they flooded her face, and the world was a blur as she ran. "Swey!" *He's gone. He's gone.* She fell to her knees. And pounded the earth with her fists until they would surely be bruised, and she let herself sob. "Swey!" she screamed to the moon and the stars, but only the bugs in the arbor made any notice of her. "I'm sorry, Swey. Braden. I'm so sorry. Forgive me, Gen. James, Maggie. Coal, Young Courtney, Holden, Benn. Forgive me..." *So many. So many. Why have so many who looked to me to save them died? Why? Am I really so wretched as this?* She sobbed so hard she felt something inside of her break, and more pain came out of the broken thing. Stabbing, strangling, burning, she screamed, moaned.

"Wulfee," came a voice from the dark. And she knew that voice. She hated that voice.

"Don't fucking come any closer to me," Etta said. Tears rolled down her cheeks. *By the gods, Crow, take me.* "You're the last person I want to see right now."

"Please, Wulf," Baerd said gently. "They took more than a hundred people."

Etta made a fist and swung it at Baerd but missed badly through blurry, wet eyes. Baerd grabbed her arm and pulled her in and wrapped his arms around her for a hug. Etta pushed him away and spat on him and pounded her fist into chest and arms, and when he grabbed her again, she fell into his arms and sobbed. She cried like a dam had been punched open inside of her, and when Baerd held her, she felt safer than she could remember. "You fucked up my life," Etta said. "You fucked it so bad."

"Then let me help you fix it, Wulf," he said, and let go of her. Etta stood back and stared into his brown eyes and saw Braden there staring back. "They took more than a hundred people. But they took them alive. Tara, she's been badly injured—the shamans took her. She said she was trying to stop them from taking Swey, and she took an axe to the shoulder."

Tara... Etta's heart froze. *Your daughterbound.* Etta shook her head. "I can't. I won't."

"You don't have to touch a weapon, Wulf, but come with me. Come with me and let's go save our grandson. Come with me to comfort Tara. Tell her we're going to go get him. These Demhoni have been a problem for too long. Let's end it. You and I with an army at our backs." Baerd was smiling.

Etta hated his smile. "If you think I'll get a taste for it again... Sweyne, I will not lead this army. I won't be a part of this prophecy shite. I'm *done. Broken.*"

"Right," said Baerd. "But you already are a part of it. You don't have to lead an army, Wulf, but prophecy laid its spindly fingers on you long ago. And now it's got our grandson."

Our grandson. You fucking shite head. You left us, you left. But Wulfee left too. She was no different. *You're no bloody different.* She killed their son. Sweyne did none of that. The thought nearly broke her all over again. *You're* worse *than him.* "You really think we can save Swey?"

Baerd shook his head yes. "I think we have to, or die trying. I owe that much to my sons." Baerd looked up at the moon like that big ball was what kept him from being a father. Etta wanted to say more, *fuck you, and your sons hated you,* but she knew it wasn't helpful, and it wasn't even true. Braden and Tarek had both looked up to him. That reminded Etta...

"How did Braden get the mask?"

Baerd paused what he was doing. "I don't know. I wasn't lying before." Baerd clenched his fists. "I lost single combat to some bastard named Colhran shortly after I lost the war to you. He spared my life because he feared taking such an eldritch mask from a dead person. He cut my hair and left me arse naked in the Fell of autumn. Braden must have found Colhran and killed him. Or someone else who had it."

Etta hated that explanation. Part of her had blamed Sweyne for Braden's going mad this whole time. It helped her to have someone else to blame. *There is no one to blame but you. You killed your son. You left him when he was young and shattered him, and he turned mad. He was cursed, sure, but he was mad before that—battle drunk, just like you were.* She hated that explanation, but she had to accept it. There was nothing else. It was easier to believe. She nodded and sobbed and listened to the stream gurgle on and thought of young Swey playing in it just hours ago.

"I have been a better person since I let that mask go, Wulf. I've fought only in defense. I came out here with these people, and I changed my ways. And when Bazal came along, I knew what it was all for. I knew I needed to find you again to lead this army. I needed to say I was sorry."

Etta laughed through her tears because that word, *sorry,* cut into her like a knife when it fell from Sweyne's lips. Sorry could never make the thing he did go away. Sorry could never make it right. But it showed he wanted to try. *And what else can you do but fucking try?* In her heart she wanted to cry out to Sweyne for help. *I killed him, Sweyne, I fucking killed our baby boy. I did it, and it's my fault he became the way he did because I should never have left him. I never should have left him, and you never should have picked up that fucking wolf mask, and nothing should be the way it is, but it fucking is.*

Sweyne watched her, waiting patiently for her to speak. She wanted to cry, and she absolutely hated that she wanted Sweyne to hold her. She hated that his smell reminded her of a time more comfortable. She hated that his smile still made her burn inside from his fire. She hated who she was, and she hated the person she was trying to hide from. Wulfee wanted nothing more but to kill this man, but Etta could do nothing but crave his familiarity.

"Love and hate are two sides of the same axe, Wulf," Baerd said. "One for each, and a sharp and deadly blade separates them. Whatever side that axe lies on at the moment, you and I both know it exists between us. Let's each grab the handle, eh? It's strong enough to get Sweyne. It's strong enough f or *anything.*" Baerd had a look of pride on his face. *He likes saying his own name referring to his grandson.*

Etta nodded, the old northern sign for luck, and Baerd returned it.

From the valley Etta heard folk crying out as more and more of them were realizing their loved ones were missing. "Your words don't mean a fucking thing to me. Show me you're sorry by getting Swey."

Sweyne nodded and unsheathed his axe. "I haven't attacked a person in eleven years, but I would for him. I would for young Swey, and I would for *you.* And I've got a thousand folk that will come with me."

"No," Etta said. "They will expect a big party to come after them and probably have traps set. I need twenty folk. Your best fighters." *And Pike. I need Pike.*

Baerd smiled and licked his lips. "Twenty?" He loved this. "Okay, what will we do?"

"We're going to build a dam."

GIVING IN

MAGGIE STOOPED ON A log just long enough to remove her boots, and then she was off again. She wanted to feel the leaves and the loam and the dirt on her skin so she could understand the earth's impulses should they try to send her a message. She could feel the whole world around her as she ran through it. The bats and owls, the bugs and the worms and the critters. Their lives hung in the air like fog in a storm and Maggie splashed through it, knowing if she took a big enough breath and allowed herself to become herself, she could kill this entire arbor and all of the Hallow Hills. Every soldier and peasant in Foulds, down to the ants and mites crawling in the wood of the houses. She could kill all of them, and she felt herself getting stronger.

"*It's almost time,*" the woman in her dreams had told her. *Na'reen was her name.* Maggie had come to miss Na'reen when she wasn't dreaming of her, even though Na'reen sometimes gave her dreams that were so vivid it terrified her. "*If you don't find us, a great tragedy will befall you.*" Na'reen had preached that same sentiment over and over, and every time Maggie looked at James, she worried she was going to kill him by accident. *But his life is so dull, you can hardly feel it. It is a small candle to your clanfire, but that is why you need him. Sometimes all you need to light the way is a candle, and a clanfire becomes destructive.*

Sticks and dried leaves crunched and cracked beneath Maggie's feet and the dirt, and grass tickled her bare skin. She had run away when the fighting started in fear of fulfilling Na'reen's premonition of a tragedy. She couldn't do life without James. If she took his life, she would find a way to follow. *In death we will be fucking glorious.* She loved it when James talked to her like that. She put a hand on her stomach and traced her belly button. Maggie had been feeling different for weeks, but yesterday she *really* sensed the new life inside of her. *It's not false. That is a life that grows in your belly. A child...*

Maggie almost couldn't believe it because she and James had hoped for a child for eleven years now and nothing ever came of it. *But something was alive beneath the nihr'el—old magics of the Druids, and it clung to James and me like skitters. Nature has come alive...*

There was a magic awake now that had long been asleep, and Maggie felt it in her bones. The trees and the stars felt it, too, and they cried out for her to protect them from it. *But how?* She had always felt out of place in this world but never so much as now. *If anyone knew what I really felt, they would kill me.* Her first father had reminded her of that repeatedly, after she had told him that she could feel the souls of the trees and all of the people. *"Don't you ever say that to anyone. That is the talk of Druids and mages. Do you have any idea why there are none around anymore? They were devils. You'll be killed for talking like that."*

There was a time when the world was overrun by eldritch magics. Not only in Yehven, but in Ardura, too. The Druids, the Draku and the Dagglanders. All of them abused the words of Karaat. All of them. It was only because the entire world supported Him that Karaat was so strong. *"The Warlocks will hunt you. They'll kill you, or worse. You're a danger, Maggie. Not just to us but to everyone. I'm sorry."* Maggie's first dad was terrified of what she was—the legacy her blood implied. He told her these stories often, and he had no interest in being a part of them. *"We live in a clean world now. Magics have become but a whisper. I'm so sorry,"* he said as he turned his back and left her exposed in the arbor.

But she didn't die then, as her dad had thought she would. And she had spent her life in silence, never revealing who she was or what she felt. She repressed everything until one day she couldn't hold it in anymore, and she walked in the woods and felt her powers. And when she was caught there, she was banished.

Her first dad left her in the woods with a load of hardbread and a fur cloak. Her mom cried horribly and refused to look at Maggie on that trip, and so Maggie knew something was off. *"I'm so sorry. I'll be back, dear, wait here. Don't you leave now,"* her father told her, and kissed her on the forehead. She thought she saw him wiping tears from his eyes as he left but wasn't sure. *Why are you sorry? Why did you say sorry so many times?* Maggie had thought.

She ate the whole loaf of bread on the first day and spent that night shivering in the dark and crying, hoping she would hear her father's footsteps in the arbor. She waited the whole next day and through another cold night until she realized he wasn't coming back.

She walked for two days alone in the arbor and on the old Lovasi road she now knew as the Northroad. She cried so much that she ran out of tears, and she walked until her heels were blistered so bad she couldn't walk anymore. She sat down on the side of the road and figured that she would probably die. That was when her second mother and father found her.

"By the gods, are you alone, little girl?" her second father had said, aghast, and Maggie burst into tears when she heard his voice.

Maggie promised herself that she wouldn't use her powers ever again. But every day she didn't extend her touch to the earth and fire, water and wind, she felt empty. The living things around her mocked her with their vibrancy. They were beautiful and full of colour, and she was dull and grey and dead inside. But when she reached out and felt the souls of things, she felt alive again, like part of something bigger. She felt the mycelium and the fungus and the bones of things and could see them all woven together in a beautiful mosaic that was called life. She could see all of the pieces and how they fit together. And she could remove a piece if she wanted. Or two, or more.

She struggled for years and years to find out where she fit into it all, but now, she could finally see that she wasn't just a thread in the weave, but the *weaver*. She could pull the strings of life wherever she wanted, and to kill was as easy as shearing a thread. *Mage.* They called her. *Magi. Maggie.* A Druid of Old. *A weaver.*

Maggie stumbled through the arbor and felt the lives of things and murmured, "Tell me where to go, just tell me," but no one answered her.

In her dreams, Maggie always found that her tongue was missing. The Abori woman Na'reen could talk to her, but Maggie couldn't talk back. Na'reen called herself a dream nymph. She never answered Maggie's questions. "Tell me how to get there and I will come." Maggie murmured into the arbor.

"Mag!" a familiar voice came from the wood, and Maggie's eyes flicked open. For a moment she thought the gods had answered her. "Mag!" the voice came again, and she knew it for James.

"I'm here," she said, and in a moment, he was there and she fell into his arms sobbing. Thinking of her past lives and all the people who abandoned her. *But he never has, and never will. Eleven years he has stuck by you.*

"By the gods, Maggie." He was out of breath and covered in battle gore, blood and slime, but Maggie didn't care. In that moment she could see her destiny so very clearly. *He is a thing of death, and I am a thing of life. Together we are whole. Together we are everything.*

Maggie jumped up and kissed James's wet lips. She smelled the sweat off him, felt the warmth from his chest on hers. His tongue, his neck, the veins on his hands as he held her. "I couldn't fight another battle, James. I couldn't wear that damned armour anymore. My fight is not here." Maggie sucked a deep breath through her nose and tasted the summergrowth.

"I found your armour and I feared…" James cut himself off, but Maggie knew what he was going to say. *He feared you'd left him. He fears that more than you dying. At least in death he can join you.*

"Leave with me, James," she said. "To Edura, to the Abori." James looked like something was tearing him in two from inside of his head.

"I want to, Mag," he said, "but I have to make sure my country is safe."

Maggie understood that. The Glennish wouldn't stop with this singular attack, especially not now that so many had been killed. This would be another war. And Toren and Eridan would be very difficult to reel in now that they'd broken off from the group and gained power and land of their own. Their only chance at winning would be to return to Rosen and beg the help of Brinley and Ruwen and the other Daggland rulers.

"That Ranger tried to kill me," James said. "He could have, I don't know why he didn't. I should be dead right now, and it made me realize that Mal Hallow is barely hanging on. If I died today, the Culdaine name would die. I have let my family and my people down. I hid away up there in the mountains for ten years with Wulfee. I should have left with you and faced this. I should have *been* here."

"The spirits won't let you die, James, not yet." Maggie didn't know if that was true, but she had a feeling, and seeing the look of fear on James's face, she figured that he had that same feeling. *Because the only thing worse than death would be to be the only person to live forever.* She thought of Maggie of Old Grove and could hear the tune in her head and she shivered, imagining a living James visiting her ghost in a place that she would never leave. *Because I will wait for you, my love. I will wait here until our souls can leave together… Just like Maggie of Old Grove.*

"I can't lose you, not again," James said, his eyes were sunken grey. "If you die, Maggie, promise me that you'll haunt me."

"I promise," she said, and she meant it.

They lay there in the arbor as the light slipped out of day, and the summer green wilted as autumn crept in and claimed it. Maggie's chest rose and fell from each breath and below her, the earth heaved, too. Deep, full breaths summoned from the rocky molten core. And from those depths came a soft whisper. *Hello,* it said. *Hello,* Maggie responded.

To James, she said, "Let's go back to Rosen."

"Now?" James said. He seemed comfortable here in the arbor, or at least comfortable to be away.

"We need to face this, whatever it takes," Maggie said. She was more ready than ever to use her powers. *But this time it will be my plan. Start to finish.*

"Maggie..." James reached for Maggie's hands, and she let him have them. "I'm scared. I'm so scared to fail—to ruin everything."

"We won't fail, James," Maggie said. "We can't." In her heart she knew that if she asked Nature for the power to beat this, Nature would respond *yes.* "Let's go home."

"This is home."

James's arms *did* feel like home, but Maggie pulled away and said, "Home to our people."

"Aye," James said. Maggie was happy to see him smiling. *My king.*

For two days James and Maggie rode through the craggy, wooded hills of Wick Arbor. They rode through lowlands over a rainbow of wildflowers. They crossed throbbing streams and rapids, side by side on two beautiful black stallions that had run off from Eridan's army. They drank from clear flowing streams and ate blueberries and raspberries and lindon berries. Twice Maggie had eaten the life from a fat rabbit, and they'd cooked it on a small wooden spit over a crackling fire that Maggie had started with help from the spirits. They slept beneath the stars beside a nytewood and made love there.

Tell him of our child. The thought pestered her the whole time, but she couldn't find the words. *Let him deal with the Ayelish first,* she thought, but knew it was more than the Ayelish that troubled him.

The rain pissed down on the third day, and Maggie and James arrived in Rosen looking haggard and wind-worn. Their horses had clumps of mud as thick as apples on their hooves. The stable master gasped, glared at Maggie and James, then back at the hooves like she had never seen shoes so dirty in all her life. She snatched the reins, and Maggie and James went to the great motte hall of Fort Rosen.

The wood was moss-covered and dirty and the thatch was rotting, but it was still a hall and in it sat a ruler. Ruwen was perched on her dais eating a bowl of brown stew with a thick wooden spoon. Her hair was tied in a knot, and her braids hung neatly on her back. She was wearing her gold arm rings stolen from Kallahorn and even a gold crown with a red ruby in the centre.

"I see you've taken your crown back," James said.

Ruwen spat. "Never got rid of it. The crown that Ayelish bastard wore was merely a prop."

"So, I guess I am no longer your king?" James stood firm, and Maggie was proud of him for that. She knew it wouldn't have been easy for him to say that. Ruwen squirmed in her chair. Maggie could sense her mind swaying back and forth from multiple ideas. But she had no fear.

"Aye, you're my king," Ruwen said. "The bull moose still means something to me, but I rule Rosen—House Ruwen—and the ruler of House Ruwen wears this crown. My great uncle plucked this ruby here in the crown from the eye of a demon bear. A beast of the Old Gods ilk, I tell ya. I don't care what title you give me. Lady, queen, I rule here."

"And can you tell me why Brinley is assembling his army in your courtyard?" James said.

"Ask him yourself, King," Ruwen said.

"I'm asking you," said James.

Ruwen squirmed again. "He means to attack Dawning. Take his home back."

"He means to fight Toren?" James asked.

"Toren won't stay at Dawning for long. He will be moving on to kill more people and please the Dead God," Maggie said. "Brinley could take Dawning without a fight if he would wait."

"*You* tell him to wait. I already tried." Ruwen drank deeply from a wineskin, and Maggie thought by the redness of her nose and cheeks that she had been drinking a lot lately.

James and Maggie found Brinley and Sessely sitting with Brigid and Aione around a small fire. Squirrels were roasting on small wooden spits and Aione turned them gently. When Brinley saw Maggie and James coming, he spat. "King Reaper returns!" he said, and put his arms in the air.

"Oh, sit down, Brin," Sessely moaned.

Maggie wasn't interested in wasting any time. "Tell me why you're assembling an army when Toren will surely not stay at Dawning for long," Maggie said, and the abruptness of it startled Brinley.

He was a calm man who'd seen many battles and even slain a drayke, so Maggie wasn't surprised when the old warrior scratched his scarred eye and grinned. "Because even a minute is too long for that fish-fucking bastard to be in my hall," Brinley said.

"Woah." His daughter Brigid made a face at the aggressiveness of Brinley's words.

"Easy there, my heart." Sessely put a hand on Brinley's shoulder.

"When I bent the knee to that bastard Calen Alder," Brinley said, "he promised me something for my daughters and my grandsons. He promised us a name. The House of Brinley. To uphold that name we would bury our dead at Dawning and maintain the land there and pass it down to our daughters and sons. I won't let that bastard stay there."

"We are going to bury the bones of Tilly there," Sessely said. "You aren't going to stop us from doing that."

"I'm not trying to," James said. "I'm just asking for patience. Togetherness."

Brinley spat.

"And what will you do when the Ayelish come back?" said Maggie.

Brinley laughed. His maps were laid out, and he pointed to a cluster of small red stones placed at Tusk. "You see, they're finally coming. My outriders have spotted them leaving Tusk, up the Northroad. They'll be in Oldwood in a week. They have ten thousand or more this time. Double the Wolf's garrison, and these aren't just brigands and sellswords, these are knights and their retainers. Aspiring knights and trained warriors from all across Ayeland. It seems to be a mixing of folk—a gathering of sorts."

"And when they attack you at Dawning, you will be crushed if you're by yourself. You don't even have food stores in the granaries," said James.

"They won't take Dawning, not this year," Brinley said. "It's too late in the year for them to do anything but march straight up the Northroad. I'd reckon they're planning on holding up at Tide for the year. I'd reckon they're headed straight there now like an avalanche. They'll cut off our access to the sea and go from there."

"Even more reason for us to band together! Surely the Ayelish will attack Dawning eventually," James said.

"The Glennish bastards grew corn in my fields, that will bring a good harvest. And when they attack, I'll bend the knee like I did two years ago. I'll uphold my word and hope the Queen Ianna upholds the word of her dead father and lets us live. We stand no chance, anyway."

Maggie couldn't believe what she was hearing. "You'll give up after all of this? The people of Mal Hallow came together to survive this winter, and now that summer has passed, you've forgotten how cold and dark things were." She pointed at James. "This man fought half gods to save you all and you've forgotten" She slapped the scars on her face like a madwoman and really made a show of it. "You see these scars?" She slapped her own face hard. The rulers of the Hallow already feared her after what she had done at Rosen and now she wanted Brinley and his family to think she had gone mad, so she slapped her scars even harder to make sure they could all hear the smack of flesh on flesh. "You see them? I got these fighting to save you and your daughters and their sons."

"I would die for the Hallow." Brinley muttered.

"Die fighting!" James said. "And I would rather die than bend the knee and lower that flag." James pointed to the yellow flag of Mal Hallow hanging from the walls of Fort Rosen, and the brown moose emblazoned on it seemed to dance in the wind.

That seemed to get Brinley's attention. He stared at the flag awhile and scratched at his eye. "There was a time," he said, "that I would have died for that flag, too." He looked to his daughters and grandchildren, who were on the far side of the hall paying little attention to the discussion going on. "But now I only care about *them*. I don't want to be on the wrong side of this war. If I get to keep my land and make a name for my family, that's all that matters. If I'm remembered as a traitor or a knee bender, then so be it. I won't let my family die for a cause that is already lost. Hell, it was lost when Claydon turned on us. I should have turned home back then."

"It's not lost while we breathe," said James, and Maggie knew he'd say something predictable like that. He liked to sound heroic, and Maggie loved that about him.

Brinley smiled at James like he was a child, and Maggie figured that to Brinley, James was. "If I'd known the Ayelish hadn't invaded Mal Hallow over the winter, I never would have stayed in Kallahorn for as long as we did. There's a curse in that castle. My girls and I all felt it. This whole thing has been tinged with darkness from the very start. I put my family in danger by following Derudin and you, and I won't do it again."

"Fight with me, Brinley. For the Hallow. We can win. We can beat these Ayelish," James said, though there was little conviction in it.

"You need to shine a light on that darkness inside of you, James, before anyone will fight for you," Sessely said.

Brinley nodded, the old sign for luck. "You're not your dad, James. But I hope you find whoever you are."

James said nothing to that, and after a moment Brinley and Sessely walked away, and Maggie said, "I'm ready to leave, James. The dream nymphs have told me it's time. Na'reen says we will be welcomed."

"Na'reen?" James said, and Maggie saw doubt in his eyes. "The Ayelish are marching. I can't leave, Maggie. I can't abandon my mom and dad like that. I can't abandon our home. I have to form a shield wall against these

Ayelish and stand in it." He touched her hands. Maggie loved the roughness of his calluses and the ridges of his scars, and the thick veins. She smiled at him.

Maggie knew that the shield wall they were capable of putting together would be crushed against a force the size of what Brinley described. *Ten thousand this time, maybe more, and without Wulfee to lead.* Maggie felt a yearning like she'd never experienced. She *needed* this. If she didn't at least try, she was afraid that what was inside of her would kill her. "Then let's take care of the Ayelish and then leave," she said.

James's face turned even more doubtful. "Mag..."

He fears losing you. "We can meet them at Oldwood if we go by horseback," Maggie said. "There are barrows there, I visited them often as a child and lay in the nytewood groves there. I can go below, through the barrows. I will sense the life of the army above me and when they pass, I will kill them. *All* of them."

James looked appalled and opened his mouth to speak, but nothing came out so he closed it again. *He knows it's the best plan. A clean and easy sweep. We have lost our army and have no other choice.* Maggie reached out and grabbed his thick hands. She could feel the death in him, seeping out of his sword and into his veins. *The sword will kill him eventually. It will eat his soul... will you be ready to die with him? Truly?* Maggie would have always thought yes before, but now she could only put a hand on her stomach, undecided.

"I could form a shield wall, like the Feldarra, like Emmer," he muttered.

"No," Maggie said, "I won't let you die."

James shuddered. Trembling, he uttered, "Okay."

Maggie took a deep breath. She thought that she should be terrified, but instead she only felt excitement—or relief...

Finally, she could use her powers. Finally, she could see what she was really capable of.

THE WOODLORE

Haro collapsed to the ground. His blue jay fluttered in his ear—pegging his mind.

"Hurry, would you?" Uma roared.

Grady came squirreling forth with nuts and leaves. "Here, here."

Kat and Uma grinded. Pastes of blue ander and green chicory-bead and purple carisroot. And Kat held a rock with all three smeared out in neat globs.

"This is gonna hurt," Uma said, holding a red-hot iron.

"Do it," Haro choked out. His head thumped. He was dizzy and his vision was blurred. "Hurry."

Kat spread the pastes on his open wound to clean it, and then Grady and Kat both held Haro down as Uma sealed the wound with the red-hot iron. Haro's raw and bloody flesh sizzled and smoked like meat as Uma rolled the iron over Haro's severed wrist.

After a moment Uma took the iron away and put it back in the fire, then Kat smeared more paste.

"It's almost over, don't you worry about a thing." Grady chittered in Haro's ear as he faded in and out of consciousness. Uma used the iron three or five more times, and finally Kat smeared the blue paste of ander over his wound and wrapped it with mullein and burdock leaves, then sealed it with a wet, red clay.

And Haro drifted in a fever dream. Day into night into day, and Haro couldn't keep his eyes open. The ander flowed through him, and he felt his blood boiling. Dreams and half dreams flooded his reality. *The Maw. The Maw and...James Culdaine. Culdaine. Juh-ames. Kull-Kill? Dayne...*

Haro had been fighting the memories and he couldn't breathe. *Days. Weeks.* They flooded into his mind like a waterfall. *Why?* His head was thumping. *Who?* The Maw had told Haro the truth of James, but he couldn't understand it. *Godkiller.* His dreams were a rainbow of vivid colour as he drifted through arbors in the bodies of different animals. Stag and bull. Bird and snake. Fish and beaver. He had a thousand memories, and he had none at all.

"How is he?" Grady asked.

"Getting there," Uma said.

And that was days ago she said that...

Haro awoke in cold sweat. *Dreaming?* He was breathing heavily. Above him he saw trees shooting up to the sky. He tried to scratch himself with a hand that wasn't there. He smacked himself in the face with a soggy leaf stump that used to be his hand, and the pain made him scream.

"Ahrh!" He got up and kicked the first thing he saw: a stack of logs. *Firewood?* He sat on the logs to let his head stop spinning. He got up and stumbled into the Wick Arbor and hoped the morning dew and larksong would be enough to clear his head. No matter what he did over the past weeks, he couldn't seem to settle. *Godkiller...*

He found a nytewood and fell to his knees in the soft dirt there and put his stump hand to his chest. "Tell me, Maw. Who am I?"

But there was no answer. *In my dreams you don't shut up.*

"I feel my time here slipping away. Coming to an end. I need to know what you ask of me. I need to know," Haro spoke quietly, almost in a whisper. "I fear the bird will take me one day and not let go."

Still no answer.

Haro was well aware of the strange history of Rangers and their animals. Long before Hagen the Great gave out the first greenhoods, they were still losing themselves to the animals. *How many animals are dead Rangers?* Sometimes Haro wondered if every animal was just a part of the cycle of Rangers. They were all in the same cycle of nature, and so it seemed likely to him. That kind of thing wasn't written about in the woodlore, though, and so Haro couldn't truly be sure.

The woodlore was started by Hagen the Great a thousand thousand years ago. As a Ranger, the woodlore was God. The Ranger's Green Book was written from it. It told of how the Maw, God of the Unknown Workings of Nature, claimed dominion over the Rangers so that the Old Gods wouldn't slaughter them all before the Old Gods rose up to the heavens. The Outcast God saw the beauty in the Rangers when no one else did. Saving the Rangers is what earned him his name from the other Old Gods.

And from that time of rapture, the Rangers started to unite from small bands of twelve to twenty into large bands of hundreds and sometimes thousands. Many hundreds of years after the Maw saved the Rangers, Hagen the Great wrote the woodlore. Therefore after, he was known as the Keeper of the Lore.

The woodlore was a guide to how the Rangers should live and work their magics. Hagen laid guidelines on how to not be taken by the animals. On one of the first trees of the woodlore, it was written that "One should never spend more than a few hours a day inside of their animal or else risk serious madness." Haro knew this and it ate him up. It hurt him because at times he couldn't stop himself.

Hagen the Great was the first one to attract e'daru by hiding his hair with a green hood. Soon, he made it mandatory for all Rangers and wrote it into the woodlore as a law. The Rangers would live in the hills and the arbors, and they would monitor the roads for thieving. In that way, they would form alliances with the kings and queens of the Hallow and ensure their survival through the ages. They stayed out of wars. And always, always they prayed to the Maw. They worshipped the Outcast and they thanked e'daru for their powers. And in their hearts, they wished for e'daru to appear.

"Without you we are nothing, Maw. Without you we would have been extinct," Haro said. "You told me this Reaper was a godkiller. You stood behind me and whispered it in my ear. So are you in danger? Is that my purpose? To protect you?" Haro was kneeled in the dirt below the nytewood praying in the dark, and just as he was about to break down and cry, a voice came to him.

"Yes. It is that and so much more." The voice was deep and snarling.

Haro trembled. He looked around and saw nothing. It was the voice of a god. The voice of the Maw. "Help me. Tell me, how? How can I help you?"

The Maw spoke through the wind. "Woodlore," the Lupin said. "Your journey is written in the woodlore. It's time you learned who you once were—who you still *are*."

The woodlore... Haro had known the laws and dictums of the woodlore well, but there was more to it, more that he had forgotten. There were children's fables, histories. *Aonis...* Stories of heroes and villains. Good and evil. Haro used to know them by heart, but the memories were gone now that he tried to recover them, stripped away most likely, little by little, by each body that he took. *And how many have you taken now? Twelve? Twenty? More?*

Haro clenched his fist, and when it started to rain, he looked up to the sky and opened his mouth to drink. *Who are you? What are you?* As the rain soaked his hair and rivers ran down his face, Haro tried to summon the memories that had given him so much comfort before. Of Ifanie and of Owen. Of a brother, maybe, or was it a mother? He tried to summon the feelings of love, but they were so distant he couldn't grab them. They were like a setting sun, and all he could do was watch them fall away from him into darkness. *Only Dalla.*

And there were other memories. Less pleasant and far less comforting than those of Ifanie and of Owen. Memories of a dead mother and father—murdered. Memories of months and years spent starving and anxious, living hand to mouth in the wild. Being hunted by Hawka and memories of his sick wife. *Of Dalla.* Haro thought of Dalla often, *she was strong,* and the remorse he felt was worse than the pain of burning his arm, and then losing that arm. *I couldn't save her... Dalla, I couldn't—I killed you, it was me.*

"So who am I?" Haro spoke the words out loud to make them real. To make them more than just thoughts. "Haro," he said. *But what's in a name?*

Haro looked out to the Wick Arbor. *The woodlore.* That was his purpose now. *So what then?* "Who am I?" he spoke again. And though he knew the Maw would not answer him, the Outcast's words hadn't left him. *The woodlore.*

It was time Haro went back to Place, the grove of white pines in the Wick where the woodlore was written. *Aonis...* He needed to read his story.

But do you still know the way? This man had never been to Place. Wick is a big and thick arbor.

Haro the blue jay twittered from a nearby tree in the rain and swooped down to land on Haro's wet shoulder. His little feet were like small sticks stabbing and poking into Haro's skin. It chirped and carried on, and Haro knew that it would take him there. The blue jay's memories went back to the pure times, when the skies were new. They knew wood and earth and water instead of the names of things. *But what's in a name, anyway?*

As long as it was made of wood and earth and water, the bird knew, and the bird could remember where it was and the colours of it and what made it special. Rocks were no good. Rocks were grey, and their memory was tightly sealed inside of them.

But the bird knew wood, and Haro would let it guide him.

I N THE WICK ARBOR, Haro saw shadows come alive. He traipsed deeper and deeper into the thick and tangled wood. Pine and birch and aspenwood, yellow and gold and green, thick, and all around him. The gurgling of small streams and the crackle of fallen leaves and needles beneath his feet as he walked was hypnotic.

"There's a shite-load of ticks in here, eh?" Grady held a squirming sharp-toothed bug between two fingers. He had just removed it from his flesh.

"There's more than ticks," Haro said. He remembered getting stuck with the reaper fist once as a child—a plant with sharp sword-like needles that get stuck up in you.

"Are you sure it is this far in?" Uma was miserable. "It's nearly been a week of this."

"It's at the very heart of the arbor," Haro said. His blue jay flew circles around his head, and for a quick moment he slipped inside of it. At once he could see that they were on the right path and it was only a couple of hours away by the way the bird flies. "We are close."

But it wasn't as close as Haro hoped. Travel through the arbor was slow, even with a bird to guide, and so they spent another night sleeping by a stream that babbled with the bugsong in the night.

The next morning, they woke before the sun and Kat had already caught three squirrels for them. Uma started a fire while Grady and Haro gathered pine nuts from the fallen cones, and when the fire was hot and snapping, Kat cooked the squirrels and Grady fried up the pine nuts on a flat rock.

"I don't really like the taste of squirrel," Grady said, eating his pine nuts. "It's a preference sort of thing, you know?"

"I get that," said Uma, chewing loudly. "I could never eat bear again."

They walked all of that morning and through midday, and by the time the sun had begun its downward path, Haro started to worry it would take yet another day to get there.

But then he saw the first shaved tree. The bark had been removed all the way down to the roots. In the bare bark, blue letters were carved deep into the wood. Haro touched the tree with his hand. *The woodlore.* He looked through the brush and found that the bare trees were everywhere.

"By the gods," Uma said. She touched one of the bare trees and started to cry. "It's beautiful."

Grady and Kat had dissolved into the woodlore and Haro felt that call, too. The woodlore would give answers, safety, a connection to the past. It called everyone that came in their own way, to their own tree.

The same things were written in different clusters of trees, mostly. The laws of animals—which types were easier to take as familiar and which posed more difficulty. Bears, for instance, were temperamental and it took a strong sort of person to tame one. Squirrels on the other hand were inherently chatty, and a few good words would be sufficient. The woodlore told the laws of the arbor, the seasons, what to eat, and how to get it. The constellations and the names of trees and plants and what they can be used for. How to forge weapons, and how to make blue dye from boiled deer hides and copper ore dust to re-trace the letters on the trees. There were two hundred or more trees on the different properties of mushrooms and fungus. *And there.* The trees of fable—children's tales, or so Haro thought. He put his hand on one of them and felt the life of the tree. He started to read. It wasn't difficult to find the story he was looking for.

Aonis. The traveller. The hero with a thousand thousand faces.

"I needed you to remember," a voice came from behind Haro that made him jump. He turned and saw nothing.

"The hate and the pain that the Creators caused us, you are the embodiment of a thousand thousand years of hatred from Nature towards the Creators. We needed you to remember," the voice came from behind him again.

This time Haro turned and saw the woman it belonged to. She was sitting on the roots of the fable tree; she wore a dress of hoary moss and spiderweb. Her thick, grey hair was a matted mess of sticks and leaves, and her round face was dirt-smeared and kind. A red spider crawled up her dress and around to her back. Her hands were stained blue, from the dye she used to trace the letters of the lore, Haro figured. Bright green eyes pierced Haro, and he knew right away who he was looking at.

"The Keeper?" he said. "The Keeper of the Lore?" *The very blood of Hagen the Great, perhaps...*

"They told me Aonis would visit in my lifetime, but you never know with these things," she said. She grinned to reveal a few yellow teeth poking out of bloody gums. "Somebody is *always* lying, you know?"

Aonis... "So it's true then?" Haro said. "This is my journey? Whatever this tree says?"

The Keeper laughed a crooked sort of squeaking laugh that sounded like steel grinding on a whetstone. "It's not Humans who will save this land. They will squabble and kill each other, time after time, age after age. It's the Rangers and the Giy'er. The Earth Faeries and the Nymphs. The Children of Nature. It is only us we can depend upon for our future. Is this your journey? Only if you believe in magics, boy. Can it be true? The sky has fallen before. How could it have ever been new, otherwise? Nothing is truer than a story we all believe in."

Haro was confused. "I have mixed up memories. Like past lives are melding together."

"That is the curse of a Ranger."

"So how far does it go back? How can I know?" Haro begged.

The Keeper laughed. "Are you Aonis? Well it certainly seems that way, doesn't it?" The Keeper sniffed at the air around Haro and cringed her face. "You've been led here. Your soul smells older than dirt. I would say you're the closest thing to Aonis we've seen. The woodlore speaks of it. The Children of Nature believe in the woodlore so if you believe you're Aonis, they will, too."

"I'm confused by these memories and the vague messages I get from the Maw," Haro said. "I don't know how to read them. I don't know which memories are mine and which are others'. I had a wife... Ifanie and Owen, they were everything to me, and now... now it's like they've slipped away into the shadows. James Culdaine, he killed them. I hated him so much. So much. But all I think of is Dalla. The woman that the man whose body I'm in now was heartbound to. Dalla and all of the mistakes I've made."

The Keeper put two fingers on her chin and raised her lower lip. She seemed curious. "Go on, boy. What has the Maw told you?"

"He told me my journey was written here, in the woodlore. That I will find what I need here."

The Keeper smiled. A big, all-knowing smile that Haro immediately understood. "Yes. Yes, it *is* you. It must be. The Maw. Oh, yes. The Maw knows." The red spider scuttled onto the Keeper's shoulder as she scanned the fable trees, tracing a line below each word as she read. "This." She slammed her finger down over and over. "This, here, look. You've had a hundred bodies or more. Starting in the first year after the Starfall. It was an old tradition started anew."

"So what? What does it mean?" Haro was intrigued. He always sensed he was destined to be great. *But at what cost?*

The Keeper sighed. Her face was one of empathy. "Your memories of Ifanie and Owen, they aren't yours, Haro. You stole them. In your last body you stole them. You were with that man's body for a long time though—so long, that his hate for James Culdaine seeped into you. Just as your love for Ifanie and Owen had seeped in. Just as if you stay with this body long enough, your love for Dalla will grow more real. It is dangerous to move bodies too much and dangerous to stay too long. Every time you take something, and every time you leave something behind. You are just pieces of all the people you've been. Like I said, Haro. Nature needed you to remember. All of these things—hate in particular."

I've been tortured for centuries—never knowing who I am. Confusing memories. Ifanie and Owen weren't mine... they weren't mine... but they felt so real, Haro couldn't believe it. He smelled them. He tasted Ifanie's lips and he *remembered* them.

"No." Haro fell to his knees. He was crying so hard his stomach cramped. He was short of breath and heaved to catch it between sobs. "Ifanie. Owen. They were my everything. I missed them so badly. Everything. You can't tell me it wasn't real. You *can't*." Spittle hung from Haro's lip.

"They were the memories of the man whose body you stole, Haro. His name was Daryll. By the time you stole him, his wife and child had already died in the war. It's written here. It's in the woodlore. Their sacrifice is duly noted, and they would have received great honours from the Old Gods upon their passing."

Haro's head swung towards the fable tree viciously. He read. And there it was. His life. Up to the point when he took the body of Grig, Dalla's heartbound. Hardly a thing about James Culdaine other than their brief encounters. "Who?" Haro caught his breath. Tears had flooded his vision. "Who's writing this?" Haro was horrified. He was being watched. Monitored. *Like a bird. Like a bloody bird.*

The Keeper stood tall and straight faced. "It is the way of things, Haro. Everything you do is written in nature. It can't be undone, but you control what is still to come. Ifanie and Owen weren't yours, they never were, but you can fight for them still. *Someone* loved them, and love like that exists all over this cold world. *You* can fight for that." The Keeper looked wise and kind and good.

"Is my name even Haro?"

"Of all the things that have come and gone, Haro has stayed. It is the Old Mal word for *hero* or *help*. Aonis means union in the Old Language."

"So why? Why am I here? Why do you keep me around."

"You are a Child of Nature, Haro, Aonis, one of Her last true servants. A soul as old as the skies, and we have carefully preserved you for this moment."

"For what? For what? Please tell me."

"To rescue us. To form a band. Bigger than any ever before. All the Rangers, and the Giy'er and the Druids. The Earth Faeries and the Nymphs. A band of all Nature's Children. It will take everything. *Everything* to win this war—to protect this land and the lore that makes it ours."

"War? What war?"

"The Last War. The War to End All Others. Nature will either finally defeat the Creators or die. You have fought this war before, Haro, Aonis, and you have won. The stories were erased from history in the first Starfall, but they happened. And these trees grew back and we kept the new woodlore alive, for this. Just for this, Haro. Bazal and Hendurinn fought against the Black Summer, and the Rangers and the Giy'er and the Faeries fought against the black hordes that rose with it. Now you must do it again."

Haro scanned the tree, taking in his own history. *Your life is a lie.* He noticed one word was crossed out over and over again. And below, it was written "Mother's Heart."

Haro looked closer and made out a couple of the other letters. "L. S." He saw a few more.

"I. N. D. Lidn-Lindis," Haro said. "Lindis is crossed out hundreds of times."

"Quiet." The Keeper wasn't grinning, and her voice dropped to a hushed whisper. The red spider scuttled behind her back. "Quiet. I know what it says."

"So what of it?" Haro pointed to the trees.

"I said *quiet*."

"Lindis is where the Warlocks tried to break the world. That is what the cycles say..."

"That is where history made a mistake," the Keeper said. "It didn't happen like it was written. Not like it was supposed to. And Lindis is an awful, monstrous name. Mother's Heart is a better name. Oh, yes. More fitting."

"So, it was you? You crossed it out?" Haro almost couldn't believe it. There must have been a thousand fable trees in this grove alone. *Did she cross out every one?*

The Keeper scowled. "You wouldn't understand. You wouldn't get it. The names of things, boy, the names of things have meaning. Without meaning, things just crumble. Without a good, strong name to prop them up in history, they fade away. Mother's Heart is strong, pure. Don't you understand? It's a better meaning—a stronger beginning."

"And Lindis isn't?" Haro asked. "What does it mean?"

"No," the Keeper said. "Lindis is a word from a tongue so old its speakers have long since left this place. The same as *Kallahorn.* Its speakers were killed in a cataclysm long before the Creators fell into this world, but Lindis was their masterpiece—a letter to the gods and all of the future expressing that they were here. But that word ties us back to a history we don't understand—a darkness so terrifying it is beyond belief. Don't you see? We can give the world new light with names. Names with good meaning."

"So what does *Lindis* mean?"

"It was written here." The Keeper pointed to a section of the fable tree that was completely sanded over. "I removed it. From every tree. It's dangerous."

"What does it mean?"

"The translation is difficult, but it seems that the Old Mal language is a bastardized version of this old language. It means Last Heart, I think. And for some race long ago, it was their last place."

Haro couldn't take his eyes from the smoothed-over chunk of wood where a piece of history had simply been removed. *Last Heart...* Suddenly, a fire flared up inside of Haro and he stood tall. *This is my journey. This is what it was all for.*

"So what does it mean?" Haro asked.

"There is something there. Something you must discover," the Keeper said. "That is where you must go. But not until the end, Haro, not until you have gathered your band. You will need them."

Lindis...

Haro and his band left the woodlore grove as one, and none of them spoke. All of them knew their purpose, that Haro understood. All of them had seen things that would change them.

Haro tried to flex a hand that wasn't there and reached for the memories of Ifanie and Owen to find they were only tiny little embers that barely lit the whole picture. *You can fight for them, for a love like the one you wished you had. You can fight for that in others.*

And he would.

A Gift from Karaat

JULIEN SAW THE FIRST signs of winter in the trees. The maples were slowly turning orange and red, and the oaks turned bronze in the Fell autumn air, and soon the birches would yellow. He had never been far enough north to see the leaves change colour. It was one of those things that he had heard about before but never really thought of. Now that he was riding through lush green lands along rushing rivers and looking at the leaves in so many shades of the earth, he felt like he had entered some kind of dream land.

You must have died somewhere back there. You are dead. But he knew he wasn't. Julien felt more alive than ever. His army had grown to twenty thousand. Rabble and sellswords and followers of the Red Eye of Letharr. They wiped the Hesterlands like a tidal wave as they marched through, eating everything they found and taking with them everything they couldn't eat.

They shouldn't have survived Darry, but by pure willpower, they overcame that obstacle. More than two thirds of the three thousand who attacked had been killed. And after the battle, more than twenty times that number had come to join Julien's cause. *Any other day, behind any other person, these folk would have deserted.* Sellswords didn't have a reputation of fighting to the bitter end. When they think they might lose, they desert. *But these folk stayed. They stayed for Karaat. They stayed for* you. *And it spread...* The rabble of five-hundred that followed him into the desert and lived to make it out were still by his side.

When the battle of Darry was over, the army swelled. Folk came from all over Esher and Lavesh and the Bone Islands. They came from Epithos and Kertann and Neira. Julien had met an entire rabble of hairy-faced people who came all the way from Arish Pura on ships made of silver wood. They came to serve their god, Karaat. To make a better world—a new world that finally saw an end to the Warlocks of Yehven. And they came to pay respects to Draku. They bowed down to Julien and said prayers in many languages. When he kissed their foreheads and told them all was well and good, many burst into tears. He was Draku, and these folk had served the Draku of Old when times were better. They wanted Julien to make it better for them again. And every day more and more arrived to join him.

"Cleanse these lands," a priest of Karaat begged him, "with fire."

"I will," Julien said. His chest was full of pride, his lungs sucked in destiny. "I will."

The Blackshire Inn had been a fat and juicy prize for them. Thirty knights of the Golden Lion had garrisoned themselves in there to protest the wars. They were sitting on a fat hoard of provisions including three thousand pounds of salted mutton and pickled eggs. Corn and barley and golden wheat. Beets and turnips and squashes and apples and pears. Ale and cider and even shine.

Julien feasted and drank himself near blind alongside his people, and helped them load the food into wayns, and they burned the bodies of their victims on great pyres and prayed to Karaat and howled at the great golden unicorn in the stars and at the silver moon.

Folk sang Words, and magics sparked and whirled in bright colours in the sky. Dark holes opened in the sand that led to God knew where, and rivers broke at the banks and waves rolled and crashed like thunder.

Unnatural fires burned in the black night, and Karaat's Words danced like a thing alive. *And he is alive.* The birds were upset and squawked in a mad fury, and the bats and the owls had fled so the nights were silent. Only the nightingales sang, rapining the night. To the Esheri, the nightingale's song was a curse that signalled death would come the next day. To Julien it was a reminder that even when you sleep, the world stays awake. Magics made the stars hazy, and Julien knew that this would only amplify. *Mother, Father, you would love this song. You would be dancing in the street to the sound of it.*

Julien had seized weapons that the Hesters were stupid enough to haul down south, and he ordered some of his rabble to fire them off into the night sky.

Great balls of stone and flaming thatch flew into the darkness, like mountainous versions of the flaming bats of Letharr. Julien watched as his people launched massive stone-pitchers, scorpions, ballistae into the night sky, and the not too far off Talon River twinkled brightly in their glow. He helped his people rope up and drag battering rams, siege towers, and slings behind mules and pack horses that were Hester-bred. They had found everything they had lost at Darry. Everything and more, because of the Hester's ignorance—the Warlock's ignorance.

Ambition killed the cat. The saying hadn't left Julien's mind since he had watched Rolan turn over to the dark side of his own mind. *The Hesters stretched themselves too thin. Like too little boot polish over too much boot.*

Julien could only think of Hest now. It consumed him like the flames of Draku consumed air. *"The book, Julien."* The words of his mother still rang in his ears like she spoke them new each day. *"The book has all the answers. It tells of our origin—of our Creator. It is the life story of our people, Julien. To find it would be everything. To find it would be to shine light on a millennium of darkness. It would be the rebirth of our culture."*

Julien breathed deeply of the good, open air. If there was going to be another Hester resistance, it would be at Talonsford. His outriders had informed him that it didn't look to be heavily garrisoned, but Julien knew that was an easy enough trick to pull off. Hide your army and lure the enemy into your cooking pot before you fire up the oven and put the lid on.

Talonsford was a big enough fort to hide a couple thousand soldiers; it was Lovasi built and sturdy as a mountain. *But why hadn't they sent more? Are they giving up? Are they really that incompetent? No Carlin? No Haven or Friars?* He had to keep his wits about him, but he currently walked with a drunken stagger that he couldn't correct for.

Rolan was gone now, just as Bones and Trist had gone. Julien had given them a new life and they took it gladly. All three refused to come to this battle, opting instead to send armies to represent them, which Julien couldn't really complain about. He was just lonely. Canri was dead, and Julien wasn't certain Ashan would survive much longer the way he had grown accustomed to climbing high places. And besides, Ashan had never been much of a talker.

Julien was all alone in this. He'd been alone, truly alone, since the day the Warlocks sank his ship and tried to exterminate his people like cockroaches. *My baby sister was on that boat. My mother went into the sea holding her. But cockroaches don't all die, do they? No, they live between the cracks and they always come back, always. And when they do it's never pleasant.*

He was tired of being alone. He missed his family—anyone.

"They are ready." Ashan approached calmly beside him as the sky bled pink in the east. "Say the word and the attack is on."

Julien looked out at the ragtag group he had assembled. The rising sun glinted off armour of a hundred different shapes and metals. Some of the army boasted shield and helm where some, including the hairy-faced folk from Arish Pura, wore almost no armour at all. *Each of these people have a dream, a want. Some of them are even as big as yours. So give them what they want. Give them a kingdom, give them glory, give them riches beyond their beliefs. Let them die for it, if that is what destiny requires. Smash Talonsford like a fist.*

Julien mounted and rode up and down the ranks. He raised his sword and shouted to the sky, and the people shouted with him. "For two hundred years, we have lived in the shadow of the Hesters and their Warlocks. For two hundred years, we have been fed scraps and forced to fight. Generation after generation of our children are dying to defend what little culture we have left." The rabble shouted in unison, and the echo of it shook Julien's chest and rattled his helm. "I was sent by Karaat to bring you back to the Old Kingdom. Back to when the Draku ruled and peace flooded the lands instead of war. Karaat is sick of watching His people die. So He has given us the strength to end it. This is our ancestors' country, our land. There was a time when Draku and Esheri lived in peace from the Bay of Lions to the coasts of Sothura. It's time we go back to those times of peace and harmony. Let's force these Hesterland-born bastards out of here!"

The rabble exploded and Julien dug his heels into his horse, and all at once the army charged.

Only when they were close enough to be in range did the archers appear on the walls of Talonsford. But only three waves of arrows fell before the front lines reached the walls of Fort Talon. The battering rams and the siege towers were right behind them, and all the while the archers on the wall were being assaulted by scorpion bolts and slings of rocks and burning tar and thatch. Julien watched balls of hot, black oil explode on the battlements and all over the archers, and the archers appeared to melt.

Thud. Thud. The battering rams echoed like thunder claps against the cedar gates. *Thud. Thud. Craaaaaacccckkk.* In a blur the gates were busted through, and Julien watched his rabble pour in like an angry spring river.

Before Julien took a step inside the fort, he watched the banner of House Norris, the black bridge and tower on river blue, get pulled down and the purple dragon on black rise in its place.

It had become too easy. *Was it this easy for Kassius? Is this why he grew bored in his old age and killed himself wandering the world?* Julien was starting to become too comfortable, and he didn't like it. He was waiting for it all to crumble to ash and drift away between his fingertips, but it only felt like his grip was getting firmer. He knew when and where he would die, and that gave him a blind confidence. *The confidence gods must have. Immortality.*

But Julien was only given immortality for a short time. *Is that even immortality then?* He didn't care about the words that represented the thing, he only cared that it was happening. He couldn't die. Not here, not yet. And that meant he could do anything. *Anything. But you remember those green eyes. You remember the fire. You remember how you die...*

Julien walked through the town of Talonsford with Ashan at his side, and when he came to the river, his jaw dropped. Two massive trading cogs had been dragged ashore; ropes bigger than Julien's legs hung from the bows like brown snakes. They were made of white pine and spruce, and Julien knew from the black sails with cross bones that they had come from Brey in the north Hesterlands. The captains seemingly came too far inland and got stuck, or someone stole these ships and sailed them here to do this purposely. Their hulls had been stripped, and folk must have been busy emptying the cargo because things were strewn all over.

Julien saw barrels of apples and pears and cider. Bags full of bread and bundles of potatoes and carrots and cobs of corn. Barrels of salt cod and pickled herring and sprat, smoked river pike and trout and salmon. Barrels of clams and muscles, cockles and shrimp. Smoked venison, moose, and elk, and haunches of smoked boar and full boars on spits. He saw furs of beaver and otter and lynx, barrels of cod oil and salmon oil and whale oil, mounds of ambergris and scarlet coral and mermaid tails. And it was all being stored in a big barn warehouse, which was a simple structure of wood and thatch. There weren't enough granaries in Darry to support that kind of food. Usually, in small towns like this, the folk would store just enough to get by and Hest would come to take the surplus. *These traders, surely, must have wanted to sail east to Edura. What forced them inland here?*

"You see this, Ashan?"

Ashan nodded. "They could have lasted that siege forever. There is a well here, too."

"That they could have. This was a gamble bigger than we even knew."

"We're going to feast well for the coming weeks," Ashan said with a grin.

"We can feast tonight, Ashan, we've earned that, but this treasure isn't for us," Julien said.

Ashan looked at Julien sideways.

"Bones has his throne, and Trist has his, and now Rolan, too, rests his ass on a throne. Only mine awaits in Hest. We all know Hest won't be this easy." Julien looked around the town and was completely ashamed that so many died at Darry to take such a shit hole as Talonsford. *No one came to assist these poor folk. The king just let it burn.* "Folk don't want to follow someone who got that many killed, Ashan. So, instead of my sword, I will use my mind. *Knowledge* is power. The people of Hest are starving while their king feeds *his* army instead of them. Look at how much food we have stolen from them. The smallfolk are ready to rebel, ready to riot. One egg would break the lion's back. Audacio said that."

Ashan just stared. Julien figured it was very possible Ashan had been hit in the head too many times. "I want you and the rabble to pack this food on wayns."

"Then what?"

Julien smiled. "Send it all to Hest. For the starving people, as a gift from Karaat."

STARVING

ON THE OUTER BAILEYS of Kelson's Keep, Aldred stood and watched, for there was nothing else he could do.

King John refused to address the people; he and Adora were otherwise occupied with their effigy, so William came to the parapets to try and make peace with the city. He was dressed in gilded armour, shiny and golden under the fat, yellow sun. His black hair flowed; his jaw looked chiselled beneath his firm beard. He looked kingly, and Aldred hated it. He felt cold and wasted. But he stood tall and watched the ceremony anyway.

The crowd below was raucous, chanting "Fuck the Lion" and "Burn the city" amongst other things. Small fires flickered throughout the city, some of crude colour, and there were twenty thousand or more Esheri headed straight for them. The army led by Brooton got into a brawl with the rioting cityfolk on their way out, and the entire garrison dissolved into the violence. They either joined it or were swallowed up by it. Not a single unit of soldiers even made it to the southern gates. Brooton was missing amongst them. *And that was weeks ago...*

Bishop Sparo stood beside William and said something quietly in his ear. Cityfolk saw William and started to yell in broken voices. They threw stones and broken bottles weakly, their projectiles falling short and smashing into the walls.

"Good people of Hest," William said. "We all face these tough times together." William stopped. His voice was lost under the yells. The people didn't want to hear him. He coughed from shouting too loud. To the council, he said, "We must remain strong and prepare for an attack. We may be under siege in the coming months, and we will need to work together to get through it."

Aldred gazed at the people as they screamed "Let them come!" He mulled over their desperation. He remembered the people of Soren. Their sunken faces begging, the inhumanity of their tortuous last months. Inside of those walls, the people had started eating the dead when there was nothing left. They ate their fallen knowing that an army waited for them outside their gates if they tried to find some place better or safer. *There wasn't even a bloody flame to stay warm by.* Even the rats had abandoned the town in fear of being eaten. *And the rulers abandoned them. Lady Taya Marwen of Sareen had left before we even arrived. Natt Floyd arrived to an empty castle after we finally opened the gates.* Aldred looked at William and thought of their father. *Will you abandon this city, father? Will you let them all die while you run off to hide?*

Bishop Sparo whispered something in William's ear, and they walked off together without saying a word to Aldred. He liked it better when they ignored him, anyway. He stood at the parapets alone and watched the once happy and prosperous folk of Hest bludgeon and trample each other. He listened to their screams and shouts of panic and rage. *Seeing is believing.* Aldred saw a whole lot of darkness.

What would the Lion, Gavyn Hester do? What would Kelson do? Aldred was ashamed that he wasn't more like the great war heroes of the past. That he wasn't more of a warrior. Aldred was more interested in the philosophers. *What would Benecio do? Benecio would remain until the last moments and then run into exile and write about what he had witnessed.* Audacio, Angelico, Phosphone, all of them would have done the same. Aldred envied that kind of freedom. None of the great authors were bound by name to serve their family. Aldred was reminded always that he would be nothing without the Lion, without the Hester name.

"*The power to stop this lies in a different book, child, not those of your youth.*" Roqeda's voice was like a rainstorm, patting down on Aldred and smothering him. "*You know which one. The boneman found it for you. Take it to the library and translate the words. I will help you to understand. I just need you to say the words, child, now go. Don't let me down.*"

Aldred stood at the parapet and felt the smooth stone of the crenelations. *Four thousand three hundred sixteen.* He thought of the library and of his mother, and his stomach ached. He knew he would go and get this over with, but something about lingering and taking that small bit of control over his life felt good. He hadn't been to the library more than a handful of times since his mother had died. It just felt too empty to him. He had thought, upon his first few visits, that he may hear the ghost of his mother's voice bouncing off the walls, caught up in the rafters, singing the fables of Phosphone and passages from Audacio. But there was nothing. Nothing but a big, fat, hollow silence that swallowed Aldred like darkness. *You told me I would have a wife, mother. Kids, too. You told me the people would love me when I returned home from battle. You told me—*

"You lied to me!" Aldred shouted. In that moment he didn't miss his mom—he was mad at her for leaving, for promising him that he would have a better life than he did. *If she hadn't died, it would be better. It would all be better. I would have the life she promised. The life I was supposed to have.*

"*The library, child. You are so close. Once you say the Words in that book, you can have anything. Anything... you can resurrect the past, child, and mould it to your liking. You just need to trust me.*" Roqeda's rainstorm of words started to crash like thunder. "*Don't fail me!*"

A hand on Aldred's shoulder scared him so badly he nearly fell from the wall.

"It's me, Aldred," Rober said.

Aldred turned around in a fury. "Praise, Eralis, Rober, shouldn't you be—"

A loud crash from below took Aldred's attention. The excitement of the rioters seemed to flare up again. Folk rushed towards the gates. Aldred left the upper walls and ran down the stone steps to one of the lower windows, where he could see the gates more clearly. There was a madness brewing down there, and many others followed Aldred to witness it.

Folk were running through the streets holding loaves of bread and bundles of potatoes and carrots and cobs of corn, and Aldred saw one man carrying a barrel of apples over his shoulder with apples spilling on the ground behind him. Two others were carrying a hog, one holding each end of the spit.

Then, black flags with the flaming red eye of Karaat began to spring up like mushrooms. *Praise Eralis... the eye of Karaat...* Seeing it again gave Aldred chills. Shouts of "*Karaat!*" began to echo through the streets. "*Karaat has sent us food!*"

"Praise Eralis," Rober said. "What's happened?"

A purple-cloaked guard of the City Watch burst through the tower door. "The priests of Karaat are arriving with wayns full of food to our gates. There are hundreds of them. They said Karaat sent them because they were starving. They said Karaat wants to save them—to liberate them. The people have let them in."

"We need to stop this," Rober said. He drew his sword as if that would do anything. Other guards gathered around the windows of the keep to watch.

"Praise, Eralis," one guard said. "The king won't stop it. He and Adora are planning to make a sacrifice to Karaat and burn an effigy in His honour. They are planning on welcoming this new god."

"Who told you that?" Aldred said. He felt like pulling his sword out himself now.

"No one," the guard said. "I heard it from the Warlock's own lips."

"This is madness," Rober said. His eyes lit up from the glow of the many fires. Aldred could see a sadness brewing in him. "We're going to lose this city."

Aldred watched those flames and he remembered his mother. *If you hadn't died... If you hadn't lied to me... none of this would be happening. None of it.* He remembered the time before his mother had died, when *she* was the advisor to King John. *She* made the decisions, not Adora, and things were right. She never would have led them down this path of ignorance. *But the other rulers should be here. They should be here to help us defend.* Aldred almost couldn't believe that none of their allies had shown up. *They came in troves for Lena Hester. They came by the boatload when she was the one who called them.* All of the Hesterlands had abandoned the Hesters. Not a single lord or lady came to their aid. *They'd watch us fall and fight over the throne.*

Aldred paused for a moment. He turned away from the window and sat down on the steps behind him. He put his head in his hands. *I just wish she could tell me it wasn't my fault. That she knew it was an accident. I just wish she could tell me.*

Aldred felt totally hopeless at that moment. He had nothing in his life to lean on, nothing to provide hope. He needed some kind of closure. He was scorned by Eshlynn. He was scorned by his brother and his uncle, and most severely by his father and the Warlock. He missed his mother more than anything. He wished he could ask her what to do. Where to go. *You could ask her.* Aldred felt a chill roll through his body at that thought. *Yes. Oh yes. You could ask her. You* should *ask her.*

"No," Roqeda thundered. "*Listen to me. There isn't time for games.*"

Without saying a word to anyone, Aldred went down the stairs of the barbican and came out into the inner courtyard of Kelson's Keep. He took a torch from one of the sconces that hung from the centre fountain. The people that were moving about the courtyard stopped to stare at Aldred as he shuffled across the cobbles carrying the torch. He felt their eyes burning him.

"They mean nothing to us, child," Roqeda said.

"No!" Aldred yelled. *They mean something to me.*

And now a knight, golden lion shining brightly on his purple cloak, quickly turned around. He saw Aldred's face and stepped forth. "Aldred?" It was Sir Kenney Norris of Talonsford. "Is that you?"

Aldred turned his head away and carried on through the crowded courtyard. He shoved past servants and house maids and cooks and smiths. Tanners and bowyers and cartwrights and stablers. All who kept the Keep a living thing, and not just a hunk of stone and wood and linen, were gathered here now, waiting to be saved. Waiting for it to be over. *I am starting to fear this won't end.*

Aldred stopped and put his hands on his knees. He took a deep breath and whispered verses from Angelico to himself. When he had calmed, he stood tall and looked around—at the panic, at the desperation. *You could have stopped this, Mother! You could have stopped it! It wasn't my fault you fell. It wasn't my fault your neck made that noise. That sound echoes in my dreams every night, Mother. Every night...*

Roofs and spires twisted up around Aldred at odd angles as he made his way to the massive basalt statue of Eralis and its sister white oak that, together, brooded over the courtyard of Kelson's Keep. The spindly white fingers of the oak spread out across the black stone of Eralis like lightning bolts in the night. To the yellow, twilit sky, the oak stretched her limbs, laden with wine-red blossoms that illumined the air with appleberry. And to the grey cobbles below, Eralis pointed an ebon finger to indicate that the memory of his followers lay there.

Aldred touched the trunk of the white oak and the basalt finger of Eralis and walked behind them. A cracked stone arch laden with bluevine vaulted over the steep staircase that led to the crypts of Kelson's Keep.

Aldred followed them, winding down and down. The dancing torch-light offered him a small circle of vision. He had heard many stories of the crypts of the Keep. That twisted chimeras and worse were buried down there. That wights from the ancient world still roamed the lowest levels. Dragons. But he had been down there enough times to know the stories were false.

He used to visit his mother three times a week. Then once. Then once a month, once a year, then not at all. It wasn't that he didn't want to visit her, it was just that it didn't feel like she was actually *there* in the crypts. It was just her dead body. Her soul danced elsewhere, in the forests of the north maybe, but not in those crypts.

When Aldred's feet touched flat ground, he held the torch up to either side. The ruddy light revealed hunks of rough-hewn stone that resembled people. He held the torch in front of him and saw dozens more, lining the barrow hall, as far as the light would show him. He inspected one of the statues and saw a name carved into the base in a language he couldn't understand. And beside that there were dozens more. Each statue stood guard in front of the long stone tomb that lay behind it. Each tomb was sealed with a solid stone lid and closed with tar and wax.

And on and on. And there, right in the middle of the hall, was the empty tomb of Kelson the Conqueror. Golden tassels still hung from the tomb's handles. Red carpets surrounded it, and a horn of plenty with fruit and vegetables and bread rotting in it sat on top of the tomb's lid. Waxy candle stubs lay scattered around the ground, remnants of a ritual. *Who's leaving food here?* Aldred poked at the soft, brown fruit and judged it to be only a few weeks old. He figured it could only have been the Wise Ones. They did all sorts of strange and secretive things in the tunnels and the dark places of the Keep. They performed rituals day and night, most of which nobody understood but them. *"It's the way of Old."* That was what High Wise One

Gavyn told Aldred when he heard the High Wise Ones chanting eldritch rhythms in the tunnels on his way to visit Eshlynn one night. He swore to this day, on the soul of Eralis, that he heard someone being killed down there, and that it was the Wise Ones who did it.

Further down the hall, the names started to get longer. Kelson's descendants began to stack their names on top of old names to try and gain prestige. And so the carvings started to show names like *Greginn Hoster Yuri Hurangan Kelson,* and *Tylo Agrecia Delmono Kleronomas Kelson.* A testament to how strange things got were the smaller stone statues that appeared alongside these rulers. Cats with the heads of humans, dogs with the bodies of rats, even one with the body of a male's lower half, a female's upper half, and a dog with the head of a horse. Aldred shivered and carried on until he found a familiar statue.

He stood before the statue of a young man, who was actually so old when he died that he couldn't even walk anymore. A man who taught Aldred to listen to his mother and to respect the words he read in books. Aldred ran his fingers over the name carved into the base of the statue. *Richard Hester.* It was his grandpa's name. And he was proud of it. *The only damn Hester I can truly say that about.*

He carried on down the line. *Charles Hester,* then *Galen Hester, Aislin Hester, Preen Hester. Ruby Hester, the Red Kitten,* the twelve-year-old queen who slaughtered ten thousand Ayelish at the Battle of Lost Arbor. There were fifty Hesters or more and all of them with stories to live up to their names. *And what's your story?* There were statues of maned lions, and of crowned lions, and a strange horned lion with bulging eyes, and one of them appeared in the line every ten statues or so, as if they were standing guard. Aldred felt more in kin with the strange horned lion than he did with any of the others.

On and on Aldred walked, and finally to his mother's statue he came solemnly. In Kelson's day, the crypts were reserved for the rulers only, not their husbands or wives, but Lena Hester was an exception in every other area of her life, so King John made her an exception here as well. King

John had her statue built down here and her body placed. Aldred still remembered that day. It was his first time in this crypt, and he could have sworn he heard the voices of dead things.

By the time he was ten steps away from the statue whose base read *Lena Hester*, Aldred was already sobbing. "It wasn't my fault." For the first time, Aldred started to question if Roqeda was real, or if he truly had just gone mad. Everything that had happened to him since that day felt like pure madness. His face had sunk in, and his heart had been sunk, too.

"Am I mad, Mother?"

He rested the burning torch on the ground, standing against the wall. With both hands he gripped the heavy stone lid of his mother's tomb. He heaved on it but it wouldn't budge. His father made sure the tomb wasn't sealed with tar and wax like the others. *He made sure.* He wanted to be able to look upon her if he chose to. Aldred knew it would open, it was just heavy. "I need you to tell me it wasn't my fault," Aldred spoke. He expected Roqeda to speak back, but there was nothing. *You're mad. You've lost it.*

Aldred was completely alone. *I need you to tell me it wasn't my fault.* He heaved again at the lid of the tomb, and this time it moved. With all of his strength he pushed. The heavy stone moved slowly. With all of his hate and all of his rage he pushed, and the lid to the tomb slid enough for him to see inside.

No. no. Aldred held his hand to his mouth. He sobbed, then started to cough and dry heave. He hadn't eaten or drunk anything so there was nothing to vomit.

Inside of the tomb, he saw only bones and hair. Grey and dust-crusted bones and dried hair. *Dead, dead, so dead. Dead, so dead there isn't even a body left.* "No!" he screamed, and his voice echoed painfully off the stone walls of the barrow. *It's not how it's supposed to be. It's not...*

Aldred brought himself to the tomb and gripped the cold stone edges and looked inside. The smell really hit him now, but it was nothing compared to Soren. The bones were there as they were before. Grey and dead. Aldred reached inside and stroked his finger across the skull. *It's so small.*

Aldred imagined his mother having a brain twice the size of other humans. Blotches of straw-like brown hair crusted the top of the skull. *Her skull is so small without any "head" on it.* He stroked the arm bones, and the ribs. They were brittle—like dried corn stalks.

Aldred took a step back and looked around. He gritted his teeth, clenched his fists and jaw. There were no flowers, not even the dried old stems of them. There were no gifts, no candle wax, no ribbons. No rotten, bloody horn of plenty. Nothing. There was nothing here for his mother. No one had come down here to visit her for thousands and thousands of days. *Four thousand three hundred sixteen... that's how long you've been gone, Mom.* Aldred wondered for how many of those she had been bones.

Aldred remembered the day of his mother's death. She had just mounted her brown-hooved beige mare that she loved so dearly. She was going to go out for a ride. Aldred and William were in the stables, playing around the massive Lovasi bell, which had been removed from the Keep to be put in the Cathedral of Light, and was being stored there in the stables for the meantime. His mother had started yelling at them to be careful around that bell. *Her mare spooked easily, William knew that, so he never should have thrown me that hammer.* When William threw a shoe hammer at Aldred, Aldred fumbled it. It clanged the bell so loudly it shook the stables—those Lovasi bells held magics in their shape.

The horse wailed. Jumped on hind legs. There was a horrible snap. Aldred fell to the ground, his head clanging from the bell, which was still ringing profusely. He lay there for a good few minutes, waiting for his mother to come to their aid. To smack them both upside the head. *I lay there for a bloody half nap while Mom lay dead. She lay dead on the same ground, and I didn't know.* Then he heard the screams. It was his brother's first. *"Praise Eralis!"* he had yelped. Then more.

"The queen!" they said. *"The queen is dead! Get help!"* And Aldred was never the same.

"He clanged the bell," William had shouted. *"It was him. Him. Him."* Aldred wanted to kill him. He wanted to smash his head open with that

shoe hammer. Instead, he summoned the strength to look at his mother's body. Her head looked like a broken red melon.

King John had the beige mare killed that very evening. *And he killed you in his heart.*

Aldred felt that tickle of life flowing through him and pooling in his fingertips. *Is that you, Roqeda? Or am I totally mad?* When there was no answer from his own head, to his mother, he said, "I need you to tell me it wasn't my fault. Mom. Please." And he stepped forward again. He touched the bones of his mother and let life flow out of him and into the bones. The marrow, the muscle, some of it still stuck to her in small, sinewy strands, and those started to move—crawl like worms. "Please Mom, just say it. Say that you know it wasn't me. That it wasn't on purpose."

The bones rattled against the cold stone as the shreds of sinew and muscle and marrow grew long and ghastly, like the legs of insects, and wrapped themselves around the bones to secure them together. Like thousands of tiny snakes, the sinews slipped and slithered their way around the body. The bones made horrible grinding sounds as the skeletal figure struggled to stand. Like a baby fawn, the thing that would have been Aldred's mother fought to gain its footing.

Aldred watched in horror as the thing cocked its neck and aimed its hollow skull eyes at him. They were gaping black holes with a strange red glow coming from a distant place inside. *Too distant.* "Mother?" Aldred whispered. He was sobbing so hard it came out as a whimper. "Are you there?"

A horrible, boiling hiss answered him, and the red glow in the things' eyes became piercing. It squealed at him. Eldritch squeaking sounds, like burning bats, spilled out of its skull mouth.

And it stood. And it walked. It came for Aldred. He was frozen. *Why?* The skeleton stood, disfigured, rotten-smelling and falling apart. It reached its skeletal fingers towards Aldred, squealing like a dying animal all the while, and Aldred fell backwards. He pushed himself away with his heels as the thing walked him down. Its crooked head slipped out of place and hung like a ripe fruit, ready to fall. And it began to laugh.

Aldred unsheathed *Phantom* from the ground. He swung weakly and missed, nearly cutting his own leg. The skeleton shrieked in laughter. It ran at him now. Aldred rolled and felt his own blade dig into his arm. Warm blood flowed down his wrist and dripped from his fingertips. He stood, gripping *Phantom,* and when the skeleton charged at him, he took one step to the side and smashed the thing into pieces with his Daggland steel.

The skeleton collapsed into a heap on the ground, and Aldred kept smashing it. He smashed it to dust. *From dust to dust, right, Mother? Just like Audacio said!* He screamed and he sobbed, and he stomped the ground as the dust of his mother's bones covered his boots. He let *Phantom* slip from his hands and clank to the cold stone, and he fell with it.

"What is this good for? What is the purpose of this power?" Aldred raised his hands to the vaulted ceiling. His necromantic hands, stained with black magics from beyond this realm. *Stained and can never be unstained.* Aldred looked at his hands, disgusted. *What have you done? Who are you?*

Slowly, Aldred picked himself up. Slowly, he walked through the hall and paid no attention to the statues or the empty tomb of Kelson. And as he left the crypt and past the statue of Eralis and the white oak, Aldred had a strange thought that no tomb could hold down the body of Kelson. That whatever soul was in him had returned to this realm or else never left. Anything that was left of his mother wasn't in those bones. It wasn't in that grey, dark tomb, it was inside of his own memories for her—inside of all the things she loved. *She's gone.*

Aldred made his lonely way back to the Keep's chamber tower. On the balcony where William had addressed a small portion of the city, Aldred brooded over the stars. "She's gone," he said to the sky.

"What is it?" came a voice so familiar it made Aldred sick to his stomach. Aldred could hear her footsteps approaching, they were equine-like. Soft and clopping. "What are you staring at up there? Do you see the comet?"

"There's no comet," Aldred croaked. His mouth was so dry that his tongue stuck to the roof of his mouth.

"No? Not yet? Well, we still have time then," Adora said. Her voice was like acid.

Aldred tried to dip his head and walk away, but a claw-like hand on his shoulder stopped him. "What do you want?"

The Warlock wore a smooth black robe with the crest of an orange comet stitched onto the breast. *"It's of the Ailaryan Order,"* Rober had whispered to him once. *"It's as old as the sky, that robe."*

Adora stood six and a half feet tall, at the least, and she stared down at Aldred. Always. "What were you doing down there in the crypts?"

"I was praying."

Adora puffed out a laugh. "To the right god, I hope." She reached into her robe. "Your father wanted you to have this back since it clearly meant so much to you as to give it to your little whore."

Aldred's heart stopped beating for a moment. His head was a blank space and in that hollow emptiness, he was screaming. Adora's bony hand held Aldred's mother's necklace. The snow-white stone with blue veins glowed in the dark. "What did you do?" Aldred couldn't breathe. *Eshlynn. Oh, Esh. Oh, no, no.*

"I will do anything your father wants. *Anything.*" Adora licked her lips. Aldred felt sick. "You know I was sent here by the Ailaryan Order to serve him—however he sees fit."

"It's you!" Aldred screamed. "You twist his thoughts!"

Adora shook her head. She moved in so close to Aldred's face that he could smell her meaty breath. "Every decision the king makes, he makes of his own free will."

King John Hester appeared in the doorway, as if summoned. He was naked underneath a silken purple robe trimmed with gold. The brown bush around his member was the closest thing Aldred had seen to a mane on his dad. "I told you I'd make you feel the way I did. I told you I'd make you hurt," King John said.

Aldred unsheathed *Phantom*.

Adora whispered a Word, and the very air twisted in front of Aldred's face like the whole world was being rung out, and suddenly Aldred couldn't move or breathe and *Phantom* fell to the ground.

"She was wearing this necklace in plain daylight, Aldred," John Hester said. "What were you thinking? Do you think I'm so stupid to not find a blacksmith from the slums of Rattrap wearing my dead wife's precious stones? You think I'm so stupid?" The king spat at Aldred's boots. "Go down to the city and find her, eh? This woman of yours. Maybe she's not quite dead yet? Or forget her. I don't care either way." The king laughed. "Don't get lost in those riots, though, if you decide to go."

"And you'll be in court tomorrow or I'll cut your head off myself, Kinslayer," Adora said. "I think I'll have you shine my new collection of pretty stones. That woman of yours had a real talent. It's a shame she got tied up with *you*. That mistake cost her dearly."

"You fucking bastard." Aldred was sobbing. "She wasn't even with me anymore. She wasn't even—"

Adora was rubbing the king's bare chest and laughing. "Hurry along," she said. "We want this room to ourselves."

"I hate you. I hate you so muc—" Aldred was slobbering all over himself.

King John unsheathed his sword *Saynomore*. The black Daggland steel glistened.

Aldred knew he couldn't defeat his father in single combat. There was no way. *You can fix it. You can fix it.*

"You go now. Get out of here," his father told him.

He listened.

ENDURE

Eᴛᴛᴀ ᴄʀᴏᴜᴄʜᴇᴅ ʙʏ ᴛʜᴇ stream and clenched her fists.

The footsteps were getting louder.

She looked at Pike, who nodded back at her—the old sign for luck. If this was one of the Demhoni creeping up on them, they could be discovered. Their plan could be over before it even started. *Swey, little Swey, I'm sorry. I'm so sorry.* Etta clenched her fists and wanted to scream. She hated herself for being so weak, but the thought of touching a weapon made every muscle in her body turn into hardstone. She weighed ten thousand pounds, so all she could do was kneel and listen to the stream gurgle, and wait.

The footsteps walked past them. They stopped and doubled back. "Etta?" a voice said.

By the gods. "Fiora?" Etta stood up. Fiora was covered in mud.

"Aye," said Fiora.

"We thought you'd be coming back as your wolf," Baerd said.

"Wolf got spooked," Fiora said. "She's run home, to Elwyd."

"What happened? Did you get eyes on them?" Etta asked.

"Aye," said Fiora. She scratched the back of her head. "There are more than we thought though. Maybe a thousand. They have wooden cages. I got too close and they shot at me, and after my wolf had returned me to my body, she ran off. She dislikes arrows. It's the feathers on 'em you see?"

"It doesn't matter how many of them there are. We're not going to fight them," Etta said. "Did you see young Swey? Anyone else?"

"I couldn't get close enough. They shot at me," Fiora said.

"I don't know about this, Wulf," Baerd said. He scratched the back of his head. "We'd have a better chance attacking—"

"No," Etta said. "These wild folk may be mad but remember they are Ayelish—probably generals amongst them, trained in warfare from books. They will be waiting for us to swarm out of here with an army," Etta said. "They will be waiting along the river with traps, ready to ambush. But look." Etta pointed to the small stream. "This leads us to a place in the river further down. Three or four miles. We can clog the river down there and flood them out up here. When the river backs up and they're scrambling, we ram into their camp and start busting open the cages." Etta pointed to Baerd. "You and I find Swey."

Baerd smiled. "You really think this can work?"

"It has to," Etta said. Twenty folk came with her. Armed with shovels instead of axes. Tara had to be physically detained to not come along, but with the axe bite she picked up, Etta couldn't allow it. Her skin was milk white and she could hardly stand from the loss of blood. *"Get my baby,"* she had said. *I will...*

"I've seen crazier things." Pike ogled his shield, fingered a chip in it. "And if Wulfee dreams of it, it's possible."

The trek up river was nothing for Etta, and she loved this land well. Even her back had started to loosen a bit. She savoured the birdsong and the insects and the critters calling. She loved the babble of the streams and the whisper of the leaves in the wind. This was *her* land, and this is where she belonged. *Not fighting. Not fighting. You wretched beast.* But the fighting always caught up with her. Peace was a far-off land—like Ni'an or Arish Pura or somewhere else Etta would never and could never go. *Maybe I'll be a spice trader in peacetime.*

She led her crew down the stream to the river, where Fiora slowly approached on foot.

"Clear," Fiora said upon returning, and so they went to the river.

"How we going to clog this thing?" Baerd said, and Etta pointed to the pile of wooden spades they had carried.

"Start digging," she said. "Take from here and start narrowing the banks."

"This could take days," Owyn said. "I'd rather fight."

The others echoed agreement.

"Anyone is welcome to leave. Just send another in your place when you return to camp," Etta said. Baerd looked at her, grinning and nodding. "It will take as long as it needs to." Etta sank her shovel into the soft, black soil of the valley and walked it over to the river bank. The river outlet was fifteen feet wide, maybe sixteen. Etta could see the bottom, which gave her hope. "We can do this," she said. And sank her shovel into the dirt again.

So she dug and her people dug with her. And they kept digging. Etta sent folk up and down the banks to make sure the Demhoni weren't catching sight of them. They kept digging and tried to stay quiet, and by the end of the first day, Etta reckoned they were nearly half way. She reckoned that the Demhoni might notice the river moving faster, but probably wouldn't think much of it. *Rivers clog all the time this close to winter.*

As the crew slept and dressed their wounds, Etta caught a glimpse of her underself in a moonlit puddle, and she forced herself to look. *That's you. Your underself. Wulfee's underself. She hasn't changed, and neither have you. Not really. It's Wulfee. You're Wulfee. You have done things you can't take back. You have to face yourself.*

"*No one but you,*" her underself gurgled, and Etta knew it was true. No one could save her from herself but her.

"But how?" Etta asked the face in the water. It didn't answer her. *Wulfee.* She would know. Her underself looked back at her sagely. "I'm sorry," Etta murmured.

Then she was falling. Then she was wet.

"You alright Wulf?" Baerd put his hand out for Etta, and she noticed the thick veins in it. She *remembered* those hands.

"I killed him, Sweyne," Etta said. Something inside of her thought that he needed to know. Baerd watched, waiting for Etta to speak though she suspected he might have made an assumption about who she'd killed already. She was already sobbing so badly that she couldn't get the words out. "I killed our boy. He—the mask. I didn't know. Not until it was too late. I didn't know. I—" Without processing the moments between, Etta found herself pressed against Baerd's chainmail. She felt his beard on her head, his hands around her back. It all felt too familiar. Like coming home. *To a burning house.* "I killed our boy. I have to live with it. I have to carry that with me, but I have to go on."

Etta saw Pike watching. She wasn't sure how he felt about Baerd after all these years. *By the gods, it's all moving so fast. So fast.* So many people had come and gone. *Gen, Braden. James, Maggie. Benn, Holden. How many who touch you will die?* "We can't let them get, Swey. We can't."

Baerd held an axe by the blade and offered the handle to Etta. Etta glared at the hilt of that axe like it was on fire and her hand would burn to bloody ash should she touch it. Her body became stone. Cold and unmoving. And her lungs struggled to fill with air against her rock chest. Baerd's hazel eyes caught hers, and at once he took the axe away.

"I won't let them take him," Baerd said. "By the gods, Wulf, if I have one deed left in me it's to save our boy. Our grandson. He's going to grow old, Wulf. He's going to find someone he loves, and he's going to live a long life and be happy. He's going to have all the things that we had, Wulf, and the things we dreamed of, too. And he won't be damn fuck dumb enough to lose it all. By the gods I promise you I will give him that chance to grow old." Baerd was crying now, too. "And *you.* No matter what happens here, promise me you'll make it out of here with him. Promise me, Wulf. Promise!" Baerd slobbered onto his black beard.

"I promise." Etta was sick of crying at this point, but Baerd had shattered a well inside of her. *He wants to make up for it. For all of it. Is that possible? Is it even possible? Does he really deserve redemption? Do you?* "I promise."

"You don't have to accept it," Beard said, "and to be honest, it doesn't do a damned thing to change the past, but Wulf, I need to tell you that I'm so fucking sorry. My biggest regret in life is losing you and the boys. Losing myself. And it wasn't just the mask. The mask brought out the demons that were already inside of me. At their height, I couldn't stop them. The things I did—they don't deserve forgiveness. I'm not looking for that. It was my fault for letting the demons live so long. It was my fault for letting them beat me. I should have killed them. I should have fought with *every fucking thing* I had and killed them for you. Wulf, and I can never make it up to you for falling short on that, but please just know that I'm sorry."

In that moment, Etta could see the person she had once loved and was also reminded of the monster he had become. "People make mistakes. But you kept making them." She shook her finger at Baerd. "For too long you kept on. Folk deserve forgiveness, sure. But I can only forgive so much. I'm glad that you're sorry, and to be honest I'm glad that it eats you up. You remind me of the man I fell in love with, Sweyne, and I thank you for that because now I see that I wasn't crazy. You *were* good once and kind, and everything a person should be. But then you changed, and it took you losing everything and running off to hide in order to change back. You're a coward, Sweyne, you fucked up everything and then ran up here and hid yourself away. I'll never forgive you. But by the gods, you go get our grandson from those fiends, and I can at least bloody well respect you."

Baerd nodded, for more than just luck. "I'll get him, Wulf. I'll get him."

The next morning, Etta's arms felt like they were going to fall off. But she picked up her shovel and knew that when others saw her, they would do the same. She wasn't digging for herself or for anyone but for young Swey. Each time her spade sank into that soil or clay, she thought of him.

Of his small face and his tiny voice that would grow and keep growing. She dug for him, for his father. *Your son...*

She saw Braden's face in the clouds, but it wasn't miserable. It was happy and smiling, and she saw Tarek's face there, too. And the boys played together, rolling through the sky.

And she saw their father, digging harder even than her, dripping sweat in the late Fell of autumn, muscles working, grunting—hard digging to kill the hurt. Etta imagined his demons were nearly as bad as hers. *You're the same as him. The same... you both fucked up. You may be worse.*

By midday, the task that had seemed so hopeless and mad the day before was nearing completion. The banks were already starting to swell. By the time the sun had started its descent, the flood started. The river was dammed and a few more shovelfuls sealed it completely. The banks swelled, slowly at first, then all at once. Water spilled up over the dam.

"Make it higher!" she yelled, and kept shovelling. And they made it higher, and the banks swelled further. Etta knew the water would break the dam eventually, but they only needed a short time.

Baerd stood in the river and kept working to make the dam higher. Owyn by his side.

They would be ripe for an attack soon. Etta didn't want the Demhoni's bewilderment to settle. "Get your weapons!" she yelled.

Pike smiled; he already had his weapons, and he held his shield high to the blue sky. "Here's to death, should it be our time to meet her!" he roared, and the folk roared with him. To Etta, he said, "This could be the one that gets us, Wulf."

"Aye," Etta said, "but not young Swey."

Pike's smile slipped away. "No," he said, "not him."

Etta grabbed Pike's hand, and they gave each other the old sign for luck. "Don't let it be the one that gets you, Pike. Not yet."

Pike grinned. "Aye," he said, "death, you see, she's having a hard time getting a hold of me. Reckon I can see out one more. Tess would be pissed should I not make it to the last battle."

"I need you, Pike, if I'm going to see this through to the end." Etta could tell that Pike knew that she meant more than just this battle and that she was referring to everything.

Pike banged on the tree of his shield. "To the very end, Wulf." His ice-blue eyes ripped into Etta's heart. "To the very goddamned end."

Through the arbor crags and up the flooding riverbank, Etta and her small crew ran.

The Demhoni were scattered. Dragging wooden cages out of the rising water with fraying ropes. Taking torches from the fires to keep them going further up the bank. They were shouting. Scrambling every way.

Etta saw the cages that held the people. *He's there. There.* She pointed to it. "There," she said. "Go!"

Baerd smiled at her. He gripped his axe and looked at the blade, and then to the folk that he was about to lead and said, "Let's send these daemons to Hell, eh?" And he charged, his beard thick and full and bouncing with each long stride. His arms flexed, strong with his axe in one hand and shield in the other. His shield held the symbol of Feldarra, just like Pike's. *These are my people,* Etta thought. *And they will rescue Swey. Just as they have rescued me.*

"Hey!" one of the Demhoni yelled before Baerd sunk his axe blade into the man's neck. Blood bubbled from his throat and even amongst the scramble, folk were starting to take notice.

There were archers in the trees. Wooden grates and spikes in the river. Nets, holes, snares, rope traps of all kinds set all along the river. *They were ready for the si'darra to attack. They would have killed us all...*

Etta hurried to the cages. Pike battered two folk down with his shield and slayed two more with his axe. Etta checked each cage as Pike fought, and when in the last cage she didn't see Swey, she ran to the next cluster. "Hurry, Wulf, we won't last long," Pike said. He was fighting three people at once now. Blood sprayed, flesh tore, bodies flayed, Pike roared.

Folk were moving all about, dragging supplies, bags of flour—*crusted Human?* cages, dry wood, chains, hooks, weapons. The water from the river was ankle-deep and rising and it was so cold that it tried to seize Etta's heartbeat.

Baerd was fighting a cluster of people in front of another group of cages. Etta ran toward them. No one noticed her. She was like a small stone in the river—everything flowed around her. *You did it, you actually distracted this lot. Now get him out. Get him.*

"He's there, Wulf. Ahead." Baerd pointed his bloody axe to the cages being dragged further on, surrounded by the bulk of this Demhoni army. There were so many people that Etta reckoned the only thing keeping Baerd, Etta, and their crew from being killed completely was that most just weren't paying attention in the din and clatter of the flooding river and the scramble to move their camp.

Etta ran and Baerd followed. At the cages, Etta saw him through the slimy wooden bars. His small face and his big hair, so long now it was hanging down to his nose. He was crouched down, hugging his knees. But there were too many people around. Too many. Etta looked around frantically for something—*anything* to make it work. Baerd caught her gaze. "You remember what you promised me?" Baerd was panting, veins thick throbbing in his arms, blood dripping from his knuckles. He held an axe in each hand.

Etta watched, silently. *By the gods...* "Aye," Etta said. "I do."

"You and Swey get out of here," Baerd said.

Etta counted five. Five folk in front of the cage and around it, trying to move it with ropes.

"You hear me? You and Swey live." Baerd's eyes ate into Etta's heart and in that moment she could only see the father of her children. "You promise me that you and Swey live."

"Aye." Wulfee uttered. "I promise."

Baerd smiled—a smile from another life—and lifted his axes and ran at the Demhoni, snarling and howling. He axed the first one across the chin, and they fell like a sack of flour. He danced between them with lupine grace. Etta moved behind Baerd as he lowered his shoulder into another Demhoni and tumbled over. Baerd rose and sliced and hacked, and Etta used a sharp rock to cut the ropes that held the bars shut.

Swey came to her. "Etta?"

"Aye, boy. It's me," Etta said. Baerd screamed from behind her. "Come on." Etta took Swey's hand and ran.

Past the drooping pines fat with cones, the golden-brown birch leaves and sun-yellow aspen and needles crunching below foot, the din of chaos behind her—somehow, amidst all of that, she could hear the jays singing. Somehow, Etta saw the blue sky and the white clouds and the god-like mountains. She smelled the dying leaves and damp mud. *You're alive. You're alive, and you can't take that for granted any longer.*

It was then she heard the rutted footsteps and knew they were being followed.

"Run, Swey," Etta told the boy, "and don't ever stop."

Swey rocked his head in agreement and they toed on. Somehow Etta knew Swey would live. She knew he would live because he *had* to. He had to because the world and all its beauty was there for *him*. One day when Etta was dust, he would live here, and his kids and grandkids would live here. But only if it wasn't overcome by darkness.

Etta had made it back to the dam. The water had already carved a path through the middle, wide enough for a horse cart. And it flowed faster than a running hare. She stopped to catch her breath. The earth thumped beneath her feet from the footsteps behind her. They were close. She needed to get back down the mountain, but she was being chased in the wrong direction. She needed to cross the river somehow and—

An arrow came out of the woods and landed in the mud a few yards from where Etta stood. Suddenly, Etta heard her dad's voice. *"Endure."* She was transported back to a time when she really was *Etta*. A time when love hadn't broken her heart. She had fallen through the ice and when she came out half frozen, teeth chattering, she wasn't met with love but with harshness. *Endure.* Her dad had taught her on that day. And she had endured more than any person should have to. She had endured it all, and she was still here. *I'm still bloody here... Swey* was still here.

The Demhoni came out of the woods slowly, smoothly. Surely, they moved, like they had already caught their prey. And they came from both sides of her now, trapping her against the river. They wore filthy, leather rags with rusted pieces of armour like patches on a quilt. A helm here, a chestplate there. One Demhoni was naked but for a necklace of Human ears and a pair of rusted iron gauntlets, with which he held a crudely crafted mace. Their hair was greasy and matted, their mouths frothed. *Rabies?* Etta thought for a moment before one of the Demhoni moved quickly towards her.

"Etta!" Young Swey screeched.

As if to get her attention, the dirt and gravel dam collapsed like a sand-castle, and the river burst forth in a frothy rage.

"Endure, Swey, don't let go of me," Etta said, and for a brief moment before she jumped into the river, she saw a look of unbridled fear in Swey's eyes. A look that had voided all trust and all affection.

And when the cold autumnal waters bit into Etta, it turned the air in her lungs to ice and forbade her to inhale any more. Swey fell away, his small hands feeling, grasping—slipping. The water crushed her, pulled at her and beat her against the rocks, and she held Swey's small hand and it was slipping.

She tried to swim up and hit the bottom of the river, and then his small hand was gone. Etta turned her body and used her legs as a spring off the riverbed, and when she burst through the surface of the white water, Swey was nowhere.

"Swey!" she shouted. Arrows pierced the water around her. Shouting. She was okay. "Swey!" The water ripped her away. Down, away. "Swey!" She dove.

Bubbles up her nose, and her eyes burned in the silty water, but she dove and looked, and there he was. Her chest loosened, and she swam to him. His eyes were wide. He was panicked in the undertow. Etta took him in her arms and used her legs to spring off the riverbed again. They burst through the surface of the white water, and Swey gasped and Etta's heart returned from her stomach to its normal spot.

With one arm she held Swey, and with the other, she clawed for the bank. When her fingers dug into the sandy wet soil, she felt a palpable relief, like removing a large stone strapped to her back. Immediately, the cold autumn air took hold of her wet body. Swey's teeth were chattering. "Endure. You won't die. You can't. For many hours yet. Endure. Come."

Too weak to carry him, Etta took Swey's hand, and together they walked into the arbor and back towards the mountain valley of Elwyd. The river, Etta reckoned, had taken them a half mile or more, and it would take many hours to get back, but she had no other choice but to endure and walk. *You made it once. You made it and so can he. So can he.*

"I-I-I'm c-cold." Swey's lips were blue. His teeth were chattering like a woodpecker.

"Hurry," Etta said. And in that moment, she felt closer to her dad than ever. *Wolton... He felt this pain. He felt this pain, too, as he watched me suffer, but he couldn't show it. He couldn't show it because he didn't want me to be afraid.*

They walked, and Etta heard the Demhoni hooting and carrying on in the distance on the other side of the river. She smelled their fire—their meat. *By the gods, Pike...* She had left him. *You left him...*

The cold nipped at her like a thousand small dog bites as night fell. Young Swey's eyelids were blue now. His hair was frosting at the tips. *Endure.* Their breaths were smoking in the air. The wolves howled in the forest. *They're following us. They're waiting for us to die.*

They walked and soon they climbed. Etta, careful not to slip on the cold rocks, carried Swey now. His eyes were closed. Etta put her shrivelled, numb hand on his small chest. His heart still thumped. His chest heaved frigid breath. *Endure...*

She climbed.

When hooded figures appeared above her and two of them picked her up, one by each arm, Etta screamed. "Swey!" And she saw his small, limp body being carried by a shaman. They were elders. *Elders, healers, helpers.*

"By the gods, Etta. You live." Annie and Fiora stood arm in arm. A wolf licked Etta's face. Lick, licked her.

"The boy," Etta murmured. "Where—"

"He lives, Etta." Fiora said. "He lives."

A Deal with Offa

Halda had never craved anything more in her life than she craved sunlight now. She clutched her stone and waited. Aunt Thora had taught her immense patience, but it was being worn thin down here.

It had been weeks since she had seen the sky, smelled the wind. Weeks since she had felt sun on her skin. Her eyes had grown tired and weak, and she feared they might stop working if they stayed in total darkness too long. Her stomach pained in ways she didn't think possible, ways even Ugga, the Woman God, couldn't make her hurt. *Were they starving her on purpose? Or because they, too, have no food?*

A rat scurried and Halda threw her stone. The stone scudded across the dirt and shattered against the wall into pieces. It was an old and weak rock. The rat scurried away and squeaked as if to say *"Fuck you."*

She hated this place. Never had she felt so far away from home as in this cell on this island. *Did the raven lead you here on purpose?* The thought ate at her. *No, the look of terror in his eyes when the other raven appeared was real. They've captured him, too.*

Vague memories of a plan to find the soothsayers still hung in Halda's mind. *Why was the truth so important to me?* Now all she cared about was water... food, maybe. Warmth if she was really going to beg.

The Nith's guards were gaunt, bickering with each other in their bulky armour. The people of Blackstone had all watched her like a caged monkey as she was dragged into the castle through the town and small courtyard. When the guards threw her in the cell, they had laughed at the fact she was Dagglandic. *"Heard you liked the cold and ice. You'll like it here then, lass!"* The guards laughed and patted each other on the back, and Halda had wanted to kill them. And the thought stayed with her the first couple of times the guards left water for her. But the guards had stopped coming.

How long has it been? Two weeks? Three? Her days and nights were the same—dark, cold, miserable. *Where is the raven?* They had taken him in a separate cage—a raven's cage. The gods knew his fate would be worse than hers, but where was he? She spent many long hours in the early days screaming as loud as she could, but it was to no avail. She heard no screams back. *They've probably killed him.* She screamed until something in her throat tore, and still she screamed, even when no sound came out. *Ox'olin is coming. It will all be over soon. It will all...*

Halda heard scurrying in the corner and she scrambled to find another rock, but there was nothing in her cell but dirt. She was lucky to have found that old, crumbling rock, and she should have been more careful to take care of it. *Careless... you've always been so careless.* Aunt Thora used to tell her as much. *"You should be a wife to that man, not cooped away in your den."* Aunt Thora had understood that the work Halda did was important, too. That she saved lives. Her work was bigger than herself. She served Offa and Oade. But still Aunt Thora liked to bitch about Halda not going down the same path as her.

It was Halda's life's work to look for signs, and now she had found the biggest one of all. *And you don't know what to do about it. You got yourself stuck in this hole… you read but a small piece of the sign and claimed you had it all. You sent Toren and the other rakkarren on a mission of cold murder.* She had to stop it. Stop Ox'olin. *Find a way—the answers, the truth. The soothsayers…*

The scurrying sound got closer and with a primitive quickness that came from a place of starvation, Halda snatched the rat between her fingers. She felt it squirming, its muscles working, its teeth gnawing her fingers and grinding the bones, her blood running down her arm, drip-dripping from her elbow. She tried to squeeze the life out of the rat, but it wouldn't die so she bit a chunk out of the back of its neck, and finally it stopped moving.

And finally, she chewed; the meat was hot and wet in her mouth, slaver running down her chin. *Or was it blood?* She didn't even taste the meat, just felt the hot, nourishing chunks slide down her tongue and the fur tickle her throat. She picked the hair off the back of her tongue and out of her throat and took another bite. She wouldn't die today. Not today. *Sweet, Offa, let me out. Let me out and I will find the answers.*

She chewed and cried, though she always cried these days, and she remembered. Remembered the fires, her runes, her rakkarren. *They will come… they have to come.* But she knew they didn't have to do any such thing. She was a bad rakkar to her people, she spent too many hours away in the Witch Den with her fires and her runes and her scrolls. They sailed the coast of Massey Rock waiting for Halda to untie their leash, to let them go, to reave with the others, but she kept them close and inactive—always waiting for her and her antics. *And now they have come to resent you for it. They will let you die here. No. Yes. Olrick… Offa. I've fucked it all up.* Her mind conjured tricks on itself in this lonely dark. *Yes. No. Red. Dead. Dying.*

Halda had devoted her life to waiting. Waiting for a sign from a god who refused to wait for her. *You could have married Olrick. You should have, he loved you, he was good to you, he wanted children by you—dawters, he had said, so they looked like you. He made you happy and that scared you.* Halda had thought many times what her life could look like had she stopped watching her fires earlier. She would be settled on a rock somewhere in Daggland. *Would this army have gathered for anyone else? Are they even still gathered?* Halda knew how Toren could be when bloodlust fell upon him. *You've been gone too long, and you gave them no direction but to kill. They could have broken into many small armies again by now...*

Halda had earned her reputation by never leaving her fires, by always having the answers. By *knowing*. If she had left those flames, she never would have had her visions. *But what* were *those visions?* She questioned everything she had seen and heard. Her gods had left her and their voices seemed wee and far off. *No one but you could have seen Ox'olin coming and—*

It makes no difference. You're going to die here. Just as everyone else is going to die. You can't stop Ox'olin. You can't. And at least if you had left your fires, you would have something to be happy about. Something worth living for—love.

"What have you done, Halda? What have you done?" she whispered to herself, or to some ghost—they were the same. She had uprooted her entire country on a hunch. The gods had told her true, and she uprooted the country. She was sure Offa would continue to guide her. But Offa had left her. *Sweet Offa.*

Halda reached for the pouch around her neck, but it was gone. She was naked even with the dirty trousers and tunic she wore over her body. She was naked.

A loud crash and the clanking of chains echoed through Halda's cell. The hardened cedar door swung open, and two large women stood in the doorway holding spears. They wore sea-green cloaks and their armour was rusty around the joints.

One of them whistled. "Wooo-eee. The reek on this one, eh?"

The other probed the ground with her glare. *Don't find my rat. Please don't find my rat.* "King Owin wants to see you, but we're to shower you first. He says you've been down here awhile."

Please, don't. Let me eat first. Please, let me finish. "How long have I been here?" she asked, though her rib bones marked the emaciation at weeks, a month maybe... *If I could only see outside. If I could only smell the season...*

"Three weeks, maybe more," the guard said. "Hard to keep track of time these days with what the king and queen have going on. These old rituals and such. Ain't been getting much sleep."

Three weeks... Halda was closer to death than she realized. She had eaten less than a pound of food in all that time, and only twice was she given clean water. The guards had offered her piss every day, and she was getting closer and closer to accepting each offer. *Please, let me finish the rat.*

"Come on, you." The guards moved in. They hooked their arms under Halda's armpits, one guard on each side, and hoisted her up.

Halda's stomach growled. She was going to be sick. Just then she vomited all over herself and on the left guard's boot and merling cloak, too.

The guard jumped back and let Halda fall to the ground. She hadn't realized how weak she had become. "Oh, for fuck—" The guard dragged her boot in the dirt to clean it. *My rat.* Halda was horrified with herself. Horrified to be found out, horrified to lose her first meal in nearly a full turn of the moon.

The guard stopped, standing directly over the carcass of the half-eaten rat. She knelt down. "Have you been eating rats?" The guard looked at Halda, disgusted. Halda shook her head. The guard shook hers. Then made a sickened face at her boot as if realizing that it was rat vomit. "Come on, you. Lord Nith wants you."

"Where am I?" Halda muttered, she thought she knew but needed reminding. She held out hope that it was all a dream, that she was still in Daggland.

"Castle Blackstone."

ASTLE BLACKSTONE'S THRONE ROOM was lined with eerie statues of beasts and chimaeras carved out of oily, black stone that Halda thought looked like the night sky. In the shadows, she saw yellow eyes watching her, unblinking. Torches flickered dimly in the wet hall. It was dark, even during the day here. Halda looked up to the small windows carved into the stone hall and tried to breathe in the grey light that came through them. The hall smelled like woodsmoke and mould and fish.

King Owin Nith sat on a throne of the same black stone, and crude entities were carved into the driftwood dais. A fire blazed in a blackstone hearth, and the flames seemed to bring that dark rock to life. Halda saw worlds on worlds inside of there, stars and more stars. She stared so long that it sucked her in, and soon she imagined herself catching a falling star and that star taking her somewhere else.

"You're still alive!" King Owin Nith said. His heavy armour clanked as he sat forward in his throne. Despite being a king, his armour was just as rusty as his guards'. *It's so wet here...* His sea-green cloak was dirty and wrinkled. Halda hated the merling that was etched into his chestplate.

She coughed. "So?" she managed to say, and was proud of herself for not breaking down. *Does he know about the rat?*

"I thought I might use you to my advantage today," Owin said. His eyes were so grey they were almost black. His thick beard was black, and Halda reckoned his heart was black. She remembered what Eurick had said. *King Owin Nith is an evil man. Half bred with the darklings that inhabit the mountains. The kin of draugr and their ilk.* His skin was blue-silver.

"You've got the wrong person," Halda said, hating how weak her voice sounded. "I've got nothing to offer but ill luck."

"Halda, right?" Owin said, casually producing Halda's worn-leather sack of runes.

Halda's eyes gaped. Her stomach growled. "Rakkar Halda of Massey Rock, dawter of Hemon and Harla." She reached for the sack.

King Nith pulled it away. "Do something for me. Do something and you can have your freedom back. All you need to do, Halda, is ask your god some questions and roll these runes."

Halda nodded. She reached for the runes.

King Nith pulled them away again. "Tell me you understand, Halda. You ask whatever questions I tell you to ask and you don't resist." King Owin Nith nodded to his guards, his small standing army, and they all touched the hilts of their swords. *They're ready to pounce like rusted steel walruses.* The thought made her laugh somehow. *Twelve Iron Blades of the Merling King.* She hadn't laughed in longer than she could remember. *Is this Offa laughing through you?*

"I understand," she said, and reached for the runes again. King Nith let her have them this time. She untied the hemp lace that she'd dyed yellow with dandelions. She dug out the ivoried knuckle-bone runes and held them in her hand, coveted them against her chest. Her hands were weak, but the rat had given her some strength, and she felt now that she would survive this somehow.

"Tonight," King Nith said, "we have our rituals. Tonight, you roll the bones and ask your god our questions."

"Tonight," Halda said, though it was all a blur. She had her runes. Offa had answered her prayers and given Halda back her only means of communication with Her. The runes. They had been passed down to the Witch Queen of Massey Rock since the skies were new, so Aunt Thora had said. "These runes were the knuckle bones of Yddra," Halda said, and King Nith seemed surprised she was talking. "She was one of the first Dagglanders to be born out of the sea. She was the first prophet of Offa and was given Offa's own voice through her spirit. Before she died, she cast her spirit into these bones, and even today they are alive with prophecy. They speak the truth. But it isn't always easy to interpret. And sometimes the answers to your questions aren't clear." Halda thought of the soothsayers. *The raven...*

Owin Nith studied Halda and studied the runes. He clenched his jaw and took a deep breath. "We will see then," he said.

Halda agreed.

"Take her to eat something more than rats, and to wash. I don't want her touching the food at the feast with those hands," the king said to his guards, his black eyes glistening. "Tonight," he said to Halda.

Halda had never felt smaller or more degraded. She would roll the runes. She would ask the questions. She would eat whatever they gave her and be happy for it. *Offa, if this is my punishment, I will serve. But show me the way out. Let my rakkarren come.*

THE FLOOR OF BLACKSTONE's feast hall was thick with sawdust and fresh rushes. A great fire crackled and smoked from thick logs in a high blackstone hearth and lit the feast hall with a dim, ruddy glow that somehow made the gloomy grey Rynish air even gloomier.

Down the centre of the hall ran a trestle table of spruce that was as long as the spruce was tall. Halda reckoned there were two hundred or more chairs, and only about twenty folk sat sparsely around them. Halda saw those yellow eyes creeping in from the corners of the room again, unblinking. And on the driftwood dais, there sat not a throne but a cage. In the cage there was a beast with mangy, black fur. *Or were they feathers?* Halda would have sworn it was a crow if it wasn't so big. *What is it?* Halda shivered and thought of the draugr. *One of its ilk?*

On the table, they had laid out roast mountain goat and mutton with applesauce, river pike baked in goat's milk and honey, and steamed brook trout with carrots and squashes and peas, potatoes baked with onions and garlic and smothered in goat butter, roast snake and squirrel and cubes of beaver, and Halda thought she would break down in tears when they placed a hot, steaming loaf of wheat bread baked with rosemary and thyme in front of her. *Sweet Offa it smells so good.*

Halda was shown to her seat, the bench by the salt. *The nobles want you close, but not too close.* She didn't blame them. She had grown used to her own stench down in her cell, but even after the guards bathed her, Halda still smelled like shit. Like grime and rats.

The King and Queen of Nith entered through the hall to the applause and adulation of their folk. King Owin wore his rusted steel armour trailed by a sea-green cloak. The merling of House Nith was etched into his chestplate, and it had been re-laid with gold leaf since the last time Halda had seen him. His black hair was tied up, and his black eyes stared at nothing.

Halda found Owin incredibly emotionless at times, as if everything inside of him just shut off and he was nothing but a stone statue without feeling. The queen, Ethil, was resplendent in a dress of green scales. Her hair was black, eyes grey-black, and her nails were long and painted black. She smiled and her skin seemed to fold like duck feathers. Halda felt sick. Something about the queen made her think of the raven, Eurick. But only the worst, unknown parts of him.

They approached their dais and the royal children filed in, three girls and two boys; Halda knew not their names and they weren't introduced, and the guards came in behind them. They took their seats on the dais. Owin and Ethil stopped by the salt.

"Ahh, my dinner guest," King Owin said, his eyes never leaving the pouch around Halda's neck. "My dear, this is Halda, the one I told you about."

The queen's eyes went deeper than even Owin's, and Halda was lost in them. They were bigger than the night sky. "Ahh," the queen said. "The squid..."

"She was a queen there, once," Owin said. "Only the gods know what kind of darkness has fallen on those islands that so many have abandoned. The wretches are probably carving themselves—"

"Don't you talk about things you know nothing of," Halda said. She was so weak she didn't even have time to think before speaking.

The queen smiled.

Owin's eyes flicked open. "Anyways, I brought you here for a reason."

"I like this one, dear. You don't find too many people this tough these days."

"Can you roll them here?" Owin changed the subject. "Or do you need to be outside?" King Nith sounded like Halda did as a small girl.

"I can roll them anywhere," Halda said, her stomach rolling. The smells, the flickering light, the noise—it was too much. Halda sunk her head into her arm on the table. *Offa save me.*

"Leave her be, Owin," Queen Ethil said. "We've had her locked up for nearly a month and now you expect her to be excited about your little games. Treat her like a Human for a few hours, then ask her questions of gods."

King Owin's face went red.

Halda raised her head and squinted. She didn't want to die, but she would face Offa if she had to. "Ask your damn questions and let me go, or kill me, but don't send me back to that fucking cell," Halda said. She thought of her Aunt Thora at that moment. *I may be seeing you soon.* She thought her aunt would probably smack her for being so thin.

Queen Ethil shook her head. "You brought her up here, get this over with."

Halda took the pouch off her neck and took the runes out. She rubbed the smooth bone with her thumb and thought that if it was the last time she ever felt them, it was okay.

Owin cleared his throat. "The draugr is cursed. Ryne has become unpredictable since the Old Gods have started dying. The Old Gods were fighting a war here, long ago, against a mysterious race similar to them. A race with darkness in place of blood. Without the Old Gods to hold them off, that ancient darkness has crept back into Ryne. Older even than Yehven—a Sorcerous darkness left behind like a stain that won't wipe clean. We want to ask your god what happened to our own gods. Why have the Old Gods left us to our own devices? Why won't they answer our prayers any longer? Why is the draugr angered?"

Halda laughed. He wanted to know the same damn thing as her—what the fuck was going on? "Why wouldn't you ask the soothsayers? That is why I came all this way. To speak to them."

"Soothsayers?" Owin was surprised. "Halda, the soothsayers don't *give* answers. They give warnings."

"They will answer me true," Halda said.

"What makes you think that?"

"I know their names."

Owin looked at Halda like she was mad, then slowly Halda saw contemplation in his eyes as he and Ethil stared at each other. She could tell they were struggling to know whether or not to believe her.

"Demi, Torcan," Halda started. Owin's face turned to horror. "Lan—"

"Stop!" Owin shouted.

To know the names of the soothsayers was to tempt destiny. Not everyone wanted that kind of power. Not everyone could handle it.

"Enough," he said. "Even if those names have any meaning, I can't let you go. The people have been promised a beheading tonight to honour the draugr."

"You're a king, can't you do what you want?" She hadn't realized she was staring at her hands—her bony, wrinkled hands. *How old are you? You were only twenty ten years ago.*

"No, because I'm not just a king, I'm a *good* king. I do what my people want."

Halda could respect that. She wished she could be half the leader to her rakkarren that the Niths were to their people. Halda thought they were absolute bastards, but the people loved their queen and king, and intruders feared them. Their castle was clean and well run, and they had a feast on the table and a trough full of salt. They ruled their kingdom with two iron fists that often extended into two arms that gave the warmest and safest of hugs to their own folk. *And starve their prisoners to death.*

"What is it that you've seen in your runes already?" Queen Ethil asked. She toyed with a silver ring on her finger, and Halda wondered about it. *It reeks of magics, that ring.*

"I've seen the sky fall," Halda said, "I've seen Ox'olin. I've seen Mother Earth rise up to meet Father Sky. Fire and water and ice and so much darkness. I've seen the end." Suddenly, she felt a small spark somewhere inside. She started to remember her people.

Ethil opened her mouth but didn't speak. She nodded her head and toyed with her ring. "I've seen such things."

"Woodswitches have been singing Words to summon replacements for the hermits that had been killed in the wither year." King Owin said, "Folk are assimilating into the earth. We hear them singing. We've seen folk turn into Fae, their skin turn into slippery eel skin and their hair turn straw—their eyes bulging out of their heads. They crawl on all fours and run into the woods and slip into holes between roots and find their way to the deep places, each to protect a stonehead below the ground. They serve the dead down there, they help the souls pass... the earth is coming alive. *Nature* is coming alive." King Owin put his hands together and rested his chin on them; this had seemingly been bothering him for a long time.

"It's getting worse. I fear the end is coming faster," Queen Ethil said. "The beasts... of draugr's ilk, they—"

"Roll your runes, Halda." Owin nodded his head at the bench in front of Halda. "Please. Ask your god for us. We are not willing to pay the price the soothsayers will ask of us."

Price? Halda hadn't thought about them asking a price. "Let me go when it's done."

"You won't make it alone, and I'm not willing to spare anyone to escort you," Ethil said.

"Let me at least try. Give me a damn chance," Halda said. She rolled the runes on the table just to warm them up. Owin watched with eager eyes. "Just warming them up." They needed that after so long in the pouch. Just a little roll to get the magics going. *What has happened to the Old*

Gods, Offa? Why won't they respond to these people? Halda rolled the runes again. She couldn't believe her eyes. The runes showed two circles and a crow. Halda couldn't believe her eyes. Death was coming for them all. *Sweet Offa...*

"What does it mean?" Owin was eager.

"The death of two worlds," Halda said.

"What worlds?" Ethil said eagerly, almost angrily.

"This, and the Otherworld."

"By the gods..." Owin said, eyes wide.

Ethil took a deep breath and grabbed for Owin's arm. Halda saw her silver ring again and the strange green runes on it. "The gods are dead?"

"Not all," Halda said, staring at the ring.

Ethil covered it up with the sleeve of her dress. "I know the Owl still lingers, and the Maw, too. Father Tree is hiding. Gods help us if the Stag has been killed."

Halda had never understood why someone needed so many gods. *One for the sea, one for earth, and one for sky.* The rest were mere vassals in Halda's eyes. "There are too many gods these days." Halda remembered her Aunt Thora's stories of the Druids, the Lovasi Empire, and the Yehvenki Empire before that. All of them thought *their* god was the only god. *Ox'olin will prove them all wrong. Ox'olin will prove that* our *gods are the only gods.*

"There are just as many gods as there should be," Ethil said. "And the Stag has been upholding the rules of war since the Druids were born. The Stag tried to add order to a world of chaos."

"Rules of war?" Halda had never heard of rules of war. These southern bastards always wanted to write down rules and laws, and it made Halda sick. "The rules are kill and don't get killed."

Owin laughed as if he had expected Halda to say that. "Aye, but what if you kill and that person doesn't *stay* dead?" he said. "That is what I mean. The Stag took care of that. Him and his ilk collected souls, distributed them accordingly, and wouldn't allow them to return from the Otherworld unless, you know, they were alive. He banned demons from fighting in

Human wars. He even kept the dragons sleeping. Father Tree kept the order of things, He kept the justice, but Father Tree has not been answering prayers."

"I can ask the soothsayers for you," Halda said without realizing the thought had crept in. "Let me go and I will ask them who or what is killing the gods. I will ask them if this is the end or if there is some way to stop it."

"What makes you think they will know?" Ethil said. "They are beasts from another time. They are mad creatures that live in shadow. Why should I trust what they say?"

"I have seen it in the runes and in my dreams. I saw their yellow eyes, a star falling, and a raven. I have heard their names."

Owin and Ethil looked at each other as if they were talking without words. Around them, folk ate and drank and the bard sang songs Halda had never heard. She thought of her rakkarren.

"I have also had dreams of starfall," Owin said.

"Let me go. Let me go with my raven and I will get answers." Halda begged.

"Raven?" King Nith seemed genuinely confused.

"The raven you captured me with. He was my guide—my friend," Halda said. *Sweet Offa, he was, wasn't he—a friend.*

"Halda, he was taken by the ravens. Surely they will have killed him," Ethil said.

Halda didn't want to accept that. She couldn't find the soothsayers without him. She had come too far... "Where is the Guild?"

"Halda, the ravens—"

"Where is it? Tell me if you know." Halda knew enough of the ravens to know their Guild wasn't on any map. It was just as much a mystery as the soothsayers.

"Below," Owin sighed.

"Below what? Where?" Halda suddenly found that energy was surging through her.

"Below this castle. Through the tunnels."

"Tunnels?"

"They're underground ravens," Ethil said. "Partially."

Well that explains why they are so hard to find. Halda had heard stories that the ravens always seemed to pop up out of nowhere.

"Can you take me there?" Halda tied her rune pouch around her neck again.

Ethil grabbed Owin's hand. "Aye," said Owin. "But we have to go now. These folk think you're getting beheaded tonight for our sacrifice. I guess we'll need to kill someone else."

Sweet Offa... thank you.

CITY STREETS

"P LEASE," ALDRED PLEADED WITH the city people, but they kept coming at him with various weapons. "I don't want to—" Aldred swung *Phantom* and sliced through a torso, flesh soft as butter. Blood splattered the others, and it shocked them long enough for Aldred to slice them down, too. Four lay dead, the fifth one stood before him trembling. They had come at him with sharpened iron rods. This last fellow had dropped his. "Go," Aldred said, "I never wanted to kill a single one of you."

The person ran off into the sprawl of people.

Aldred was trembling. His hands were shaking, covered in blood.

"What are you doing down here?" Roqeda thundered. *"You shouldn't be down here. You should be in the library. Do you not realize what power awaits you, child? Are you that stupid?"*

Aldred had tried to take the tunnels, but city people had found their way into them so the Hester guards were holding the Keep's tunnels with the guidance of the Wise Ones. Aldred saw vats of steaming oil being hauled through the basements and heard the Wise Ones singing strange songs in old tongues. He didn't know what kind of magics they would use down there, but he couldn't use the tunnels in and out of the Keep, so he was forced to walk down into the city of Hest like a beggar.

He had gotten out of the Keep by riding in the back of the coroner's wayn, lying with corpses in the back. When he was free of enough watchful eyes, he slipped out of the wagon and found his bearings. He was dressed in a light chain shirt, trousers, and worn leather boots he borrowed from the scullery master. He wore *Phantom* at his hip and draped an old, ratty grey cloak over all of it. He held the cloak shut at his neck and crouched over to appear weak. He had hoped he would avoid any confrontation that way.

Now he stood trembling over four corpses that he created and had to bite his lip to stop the urge to animate those dead. His ratty cloak had fallen to the ground, and blood was pooling beneath it. Aldred was exposed in weak armour. *You should have worn all of your armour, or none.*

The city had turned into a battlefield, and Aldred found himself becoming violent. More and more people attacked him, and more and more people he killed. Two, three, four corpses. Seven, eight. *They want your sword. They see the blood on it, they see your armour, you imbecile. Daggland steel would make them richer than they could dream.*

Soon he was slicing folk down even if they seemed to mean him no harm—if they held a weapon, he killed them. *You did this. You did this to me, Father. I should never have spent so long at war with Brooton. You should have kept me from him. Why couldn't someone keep me from him?*

"*I*"—Roqeda's voice crashed like a flaming thunderbolt—"*kept you from him.*"

Aldred was scared now because he knew it was true. Roqeda had given him more than he had received in nearly all of his life.

Aldred moved into the slums of Rattrap by way of the Wood Road. "You lied to me," Aldred said to Roqeda aloud. "Just like everyone else, you lied."

"I told you more truth than you deserve to know. All I asked of you was one thing. One! And you don't even care to do it..."

Aldred was on the Smith's Road now; he saw the fountain of Eralis, he saw Eshlynn's sign with polished chains. *Who's going to polish her chains? Sebastian, you better fucking polish the chains, you bastard.* "I've obeyed you. I got the books. I got them," Aldred told Roqeda.

"You need to say the Words, child, don't you see? You need to say them!" Roqeda's voice was less like thunder now and more like an angry wasp's hive. *"You could Ascend, child, to the world beyond gods. We could Ascend. Don't you see? Can't you see you're making me suffer? And after all I've done for you?"*

Aldred burst into Eshlynn's shop. He was driven by something primal—something above himself. *Two things you can't choose are love and death.* Benecio's words had never held so much meaning for him. The place was torn apart. Eshlynn's shelves were tipped over, forge extinguished, and the wetted ash was strewn all over. Cookware and coal bricks and shattered pots stuck in the muddy ash like fossils. Aldred saw no sign of Eshlynn.

"Turn around, child. Go back to the castle. There is so much more to life than love, can't you see? I lost the ability to love when the sky fell. I traded love for long life, and you know, it's not just the love of people I lost. It's all things. I love nothing. I never will. And so you learn that life is about more than people. You can become a god, Aldred, you can leave all these people who have mistreated you behind." Roqeda spoke softly now, like waves lapping against a sandy shore. *"Come, child. Trust me. Leave her. Turn around."*

Aldred looked around the forge and felt a strange relief. *She made it out. She lived.* He remembered her words to him. *It wouldn't be the same me up there...* Aldred thought those words hit him so hard for a different reason before, but now he realized it was because he was not *him*, not truly. *You could be the author of your own life. Make the right decisions from here on. Save this city from your father, Adora—all of them. Give them a new ruler.*

Aldred pulled the lightning flower he had found for Eshlynn out of his boot. *Reibloom, she called it. A new beginning.* He put it back in his boot and left.

Aldred dragged himself out of Eshlynn's forge and into the streets once more. He couldn't pull himself away from the madness. He saw the Cathedral of Light burning, and he ran towards it. The flames licked the sky, and the black smoke looked like a great nytewood stemming from the wreckage. Many folk were on their knees praying to the burning cathedral.

"It's over!" a woman yelled at Aldred as he walked past. "It's over!" Spittle fell from her mouth and hung from her chin. "Two temples down in one day. In one day... Eralis is dead. *Dead!*" The woman collapsed to her knees again and started to pray with the rest.

Karaat is mocking the old gods and the new alike. The folk are praying to the wreckage of dead gods...

The cobbled streets, lined with trees blossoming in their full autumnal beauty, were filled with blood, and corpses and hedonistic folk were committing debaucherous acts. Statues had been draped with discarded clothing and smeared in feces. Small fires burned everywhere, and larger fires expunged their black smoke towers to the sky on each horizon. The flower beds that lined the roads had been trampled, but the flowers still held their colour, even crushed into the ground. *They'll grow back, those, with a little sun and some rain.*

Aldred had hoped to bring Eshlynn back in the same way. He had hoped that if she hadn't been dead very long, the soul would still live in there somewhere, that she was lingering. *She made it out. She got out of here alive. Did you save her, Sebastian?*

Aldred had hoped he could bring something of his old life back, but all he could do was bury himself in more pain—in more horror. *You can't bring back your old life. Not even with this power. You can only move on, author a new one.*

"*You're so wrong.*" Roqeda's thunder-blasts boomed in Aldred's head. "*You are such a coward.*"

Aldred approached the gates to Kelson's Keep and saw that the riots had really picked up there, and the only guards left were high on the barbicans above. He knew they wouldn't open the gates for him. Slowly, as the sun dipped away and the night began to rise, Aldred made his way to the Keep's second gate.

He walked through a neighbourhood where triple-storied daub and wattle houses roofed with thatch leaned over the streets and towered above him, blocking all of the sky but for a sliver down the centre. It was dark there, and Aldred didn't entirely recognize the smell coming off one of the pieces of meat that a person was roasting over a spit. People eyed him wearily with gaunt, grief-stricken faces. They watched him come, and they watched him go as he walked up the streets that surrounded Kelson's Keep.

He saw dead and dying clung to walls with crude shelters erected over them. He saw young children coughing and crying sickly with broken voices, calling for parents who weren't coming. *This is what the Hesters have done. This is what your* father—*no, what Adora has done... and everyone around the king has sat by and let it happen.*

"Help us, Prince," came a broken voice from the dark. Aldred saw a haggard old woman leaning over a fire with three young ones huddled around her. Aldred didn't recognize her, but on her, Aldred projected the entire Human race. Each of her children were future generations—Humankind's children. And all of them were dying. "Help us," said the woman once more. The children looked at Aldred with glowing, sad eyes, and those eyes and their dirty faces said more than their words ever could.

Aldred thought about giving her *Phantom,* he even reached to his belt to grab it, then realized it would probably only get her killed. Instead, he grabbed the lightning flower he had picked for Eshlynn. *The reibloom. It's not to give.* Eshlynn had said. *Fuck that.* He held it out to the woman, and the woman looked at him with fear in her eyes. "Take it," Aldred said. "That's all I have to give. It's a promise. I will save this city. I will make this right."

The woman took the flower. She gave it to her children, and they all wondered at it.

"It's a lightning flower," Aldred said. "In Esher they call it reibloom. It's from the Behruvian Desert, made when lightning strikes the sand. It represents change, this. A new beginning."

The children passed it around, girl to girl to boy, and they beheld it equally. The woman stared at Aldred with a strange wonderment in her eyes. "Thank you," she said. "I believe you. I believe that you will save us. Your heart isn't like the other lions."

Aldred carried on to the other gate and saw that it too had been abandoned by the guards. *Praise Eralis.* A great panic grabbed hold of him for a moment, and he sat down on the hard cobbles behind a barrel and rested his back against the wall of the Keep. *They will open the gates come sunrise. You will be okay.*

Aldred thought of his mother, and of William. He thought of Brooton alone in those cells. His father. Everyone was affected by the death of Lena Hester in different ways. And he thought of Adora. A Warlock from the Far East. *And for what?* Aldred had heard there were one or more Warlocks in each of the Lovasi castles in Ardura, and one or more in every other ruler's court, as well. *But why?* They had no open agenda, no literature explaining what it was they did. Aldred only knew he wanted Adora dead. He wanted her dead more than anything.

"Let it go, child. She will kill you should you try. You have bigger things on your horizon. You can be a god." Roqeda's voice turned into a dark tempest. *"Don't make me have to force you, Aldred. Don't make me."*

He leaned his head against the barrel and mumbled the dictums of Angelico to himself softly.

That night Aldred dreamt that all of Hest had turned into living skeletons. They swarmed him and picked him apart like carrion, and he felt every moment of it. When he had been completely eaten to bones, he himself rose up to join the bone army, and together they killed a lion and a dragon.

He awoke to the sound of a bell ringing, and somewhere deep in his mind, he heard a horrible cracking sound. The sun was white and hot and Aldred figured it must be halfway through morning already. His back was screaming at him, and in the daylight, Aldred could see how filthy his spot behind the barrel truly was. *What's even in this barrel?* Aldred tried to move it but it was heavy as anything. *Grease?*

A host of guards stood in an arrow formation in front of the small gates. Aldred approached them, and they bared their spears at him for a moment before the head guard recognized him and let him in the gates. "Praise Eralis, Prince, the city is no place to be right now."

"I had to see it with my own eyes," Aldred said on his way in. The castle was colder than he remembered, and all he could think of was those children and the haggard old woman. *They're suffering far beyond anything the king can even begin to understand. But I can save them. I can save the people from this.*

"When you translate the words in those books and say them aloud, you can save the world, child," Roqeda said as Aldred entered the courtyard.

"What were you doing down there, brother?" William seemingly came from nowhere.

"Fuck!" Aldred jumped. "I was warming myself by the fires. It's so very cold up here."

"Something changed in you, Dre. I'm not sure I like it," William said. Aldred walked past him.

"Is it that woman you go to see down there? Is she one of those witch-priests?" William said. Aldred stopped walking.

Aldred turned around faster than a lion and thrust his palms out to clutch under the arms of his brother's chestplate, and pushed him against the stone castle wall. Aldred held him there with all the strength of four thousand three hundred fifty nine sunrises. His blood boiled, and Roqeda seeped in.

"You know the truth, don't you, child? You remember what happened, deep down, you know what he did. He threw that bloody hammer at you. He knew you would drop it, so what did he think would happen? He's a fool who doesn't think things through. He let you take all of the blame. All of it. Now, pull your

knife and stab his fucking throat! Take control of your life. Do your fucking job!"

Aldred bared his teeth. He refused the power Roqeda offered him. It felt like holding in a piss-full bladder. It pained him to let it linger. "What do you want, William?" Aldred raised his voice. Aldred saw fear in William's eyes. *Good. Fear me, brother.* Aldred's face twisted into a haunted snarl. "What do you want from me?"

William trembled. "I want you to stop this! Whatever it is you have going on. I don't know if you're fucking one of these witch-priests, or reading those grimoires again, but you need to stop it. I don't want to have to watch our father fucking kill you, okay?" William said, puffing his chest out. Aldred saw tears welling in William's eyes. "I don't know what you did to Brooton, but you won't do it again. Stop acting this way and serve. That is what we were born to do, brother. No matter what. Remember the name. Don't you remember our oaths? Remember when we were boys, how much it meant to us? I won't stand by and watch you soil our family's good name."

Aldred scoffed. William had never been to war. He had never seen a person bleeding out, begging for their life. He had never seen a person starved to death. This was his idea of fighting darkness. He hadn't a clue how dark the world was. The bastard thought he was being knightly. "Our family's good name? And what makes it so good? All we do is slaughter our neighbours and subjugate smallfolk to work our fields. Then we force those same folk to fight, too." Aldred backed away from William. "You walk around a kingdom where everyone kisses your ass and calls you a lion. You've never faced a field full of people who would rather see you dead. People that are ready to risk their own lives to end yours. They spit on our family's name and call *us* the evil ones. And probably we are." Aldred shivered remembering Soren, Behru, and Sareen. "There are people who believe they would make the world a better place by exterminating the Lions of Hester."

William said nothing.

Aldred spit. He tasted sour bile where Rodeqa's words sat on his tongue: *I'll bleed you like a hog, brother, you piece of*—but Aldred left the words on his tongue. "But none of that matters to you, right? None of that affects you here in this castle."

William came forward. "You don't think I was affected by our mother's death, too? I heard her neck crack just the same as you, Aldred." William pushed his way out of Aldred's grip. "At least she *loved* you. She read you all those books and spent all that time with you, and she only shunned me. She looked at me disgusted with what she saw. She couldn't grow too attached to me because I was the heir and I had to spend so much time with father. She couldn't mother me like she did you, and I was left out of *everything* you two did together. You're not the only one who was forced down a path, Aldred. They forced me, too." William clenched his fists, his face twisted into a scowl. "And that Warlock. Adora. You have no idea what she's done to me. The things she's made me do, watch." Suddenly, William lowered his head and sunk his shoulders. He seemed to let his guard down. Then he sobbed. "I just miss her. I miss the way things were. I miss *you*, Aldred. But I don't know how to say these things. I'm sick of being angry at the world. I need you by my side. We can do this together. But if you get yourself killed, Aldred... I-I just don't know."

Suddenly, Aldred felt warmer towards his brother. He had never thought that William might be suffering in all of this, too, just in a different way. "Adora's poison. I want to kill her."

William laughed. "You can't kill her, you know that right? Warlocks are immortal."

"Time cannot kill them but blades can," Aldred said.

William looked at Aldred like he just realized Aldred had truly considered killing her. "She's wreaked havoc on our father. He's become sick with hubris, his mind is poisoned with soma and Warlock whispers. She's always in his damn ear, telling him this and that, making him believe he's more than he is." William shook his head. "You know Adora has convinced our dad that the Hesters were actually lions once. Something about the Old

Gods of the north in Hearthill where Gavyn hailed from. Creature beasts of Old."

The old gods of the north? Aldred had read something about them, that they were a race of beasts from ancient times that could walk and talk like Humans. They ruled all of the north before the Druids killed them and banned their leaders to the Otherworld. The story scared him beyond end, and he had asked his mother to never read it again. "We can't put this city through a siege, William."

William scoffed. "You really think our allies won't show up, do you? Do you really think all of the Hesterlands would see Hest besieged?"

"I think if they were going to come, they would have been here already. I think our father was more hated than loved, and that every single ruler of the Hesterlands would like to be living in this castle," said Aldred.

"So what would you do, then?" William said.

Aldred had read Benecio's *Songs of War* so many times that he could think of dozens of ways to fight back. They had the city and its massive walls. They had the advantage one hundred times to one because of that. But if the enemy chose not to attack and just surround the countryside, the Hesters could be starved out over the winter. "Build walls inside of our gates. Let the enemy in by leaving the gates wide open. Then slaughter them like pigs in a pen."

"Are you mad?" William scoffed.

"They won't attack unless the gates are literally fucking open," Aldred said. "Why would they?"

"The king would never—" William stopped himself. "Adora would never go for it. She would never allow it."

Aldred shrugged. "You asked what I'd do."

William looked concerned now. "You think we're going to lose this city?"

"I think I can keep a lot of people from dying," Aldred said. "But not with Adora still living."

William said nothing. He looked at Aldred like Aldred was a rare object he couldn't understand.

Aldred thought of his dad and how worthless he made Aldred feel—like he had died along with his mother. He thought of Brooton, and how weak he made Aldred feel. How helpless he was under his uncle's mercy. And he looked at his brother, older by two years. William should have been there for him as an elder. He should have helped him, guided him after their mother's death, but he only scorned him.

"*Remember the truth, child. You know what really happened on that day your mother died.*" Roqeda's voice rattled Aldred's skull.

"You read too much, brother," William said. "It's going to get you killed. Please don't try to kill her. Don't."

"All of the knowledge of the old world is sitting on those dusty shelves of the library," Aldred said. "In mouldy books that few can read. For two hundred years our family has done nothing but take a shit on that throne that used to be Kelson's. Our ancestors were barbarian Druids from the hills. They moved into sophisticated structures built on lands that weren't theirs. The king's order is exactly that—barbaric. Everything can't be made better by assigning plots of land to this person or that. Don't you see that everyone is just fighting over who can pile more wealth on their little piece of land, under their precious flag of arms? All the while those Warlocks whisper in rulers' ears and tell them what's right or wrong and to do this or that. None of them have realized that the wealth of the entire realm is far greater. Our father included. *That* is how this castle was built, brother. *That* is how this land was peaceful for a thousand years under Kelson and his descendants. *One* ruler. *One* kingdom," Aldred said. "A true leader could unite all of Ardura and rule them all under the same flag. *The purple and gold. Or something else.* A true leader would bring peace back to these lands, like Kelson did." Aldred looked up at the stars. The moonlight cooled him.

"*You mustn't lose focus, child. The books, the library. You must hurry. Don't fail me.*" Aldred flushed the thought out.

William was silent for a time. "I worry you've lost your mind, brother. I worry you've gotten yourself into something, and you're too deep to turn back. I can't help you, Aldred. I can't help."

"I don't expect you to," Aldred said.

"Just be careful, Dre."

"I will."

They both left in separate directions. Aldred knew he needed to go to the library and get this over with, but there was still one thing to do. He had to save his city. He had to do whatever would save the most people, not just what was best for his family. *That's really what it comes down to. That's what Mom would have wanted. I can be my own author and start with a deed that will be sung of for the ages. I will save the people of Hest from annihilation. I will give them a new king.*

He strangely thought of Phosphone's fable of the dragonfly. The little dragonfly could fly full speed in one direction, then, in no time at all, turn around and fly just as fast in the other direction, always avoiding the frog's eager mouth. *Are you changing directions now?*

Aldred walked through the castle and up the stairs to his bedchamber. *Praise Eralis, it reeks in here...*

Aldred's eye twitched, and after some time he realized he was glaring at himself in the Epithosian mirror in his room. He wore a sardonic grin that wasn't his and held a quill in one hand. He pulled himself away from his own eyes and found the scroll he had written out on the table. He read it over and nodded in approval and rolled it up and dripped hot purple wax from his candle on the fold, and sealed it with a pewter stamp in the shape of the lion's head of Hester.

"Egan," Aldred called, and his voice echoed into nothing. Egan would always have run a letter for Aldred. *Where is he? Someone needs to do something about this stench.*

Aldred remembered nights lying awake recently, unable to sleep from the rotten smell of something. He lay awake sweating and wake-dreaming of necromantic wishes, and the *smell* drove him mad and he thought of—*Egan...*

Aldred couldn't ignore that wicked smell anymore. *How long has that been there?* He felt sick with himself. *How long have you lived in this?* Aldred looked around his chamber—it was a small chamber. Chamber pot hadn't been emptied but the smell was worse than shit. *God damn Egan.* Aldred was pissed only because he was worried. *Where the fuck are you?*

He sniffed the air. He had checked everywhere and the smell just hung there like a rotten fart. He looked at his bed, raised on golden bedposts whose ends were carved with lion heads. *No...*

Aldred got on his knees and looked under his bed.

He whipped his head away and retched orange vomit all over his shirt sleeve and the floor. "Fuck!" he screamed. *Whywhywhywhy?* "Fuck!"

He crawled over to the bed again, and this time stood up and flipped the bedframe over. Egan's rotting face was staring back at him with a smile that was clearly put there after his death. "Fuck, Egan, what the fuck, what the—"

How long has he been there? God he looks weeks dead already... Aldred hated himself that it had been that long. *What the fuck is this? Who did this?*

He calmed himself by reading passages from *Rudea the Prophet of Eralis* out loud. He tied a scarf around his mouth and nose to block some of the smell and dragged Egan's corpse to the window and picked him up, and threw him out.

Aldred washed his hands and face in a water basin he had filled himself earlier and shook his head. *Praise Eralis...* his heart was thumping in his chest.

He felt more urgency than ever to get this over with. He re-read his letter and nodded. *They'll call me the Whisperer...*

Aldred left his room and made his way down into the courtyard. By the gates he approached the raven's den and talked to the black-robed woman crouched over the fire there.

"You a raven?"

The woman raised her arms to show that the sleeves of her black feathered cloak had wings.

Aldred handed her the scroll sealed with the purple stamp and a pouch full of coins. "Give this to Julien Esterbraun."

WAITING FOR FATE

The morning fog burned off and Hest plastered itself in the sky like a granite mountain. Towers and walls and halls of a size that was almost comical to Julien. *Who needs anything so big? They are buildings built for giants, or at least common folk who thought they were giants.*

Small fires burned in camp and as Julien walked through, folk looked at him with expectant eyes. *They want to attack. Or at least to know how to attack.* He avoided their eyes and kept up his rounds. He wanted people to see him—to know who their leader was.

Julien had no intention of attacking. He wanted to march up to the gates with his army and bust down the doors like he had with every other castle. But Hest was not the same. The plan sounded sweet in his head, but truthfully it would mean death. His grandfather had spoken much of Hest. He had been there many times, always plotting, always learning. He said the walls were twenty feet thick and a hundred tall. It was an unnatural place full of unnatural acts.

For the first time since he had left Lavesh, Julien was completely unsure of himself and what to do. *Karaat, please, show me true, don't leave me now.* He had spent every night praying to the flame, hoping to hear the voices that had guided him this far. But the voices had left him. Suddenly he wasn't sure if anything they had told him was true. *I killed the Oracle for you... why have you gone?*

Each night, Julien lit a pyre with a Word and he and his rabble sacrificed their victims to Karaat. The black magics danced beneath the stars and moon, and the songs of Karaat echoed in the dark woods and farmlands of the Hesterlands.

"The true name for these lands," Julien told his rabble around the pyre fire, "is Rhosanti. As the Draku named it when we ruled these parts before Kelson. It means *delight* in the common tongue. And isn't that an understatement? Kelson thought it such a good name that he kept it, too. Only the Lions felt it needed to be forgotten."

Julien's rabble "Oohed" and "Ahhed" but in truth, he had lost faith in them, too. Julien had sent outriders back to Darry to ask Rolan for his support. He thought about sending them all the way to Sareen to ask Trist Serahnon but opted not to, for he didn't want to wait the weeks required for an answer to return, and Julien also knew that, now that they had gained power back, the Serahnons would be gearing up to fight the Marwens, as they have always done.

Julien prayed to Karaat that Rolan would answer his call and come back. Rolan was good to talk to, and Julien hated to admit it but he missed him. He missed the company, the banter. He missed anyone at all who wasn't just a sword in his army. *Mother, Father, Grandpa, my brothers and baby sister, you would be so proud of where we are. This song would be so sweet to your ears. The return of the Draku.* He could see his mother and father dancing in the streets, smiles on their faces, music bursting out of the bard's lute and mouth, his grandpa clapping his hands and stomping his feet. Julien wiped a tear from his eye.

Julien had been having the same dream over and over lately. In it, he was with his mom and grandpa, and they were walking through the palace of Hest. Julien's grandpa always wore the finest Tiago Dilario boots, and the tap-tapping they made on the rich marble of Kelson's Keep was a sweet sound indeed. His mother was so excited to show Julien and his grandpa what she had found. She led them through the palace courtyard and through the library and down a stairwell. The stairs kept going on and on, and at this point in the dream, it turned into a bit of a nightmare as he descended deeper into the dark where he could see nothing and hear nothing but his own thoughts. His ears popped as he went deeper, and the air became wet and colder, and he felt like if he screamed no one at all would hear it.

But the tap-tapping of his grandpa's boots echoed, and Julien knew that his mother still led them and that he had to keep going deeper. He wanted his dragonbone but it was gone, he reached for his rapier but he was wearing no belt. It was him in the deep dark, and he kept going deeper until finally he saw two eyes burning bright and green. He carried on, deeper and deeper, and the air became thick and rank with sulphur, and his lungs filled with steam, and he coughed and kept coughing.

The eyes became wider, like they were only slightly open before, and the horrible greenness of them made him choke. He had no breath, his lungs had been stolen, and the green eyes stared and finally its mouth opened, a gaping maw with teeth like shattered rocks, and from deep in its throat a flame appeared. Small at first, then larger, then he and his mom and grandpa were in flames. Burning burning, so deep down that his breath iced.

The dream came every night lately, and every night Julien awoke cold and shivering. He would swing out of bed and warm himself by the fires and try to erase the image of those green eyes and the sulphur smell of the thing that owned them from his mind. *That is your death—sulphurous, torturous, and those green eyes...*

The dream scared him more than anything because it felt so real. *Karaat told you he would show you not just when you died but how. Is this how you die?* Julien hated that Karaat had left him, but as soon as he did, the dreams came.

Julien threw up smoking black bile and refused his breakfast. *Why have I heard nothing from the city? What came of the food I sent? Where is Rolan?* Julien hated himself for not knowing the answers to any of these questions. He had no reliable outriders. No reliable generals. *Alone.*

"The people want to know what we're going to do," Ashan said. He was a fighter and fighters want to fight. Julien couldn't blame him for that.

"Nothing. Not yet," Julien said. He gritted his teeth. *If I fucking knew I'd be doing it...*

"They want to fight."

"Tell them to fight each other." Julien said out of anger at first, but then realized that his idea wasn't all mad. "Blunt weapons only. Winner gets a pot of gold," Julien said. He had many pots of gold that he had stolen and could think of no better way to put it to use. Ashan's face lit up at the prospect of winning himself, even though Julien had already made him richer than he could ever imagine. *This would distract them. And more, this will please Karaat in the end.*

THAT AFTERNOON, WITH THE sun blazing, Julien and Ashan dragged a steel kettle full of gold coins, stamped with the blazing suns of House Marwen, and plopped it down in the sand for all to see.

"This," Julien said, "is your prize."

The rabble of sellswords made a ring by placing branches of cypress on the ground. They stood around the circle and watched as two people fought each other in the middle using blunted wooden swords. The fights would last until one person either gave up or was pushed outside of the boundaries made by the cypress branches.

It was hard to kill a person with a sword like that, but Julien watched many stagger out of the pit dripping blood from black and purple faces. They weren't dead, but they were certainly incapacitated.

Julien looked at the windswept, sunbaked walls of Hest and shook his head. He had sent word to Rolan weeks ago now. If he didn't arrive soon, he wasn't going to arrive at all. *So how long do I wait before I attack Hest myself?* Julien didn't know. His faith in his own actions were dwindling without the voice of Karaat in his ear. *How long do I wait?* If Karaat didn't come back, Julien was going to have to find a way to make his own luck.

The fights lasted for three days, and Julien carried on and drank wildly with his rabble from the crowd as a spectator. He smoked raw soma and howled at the moon like a jackal along with his people.

Finally, one person came out the victor. He was a round man from the Spice Isle of Lisi, his skin was as brown as his sprucewood sword, and he had won twenty-two fights in a row before no one else dared to face him.

Julien sat upon a dais of piled up chests full of treasures. Ashan and the champion stood before him and the champion knelt.

"My pleasure, Sir Esterbraun." The warrior had purple eyes and many gold teeth. "I won this tournament in your honour."

You won this tournament in honour of killing time. "You won in Karaat's honour. Don't forget who we truly serve."

"True, sir."

"What is your name?" Julien signalled for the warrior to stand.

"Mulu, sir, from Lisi."

"Well, Mulu from Lisi," Julien pointed to the steel kettle full of gold coins. "There is the treasure you were promised." Mulu took three big steps forward and seized the kettle. Grinning, he grabbed both handles and hoisted it himself. "I want to offer you more than gold, though, Mulu."

The warrior's purple eyes twinkled in prospect. Julien knew the look well enough. "Mulu doesn't need much more than gold. This much gold means I don't have to fight anymore."

"You don't want to fight?" Julien couldn't comprehend why someone wouldn't want to do the thing they're best at.

Mulu just shook his head.

"I want to make you my personal guard, Mulu. I'll pay you that much gold every single year just to stand by me. You don't even have to go into battle anymore. Not if you don't want to."

Mulu looked up, his eyes wide. He looked back at the gold. "I can do that."

"Good, Mulu, great." Julien looked out to the southern horizon hoping to see Rolan, but all he saw was the black shape of elm trees in the twilight. *How long do I wait?*

Julien had become worried that someone would try to kill him in his sleep. This army was in a precarious position. They were in line to capture one of the richest fruits in all of the Remembered Lands—maybe the richest—Hest. And at this point, Julien had instilled all of these folk with a righteous confidence that was unwavering. All of these folk believed they would take Hest. Many probably believed they could do it without Julien, and those who believed that would start thinking about taking the glory of this incredible victory for themselves. All they would have to do is kill Julien and claim captaincy over the rabble. *"The thing about a rabble of sellswords"*—Julien could remember the words his grandfather had told him—*"is that they follow strength, not blood. That's why any person with enough grit about them can become a leader. A leader based on merit, not who their mommy or daddy was fucking."*

Mulu put down his kettle of money to retrieve his blunted weapon from the sand. Julien looked at the blunted wood sword in Mulu's hand. "Do you have a real weapon?"

Mulu threw the sword and held up his fists. "Mulu has these."

Julien couldn't help but laugh. *He will do. He will have to do.* Julien couldn't attack Hest until Rolan came. He simply didn't know how to breach the walls. *Rolan will know a weak point, a strategy—something.*

Julien cursed the skies for getting dark. Karaat would not talk to him anymore, but he insisted on sending him dreams. Horrible, incomprehensible dreams. He cursed the skies for making him have to do this. "Come Mulu."

"Where?"

"To feast, Mulu. We have to wait for a sign from Karaat, and what better way to wait than to feast?" Julien said. *Karaat won't abandon you. He will send you a sign. He will guide you through this last step. He has to. He just needs a payment. Something meaningful. He needs to know I still need him.* Julien held the Oracle's ring in one hand. There were magics in that ring that he couldn't comprehend. Black, twisted magics that tortured one's soul if they were too weak to wear it. He gripped the ring firmly in one palm. *With this ring and this champion, Karaat will hear him. He has to. He has to.*

THE MOON WAS FAT and golden in the autumn midnight as Julien stoked the fire with a Word. "*Dagdora,*" he sang, and the flames danced. They licked the high branches of the cottonwoods in the grove. Julien and his rabble had built a modest pyre of wicker, beech, and ashwood.

"Mulu, sweet Mulu," Julien said as he tied the champion's limp body to a plank. He tied bowline knots he learned from Hild to ensure that Mulu couldn't break free if he woke up once the flames started to tickle him. If Julien had learned one thing about sacrifice, it's that they always wake up when the flames touch them. The old medicine of snake oil and scorpion tongue worked well to keep the consciousness at sleep, but the rest of the body still felt pain, and too much of it would override the effects of the snake oil.

All Julien had had to do was slip a few drops of oil in the gravy and Mulu was out. For a brief moment, Julien had thought that Mulu wasn't going to touch the gravy as he had avoided the lamb and potatoes and had gone directly for the sugarcane cakes and buttermilk pie. Julien cursed himself for putting those delicious things out on the table. But as soon as the desserts were exhausted, Mulu finished his dinner.

Karaat, please show me true. Let Rolan heed my call, or show me some other way. Please, Karaat, show me true, one last time. I will not let you down. Help me on this last step.

Julien and five of his rabble raised the plank with Mulu's big body and slid it on the rack of logs in the burning pyre.

A priest of Karaat sang a song to the moon and stars while twenty thousand folk joined in. The cottonwoods shook as the songs of Karaat echoed in the grove, and the moon shone beams of silver light through the cracks in the canopy. Mulu burned and smoked as the rabble danced around him, and in just an hour or so, all that remained were ashes.

Julien slept dreamless drunk in his pavilion tent that night.

He awoke the next morning to a steady rumble below him. He laid his ear to the dirt in his tent and listened. The ground shook from what Julien knew had to be people marching in unison. *Rolan...* Julien thought. He hated to admit it to himself but he missed the bastard. *Karaat has seen your sacrifice.*

Outside of his tent, the air was still rank with smoke and magics. The ground was flat and trampled from their dancing, which they kept up to the small hours of the morning. Julien's eyes burned from lack of sleep and too much drink, but the rumbling was clear. Someone was coming from the south. It was another foggy morning so all Julien could do was watch the wall of fog and sit in the rankness left from the night past and wait. *Rolan. It has to be Rolan.*

But it wasn't Rolan. The red scorpion of Serahnon waved madly in the wind. *Serahnon?* Julien's mind went wild with possibilities. He hadn't even sent a message to Trist. Had his messenger been killed on their way to Darry? Had Rolan himself killed the messenger when they arrived? Did the messenger fear stopping at Darry so they rode all the way through to Sareen? It didn't make sense.

Julien was standing alone in the fog when Trist approached. He rode in front of his army, and when he was close, he dismounted and came to Julien on foot. "Hell of a fog in these parts, hey?"

"Where is Rolan?" Julien said.

"Rolan?" Trist seemed upset. "Are you not happy to see me, Esterbraun? Have you forgotten our goodwill so soon? I helped you take Sareen, remember? Or was it the other way around?"

"I have one more city to take. One more and it's over." Julien wasn't in a joking mood.

"Well, that's why I've come, Julien, because I have to be the one to tell you it's already over." Trist put his hand on his sword. Julien hated how magnificent he looked in his splendid armour. His brown hair draped his shoulders and his brown eyes twinkled with youth. Not at all the sellsword Julien had met. "I'm willing to give you all the land south of Darry all the way down to Lysses. You can be a king, Esterbraun, give the Draku a home. But I can't let you assault Hest. Too many people would die. Leave it to the Hesters. Haven't you heard the old saying, ambition killed the cat?"

Julien laughed at his circumstances. *Has Karaat truly abandoned me?* "You don't understand, Trist. This is my destiny. I need what lies in the libraries of Hest." *And this isn't his land to give, anyway.*

"You don't need to invade the city to do that. Build up your kingdom and keep good standing with the Hesters. You can earn favour by reminding them you never attacked their city. Then ask them for what you seek, Julien. There are other ways to accomplish what you want. You don't just have to burn it all down."

Julien grinned, and whether it was his grin or the grin of a million dead Draku flowing through him, he didn't know. "You can't stop this, Trist. Join me. You can have Hest when I'm done with it. I will give orders for my people not to harm anyone who isn't trying to harm them. I want to give them peace, not war. But you know as well as I do that the Hesters won't give me anything I ask for. Especially when they find out who I am. They will come to kill me and all of mine. It's now or never for me Trist. So, join me." Julien held out his hand.

Trist looked at the hand like it was filth. "Only one has ever taken this city, the Lion, Gavyn Hester. And he had an army of sixty thousand and inside knowledge of the tunnels. You can't do this, Julien. This is where it ends."

Julien was about to say something when a voice boomed through the thickness of fog that drew everyone's attention.

"Esterbraun!" The voice came first, and then she appeared. The raven looked like a feathered wight as she emerged through the fog of morning with her hood up and her face shadowed. She held a lantern that creaked, and its light shuddered with each step. Julien smelled sperm-whale oil. She stood before Julien and pulled her hood down.

"Esterbraun?"

Julien looked at her with his mouth gaping. He had heard stories of the ravens from the Transporter's Guild, but he couldn't believe this was one. "Who wants to know?"

The raven smiled a carrion-like grin and held her dirty calloused hand out. She was holding a rolled parchment. "From Aldred Hester."

"Hester?" Julien was sure this was a jest. Kelson's Keep was hidden just behind this fog; he was only a few miles from the doorstep of Hest. This had to be a trick. Julien didn't take the parchment.

The raven shrugged. "I'll read it to you," she said calmly. "Then the job is complete." She unrolled the parchment carefully, precisely, and read, "Welcome, Julien, I've been expecting you."

"Give me that." Julien snatched the parchment. The words were written in Esheri, in choppy block letters. Julien was relieved because he couldn't read in any other language.

Welcome Julien, I've been expecting you,
I would like to formally invite you and your entire army to a feast.
The whole city is the meal! Unfortunately, no one else but I know you're
coming, so you won't be able to use the front gate. Please use this
convenient map to navigate below the walls and come right into the
castle! You can even open the city gates from inside to let in the
rest of your army once you've made yourself comfortable.
Thank you for this consideration. Please enjoy the Lion's Throne.
You may need to wash it.

"What is this?" Julien said.

Trist snatched the note out of his hand and studied the purple wax on the backside. "The seal looks legitimate."

"That's a letter, sir, from Prince Aldred Hester," said the raven. "It's legitimate." She cocked an eyebrow at Trist.

"Aldred Hester?" Julien wrinkled his brow.

The raven said, "He's a prince of—"

"I know who Aldred Hester is." Julien couldn't decide whether this was some kind of ploy or if Aldred had truly gone as mad as he sounded in his letter. *Ambition killed the cat, and Aldred's dad and uncle had an awful lot of ambition...*

"Is this a joke?" Trist said, he crumpled the note in a closed fist.

"It's no joke." The transporter raised her arms to show her raven wings as if her credentials were enough to prove she was telling the truth. "But the job is complete and I now must leave," she said, and disappeared into the mists from which she came.

"This is mad," Trist said. "It's clearly a trap."

"It's destiny, Trist." Julien grinned because now he truly understood. Karaat was testing his will and he held firm. He looked at the map that came with the letter.

Trist stared at him like he was some kind of rare animal he was trying to figure out. "Who—" Trist started but went silent, like he couldn't get the words to come off his tongue.

Who am I? I am Draku. I am Karaat's prophet. I am the new ruler of Ardura. I am destiny come. "I had no idea how I was going to breach the walls of Hest. They are a hundred feet tall and twenty feet thick. Hest and the Keep were Kelson's pride and joy, his crowning jewel of achievement. And now this... it's too good *not* to be true."

"It's a trap. It's clearly a trap," Trist said, but Julien knew Trist was in some kind of shock now. Good luck of this magnitude would seem like a miracle to any who hadn't worked for it.

"It's destiny, Trist. Aren't you familiar with the story of Gavyn Hester, the Great Lion?"

Trist nodded. "He conquered Hest from Kelson's descendants."

"You've got it, and you know how he got in?"

Trist rubbed his temples and paced. "This is madness. It... it can't be. How can it?"

"Gavyn was given maps to an underground tunnel by someone on the inside. An angry guard or jealous cousin. They called the person who sent the note *the Whisperer.* Gavyn was given the maps by the *Whisperer,* and he went in and killed everyone from the inside. History has sucked us into its current, Trist. This is more than mere coincidence. This is *destiny.* I have received a message from the *Whisperer* now."

By now the rabble had heard what was going on and the story had been passed around, and so near twenty thousand folk were crowded around, and when Julien said *Whisperer,* the rabble started to whisper.

"*Psss psss psss psss.*" The wave of whispers from twenty thousand voices was haunting.

"I know the god damned story!" Trist shouted. He unsheathed his sword and gritted his teeth. "I should kill you right now. I should kill you before this goes too far."

"*Pss pss psst.*" The wave of twenty thousand whispers rolled on.

"It's already gone too far, Trist. Look at Esher. And I'm sure you've heard the same stories I have about the north. The Warlocks will kill us all if someone doesn't do something about it." Julien glared at Trist's sword and felt something rise up inside of him. It was a laugh. A full-on belly laugh that he couldn't control.

Trist glared wide eyed at Julien Esterbraun. "Why? Why are you laughing!"

"Because I prayed to Karaat for Rolan Wence and he sent me you. You're tied up in this now whether you like it or not. This is *your* destiny too. Can't you see Trist? I found you pretending to be a sellsword, licking your wounds. Karaat sent me to you and now he's sent you back to me."

Trist's thoughts seemed to move inwards, and Julien knew the words had hit him. *The truth usually does.* "Are you really going to go?" Trist asked. "Through the tunnels?"

"Of course I am," Julien said. He had the Oracle's ring around his finger, and he spun it around with his thumb. In his front pocket he felt the weight of his snowstone key. "*This will open something down there.*" His grandfather had said. He had stolen the keystone from Hest and only vaguely knew its origins and purpose. "*It's important, somehow.*" Julien noted his dais of chests, including his dragonbone that represented so much. He studied his rabble of twenty thousand and now Trist and his son Coran's three thousand. All of them were hanging on his every word. Staring at him with wide eyes and gaping mouths, waiting to hear where *destiny* was going to take them.

Trist was seemingly in shock and had no words. To the rabble, Julien cried out, "I am destiny, and I will take you all with me." The rabble erupted in celebration. Elated cries of victory before the battle had even begun. "I killed the Oracle, and I have seen the future. This only ends in victory for us."

"This is madness. I thought you were a bloody fool. Maybe you *are* some kind of prophet..." Trist spoke so low Julien could hardly hear him.

"So are you coming with me?" Julien said. Trist's head shot up. Julien held out the maps that he had received from the raven and tapped his finger on the entry point to the tunnels. About three or four miles south, away from the wall of Hest, and far out of sight in a grove of elm.

Trist shook his head and mumbled to himself, but after a moment he smiled. "Praise, Karaat, Esterbraun, I can't fucking believe this but here we are. This is the fall of Hest. I wouldn't miss it for the world."

THE RAVEN'S GUILD

"RAVENS," KING NITH SAID, "are of Old Blood. As old or older than the Warlocks."

Halda traced her hands along the carved walls of the tunnels. So smooth as not to be done by any chisel. It was the work of magics, undeniably, and it made Halda feel so small. *The Warlocks who made these tunnels must have controlled their magics like a rider controls a horse.* She had little control over her own powers, and they often failed her when she needed them most.

"They control the passage of most messages between kings and queens throughout Ardura," King Nith continued. "From the Fell Mountains to the Bone Islands, they deliver their messages marked with their own seals. Many of the people whom they deliver to can't even read, so the ravens read for them. Only the Owl knows if they tell the truth or not. The Owl will tell Father Tree, and surely, upon death they will be severely judged."

"They send the wrong medicines, they meddle," Ethil continued. "But we, the people of Blackstone, know their truth. We hear their chantings and callings, and we have seen their sky rituals in which they make the clouds dance greenly. They use magics and witchery to alter themselves in ways. They see in the dark and remember *everything*. They are dangerous. But our people, the first Rynish that were born unto this land, made a pact with the ravens and the pact stands today—we of Blackstone protect this ancient castle, the most sacred of entries to their Guild because it was the very first. We protect their secrets and farm for them. In turn, a Warlock has never ruled us here. We are truly free on this island to do what we will. So long as we hold our pact."

"So, why break it now?" Halda was confused. Suddenly, her gut turned and she felt like an idiot. *They're going to kill you down here.*

"We're not, Halda." King Nith handed Halda a torch. She took it. "We won't be going any further."

Queen Ethil handed Halda an old map on a ragged, old beaver skin. "There are hundreds of entrances to the guild. Usually if someone wanted to hire a raven, they would go to one of the many outposts the Guild has set up, and one of the many ravens living there would deliver the message. But many folk travel here to Ryne to hire a specific raven for a specific job. They would get in using one of the many entrances, which is knowledge that is passed down amongst the wealthiest families in Ardura. Many of the best ravens with the longest records live at the Guild and are ready for hire from a more prestigious lord or lady, king or queen."

"So what are you saying I do?"

"You will stand out there, but if you tell the ravens who approach you that you are there to hire a specific raven for a specific job, they will take you to the nest. If you tell the Passerine what you're there for, they will at least hear you."

Halda was feeling like an idiot. "What is the Passerine?"

"Who," Owin said, "you should be asking. The Passerine is the leader of the Raven's Guild."

"So are they nice, then? Or what?"

"Haha." Owin almost choked on his tongue. "Do you have gold?"

"Yes," Halda lied.

"I know you don't have gold. So be careful, okay?"

"So you're going to send me without hope? Can't you give me some gold?" Halda said. She tried not to sound like she was begging.

"Halda," Ethil Nith said, "we were ready to behead you an hour ago."

"You said to give you a chance, and that's what we're giving you, a chance," Owin Nith said. "If not only to earn a small favour from the gods."

"Okay, yeah." *Fuck, fuck. Sweet Offa, is it too late to turn away from this?*

"Three miles," Ethil said, "and then you must make a turn to your left. There is a marker on the wall, a thick line about two inches deep. Walk with your hand trailing against the left wall so you don't miss it. These tunnels go on and on and on. From there it is less than a mile to the stairs. From there, well, I'll let you discover that for yourself."

"Aye." Halda tried to turn away but was stopped by a hand grabbing her arm.

"One more, before you go." Owin nodded to Halda's runes around her neck. Halda agreed.

"What do you want to ask?" Halda toyed with the runes in her palm and felt a childish joy.

Owin and Ethil held hands and both looked ashen. "Listen, Halda," Owin said, "I want to ask *who*. Can they tell me who is killing the gods?"

"Who?" Halda hated this. Sometimes, when she rolled the runes, she couldn't wait to see the answer they might give. "I can try."

Halda shook the runes between her two hands and felt them tumble around in the little cocoon of flesh she made for them, and on the dirt floor of the tunnel lit by the ruddy glow of a flickering torch, she rolled the runes. She looked on eagerly. The runes bounced along the dirt path, hopping over small stones and sticks, and when they came to a stop, Owin shone the light closer and Halda had a good look.

A stag and three crows. All of them could see the markings on the runes Halda pointed to, but only Halda could read them.

"What does it mean?" King Nith said. Halda got the feeling he was sensing her displeasure.

"It's a stag and three crows." Halda rarely saw two crows let alone three and her heart was thumping. "Three crows means death of the highest kind. Death of the soul. Total annihilation of being."

"By the gods," King Nith said, and reached for Ethil's hand.

Halda snatched up her runes and put them back into her pouch. She was sick of looking at the triple crows.

They said goodbyes after that. Halda had a wretched taste in her mouth from the reading. Offa had a way of doing that to her. Tearing her down and building her up.

But it was only moments before Halda was walking through the dark with only a small cone of light from the torch and a hand on the left wall to guide her. And it was only moments before her thoughts crowded in. Once she was alone there was nothing to stop it. *Your rakkarren should be here. If you were a better leader they would have come. They would have come, but it's your fault they didn't.*

Halda had come to the conclusion that she had fucked up most of her life. She had traded a great deal of love and happiness for mystery and seclusion. Chasing prophecies in the fires. *Aunt Thora warned you. She said if you watched the fires too long eventually you couldn't look away.* And Halda had done just that. Harald and her rakkarren begged for her to let them go, to let them go off and explore the islands like the other Daggland mariners. But Halda had selfishly kept them close. *What if Offa needed them...* If she needed to warn someone of something she had seen in the fires, she would need them to be on hand. *And you're a queen of that Rock they call Massey and so you make the rules, right? It was given to you as a gift for your parents dying. You are a great prophet from the Witch Den, and you are above all others because the gods chose you to talk to, right? You damn fool.*

Halda's hand scraped gently against the wall, and the torchlight revealed a small ring of light in the darkness, and in that ring Halda saw faces. Her parents, her lover Olrick and a child—*is it our child,* my *child?*—she saw the faces of her rakkarren and of Toren and Erik and Sera and Gunnar. *Judging you, they're judging you. If you fail this... if you got this wrong...*

Halda hated the growing feeling that she wasn't supposed to bring Ox'olin but stop it. *Your rakkarren wouldn't come because they are too damn loyal. If they had come searching for you and you didn't need help, you would have scolded them, made them feel small... they knew that and so they didn't come. Some maybe even hoped for you to die. It's okay to ask for help. It's okay. You need to stop being so stubborn and wanting to do everything on your own.*

Halda remembered the feeling of complete loneliness in the cells below Blackstone. She remembered the rat, and the starving hunger—the embarrassment and shame that followed. *You don't want to be alone, not ever again, not truly.*

Finally, her hand brushed the wide carving in the wall, and Halda turned left and went up the stairs.

Halda emerged from the tunnels out of the same kind of gaping mouth she'd entered through. Moss-fuzzed pillars and hanging lichen stretched out to grasp her. The stones, and the tunnels they opened into, showed their ancient bones. And what she walked into was unlike anything Halda could ever even dream.

She was in a long and narrow flat valley with the Blackrock Mountains forming steep and unforgiving walls of jagged, mean-looking stone on every side of her. The beauty was unreal. In the glorious midday, light waterfalls sparkled as they cascaded down the face of the black rocks and into streams of crystal-blue water that spread through the valley like veins to unseen basins. The leaves of aspen and pine and birch and whitewood burst in silver-white and honey-yellow, and the songs of a hundred birds rang out in a choir that left Halda completely unable to speak.

She scanned the sun to take her bearings and walked through the valley northwards. She soaked her cake of tack in a wooden tankard the Nithss gave to her. When it softened enough to eat, she chomped into it and then soaked and washed her saltfish in the same water. She ate the fish and the tack and added the water to a small bit of broth that she boiled of nettles and dandelion. When the broth cooled, she drank that and still, her body felt incredibly weak. Her legs wobbled and her head was flushed. *You were down there in a dungeon for a moon cycle and you expect to come out clean? Offa has punished you for not recognizing that you're not alone in this. Offa wanted to remind you that you have people—you have your rakkarren... and Olrick... it's not too late. It's not...*

Halda's thoughts trailed. She had come out of a small patch of arbor and into a valley where a pond sparkled in the sun. And there, in the trees and built into the black rocks of the north-facing mountains was the Raven's Guild. *It has to be.*

Wooden bridges hung high in the trees and connected one canopy to another. An interlocking chain of them, bigger than Halda could even see. They were so high up the bulk of the buildings were lost in the fog in that low valley. And from the holes in the rocks, Halda saw lights flashing. Small fires or magics, she couldn't be sure.

Soon she saw the entrance hall, and the sound of birds was replaced with the singing of people. A haunting, low hum came from the windows of the hall in unison. The hall was made of riverstone and some kind of coal-black mortar and roofed with timber. As grand a structure as Halda had seen in Ardura that wasn't the work of the Lovasi. A weather vane raven turned and creaked atop a thatched eave below which two massive aspenwood doors stood tall. The doors were carved with the symbol of the Raven's Guild, a spread-winged raven, in high relief.

Halda tried to open them, but they seemed to be barred from the inside.

She pounded on the doors with a fist.

She remembered what King Nith had told her. *They receive lords and ladies and even kings and queens in that hall. Tell them what you're after, and they will at least hear you.*

Yeah, Halda thought, *and how the fuck are you going to pay them for this? What's your plan Halda?*

No one came so she pounded again. Inside, she could still hear the singing. She sat and waited. She studied the hanging wooden bridges and the balconies in the rockface. What a peculiar type of people these ravens must be to live in a place like this. *They try to live like birds here. Are they truly mad?*

All seemed quiet outside of the hall. Far too quiet for Halda to sit comfortably. On the sea, quiet like that meant a storm was coming. Halda readied herself for a storm. *If I make it out of this, I will be better. I will be better to my people. Whatever answers the soothsayers give me will be received as news for all. I will not hold it over them as a prophet. I will not act like a god over my own people any longer.*

Halda thought of Eurick and how the bastard could so easily be himself—so easily to express his heart. He was so damned aware of himself it made Halda sick, but now she realized that she secretly admired his virtues. That she *needed* him to find that same quality in herself. *You are wise, Halda, but you are no god. You were foolish to guide this many people into Ardura. They could wreak havoc that you can't stop, no matter what message you have from a god. You led them here, and you left them to their own devices. You were unwise but you can make it right. Make it worthwhile. Sweet Offa, I hope it was worthwhile.*

Finally, the singing stopped, and before Halda could even stand up again, the aspenwood doors flung open and a flock of black-cloaked ravens came rushing out.

She told them she was there to hire a raven.

She was escorted to the Passerine by two ravens.

The chamber was so tall that Halda couldn't see the roof. Part of her wondered if there was even a roof or if the darkness above was just the new world she had entered. The two ravens guided her calmly to a where a woman sat cross-legged on a large wooden chair. The chair was a round mess of woven sticks between two aspen trees, whose canopy was golden-yellow. The leaves were brighter than those of the aspens outside, though, and Halda reckoned they stayed that golden colour all year round from whatever earth magics the ravens had cast on that throne.

Beneath them, and in her chair, the Passerine looked magnificent. Her hair was coal-black and tied in a crest upon her head. Her eyes were blackened with some kind of mud or paint, and her cloak of feathers was thicker and longer than those of ravens, but she almost looked like whatever was in that cage at Blackstone... the blackbird with no eyes and ragged, holy wings. *That bird came from some other place—the draugr's ilk.*

It came back to Halda now like a nightmare. When she was deep in the cells of Blackstone, she had dreams of the bird—dreams of wearing its face like a mask. And when she *did* wear it, she didn't need her fires anymore. She didn't need *anything* but the mask—the face of the bird. And now the Passerine's cloak burned that bird's face into the back of Halda's eyes.

"A visitor!" The Passerine's voice was high and emotionless.

Halda bowed. *Is this what I'm supposed to do?*

The Passerine laughed. "Get up, get up. First, my name is Ydril. Who are you? What family?"

"I am Halda, dawter of Hemon and Harla, Rakkar of Massey Rock," she said proudly. It also made her sad to think she hadn't produced an heir to her Rock, and when she died some other ruler would come and claim it as their own after a kingsmoot at the Isle of Offa.

"Ahh, Halda. Of Daggland is it?"

Halda nodded.

"Haven't been to Daggland much, personally. Too cold. What is it you come for? Delivery? Pick-up? Something else entirely?" Ydril sat forward with her elbows on her knees. Around her, the eyes of ravens appeared from shadows and in high places, and all of them, she knew, were armed and armoured in their fashion—chainmail and sword, both of hard steel.

"I came to hire a specific raven for a specific job," Halda said. Her voice was weak. Somehow, she thought that Ydril would find out about the rat she had half-eaten and be too disgusted to do business with this animal before her.

But the Passerine smiled a sinister sort of grin and said, "Honey, you've come to the right place. Name the raven and name the job, and I will name your price."

"I want Eurick to take me to the camp of the soothsayers," Halda said.

Ydril's mouth dropped, and a few of the ravens stepped forward and unsheathed their swords before the Passerine whistled to hold them off. "Easy, ravens," she said, and to Halda, she scoffed. "I don't know much about Daggland or your customs, and I'm not quite sure if you're just trying to be funny, or if the stories you've heard of us over on those frozen islands are as mad as I know your people are. But I'm going to let that go and give you one more chance to answer me seriously before my ravens slice you into food for the birds. Ravens, of course. We have thousands."

"I had him as a guide when I first came to this island, and I want him to finish the job he started. I have faith in him, that he is the only one."

"*You're* the one he was with?" Ydril looked at the ravens around her, and they started to move towards Halda again. "We have an escaped prisoner here. Take her back to Blackstone. I'll have to talk with Ethil..."

"No, they let me go. They let me go—" Halda jumped back and ripped her rune pouch off her neck. She held them out as if they were a weapon. *And they are.*

The ravens stopped moving towards her. She knew from Eurick that they were weary of witch magics. They were stuck in their ways, and unknowns made them afraid. "I'll summon demons in here if I have to, if that's what it will take for you to hear me."

The Passerine looked worried, and Halda couldn't help but feel joy. Many folk from Ardura had heard stories of Daggland that involved the Blood Words and the madness that took place during those decades. Most didn't know that those days were long gone, that Daggland was merely a trickle to the white water that was the Dagglandic Empire. But the mystery still held power, enough for Halda to gain footing. "Answer me four questions," Ydril said, "and I will hear your words. What is it you would ask the soothsayers? Why have you come so far? And what makes you think they will hear you?"

"I need to ask the soothsayers what role I play in Ox'olin—the end of the world. My god has spoken to me and led me here, and I will go to whatever great distances my god asks of me. The soothsayers will hear me." Halda took the knuckle bones out of her pouch, and all watched her with beady, nervous eyes. "Because I know their names. Demi, Torcan," Halda said, "Lan, Os—"

"Stop!" Ydril shouted. "Stop it now. Don't you dare say their names in front of us. That curse is yours and yours only."

Halda couldn't help but smile. "That was only three questions," she said, and the Passerine seemed to almost forget what Halda was even there for.

"Right, yes," she said. "Why Eurick? What do you want with a lying, unreliable piece of raven's shite? He is not a first-time offender, you know? This is his third time. Three strikes is death to a raven."

"Death?"

"You don't understand. He lies. He says one thing and does another. Eurick has no loyalty to the Guild and therefore he cannot be trusted to complete work on our behalf. Despite his flawless record. He can't be trusted not to flee on a whim when his emotions flare up. We work hard to quell those emotions in our ravens. Eurick is but a failed cause."

"Then let me take him."

"Take him?" The Passerine seemed genuinely confused. "No, you don't understand. He is dead. Or as good as. If he's not been killed, he is being held in the Talons, and our very best is torturing him for what he's done as an example to the others. We are an ancient guild, Halda, older than Kelson, older even than Daggland perhaps. Our blood goes back to old Yehven and beyond, and we haven't maintained our order for so long by breaking our own rules. Eurick is a dead man. If you want help to get to the soothsayers and you have the gold to pay, I won't stop you. But you ask too much, Halda, dawter of Hemon and Harla, Rakkar of Massey Rock."

Halda bit her lip. She rolled the runes on the ground, and the ravens jumped away. One even squawked in fear. Halda looked at the runes and couldn't hide her genuine amazement. "An owl, a hawk, and an eagle," she said. "The natural predators of ravens. It would seem that Offa has marked you. Marked you as part of this journey. Eurick was marked too."

The Passerine's mouth gaped, and her eyes were wide with terror. "Who the fuck are you?" she said. "What is this black magics you bring in here? Have you cursed us?"

"Just give me Eurick and the curse will be broken."

"You want Eurick, you can have him. But he is not the man you knew. He is no raven now," Ydril said, and the swords were out again. "You can take the same fate as him. Take him and your curse with you." To the other ravens, she said, "Get this filthy Dagglander out of my nest."

The fear Halda had conjured in the ravens was fading. She wanted to keep them away from her. "Demi, Torcan," Halda started, "Lan, Os—" She saw the club coming from behind her at the last second, and in an instant, there was only darkness.

Nature's Child

MAGGIE LOVED THE TOUCH of old, cold stone on her bare feet. The barrows were dark, dismally so, and each breath brought in as much dirt and dust as air, but she had never been so sure she was in the right place.

Cobwebs crusted her face, arms, and hands as she moved through the darkness. She could feel the roots of the nytewoods writhing in the earth around her, and she felt the worms and the moles that had nestled in with the bones of long-dead warriors in their final resting places.

She couldn't see the cold stone cairns of the old Druids, but she knew they were there, watching her. This was old land, she knew, older than even the elders at clanfires made it out to be. *The spirits were here long before any Druid or Human was birthed from the land.* And she comforted herself in knowing she had the spirits close at hand now. Something had come alive in the world after James had opened the Gateway. It was like Nature was coming alive, preparing for some great battle, and it was coming alive through *her*.

Now, she walked in pure darkness with her bare feet stroking the ground, and she let the spirits of earth guide her. It was as easy as walking and letting the spirits share her mind; she didn't have to think, her feet just moved in the right direction. *Hagel told you not to do that—that sharing your mind with the spirits was witch work and it would turn you dangerous.* But Hagel wasn't here anymore, and neither were any of her other variations of parental figures, all with their own variations of rules and beliefs. All of which abandoned her in one way or another.

Wulfee was the only one, the only one not to leave you when she found out who you were. It hurt Maggie to think of her now. She knew that in reality Wulfee had probably been killed in the war. Especially when no one, not even Pike, had found her. *The only mother that loved you is dead.* She put a hand on her stomach. *For you, I will never leave. I promise you I will never abandon you, baby girl.* Somehow, she knew that, too—that it was a small girl growing inside of her.

Maggie called a spirit of flame and let it rest on her fingertips for a while before throwing the ember into a wall. The flame revealed the beauty of the barrow, the underground space paved in rock and adorned with carved stone statues. Beautiful art and craftsmanship buried underground.

The Druids were a curious people. Maggie thought before calling another flame to her fingers. The small ball of fire danced from finger to finger, and Maggie smiled. She had always known one day it wouldn't burn—at least not so bad. After a few moments she couldn't handle the heat any longer and threw the flame away to extinguish. *I am the fuel that gives it life.*

Maggie hadn't had the heart to tell anyone that it was she who called the rain two nights ago. And it was she who called the lightning, too, and a wind so strong it moved the roots of the trees, and the whole earth reeled beneath her toes. *Your baby knows, she gives you the strength to do it.* When Maggie called the flame and danced it on her fingers once again, she could feel the power surging from inside of her.

She felt safe to be herself in the barrow. It was the reason she had spent so much time down there in the first place after her third family had left her to die in the Dark Arbor. She had stumbled into Oldwood cold and hungry and was greeted with locked doors and people turning their heads away. Clearly her mother and father had told the people in the village what she was, so she kept walking. *Walking, where I found this place. The pillars crusted with moss and lichen and crumbled half into the ground. This place that was so dark as to hide my face and body from existence and allow me to be myself—to find what was inside of me.*

Maggie found herself at last in the place she had been searching for. A wide chamber where the barrow opened up into an almost cavern-like room with a stone fountain in the middle as long and wide as a nytewood. The water inside was silvery, a liquid metal that shone its own dreary black-light. The roof drip-drip-dripped constantly from all over, and the falling drops made an unmatched choir with their echoes.

It was in this chamber Maggie sat as a girl and first reached out and felt the lives of others freely, without fear of discovery. This chamber was directly below the well in Oldwood; the reservoir was right above her head, and she often heard the bucket *ker-plunk* into the water.

It was here she first found that her powers extended beyond the elements; they extended to life itself, in all forms. The spirits were everything. When they had died last year, Maggie had nearly died with them, but when they came back, they were stronger than ever. Perhaps it made her more confident than she should be, but she was proud of herself for finding a way out.

This will give the Hallow time—time for Ruwen to raise her cattle and sheep and gain strength over another season. Time for Brinley to take his home back and realize he still needs to defend it. Time for Halda to return and reassemble the Daggs. Maggie was sick of war, sick of blood and the screams of dying people. She was sick of meeting folk who had lost loved ones in battles that could have been avoided. *Avoided if they would just let you be you and use these powers. Like Wulfee wanted. So you're just going to wipe them all out and run off into the sunrise with James? You really think nothing will happen?*

Things had happened before. When Maggie had let herself take too much life, she had a hard time displacing it afterwards. *Like Rosen.* But she had learned from Rosen. She wouldn't take the lives all at once but rather in bursts. There was plenty of room in the barrow to throw the energy, just like she threw the flames from her fingers. *And the Druids built this as sturdy as a mountain. It won't cave in,* Maggie told herself, but part of her couldn't shake the fear that all of the rock and earth above her head would just bury her.

But there was no other way. *You and James failed to keep the Hallow army together, and this is all that is left.* She told herself that but she was still afraid. Part of her wanted to run from this. *James would understand, he would be upset and heartbroken to betray his people, but he would understand.*

But Maggie couldn't run and she knew it. If she was going to leave this country and find the Abori, she would need to do it with a clear mind. She couldn't have the guilt of leaving her country to die hanging over her. No matter how much she felt like she didn't belong, she was still queen. *Too many battles, too many. I could have saved so many people over the years if they had just let me be myself. If they had just let me be mage.*

Maggie sat on the brim of the fountain and touched the cold, metal liquid. *The Druids lay in these pools and talked to the gods before they died. They actually came down here to look at the place they would forever rest in and meet their gods in preparation.*

As she awaited the coming army, Maggie ate her standard fare for the barrow: bugs and worms and small, blind fishes from the pools around the edges of the room. She placed a small bowl-shaped stone below the dripping water and drank when it was full. She ate moss and groat-weed and algae from the pools.

She slept each night on a raised dry spot in the barrow and covered herself in her white fox fur for warmth. And each night Na'reen visited.

"I'm leaving," Maggie said. "I'm coming."

Na'reen had a way of smiling that made Maggie's skin crawl—like it was worming its way into her, manipulating. "Oh?" she said. "Really?"

"Yes," Maggie said. She had thought Na'reen would be happy.

"Why now?" Na'reen seemed to be mocking Maggie, and she hated how unsafe she felt inside of her own head.

"Because," Maggie said, "I want to learn."

"To learn?" Na'reen laughed. "What would you learn that you don't already know? Look at you. Wielding fire, feeling earth, capturing whispers from the wind. You play with life like it's a child's toy. What could *we* possibly teach *you*?"

Maggie felt sick. "You can teach me what it's all for. About the star."

"The star?" Na'reen turned angry. "You say you want to learn about the star? Do you know what the Mother of Nature was, Maggie? The woman who James killed last autumn?"

"The Mother?" Maggie was confused, she had tried to forget about all that. "The Mother was a god."

"No, Maggie. And as powerful as you may be, you should never think of yourself as a god. You are not that. She was not that. The Mother of Nature was a mage, just as you are. You say you want to learn about the star, find out what it's all for, then you need to understand that the Abori have been fighting a war for millennia. A war that keeps coming back, time and time again, in different shapes and forms, with different names and peoples and races, but it always comes back. Nature has been fighting a war against the Creators since the skies were new. Nature made this earth, and the Creators fell into Her and tried to steal it—*are* trying to steal it. They destroy, She rebuilds. But She's tired, Maggie. She's sick and infected with dark magics that have seeped into the very deepest cores of Her. This could be Nature's final song."

Maggie was awestruck silent. Na'reen had never spoken to her this directly before, and she felt truly invaded. *Are we really in my dreams?*

Or somewhere else? Maggie couldn't move, couldn't speak. She felt like an infant, wiggling and wanting to cry.

Na'reen continued. "You say you want to learn what it's all for? It's for *everything*. For all of existence as we know. Another god is trying to take over these lands in the name of the Creators. They are trying to make an alternative to Nature—something just for Them. Something more easily controlled. If you keep using your powers at scale, Maggie, the Warlocks will come for you, and they will find you. They will seek to control you as they controlled the last Mother of Nature. If you come here and become *mage*, you can never go back to the life you know. But if you come here, you will have a home. You will have a family in us that loves you more than anything."

"James," Maggie croaked. "What of James?"

"He will come with you because you two will never again be apart. We know this. But Maggie, if you become *mage*, you will not see your child grow old."

Maggie's hand shot to her stomach. "But she *will* grow old?"

"Your daughter will rule Ardura and know many years of peace. But first, she will know many years of darkness. *Below.*"

"I will come. I'm not afraid."

"You should be, Maggie, but you will be received here with great joy. Look to the Lovasi lighthouse at full moon on the fourth Rise of winter to find your way. Be careful." Na'reen's voice got further away as if it was being carried on the wind.

Maggie awoke to a drop of water splatting on her forehead. She was freezing, drenched in sweat and shivering. *How long have I been out?* Sometimes, as a girl in the barrow, she slept for what felt like entire days. *Did I miss the Ayelish?* She felt sick, but missing them would have been impossible. *They are too big a force, and they will linger at the well.* She more likely felt sick from the dream. *Was that real?*

It was another full night in the barrow before Maggie sensed the Ayelish, and as much as she hoped for Na'reen to visit her again, her sleep was dreamless.

She felt just a few of the outriders' horses at first, and then as she reached out, she could feel the sea of lives behind them. The ground rumbled above, and Maggie could sense everything about the people there. Men and women, young and old. She sensed their leathers and furs and chain and steel. She sensed their axes and swords and maces and cudgels. She sensed black and brown and white skin—all, and as she grasped tighter and pulled herself deeper, she started to feel the lives that we re *connected* to these. The sons and daughters and grandchildren. Her mind was flooding, her eyes started to bulge. Maggie let go of her powers and collapsed to the ground. If she was going to do this, she had to do it all at once. *Like yanking a hair out, fast and easy.* Her idea of taking it in small bursts wouldn't work.

More and more of the Ayelish gathered, and Maggie remembered what Na'reen told her. *It's for everything.* Maggie had to remember that this wasn't about just her and James. He had kept reminding her that they were fighting the wrong fight, that this was bigger than they knew. *And you were right, my love.* She hoped he was waiting for her, far enough away from Oldwood that whatever she was about to do didn't affect him.

Hour upon impatient hour went by as Maggie waited for all of the Ayelish to gather. Every time she thought they had stopped coming, another wave rolled in. She started to think that maybe this wasn't an army at all, but some kind of refuge. *A refuge from what?* But they kept coming and coming until finally Maggie sensed that something had changed.

The rumbling of the earth had become less distant, and as she reached out, she finally felt an end to it. What scared her is that each time she felt around, she was overwhelmed by the density of life above her. As a girl, when she felt the lives of the people of Oldwood, it was no more than a few hundred. But this... *this* was thousands. Ten thousand, maybe, if Brinley's scouts were right. And those fuckers were usually right.

One grand swoop, right? And you and James can run off and be safe, at last. But Maggie remembered what Na'reen had said. *You will never go back to the life you know. You will not see your child grow old.*

Maggie always knew she would die, but willingly dying was a different thing. *But your child will rule all of Ardura,* she thought, choosing to forget the part about darkness. *What was the alternative? To die fighting a bloody war? To die running, exposed in the harsh north? What?*

Maggie listened to the roots writhe and the insects buzz, and she took a deep, cold breath and she remembered all of her pain. *You can keep others from that pain. You can turn your freakish gift into something good. Then all those who abandoned you will be proved wrong, because you're special, Maggie, not just different. You're the Queen of Mal Hallow, and the Mother of Nature was your kin. Avenge her and make it right. Nature is calling you, it has been all your life, this is your chance, finally, to belong. You can stop the starfall. You can stop it—save the world.*

With everything inside of her, the heartbreak, abandonment, and guilt, the hate, the sorrow, and the overwhelming love, with all of it, Maggie reached above. She felt the lives of so many thousands and held them like a thread of hair. Without overthinking she yanked the thread with one mighty pull.

And her mind exploded.

A Princess of the Hallow

*T*HIS IS WHAT IT'S *come to,* James thought as he sat alone on a boulder north of Oldwood. He was high on a cleft that required quite the climb to get to. From the cleft he could see all of Oldwood and beyond, as far as his eyes would allow.

And he sat all alone.

Bren Culdaine had once assembled four thousand Hallow folk to fight against Calen Alder. Just last year, James had gathered a thousand at Rosen to make a last stand for their country. They had even won that battle, but war was not a single battle. Now, James sat completely alone on a boulder and watched the Ayelish make their camp in the rising sun.

With *Essikah* firm on his back, his hands were bare and he fidgeted with his own fingers in anticipation. He hated being away from Maggie again, it reminded him all too much of his strange odyssey last year with Eurick and the wizard. *How are you, Eurick? I hope you're doing better than me.* James had lost his country, lost his clan leader, and now he was facing the prospect of another loss.

James couldn't shake the thought of losing her. *She doesn't know that I've seen our child. Maggie doesn't know what she's putting at risk.* But Maggie had nearly begged James not to stop her from doing this. James tried to understand. Since the day he had met her, she was torn inside. She had been abandoned her whole life and tossed away for who she was, and now she was afraid to show it. This was her chance to let it out, and for a cause that seemed meaningful. James understood that and he wanted to give that to her. *James and Maggie Culdaine, the Reaper of Death and the Mage of Life, saving Mal Hallow from the bad old Ayelish.*

But it couldn't actually work, could it? James had never heard a song like that in the cycles. There weren't many tales of mages, and the few that James had heard weren't anything nice. *What are we doing, Mag?* James was terrified, but somehow, he knew it was right. He prayed to the Bluebirds for a bit of luck on behalf of Maggie.

From his high hill, James watched the Ayelish army march, and birds flocked out of the trees. Thick armour, iron and furs, and chain covered the bodies of these soldiers, and in their hands were heavy weapons. James wondered again what in the name of the gods he and Maggie were thinking. *But you'll get away with it—you two always get away with it.*

Red eagle banners flapped in the low wind, and amongst them, James saw many banners bearing the seven-pointed star of Eralis. When they reached the town of Oldwood, the horses split into two groups and circled the wooden palisade walls while the remaining bulk filed in through the front gate and into the motte hall.

"If you don't kill them all and they find us... it's too risky, Mag," James had said to her.

"What other choice do we have?" Maggie was relentless. "Let them come? Let them kill everyone?"

"The other rulers won't listen to me," James said, "I've tried to—"

"James, you tried to tell them things that made no sense and had little urgency. You tried to tell them nonsense of magics and prophecy when all they wanted was someone to tell them it would be okay. Let's make it all okay, James. I will be okay. I want this. I *need* this," Maggie had said, and James didn't know how it all made him feel, but he truly didn't know what to do. He needed to save his country from being swallowed up. *End it and leave. Go with Maggie, her dreams will guide us,* he had thought.

James had tried so hard to hold his father's kingdom together, but he just wasn't the right person for it. *There is a monster in me that shouldn't be anywhere close to a throne.* A ruler could only maintain control with respect. Blood and history meant nothing if the folk didn't want to follow their leader.

James had lost his army and most of the civilfolk, lost the other rulers of the Hallow, and he was losing himself. He prayed to the Hare for a little bit of mercy, that wherever Maggie's dreams were taking them, he would find salvation. It made sense that the farther away from Kallahorn he got, the better his life would be. He had nothing left here. Nothing but Maggie. *No one will even miss you. Either of you.*

But Maggie could hardly use her powers in a clean way. At Rosen she had made a mistake. It didn't go as planned, and it could have turned out a lot worse than it did, but they had a lot more room for error at Rosen. They had a whole army then. *Now it's just you. If she fails and this army finds you, you're both dead.* She had told James countless times that she couldn't control her powers, that she didn't even truly know what they were.

"She won't fail," James told himself. He remembered when Maggie saved him from Calen Alder and truly believed that she wouldn't fail at this. *"Nature has come alive for me, James,"* she had said. And James thought that she was right. It had. He was only worried it would kill her in the process.

It was hard for him to make out any detail, but he could see that the mass of soldiers was moving. They carried white banners with red eagles on them and white banners with yellow seven-pointed-stars on them, and when James really strained his ears, he could hear them singing songs of Eralis.

He watched them march and thought of Maggie. *Can you feel them, my love? Are you waiting?* It had been two nights and now a third day since Maggie had gone underground, below Oldwood. James had been fighting the urge to go under ever since. But Maggie had asked him not to. For every bit he was afraid, she was five times that.

James thought about the Maw God mocking him. *"This will eat you."*

Have you ever had the weight of an entire country on your back?

The Ayelish army looked like a sea, their weapons and armour glinting like a thousand small suns beneath one mighty mother. The Ayelish had figured out that an easy way through the Mal shield wall was to run it down with war horses the size of cows. And he saw plenty of those in front. *Knights,* they called them. All James saw was a steel pot on a massive horse holding an oversized stick they called a lance. It was a fighting style that the Ayelish had been using more and more over the years. It was like taking every tool out of the smith's forge except for the hammer. And the Ayelish used that hammer to smash through the walls of Mal shields and take their country.

James saw the knights now, riding in front, waving their banners and circling the moss-blanketed wooden palisade walls of Oldwood.

As the wave continued to roll in, James noticed that the banners became thinner and thinner. As the middle of the mass started to file into Oldwood, James saw they weren't armoured. They weren't carrying weapons. They were moving slowly, alongside supply carts. The carts were covered over in dirty canvas and didn't look to James at all like the Ayelish supply carts he'd seen behind countless armies.

Near the end of the mass, the folk were nearly limping. Old greybeards and mothers with babies or with swollen bellies trailed slowly behind. What seemed like a massive army was no more than a wayward band of pilgrims. They were no different than the sorry lot that had traipsed through the Fells behind James and the rulers of Mal Hallow. *But why have they left Ayeland? What is this? Who is this?*

Then James remembered what was about to happen. *By the gods, Maggie.* She wasn't going to kill an army but a group of refugees.

He started to scale down the cleft. He had to stop her. He had to—*but you can't. You can't go near her or she may kill you too. They're too far along. She's going to use her magics any moment now. You promised her you'd stay away. If she finds out that she killed you by accident, what then?* James really didn't know. Part of him was worried that she might go completely mad and let her magics take over, then.

A stream ran down from the hills and it trickled past James's feet softly as he stopped dead in his tracks. He felt something in the air, something like fog or mist. He smelled peonies and honey. *By the gods.* Around him, the stream stopped moving, as if something was strangling it. Rocks tumbled down the cliff and crumbled into the arbor below.

James ran to the edge of the cleft to try and get a glimpse of Oldwood. The light of day had dimmed and the whole world was a strange half-glow, and everything was quiet. Completely silent.

Bands rode forth from Oldwood carrying all white flags—banners of peace. *Peace...* They rode out in many directions. *These folk are fleeing Ayeland... they're looking to ally... they may have been fighting a civil war, as Sessely thought...*

Then James felt his stomach cramp. And the birds started to fall from the sky and land on the cleft around him with heavy *thuds.*

James's head buzzed from an unseen sound, and almost like a dream, Oldwood turned from a collection of wooden walls and thatch shacks into a single beam of light—heavenly. A tree of light that stretched from ground to sky unbroken, as if the sun had fallen from the sky and left its tail behind in the clouds.

The sky shook, and the sun looked like it was just hanging on, about to fall out of its high place and burn all below it. Splinters floated in the sky like black swarms of bugs, and over the trees James watched a wave of magics spread and keep spreading. Getting closer, and then it hit him like a throat punch. A shockwave of sound and energy that knocked James off his feet and into the dirt.

Maggie! James could hardly think of anything else. The birds squawked and kept falling, the bugs scattered in great black clouds, and leaves fell from trees, traipsing. *Maggie.*

Dead souls rushed to James, they filled his lungs, swam through his blood, breathed into his heart. He sat up and dreaded looking out at Oldwood, but he *had* to look, he *had* to. James pulled himself close to the edge of the cleft again, amazed at how far he had actually been flung from where he stood.

The dead stood with him as he peered out at the valley where Oldwood once was, and James only saw greyness. Dead grey trees, grey soil, and grey sky. There was no smoke, there was no char. Only grey dust. James almost wished to see the blackened burned bones of things, that would have made it feel more natural, but there was nothing but grey. As if life had been completely drawn from everything so all that was left was an ashen residue. *Maggie...* Some folk were scattering away from the circle of death, but not many—not enough to make James worry.

James tried to stand but found himself weak. *Had she sucked life out of him, as well, even from this distance? By the gods... you have to find her. Find her.*

James willed himself to stand and his legs started moving on their own. He was running like a Hawka through the brush and arbor, out to the Northroad, where he kept running.

The entrance to the barrow was a mossed-over stone outcrop that had been all but taken over completely by the surrounding arbor. The stone pillars were carved with runes of Old Druid, and the way down was as dark a hole as James had ever seen. As he descended, he thought of Kallahorn. *How many dark tunnels run below these lands?* And an even scarier thought came. *What if they're all connected?* And his thoughts got even darker. *What might live down here? Wyrms and draykes and snakes of sizes beyond belief?* James knew tales from the cycles that involved great heroes of the

Mal and the Fells fighting mountain wyrms that flew out of the ground and devoured entire villages. Old Gran had largely played them off as false, but many times she spoke as if the stories were fact and not just made up. And she told him of dragons that lived below the great Lovasi castles in the south.

It's dark, too dark, you should have brought a torch. But James's cook fire had been extinguished when Oldwood was devoured. James walked in the dark and yelled out to the Maw.

"Find me now, why won't you? Guide me through this! You're not done with me, so *help* me!" James heard the echoes of his own voice bouncing off the narrow walls and swarming him like flies. *Me, me, ee, ee, e.* He swatted at them. *You're mad?*

He was running now, completely blind, unafraid of whatever might stand between him and Maggie. His boots crushed bones and debris, and his nose was dripping snot from the cold. *By the gods, Mag, where are you?*

And then a soft blue-green glow lit the chamber ahead. James had seen that glow before. He had danced in it beneath the moon and stars countless times. He had slept in it and bathed in it and lived in it for eleven years. Maggie brought that glow to the world, and he knew it could only be her. *Crow, not yet. Please, Crow.*

She lay delicately on the ground, the dust and the bugs glowed green and blue and purple as they danced around her. The cold, dead barrow was alive with Maggie's energy, and so James knew she couldn't be dead. *She can't be. She can't. The magics...*

"Maggie," he whispered, afraid to startle the magics maybe. She didn't answer. "Maggie it's me. It's James. You did it. You really did it."

She stirred slightly. "James?" she murmured.

"Ai mair Darra, my love, I'm here. I'm here." James brushed his cold hand against her red-warm cheek. Her eyes flung open, glowing. James tried not to show his shock.

"What's wrong?" Maggie asked. She started to look worried.

"Your eyes, my love, are glowing. Like the magics around you," James said, and the fear had already been flooded by his love for her. The scars on her face and her glowing eyes only made him love her more. *I will love you till the stars burn out and even after, Maggie. By the gods.* James hated how vulnerable he felt.

"James. What happened?" Maggie looked around, at her hands, at her body. She pulled herself up.

"You did it, Mag." James slid his arms around her waist, and she slid hers around his torso. "You really did it." And the true power of the woman he held in his arms—*or is she holding you*—truly sunk in. *She could kill the world, and would, if she was pushed to it.*

"James, I had a dream," Maggie started.

"Of a child," James finished. Maggie's face turned soft, her hands slid to her stomach.

"It's stronger in me now, James. She's strong as all hell. The power... Nature, it feeds her."

"She? Now?" James's heart seized. His body tingled, hair standing, eyes welling. *By the gods.*

"Aye, I feel her now, James, I feel her."

"You feel her?" James put his hand to Maggie's stomach. James thought of his mom.

"A girl, James. *Our* girl."

By the gods, baby girl... "We'll build a house for her, on a lake. A beautiful lake in the woods, with a view. It'll be safe there, Mag. We'll make it so," James said.

"We need good rocks to jump off. I loved so much to jump as a girl. And rocks are good—hard to move—they don't leave." Maggie pulled away, seemingly distraught. "But that wasn't my dream, James."

"You can tell me if you need to," James said, "I'm here."

"The Abori..." Maggie put her head down. "Mage, they said... it's—"

James put his hand on Maggie's cheek. "It's okay, baby. Ai mair Darra."

"Ai mair Darra," Maggie repeated. "They're going to come for me, James. In my dreams, Na'reen tried to warn me."

"Come? Who?"

"The Warlocks. The Mother of Nature, she—"

"Maggie let's not talk of that."

"Listen, James," Maggie pleaded, "the Mother of Nature was a mage, just like me, but the Warlocks, they—"

"Tortured her." James said, "I felt it in her soul."

"They'll come for me, too, James."

That made the monster flare up in James. "Then let's go. Now." *Or I'll kill the whole world to save you.*

"The lighthouse at Tide. We have to go there. I'm absolutely sure of it. Na'reen... The Abori will help us, James. They told me they would help us. Our daughter can *live* James, but we have to go."

"Aye." James's head swam with questions. *Na'reen? Abori? By the gods what am I doing?* But in his heart, he wasn't afraid. He had run all his life and now he just needed to run a little more. *A little more and I will find peace. I'm sorry Dad, but I'm just not you.*

Maggie had bought Mal Hallow time. Time to organize themselves against whatever is to come. *But the white flags, the unarmed people. These were refugees. A civil war... was there a civil war in Ayeland? Sessely thought there might have been. You made a mistake, a mistake...*

But Maggie lived, his child lived inside of her, and they were all three together. They could leave now, and folk would think them dead. When word of whatever happened here spread, they would be free and clear. Ayeland would surely think twice about attacking again. *Or would they just double down? Would they come at all? By the gods, did they wait a year to march to let us destroy our damn selves?* James could argue with himself all day, but for now he needed to leave.

"They will be searching for us, Mag. There were survivors. And the Warlocks..."

"They will search for me. I have seen it," Maggie said, "so we have no time to waste, James."

"Aye." James thought of Adeqor. On his back, *Essikah* pulsed. *I'd kill the whole world if it meant you'd live.* "Let them come."

SOOTHSAYERS

"**H**EY." A VOICE FROM the darkness. "Hey, man, you awake?"

"What?" Halda croaked, opening her eyes. Her head thumped and her vision was foggy. "Where am I?" Brief glimpses of a wooden club flashed in her mind. Above her she saw the half-bare limbs of aspenwood and birch stretching out to a grey and flaxen-gold sky, their amber-yellow leaves fluttering to the ground all around her. The dove-coloured clouds were fat and fleeting.

"We're still in Ryne." The voice sounded far-off. "Something just happened across the channel. Some magics. It doesn't sound good, man. Can you see?"

Am I awake? "Eurick?" She strained to see the raven, for he looked much different without his beard. His face was covered in dirt and grime, and a red scarf was tied around his head, covering his eyes.

"Halda? Halda is that you? By the gods," he said. He didn't seem the same Eurick that she knew. *He's only half that man now... they stole something from inside of him.* "I didn't- I- Halda, I'm sor-"

"I know." Halda didn't need to hear it.

Eurick nodded. He hung his head. "Something is happening over there in Mal Hallow. It sounded like the sky falling. Do you see anything?"

Halda sat up. It was getting late and it was just the two of them. They were somewhere in the deep arbor. Her head was thumping. It felt like something had been knocked loose inside of her skull. She could hardly comprehend what Eurick was saying. "What are you doing? Why are you wearing that scarf."

Eurick turned his head towards her. He was skinnier now. He unravelled the red scarf and revealed gaping red holes, raw and blood-crusted where his eyes should be. He held the woollen red scarf up in his dirty hands, and the loose threads dangled and swayed in the wind like hair. "This is the mark of the Scorned Raven." Eurick began putting the scarf back around his raw red eyes. "And it keeps the infection out."

"Sweet, Offa." Halda held her hand to her mouth. "What happened?"

"The ravens happened. This is the mark of a transporter who disobeys. The red-scarfed beggar. The Scorned Raven. I was surprised to see the red... I thought for sure they were going to kill me," Eurick spat. "Too kind, that, I guess. By the gods, I wish they had. Eronel will never love me like this. How could he? Didn't think the last thing I'd ever see would be a ragged red piece of cloth. I wish it'd have been him."

"I begged for your freedom. I came for you Eurick." Halda had almost forgotten what she'd done. As much as she could tell herself it was for Eurick, her real motivations lay in her own need to communicate clearly with the soothsayers. *Or is it more than that?*

"You?" Eurick said. Halda thought she sensed contempt in his voice. "You begged?"

"Our job is not complete, Eurick. The soothsayers await our arrival."

Eurick scowled. "I would have been happier to die. I'm nothing now without my eyes." He stood up and Halda could really see the weight he'd lost now. He pointed a bony finger at Halda that reminded her of a talon. "You should never have gotten involved. You should have left me."

"I made a promise to you when we first started this journey, and you made the same to me. That we would see this thing through to the end. Remember? You wanted to do something—to help change the world for the better. Offa has woven your thread with mine, and you will play many more important parts before it is over."

"By the gods," Eurick said. "We failed, Halda. We failed. Look at me. I can't take you anywhere. I can't—"

"Then I will take *you*," Halda said. "You've never failed a job, and I'm not going to be the one in your company the first time it happens."

"I'm not a raven anymore, Halda. I'm nothing. And you *can't* take me. They live in a cave through a maze of tanglewood and dogwood with pits of quicksand and reaper fist plants with stinging needles the size of daggers."

"We've come this far, Eurick." Halda reached out and touched his arm, and that made him jump. "It's just me, don't worry. I want you to know we've come this far because it was Offa's will. The gods are dying, and I believe Ox'olin is coming. The sky will fall, but my god has been trying to communicate with me—trying to guide me. I think She wants me to stop the sky from falling, Eurick, but I don't know how. I don't know how, and I need you by my side as we walk through that maze and find the soothsayers."

Eurick turned away. "I don't have anything left in me."

"I have enough for both of us. I will carry your skinny arse if you make me. The spirits will guide us. If Offa hasn't swept our souls into the Blood God's sea yet, I don't think it will happen now. Not here on this island."

"What good am I?"

"You're a friend, Eurick, okay, and I haven't had many of those. I want to be better to those I care for. My rakkarren, they—" Halda didn't want to think about what they were doing. They were most likely tucked away somewhere in an inlet off the Lake of Scales. Either waiting worried, thinking she abandoned them or got killed—*the draugr*—or what she feared far worse, that they hoped she was dead so that they could finally be free to leave the Rock and find a new rakkar.

"They respect you, Halda. I saw it in their eyes."

"When we find our way out of this and I get back to them, I won't leave them again so easily. I didn't know how much they truly meant to me. I didn't know life outside of that Rock—outside of my fires," Halda said.

"I'll get you back to them, Halda. If I can promise you one thing it's that I will get you back to them, or I will give my life trying. I owe you my life. It's more than any other person has done for me. I won't forget that. Not ever." Eurick lowered his head. "Guess I won't know much of anything now. By the gods, Halda, it hurts so much." Eurick rubbed his forehead. "It hurts so, so much."

Halda put a hand on his back. "It's getting late. We need to hunt."

"I'm afraid I've lost my appetite. Seeing the inside of an eye will do that."

"Not for us," Halda said. "For the draugr."

"**I**S THERE A RASH?" Eurick had his bare arse in the air.

"Hold bloody still so I can—no, there's no rash there," Halda said. Eurick had taken a seat on some reaper's club and just got through picking the dagger-sized needles out of his arse.

"Yea, not yet there isn't, it's gonna be nasty, man." Eurick yanked his pants up and adjusted the red scarf around his eyes. He spat. "It's gonna be nasty."

Halda and Eurick had been a full seven days on the road since they had left the premises of the Guild, and Halda feared that they hadn't travelled more than a few miles. Eurick mumbled things about moss and tried to sniff at the wind, but for the most part, they followed Halda's judgement. She took their bearings from the sun and kept a straight line by marking trees, and she did her best to gather nuts and berries and mushrooms when she saw them, though the berries were slim pickings this late in the Fell of autumn.

Winter is coming and your rakkarren will leave before they get iced in the river. She hadn't had that thought before. That with each setting sun, the sky got closer. With each sunrise, winter clawed itself closer with icy wet fingers, threatening to leave Halda abandoned on this island to bear the winter months exposed. *That is the true Hell.*

Halda looked around at the thick trees, and through the canopy, she marvelled at the black mountains rising up like so many daggers towards the sun. *Draugr probably lives in those mountains. It's probably watching me right now...*

Halda got the fire going one night and watched Eurick stumble his way down onto a log to stretch his feet out. The red scarf around his eyes was already sooty and grimy, and he hadn't gained much, if any, of the weight that he'd lost back. He looked ragged, haggard as all hell, and Halda worried a stiff wind might take his torso off like a loose sail. Then she remembered what the Niths had told her. That the ravens twist messages and meddle.

"I heard stories about the ravens. Stories that say they've been there in that valley a long, long time."

"Aye," said Eurick. "Since the skies were new, and even before, so the stories say."

"Aye. And I heard stories that the ravens are pretty friendly with the Warlocks. That the ravens meddle."

"Meddle?" Eurick sat up on the log. He looked like he wanted to get up but was fighting the urge.

"That they twist messages."

"Twist messages?"

"That's what I heard."

"Halda, the ravens are into so much shite you wouldn't believe. I would believe any story I heard of their dealings. But if you're asking me if I've twisted messages or meddled with any plots, the answer is no." Eurick rubbed at the spot where his eyes used to be. He seemed to be in pain. Halda felt bad for bringing all this up. "I always tried to be a good person—best I could be. I never knew my mom or dad, many of the ravens don't because the death rate of ravens is high, but I always had a feeling they were *good* inside. That their hearts were full and good, and that I came out of that. I dreamed of seeing the world, falling in love, of seeing the Mother's Shrine one day. I did all of those things, and they ended in darkness for me. The only constant light I have in my life is imagining those big, full, good hearts of my parents and knowing Eronel is out there somewhere, alive, and safe from me. And I know that he loved me once, and I him. I got to feel that."

Halda felt stupid for even bringing it up. "Aye." Halda remembered Olrick. "I've felt it once, too."

"But the Raven's Guild is not a good place. *That* I know. I denied it for a long time but I can't any longer. I don't even know half of what they've truly done, and they have been getting into more and more shite. Involving themselves with this lord and that. I do believe they were twisting messages. I do believe they meddle with the affairs of rulers and cause war after war. Could I have done a thing to stop it? No. The Guild is bigger than any one person. It's a living thing." Eurick adjusted the red scarf. "One generation trains the next, and on and on. They have traditions that will never die. Like cockroaches," he said. "I am a red-scarfed beggar, the Scorned Raven. A red-eyed crow—death walking. I have a hundred names and more now."

Names... "The ravens were afraid of the soothsayers. Afraid to hear their names. Why do their names frighten people? Why do they frighten you?"

Eurick rubbed at his temples. "Because to know the name of a Sorcerer or wizard would mean to control them. The Soothsayers represent secrets, unseen truths, future sorrows—most people don't want control over that kind of thing. They leave that to the gods. The soothsayers don't speak of happy endings. They don't speak of birth and marriage and love. They speak of death, and dying, and foreboding."

"Ah," Halda said. It was all she could say. *What kind of answers will they have for you? Of death and dying?* She hated how grim her future looked but she carried on through the brush anyway. *You can't turn back now. You've gone too far. You brought all of Daggland together and led them away from their homes. If Ox'olin doesn't come, they will turn unruly… it will get ugly.*

But Ox'olin had to come. Halda had seen too many signs now. She just needed to know how to deal with it. *They will know. Death and dying, right?*

In the maze of rock and wood and water, Halda thought she might perish. "Here."

"I can't hardly hear you, man. Yell a little louder." Eurick was twenty feet behind her and headed on the wrong trajectory.

"Here!" Halda was using more energy yelling after the raven than she was finding her own damn way. Part of her was cursing herself for going back for the raven. *You would have been better off on your own at this point.* But she fought those thoughts away with the memories of Sig Arfa, the legendary Dagglandic hero who led all of Daggland against Kelson and the Lovasi. *Sig Arfa sacrificed himself to save the closest members of his rakkarren. He said the true quest is the people you help along the way to your final destination. It's not how many you killed, but how many you could bring with you to the top. That was Sig Arfa.*

The raven cracked his way through the brush, adjusting his ragged red scarf up over his eyes every few steps, and when he reached Halda she started on again. The raven sniffed at the air, he touched the dirt and leaves, and at one point smelled mushrooms and ate them. He touched tree trunks and drank from streams and stagnant pools that shouldn't be drunk from. "We're on the right track, man," he said, "you just keep us straight."

When it became obvious they would be spending another night out in the mountains, Eurick suggested Halda start hunting.

"Draugr?" Halda asked.

"Aye."

"Still? This far into the mountains?"

"You don't understand, do you? It's all places. Maybe there is more than one, I thought. But the Rynish swear there's only one. I've had folk argue with me till they were blue in the face talking about how it has the same markings, the same crooked antlers and the same skinned horse legs. There's only one and it's everywhere. A Sorcerer's Creation—Hellsent, man."

So Halda hunted. She killed a red squirrel with a rock and set snares along the small game trails she found. She took a drink from the river and got the fire started. She caught a rabbit in a snare while getting the fire started. She gutted the squirrel and the hare and cooked the squirrel on a spit for her and Eurick. She left the hare skinned and staked in the ground for draugr. She didn't want it to think they took more.

Birdsong woke Halda that next morning, and Halda knew the song immediately for that of a lark. She burst up from the damp ground and tried to find it. She moved through the dew, sticks snapping beneath hurried steps, and there, on the bough of the most perfect pine, was the most beautiful golden skylark. Almost as soon as her eyes touched it, the skylark flew to her and landed on the ground in front of her and continued to sing. Then it flew away, spread-winged and carrying the tune merrily. *The skylark is a perching bird. It perches and sings songs, the most beautiful songs in all the land, for all to hear. Just like you, perched high in your Den, singing songs that no one else can sing.*

Halda started crying. All at once, and she didn't know why, but it came on hard and fast and she couldn't stop the tears. *You can't be a lark any longer, you need to be a kraken... a kraken is who you are—who you're supposed to be. Your Aunt Thora warned you of this, of the isolation and the loneliness. She told you not to let it happen, to bind your heart to Olrick, but you chose the perch and the songs—you're a bird when you should be a kraken.*

When Eurick awoke, he didn't speak, he only put his arm on Halda's back and stood with her, and that was more than she could ever ask for. It was all she needed and more. It was then Halda realized that maybe Eurick was crying, too. *But he can't cry anymore, not truly, not without eyes.* But the tears didn't mean a thing, a person could cry on the inside, too, and Halda felt that in Eurick, and she wanted nothing more than to make him feel okay.

So they stood, and Halda watched the sunrise up through the canopy and Eurick gazed up there, too, perhaps remembering what it may have looked like. And after some time watching the trees sway and listening to the streams gurgle down into the river and the birds sing, they turned and walked towards the black shadow of the sun burning into the Blackrock Mountains.

Without speaking, they walked for an hour or more. Eurick picked some pine needles and sniffed them and let them flutter away in the wind. He nodded, and Halda knew they were close. She could feel something changing in the ground. It was becoming spongier, and she could see the mushrooms, too. Blue and purple and black, they sprouted from trees and logs and earth and rock. There were more and more of them the farther Halda went, and Eurick picked many of them and stored them in a small hempen sack.

"What are they?"

"Mushrooms," Eurick said.

"How do you know they're not poisonous?"

"Smell, man. Feel. But these ones are certainly poisonous. I'm not keeping them to eat."

It was midday when the fog rolled in. The pines and birch and aspen became so thick that they muted the sun a dull green colour. In the foggy dew, Halda smelled the sea.

"You smell that, man?"

"Yes. We must have gone the wrong way. It's the sea." Halda breathed it in. The salty, fish smell of it. The damp, slimy taste of it at the back of her nose. She missed the sea more than she knew. More than she even understood.

"No, no. It's a trick. Earth magics or something of the like. We keep going." Eurick adjusted his dirty red scarf and scratched at his beard. It was as thick as an arbor now, and his hands were skinny and talon-bony. Halda hated to think of what she might look like.

"We keep going." She agreed, for she knew the soothsayers were close. Their names flared up in her mind as if the soothsayers could feel them there and were trying to steal them from her. But she held them close. *Demi, Torcan, Lan, Oswe.* She repeated them in her mind and made them hers. *Demi, Torcan, Lan, Oswe.* The soothsayers could change threads of the future. They could weave a variation of what is already written. And Halda knew their names.

Halda and Eurick carried on, and the streams gurgled and the wind blew softly but the birds had gone, or else they had finished their song. And here, in this fog, Halda saw flowers blooming verdantly despite the cold whisper of winter blowing its gentle reminder on the wind. In pink and in purple, they bloomed happily. In all shades of blue and the brightest of yellows. In orange and red and snow-white. And they grew in neat little rows, as if they were planted there. A forest or a garden, or perhaps it was both.

At once, the soothsayers made themselves known.

It was by their singing at first—*or was it chanting?* Then the strange lights in the sky and on the trees. And then the water. The river nymphs rose up from the rippling surface of the streams like fish jumping. And when they beckoned Halda, she grabbed Eurick's arm and followed them.

The spirits will guide you. The singing got louder until the aspenwood and pine cleared out to an opening where there was only silence. A quiet place of a kind that Halda had never known, and she got an overwhelming feeling that she would never know a place so quiet again.

Eyes, yellow and knowing, watched Halda from the hidden places, but she kept walking and Eurick puffed his chest out. Halda admired him, his bravery. It helped her keep going despite being scared shitless of those *eyes. They see* into *you and through you. They see all things about you with those bloody* eyes.

The soothsayers made themselves seen.

They slinked out of the shadows to reveal crouched, shrouded figures. Their ragged cloaks were stained sticky with filth, and their greasy hair clung to their faces and only their *eyes* were visible beneath the hood. The stench of them was enough to make Halda step back and shield her nose. *They live out here in their own filth and* watch, always watching.

Eurick's mouth was moving but no sound came.

"Who would pass through the Gwendarian Garden?" one of the soothsayers spoke, its tongue slobbering out of its mouth. Halda knew it for Demi.

"I am Halda," she said at once. "Dawter of Hemon and Harla, Rakkar of Massey Rock, I've come for the soothsayers. To ask questions."

"Questions? That would imply we had answers for you." Demi grinned.

"I was hoping you would."

"We give answers to no one. To nothing." Demi scowled.

"You have to give me answers to what I ask. I know it is the way of things, for I know your names."

"We owe you nothing. You know nothing. Nothing at all." Demi frowned.

"You owe me everything, Demi." The soothsayer sucked its teeth. Its face froze, eyes open, mouth gaping. Halda looked at the others.

"You owe me your lives, Torcan, Lan, Oswe. I am Offa's prophet, and you must answer me."

The soothsayers were completely silent. They looked at each other with shocked gazes on their faces.

"Answer me, Demi! Answer me, Torcan and Lan. Answer me, Oswe!" Halda shouted, and her voice was full and proud and loud.

Only their eyes appeared from the darkness beneath their hoods, blinking, watching, knowing. "What would you want to know?"

Halda sensed fear in them now. *They haven't heard their names in far too long.* But it was Halda who was most afraid. There were stories of the soothsayers in the sagas. In Halda's fires she could get a brief glimpse of the future, the soothsayers, through their magics, can see the past in crystal clarity. And from the past they discern the future. From the past they *know*. And with that knowledge they *change*. They tear and remove threads when they need to. "I need to know of Ox'olin," Halda said. "The sky is falling. I need to know if I am meant to stop it or to assist in its coming."

The soothsayers were silent, but they seemed to be thinking. Eurick stood just as silent, his mouth open, Halda assumed out of anticipation. "Starfall is coming. *That* we know," Demi said.

"And the Reaper." Oswe came forward, her voice creaking like a rusty wheel. "You want to know of the Reaper?"

"Yes," Halda said. "Yes, please."

The soothsayers conversed in a strange clicking tongue, and when they were finished, Oswe said, "Three stones will open the door. Circular white beneath towering black. Neither put there by Nature. Three keystones, not one, and the Reaper." Oswe took a deep breath.

"And the sword," Lan said.

"The sword," Demi and Torcan echoed.

"And the sword," Oswe said.

The sword... Halda remembered the big thing James had been carrying. "Is this my duty? Is it my duty to find these stones and prevent this?"

"The skylark has made it so. It has judged you to be the choir of this song," Torcan said. Their voice was like bat wings flapping. "The World Walker must walk again."

"What are you talking about? Tell me true, is this my task?"

"Not yours alone," Oswe spat the words. Its eyebrows furrowed. "You have a part to play. You will meet the Reaper thrice. Once at the stones of Grave, once at the lighttower at Tide, and once at the place you will die. When and where cannot be known, but it will happen and you will be there. And you will have a keystone to give him upon your third meeting."

"This is what we have seen," Lan said, and Halda thought that its voice was so gentle, she wished that only Lan spoke. The soothsayers spoke softly together in their clicking tongue, then Lan said, "We cannot tell you what we have not seen. On the fourth day, Rise of winter, look to the lighttower at Tide. There is a great cloud over that time and that place, and that means your destiny awaits there."

"And what of the raven," Halda said, last minute.

The soothsayers stared at the transporter and whispered to each other.

Eurick looked uncomfortable. "I don't want—"

"You will see again," Oswe said.

"You will see more than you ever have before," Torcan finished.

"What will I see?" Eurick said, hopeful now, almost righteous.

"The truth," Demi said. "And more than that, too. *Your* truth. But you will see horrors beyond comprehension first." Then to Halda, it said, "Would you like some milk?"

"Milk?" Halda said.

"Not ours."

"No," Halda said, and after a moment, "thank you."

"Right," Oswe said. "Then take our names and leave this place. Don't dare threaten us like this again. We will know about you next time. Next time you will not make it here."

The soothsayers hid themselves in the shadows. Only their eyes watched, yellow and wicked from the darkness round the edge of things, and from that darkness, Halda heard them drinking—gulping.

Milk? Halda and Eurick only stood, unmoving. Perhaps both thinking variations of the same thing. *This is madness. True madness.*

"They've been on this earth since the skies were new," Eurick said. He was still in shock, it seemed.

"So I've heard," Halda said. Her skin was goosepimpled, and her hair felt thin and straight like a cat that had been scared. She had heard about the soothsayers, all kinds of things, and now she knew that every one of those stories was false. The soothsayers were something darker than any story had told. The things they knew were the shadow-thoughts, the silent whispers of things that folk can't say in full. The darkest depths of the heart that only a few mad folk in all of history have ever treaded on or explored. The soothsayers knew all those things and they knew all of those people and the things they will do. They knew how it was.

And Halda knew their names. She made them hers, but now she left them. She left them in that room with those eyes because she had never been more afraid to possess a thing in her life.

"Sweet Offa, Eurick," Halda said as she noticed the big red thing in the black sky. "The blood moon," she said. The moon was bigger than she had ever remembered, and bleeding red. *Darkness is taking place in the world on this night.*

"That's two blood moons this year," Eurick said. "Glad I can't see it. That's a bad omen in Mal Hallow."

"What does it mean?"

"Slaughter," Eurick said, and it seemed to Halda that he was hurting inside thinking about it.

Halda left that place of the soothsayers, and with Eurick, she left the strange valley and the strange trees and hills behind. Through the garden with the most beautifully flawed flowers she had ever seen. In every colour and every shape—shapes that shouldn't be. Jagged little things, pretty as all hell. Back through the Black Mountains and the Black Arbor and through many black nights, Halda treaded and she guided Eurick through all of it with a careful hand and gentle words. And she made her sacrifices to the draugr.

"They've been here forever," Eurick said. "The soothsayers. Since the skies were new. What do you think they were drinking? Milk? Of what?"

"Leave them," Halda said. "Leave them there—forget them." And suddenly, Halda realized why folk were so afraid of their names. Because after seeing them, all you could think of was shaking that thought. But a name brings meaning. A name brings a thing to life and anchors it to others, and in Halda's mind the soothsayers lived. They took a small spot and called it theirs. They knew her secret whispers and her unseen truths. She couldn't shake them but she couldn't ever say it. She had asked for this. She had used their names as weapons, and Offa had given her this burden as a consequence. Her visions and her power would come at a price, she knew, and she hadn't paid it in full. Not yet.

The Lake of Scales, white and rippled and glistening in the sun and the wind, healed Halda's soul with a single glance. The hurting, the uncertainty, those dark whispers were all silenced when the freshwater caught the wind and she breathed it in with the gulls' song.

"They won't be here," Halda said. "They'd have gone to the river."

"It's a big lake," Eurick said. "It will take us a while to find the river."

Eurick sniffed at the air and touched a large boulder close by. "These boulders were dropped here by a great ice giant, you know that?"

"Aye," said Halda. There were stories of it in the sagas. "Yuri Smokeson killed one of those ice giants with a slingshot big enough to hold a star. He missed the first time and that star is still stuck in the sky now, but he hit the great ice giant with the second shot and brought him down. When the ice giant melted, they found that his heart was a massive stone boulder, just like this one, eh?"

"Aye. I wonder if *they* were here, even then."

Halda knew Eurick was talking about the soothsayers. Of Demi, of Torcan. Of Lan and Oswe. Halda knew their names. She couldn't shake it. "May well have been," Halda said, and thought that this world was far more complicated than she cared to even try and understand.

They camped for one night on the north coast of the lake, and by midday the next day, they had reached the southeast coast and Halda saw the river outlet.

By evening, as the sun started to set, Halda saw *Red Morning*. The sails were relaxed, the ship sulked cooly in the river. Her rakkarren had a big fire blazing on the beach, and when she and Eurick approached, loud yelps spilled from the rakkarren wildly.

Harald stood in front of the rest, tall and proud and beaming with a smile as thick as his beard. "You bloody made it," he said. "You found them?"

Halda smiled and hugged him. She forgot how haggard she had become until she felt Harald's strong arms and back. "*We* found them. Eurick and I."

Harald glared at Eurick for a moment then back at Halda. "Let's get you some food, eh? You're skinny as a damn oar." To Eurick, he said, "You too, raven, welcome."

"I'm not a raven any longer, man," Eurick said.

"Whatever you are or aren't, tonight you're one of us, and you need some food, guy."

Eurick didn't argue.

They feasted that night around the long table in the ship's dining room. Small tallow candles flickered and burned pungently to wade off the coming dark, and Halda's rakkarren crowded round her.

Their meal was smoked herring and fresh baked lake trout with fat fried chaga mushrooms and vinegar. When the fish was finished, Halda's rakkarren served baked apples and honey with goblets of cranberry sweetwine they had stolen from a small village. They told stories of the draugr and of the snow-white trees, and Halda avoided questions of the soothsayers, but in her mind their names cycled. *Milk of what? They were gulping it...* And their *words* danced on the names like tiny butterflies. *Three stones. Three stones and the reaper.*

Halda hated those words. *Aunt Thora had a stone. She had an awful, awful stone that was full of magics. She showed it to you. She told you the secret of it—that it came from the sky long, long ago. That it had powers—that it was a key of sorts.* Halda shook the thought loose. She would deal with that after. *After the lighttower.*

After two goblets of sweetwine, she raised her cup and said, "To Tide. We sail to the lighttower there and find our destiny. And to you, for still being here. For not leaving me. I haven't told you how much I appreciate the hell out of you. Haven't said it near enough. So, here it is. You're my rakkarren. I wouldn't trade you for the bloody world. We're family. A family that has no other. You're my people."

And Halda didn't know if it was her words or the wine, but *Red Morning* shook that night from the revelry. Halda and her rakkarren celebrated together and they forgot all things. Halda was safe. She had made it to the soothsayers and back again with answers to her questions.

Then why are you terrified?

A New Beginning

"**W**HAT DO YOU MEAN, dead?" Aldred was still half asleep and was sure what he was hearing was false somehow. He rolled out of bed to face Rober and the other purple cloaks who had awoken him.

"He no longer lives," Rober said. "The cityfolk found his body below the castle wall this morning."

William, what happened? Aldred had been with him on top of that wall just weeks ago. "So what does this mean?" Aldred asked.

"Your father is... upset," Rober said. *Bloody mad more like.* "I think you should make plans to leave."

"To leave?" Aldred said. "The castle?"

"The city altogether. This is a sinking ship."

"I can't, I—" Aldred thought of Eshlynn. *She's gone. It's all gone. There is nothing here for you.*

Outside of Aldred's window, he saw flashes of unnatural light. In the sky, the moon was fat and bloody. *A blood moon... second of the year.* A mass of city people was raucous, chanting, and jeering wildly at the front gates of Kelson's Keep. On the barbican, Aldred saw a grand pyre. "What is going on down there?"

"Adora," Rober said. "She's lost her bloody mind. And... praise Eralis, another blood moon. The priests were saying that it's a sign of the end times."

Chanting echoed up from below. The cityfolk were ecstatic. "They're roaring down there. What is it?" Aldred asked.

Rober sunk his chin into his chest. "She's burning Sparo."

"Priest Sparo?" Aldred almost couldn't believe what he was hearing.

"Yes, Prince, and he will not be the only one to burn. Adora is trying to gain favour from Karaat to win this battle. All of the priests and any who don't renounce Eralis will burn, too. The priests of Karaat claim the second blood moon is a sign that Karaat is rising."

The people have lost faith in their god... "What is this?"

"Esterbraun is at the gates with twenty thousand or more," Rober said. He was smiling now, as if he knew it all sounded unbelievable. "I'm not sure how long we can hold them if reinforcements from the other rulers don't arrive. You should really consider leaving, Prince. This is your warning. I've always cared for you, your mother was a good person, I loved her dearly, Aldred, and I see her in you. Get out of here. Take your family's coin and go—get a ship across the Old Sea. This life is not for you. It will tear you down like it has the rest of us."

Aldred considered that. *You could go.*

"*No, child,*" Roqeda intruded. "*If you stay you will be a god. You will have the knowledge of all the worlds at your grasp. I will make you undeniable.*"

Aldred smiled. In the mirror he saw the crooked, mad kind of smile it was, but he held it just the same because it was *his* smile. Not the twisted thing inside of him. *I will go.* He thought and it felt so good. *Be the author of your own story. Just be* you.

"Kallahorn," Aldred said.

"What?" Rober answered.

"Kallahorn. That's where Kelson retreated to. There is a library there, I've heard. Kelson moved his books there."

"The whole continent is at war," Rober said. "Ayeland is at war with itself, the north is in shambles. Find passage to Edura, Aldred. You will be safe there."

"No," Aldred said. "No, that's not where this ends. Nowhere is safe. Not now." He held the books Dustey had procured for him. *Necromanse. Nekk-row. Roqeda's using you for the spells in these books. He's using you...*

"Stop it, child, that is nonsense. Do not doubt me," Roqeda thundered.

You will gain from the spells in these books, not me. No. I can feel it. They will destroy me. Suddenly, Aldred knew what he had to do. He was going to be the author of his own story. He gathered his knife. "Thank you for this warning, Rober."

"Don't linger here, Aldred," Rober said.

"I won't." Aldred hurried out of his room.

He wound his way down the tower stairs and stopped at a window to view the city. It was engulfed in flames and shrouded in blood-light. All four quarters of Hest were alight from somewhere. *Four thousand three hundred and sixty one days,* Aldred thought. *That is how long it took the city to fall after you died, Mother...*

People moved around like flies and many didn't move at all. The screams were scarcely heard over the flames gorging on the fresh air. Great black towers of smoke rose from the city, making all of the world look like a palace with basalt pillars. The pyre was burning now, too. The High Priest, and soon, every other priest in Hest, would burn.

What kind of Hell did you fall into? Aldred wished so bad that he could bring back what was—that he could change the past. *But the dead should stay dead. Their voices live on in books, and that is enough. But you can break away from this name—this family.*

Aldred carried on down the tower steps and made his way through the tunnels to Dustey's lab. He waded through the swarms of rats evading the fiery city streets and winded around dozens of corners—*so many cor-*

ners—until, at last, he came to the large circular sprucewood door carved with old runes. *Dragon runes,* Dustey had called them.

Aldred shivered. He opened the door without knocking and the bone-man didn't even flinch. He was nose deep in an old text, a flickering candle the only light. "It's over, Dustey, we need to leave." The ground was sticky wet.

"Over?" Dustey grinned. "No, no. It has just begun."

"Come on." Aldred rummaged through Dustey's shelves, his feet sticking to the ground. "What did you spill here, Boneman? This isn't Yehvenki blaze, is it?"

"No," Dustey said. "What are you doing, Aldred?" The witch-priest stood up, still holding the old book.

Aldred grabbed a wineskin of Yehvenki blaze. A stench struck him. *Bodies?* "Help me with this. Grab more."

"Aldred!" Dustey said. His face was malignant. "You take what you want, but I'm not going."

Aldred hadn't even considered that the boneman might not want to come with him. *Alone. You're going alone.* "What do you mean?" Aldred said. "Dustey, I'm going to kill her. I'm going to kill Adora."

"Good." Dustey was still straight-faced. "Aldred. When you finish with that, you get far away from here, okay?"

Now Aldred began to sweat. His chest felt loaded with stones. *What is this?* His feet were sticky.

Sticky with... *no.*

Aldred looked at the book Dustey was holding. *The Dragon Peoples.* "What's going on here?" Aldred looked all around the dark room.

Books on books on books. Leatherbound, paperbound, papyrus scrolls, hide coverings. Bottles. Mortar and pestle. Tincture jars and herbs hanging, and bowls oozing pungent jellies. Blood. Blood on the floor. And, *praise Eralis,* bodies. In the corner. *How many? Leaking, leaking... blood.*

"What are you doing, Dustey? What is all this?" *Five, six, seveneightnine piled up. I'm standing in their blood.*

"Here." Dustey offered Aldred a key. "It's your mom's library key. I needed to borrow it."

Aldred looked at his key ring. There was another key on there that looked identical, but now that Aldred eyed it closer, he realized it was a fake. *He stole it from you...* "What have you been doing, Boneman?" Aldred felt a lion roaring inside of him.

Dustey smiled, his teeth stark white against his blood-red skin. "I've been called to something higher, Aldred. Roqeda has guided me, and I found it—Kelson's secret. I found the dragon husk, in the tunnels directly below us. The tunnels open up into a glorious cavern and there it lies. Eternal beauty awaiting a reawakening."

"How?" Aldred remembered a passage somewhere in Kelson's journals that mentioned a dragon husk. He couldn't resist his own curiosity.

"Kelson knew of it, and others, too," Dustey said. "Kelson became obsessed with Insa Rolin near the end, you know? I would kill to see what kind of books are sleeping below Kallahorn. And whatever else is down there, too," Dustey said.

Aldred saw the other books spewed across Dustey's desk. *Necromanse. Necromantis. The Truth.* All by Insa Rolin. Insa Rolin. *Insa Rolin...* "It was you from the very beginning. The Army of Truth... you planned all of this? You put this *thing* inside of me."

Dustey laughed. "Not just me, Dre. Roqeda has guided me every step of the way—in dreams I speak to him. It was He who formed the Army of Truth years ago, I just simply showed up and gave their priest, Miri, the necessary spell from our library."

Aldred unsheathed *Phantom* and held it to Dustey's face. "Why shouldn't I kill you right now?"

"It was for a purpose, Dre, a grand purpose."

"Don't you call me that." Aldred pressed *Phantom's* tip into Dustey's cheek to make him sprout a red blossom of blood. "What are you going to do with that dragon husk?" Aldred nodded at the books. "You were testing this on me, weren't you? This *necromanse?*"

"I didn't think it would actually work. I just wanted to test it before I used the spell on myself. Just like you, Dre—"

"Don't you call me that, Boneman." Aldred pressed *Phantom* to Dustey's other cheek now. It made him angry how unafraid Dustey was.

"Just like you, Aldred, I want to be the author of my own story. I'm of Draku blood. It wasn't a coincidence that I met a priest with *this* book. Insa Rolin's masterpiece. His final work before he Ascended. *The Necro.* Eternal life." Dustey beheld the book in his hands. Admired it like a baby. "These are all copies of copies—translations of translations, but I've taken what I needed to decipher it all. I have." Dustey was clenching both fists in the air. "I did nothing but coax you along, allow you to discover yourself through this curse, and learn from you along the way. I kept you safe. Now I can use what I've learned and bring back what was lost, Aldred. I can help to bring back the Draku, our culture, our beliefs, our mythology. Our *dragons...*

"This Esterbraun is the closest thing I've had to a proper ruler in the time I've been on this earth. And Aldred, I'm going to wake the dragon husk for him. Haha!" Dustey began to laugh. His malevolence faded into a twisted sort of happiness. "Give me the curse, Aldred, I know you don't want it anymore. I see what it's done to you. I see it in your face, your eyes. Give me the power, Aldred, it's right here, just stand right here. I've been working on something even better, just for you."

Aldred glared at Dustey. *Praise Eralis.* Aldred's gut twisted—it all connected. *The blood, the bodies, the blood moon. He's going to bloody kill you.* "No," Aldred choked out. He felt like he was going to shit himself.

"What other choice do you have?" Dustey said. "To let Him slowly take over while you resist the true power He could provide?"

"Give me to him, child." Roqeda was a tempest. *"Or I will fucking kill you, too."*

What?

"Be rid of me," Roqeda thundered.

"The spell is so beautiful, Aldred," Dustey said. "It will fill the world with magics when it is sung."

"Sung?" Aldred lowered *Phantom*.

"A sweet ballad of dragon rising; golden like the sun from the burning red sky, it will rise, Aldred. Just stand right there. Let me do the rest." Dustey pulled out a long wooden straw, and by the time Aldred realized the boneman was going to shoot a dart at him, the dart had already struck. It was warm at the point it pierced flesh, and all at once Aldred couldn't move.

"This is madness, Boneman, what have you done?"

"It's a time of madness, Aldred, and I've told you before, my name is Dustey," the boneman said. "There are thousands and more dead in the streets. Hundreds dead in the castle now that Adora has started her purge. There is enough hot blood around us to bring black magics to life." He took a deep breath and sang, "*Akovha Liet Neia.*"

Aldred felt something happening; his blood was bubbling.

"*Akovha Liet Neia,*" Dustey sang, and pulled out the eldritch green knife that Aldred had killed the priest in the desert with. *The knife of Albalalsami.* Aldred's stomach twisted into a knot. Suddenly Aldred couldn't move, his body was seized by unseen magics that flowed through his blood. *He's going to kill you. Praise Eralis he's going to bloody kill you.*

Dustey thrust the knife at the left side of Aldred's chest, and the last thing Aldred saw were the runes on that twisted green knife blade glinting in the candlelight.

ALDRED OPENED HIS EYES.

The white teeth, red face, and bone-white hair of Dustey was overwhelmingly there. "Yes," said Dustey, "it worked. Drink this." The boneman thrust a wineskin at Aldred.

Aldred drank. It was wine. He took a deep breath. He was lying shirtless on the boneman's table. Wares and odds scattered all around him.

"How do you feel?" Dustey said, still smiling widely.

"What?" Aldred looked down; his chest was bandaged. His skin was blood-stained, wiped clean with towels. "I feel... fine. What happened?" Aldred suddenly remembered a green knife. *Albalalsami.* "What did you do?"

"Gave you another chance," Dustey said. "*Resurrecti.* Now hurry, get dressed." The boneman gave Aldred a tunic and a chain shirt unmarked with heraldry. "Take your sword, the sheathe. Hurry. Do you remember what you were going to do?" Dustey said.

Aldred remembered blood. He remembered... he strangely remembered very little. He felt incredibly cold. He looked at his arms and hands—milky blue. *The library. The books.* "I'm going to kill her," Aldred said.

Dustey smiled. "You were always fearless, Aldred, for that I respect you. Here, take this before you go." Dustey produced a brass key and opened the gold latches on a cedarwood chest beside him. With both hands, he pulled out a strange looking bow. "Lovasi made. Tee-bow they called it. That thing will take the head off of a person. It's faster even than magics, that."

Aldred took the bow—put his hands around it.

"Ah, be careful. That button there will trigger it. Be careful, it's loaded," Dustey said, "Take it. Go. Kill her. End this." The boneman's eyes were twitching.

Aldred strapped the bow to his back and left.

Through Kelson's Keep he ran towards the tower. Wall sconces flickered in the night and cast Aldred's long shadow in the white stone before him. *Alone. You're going alone...*

He ran and *Phantom* slapped his leg with each stride, and for the first time in so many years, he felt sure of something—*I'll kill her.* He noticed the stars, and by the stars—*the blood moon.* Suddenly, Aldred remembered Roqeda. The blood, bodies. The knife. He looked at his hands, clammy white. *What is this?*

In the courtyard, it was madness. A massive, ripping fire marked the centre, where the Lion's Oak once grew, and Aldred could see the blackened wick of the great tree through the flames. People everywhere, jostling about and screaming. Scared. Panicked. Hands reached for Aldred as he made his way through the throng.

"What are you going to do about this?" a man with hands like bear paws grabbed Aldred by his chainmail and shook him. "Do something, man!" The man threw Aldred to the ground and disappeared into the crowd. In a normal time, that man would be hanged for laying hands on a prince. *Nobody recognizes you anymore...* Aldred hated to admit it, but he knew it was true. He had seen his reflection, though he had been avoiding it, and he knew what kind of blight had befallen him. He looked like a mongrel, a leper. And now he looked even worse.

Aldred brought himself to his feet.

"Take it, man!" A woman thrust a wineskin into Aldred's chest and staggered away. It smelled like leather tanning oil. Aldred tossed it.

The blood moon boiled him as he moved through the courtyard. He climbed the stairs to the throne room. Its magnificent black slate ceiling sloping at an impossible angle up to that bleeding sky.

Adora. She's in there. I know she's in there. She had been the root of all his pain. It was Adora who first cursed Aldred's name after his mother's death. It was *her* who put the idea that it could possibly be Aldred's fault. *She has taken everything from you.*

Aldred wept. *Alone. You're going alone.* And this time it didn't scare him. He was the author of his own story and it didn't end here. *No, no it's just beginning.* The boneman's words echoed in his ear. *You're the blood of the Lion. You can be great.*

I'll fucking kill her. Aldred knew he would kill Adora. He would or he would die trying.

He stood just outside the throne room doors, holding the bow in his hands. His chest was still oozing thick blood from where the boneman stabbed him; he felt dizzy—he felt different. *Empty?* Aldred walked in slowly. No one stopped him. There was no sign of funeral, no signs of William.

A strange sucking sound echoed off the high ceiling. *God...* Aldred put his hand to his mouth. *Oh my god...*

There was Adora, squat like a toad over King John's dead, blue body. Her long fingers were prodding his open skull until she pulled out a small, pink piece of brain and held it between her fingers to admire before placing it in her mouth. *What is this? What the fuck is this?*

Aldred tried not to make a sound. *Karaat, illumine in me what is dark.* Aldred remembered Dustey's words. *Write your own story, Dre.* He felt the weight of the trigger on the tip of his finger.

Adora, still squat on her calves, turned suddenly and saw Aldred. She stood and hissed like a rabid beast.

Whipp. Aldred pulled the trigger, the tee-bow stock lunged into Aldred's shoulder, and in the blink of his eye, Adora's face went blank. Horror seeped from her bulging eyeballs, and then she was screaming. A beam of light shot from her mouth as she screamed a Word and crumbled a portion of the ceiling. She fell to her knees, bolt protruding from her chest, and she tried to scream again but only gurgled and choked. Aldred watched her skin turn blue then grey. *What sorcery has the boneman summoned? A poison arrow?*

Aldred watched the skin on Adora's face contract and tighten up until it squeezed the life right out of her eyes. Her hair turned grey, then withered, and fell out. She writhed on the ground and Aldred could only see his mother. *Bones. She was bones. Living bones...*

Aldred unsheathed *Phantom.* Adora was a decrepit thing, fetal on the ground. Her chest heaving. *The Warlocks were strange creatures. They are holding on to something long dead—like you.*

With one clean swing, one his father would be proud of, Aldred took Adora's head off. *A mercy, by god.* When it toppled to the ground, black blood oozed out of her, and the stench was like stagnant water.

Aldred stood over Adora's dead body and shook his head. *Don't become this. Don't ever become this...* he felt sick. *You should have killed that boneman.*

Aldred looked at his arms, his hands. *Cold blue.* What are you? He couldn't bring himself to think deeply on the things Dustey must have been up to in that lab. *I'm going to wake the dragon husk, Dre,* the boneman had told him. *By god, is this world lost?*

Aldred couldn't help but think someone like Angelico or Benecio could save this world. *Someone like you...* he felt the wound on his chest. *But what are you?*

Aldred brought himself to look at his father's body. He was almost surprised when he felt no sadness. *You should have protected me. You should have done your duty as a father but you failed. You blamed me for the death of the person I loved most dearly in this world, as if it didn't tear my heart into pieces. You were a selfish prick. A fucking asshole and you deserve death. But by god, I wish I could have seen your face when this castle falls. I wish I could have watched you fall from your place of hubris and be humbled.*

Aldred saw purple light flickering from outside. Someone had gotten ahold of the Yehvenki blaze. He ran. *Alone. You'll go at it alone.* Folk were scrambling, panicking, crowding. A choir of screams held, and violence broke out amongst the courtyard. Things were burning now; folk were killing each other. *They got in... the rioters got through the Keep gates.* Aldred kept close to the walls and slinked in the shadows. And the folk burned and burned. *They'll burn it all. Why is it we get so much joy in burning the things we don't understand?*

In the stables, Aldred packed a horse and unhitched her. He rubbed her muzzle and put his foot in the stirrup.

Hands around his face and neck stopped Aldred from trying to mount. The cold steel of a blade touched his throat. Then, hot breath in his ear.

"I'm coming with you," the voice said. His dirt-smeared hand covered Aldred's mouth so he couldn't make a sound. It tasted like soot and leather. "You'll take me where I want to go, you hear?" Aldred knew that voice. He knew if he made a sound, the cold steel would warm with Aldred's own blood. "Don't make a sound or I'll kill you, nephew. You don't think I'd kill you in a second if you make a sound? You keep your little mouth tight now, okay? I'm coming with you. Getting out of here. The two of us, okay? By the gods your skin is cold, kid."

Brooton loosed his grip and Aldred squirmed away. Brooton held a sword out, threatening Aldred if he made a sound, but Aldred made no sound. Then he noticed the sword. Black Daggland steel.

"Is that—"

"*Saynomore.* Your father won't be needing it anymore. Best keep it in the family."

"Get a horse," Aldred said. "I've got provisions for a three-day ride for one, but the two of us can probably stretch it out for just as long."

"You've got coin?" Brooton asked.

"Some," Aldred said. "But I fear coin won't be of much use if the war is as bad as these riots." It was then Aldred realized Brooton wasn't even in armour. He was in a threadbare tunic and trousers with simple leather boots. *Where have you been, Brooton? What did Adora do to you down in those dungeons? What happened to you when you led that army into the streets?* Aldred knew those were questions for later.

"We'd best hurry." Brooton's voice was betrayed by fear.

"My whole life has been leading up to this moment," Aldred said, "We're following the pilgrimage of Kelson. We're going to Kallahorn."

"Kallahorn? No," Brooton said. "We're going where I tell you we're going."

RISE OF THE DRAKU

F IRE.

The heat of it made Julien joyful. The sweat on his brow was soothing. The flames danced in the sky, and the smoke rose pigeon-grey to the black clouds above. The sky was burning purple and flashing and swaying like the very air was alive.

"This is it." Ashan pointed to a weathered rock-wall that was heavily earthed over.

Julien peeled his eyes away from Hest burning long enough to answer him. "Open it," he said, and watched the flames again. The fog had rolled away and all had turned to fire.

"Praise Karaat." Trist made the symbol of the eye on his chest. "The city has already destroyed itself."

"So it will be easy for us to take. The cityfolk will welcome a new ruler who brings order," Julien said, and Trist knew it was true so he nodded.

In the back of Julien's mind, he saw the green eyes glowing beneath the flaming rock and wood and earth of the city. *Deep down where the flames can't hurt it, that's where the green-eyed beast lives.*

Ashan and the fifty soldiers who volunteered to come on the journey worked to clear away the dirt and debris that had piled up on top of the entrance. When they were finished, Julien himself opened the cellar door. It was made of heavy black rock and carved with Lovasi runes. Trist handed Julien a torch. "Let's go then," Julien said, and walked into the dark tunnel.

The fifty others followed closely behind, and when all of them had their torches lit, they seemed like a small sun moving through the tunnel. It was neatly carved so that the rock was as smooth as river stone. Rust stains lined the wall where iron sconces once lived.

"This is madness," Trist said. "What kind of sorcery made this?" He traced his hand on the wall and Julien did the same.

The first ladder they came to was carved right into the stone, nothing more than a hundred-foot rock wall with chipped-out foot holes, straight up.

"Here?" Trist asked.

"No." Julien pointed to the map. "The third one."

They kept going, past the second ladder, and came to the third. It was the same thing. Julien looked up and gulped. He had never much liked heights. He put his hands in the rock hold and a big spider squirmed up his arm. He brushed it away, looked at Trist. "Here we go, then."

Julien climbed. One foot and one hand after the other. He didn't look down. He heard the others climbing behind him. *If you fall, you'll take the whole lot down with you.* And he knew the same was true of any of the others. But he climbed and they climbed behind him. *For all the Draku that were forced down, I climb for you. Up we rise.*

Julien carefully pushed the stone trap door up and off its track at the top of the ladder. He pulled his chin up and looked around. The trap door wasn't a door at all but a tile in the slate floor. Julien saw stone walls, windows. He saw wooden crates piled up and barrels, standing or tipped on their side. He saw ropes and chains hanging from beams and on the ground in coiled bundles. He pulled his whole body up and out, then helped Trist who was right behind him.

Julien walked over and looked out one of the windows. It was the city of Hest.

"There." Trist pointed to the ropes and chains. "This is the gatehouse, Aldred. That is the front gate."

"Where is everyone?"

"They're here. Be quiet."

Slowly the fifty seeped up and out of the hole like ants. Aldred smelled the smoke, he heard the screaming, the dogs barking, children crying. *How could they possibly imagine it could get worse than this?* Julien felt awful, but it was about to. *Suffering is only temporary. It will be worth it for the generations of peace that follow.* "Your son won't let us down?" Julien said. Trist had left his son, Coran, in charge of the main army with orders to attack full-on when he saw the gates open. Julien had given them all the order not to harm a soul who wasn't trying to harm them. They were saviours here, not conquerors.

"I would trust no one else," Trist said.

Julien looked at his crew and around at the tower he had found himself in. A strange mess of chains and ropes and barrels. "We're going to kill every single person in this tower who tries to stop us, and we're going to open the gate," Julien said. He raised his dragonbone, which he had decided to use as a sword of sorts. "That's it. If it's the last thing we do, it will be the most important single moment of this campaign. If it's the last thing we do, we will always be remembered. The bards and the singers will write songs about this year for generations to come. But not if we lose. No. Not if we fail. So not only do your lives depend on this, but your memory, too. Will you fade to dust, or will you dance on the songs of time?"

The crew roared, and Julien knew that was probably a mistake, so he charged. They would hear them coming now, but Julien didn't care; he was flaring with passion. His fifty dispersed amongst the halls and stairways of the tower.

Only a few breaths before Julien found a soldier leaning against a wall. The soldier screamed when he saw Julien coming, and Julien clubbed him down and turned him to ash with his dragonbone. Two more came and Julien turned them to ash, too. Suddenly, he felt all powerful. *Like Kassius, like Karaat, like Kelson.*

Then the chains rattled and the ropes swayed, and Julien heard the grinding of steel on steel.

"Raise!" Folk were shouting—his folk. Julien saw the big, black grate rising into the tower like it was being swallowed by some great beast and he was in the belly of it.

From the south-facing windows, Julien saw his rabble. Flowing, funnelling towards the gate like it was a great big drain and they were water. On Trist's face Julien witnessed a mad grin as he watched the gate rise. Trist raised his arms in the air. "You're a bloody mad fool, Julien. Praise Karaat. Only a mad fool could pull this off."

As the army flowed in through the gates below Julien's feet, they were met with very little resistance. They entered. They slaughtered any who opposed them. Most cheered for them. And welcomed them.

Littered through the streets Julien saw Hester armour. Chestplates, helms, gauntlets all carved with lions, discarded. Purple cloaks lay in heaps. *The army gave up. They don't want to be recognized as soldiers...*

Julien slinked out of the tower and mingled with the crowd. *Darkness. This is darkness.* The blood moon burned the sky red. Julien had not seen darker things. War, he learned, was more than battle.

Naked, bleeding, dying folk rambled through the streets and in the corners and alleyways and on rooftops. *The city was in ruin before we even got here.* Stray animals bleating, screams sharp enough to cut, smells rank enough to curdle blood, Julien waded through the sickness of it. He moved like a turd in a sewer towards the burning palace of Kelson's Keep. Purple flames and red twirled like ribbons against the bright blue sky of day. And in his mind, *green* eyes burned him.

Trist was gone. Ashan was gone. Julien moved alone through the cesspit called Hest. A couple of folk, scared and desperate, lashed out at him, and he clubbed them down into ash with his dragonbone. A knight wearing a cloak of purple holding the limp body of a woman saw Julien walking and slinked into an alleyway to avoid him.

Julien opened Aldred's map and found his way to a large fountain. Around the fountain, statues of the Warlocks stood erected in a circle, watching over the fountain. Eralis stood out from the rest, holding the fountain with outstretched arms that formed a bridge over the small streams that flowed out from the fountain. Below the fountain was a small crevice. In the crevice was a small wooden door that Julien had to crawl through, holding his torch in front of him. The small door opened up into a tight, cave-like tunnel.

Julien traced his way through the tunnel, fading torch in one hand, Aldred's map in the other. *How many have used these tunnels? For ill or for better? How many Draku have crawled around down here?* The tunnels were a labyrinthine maze, with offshoot tunnels and dead ends every couple of feet. The map traced the way, and Julien followed it closely. *This alone is madness. If this map was false, I'd die down here—perhaps* that *was Aldred's plan.*

Julien emerged in a small stable facing the courtyard on the inside of Kelson's Keep. The heat from the surrounding flames was seeping in now. The sound of the flames ripping was incredible. He walked out into the courtyard and the ashes fell like snow around him. Julien spread his arms. *I've done it, Mother, Grandpa. I've conquered the ashes of Hest.*

The throne room was before him. Towers rose up around it and halls ran adjacent to it, so Julien couldn't be sure of which building was the library. But half of them were on fire, and the purple flames were licking fiercely at the rest. *Yehvenki blaze...* Julien had seen the stuff, but never on this scale.

Julien climbed the steps to the throne room and walked in the gaping wide doors. He was drawn to the sparks of green, flashes of orange. He was soothed by a strange humming, a gentle song. The entrance hall to the throne room opened up to the dais chamber, and the ceilings fell up into the sky. And there, in the middle of a room as big as a village, a man stood with his arms raised. His bone-white hair was rattling, his green eyes fiercely glaring at the limp dead bodies in front of him. A crown on his head.

"What is this?" Julien shouted. The man turned around. He looked like a man from the Bone Isles.

The man didn't respond, he continued chanting. Julien walked closer. Suddenly the dead bodies began to writhe. Their skin was white like maggots and they twitched like them too. Then they rose clumsily to their knees before fully erecting and standing tall. Dead blue eyes glared hauntingly at Julien.

Julien pulled out his dragonbone. "What is this?" he shouted again. This time he walked into view of the boneman.

"Ah!" The boneman lowered his arms. The dead things swayed before him. "You're just in time, Julien! I've been waiting for you."

Julien looked at the wights, at the man from the Bone Isles, his teak-wood skin and bone-white, dreadlocked hair, and—*green eyes*. "Waiting? Who are you?"

The boneman sang a Word and the dead bodies dropped limply to the ground. "My name is Dustey, that is all. I have no family name. Not yet."

"Not yet? I don't bargain, Dustey, not now." Julien looked at the throne.

"Take it," Dustey said. "I won't stop you."

"It's a symbolic sort of thing." Julien walked to the Lion's Throne and sat his ass on the purple down-filled cushion. He gripped the ebon handles and ran his fingers up the smooth heads of roaring lions carved into each arm. He admired the fierceness of the tapestries on the walls, Giy'er slain by Lion Knights, and krakens, and draykes. *But no dragons.* Julien admired the purple flames dancing in the blue sky. *Why is destruction so beautiful?* The flames were spreading.

Dustey held out the lion's crown. "Take it," he said. It was crusted with purple diamonds and shaped like a roaring lion's head.

Julien took it, admired the sparkle, and threw it to the ground.

Suddenly, the great tapestry on the ceiling that depicted Gavyn Hester killing Tullia, the last Lovasi queen, bubbled, and in an instant burst into flame. Hot slate rock fell to the ground, and the stars above shone down angrily upon the wreckage.

"I came for books," Julien said. "I came for the library, not this throne." He stood up and walked through the smoking ruins of the throne room to leave.

"The library is on fire, the books here are gone, but they were only copies, mostly, of the originals. The originals remain in Kallahorn."

"Kallahorn?" Julien said. "In the north?"

"Yes, in the north. But it is what is below the library that is important. What is below will help you take whatever you want in this world, for our people—for the Draku."

Julien suddenly realized the boneman was Draku. *Of course he is, the Bone Isles were one of our native homes.* The whole ceiling had burst into flame now. Beams fell from the roof. The walls engulfed; oil paint dripped from the many paintings. "Show me," said Julien. "What is below?"

Julien hurried out of the throne room behind the boneman. The roof above the throne caved in and crushed the old Lion's Throne. The hearth that had been kept alive for so many years was still burning, but it was cracked and demolished from the roof falling on it. Just as Julien broke into the courtyard, the barrels of lamp oil started to explode behind him. Purple flames roared above. Julien coughed from the smoke, fell to his knees.

"This way, hurry." Dustey helped him up. "Below the library. Down, down."

Julien was led through a door that opened onto a steep stone staircase. Dustey lit a torch from the one burning at the top of the stairs and started down. Julien followed closely behind. *What are you doing? Going to get yourself killed. You've come all this way, what are you doing?* But something told Julien he was going the right way. *Into the belly of the beast, Jules, don't be afraid.* His grandpa's words rang fondly in his ear. *You're going to bring back the Draku. You're going to bring back a thousand years of dead culture.*

But Julien knew his work wasn't done yet. *Not yet.* He knew when and where he was going to die, and it wasn't here, and it wasn't now. *Not until the falling star is burning up the sky above. Not until you can see the sky coming down will you die. And those green eyes will be the last thing you see. The green eyes of—*

"A dragon," Dustey said. "The husk of the great dragon, *Ermegal*."

And before him was just that. In a gaping scissure of rock lay a mountainous creature-shaped stone. Mushrooms and moss grew around stagnant pools resting in the crevices of the creature's body. "Who knows this is here?"

"Some," Dustey said. "The rulers know. They don't care. They don't understand the world."

Don't care? No wonder this kingdom was falling. They had lost touch with empathy. Amongst other things. Julien studied the cavern he was in. Stone statues lined the walls. *Kassius... Kassius stood right here...*

Fountains and pools and cabanas of marble filled the open spaces. Chairs and beds and chimney stoves. *People lived here once.* And in the middle of it all lay the husk of a dragon. "How long?" Julien asked. "Has it been here?"

"Longer than the Hesters," Dustey said. He led Julien closer to the thing. "Longer even than Kelson."

Julien reached out and touched the scaly stone thing. It was as cold as ice. *If there is one, how many more could there be?* It was fire that killed Julien in his dreams. *A song of fire will be your last ballad.* "I'm going to wake her."

"What are you?" Julien's heart thumped in his chest.

The boneman smiled. "Necromancer," he said.

Julien noticed Dustey was clutching a book close to his chest. "Do it then."

"I don't know what will happen," the boneman said. Julien saw not a trace of fear in those emerald-green eyes. For a moment he had a horrible thought. *It's* those *eyes that will be the last thing you see. Those...* "This dragon could raise Hell along with it."

"Raise it then." Julien unsheathed his bone and held it towards Dustey as a threat. There was no going back now.

The boneman twisted a sardonic grin and opened his book. Softly, he began to sing. His voice was deep and rhythmic, radiant. His tones were enchanting. Euphoric. His song was so serene that Julien felt rapturous joy flare up inside of him. He was alight with the flame of destiny. In him burned the lives of a thousand thousand dead and forgotten Draku. In him burned the fire and pain of a hundred hundred generations that were torn to shreds and tossed to the wind to smoulder and burn out.

The boneman's song got louder, and Julien's fire got brighter. *Yes, Karaat. I am here, Karaat, I have followed your every word. Now show me my destiny.*

Like a thunderclap, the stone eyelids of the sleeping beast flicked open. Burning green eyes, like a marshy sun, glared out at a world that had been swollen by centuries.

The boneman went silent. He clutched his book tightly. Sweat dripped from his brow. He breathed in heavy succession. His song still echoed far off in the cavernous dark.

The black slits in the centre of the dragon's eyes widened like great chasms. It cracked its stone neck to one side, and all of earth seemed to moan. It grinded its neck to the other side and saw Julien. The haunting green eyes pierced him like lightning bolts—the great black slits were windows to Hell.

Praise Karaat.

The beast stood and heat wafted off its dead body. Sticky, sulphurous saliva hung from its wicked jaw.

Is it dead?

The beast roared.

THE OLD ONE

E TTA WATCHED HER GRANDSON play.

She sat by a small fire and smoked chuff with Pike and with Calum. It had taken three days for her to stop shivering. Young Swey had stopped after only a day, and now he was already running about.

Nettle stewed mint tea on the fire in a pot. She stirred it with her ladle. She sniffed the smells. It was the first Rise of winter, Deepwinter, the Feldarra called it, and the first snow had just begun to fall. It hung on the pine boughs and on the thatched roofs and in the hair of young Swey and the other children. The valley of Elwyd was long and full of folk, and the children played in and amongst the wooden shacks and cook fires. Smoke hung like a grey-black chain from the clouds into the great forges that billowed day and night. All day, there was the din of hammers cranking, and horses rearing, and swords crashing against shields in practice ringing out and mingling with the children's laughter. And they still laughed despite the people they had lost recently. Children had a way of finding laughter—or it finds them.

But Swey didn't laugh. He didn't smile. He had barely survived, and since he opened his eyes, he was melancholic. Though he ran about, he looked deflated, like the joy had been lost in him. *The boy inside of him died and now he sees only a man's world. He's seen the darkness and it's crowding his light.*

Etta remembered the days and months after she had pulled herself out of the river when she was a girl. *They were hard days and hard nights, and you spent most of them in tears. You were terrified to leave your childhood behind. You mourned it. Terrified of what the world truly was. But your parents made you face it and you came out strong. Right? You're strong, aren't you?* This poor boy's earliest memories are of war and terror, and he had done nothing but run in all that time.

Fiora came and sat by the fire with her wolf. The big grey wolf licked Etta's hand and tried to jump up on her. "Down," Fiora said, and to Etta, "They'll be ready to march come spring."

Etta glared out at the valley and back at Fiora. *And will you be with them, Etta?*

Pike had come trailing into the camp hours after Etta and Swey had arrived. He was wet and shivering much the same as she was. Etta couldn't stop herself from breaking down when she saw the old warrior slinking in by the fire covered in furs.

"By the gods, Pike, I thought death had caught you," Etta had sobbed.

"Not yet, Wulf, not yet."

"Baerd?" Etta had asked, not knowing what answer she hoped for.

Pike had only shaken his head.

"Right," Etta said to Fiora, hardly able to believe another year had slipped away. "Spring."

Not far behind Fiora was Annie. "Ahh, the Kihl'dor Who Saved the World," she said, feeling for her seat. Fiora's wolf helped her find it.

"I'm no kihl'dor," Etta spat. She had a bad taste in her mouth.

"Of course not, no," said Annie. "Regardless. He has asked to see you. On Deepwinter, too, imagine that."

"He?"

"Him. Bazal."

Etta thought of Sweyne. He was supposed to be the one to bring her to this Bazal. *Do you still live?* He was a stubborn bastard in that way. She hated him more than anything, but she couldn't help but think of him often.

"Love and hate are two sides of the same axe, Wulf. One for each, and a sharp and deadly blade separates them," Sweyne had said to her. And maybe it was true. She hated him but she loved him once, too. Both made her flare up with passion. Both made her obsessed with him. For too long she was obsessed.

"What does he want?" Etta asked.

"To talk," Annie said, her pale eyes wide. "That is all I know. He is awake now. But not for long."

Etta had been dragged through Hell and somehow still lived. Somehow, folk still looked to her for answers, for guidance. *How do you tell them that you are a failure? A kin-slayer? Worse, what happens when they find out how much of a coward you are?* But Sweyne had told her that this was her destiny—to lead the si'darra and fight Nature's last battle. But she couldn't fight. Not anymore. She was Etta now and she couldn't fight. *But you can lead. You can lead without an axe. You can move on, and you can make good with the world.*

Etta had sworn to herself when the world died last year that she wouldn't get involved with the games of gods, and here she was about to talk to one. *But things change—people change. By the gods, even that bastard son of a bitch Sweyne changed in the end. Would it be so hard to change, too?* Etta reckoned one day she'd look at her underself and everything would feel alright. She would be able to bear it—looking upon her own face. She had to. For young Swey. For Tara.

She stood. "Well, let's get on with it then," she said.

Fiora smiled. "Aye," she said, "let's get on with it."

{F}ROM ITS SOURCE, A river trickled down the mountain, sometimes fast and white and loud and sometimes slow and blue and soft, and at the mouth of the valley, on the north side where the si'darra made their camp, the rocks were tall and thick, and the water fell like thunder there and crashed into a pool below, where it continued to flow through the valley.

"Behind the falls," Annie said, "there is a cave. Bazal sleeps there."

"He sleeps *there?* In the cave?"

"Aye."

"How long has he been here?"

"He came around the time the world died last year."

"And he's slept there ever since?"

"Aye, sometimes for weeks at a time."

"You think he's really sleeping?"

"By the gods, I don't know."

"What does he eat?"

"He doesn't ask for any fare."

"By the gods," Etta said.

"Aye," Fiora said. "I haven't been inside there before. Mom and Bazal only appointed me after—"

"Aye," Etta said. "Since Baerd died."

"I'm sorry," Fiora said. "I know—"

"He deserved it," Etta said. "Nothing for sorry."

Fiora studied Etta like she was looking for something in her eyes—some lesson. "You really hated him, eh?"

"Hate and love are two sides of the same axe, Fiora," Etta said. "Some good folk turn rotten and some bad folk turn clean. Sometimes a person sinks that axe in too deep on one side and they can't get all the way back over, no matter how hard they try. I've loved him more than the gods, and

I've hated him thrice times that. And in the end the fucker still saved our grandson. If you had asked me last year if I hated Sweyne, I wouldn't have blinked a damn eye before telling you I fucking hate him with all of my being. But now? I don't even know. But I can tell you I'm glad he's dead. For whatever that's worth. I'm glad he's gone and out of my life." *I hope he's with Braden. By the gods I hope they find peace together.*

Like rolling thunder, water fell, and as Etta got closer, she could hardly hear herself think. A winding rock path crusted with lichen led to the waterfall and behind it. The stone was slick and slimy beneath the falls so that Etta had to grip the rockface and be careful with each step. Water dripped from the cave roof into stagnant puddles on the ground; Etta avoided her underself in them and kept forth.

With a small torch of ruddy flame, Fiora led Etta deeper and deeper until the roaring, thunderous sound of the falls faded to a mere whispering breeze in the background.

Deep deep. Etta hated being so far from the sky. Suddenly, a horrid thought seized her. "Is he... *Human?*"

"Something like that. On the outside, anyway."

The tunnel narrowed so that Etta and Fiora walked in a straight line, the crusted earth and rock walls cut into Etta's arms and shoulders as they squeezed through the narrow passage. "What is this?" Etta complained.

"He's just on the other side, come on," Fiora said, and dropped the torch. Etta's heart ceased to beat at the thought of that torch going out and the dark closing in around her in that narrow passage. The torch landed flat on its side with a thump, and the flame flickered and waved but didn't waver, and Fiora snatched it up.

The passage opened up slowly and then all at once into a wide cavern. A fire flamed on the shore of a great black crevice off to one side. Its low light revealed towers of rock and of earth hanging from the roof and jutting up from the unseen ground like the teeth of some great beast. On and on the teeth went until they faded into nothing.

And at the fire sat a lone man.

Etta stood at the edge of this great cavern looking at the man, and then looking at Fiora, she said, "Is that him?"

"Aye." Fiora reached to pet her wolf, but her wolf wasn't there, and Etta saw the worry in her eyes even in the darkness. "You must approach alone."

"Alone?"

"That was the request," Fiora said.

Etta didn't like the idea of coming through all the shite she'd been through and then getting her arse killed by some strange figure in a cave. *A wizard's cave, innit?* She laughed to herself. Somehow, she laughed to herself. *You're in a bloody wizard's cave. The next thing you know, you'll have the Axe of the Moon.* "Right then," Etta said. Fiora gave the old northern sign for luck and Etta returned it.

"I'll wait for you," Fiora said, snubbing the torch to save it for the return.

Etta walked into the flickering low light, deeper into the great beast's mouth, towards the solitary figure crouching by the fire.

The way seemed to drag on, just Etta and the sound of her footsteps. The nagging thoughts of Braden, of Gen, and now even Sweyne chiselled his way in. She couldn't stand it, so instead of the dead and her mistakes, she thought of the living and what she had accomplished. Young Swey and Tara lived. A grandson and a daughterbound. She thought of her life. *What's it been for? You spent a decade trying to kill a man who gave you a decade of happiness. You've spent your whole life fighting yourself and never aspired to something more than fulfilling your own vengeance.*

Only a few steps away from the decrepit man, and he still hadn't acknowledged Etta. She kept on and stood by the fire, not saying anything, but watching.

Bazal was a miserable looking thing. His skin was white as smoke. His eyes bulged, all black, and two thin holes on his face marked the spot where a nose might have been once. His face looked like a skull. Over his shoulders, a filthy cloak of greasy rank wool hung like a near-dead leaf clinging to a bare autumn bough.

"I took this body from a wretched creature," he finally said. His voice was like rock grinding. "A moleman living in the hills here. He was so feral and rabid it took me weeks to gain my thoughts back from whatever abyss that creature had banned them to. I had to work at expanding his mind slowly. He had no family and surely would have died soon from the sickness of his stomach that I have been nursing. I tried to affect the least lives while taking this body, leaving no child or spouse without their love. Taking a creature destined to die. I just needed enough time to pass this message. Enough time to explain. This plot to kill Nature has been unfolding for thousands of years, and I've been fighting, *fighting* for it since then. The Creator God Karaat and his servants will turn this world black if we can't stop them. They will kill Nature and all of her Children. But alas, I speak too much too fast. There is much to know."

"Tell me," Etta said. "I want to know."

Bazal twisted a wan grin. "Baerd said that you would be eager. Yes, and it would seem I made the right choice in finding him here."

"You found *him*."

"I found this place, and the si'darra, and Baerd was simply their leader. But from this place we found Fiora and her mother and father, Baleth and Annie Longsongs of Kallahorn. Baleth had long been curious to decipher the knowledge he had found at Kallahorn, and I knew he would the person I needed. But I couldn't have gone to Kallahorn, not with the wars and not with Adeqor freely roaming—he so badly wanted me dead after he freed me—so I needed a place to hide. Mostly from Adeqor, who had freed me from my prison only to further his own plot of becoming god. He didn't want me in the Otherworld when he arrived. So, I needed to be somewhere safe and away. We plotted. We used the magics of Yehven to wake chimeras and rock giants from the deep and to forge this valley. Then Baleth declared himself king and Calen Alder marched to Kallahorn with his Warlock, just as we had planned. Adeqor gained his powers back and used them to transfer his soul and body into the god-realm. This is all as planned. Now

Adeqor will fight and kill the gods, he will fight Karaat. And I would not count on him losing."

"By the gods," Etta said. She had no other words.

"I knew the Ailaryan Order set up fail-safes after my death. They kidnapped a Druid mage and made her into a guardian of the Gateway. They called her the Mother of Nature as a crude insult to Nature. As if to mock Her and flaunt how high above Her they *still* think they stand. It only made me all the more hungry to succeed in my plans to rid this world of them and their god Karaat. This started long, long ago. And Eralis was the key. He has given us this time to regroup."

"Eralis?" Etta knew the religion well. He was the son of the One God that the Ayelish believed in. This was getting too much for her own belief. "You talk as if you know him?"

"Eralis was my Brother in Time. He is a hero of our ages. It is because of him we have made it this far. It is because of him we survived the Starfall, the Dance in the Dust, Lindis. He had sensed that these things might occur, and he did his best to save us from them. Karaat gained his power through worship—the stronger he was, the more powerful his Words. Eralis understood that he could craft a religion powerful enough to compete with Karaat for worship and quell the power of His Words. And he did just that. He created the One Faith and wrote the doctrine himself. He devoted his life to the spread of it. But the Ailaryan Order still had far too much power. They were slipping. Adeqor and Ellorin were crafting their own plots far beyond any convention of the Old Ways or the Book of Order. So Eralis came up with his ultimate plan. He knew that if he was killed, he would be made eternal. It would be easier for folk to accept him as god if he didn't walk amongst them. That's what prophets were for, and he couldn't be his own prophet any longer. No one else could do the deed but I. So I killed Eralis and was forever damned by Humankind as a godkiller—a devil. I was locked away in the Otherworld—sacrificed. I was helpless to prevent Lindis from happening. But after it did—when Adeqor delved into the core of our earth with his magics and the Sorcerers rejected him—the dreams started."

"Dreams?"

"The Warlocks started to receive dreams of their own demise. We've been having them for three hundred years now. Dreams of a black castle, black walls, and hordes of Abori warriors come to kill us. To make us watch as they butcher our children. To make us watch as the sky falls on us, and we are exterminated for all of time. I was not exempt from these nightmares. I am still not. Sometimes now, they take hold of me for days at a time and I am forced to live in this other dream world."

"These sound like stories. Stories from the cycles of the Starfall."

"Those are not just stories, Etta, but *histories.*"

"The histories have caught up with us," Etta said.

Bazal smiled with a twisted, skull-like grin. "They quite have," he said. "Now, Eldinian has seized control of the Ailaryan Order. He's seized the throne of Ayeland, and he is preparing for war against the Abori and now the Draku. He's killing the priests of Eralis and burning the churches to strengthen Karaat. So they can fight with His Words. They are preparing for the end. And now, too, the Draku have risen on the back of a sellsword captain. And the ancient threads of war have tied themselves in a knot once again. The Draku and the Warlocks will fight each other when they should be making peace and joining their forces. And the Abori will come and destroy them both. There is something the Abori missed when they tried to exterminate the Warlocks three thousand years ago. They missed the tunnels—they underestimated the strength of them. The Gateway in particular. At the Gateway behind Kallahorn, the god-realm lies open to influence from this world. When the Creator God fell into this world at the time the sky was born, He gained power by entering the Gateway. But the Warlocks of the Ailaryan Order will want to destroy that Gateway. Forever now. Destroying the Gateway and blocking the way to the spirit world will kill Nature forever, giving way to the Creator's wildest dreams of Creation."

"The same Gateway in Kallahorn?"

"In Kallahorn. So that is where we will make our final stand. That is where we will fight the Warlocks, and the Draku, too if we have to. That is where we will endure the starfall if the Abori get so far. But the Ailaryan Order should not be underestimated. Eldinian and the remaining Warlocks will do anything to ensure victory over the Abori this time. I mean *anything*. To destroy the Gateway would be to destroy the balance of spirits and souls. The world would die again, as it did last year, but this time it would not be a fail-safe, it would be permanent. Forever destroying Nature and Her world. Where Ellorin sought to kill the world just enough for a *reset* of sorts, Eldinian would see it all erased—as if it never existed. It would be a black and desolate wasteland of a world. In that world, the Warlocks think they will rule."

"So why me? Why did you bring me here?"

"To lead this army in defence against whatever is to come. Warlocks and dragons and Hellfire are brewing, and they will verge on Kallahorn. Some for the Gateway beyond it, some for the knowledge below it, but they will verge, as they did once before, long ago. You must stop them."

"You're mad?" Etta said. "I'm no kihl'dor. I can't lead anymore."

"Etta, this is bigger than you now. Bigger than the chips on your shoulder, however big they may be. And it's more than leading an army. It's *Culdaine*."

"James? What about him?"

"Surely you know he's not normal? Surely you sensed something."

"He's a seer. I knew that."

"He's more than a seer, Etta. He's a World Walker, half-god. *Essikah* has chosen him."

"*Chosen* him?" Etta knew of the big sword; she had seen him wearing it at Rosen when they crossed paths.

"I made that sword, Etta, and I made it for one purpose. To open the Gateway, sure, but it's so much more than a key. It's forged of Godrock. It is the only Human weapon capable of killing gods. Somehow, Adeqor knew it would accept James—that it would allow him to take it. I owe Adeqor a great thanks for that, for it would have been difficult for me to find another Hendurinn—many years of watching, studying, stalking, as Adeqor did to find James. He did it for his own selfish reasons, mind, but alas, I'll take what I can get."

"So you want James to kill the gods?" Etta thought she might shite herself.

"*A* god. One. Karaat. And whatever Adeqor has become. James and James alone can end this cycle of war forever. But to get into the tunnels and beyond the doors that seal them will take work, Wulfee. Work that is not yet complete. James cannot pass through the Gateway because he needs more than just his soul to defeat Karaat—he needs his body, and more importantly, *Essikah*." Bazal squirmed in his chair and pulled his decrepit body upright. His all-black eyes were like a cold, forever nighttime and in them, Etta saw dying moons and stars falling and fading to nothing. *A dead sky. His eyes are dead skies.* "The World Walker alone is capable of making the journey, Wulfee, but without you he will never make it. I have deciphered a message, left for us by a race that must have lived here long ago. There are old magics in the tunnels below Kallahorn. Magics that will help James to Ascend, body intact, sword in hand. Three stones, keystones from the time of Old Yehven, will be required to open the door. And not only that but James needs to be willing, for not even I know what he will face beyond those doors. There is no way to know what he will experience. The magics are too old to comprehend. But it is our only chance."

Well, fuck.

"How?" Etta said.

"I have reason to believe Kelson made this very journey," Bazal said. "How? It won't be easy. It will require great work—work I have already begun, but it won't be easy. It never is."

Etta hated that answer. *Why can't it ever fucking be easy?* "You speak of Warlocks and Dragon Peoples. Kings and queens I know nothing of. Gods and Sorcerers that are only stories to me. What makes you think I will be of any help to you?"

"You have forgotten, Wulfee. You have faced so much in your life that some parts of you are hidden in darkness. You call yourself Etta, and you hide in a tiny, dark hole blocked off from everything that brought you love and joy, as well as the things that brought you pain. You have forgotten who your parents are, your brother. You are more than your vengeance. You have forgotten who *you* are. Wulfee, child of Wolton and Kerris, sister of Lars, blood of Emmer, the Mother of the Fells. It was foretold in the cycles that the sky would fall and that the Feldarra would be there. Yours is of the oldest blood that walks these lands. The blood in your veins has been kept warm by Nature for this very moment. To defend Nature in Her most dire time of need. To protect Kallahorn and give James time. To get him there in the first place."

Etta shook her head. She was at a loss.

"Oh, and Wulfee. There is one more thing. I asked Baerd to search for this in the mountains. He found it and brought it here to me. He *actually* found it. It has been waiting in the frozen cold for three thousand years. It has been waiting for *you*, Wulfee, the Mother of the Fells, blood of Emmer."

"What? What is it?" Etta had truly turned into that small girl again, curious.

The decrepit, skeleton-like creature called Bazal stirred and moved. He reached behind him and dragged out a worn brown chest. He opened it. Inside was an axe, its blade gleaming with moon-like silver. The hilt was purple black and dotted with golden stars. Runes danced through the finely folded metal like waves. "You don't have to touch it. Not yet. Not until you're ready. But take the chest. It's rightfully yours." Bazal closed the chest and sealed the latch, and gave Etta the small steel key.

Etta looked beyond at the great teeth of the cave and back at where she knew Fiora stood. She had suddenly felt like she fell out of the earth and into some strange dream. Some strange place where she had killed her son and the people she loved were dead, and some strange skeleton had just given her the *Axe of the Moon*.

She picked up the chest.

"Happy Deepwinter, Wulfee. Come spring, we march, or it will be too late," Bazal said, and he seemed to slip into some kind of strange waking sleep. He murmured things in a soft voice.

Etta walked away from the small fire, only smoking coals now, and carried her chest in both hands. In her eyes, tears welled and slipped down her cheeks. She couldn't believe she was awake, let alone alive.

She was Etta, but a small flame called Wulfee burned somewhere deep inside. She couldn't forget who she was now, she couldn't let that flame die. Etta would *have* to remember. She was the blood of Emmer, the Mother of the Fells, and now she had *the Axe of the Moon*.

Etta needed to remember who she was—because Wulfee needed to save the world.

THE FOURTH RISE OF WINTER

I N THE PINK SKY of morning, the lighttower stood tall and black on the horizon where the sea disappeared into endless blue. Maggie closed her eyes and took a deep breath. She took the dewy winds into her lungs and tasted the salt on her tongue. With one hand on her stomach, she reached with her mind and touched the small soul of her child. Her soul was brighter than a summer day—brighter than the sheen of morning on fresh fallen snow. *She's alive, and so are you.* Something had changed inside of her. Something had *awakened.* She had given the child a thousand lives and more. *Feeding.*

"James," Maggie said. "Do you smell the sea?"

"Aye," he said, and his lips twisted into a wan smile. He had black lines under his eyes, and his skin was greying. *I am becoming life and he is becoming death.*

The trodden road to the shorefront was down-sloping and pleasant. The golden tamaracks and sun-yellow birches were still hanging onto autumn, and though James and Maggie didn't talk, Maggie enjoyed the feeling of him close, of their child in her stomach, of the smells and the sounds. She was *alive*. And for the first time in her life that she could remember, it felt like she was going home. To a place she was wanted and not reviled. *The Abori will welcome me like a queen*. But as she walked, James dragged behind her.

"If it's too heavy, why do you still carry it?" Maggie asked. She didn't see the point in that sword. Not anymore. James had done his part and brought the elements back. He saved her.

"I carry it because it is mine." James scowled. "It's not just something I can leave lying around. It is mine to bear."

"It bears on you heavily," Maggie said. "I only want to see you better."

"Better?" James said. "We've just left ten thousand corpses on the ground back there." James studied the ground, and Maggie knew he was keeping something from her.

"We *had* to James," Maggie said. "It was them or us." She didn't understand why he was so upset about it. *They hated us.*

"It wasn't—" James raised his voice and stopped himself. "I don't think it was what we thought, Mag. I haven't been able to tell you. I haven't been able to find the words. I don't think those folk were going to fight us. They were leaving Ayeland, running…They weren't an army, not the kind we thought."

Maggie felt a pit in her stomach. *He's having regrets. He thinks you're a monster now… you showed him too much. Too much.* "Leaving?"

"Or *running*," James said. "From the same thing we're running from. The Warlocks. What if they were fighting? What if they only left because they *lost* Mammoth's Head."

"James, what are you saying? That they were retreating?"

"I'm saying that I think we've fucked it all up, Mag. We've slaughtered so many people. How can anyone see us as anything but monsters—daemons from the dark depths of the world? How do we come back from this?"

"You think I'm a monster? I'm the one who killed them, James. You think I'm a daemon?"

"We both are, Mag. Don't you realize that?"

Maggie was hurt. She had become delusional again. She thought James had understood that the thing he called a monster was the very thing she called a miracle. It was the *only* thing about herself she loved. She hated her scarred face and her wonky eyes and her frail body, *why couldn't I have a strong body like Wulfee?* She loved only *mage.* Yet it was the very thing that others reviled in her. *But not you, James, never you. Don't break my heart, baby, please.* "I thought we weren't going to hide it anymore, James? I thought we were going to be our true selves." Maggie reached for James, and he pulled back.

"I don't know who my true self is anymore, Mag. I only know that I want the voices in my head to stop. I want the dead to leave me alone. I want to *rest*, Mag. I would kill the monster inside of me if it meant I could rest."

And do you think the Abori will let him rest? The journey ahead is long and hard. I need him. "We're going to find our true selves together. Remember?" Maggie reached for James again, and this time he gave her his hands. *Can you even truly imagine doing this without him?*

"I don't know if I can face it, Mag."

"We'll face it together." Maggie squeezed his hands, and they continued to walk down the winding pathway. The rooks swooped and cawed in the blue-white sky, and the golden birch leaves fell and fluttered like butterflies. At the bottom of the hill where the road met the village of Tide, Maggie saw that James was out of breath. "Just there, look." Maggie pointed. "The lighttower."

The lighttower was bigger than Maggie imagined. It stood as tall and thick as a nytewood, but it was made of solid rock. It stretched up and up to its peak that sat just below the clouds. No fire burned from the top. Maggie figured it had probably been a thousand thousand years since a flame danced there. A smaller tower of blackened and charred wood leaned up against one side of the tower, almost like a small crutch. Maggie figured it was a smaller lighttower built more recently and had burned.

Great hills of stone and moss rolled out across Tide like an angry ocean of green, stretching out to a rolling ocean of white and grey.

"These are the remains of great Lovasi forges," James said. "They look like hills in the landscape now, for they are so grown over. They used to mine iron and tin out of the Hallow Hills and process and store it here. I've seen the mines myself. Desolate."

"They're very pretty hills," Maggie said. "And they sing such beautiful songs."

"So what will happen to the Hallow?" James looked to the sky. "Will only hills remain when it's over?"

"The Hallow will roll on," Maggie said. "As it always has. Before you or me or anyone walked these grassy hills and rocky crags. Before even the first Culdaine, people were here. If we survive, it will."

James lowered his head. *He's sick. He doesn't look well.* Maggie's heart hurt. "Maybe I will feel better," James said, "when you are safe."

Maggie knew how much James was worried. He was afraid of those Warlocks more than she was, and she was starting to get worried that maybe she wasn't taking it seriously enough. But Adeqor never scared her. Perhaps that was by the wizard's own design.

From atop the pathway Maggie saw a pack of squalid soldiers clinging to the tufts of grass. Cookfires smoked amidst hovels with rotten thatch roofs or none at all, and everywhere was mud. The bones of sunken ships protruded the water's surface so that the harbour looked more like a crypt. The waves smacked about the masts and the bows and churned up a wicked foaming froth. Bones and bodies scattered, rotting.

"There are no ships here, Mag. How are we going to cross the sea? We may have to walk up to Whitewatch. We won't make it before winter," James said.

"A ship might be coming. We could ask them," Maggie said.

"Those are Ayelish soldiers, Mag. They aren't going to want to talk."

"We'll kill them then."

James shook his head. "We can't just go on killing everyone that stands in our way, Mag. We can't become the monsters we're running from."

But I'm running towards my monster, James, not from it. How can I tell you that without you losing your love for me? "We need to talk to them, to do *something*."

"I won't kill them, Mag. I've had enough of that. Death…" James sighed, took a deep breath. "Death haunts my dreams and my waking thoughts. It haunts my very existence. I can't *kill* anymore."

"Then we wait and watch. From the arbor where we are always welcomed."

"And if a ship doesn't come? It's the Rise of winter, Mag. There may not be another ship until the Rise of spring."

"Then we wait, James. You and I together. Is that so bad?" Maggie was feeling a distance between her and James, and she hated it. *You caused this. You showed him too much. Too much. He thinks you're a monster. And you are. But it's not so bad, James…*

James frowned now. Maggie didn't mean to upset him. "No, it's not—" James winced in pain and rubbed the sides of his head. "It's not bad. I'm just afraid, Mag. Ellorin. Sometimes it feels like she's still in my head, like a piece of her soul still lives in me. And Adeqor… I can't forget him. What he said to me, what he did—what we *saw*. I still hear that chant, that, that… *noise* he made as he was dying. Though I know he didn't really die. What magics did he invoke? Where is he?"

Maggie ran her fingers through James's hair. She pressed on his neck and the sides of his head. She kissed his forehead and rubbed his shoulders. "The Abori will know, James. They have told me they know *all* things from their lore, which is the lore of the Remembered Lands entire, and would teach us whatever we would want. With that sword"—Maggie took James's hands in her own—"and these hands, you will do great things James. I know it's true. Adeqor will not get the better of you, not in the end. Just give yourself the time to *learn*. Together we can have it *all*."

James swooped his head back and forth as if to shake something loose. "Right," he said, gazing at the soldiers congregating in the patches of verdure. Maggie just wanted to make him okay. She wanted to make him feel the way he made her feel. But she was powerless to that. *He fears you will leave him, and now you fear the same. He will run from this and leave you in fear of going too deep and losing himself.* "Maggie, I just need you to know that I love you. With everything I am, I love you. I won't let this thing beat me, but I'm bloody sick, Mag. I feel a darkness infecting my veins and my heart. It's coming from the sword or somewhere else, but it's getting stronger every day, and Mag, I have to tell you, I'm so scared, I have to tell y ou—I *want* it to take me. The dead would worship me, the nightmares would cease—a ghost king, and you, my queen of life, together we could sail away to any life or any death and I'd be happy. It's *fighting* the monster that's hard. Becoming him would be peace."

"Then become him, James. Please. And let me become me. Let our flowers bloom eternal."

"I *can't*, Mag. If I let it beat me, it will kill me. It's like my soul is being dragged down. Down to the Otherworld, and if I let it slip, I will never come back."

Maggie's stomach sank. All this time she hadn't considered the consequences of James's powers. She was too caught up in her own—for the first time ever able to use them in full. "Then we'll fight it. Whatever we do, we'll do it together."

They slept by the banks that night, and Maggie dreamt of stars and of the most beautiful moon lighting up the sky.

In the misty morning, Maggie walked barefoot to the waterfront and watched the rising sun slide up from the Old Sea's heart. Her breath smoked as she sang with the larks and the mourning doves. *Who's that?* A figure was walking towards her. Dressed in leather armour, tight-fitting. A vale was draped over their face, orange as the sun. Only their eyes showed, violet in the mist.

"Good morn," Maggie said, and the figure ran at her.

"*Haruka,*" the figure sang in a haunting, low voice.

Maggie couldn't move. Her muscles had turned to stone. Her tongue was ice. Her eyes felt hot with blood. The figure removed two knives as they moved towards her. They peeled the orange veil away to reveal a woman's face. "Are you mage?"

"Yes," Maggie blurted. She had no control over herself.

The woman smiled, rolled her fingers around the hilts of her knives, and sheathed them. From her cuirass, the woman pulled out a collar and chain of black steel. "This won't hurt, okay." Footsteps from behind made the woman turn away.

James. Up the shore, James charged like a rock falling. "Arh!" he yelled, primal, groaning.

"*Amon,*" the figure sang, and just as the Word slipped from her mouth, the woman was gone from sight. Maggie heard footsteps slink off up the shoreline.

"What was that?" James said.

Maggie stood in awe. *Magics.* "I don't know," she said. "That woman seemed like she was going to kill me. She sang a Word and I couldn't move—couldn't think—I would have done anything she asked me to."

James reached for Maggie's hands. "Warlocks. They're coming for you, Mag."

Maggie would have cried, but she was exhilarated from the magics that just coursed through her. *You can't die.* Maggie touched the small soul in her belly with her mind. *Together we will live.*

Then, in the pink sky, three black masts appeared, their salt-beaten grey sails were fat with the cool west wind. "James," Maggie whispered. "James," she yelled. "A ship!" It was sailing hard and fast upriver, towards Tide.

"A ship." James rubbed his eyes.

"A ship!" Maggie waved her arms. She soon realized how feeble an attempt that was to get the ship's attention. They were twenty miles downstream from Tide.

"There are krakens on the sail," James said. "It's Dagglanders."

"That's just who we want. They owe us a debt."

"We abandoned them. We made a pact with them that was broken the moment we ran. They won't be entirely friendly towards us."

Maggie considered that. She knew James was right, but she felt good energy on that ship. Good, positive energy. "We have to try, James. We have to try."

The bags under James's eyes had gotten deeper. He smiled, though, and when he did, Maggie's whole world came into colour. "Okay," he said. "Let's do it"

Maggie knew she would have to do something more than wave her hands to get the ship to notice her, so small on a coast so big and covered in rock. "We need to start a fire," she said. Maggie searched the coast for tinder. James started to help her. With each second the ship got farther away.

"We can meet them at Tide." James held his hand to his forehead and peered out at the shrinking ship.

"What if they don't stop at Tide?" Maggie shaved tinder from a piece of wood with her knife. She gathered it into a nest. She slid her knife blade up the flint rock, and a small spark landed on the tinder pile. She picked the small pile up and blew it into flame. She put it down and fed it with sticks. It was a small little thing, and the wind was exhausting it. The ship got smaller.

Maggie could feel the fire. She felt the spirits with her mind and moved around with them. *I could swim in this. I could bottle it and throw it.* She let the mage part of her reach out and touch the flame. And once her mage had it—*yes, that's what I'll call it. My mage, not my monster. It's beautiful. It's lovely. It's so wonderful.* Maggie picked the fire up with her mind. She let it whirl around in the sky, and with a whisper to the wind, she fed the fire so that it burst into something greater. *Oh, it's wonderful and beautiful.*

It wasn't a flame any longer, it was a forge, *no, it's a phoenix.* The firebird from the cycles. *A mage rising from the ashes of her own life.* Maggie let the flame grow. She ignored the look of horror in James's face because she could see through that pain, and beyond it, see the love he had for her. *He won't leave you. He won't.*

Maggie held a small sun in the sky over the Old Sea. *My own sweet little sun.* She held it there and watched the ship with the kraken sails turn around and sail towards them.

"By the gods, Mag, they're turning." James was actually smiling.

Maggie couldn't help but smile, too. The flame called to her for feeding, and for a moment Maggie considered taking the life of just a few trees, but then she turned her mind away from the mage and ignored the will of it. She lowered the flame and extinguished it on the water's surface. At once she felt a coldness pass over her body and, shivering, Maggie fell to her knees.

James rushed to her side. "What is it?"

"Cold," Maggie said. Suddenly her bones felt frosted over. She couldn't control her jaw from chattering. James held her, but his body gave little warmth, and the sword's strange shimmer was giving Maggie a bad taste in her mouth. She could feel something inside of it *reaching* for her. "The ship?"

"It's Daggland, Mag," James said, "and by the gods, it's Eurick."

A wave of warmth rolled through Maggie's body to her toes. "Eurick? And Halda? They made it..."

"Aye," James spat. Maggie saw worry in the lines of his face. "But something's different."

"**B**Y THE GODS, MAN, it's good to hear your voice," Eurick said. His voice was choked. He and James held a tight embrace. The raven slowly untied a red cloth around his head.

Maggie turned her head. She heard James crying.

"It was the will of the gods, man. Will of the gods. Praise the Hare for showing me mercy." Eurick's voice sounded stronger now. *He aims to ease worry with that strength, and by the gods it's working.* Maggie knew Eurick was going to be okay. Somehow, she knew.

Maggie caught Halda's glare. The Dagglandic witch was standing in front of her crew with her arms crossed. She seemed like a skeleton netted in flesh. Her eyes were a tempest. "How did you know we'd be here?" Maggie said.

Halda's bony face twisted a grin. "Same way you knew I'd come, I reckon," Halda said. "Or something of the same force."

Maggie felt a chill roll over her body. "The soothsayers?"

Halda dipped her chin. "Aye."

"What did they tell you?" Maggie said. James and Eurick were listening now, too. Maggie reached for James's hand and squeezed it. Some part of her felt that Halda was going to tell them something that would keep her from going. *Going home, right? That's what you're calling it? Paradise?*

Halda spat. She looked at James and back at Maggie. "That I would find my destiny here."

Maggie burst into tears. She threw her arms around Halda, her bony figure. Halda tried to squirm away at first but then accepted and embraced it. "Take me to Edura." Maggie fell to her knees. "Please. Take us. Destiny awaits us there."

"It wasn't all good, what they told me... There was much to decipher. Stones, and doors and prophecies." Halda looked up at the blue sky. "And we don't have a lot of time..." she said.

"I don't need a lot of time. I can help," Maggie said. "I promise you I can help, but I need to get there. *We* need to get there." Maggie signalled to James with her thumb.

"Then my rakkarren will take you," said Halda. To Eurick, she said, "And you can make sure they get home to Ardura safely, Eurick?"

"Wha- I... I'm blind."

"You don't have eyes. Not entirely the same thing, but yes, I didn't ask you to guide them. I asked if you could make sure they get home safely. That requires only your heart," Halda said.

Maggie watched Eurick, the red cloth around his eyes, the black feathered cloak on his shoulders. He slouched, pouted. "James, I, I—"

"I wouldn't want anyone else in the world as a guide," said James.

"Nor I," agreed Maggie.

Halda's rakkarren helped Maggie and James board the ship. The smell of the salt- stained wood and the wind-washed sails made Maggie excited. She hadn't been on too many boat rides. The waves lapped at the hull and a breeze tugged gently at her clothing, messing her hair. *Hello wind, sea.*

They sailed all that day, and opposite the sun, they slipped down into the eastern horizon. As the sun set at her back, Maggie found a moment alone to gaze out at the sea.

Na'reen. I'm coming. I'm really coming.

And in that twilight the sea nymphs twirled on the sea alongside the boat. Their small feet forever moving, forever dancing, and their upper torso was completely still. *"Yes, and you will save the world,"* the nymphs spoke without words or sound. Silver with moonlight, they danced.

Maggie was overjoyed. The spirits of sea and wind rolled with her, forever dancing. *"I'll save the world from the starfall?"*

"No, dear." The nymphs were of a darker shade now—of shadow and crude oil. *"You will bring it."*

PLEASE READ!

Dear Reader,

We did it. We're here, at the end. I wholeheartedly hope you enjoyed *The Second Verse of The Last Ballad, A Chorus of War*. Writing this one was incredible, knowing that people had read and enjoyed book one made the drafting of the sequel very fulfilling. Taking these characters down the next stretch of the road has been one of the greatest joys in my life, and having you along for the ride makes it infinitely better. My promise is that to pay you back for being here with me, I will work endlessly to improve my craft and to finish this series as strongly as I humanly can. We're halfway now, so let's take it home together.

If you enjoyed this book and you would like to support the series further, it would mean the world to me if you left an honest review on Goodreads and Amazon. Honest reviews help books reach a wider audience and give indie authors like myself a chance to grow. Your words might just inspire someone to pick up the books, and what better way to use words than to inspire?

Until the next Verse,

Scott Palmer

JOIN THE FELDARRA!

Sign up for my readers list at scottpalmerauthor.com/freenovella and be the first to receive news, offers, and exclusive content from *The Last Ballad* series! But that's not all! When you join The Feldarra, you will receive a digital copy of *The Sound Of Starfall*, a multi-part prelude Novella to *The Last Ballad* series, as a welcome gift.

And I would love to hear from you! Please, reach out. Let's chat about magic, and cats, or whatever...

Website
Instagram
X
Goodreads
Amazon
Discord

Acknowledgments

To...

Syd, who made it all possible. Who picked me up on the days when I didn't have the strength to do it myself. Who fills me up when I am empty, inspires me when I lack hope. Who makes me believe in myself again when I am low. If I could put even a small fraction of what you truly mean to me into words it would be longer than this book, so instead I will just tell you I love you all the way. Walking beside you in this life has been my greatest privilege.

Indie, my baby girl, who makes me slow down and appreciate each moment. Who makes me look out the window and watch the leaves grow each day. Who makes my life infinitely better just by being here. Who's growing so fast into the most incredible person. It's all for you, sweetheart, anything you dream.

Mom, Dad, Nan, who allowed me to dream, play, and make mistakes. Who gave me everything I needed and more. Who taught me to love and care for people. Who showed me that who you were inside was more important than what you had on the outside. Who I could always count on to be in the crowd. Thank you for always showing up for me, and now my daughter.

Brando, my brother, I am so proud of the man you've become. Watching you grow up has been an absolute honour. I am so happy you didn't chop any of your extremities off with that axe you were swinging around in the front lawn when you were seven.

Jimmy, Bella, Jamie, Meghan, Rich, Jen, and Jake, for being our web of support. For helping us when we were sick, tired, had no time. For your never ending support and friendship, I couldn't have written this one without you.

Lisa, Tim, Carol, Sandy, Debbie, Coulton, Tasha, Tom, Kristen, Liam for being my second family and making me feel loved and accepted as one of yours. For being yet another web of support in this world, thank you.

The people who helped me make this book into what it is. Kelley, who has looked over every word in this series (more than once) and turned my lumpy rock shaped manuscripts into polished stones every time. I still feel awful about the bats LOL. Dom, for lending me his eyes for a few weeks to proofread this book. To Joshua, for yet another map and yet another burst of inspiration. Filling out and detailing maps for you has filled the nooks and crannies, and far-flung corners of this world with life and stories. Brian, for pouring his heart into the chapter headings for my characters. For taking the time to understand each one, and to create a story with the symbols. Joe, for being an absolute badass with a pen. Your illustrations of my characters have brought new life to this world. Robert, whose illustrations of Ardura have added another layer of depth to a world that was already so deep in my mind. Stuart, for creating yet another masterpiece with the cover. My Beta Readers, Petar, Alex, Jade, Stephen, Michael, Ella,

Rob, Kaley. Your feedback and support really brought out the full potential of this book and gave me the confidence that it wasn't complete shite. And, of course, my wonderful ARC readers!

And a very heartfelt thank you to my friends, and author family, The Break-Ins. Josh, Calum, Kaden, Isaac, Adrian, Rob, Louise, Sam, Bryan, Andrew, Jonathon, Nicholas, Zac, Francisca, Aaron, each and every one of you inspires me daily. Your work ethic, creative skill, and genuine kindness are of the very highest class. Without you all, I may be wandering lost in the deep woods of publishing with no food or water, all I can say is thank y ou.

GLOSSARY

CALENDAR AND SEASONS:

THE MEASURING OF THE seasons was mastered and recorded long ago by the Druids of Old. Their teachings were passed down, and then later picked up by the conquering Lovasi. Soon, the Druid Calendar spread as far and fast as the Lovasi themselves, believed by most cultures of the world to be the superior way of organizing the year.

There are four seasons. Spring, summer, autumn, and winter. Each season contains three stages, Rise, Wayk, and Fell. Each stage contains a set number of days. Every fourth year, an extra day is added to the Fell of summer. Across Ardura and most of Edura, that day is known as Summerfell, or Kelson's Day.

Spring
Rise of spring = 30 days
Wayk of spring = 31 days
Fell of spring = 30 days

Summer

Rise of summer = 30 days

Wayk of summer = 31 days

Fell of summer = 30 days (Summerfell, every fourth year = 31 days)

Autumn

Rise of autumn = 30 days

Wayk of autumn = 31 days

Fell of autumn = 30 days

Winter

Rise of winter = 30 days

Wayk of winter = 31 days

Fell of winter = 31 days

<u>Place and Events:</u>

Ardura - (ar - dur - ah) The continent of Ardura. The westernmost of the three known continents of The Remembered Lands.

Edura - (eh - dur - ah) The continent of Edura. The easternmost of the three known continents of The Remembered Lands.

Daggland - (dayg - land) A group of islands to the far north. Inhabited by an ancient race of reavers and warriors who once crafted unbreakable steel and have since fallen to a lesser state.

The Fells - The northernmost kingdom of Ardura. Mostly inhabited by nomadic, warring clans. Dominated by the overwhelming shadow of the ancient castle Kallahorn, and its dark secrets.

Mal Hallow - (mAL hAL - oh) A land of haunted arbors, magic hills, Standing Stones, and rushing rivers. Protected from the south by the great Lovasi castle of Mammoth's Head, built at the crossing of one of few passable fords in the rushing White River. The Mal people have lived here since the start of time. The kingdom is governed by many ruling Lords who have sworn fealty to the king of Mal Hallow, James Culdaine.

Ayeland - (AIL - ind) The largest kingdom in Ardura. A land of bounty and abundance. Ruled by the Alder dynasty for the last seventy years from the Lovasi castle known as The Bloodwall, in the city of Solace.

The Glenn - A kingdom in the northwest of Ardura. Known for its lush arbor and the Lovasi castle Stone Tree in the city of Elurra that was built therein. The Brynmor dynasty has ruled the kingdom for the last sixty years. The Glenn is also well known for its massive destrier war horses that feed on dead flesh, and the speed and strength that the beasts give to their army.

The Hesterlands - The Hesterlands, formerly known as Rhosanti, are the crown jewel of Ardura. Located at the Bay of Lions, at the mouth of the Roaring Sea, The Hesterlands, and their rulers, the Royal Hesters, are able to control all seafaring trade to Ayeland, and therefore the rest of the n orth.

Kelson the conqueror called Rhosanti home, and built himself a fortress there that is considered his masterpiece. Known as Kelson's Keep, the castle stands thousands of feet tall, and looms over the grand city of Hest, overlooking the strait of Lions and the Roaring Sea. Though it is the most fortified castle in all of the Remembered Lands, it has long been the target of conquest and has seen many rulers over its long centuries of existence. In those years, many secrets were lost and found behind the walls and in the dungeons of Kelson's Keep.

Ryne - The Island of Ryne has long been shunned by the mainlanders, considered strange and dangerous, and too much of a risk to mine the abundance of tin and iron in the hills and mountains there. The Nith dynasty has ruled happily on the island for a few hundred years, co-existing with the strange race of transporters from the Raven's Guild, and working eldritch rituals with the Warlocks to ensure their safety from the outside world. The Niths have never been involved in any major war, and only Kelson was able to conquer them.

Esher - The southernmost kingdom of Ardura, Esher is known for its hot and dry weather, and the incredibly lush valley along the Esheri Rush. A long history of infighting between the ruling Houses of Serahnon and of Marwen has left Esher wartorn and grief stricken. Long centuries of famine and corruption have destroyed what was once Ardura's richest, and most beautiful kingdom.

Lavesh - An island off the southern coast of Ayeland and the west coast of Esher. Known for its tri-magistrate ruling structure and an abundance in gold, salt, and jewels. Lavesh is a peaceful state, never involving itself in foreign wars but to trade and profit from them. Though the same cannot be said about civil wars, for Lavesh is famous for its bands of sellswords, a business that rose up around the constant warring of the magistrates. Though constant, these civil wars rarely result in any significant loss or gain.

The Starfall - An event that destroyed the great empire of Yehven around four thousand years ago. An Abori mage used magics to bring a star down on the Golden City of Ailar, in Yehven. The impact turned the area around Ailar to dust and sent the world into many years of darkness.

Ox'olin - A future apocalyptic event that the people of Daggland have feared for centuries, resulting in Father Sky falling down to meet Mother Earth once again. The Dagglandic prophets fear that it is closer than ever.

CHARACTERS:

The North:

Rulers of the Hallow and Their People:

James Culdaine - (jaymz - kULL -dane) Known as the seer, or world-walker. The king of Mal Hallow. Heartbound to Maggie Culdaine of the Wick.

Bren Culdaine - (bren - kULL - dane) Father to James Culdaine. Former king of Mal Hallow. *Killed by Calen Alder.*

Nara of Oster - (nar - ah of aw - ster) Mother to James Culdaine. Former queen of Mal Hallow. *Killed by Calen Alder.*

Bren - James' horse.

Maggie Culdaine - (may - gee) A mage of unknown origins. Queen of Mal Hallow. Heartbound to King James Culdaine.

Hagel - (hay - g - el) Maggie's former mentor. A strange woodsmage who had the Old Blood. *Killed by Maggie.*

Flora - (flo - rah) Maggie's big sister from her third family.

Nareen - (na - r - een) A dream nymph who visits Maggie and claims to be an Abori prophet.

Eurick - (yurr - ick) A former transporter of The Raven's Guild. Run-away from his place at the guild to try and help James and Maggie do something of importance in the world.

Mineera Mori - (mih - nEER - a mOR - ee) A scholar from New Lovas. Travelled to Mal Hallow to record the events of barbarians.

Itchy - (ih - chee) An old bard who seems to know more than he says, and he says a lot. He is loyal to James and Maggie.

Adeqor - (a - deh - kor) A warlock of Yehven. Cast out from The Ailaryan Order — a group of Warlocks that survived The Starfall. *Died at the Mother's Shrine.*

Ellorin - (el - oh - rin) Known as The Banshee, or The Hunter of Souls. A former member of The Ailaryan Order. *Killed by James Culdaine.*

Lord Brinley Scareye, the Dragonslayer - (brin - lee) Former lord of Dawning. Heartbound to Sessely of Fever. Father to Tilda, Brigid, and Aione. Fealty sworn to King James Culdaine. Coat of arms is a black crow on a field of gold.

Sessely of Fever - (seh- sih - lee) Lady of Dawning. Heartbound to Brinley. Mother to Tilda, Brigid, and Aione.

Tilda - (tILL - dah) - One of The Three Black Crows of Dawning. *Killed in the Battle of Rosen Bridge.*

Brigid - (brih - jid) - One of The Three Black Crows of Dawning. Heartbound to Corwin of Wick. Mother to Corbin and Ais.

Aione - (eye - oh - nee) - One of The Three Black Crows of Dawning. Heartbound to Ludin.

Lord Eridan - (AIR - ih - dan) - Rightful ruler of Ockam. Heartbound to Ura. Father to Iradin.

Ura of Ockam - (oo - rah) Heartbound to Eridan, mother to Iradin. *Died in childbirth.*

Iradin - (eer - a - din) Son of Eridan and Ura. *Killed by winter sickness.*

Derudin Deadmaker - (deh - roo - din) Former lord of Ockam. Heartbound to Aylee of Oldwood. Father to Eridan. Coat of arms is a white flag with a bloody red handprint. *Killed by Adeqor.*

Aylee of Oldwood - (AIL - ee) Former Lady of Ockam. Heartbound to Derudin. Mother to Eridan. *Killed by unknown causes.*

Lord Claydon Coldfoot — (klay - din) Former lord of Tusk, and former castellan to the Lovasi castle of Mammoth's Head. Fealty sworn to King James Culdaine. Coat of arms is a grey mammoth on a field of green.

Heri Doe - (hair - ee - doe) A mysterious woman who came and went without warning, and disappeared forever after giving birth to Macts. Some folk believe she was a river nymph.

Aron - (ar - on) The oldest son of Claydon Coldfoot and Heri Doe. Heartbound to Mery of Tusk. Father to Camdin.

Macts - (sounds like max) The youngest son of Claydon Coldfoot and Heri Doe. Heartbound to Tana of Oldwood.

Lady Ruwen, The She-bear - (roo - win) Lady of Rosen. Heartbound to Yaren of Rosen. Mother to Gareth and Jon.

Yaren of Rosen — (yah – rin) A man of Rosen. Heartbound to Lady Ruwen. Father to Gareth and Jon. *Killed by the Ayelish.*

Gareth - (gAIR - ith) The oldest son of Ruwen and Yaren. *Killed by the Ayelish.*

Jon - Youngest son of Ruwen and Yaren. *Missing in battle.*

<u>Rakkars of Daggland and Their Followers:</u>

Halda of Massey Rock - (h - all - duh) Dawter of Hemon and Harla. Niece to Thora Witchheart, the Knower. Rakkar of Massey Rock. Hearthane to Witch Den. Her banners are the same as those of Sig Arfa, a black kraken on a sea of blue.

Harald - (hair - uld) Son of Bannen, heart to Kari.

Ria, Den, Barret, Haron - Other members of Halda's rakkarren.

Thora Witchheart, the Knower - (thor - ah) Halda's aunt, sister to Hemon. Thora gained the reputation of being a sorceress, conjuring magics to shape the future at her will. Thought to be a danger, the rakkars of Daggland voted to exile Thora and strip her of her influence over the realm.

Olrick - (ol - rick) Halda's ex-lover. She still thinks about him from time to time and what they could have been.

Sigrid Windharp - (sih - grid) Halda's rakkar's Bard.

Toren of Morden Vale - (tore - in) The rakkar of Morden Vale. Hearthane to the Grimholt.

Haron, Samuel, Dirk, Rora, Kaley, Barth, Mantha, Jax - Toren's rakkar.

Hegglund of Ash River - (h - egg - lund) The rakkar of Ash River. Hearthane to Omenhall. His banners are two black ravens flying in opposite directions on a field of dark green.

Erik of Smokestone - (air - ick) The rakkar of Smokestone. Hearthane to Elderwold Hall. His banners are two crossed axes on a grey field.

Sara of Farrock Bay - The rakkar of Farrock Bay. Hearthane to Hearthspear Hall. Her banners are a single brown spear pointing downwards on a white field with a red border.

Gunnar of Oldstone - (gun - err) The rakkar of Oldstone. Hearthane to Ironhowe Hall. His banners are a black hammer with Dagglandic runes on a field of mountain grey.

Asmund of the Cape of Krakens - (az - mund) The rakkar of the Cape of Krakens. Hearthane to the Lighthouse.

<u>Rangers of E'daru:</u>

Haro - (hair - oh) Leads a band of Rangers and is a highly respected member of The Fellowship of Rangers. Other band leaders take his word as law. Hearthbound to Ifanie. Father to Owen.

Ifanie - (iff - a - nee) - A crofter's daughter from a valley near Oster. Heartbound to Haro of the Wick. Mother to Owen. *Killed by James Culdaine in the Ayelish wars.*

Owen - (oh - win) - Son to Ifanie and Haro. *Killed in the Ayelish wars.*

Grig - (gr - igg) - A strange crofter living in a secluded wood in the north. Heartbound to Dalla.

Dalla - (d - al - ah) - A strange crofter living in a secluded wood in the north. Heartbound to Grig.

Timmon, Rend, Elley - Known Ranger band leaders in the area.

Hagen the Great - the first Keeper of the Lore.

<u>People of the Glenn:</u>

King Richard Brynmor - (brin - mOR) Ruler of Elurra, Castelan of Stonetree, and King of The Glenn. Usurper of Ockam, Dawning, Lorne, and Fever. Heartbound to Queen Grace. Father to Princess Gwen Brynmor. *Missing after the battle of Dead Rising.*

Queen Grace Brynmor - The Queen of the Glenn. Heartbound to King Richard Brynmor. Mother to Princess Gwen Brynmor.

Princess Gwen Brynmor - Princess of the Glenn. Daughter of King Richard and Queen Grace.

Ossian, the Blue Knight - The Blue Knight is a living figure of Glennish renown, donning mythic blue armour that is passed down from one knight to the next, generation after generation. Little is known about the training rituals and routines of the Blue Knight, and less is known of their origin. No one truly knows how a new disciple is chosen and no one cares to ask. The King of the Glenn simply accepts Ossian's help and leaves it at that.

Don Ryatt - (ry - it) A knight of the Glenn, serving under Ossian.

Don Gordon of Beauty - (g - ore - dun) A royal knight of Beauty. Sent to Dawning to assist Queen Grace Brynmor in the search for King Richard. His banners are a white horse on a field of green.

Don Kenzy of Maple - (ken - zee) A royal knight of Beauty. Sent to Dawning to assist Queen Grace Brynmor in the search for King Richard. Her banners are an orange maple leaf on a field of brown.

Don Martyn of Till - (m - ar - tin) A royal knight of Beauty. Sent to Dawning to assist Queen Grace Brynmor in the search for King Richard. His banners are a silver chevron on blue centred by the black sword of Baynard. Baynard was a legendary warrior of Old Till.

Aelia, the Warlock - (ale - ee - AH) Aelia is a Warlock of Old Yehven who lives and works in the castle of Stone Tree. She arrived only days after the death of Ellorin to replace her in the courtroom.

The Isle of Ryne and the Raven's Guild

Owin Nith - (oh - win n - ith) King of Ryne, Castellan of Blackstone. Heartbound to Ethil Nith of Ardeen. Father to Amin Nith, and Yara Nith. House Nith's banners are an aqua green merman with a black sword on a field of rocky grey.

Ethil Nith - (eth - il) Queen of Ryne. Heartbound to Owin Nith of Blackstone. Mother to Amin Nith, and Yara Nith.

Ydril - (ih - drill) As the first Passerine of the Raven's Guild, Ydril decides which ravens go where, when, and for who. She is expected to uphold the ancient traditions and customs of the Guild and keep order amongst the transporters.

The Fell Mountains

Si'otha, the peaceful folk:

Etta - (Ett - ah) - Formerly known as Wulfee. A former kihl'dor of the Fells, now finds herself a refugee searching for peace. Heartbound to Sweyne. Mother to Tarek and Braden. Grandmother to Young Swey.

Braden - (b - ray - din) Son of Etta and Sweyne. Formerly known as the Wolf, a brigand general who was feared and renowned in the north. *Killed by Wulfee.*

Tarek - (t - ar - ick) Son of Etta and Sweyne. *Killed in single combat.*

Lars - Etta's brother. *Missing.*

Wolton - Etta's da. *Killed in combat.*

Kerris - Ettta's ma. *Killed in combat.*

Young Swey - (s - way) Son of Tara and Braden. Grandson to Etta.

Tara - (ter - ee - sah) Heartbound to Braden. Mother to Young Swey.

Benn - A healer who learned some medicine magics from his father, who in turn had learned it from a deathstealer.

Sweyne – (s – wayne) Heartbound to Wulfee. Father to Tarek, and Braden. *Missing.*

Calum, from the Scale Isles - (cal - um) A lone traveller from the Scale Isles. Searching for peace in the mountains of the Fells.

Holden - (hole - den) An orphaned warrior from a small northern mountain tribe in the Fells. Searching for peace.

Aris - (arr - is) An orphaned warrior from a small northern mountain tribe in the Fells. Searching for peace.

Cullen, the Cook - (cull - in) A cook from the mountains of the Fells. Searching for peace.

Young Courtney - An orphaned warrior from a small northern mountain tribe in the Fells. Searching for peace.

Gwynn - (g - wIN) The leader of a band of misfits in the mountains of the Fells. Hoping to find peace one day.

Ryatt - (ry - it) An orphaned warrior from a small northern mountain tribe in the Fells. Searching for peace.

Baerd - (bare - d) A mysterious, cult-like leader from deep in the Fell Mountains.

Yessa - (yes - ah) An elder of the Feldarra. Known as the child of the stars.

Tana, Relia, Caden - Orphaned warriors of the Fells.

Si'darra, the shield people:
Annie - The rightful Queen of Kallahorn. Heartbound to Balen Longsongs. Mother to Fiora.

Fiora - The Princess of Kallahorn. Born with the taint of the half-blood of Rangers, Fiora has always been feared and forced into isolation from the outside world due to her strange keenness towards animals, specifically a wolf. Daughter to Balen and Fiora Longsongs.

Nettle - A member of the si'darra. Maker-of-the-stew. Keen to make a batch of food for the lot, but she could hardly be called a cook. Best friend of Rat.

Owyn - A member of the si'darra.

Bazal - (bah – zil) A wizard of eldritch renown.

Oris - A member of the si'darra.

Rat - A member of the si'darra. Best friend of Nettle.

Owyn - A member of the si'darra.

The South:

<u>**Ayeland**</u>

King Calen Alder - (kale - in) Former king of Ayeland. Usurper of Mal Hallow. Heartbound to Helen Alder. Father to Ianna, Sammil, Dredrik, Helena, and Sherri Alder. *Killed by James Culdaine.*

Queen Helen Alder - (hell - in) Queen Mother of Ayeland. Passed Queenship of Ayeland onto her eldest daughter, Ianna, upon the death of her heart, Calen. Heartbound to Calen Alder. Mother to Ianna, Sammil, Dredrik, Helena, and Sherri Alder.

Ianna Alder - (eye - ann - ah) Queen of Ayeland. Heartbound to Robert Crowen of Glavelin. Mother to Kevan, and Trina Alder. Eldest daughter of Calen and Helen Alder.

Sammil Alder - (sam - ill) Eldest son of Calen and Helen Alder.

Dredrik Alder - (dred - ick) Son of Calen and Helend Alder.

Helena Alder — (hell - ee - nah) Daughter of Calen and Helen Alder.

Sherri Alder - (share - ee) Daughter of Calen and Helen Alder.

Eldinian - (el - din - ee - in) A Warlock in the court of Queen Ianna of Ayeland. Arrived unannounced after the death of Ellorin to replace her. A surviving member of the Ailaryan Order.

Vincint Garrish of Leveny - (vin - sint of lev - in - ee) The Lord of Leveny. Castellan of Castle Leveny, a stone motte and bailey. Heartbound to Lady May of Leveny. His banners are a yellow cheese on a field of milk white.

Alyce Florhen of Severn - (al - iss of floor - in) The Lady of Florhen. Castellan of Fort Horn, a stone motte and bailey. Heartbound to Lord John Florhen. His banners are a white unicorn on a field of sky blue and pink.

Hest

The Royal Hesters:

Aldred Hester - (all - drid) A prince of Hest. Son to King John and Queen Lena Hester. Has a Lovasi sword called *Phantom*.

Brooton Hester - (broo - tin) Brother to King John of Hest. Heartbound to Mary Rose of Timpany. Father to Marton, and Lexis Hester. *Heart and children deceased from natural causes.* Has a Lovasi sword called *Nail.*

King John Hester - The Ruler of Hest and King of the Hesterlands. Castellan of Kelson's Keep. Heartbound to Queen Lena Hester. Father to Aldred, and William Hester. Has a Lovasi sword called *Saynomore.*

Queen Lena Hester - (lee - nah) Queen of the Hesterlands. Heartbound to King John Hester. Mother to Aldred, and William Hester. *Killed in an accident.*

William Hester - (will - yum) The First Prince of the Hesterlands. Next in line to be king. Brother to Aldred Hester. Son of King John, and Queen Lena Hester.

The King's Court:

Gavyn Hester - (gah - vin) The High Wiseone. Tasked with acquiring knowledge and presenting facts to the court. A distant cousin of King John.

Rober Hester - (ro - ber) Commander of the city watch. A distant cousin of King John.

Vinsent Carlin - (vin - sint) The Master of Coin. Brother to Robbert Carlin, Lord of Carlin.

Adora - (ah - door - ah) A Warlock of the Ailaryan Order. Tasked with informing the King on crucial decisions.

Sparo - (spare - oh) The King's Bishop, devout follower of the One Faith and prophet of Eralis.

The People of Hest:

Dustey - (dust - ee) A witchpriest from the Dead Isles. Found wandering the Bone Islands and taken in by Brooton Hester as his assistant.

Egan - (ee - gin) Aldred's scribe.

Jerith - (jair - ith) A bishop of Eralis, preacher of the One Faith.

Kirt - A wiseone—a cult of mysterious robed figures who roam the underways of Hest.

Eshlynn - (esh - linn) A blacksmith of Hest. Former lover of Aldred Hester.

Sebastian - (seh - bast - chun) A bellmaker from Hest. Lover of Esh-lynn.

<u>Esher</u>

<u>Julien's Rabble:</u>

Julien Esterbraun - (joo - lee - in est - er - brawn) A sellsword brigand from Lavesh. Born in and exiled from Esher. Claims to have the blood of Old Draku.

Damen Esterbraun - (day - min) Julien's dad. *Killed by Hesters.*

Iris Esterbraun - (eye - riss) Julien's mom. *Killed by Hesters.*

Lucien Esterbraun - (loo - see - in) Julien's eldest brother. *Killed by Hesters.*

Darian Esterbraun - (dare - ee - in) Julien's younger brother. *Killed by Hesters.*

Kalila Esterbraun - (kah - lie - la) Julien's baby sister. *Killed by Hesters.*

Elario Esterbraun - (ih - la - ree - oh) Julien's grandfather. *Killed by Hesters.*

Tiago Dilario - (tee - ah - go dih - lar - ee - oh) A famous bootmaker from Lavesh.

Magister Libby - The magister of Odessa. Known in the tri-archy of Lavesh as the Magister of Jewels. A past mentor of Julien Esterbraun.

Canri - (can - ree) A large albino soldier loyal to Julien for many years.

Ashan - (ash - an) - A skilled sellsword warrior loyal to Julien Esterbraun.

Folk of Esher:

Bones - A mysterious pirate-sellsword who frequents the ports and inns of Saltsan. He has one eye and wears an eye patch.

Rolan - (roe - lin) A former nobleman of Darry who now sells his sword for a living. Loyal to Bones.

Hild - The shipmaster of *Saltspray*. Loyal to Bones.

Mulu - A masterful sellsword warrior from the island of Lisi, in the Spice Isles.

Odius - (oh - dee - us) The prophet of Lysses. Known for conducting eldritch, mushroom fueled rituals to invoke the spirits of the gods and communicate to them.

Miri - (meer - ee) A prophet of Karaat and leader of the Army of Truth.

Former Rulers of Esher:

Caris Serahnon - (care - iss sir - ah - nin) King of Soren. Seneschal of Palace Soren. Heartbound to Katee of Soren. Father to Trist. His banners are a red scorpion on a black field. *Killed by Brooton Hester.*

Trist Serahnon - Lord of Behru and Prince of Soren. Seneschal of Palace Behru. Heartbound to Miralys Serahnon of Behru. Father of Coran, Lexa, Cleo, and Aldin Serahnon. His banners are the same as his fathers, a red scorpion on a field of black.

Coran Serahnon - (core - in) Eldest son to Trist and Miralys Serahnon.

Lexa - Eldest daughter to Trist and Miralys Serahnon.

Cleo - Daughter to Trist and Miralys Serahnon.

Aldin - Son to Trist and Miralys Serahnon.

Taya Marwen - (Tay - ah mar - win) The Queen of Sareen and seneschal of Red Sky Rock. Heartbound to Ramiro Marwen. Arch rival of House Serahnon. Mother to Neferi, Elira, Azara, and Velira Marwen

Usurpers of Esher:

Natt Floyd - The lord knight of Friars. He left Fort Friars to his son, Cane, upon usurping Sareen. His banners are a round brown shield on grey.

Leonil Hester - (lee - oh - nil) A prince of the purple lion Hesters. Usurper of Saray. His banners are a purple lion on a field of gold.

Jonathon Rose - A prince of Timpany. Son to William and Brienna Rose. Sister to Mary Rose. Usurper of Soren.

Katelyn Merris - A princess of Bralter. Daughter of Henri and Jade Merris. Usurper of Lysses.

GROUPS AND GUILDS:

The Feldarra: (Symbol - The Nihr'el) A group of folk sworn by sacred blood oaths to protect the lands of The Fells and Mal Hallow from foreign invaders.

The Si'otha: (Symbol - none) The peaceful folk. A group of misfits and orphans banded together in the mountains. All of them are seeking to avoid war and find some form of peace.

The Si'darra: (Symbol - The Nihr'el) The shield folk. A group of folk sworn by sacred blood oaths to protect all of the world from darkness.

The Ailaryan Order: (Symbol - The Flaming Star) A group of warlocks from Old Yehven who survived the Starfall. They have used their magics to influence the world, and the people in it, ever since.

The Rangers of E'daru: (Symbol - The e'daru, a black horse with long human hair and no eyes.) A band of Rangers actively seeking E'daru. They live in the arbors and steal from folks passing through. They are all hoping for a meeting with E'daru. There are many Rangers who are not active in a band, and have settled down as a crofter, or in a hamlet somewhere. Because they have already had an encounter with e'daru, or they simply choose to walk away.

The Raven's Guild: (Symbol - a spread-winged raven) The transporters of Ardura. The Raven's guild can send one of their Ravens to retrieve anything, or anyone, anywhere in The Remembered Lands. And then deliver that thing, anywhere. For the right price, of course.

Sellswords of Esher and Lavesh: (Symbol - ever-changing to suit their needs) Many misfitted individuals banded together in various factions who have chosen to sell their fighting skills for some form of payment.

The Wise Ones: (Symbol - a grey robe for novice Wise Ones and a blue robe for masters.) A mysterious guild which lurks beneath the castle and city of Hest. Their order is believed to go back to times even before Kelson arrived to Ardura, and many of their secrets are reserved, though not privy to anyone outside of the guild. They are renowned for getting information and learning secrets.

The Demhoni: A group of fungus-infested cannibals from the deep north. Shrouded in ancient myth, the Demhoni believe they must eat the bodies of other Humans to absorb their strength.

NON-HUMAN RACES:

Druids: The Old Blood of the ancient Mal. Even The Mal know little about the druids, other than they built the Standing Stones using magics they stole from Old Yehven. Mages and seers were once common amongst the Druids when their blood was pure, but as they have diluted their blood over generations, folk have forgotten them.

El'vie: (Ell-vee) Merrmonsters that live in the Lake of Pool. They are almost more fishlike than they are human. They speak in a twittering tongue lost on most ears. The druids said the el'vie have always been there, born out of the waters that surround the World Tree. Their souls are bound to it. They pay no attention to others, and they rarely leave their Pool except to mate with humans or if they feel threatened.

Giy'er: (Guy-err) Massive, giant-like creatures that live in wide open spaces, usually at the foot of mountains or hills or at the mouths of arbors so they can easily catch game animals. Faster than a horse, with leathery skin and rock-like bones. They start enormous bonfires that often spread out of control while cooking their mass haunches of meat. They are unpredictable.

Hawka: (Hah-kah) Wolfish, elk-like carnivores that roam the mountains and the hills. They eat what they see and they are always hungry. They are afraid of arbors and the dead souls that lurk in them.

Rangers: Descendants of the E'daru–the first skinchanger. (Also known as, greenhoods, skincrawlers, skinchangers, bodysnatchers.) Rangers have the ability to warg into animals. Common folk know little about the details, for most fear going near them. They worship the Maw god, and practice sacrifice regularly.

THE PEOPLES OF OLD:

Warlocks: The survivors of Old Yehven. A race of folk known to have used dangerous and unpredictable magics to build grand empires. They seem to have used their magics to alter their lifespans and can live for many thousands of years.

Draku: The dragon peoples of Old. Thought to be extinct. A race so similar to humans that there is no difference in appearance. What separated the Draku from regular humans was their resistance and seeming insatiability to flame, and their ability to communicate with the great wise dragons.

Sorcerers: A race believed to have existed even before the Warlocks of Yehven. Little to nothing is known of them.

The Soothsayers: A mysterious group of truth seers with eldritch origins surrounding their existence. Rarely ever seen, the soothsayers spend their time hidden in wicked groves and crooked gardens enriched with their black magics to protect themselves.

The Oracle: A thought-to-be Sorceress hidden in a strange and ancient shrine in the middle of the Behruvian Desert. Rumoured to be old enough to have seen the old skies.

The Abori: A cult of death worshipping warriors in the deep north of Edura.

LANGUAGES:

Runish Tongue of the Ancient Mal:

Ai'mair - (eye - mare) means *love.*

Darra - (dar - ah) means *protection.*

Karl - means *free.*

Kihl'dor - (keel-dore) means *leader.*

Nihr'el - (neer-el) means *World Tree.*

Nihr'el nur amo ruso – means *World Tree save my soul*.

Aku'mar - (ah - koo - marr) means *lost one*.

Runish Tongue of Old Daggland:

Ox'olin - (ox - oh - lin) A word used to describe the end of the world—when Offa, the Earth Mother, rises to meet Father Sky once more.

Rakkar - (rack - arr) means *leader*.

Rakkarren - (rack - arr - in) means *loyal-follower*.

Lovasi:

Ti arda montë - (tee-ar-dah monn-tay), means *How is your heart?* - old Lovasi greeting.

Ênalia dura - (ee-nah-lee-ah dOOR-ah), means *My heart is home* - Reply to the old greeting; means my heart is happy, safe, warm—feelings of home.

Di ạrda illientë - (dee - ar - dah ILL - ee - en - tay) means *Where is your mind?* - Old Lovasi insult; a way of calling someone stupid.

The Old Tongue (Yehvenki)

Amon - (ah - mun) means *stop*.

Dagdora - (dag – dOR - ah), means *fire*.

Haruka - (ha - roo - ka) means *obedience*.

Ventes - (ven - tez) means *Destroy.*

Iril tur sa'illes - means *speak true and enter.*

Akovha Liet Neia - true meaning unknown—involved in a strange necromantic ritual.

<u>GODS AND RELIGIONS:</u>

The Old Gods:

The Spirits - Fire, Air, Water, Earth.

Father Tree - Divine justice, and ultimate judge of the souls of the dead.

The Hare - Mercy, peace, fertility, childbirth, life - blesses with bountiful harvest (or eats the harvest)

The Owl - Wisdom and foresight.

The Stag - Courage, and strength, fortitude in battle

The Crow - Death, decay, and mystery.

The Swan - Innocence, love, beauty, protects the innocent

The Bluebird Twins - Ayla: Arts and music. Firo: Crafting. Luck.

The Lupin (The Outcast) - Darkness, the moon, and the unknown workings of nature. Referred to as the Maw God.

Other Gods:

Eralis: (Eh – rah – lis), The One God. Worshipped throughout most of The Glenn, Ayeland, and The Hesterlands. A religion founded in Lovas, and spread by their empire.

Karaat: (Kah – rat), The Creator God. Worshipped throughout Esher, Lavesh, and most of Edura. A religion that has roots back in the days before the Starfall. Created by small folk and slaves, there are no places of worship for the followers of Karaat. They pray to the sun and the moon below the great sky sea. They usually centre their prayers around sacrifice, morning or night, and fire.

Roqeda: A strange new god who speaks to his disciples backwards.

Creators: The Creators fell into the earth before the sky was born and only rarely surface.

The Gods of Daggland:

The Dead God, Offa: Also known to the Dagglanders as Mother Earth. Believed to have created all of the land, water, and mountains in the world.

The Blood God, Oade: The Dagglandic god of water. All of the water is believed to be the blood of Offa, and Oade is believed to watch over it.

Father Sky: Mother Earth's mate. Had his Name eaten by Tulu, the Great Serpent. Father sky created all of the skies, the clouds, and is responsible for great storms. He is generally revered amongst the Dagglanders.

Tulu, the Great Serpent of Hell: A serpent large enough to have once wrapped its body around the sun in an attempt to pull it out of the sky. As a result, Father Sky relegated Tulu to the greatest depths of the frozen deep realm of Hell,

STARS

The Lovasi Zodiac:

Wolf Star - **Deepwinter**

Bouncing Bear

Kassius' Bow

Karaat's Eye (sometimes called Eralis' Eye, or Crow's Eye) - **Springtide**

The Boar

The Snake

Giy'er's Belt - **Summerhigh**

Raven's Wing

Stag Head

Golden Unicorn - **Autumnwane**

The Bearded Tree

Heart Star

ITCHY'S SONGBOOK:

Your Name Upon the Moon

The Flowers Burn Blue For Dixie

The Dead King Rises

The Hand and the Heart

The Bells of the Fells

Down and Down and Back Again

Twelve Iron Blades of the Merling King

Cook Me Up A Rabbit, Cook Me Up A Hare

The Rack of the Mal

What's Next?

Third Verse of the Last Ballad
A Melody of Madness
Coming 2026